Praise for
THE LAST TR

'Petronella McGovern consistently delivers smart, twisty page-turners guaranteed to keep her readers coming back for more.'

—Liane Moriarty, author of *Apples Never Fall* and *Big Little Lies*

'Two stories about different worlds collide in *The Last Trace*, an enthralling, brilliantly plotted novel of suspense. With contemporary themes, rich characters and an ending that I can't stop thinking about, Petronella McGovern has written one of the best books of the year.'

—JP Pomare, author of *The Wrong Woman* and *The Last Guests*

'Well done to Petronella McGovern on another binge-worthy read. I loved the way several mysteries ultimately tied together—a DNA test, a series of murdered women, and a major player with frightening blackouts. There were heart-racing moments as I tried to figure it all out. A clever and compulsive novel, *The Last Trace* covers a number of meaty themes with accuracy and sensitivity. It had me completely hooked.'

—Ali Lowe, author of *The School Run* and *The Running Club*

'Part family drama, part high concept thriller = 100% compelling. A highly original mystery peppered with family secrets and truths. Petronella has created her own genre and never fails to impress. *The Last Trace* is the perfect book to curl up with. Prepare to be hooked!'

—Sarah Bailey, author of *Body of Lies* and *The Housemate*

'Tightly plotted, atmospheric and poignant: Petronella McGovern has done it again.'

—Charity Norman, author of *Remember Me*

'Emotionally charged and wholly compelling, *The Last Trace* is a brilliantly twisty tale about the slipperiness of memory and how our past is never truly buried. Strap in and enjoy the ride because you never quite know where this story will take you.'

—Anna Downes, *Red River Road* and *The Safe Place*

'Petronella McGovern's band of clever, family-centric thrillers just got even better. *The Last Trace* grabbed me from the first sentence and didn't let me go. Highly recommend.'

—Pip Drysdale, author of *The Next Girl*

'Petronella McGovern's unerring knack of dissecting and upending families and friendships is cleverly showcased in *The Last Trace*, a compelling tale of secrets and lies, memory and fear, deceit and redemption.'

—Suzanne Leal, author of *The Watchful Wife*

'What first appears to be a contemporary family tale unfolds into a fascinating murder mystery. Petronella deftly explores how the mistakes of past generations reverberate through the lives and actions of their children and grandchildren, and weaves together a modern criminal investigation and a cold case. *The Last Trace* is an intriguing tale of mistakes, redemption, and the futility of trying to outrun your past.'

—Genevieve Gannon, author of *The Mothers*

'Opening in the scenic wilds of the Snowy Mountains, *The Last Trace* is full of gripping twists, family secrets and endearing characters. This perfect blend of crime and heart is McGovern's best novel yet!'

—Ashley Kalagian Blunt, author of *Dark Mode*

Praise for
THE LIARS

'*The Liars* is a propulsive thriller that covers some serious subject matter. Switching perspectives between a number of characters—including a killer—it keeps the reader guessing about motives, secrets and how it will all end.'
—*Weekend Australian*

'A timely psychological thriller that will open your eyes.'
—*Who Magazine*

'A textured psychological thriller that encompasses voices of truth, lies, deceit, deception and benevolence, *The Liars* is a first rate read that I mightily recommend.'
—*Mrs B's Book Reviews*

'A heart-stopping tale told across different generations.'
—*Canberra Times*

'Petronella McGovern has woven a story of unfathomably good twists, turns and unforeseen outcomes. Her intelligence, wisdom, insight and understanding shine through on every page. Yet again the bar has been raised in terms of writing excellence by an Australian writer. I loved this book, and shall be on the lookout for her future books.'
—*She Society*

'A psychological thriller that is about much more than crime.'
—*New Zealand Women's Weekly*

Praise for
THE GOOD TEACHER

'An emotionally charged and intriguing novel that goes down some unexpected paths. Jolting surprises and a strong cast of characters will keep you reading well into the night.'

—*Canberra Weekly*

'A fast-paced, heart-stopping thriller full of gripping tension, twists and turns from bestselling author Petronella McGovern.'

—*Who Magazine*

'Intriguing . . . a lively, well-plotted tale about generosity and betrayal.'

—*Sydney Morning Herald*

'I loved this book . . . absolutely engaging from start to finish, and kept me reading into the wee small hours.'

—*Living Arts Canberra*

'Taut, tight and terrific, an addictive read.'

—*Blue Wolf Reviews*

'McGovern has created a compelling and well-plotted second novel . . . deserves a place at the top of your must-read list.'

—*Pittwater Life*

'McGovern's books take us to people and places we know, the characters ringing so true. And the books are addictive, leaving you guessing to the very end and wanting more.'

—*Canberra Times*

Praise for
SIX MINUTES

'Super tense from beginning to end, this is a great read that will spark plenty of book club debate.'
—*New Idea*

'Well crafted and twisty, an accomplished debut novel.'
—*Canberra Weekly*

'Ostensibly a mystery story, with a complex plot and cliffhangers aplenty, *Six Minutes* is also a beautifully drawn look at parenting and relationships. McGovern invites the reader to recognise some of the unnecessary pressures we put on ourselves as parents, as well as the terrible guilt we sometimes carry over things that are outside our control.'
—*Charming Language*

'The perfect read . . . keeps you guessing until the very end.'
—*Manly Daily*

'*Six Minutes* is a book woven from unease, threaded through with an air of creepiness that starts even before the drama of Bella's strange disappearance. As with *Broadchurch,* a TV series also set in an isolated community and involving a missing child, the central drama is really a frame from which to examine the effects of such an event on the local community, and how tragedy can draw out the best and worst in us all.'
—*Newtown Review of Books*

Petronella McGovern is fascinated by what makes us tick, the lies we tell, and the secrets we keep. She is the bestselling author of *Six Minutes*, *The Good Teacher* and *The Liars*. Her books have been nominated in the Ned Kelly Awards, the Davitt Awards and the Australian Independent Bookseller Awards. *The Liars* was selected in the Top 100 Big W/Better Reading list for 2023. Petronella has a Master of Arts in Creative Writing and tutors in creative writing. She grew up on a farm in central west New South Wales and now lives with her family in Sydney, on Gadigal Country. Among other adventures, she has worked on a summer camp in America and travelled in eastern Africa, which partly inspired *The Last Trace*, her fourth novel.

www.petronellamcgovern.com.au

THE
LAST
TRACE

PETRONELLA McGOVERN

ALLEN&UNWIN
SYDNEY · MELBOURNE · AUCKLAND · LONDON

First published in 2024

Allen & Unwin
Cammeraygal Country
83 Alexander Street
Crows Nest NSW 2065
Australia
Phone: (61 2) 8425 0100
Email: info@allenandunwin.com
Web: www.allenandunwin.com

Allen & Unwin acknowledges the Traditional Owners of the Country on which we live and work. We pay our respects to all Aboriginal and Torres Strait Islander Elders, past and present.

A catalogue record for this book is available from the National Library of Australia

ISBN 978 1 76087 925 9

Set in 13.2/17.2 pt Adobe Jenson Pro by Bookhouse, Sydney
Printed and bound in Australia by the Opus Group

10 9 8 7 6 5 4 3 2 1

To my siblings, Fiona, Icara, Hamish & Shelalagh.
You're each inspiring in your own way.
Here's to our shared family memories.

And to my extended Australian & English family,
from my oldest uncle to my youngest niece.
Love you all x

PART ONE
FORGETTING

DNA:Match

 ### Take your DNA test now

Explore your maternal and paternal heritage.
Spit into a test tube. It's that simple.
Your DNA will unlock your personal history.

Note: We work with the FBI to identify missing persons and catch
violent offenders. Click here to read our privacy statement.
Your DNA can help too! Tick the box to opt in.

1

LACHY

MEMORY'S A SLIPPERY BASTARD, LACHY THOUGHT. HIS FACE HOT WITH shame, he blinked and tried to focus on the teenager sitting opposite him. Kai was devouring a hamburger, elbows propped on the table, a soft groan of delight accompanying each mouthful.

Lachy took in the long bar, a sprinkling of diners at wooden tables and the historic photos on the walls. They were at the Dalgety pub. Bloody hell, he must have had a blackout. That had never happened before with his son around. Oh God, had he driven here from the cabin?

Kai licked a blob of barbecue sauce from his lips and continued their conversation. 'So, if the ski fields open in June, when can we go snowboarding?'

On Lachy's placemat sat a half-eaten bowl of vegetarian nachos and a schooner of sparkling water. He lifted his glass, desperate for something cool to douse the burning shame. But when the liquid fizzed on his tongue, he was surprised by the sugary taste of lemonade.

'We can drive up any time,' Lachy said, relieved his voice sounded normal. 'Apart from opening weekend. It's always too crowded then.'

How the hell had they ended up at the pub for dinner? His last memory was from hours ago, just after lunch. He'd opened the package with the DNA results, alone in the cabin while Kai was at school. A short report had already been sent to him online but this package contained extra detail and a few brochures, including one on counselling. His mouth had been as dry as four months ago, when he'd been trying to work up enough saliva to fill the tube. Even though the report told him little more, the physical sight of it had him reaching for the whisky bottle. With the alcohol burning in his throat, he typed out an email, double-checking each word, hoping Juliet would answer this time. She must have received her report by now—it would indicate if his DNA was a match. Pressing send, he noticed a new message from head office pop up. He slammed the laptop shut, but it was too late: the sounds from the Kenya project flooded his brain. He'd slugged another whisky, blocking out work. And another.

Those moments, and the forgotten ones in between, had led to here, now.

'What about the July school holidays?' Kai was asking. 'Is that a good time to—'

'Yeah, great. Sorry, just have to use the loo.'

In the men's, he locked the cubicle door and slumped on the toilet lid. How was it that the things he wanted to forget wouldn't leave him alone while other stuff vanished into the ether? Jesus, he was a mess. A shit parent, shit employee, all-round failure. He must have driven along the twisty road, lined by gum trees, in the windstorm. They were lucky a mob of roos hadn't leapt across their path. Idiot. At least he'd only driven as far as Dalgety, fifteen minutes from home, and not all the way into Warabina.

A knock on the door startled him. Had his son spotted something wrong?

'Just finishing,' he shouted and flushed the toilet.

Waiting outside the cubicle stood an old bushie, sporting an impressive beard and a huge bruise on his forehead.

'It's you!' The bushie clapped him on the shoulder. 'I owe you one, remember. What's your poison?'

Normally Lachy wouldn't forget a face like that but he'd spent the last five hours in a blackout state. Had he been chatting to this man at the bar and bought him a drink?

'Don't worry about it,' Lachy said. 'I'm here with my son.'

'Yeah, good lad, Kai. I'll get him one too. He's not on the beers yet, though, is he? Reckon I was drinking at his age.' The bushie winked. 'What does he like? Coke?'

Head spinning, Lachy stared at him for a beat too long, then rushed out an answer.

'Yep. Coke.' He cleared his throat. 'I mean, you really don't have to . . .'

'I owe you heaps, but I'll start with two drinks. I'll bring 'em over after.' The bushie nodded towards the toilet and Lachy hurried to step out of his way. As he did, he felt a hand on his wrist. Gentle, surprisingly intimate.

'Hope you don't need stitches. You've had a big night, mate.'

Lachy pulled up the sleeve of his jacket and stared in shock at the bloodstain on his shirt. After the bushie had gone into the cubicle, he took off his jacket and rolled his shirt cuff back.

An angry, red graze covered his forearm with two deeper gashes. Shit, he had to clean this up. What had he done to himself?

Was Kai injured too?

Surely, he'd remember that.

No, he wouldn't.

He splashed water over the cuts, grimacing at the sudden pain, watching droplets of blood swirl down the plughole. When he turned the tap off, it kept dripping: clean water going straight into the drain. Tomorrow morning, he'd drive back and replace the O-ring and the jumper valve. He should be doing more; he should be in Kenya right now setting up a water system. Instead, he was hiding out here in the mountains, being absolutely useless. He rubbed the tattoo around his left bicep, a circle of interconnecting lines, tiny waves of never-ending water. A symbol of everything he believed, and yet he didn't recall getting it.

These goddamn blackouts, he'd had them when he was younger then got them under control. For the past decade, his memory would only slip once a year, when he finished an aid project and flew back to head office in Washington DC. He drank fast to ease the transition from the drought-stricken communities in Africa to the wasteful West. The blackouts were never intentional but he couldn't seem to avoid them on those particular nights. The rest of the time, he prided himself on his excellent memory, his responsibility and moral code.

Years ago, he'd read up on the science: he was drinking too fast for the alcohol to be absorbed and his brain couldn't form new memories; they'd last three minutes then whoosh, disappear into nothingness. Some people, like him, were predisposed to blackouts and didn't always appear intoxicated. A surgeon had done a successful operation in a blackout state: his brain accessed his skills and experience but he had no memory of the procedure. His nurses didn't even realise because he presented as sober.

God, Lachy hoped that he'd presented as sober tonight, that he'd made good decisions. Although if he'd driven the ute, that was unforgivable. Had he endangered his son when he'd wounded himself? Fucking hell, this wasn't supposed to happen back home in Australia.

Checking his watch, he reorientated himself. Seven-thirty, Tuesday, the fourth of April.

Sheridan, Nick and the girls were arriving on Friday for the Easter family gathering at Mimosa Hideout. His big sister would be checking that he was properly looking after Kai and the farm. Sheridan already thought he was a crap dad. If she found out about tonight, she'd be ropeable. But they'd been doing okay—he'd settled Kai into the local high school and taken him hiking in the mountains. Sure, he wasn't strict, but Kai didn't need another adult telling him what to do; he already had an enthusiastic mum and a follow-the-rules stepfather. Lachy had always been the good-time dad, cramming all the fun into one adventurous week when he came home between projects. Until this year.

A phlegmy cough from the cubicle snapped Lachy from his thoughts. He stared at his bloodstained sleeve. If only he could just ask about the missing hours but then everyone would learn the truth: he wasn't the man he made himself out to be.

When Lachy returned from the bathroom, Kai raised his eyebrows at the extended absence.

'I just ran into'—was he supposed to know the man's name?—
'the old bushie. He's buying us drinks. And he asked about
my arm.'

'Is he all right?'

'Yeah, I'll put some antiseptic on it when I get home.'

Lachy realised he'd misheard the question. Could it possibly
be *his* fault that the bushie had a bruised head?

He was totally against drink driving; never, ever did it. Except
one other time. During his very first blackout, nineteen years
old and working at a summer camp in Pennsylvania. They'd
partied hard on a night off without any kids. Apparently he'd
borrowed a pick-up truck and driven Tiffany, another camp
counsellor, to meet a friend in the middle of the night. He
never saw her again.

His first blackout had been in America and so had his last,
six months ago. The reason for his DNA test.

No, his last blackout was today. Here in Australia. *You've had
a big night,* the bushie said. What had Lachy done? And what
had his son witnessed? A familiar shame washed over him. He
wanted to curl up in bed and hide from the world. Hide from
his son. Hide from himself.

Because Lachy never knew how he behaved when he was
a stranger in his own life.

2

KAI

KAI COULD HEAR SLOW BREATHING COMING FROM DAD'S BEDROOM. He must have been asleep already, even though it wasn't nine o'clock yet. When they got home from the pub, Kai thought they'd sit in the kitchen and debrief, but Dad went for a shower and never returned.

He rang Mum. She answered immediately, speaking fast.

'Hi, honey, I'm packing. The girls are already with their grandparents. We're leaving at six in the morning.'

Mum and Simmo were flying away to a remote island in Indonesia. He wished he could go too, the island had awesome surf breaks. But this was their first trip without kids and also, of course, they'd sent him to the sin bin.

When Mum asked Simmo to fetch her toiletries bag, he could picture them in their house in Narrabeen, a few blocks from the beach, breaking waves the soundtrack to their lives. Exactly thirteen and a half weeks ago, he'd been banished from there to this wooden cabin in bogan mountain country, five hours from Sydney, a million light years from home. The only good thing about it was hanging out with Dad; this school term was the longest they'd ever spent together. And Dad was nothing like Mum and Simmo with all their rules and nagging and curfews. Dad had said, *I don't buy into all that. We're mates.*

He'd planned to tell Mum about Dad's strange behaviour, but he couldn't do that when she was flying overseas.

'Well, have a great time.' He tried to sound enthusiastic.

'Thanks, honey—' She paused. 'Remember—'

He said it for her: 'Stay out of trouble.' The loaded sign-off for every phone call.

Next, he rang Aunty Sheridan. Since he could remember, she'd been Dad's stand-in. While Dad was away for months and months, Kai would have regular sleepovers with Sheridan and Nick. Mum refused to go to the zoo because of the locked-up animals, but his aunt took him whenever he asked; the dolphin show had been their favourite. She'd brought him down here for weekends. Back then, he'd loved the wilderness of Mimosa Hideout.

'Can we have lots of meat over Easter?' he asked her.

She laughed. 'Is Lachy feeding you too many vegetables? We'll have roast lamb on Sunday. I could do steak one night and chicken casserole on Saturday?'

'That'd be great.'

There was a short silence. Was she writing a shopping list or wondering why he'd really called? His aunt phoned him once a week, but he rarely rang her.

'Is everything all right down there?' she asked.

'Yep.' He didn't know what to say. 'Dad cut his arm, but it's okay, I think.'

'Do you want to put him on?'

'He's asleep.' Kai stared out the kitchen window into the pitch-black darkness. The cabin was in the middle of nowhere. No city lights, no traffic, no people. He still wasn't used to it.

'When do Amber and Simmo leave?'

'Tomorrow. They're excited about going on holiday.'

'Well, I'm excited about coming down to Mimosa to see you.' Aunty Sheridan always said nice things like that.

'You should come early,' he rushed out the suggestion. 'Come by yourself tomorrow.'

'What's wrong? Are you okay?'

'I'm good. It's just . . .' Explaining it over the phone wouldn't work. But Sheridan knew Dad better than anyone—if she could see him in person, check him out, then Kai would feel a whole lot better.

After a brief pause, she said, 'Let me talk to Nick.'

Ten minutes later, her text came through: *I can come tomorrow! Meet you at Warabina FoodWorks after school.*

Phew. He wouldn't be solely responsible for Dad. What if his father had the same disease as Glamma? The last time Kai visited his grandmother, she thought he'd been sent to fix the toilet. Sheridan said to go along with it, so he spent five minutes in the bathroom on his phone then came out and told her that he'd replaced some screws and it was all good now. But Dad was only thirty-seven, heaps younger than all the other parents. Too young for that crazy shit. Right?

Collapsing onto the couch, Kai switched on the Xbox and joined a game of *Fortnite*. But even as he scavenged for weapons and pickaxed through buildings, he couldn't stop thinking about Dad's behaviour. By themselves, they were all little things, but then they kept stacking up all afternoon.

First, Dad hadn't been waiting to collect him at the front gate when the school bus dropped him off. Mimosa Hideout was the last stop on Mr Suttor's run and he'd complained about the windstorm. 'Look at those branches bending. They'll be falling on the road any minute now. Widow-makers, they call 'em.'

Dad had been late before, so Kai wasn't worried, just annoyed at having to walk up the track in the howling gale. His leg still hurt. Grug had slammed the convict ball-and-chain into his calf muscle on their school excursion to Cooma prison museum. When Kai cried out in shock, Grug and his gang laughed and fist-bumped each other. Arseholes, the lot of them. Grug, aka George Rupert Gallagher, came from merino sheep royalty, with eight properties, a big old house and a colonial history. He should have been sent away to an expensive boarding school in Sydney, but times were tough. Instead, Grug was at Warabina High, torturing his latest victim. *Kai will end up in the slammer one day*, he'd taunted as they peered into a jail cell.

Kai stopped to rub his calf and then kept trudging up the track. Only two more days until term finished. Freedom from school and from Grug. He was wondering how he could convince Dad to take him back to Sydney for a few days to see his mates. Dad had a tenant in his Sydney apartment, so they couldn't stay there. And Mum had said he wasn't allowed to come home in the holidays—the whole point of sending him to Mimosa was to keep him away from Hudson and the rest of their friends.

When Kai finally reached the cabin, the ute was parked in the shed. He figured Dad must be stuck on a Zoom meeting or finishing a report. Starving from the walk, he went straight to the kitchen and dumped six Weet-Bix in a bowl. When he carried his cereal to the dining room table and noticed the shape in the chair by the window, he'd freaked out.

His father had turned towards him slowly, then grinned. 'Oh, hi, mate. How was school today?'

Even though Dad was smiling, his eyes seemed glazed. Shit, had he found the pills and taken one?

'School was okay. We had the excursion to Cooma prison. You weren't at the front gate.' Kai didn't mean to whinge, but his leg hurt.

'Sorry, I had a meeting about a desal plant for a hospital in Tonga. Hey, what's the capital of Tonga?'

Kai had been mapping his dad's journeys since preschool. It had become their game to learn the capital cities. Kenya: Nairobi. Tuvalu: Funafuti. Nepal: Kathmandu. Ethiopia: Addis Ababa. He had so much geographical knowledge in his head but it wasn't useful for any of the topics at school.

'Nuku . . . something.' He couldn't remember the rest. 'I thought your projects were all in Africa now?'

It wasn't a trick question, but Dad frowned and took a moment to answer.

'They asked me because I worked in Tonga years ago. When you were just starting school.'

Apart from his glazed eyes, Dad looked normal. His dark wavy hair was slightly mussed, and he was wearing jeans and a green t-shirt. Kai's own hair was a bit lighter and longer; Mum wanted him to get it cut before the beginning of term, but he'd refused. Dad's tattoo peeked out from under his sleeve. As soon as Kai turned sixteen next year, he was going to get a tattoo; he just needed Dad's consent.

'I'll forgive you for not picking me up if we can go to the pub for dinner,' Kai said.

Dad laughed. 'Had enough of my cooking for the week?'

'I need a burger with the lot.' That was the only bad thing about Dad—vegetarian meals.

'Fair enough.' And then Dad asked, 'So how was school?'

Weird, he'd already asked that. Kai went into more detail about the Cooma prison museum, and then Dad told him about a friend's trip to the Okavango Delta. But as Dad stood to leave the room and go back to work, he said, 'Hey, what do you want for dinner? I could do a chickpea and pumpkin korma.'

For a second, Kai wondered if his father was pranking him, but neither of them laughed.

'Aren't we going to the pub for a burger?'

'Sounds like a plan.'

An hour later, Dad went into the kitchen to start preparing a curry and Kai reminded him one more time. Driving to the pub, Dad occasionally repeated the same comment but then the accident had distracted them both. After that, all their conversations had been disjointed.

He'd just been killed again on *Fortnite*. His mind wasn't on the game. Maybe Dad had taken his stash because he was bored of the quiet life, bored of not travelling, bored of his own son. No, Dad didn't do drugs. In addition to them being 'bad for your brain', Dad said the cultivation of illegal drugs caused deforestation and water pollution. Classic. What other father would say that? He'd had a good laugh about it with Hudson.

Kai switched off the Xbox and walked over to the games cupboard where Glamma had kept her jigsaw puzzles. He pulled the bottom box from the pile. The cover showed an old-time painting of Philadelphia's Independence Hall: a horse and cart trotting along the street, a white tower against a blue sky. Dad had given it to Glamma because she grew up in America. Hidden in the box was an envelope. Kai opened it and counted eight pink-and-blue pills. Exactly the same number as before.

So the pingers hadn't caused Dad's confusion.

Tomorrow he'd watch Dad over breakfast and then tell Aunty Sheridan everything when she arrived.

3

LACHY

LACHY HAD BARELY SLEPT, TOSSING AND TURNING, BERATING HIMSELF. Scumbag, loser, irresponsible dickhead. In between those thoughts, he tried to piece together the missing hours. How had he behaved in front of his son? Of course, none of the memories returned. Whoosh, gone after three minutes, gone forever. The fear that he'd done something terrible made him jittery, craving a whisky to calm his nerves. But no, he was never touching the stuff again. Shit, how could he have had a blackout with Kai around? How could he have driven in that state? He knew he was in a bad way but moving here was supposed to make him better. Not worse.

Sitting in the ute with Kai, waiting at the front gate for the school bus, he told himself to focus on the present, look at the layers of cloud in the valley. But that reminded him of climbing up Mount Kenya, dawn breaking to a blanket of mist. And that reminded him of Henrik. Fucking Henrik. This was all his fault.

'Can you teach me to drive in the holidays?' Kai's question interrupted his spiralling thoughts. 'Then you wouldn't have to bring me to the gate each morning.'

16

'The other option is that you could walk.'

'It's three kilometres, Dad. And it'll be freezing in winter.'

Actually less than three kilometres. And Kai was a healthy teenager with no concept of how far some kids had to trek to fetch water for their families. Across dusty, dry plains with no shade from the scorching sun. Those kids in Kenya didn't have the privilege of going to school, they were too busy trying to survive, carrying their containers back and forth. And the girls had to avoid . . . no, don't think about that. Gritting his teeth, he suppressed his anger and forced out an appropriate reply. 'What if I need the ute during the day? I'd have to jog down and get it.'

'Downhill's easy. Going up is the hard part,' Kai said, smirking.

Lachy wondered if they'd had this discussion already. Maybe after he'd forgotten to collect Kai from the bus yesterday. 'I promise I'll be here this arvo,' he said.

'Nah, it's okay. I'm meeting Aunty Sheridan in town, and she'll bring me home.'

'I thought they weren't arriving till Friday?' Bloody hell, had his sister called in those missing hours and made new arrangements?

'She's coming early, by herself.'

Presumably he should know why. Beneath every conversation lay a landmine. He'd re-traced his steps as much as he could from yesterday afternoon—the DNA report was by his laptop, the counselling brochures in the lounge room. He'd checked the paintwork on the ute and there was no sign of damage. Thank God, he hadn't crashed into anything on the way to the pub. Driving with Kai in the passenger seat, that was the lowest of lows.

He wasn't an alcoholic. He drank in moderation ninety-nine percent of the time. Last night's blackout was unexpected; perhaps his tolerance had become lower with age or he'd been affected by the sleeping tablets.

As the minibus approached, Kai opened the door and ambled over to meet it. When Lachy lifted his hand to wave at Mr Suttor, the bandage caught against the graze on his forearm. A stab of pain. He deserved that as punishment. Probably needed stitches, but he couldn't face the shame of visiting a doctor when he didn't know how he'd been injured.

With Kai gone, the day stretched before him. He should drive to the pub and fix that dripping tap. He should do the food shopping for Easter. He should check in with work, figure out his next step. But contacting work would bring on that memory, which would lead into a murky replay of yesterday. All he wanted to do was go back to bed. If he didn't have to wake Kai for school, he would stay asleep. Every day. What was the point of getting out of bed? Of doing anything? He was a waste of oxygen, the world was imploding, and they were all doomed.

No other cars had passed by the gate since the school minibus had come and gone. The road was only used by a few locals, it led higher into the mountains, then petered out into dirt. Lachy stared at the black tarmac, willing himself to start the ute and drive towards town. Do something useful.

He shifted his gaze away from the road. Debris from the windstorm lay strewn across the paddock but now there was barely a breeze. The mist had burnt off and soft sunshine shimmered through the cloud, opening up the sky. He could hear his mother's voice urging him: 'Come on Lachy, this glorious day should be spent outside. We must enjoy the glory of the world and that's not just because I'm called Gloria.' That had once been his mantra too: make the most of every day.

'This glorious countryside.' Speaking aloud, he tried to inject Mum's enthusiasm into his miserable thoughts. He started the ute and turned it away from the main road; he couldn't face driving to the pub or into town but he wouldn't go back to bed either.

He rolled down the window and caught the scent of eucalyptus, damp grass, soil. The scent of rejuvenation. An opportunity to reset. He and Kai both needed that.

Bumping over the rocky terrain, he slowed to appreciate the view from the ridge. This vantage point had always been Mum's favourite. She'd been raised in an American Bible-thumping family, but when Dad had brought her to Australia she began worshipping nature instead. He wished she could see its beauty today. The biggest sky imaginable—gradations of blue from aqua to the deepest cobalt, an ocean in the heavens. The nearest mountains had a green-brown hue, while those in the distance matched the peacock blue in the sky. Peaks and ranges nestled into each other, thin slivers of cloud draped over them like a lacy shawl.

By the end of next month, the ranges would be stark white, the snow reflecting the sunshine. Or, depending on the weather, barely visible in a blizzard of cloud and ice. They'd been stranded a few times at Mimosa Hideout. If they were staying all winter, he should get organised, stock up with food and sort out proper heating. He'd been planning to install solar panels and a battery system to take the cabin off-grid, but he hadn't had the energy to do anything about it. He assumed they were staying; Amber hadn't discussed Kai returning home to Sydney.

The mountain vista vanished as he drove down towards the creek. The small bushes of the higher ground gave way to tall snow gums and the sides of the valley closed around him. He could hear the creek before he saw it, water cascading on a furious descent from the alps to the basalt plains of the Monaro. He'd inspect the wooden bridge to Ronnie's place for any wind damage and then sit for a while by the rushing water. Dip his hands into it. Splash his face. Taste the snowmelt. Experience the circle of life through rain, clouds, snow, this headwater stream. Consider the next step in his own life journey.

It was even cooler out of the ute. He crouched on the damp rocks and brought a handful of icy water to his mouth. The shock of cold made him gasp.

On the other side of the creek, Ronnie's old truck was pulling up. Her dogs jumped from the tray. She began speaking before she'd even shut the door, shouting to make herself heard over the gushing water.

'Where were you yesterday?'

Shit, he'd let her down too. 'Sorry. Got caught up with work. Big project.'

'The water tanks in Tanzania?'

'Uh, yep.'

She unlatched the gate and strode across the bridge, her white ponytail swinging in time with her steps. Her posse of five dogs threaded around her purple gumboots. As they neared, one broke free from the pack, sauntered up to him and licked his hand.

'That wind last night . . .' Ronnie gazed at the clouds high above them. 'It brought something bad. I can smell it. An ill wind.'

He couldn't smell the wind, only Ronnie herself, a combination of deodorant, sweat, horse and dog. The tang of the country. But he could feel the ill wind—it swirled inside his brain, his heart, his bones. He shivered and the panic he'd been fighting since the pub ratcheted up another notch. Sheridan would tell him to ignore her strange ramblings, but Ronnie had become a friend over the last few months.

She moved closer and peered into his eyes. 'You're lookin' a bit pale. What happened?'

'Nothing. Just a work deadline. I can help you on Monday.'

'Good.' She nodded. 'Bring your boy. He can lift a few planks.'

Ronnie had been a loyal neighbour to Mum and Dad for decades. These days she'd visit Lachy but she avoided going into town. An original prepper, she'd been prepared for a global catastrophe years before the pandemic.

'Do you want to come for Sunday lunch? Sheridan, Nick and the girls will be here.' The invitation popped out before he had time to think it through. His sister wouldn't be happy.

'Ripper idea. I haven't seen Sheridan in yonks. She can give me the latest news on your mum.' Her smile turned into a grimace. 'But you'd better warn her about the bad wind. It's bringing disaster.'

Her words had shattered Lachy's attempt to appreciate the glory of the day and sent him reeling home for strong coffee. Goosebumps pricked his arms, and the bandage felt too tight against his wound. He knew he should see a doctor, take

antidepressants, speak to a counsellor, contact head office . . .
he knew what he should be doing but he just couldn't. The
little energy he had was spent on Kai, getting him to school,
cooking dinner, pretending everything was okay. Right now, he
would finish his coffee then concentrate on cleaning the house
for the family.

As he walked down the hallway, he ran his hand over
the wood panelling. His grandfather had bought the cabin
while working as an engineer on the Snowy Hydro scheme in the
1960s. He'd inspired Lachy's own career. Not hydro-electricity
but water itself. He could still recall the buzz of setting up
a reverse osmosis filtration system in a remote location, and
watching the community's reaction as they turned on the tap:
tears, laughter, utter relief, and renewed plans for a future.

The opposite of how he felt now.

He hadn't told Sheridan, she wouldn't understand. She'd
want to life-coach him back into his job. But even though
he'd been good at his work, there was no future. His optimism
had vanished, just like his memory of last night.

Dragging the vacuum cleaner around the lounge room, he
spotted a blue jigsaw piece in a dusty corner. The sideboard
contained a haphazard stack of puzzles. He could take up Mum's
old hobby as a way to pass the time while Kai was at school.
He wasn't doing anything else. Not working, not farming, not
setting up a solar unit—just feeling sick about the world. He
squatted down, opened the doors and tried to guess where
the piece belonged. He considered pulling out the boxes and
going through each one, but he'd have to do all the puzzles to
figure it out. A mission for another week. Instead, he found an
envelope in the kitchen, wrote BLUE PUZZLE PIECE across it and

popped the shape inside. He placed it on the stack of boxes and shut the doors.

Photo frames crowded the top of the sideboard. When he picked up the nearest one, its timber edge came apart in his hand. Terrible workmanship. Ha! He'd made it in wood-work class at fifteen and given it to his parents for Christmas. More than two decades later, the photo had a mottled tinge. It showed his family, frozen in time, the four of them standing next to the Liberty Bell in Philadelphia. In another frame was a freezing Pennsylvanian Christmas with Mum in the centre of her extended family. A slideshow of American moments flicked through his head: his aunt's house with its red mailbox; kayaking at summer camp; drunken nights with his cousins; his last difficult work meeting in DC, waking up disorientated the next morning, unable to remember the night before.

His arm throbbed after vacuuming. Blood had seeped through the bandage. A blotch of maroon on the white fabric. A reminder of his missing moments.

Half of him wanted to know what had happened yesterday; the other half was too scared of what he might find out.

4

SHERIDAN

SHERIDAN LUGGED HER BAG TO THE CAR THEN RAN BACK INTO THE house for a quick once-over. The logistics of leaving early had been complicated by the school's Easter hat parade, donate-a-can for the food drive, Eloise's family tree assignment, Mabel's end-of-term morning tea, and organising for ten days away. Five days at Mimosa, then five days at Jindabyne . . . as long as the nursing home didn't call with an emergency. She'd packed the girls' bags and placed them in her own bedroom so they wouldn't take out any clothes, and she'd put the snacks for their trip on Good Friday on a high shelf in the pantry so they wouldn't be eaten beforehand.

Good Friday. The old Wilson family tradition. Mum and Dad used to load the car on Thursday night, then they'd all go to bed in their clothes and wake up at three in the morning to begin the drive from Dural. *Outsmart the traffic*, Dad said. Mum brought a picnic of hot cross buns and hot chocolate in the thermos. The sun would rise somewhere near Canberra, reflecting off Lake George when it was filled with water. Years later, in the throes of courtship, Nick followed the early-morning tradition with her, but when the girls came along, they couldn't manage it. Their new tradition was breakfast at home, bumper-to-bumper traffic on the highway, punctuated with stops at McDonald's.

Even though she felt silly rushing down to Mimosa with no solid reason, Nick had been as understanding as always.

'If you feel Kai needs you, then go. I can sort out the girls. Don't worry about us.'

But of course she worried. She wanted to make it easier for him; she wanted her daughters to have the right clothes and toys; she wanted to keep everyone happy.

Happier than the last time she'd seen Kai, when they'd all been trying to decide what would be best for him. Amber and Simmo wanted a circuit-breaker, a change in his environment. When Lachy had offered to stay in Australia and live in the cabin with Kai, she'd almost fallen off her chair. He'd been working overseas for fourteen years and, while he took Kai on occasional holidays, he'd never had any day-to-day involvement with his son. Her brother had a knack for avoiding the hard stuff.

Tonight she would see if he had evolved into a responsible, full-time father. But before she could leave Sydney, she had to drop by Mum's nursing home; luckily, they'd been able to get her into a place not far from their home in Willoughby. Mum might not recognise her after ten days away.

✕

Her mother was sitting at a table in the residents' lounge, working on a jigsaw puzzle and humming along to a Beatles song that drifted from the sound system, 'All You Need Is Love'. If only life were that simple. The puzzle had large pieces; her daughters had mastered it when they were three years old.

Mum smiled up at her. 'Look at this puzzle. It's like Dad's horse. Mimosa.'

Sheridan let out the breath she'd been holding: Mum remembered her today.

'Mimosa was the loveliest horse,' she said. 'Dad named the cabin after her.'

She never knew if mentioning the cabin would upset Mum. Dad had renovated it so the whole family could stay there comfortably and renamed it in honour of his favourite horse and Mum's favourite drink.

'Mimosa Hideout . . . Ronnie hides out on the property next door.' Mum gave her signature giggle. 'We never knew what she was hiding from. Dad said the bikies. I thought it was a bad husband.'

Wow, Mum's brain was in top form today—she even recalled their odd neighbour. And how funny that her parents had played the same guessing game as her and Lachy.

'I think she's hiding from the whole world,' Sheridan said.

'I'm not hiding,' Mum snapped, her mood changing abruptly. 'I told Father I'm here.'

Growing up, she'd rarely heard about her grandparents, only Mum's three siblings: Theresa, Virginia and Ernest. Lately though, Mum had started talking about her parents, and when she did, her American accent became more pronounced.

'Father definitely knows where you are,' Sheridan reassured her.

'I'll be in trouble otherwise.' Mum sounded nervous. 'Where's Betty?'

Patting her mother's arm, Sheridan kept her expression neutral, hiding her shock. Why was Mum asking for her old doll. Shit, was she reverting to childhood now? Betty was made in the 1960s and falling apart; the staff would classify the doll as a health and safety risk. She'd ask around the school mums to see if anyone had the skills to patch up the toddler-sized doll.

'We're going to Mimosa for Easter. I'll have dinner with Lachy and Kai tonight.' Mum nodded, recognising the names. 'Do you want me to bring Betty back?'

'Oh yes.' Her face lit up. 'I love Betty.'

It would be strange having Easter at Mimosa without Mum and Dad. Mum enjoyed gatherings and parties so much that she'd started her own event-planning business. Back then, she'd held so many details in her head: names, numbers, venues and special requests. Mum had been so sassy and glamorous that Kai, the unexpected first grandchild, had called her Glamma instead of Grandma. And Lachy had learnt his blasé approach to parenting from her. She'd outsourced the boring, bossy part of parenting to Sheridan: *Keep an eye on your little brother, make sure he has his lunch for school, hold his hand on the pedestrian crossing.* Decades later, she'd found herself caring for Lachy's own son. If it hadn't been for her, Lachy wouldn't have much of a relationship with him now.

'Theresa called me,' Mum said. 'They're having their fiftieth wedding anniversary. But she didn't tell me any party details. She kept going on about the Casanova Killer. She's obsessed by that case. I told her to stop talking about murder and run through the menu. She's going to wear a turquoise dress.'

It was good that Mum had managed a phone call with Aunt Theresa. But had they really talked about murder and not party food? Theresa was a good cook who would do an excellent menu.

'It's a shame none of us can go over for the celebration.'

'Oh, I told her I'm coming and I won't be late.' Mum was suddenly in a different place. 'I told her I'd be home in time to help with dinner.'

This accounting for her whereabouts had become a recurring theme. It surprised Sheridan because Mum hadn't brought them up like that. The doctor said dementia patients often fixated on particular issues—she hoped the other one didn't come up today.

'Good. You won't be late.' Going along with these circuitous exchanges helped to keep Mum calm. Over Easter, Sheridan would encourage Lachy to plan a visit to the nursing home. She'd expected him to take on some of the responsibility for their mother now that he was back in Australia, but he hadn't seen Mum for months.

'Father is giving the sermon at Easter.' Mum clasped her hands against her heart and intoned: 'Christ has died. Christ is risen. Christ will come again.'

Mum had never taken them to church. When she and Nick were getting married, they'd had to convince Gloria that they really did want a religious ceremony. Mostly the pressure came from Nick's parents; Sheridan didn't really care, but she found herself in the impossible situation of trying to please her fiancé, her mother and her parents-in-law. Thankfully, Dad had sided with her, as always, and talked Mum around.

'Look after Lachy in the Easter egg hunt,' Mum said. 'Make sure you both get the same number of eggs. Count them out. His little legs can't run as fast as yours.'

Stretching her neck, Sheridan felt the bones cracking. Speaking with Mum led her down a memory lane maze; you never quite knew where you were, who you were, or what would appear next.

Mum had finished the jigsaw and was tracing the outline of the horses with her fingertips.

'Great job on the puzzle!'

'She's gone,' Mum whispered, 'and it's all my fault.'

Oh no, not this again—they needed a distraction, fast.

Sheridan opened Facebook on her phone. 'Mum, look at this cute video of a dog skateboarding down the stairs. Isn't that funny?'

But Mum pushed the phone away and began to sob.

If only Sheridan knew what her mother was remembering, she could comfort her properly. Mum had been estranged from her parents when they'd died. Afterwards, she returned to Pennsylvania and reunited with her siblings. A few years ago, her youngest sister, Virginia, had suffered a fatal stroke. But that had happened in America, so it couldn't be Mum's fault, however she imagined it.

'I'm here, your daughter, Sheridan.' She reached over to hug her mother but it didn't help. Maybe Mum would find comfort in the old doll. 'I'll bring Betty with me next time I visit,' she promised.

'She's gone.' A heart-wrenching cry shook Mum's body. 'And it's my fault.'

Sometimes, Sheridan wondered if her mother was talking about herself, if a tiny part of her brain understood what was happening. Even though Mum looked the same, decked out in colourful clothes, her white hair in a chic bob, the mother Sheridan knew had definitely gone.

One of the benefits of being a life coach was that she could conduct appointments on the five-hour drive down the Hume Highway. She had two new clients starting this week, which was great, although she wasn't sure how many more she could fit in mentally. The number of people needing her help already felt overwhelming.

She had an eleven o'clock call with her easiest client, Brendan Taylor, who had left his corporate job and set up a boutique distillery in the Snowy Mountains, an hour from Mimosa Hideout. He'd sent her four little sample bottles, all delicious—apart from the limoncello, which tasted like medicine. Brendan had followed her advice and written an action plan to achieve his business and lifestyle goals. She enjoyed their sessions because he always made her laugh. But more than that, he understood how goal-setting worked.

In early February, she'd tried to get Kai to list his goals for a good term at his new school but he refused. Despite that, everything seemed to be going well; he hadn't reverted to his bad ways. Hopefully, the reason he'd asked her to come early was just a little homesickness, and nothing more.

Sheridan was adding three packets of rice crackers to her full shopping trolley when Kai entered FoodWorks.

'Look at you!' She pulled him into a hug. 'You're towering over me. The mountain air must be good for you.'

He automatically put his arms around her, then drew back slightly, checking over his shoulder to make sure no-one had seen. 'Dunno about that. Thanks for coming today.'

She studied his face. 'Well, your pimples have cleared up. You're drop-dead gorgeous!'

'Jeez,' he groaned. 'You'll make me drop dead with embarrassment.'

Positioning himself behind the trolley, Kai started pushing it towards the end of the aisle. He looked healthy, if a little skinny, but he was so awkward.

'Have you made friends at school?'

His neck flushed red. 'Can we get outta here and talk about school later?'

Sheridan frowned. Was he in trouble at school? Was that why he'd asked her to come early?

'Okay. I need to find Easter eggs and hot cross buns, then we're finished. Does your dad still hate sultanas?'

He just shrugged.

She chose fruit-free buns with chocolate chips and baulked at the price. It would have been cheaper to do the shopping at Coles in Chatswood or even in Cooma. She'd spoken with Lachy on the way down—of course, he hadn't bought any food yet. No doubt when she unpacked the steak and lamb, he'd remind her that livestock farming meant fewer trees, a decrease in native animals, and an increase in water usage and carbon emissions.

But their mum always cooked a roast lamb at Easter, it was tradition. Anyway, Lachy could have planned his own menu for the weekend. How was it that her brother managed to travel to the most remote places, organise months of food, water and engineering supplies, but he couldn't shop for Easter?

Learned incompetence. He expected her to do it.

'I'm worried about Dad's memory,' Kai mumbled.

'His memory?' She hadn't been expecting that. What if her brother really did become incompetent, like their mum? She put a hand on the trolley to stop him from moving. 'What's happening?'

'Nothing specific.' That shrug again. 'Yesterday afternoon . . . last night, he seemed surprised by ordinary stuff. Things he should've known.'

'Like how to cook a meal or drive a car?'

'No. I can't really explain.' Kai screwed up his face. 'That's why I called you. I wanted you to check if he's all right.'

Hugging the packet of hot cross buns to her chest, she willed herself not to panic. Early-onset dementia. Please God, no. She couldn't look after them both.

Kai must have seen the fear flash across her face.

'I shouldn't have said anything. It was just once. Dad's cool. We've been having a good time together. Don't tell him.'

'Okay.' She resisted the urge to hug him a second time. 'I'll keep an eye on him over the weekend, see if I notice anything unusual.'

Seeming satisfied, Kai started pushing the trolley towards the checkout. She followed and almost ran into the back of him when he stopped suddenly. Two boys in Warabina High

School uniforms stood near the lolly section, arguing. Swivelling abruptly, Kai chose the counter furthest from them.

Sheridan nodded in their direction. 'Do you know them?'

'The tall one. Grug. He's a jerk.'

She was about to ask more when she noticed the newspaper on a rack at the checkout. LOCAL HERO IN WINDSTORM shouted the headline. Beneath it was a photo of her brother, Lachy Wilson.

5

KAI

KAI STARED AT THE NEWSPAPER WITH HIS DAD ON THE FRONT PAGE. Buzzing with pride, he handed a copy to Aunty Sheridan.

'Wow!' She exclaimed. 'What did he do?'

From the corner of his eye, he saw Grug's head snap up.

'Oh, it just happened on the way to the pub,' Kai said.

His aunt was quiet for a moment, reading the story, then she looked at Kai. 'Did he get concussed? Could that explain the memory issue?'

'Um . . . no.' It was hard to concentrate with Grug nearby.

The predator was coming towards them. Kai turned his back; he couldn't face another round with him today.

'Good afternoon, Mrs Wilson.' Grug put on the arse-licking voice he used for the principal. 'Nice to see you, Kai, and to meet your mum at last.'

'I'm Kai's aunt, actually,' Sheridan said. 'And you are?'

'George Rupert Gallagher.' He held out his hand for her to shake. 'You've probably heard the Gallagher name. It's well known around Warabina. We've held merino studs in the region for generations.'

Tosser. Hopefully his aunt would see straight through him. In the first week of term, Grug had asked about his background, but Kai refused to explain his complicated family set-up: parents who split when he was a baby; a father working overseas; a step-father; two half-sisters; Dad's relatives in America; and three sets of grandparents. Anyway, it wouldn't matter what he said. Grug considered everyone beneath him.

'Merino studs?' Sheridan nodded appreciatively. Oh no, she'd fallen for Grug's revolting charm and his tousled blond hair. 'I wouldn't mention that to Kai's dad. He'll tell you sheep farming destroys native forest and fauna. In fact, the livestock industry's emissions are equivalent to all the world's vehicles. Did you know that?'

Ha! Go Aunty Sheridan!

Grug looked like he'd been slapped, but he recovered quickly. 'With facts like that, you must be a teacher.' He granted her another smile. And then he waved a hand at their groceries laid out on the conveyor belt. 'But you're still buying a leg of lamb, though.'

'It's for our dog,' Aunty Sheridan said. 'Thanks for introducing yourself, George Rupert Gallagher. We have to get back to Kai's dad. Did you see his picture on the front page? He's the hero of the day.'

Grug sneered at the paper and walked off. Unreal! Sheridan had just put the school bully in his place. And lied. They didn't even have a dog. He'd never heard her lie before. Woah, what a takedown. Best. Aunt. Ever.

'Are they all like Grug?' she asked him.

'Nah. The others aren't as bad. There's only one Grug.'

When he'd told Hudson about the bullying, his mate said, 'Don't give Grug a reaction, then he'll find someone else to pick on.' But there wasn't anyone else. People didn't relocate to small towns in nowheresville. Warabina was so small, it shouldn't even have a high school; they'd only built it because of the families working on the hydro-electric scheme in the sixties. Dad had done Mum a massive favour by moving here, and he'd told work he couldn't travel overseas for twelve months—that was how much he was giving up for Kai.

At recess that morning, Grug had thrown a soccer ball at his head and shouted: 'I hope you're fucking off to Sydney for the holidays.'

'Nup, I'll be too busy partying here,' Kai shot back. A stupid line—he didn't even have any friends in Warabina.

Two girls from his English class were walking by as he said it; he hadn't spoken to them outside the classroom before, but Tarni yelled, 'A party? Awesome! We'll be there.'

'Come to the canteen with us,' Bronte said. 'We're getting sausage rolls.'

'If we're going to a party, we'll need something stronger than sausage rolls.' Tarni giggled. 'How easy is it to get pills in Sydney?'

Kai shrugged. 'Pretty easy.'

Walking away with the girls, he smirked over his shoulder at Grug.

More magic happened after lunch. In maths, he'd sat in his usual chair near the window and almost immediately someone slid into the seat next to him. Ethan Thompson, one of the cool kids.

'Wanna come to a party at mine on Friday night?' Ethan asked. 'Tarni and Bronte said you could bring some gear.'

'Um . . . yeah . . . maybe.'

A party, at last! But why did it have to be this weekend, when all the family was here? Parties were banned. Dad wouldn't care but Sheridan was another story. And Mimosa was so far from everywhere. At home, he and Hudson could walk or catch a bus.

And, really, was he only being invited because he'd mentioned the pills to Tarni?

'Not so keen?' Ethan nudged his shoulder. 'It'll be good, I promise. Big bonfire in the paddock.'

'Great!' He didn't want to explain: the party wasn't the issue, any party would be excellent.

Ethan nodded. 'Oh, right. I get it. You think it'll be shit. Our parties aren't like your flashy Sydney ones.'

Kai suppressed a groan. Now he'd offended the first person to invite him to anything.

'It's not that,' he said, honesty the only option now. 'I don't know how I can get there and home again.'

'Maaate, you got a sleeping bag? Everyone will crash in the shearing shed. We'll have a fry-up in the morning.'

If he told Dad it was a bonfire with a few mates, then Sheridan would never know he was breaking Mum's rule.

As they left Warabina and began the ascent into the mountains, Sheridan grilled him about Grug, about school, and about Dad. Now that he'd been invited to a party, he was regretting asking her to come down early. She'd be watching Dad more closely than ever, making sure he was doing everything properly. Before

Christmas, Kai had overheard her complaining to Uncle Nick that Dad wasn't very good at parenting, but Dad was the best. Mostly. Sometimes he disappeared out on the farm somewhere; sometimes he could be distracted and snappy. But after all these years, Dad was finally hanging out with him every day. If only he could see his Sydney friends as well, life would've been perfect.

'It's great living with Dad,' he told his aunt. 'We do loads together. He took me kayaking and he's teaching me to cook and stuff. You don't need to worry about us.'

'But this memory issue . . .'

'Nah.' He backtracked. 'I reckon you're right about the concussion.'

Dad wasn't home when they pulled up outside the cabin, and Kai freaked out. Had something happened to him? He'd seemed fine this morning.

Kai and Sheridan were still unpacking groceries in the kitchen when they heard the ute, then Dad was hurrying down the hallway.

'Sorry, sorry. I was near the creek, mending a fence.'

'Here's the hero!' Sheridan kissed him. 'You should be having a day off after all your efforts.'

'What are you talking about?' Dad frowned.

Kai stared at him. He couldn't have forgotten the rescue, could he?

Sheridan slapped the newspaper on the benchtop and Dad bent over to read it.

'Fred Whyte.' Dad said the name aloud. 'His property is on the road to Dalgety.'

Duh, otherwise they wouldn't have been there to save him last night.

'Hardly any cars go along that road,' Kai explained to Sheridan. 'It's lucky we came along.'

'You two were his guardian angels.' His aunt patted him on the shoulder. 'And how was Fred? Did he have to go to hospital?'

He and Dad answered at the same time.

'Yeah.'

'No.'

A silence as he waited for Dad to elaborate. When he didn't, Kai stepped in. 'Fred wouldn't go to the hospital or go home,' he said. 'He came to the pub to celebrate his lucky escape. He bought us drinks. He said he'd been drinking beer at my age but Dad told him I could only have Coke.'

Dad wouldn't have been drinking beer at fifteen, Kai knew; he was the golden child. He'd never done anything wrong. Kai loved having a hero for a father, but it made life tricky. When teachers heard Dad was a water engineer working overseas on aid programs, they were stupidly impressed. Their faces went soft and gooey, like when old people smiled at babies. They praised Dad for making a difference, and then they asked: 'Will you follow in his footsteps, Kai? Are you going to change the world too?' But their high expectations sent Kai whirling in the opposite direction. What was with all the pressure? He was only fifteen; why couldn't he just have fun?

Mum's threat replayed briefly in his head. *If I find out that you're taking drugs in Warabina, I'll drive you to the police station and have you arrested myself.*

He hadn't been to a party in five months. Stuff it—he'd go hard on Friday night. A beer would be just for starters.

6

LACHY

A HERO? WHAT THE HELL? LACHY THOUGHT HIS SISTER WOULD BURST in and do a military inspection of his life with Kai, yet here she was congratulating him on his heroic actions. While she filled the kettle, he leant on the benchtop and quickly read the article.

LOCAL HERO IN WINDSTORM

Lachy Wilson risked his own life in last night's windstorm to rescue Dalgety farmer, Fred Whyte. As the wind tore through the valley, shredding trees and whipping off roofs, Fred was out in the paddocks, checking his sheep and horses. While he'd gone to ensure their safety, Fred struck danger himself. A branch fell across his path, causing Fred to crash his ute into a ditch.

'It knocked me out, and when I came to I was trapped in my seat,' Fred said. 'I could smell petrol. I thought my time had come.'

Fred was lucky that Lachy Wilson had promised his son a burger at the pub. His property is on Jamieson Lane, the route from the Wilsons' place to Dalgety.

'We almost missed seeing Fred's truck, it was so far down in the trench,' Lachy said. 'We moved the branch and got him out of there.'

It was much more dramatic than that. Fred said his rescuer had risked his life as the wind continued to bend the trees, and Lachy used superhuman effort to drag the big branch off the top of the truck.

'The door was buckled but Lachy kicked and kicked until he could get it open,' Fred said. 'I reckoned he wouldn't have enough energy left to pull me out but he did. He was like Superman.'

Studies have shown that people sometimes demonstrate extraordinary strength in crisis situations. When I interviewed Lachy in the Dalgety pub afterwards, he was humble to the point of embarrassment. He refused to talk about the gash to his forearm that he'd sustained in the rescue. Nor did he wish to speak about his role in eastern Africa on water projects for organisations like the World Bank, USAID and WaterAid.

Country folk always help out in times of need but Fred's rescue was extraordinary. Lachy Wilson is a true hero.

Bullshit. Surely they'd mistaken him for someone else. Lachy Wilson was pathetic and weak, definitely not a hero. But that was him in the photo with Fred Whyte. And it did explain his injury, and why his shoulders, back and quads ached this morning.

Except the self-loathing made it impossible to believe he'd done a good thing.

He'd read that some people behaved in the opposite way when they were experiencing a blackout: pacifists became violent; introverts became extroverts; wallflowers had sex with strangers. Lachy Wilson drove drunk. He pictured his ute upside down in the ditch, Kai trapped in the cab instead of Fred Whyte. Shaking his head, he tried to dispel the image, but it was replaced by another. Punching a bikie in full leathers outside the Dalgety pub. And yet another: a girl, Juliet or Tiffany, begging him to stop. Were these actual memories or delirious imaginings?

Glancing up from the newspaper, he noticed Kai watching him.

'You were a great help, mate.' He smiled at Kai to cover his memory loss. 'But how did this make the paper today?'

'The journalist said they had no power last night because of the storm so they were printing this morning instead. Remember, he was keen to do a human-interest story. The editor keeps making him write livestock reports.' Kai was watching him, so he nodded quickly.

Lachy had imagined so many different versions of those missing hours—a car accident with Kai; a fight in the street; a fall down the steps of the pub; climbing over a barbed-wire fence. Here it was in the newspaper, but he still couldn't believe it. None of it felt real. Imagine if he had written evidence of those other blackouts—then there would be clarity. No, he didn't want any evidence of how badly he'd behaved.

That headline calling him a hero . . . if only they knew.

Sheridan passed him a cup of tea and asked if he needed to see a doctor about his arm.

'No, it's fine.' He wouldn't show it to her; she'd disagree. 'Thanks for shopping.'

'Anything for our local hero.' Her mocking was gentle. 'Mum will be so proud of you. I got an extra copy to put up on her wall. She was good when I saw her yesterday.'

He felt a twinge of guilt; he hadn't been to Sydney for months, using the excuse that Kai needed to settle in here. Really, he'd been hiding out, avoiding friends, including Nick.

'I'll visit her soon.' It would be good to see Mum; just being in her presence would calm him. Her hugs were a mug of mulled wine by the fire in winter—warm, cheering. In personality and appearance, he resembled their mum while Sheridan, with her auburn hair and rounded cheeks, was more like their dad. And that was how the family allegiances were drawn. He grieved for Dad and missed him, but Mum's death would destroy him. Although she'd already started disappearing right in front of them, the holes in her brain ravaging her memories. He understood how she must feel in moments of lucidity: totally and utterly terrified.

'I was showing her photos of Kai's third birthday,' Sheridan said. 'Do you remember that?'

'Uh-huh.' Why would she choose photos of that nightmarish party?

'Your dad had just arrived home from the Pacific,' she told Kai, 'so Glamma planned a sun and surf theme. She bought you a little Hawaiian shirt and matching ones for the men.'

They'd been so excited to have Kai stay for a week at Mimosa. Mum had set up a picnic by the creek, reimagining it as a beach, with deckchairs, beach balls, even a fake palm tree. Dad lit a fire and they grilled sausages and toasted marshmallows. And Mum had made tropical cocktails, filling huge blue plastic glasses with Malibu, coconut cream, pineapple slices and those little umbrellas.

The rest of them must have been busy cooking when Mum took her three-year-old grandson to the numbingly cold creek.

'I've seen the pictures,' Kai said to Sheridan. 'Don't remember it, though.'

Thank God he didn't. He'd slipped on the wet rocks into the water.

'Well, Nick was just like your dad in the paper today. A hero! When you fell into the creek, Nick rushed in, pulled you out and saved your life.'

Lachy had just taken a sip of tea and choked on it. 'Huh? That's not what happened!'

His sister gave him a patronising smile, like a teacher whose student had passed a difficult test.

'Dad was the one who rescued me.' Kai beamed. 'He jumped in fully clothed. I'd turned blue from the cold and Dad wrapped me in the picnic blanket.'

Back in the cabin, Lachy had run a bubble bath to warm him. He'd blamed himself for not keeping a closer eye on his son. For weeks, he'd worried that Kai would come down with pneumonia and Amber would restrict access. Neither happened. Now, thinking back, he wondered if Mum had been prone to blackout drinking too. Had she downed those cocktails fast, taken Kai for a walk and forgotten about him?

'Of course your dad rescued you,' Sheridan said. 'He's the hero.'

Lachy frowned. 'Why would you say it was Nick?'

'Just a bit of fun to test the memory.' He caught her winking at Kai. 'We need to keep the Wilson family legends straight.'

Had Kai said something to her about last night? Was that why she'd come down early? He thought he'd covered himself expertly. Except, of course, he'd forgotten about the heroic rescue. That was the trouble with memory: if you didn't know what you were supposed to remember, it was impossible to fake.

He had another moment of disorientation when he opened the fridge to find a container full of vegetable korma. He must have cooked it yesterday for dinner. Well, at least tonight's meal was sorted. He left Sheridan and Kai in the kitchen, saying, 'I just have to send a few emails before the end of the work day.'

In his bedroom, he sat at his desk staring through the window. A flock of galahs painted the sky pink and grey with their wings. The trunks of the snow gums were mottled white, brown and grey. Granite boulders reminded him of the history of the land, the rock four hundred million years old.

He couldn't reconcile himself with the hero in the newspaper. He'd done the wrong thing in Kenya, crumbled in Washington DC, stuffed up with Juliet, and been a lousy father to Kai.

Maybe he would hide out here forever, like Ronnie.

Suddenly he could picture another landscape on a different continent. Vultures circled overhead, their rasping cries sending goosebumps down his arms. Scrappy bushes bordered the dried-up creek. The land stretched out around him, yellow and dusty. Dotted across the dirt lay the carcasses of goats, leathery, contorted, mouths open as if still searching for a drink. The images were a slideshow, and he knew what was coming next. He put his hands over his ears to stop the sound inside his head.

The sound of pain. A guttural howl from the depths of a soul. Those screams ambushed him at random moments: as he made his morning coffee; when he was on his laptop; in the shower; driving the ute. A psychologist would call it emotional trauma compounded by his experiences. But it wasn't exactly *his* trauma; he didn't have to live it himself. He'd met so many locals in so many different countries facing climate disasters; their family members were dying every day from a lack of water.

Those screams. The one memory he yearned to forget.

Blinking away tears, he opened the laptop and clicked on his in-box. Carefully avoiding any work emails, he scanned the list for a message from Juliet. Three notifications from DNA:Match with names he didn't recognise. Probably distant cousins who wanted to get in touch. Nothing from Juliet. Why wasn't she answering? She'd asked him to tick the box to share his results to the DNA:Match database so she could access them. While he'd only got the hard copy yesterday, she would have received it ages ago. She was in America where their DNA had been tested. His tears turned to anger in a second. He'd done exactly as she asked. How dare she keep him hanging like this?

He couldn't bear not knowing.

If Sheridan quizzed him on the night he'd met Juliet, that would result in a hard fail.

He wouldn't drink over Easter; he wouldn't drink ever again.

Damn, Nick always brought a case of craft beer for them to share. He'd take it easy, sip slowly, tip some down the sink.

He had to get his shit together and keep up the pretence.

7

SHERIDAN

SHERIDAN HAD CHANGED THE STORY OF KAI'S THIRD BIRTHDAY TO SEE Lachy's response—he was insulted. Good; there was nothing wrong with his long-term memory. While she was frying a steak for Kai, she'd watched Lachy prepare their dinner: boiling rice, reheating the korma, serving food. He chatted normally during the meal and cleared up afterwards. He asked the right questions about Nick and the girls. A blank expression had flickered across his face when they were discussing last night's rescue, but maybe his brain was still processing it.

Was Kai really worried about his dad's memory, or was something else troubling him? The school bully or the accident itself? The crushed vehicle in the ditch, the power of the wind, his dad putting himself at risk, and the phenomenal effort to free Fred Whyte. It must have been terrifying; perhaps he'd called her for some motherly comfort.

This morning, Kai had gone off on the school bus happily enough and had come home this afternoon excited about the holiday break. She didn't know what to think.

The three of them were having afternoon tea when Ronnie's truck lumbered up the driveway. They went out to greet her near the woodpile. Sheridan hadn't seen their neighbour in so long, but the weathered face was the same, tanned by the sun.

Two of Ronnie's dogs balanced on the logs in the tray of her truck, protecting the haul. Another jumped down and shoved its nose into Sheridan's crotch. She pushed it away and leant forward to hug Ronnie, who pointedly stepped backwards to avoid her embrace.

'I had a dead tree down and heaps of firewood.' Ronnie gestured at the logs. 'Thought you could use some for Easter.'

'Really appreciate it,' Lachy said. 'But you should've told us. Kai and I would have helped cut it up.'

She could see Kai shaking his head slightly; Lachy hadn't converted him into a country lad yet. But at least the teenager was with them, ready to lift the logs off the truck.

As they began shifting the wood, Sheridan could picture herself as a twenty-one-year-old, standing in this very spot with Dad. He'd asked about her dreams. *I want to work with people and I want to be my own boss one day.* She'd achieved that, but it didn't resemble the life she'd envisioned. She had never told Dad her real dream—to work on a cruise ship on the events side, maybe as a cruise director—because that was too close to Mum's career. And Sheridan was the sensible one, like Dad, not fun and outgoing like Mum. Her brother had claimed that role. Cruise director: a ridiculous dream, incompatible with marriage and children. Funny how the memory came back to her now.

Ronnie stacked some logs on the woodpile then turned to her. 'How's Gloria doing?'

'She's okay. I wish I could've brought her down for Easter but it's too hard.'

'Well, if there's a chance of her coming for a few days, let me know.' Ronnie sighed. 'I'd really like to see her. I miss her. Miss them both. No offence'—she nodded at Lachy and Kai—'but it's not the same here without them.'

For God's sake, Ronnie had no idea how difficult life was for Mum. They'd tried taking her to their house for lunch before Christmas and it had been a nightmare; she'd become more agitated at every transition. 'Call the police!' she'd shouted to a passing dog walker. 'I'm being kidnapped!' The whole experience was heartbreaking, and it had taken weeks for them all to recover.

'You should come and visit her,' she said instead.

It was a direct challenge: Ronnie wouldn't leave her farm; she'd dropped out of life. Giving up on the world instead of addressing the challenges, breaking down the obstacles and moving forward.

'I don't do the city.' Ronnie folded her arms tightly across her chest. 'Too many cars, too many people, too many shops. Just breathing in the smoggy air costs you money.'

'Life's expensive everywhere at the moment. I don't know how you survive down here, money-wise.'

It was an off-the-cuff comment. Her farm didn't seem to provide an income, but Ronnie didn't interpret it that way.

'I survive,' Ronnie barked. 'And my finances are none of your business. Are you working for the government now? Checking up on my income? Or are you about to offer me a too-good-to-be-true investment that'll make me rich forever?'

Quashing her laughter, Sheridan bent to retrieve a log that had fallen from the truck. A spy, a scammer, the government— they were all the same to Ronnie: someone thieving from you. Where did she get these ideas? Out in the paddocks, listening to radio shock jocks?

Lachy jabbed a finger into her side, a warning to play nice; he had to live next door to the paranoid neighbour.

'Sorry,' she said. 'I didn't mean to sound like I was prying.'

Taking no notice of her apology, Ronnie barrelled on. 'Living down here on as little as possible is good for the planet. You're killing the world with your fancy houses and your swish cars and your city lifestyle. Women shouldn't even be having kids. The kids will pay the price of a doomed planet. Mothers are the worst.'

Actually, this rant was the worst. Women, mothers were carrying the weight of the world on their shoulders. Why wasn't she ranting about men and fathers? Before Sheridan could argue that particular point, Kai piped up.

'But no kids will lead to no humans—and no-one to help you shift those planks on Monday, Ronnie. Dad said you needed us to come down to your place.'

Ronnie gave a short cackle and punched his shoulder. 'You're right, mate. But at least you're going to feed me first on Sunday.'

She called the dogs, corralled them onto the back of the truck, then drove off with a wave. Sheridan felt physically winded. What the hell was that rant? Honestly. Mothers like her were the ones doing it all: bringing up the kids; organising family life, school life, the community; looking after ageing parents. She was smack bang in the sandwich generation, a decade earlier than expected, and bloody tired.

'Don't tell me you invited her to lunch on Sunday?' The thought of another conversation with Ronnie made her feel even more exhausted. 'Seriously, Lachy, why would you do that?'

He gave a low laugh. 'I thought it would be nice.'

Back inside the cabin, she couldn't stop thinking about Ronnie's words. How dare she! Sheridan tried her best, every fricking day. Ronnie only cared about herself; she didn't look after anyone else apart from her animals, who were sending methane into the atmosphere with every poo. Their neighbour was totally self-centred. She should have reminded Ronnie that everyone had a mother, even her.

Flinging open the door to her bedroom, she jumped yet again at the sight of Betty.

'Jesus, Betty, you scared the hell out of me.'

Betty sat in a chair like a toddler waiting in the naughty corner. No doubt Lachy had propped her there, hoping for this exact response. It was a favourite trick, placing Betty in a surprise spot: on the toilet, above the TV, in the passenger seat in the ute. The worst time was when Sheridan pulled back her doona to get into bed and there was Betty staring up at her, a corpse in the morgue. Maximum fright factor.

And Betty was even more frightening now: her knitted arms lumpy and misshapen, loose strands of wool shedding from her blonde plaits. The pink dress had frayed at the seams; it was one of Sheridan's from when she was four. Her tan face, made from a soft leather, had scratches across it, her lips were faded and her nose squashed.

When she'd been the same size as the doll, Sheridan had called her 'Sissy' and kissed her goodnight. She'd shared tea parties with her. But once Lachy was big enough to play games, she decided the doll, with her huge, unblinking eyes, could read her thoughts.

'Betty's evil,' she'd told Mum. 'I don't want her in my room anymore.'

'Don't be silly. Betty doesn't have a mean bone in her woolly body. Maybe *you* have evil thoughts—that's what my father would say.'

Sheridan had burst into tears.

'I'm so sorry, my love.' Mum pulled her onto her lap. 'I don't know why that came out. My daddy was very scary with his horrible words. I promised I'd never say them to my babies.'

'Am I evil?' she'd sobbed.

'Absolutely not. You're my kind, caring Sheridan.'

Letting out a long sigh, she collapsed on the bed. 'Betty, you look terrible. How can I possibly make you presentable for Mum?' God, she was talking to a bloody doll. Going loopy like Ronnie.

An alarm sounded on her phone. Time for the check-in with her clients. Sitting up again, she grabbed her laptop from the bedside table. Brendan had sent an email answering her questions about visualising success and the obstacles in his path. At the end, he'd added another line: *Fiona and I would love to host your family for lunch. Come up next week and taste all the spirits. You're part of our success story!* It was such a pleasure to work with Brendan; he committed his time and energy to self-improvement, and he reaped the rewards. Unlike Heidi with her negative self-talk, endless excuses and fixed mindset. After eight sessions, she'd barely progressed; maybe, deep down, she felt she didn't deserve success. She hadn't done the work again this week and Sheridan sent her a message oozing with encouragement. Next, she focused on her two new clients: Dom, just starting his career, and Tamara, at her peak. Dom had relocated from Canada to Australia with an international accounting firm and wanted to set some work and lifestyle goals. Tamara was currently a director with a big mining company and considering a move into the charity sector. She'd said to call her Tammy—it seemed a cutesy name for a senior manager in a male-dominated industry. Sheridan emailed them introductory worksheets about outlining their goals.

Coaching individual clients and seeing them succeed gave her such a thrill. Years of working in the HR department of a large manufacturing company had wearied her—the power imbalance between employer and employee, the pressure from both the directors and the union, the win-lose mentality. In her life-coaching business, she could concentrate on one person and help them achieve the best outcome. That was the good part. She found the rest tedious: the logistics of working from home; the juggle of school and kids and Mum; the need to find new clients and the erratic income. She logged into her bank account to find Heidi's payment was late again. Nick would tell her to postpone the next session until her invoice had been paid, but Heidi would feel ashamed and end up quitting all together.

Footsteps in the hallway made her glance up from the laptop. 'Can I interrupt for a sec?' Lachy asked.

She closed her computer, wondering if Heidi's husband was against the concept of life coaching. Some people, like her brother, didn't understand it and dismissed it as a fad. When doing her training, she'd asked Lachy to be one of her practice clients. He'd agreed at first, but then said it was too difficult while he was based in Kenya. Maybe she should offer again now that he was back. They could discuss how he was managing his responsibilities for Kai and his work, if he felt resentful about the parenting role and staying in Australia, and where he imagined his future. She loved having him home, even though they hadn't seen much of him. Mum and Dad used to worry about the risky places he was working; they'd see a media headline—SOMALIAN REBELS ASSAULT ON KENYA BORDER—and ring her immediately. Their parents would have been overjoyed about him living at Mimosa Hideout with Kai; it hurt that she couldn't tell Dad, while Mum wouldn't understand the significance.

As Lachy came further into the room, he did a double take. 'Why's Betty sitting there like that?'

She snorted. 'Ha! Now you're scaring yourself. You're the one who put her there.'

'Did I? Or has Kai joined our game?' He sat on the bed next to her. 'Sorry I didn't ask you before inviting Ronnie. It just came out when I was talking to her yesterday. I'm the only person she sees.'

'She's getting worse, don't you think? It's going to be an interesting lunch.' Sheridan thought back to their earlier conversation. 'She said she misses Mum and Dad. I mean, I know they were friends but . . .'

'Ronnie barely leaves the farm, so they were her *only* friends. Now it's me and Kai. She's all right. Just eccentric.'

More than eccentric, Sheridan thought, but she wouldn't argue with him tonight. 'What about her secret life? Have you found out more? Techno dance parties at her house? Online romances?'

They'd had so many theories over the years, trying to unravel the mystery of Ronnie.

'She's busy playing in a FIFA esports comp.' He pretended to click a gaming console. 'She's winning heaps of money.'

'When I saw Mum yesterday morning, she remembered Ronnie. Did you know she and Dad were trying to guess what she was hiding from too?' Sheridan paused. 'Mum was really with it for about ten minutes. You should come up to see her in the school holidays.'

'Yeah, I will.' His answer was too quick, agreeing without actually thinking about it. Then he moved the conversation right back to Ronnie. 'I can't believe Mum and Dad were playing the same guessing game. And they told us to stop being disrespectful!'

They had five days to discuss him visiting Mum. She decided not to push it and spoil the mood. 'Did you see Ronnie's purple boots? Her latest venture is designer gumboots. They're selling like hotcakes.'

'Hotcakes? I heard she took up baking and she'll be a contestant on *Farmer Wants a Wife*.'

The thought of Ronnie making multi-layered cakes on a dating show set them both off, and suddenly they were teenagers again, in hysterics.

'Are you two all right?' Kai called from the kitchen, as if he were the adult checking on the kids. That made them laugh harder.

'Yeah, mate,' Lachy shouted. 'All good.'

When their laughter had subsided, she rubbed his back.

'I'm sure you're missing being overseas, but you're doing the right thing.' She gestured to the doll, smiling in the corner. 'Even Betty agrees that you're a great dad and a local hero.'

8

ELIZABETH, 1968

I COULD HEAR THE SWISH OF THE BELT THROUGH THE AIR BEFORE IT connected with my thighs. *Thwack.* Flinching with the shock of it against my soft flesh, I bit my lip to stop myself from making a sound. Father did not permit crying. As a distraction, I rested my eyes on the rosebushes; beautiful red roses stood tall and straight on one bush, while another was dotted with yellow buds. Father nurtured these hedges and took bouquets to sick community members. On our birthdays, we were allowed a posy of yellow roses on the dining table. The red rose symbolised the blood of Christian martyrs. Father's belt never made us bleed; we were not martyrs but disobedient servants. Heat bloomed on my legs. I knew the red mark would remain for a whole week, replacing the one from last Saturday.

From here, I could also see the back of the wooden potting shed. Under a shelf, beneath a loose plank, I'd hidden a small metal trunk. Everything in our house was shared, but I wanted a place for my secret things, especially my library books.

'Elizabeth, what do you have to say in the presence of God and of us all?' Father demanded.

The whupping was a family event: we had to learn from each other's mistakes. Mother, Gloria, Theresa, Virginia and Ernest stood in a circle around me. We were being raised to meet God's expectations, learning how to be ladylike, how to run the house, grow vegetables, look after the chickens and the milking cow. As the only boy, Ernest's lessons focused on how to become a man and God's messenger.

All of us needed to understand how to please our father.

'I'm sorry, Father.' I held my body tense, absorbing the pain. 'I will not talk to boys on the bus again.'

'What are you?' Father deepened his voice as if he were directly channelling our Lord.

'I'm impure. Immoral.' My cheeks felt as hot as the marks on my thighs. 'I'm a slattern. I'm a Jezebel.'

Father turned to the others. 'What is she?' he asked.

'She's a slattern,' my family repeated. Gloria was the loudest. 'She's a Jezebel.'

Those boys were loose and fast, and one of them, Eddie, had invited me to the drive-in, otherwise known as the passion pit. Everyone knew what happened there—a girl's virtue was violated. Even though it was wrong, I wanted to go with Eddie and let him kiss me. I'd been talking to the boys on the way home from school for a month. Gloria had turned a blind eye but Theresa noticed last week. Of course, my little sister had told Father.

'Pray for her forgiveness,' Father continued.

'Guide her way, oh Lord.' My family spread their arms, linked hands and encircled me. 'We open our hearts to you, Jesus!'

Father touched my bent head, his warm hands carrying the

warmth of Jesus's forgiveness. I was sorry to disappoint Father but not sorry that I'd spoken to Eddie.

Each of us disappointed Father in our own way. Theresa's whupping was for tearing her stockings. Ernest was punished for gobbling three slices of cake. Virginia asked an impertinent question about the human body. Gloria was too old for a whupping, so she had 'discussions' with Father and had to pray for an hour afterwards. Not that she did much wrong.

We all had to be on our best behaviour for the upcoming nuptials of Mother's young cousin Constance to a boring man called Melvin. They were moving into the caretaker's cottage at Camp Happiness over in Montgomery County. Our parents were delighted about the wedding, the second in our church this year. Presiding over a ceremony of holy wedlock was a privilege, Father said, and the way for our Good News community to grow. Every week, Father reminded our congregation of Hebrews 13:4: *Marriage is honourable in all, and the bed undefiled: but whoremongers and adulterers God will judge.*

Gloria and I would have a double wedding when I turned eighteen, and Mother was busy expanding our home-making skills to ensure we'd be ready to manage a household. But when I had my own kitchen, I hoped to use it for parties, not canning home-grown vegetables. At the library, I'd seen an advertisement in *Life* magazine for Campbell's Oyster Stew: it looked delicious, and you only needed a can opener. I would serve onion soup dip from a packet, oyster stew and a pineapple upside-down cake. The magazine also had a recipe for a brandy alexander cocktail, but Father said alcohol was the devil's drink; it stole your thoughts.

Father was assessing potential husbands for us. They'd be Good News boys, of course, though none of them made me tingly like the bad boys on the bus. There were things I needed to do before I became a wife: go to the drive-in, kiss Eddie, eat in a restaurant, catch a train to Philadelphia. I wanted to see the films that had everybody talking. Father had preached on the evils of one called *The Graduate*, in which a young man was seduced by an older, married woman—a whoremonger and an adulterer together. I'd read an article in *Life* magazine that said the graduate was an 'archetype of youthful angst'. Was youthful angst this agitated feeling I had?

Life also had a story about an actor, Robert Redford—gosh, he was handsome with those piercing blue eyes. That cheeky smile implied a sense of mischievousness; he was a grown-up version of the boys on the bus. I'd marry someone like him in a heartbeat. But the men in our church community were nothing like Mr Robert Redford. We'd known most of the prospective husbands our entire lives.

If Father discovered I was visiting the library and browsing the magazines, there would be another whupping. He'd forbidden us from reading newspapers because the country was in a tumultuous time but I would glance at the headlines. The librarian was aghast the day that *The Washington Post* reported 'Dr King is Slain in Memphis'. The governor ordered four thousand National Guard troops into the city to stop unrest. But Father didn't want us talking about racial segregation and the rioting in Baltimore and Pittsburgh, nor about the long-haired students protesting America's involvement in Vietnam.

And Father believed women going to work was an attack on the American way of life. If he saw the library book I'd borrowed and hidden in the potting shed, he would ban every book apart from the Bible. In *The Feminine Mystique*, the author, Betty Friedan, shared her thoughts, along with those of other housewives she'd interviewed. Father would be particularly horrified by the chapter on seeking sexual fulfilment. I didn't understand it all. But I felt there was more to my future than looking after a husband and children. I loved my mother but I could not live her life.

✕

After Father had prayed for us all, it was time for me to feed the chickens. The skin on my thighs stung as I carried the bowl of vegetable scraps out to the henhouse. Gloria joined me to check for fresh eggs. She was only eleven months older but she'd changed over the past year: now, she was so sure of her place in the world, obeying our parents and the church without complaint. Last April, she would have been questioning the rules, like me.

Keen to read another chapter of Betty Friedan, I ducked into the potting shed and retrieved it from my secret trunk. If Gloria covered for me, I'd have time.

'Please can you do the kids' bath without me?' I begged her. 'I have to take this back to the library by Wednesday.'

'You shouldn't even have it.' She shook her head. 'It's a sin. If Father sees it . . .'

'Please don't tell.'

'Okay, not this time.' She gave a martyred sigh. 'But don't you see? Evil is all around us. We must choose the right path.'

'But what *is* the right path?' I asked. 'Why would God give us these opportunities if He didn't mean for us to embrace them? Women are working outside the home for the church. You have an afternoon job; why shouldn't you be paid for it?'

One of the assistant pastors had been sent on a mission to Africa, and Father had asked Gloria to take the youth class in his absence. Since then, Gloria had become utterly focused on setting a good example and a lot less fun.

'I have a calling, not a job. I'm humbled to serve the Lord.' She clasped her hands and held them to her heart.

'You're so good at teaching. Maybe we could be missionaries instead of getting married straight away? We could go to Africa or Australia.'

Oh, how I wanted to experience more than our small patch of Leeville, Berks County. Those names on the world map in the church office sounded so exotic: Kenya, Tanzania, Nigeria, Ghana, the Republic of Uganda. Was it wrong to have a selfish motive while spreading God's word?

'There are no lady missionaries.' Gloria arched her eyebrows. 'Once we're married, we can go as wives.'

'Don't you want a little freedom before you become a wife?' My cry came out more impassioned than I'd meant it to, and she frowned.

'Freedom? We will have our freedom in heaven, Betty. You know what Father says. Freedom today is a selfish shirking of duty.'

Father's latest warning had been about teenagers searching for freedom through dangerous new music, listening to bands like The Beatles and The Monkees. But the world was advancing, and my Father and my church were stuck in the 1950s. I clutched Betty Friedan's book to my chest. A woman called Betty had written this radical book and her words were changing society. Women had a duty to participate fully in life and not be cloistered at home; a duty to broaden our knowledge. And, yes, a duty to God, to experience the wonders of His world.

We heard the back door bang.

'Quick,' Gloria whispered. 'Hide your book. I'll tell Father you're locking up the chickens.'

My dear selfless sister. Even though she disapproved, she'd protect me from Father's wrath. She hadn't completely changed.

When I returned from the potting shed, Father was waiting.

'Elizabeth, I have a task for you on Wednesday,' he said. 'You are to assist with the evening meal at the Soldiers' Home near Pottstown. It will remind you of your duty and how you must resist the devil's temptations.'

The boys on the bus would slap their knees and hoot at Father labelling them *the devil's temptations*.

Pottstown was twenty miles away, just over the border in Montgomery County. Not quite Philadelphia, but closer than our house. Maybe the Soldiers' Home would have a library with interesting books. Or maybe I'd meet a boy on the bus trip there. I set my mouth in a contrite line to stop myself from smiling about my punishment.

9

KAI

KAI PROPPED ANOTHER PILLOW BEHIND HIS HEAD. IN THE BEDROOM next to him, Dad and Sheridan were still laughing. Ignoring them, he kept scrolling through his phone; Snap Maps showed most of his mates hanging out together on Narrabeen beach. Should he video-call them or would that make him feel worse?

He'd texted a photo of the newspaper article to Hudson and Mum. Hudson thought it was *EPIC*. Mum asked: *Are you okay? Were you hurt too?*

You couldn't get hurt if you stood by and watched.

Maybe there'd been a mix-up at the hospital when he was born. It'd be easy to do; newborns all had the same red, squishy face. That would explain why he hadn't inherited any of Dad's heroic DNA. Sure, he'd helped Dad a little that night, done whatever he asked—*Lift that end, Kai. Hold the rope. Watch for dropping branches*—but he'd been terrified every minute. Scared of the petrol tank exploding; scared of being impaled by a falling tree; scared of Dad getting trapped along with Fred; scared of the roaring wind. He was a freaking scaredy-cat.

He'd glimpsed Fred's truck in the ditch before Dad and thought nothing. If it had been up to him, they'd have driven straight past, and the old farmer would be dead.

Kai pressed the button on his phone and Hudson's face filled the screen.

'Barbie on the beach!' Hudson shouted, bringing a half-eaten sausage to his mouth and taking another bite. While he was chewing, he panned the camera around their group of friends. They were at their usual spot on the grass near the surf life-saving club. Jezza stood by the barbecue and waved a pair of tongs in greeting; Marley tossed a juggling ball towards the phone; Cooper and Abby lounged on a towel, inseparable as usual. Ellie, Isla and Lauren were walking on the beach. Two figures bobbed in the water, too far away for him to see properly—Richie and Tom probably.

'Still warm enough to swim, hey?' A dumb thing to say but the one which hurt the least. 'It's already cold down here.'

He could smell the sea, taste the burnt sausages, feel the sand under his feet. And Ellie: he'd almost kissed her at a party on the beach before Christmas. Her black hair hung down between her shoulders, not in a ponytail like usual. Or maybe she wore it like that all the time now. He wouldn't know. She hadn't answered his last message.

Seeing them all together reinforced his plan to talk to Dad; surely, they could go to Sydney for a few days while Mum and Simmo were in Indonesia. Kai would catch up with his mates while Dad visited Glamma.

Onscreen, Hudson, Jezza and Marley were having a convo, but he couldn't hear what they were saying. Eventually, Hudson remembered Kai at the other end of the phone.

'That was epic about your dad.' He turned to shout at the others. 'Kai's dad saved a bloke trapped in a truck. He was in the paper, and it said he had superhuman strength. He lifted the truck off him!'

'Like Thor.'

'Did he lift it with one finger?'

'That's so cool.'

'How can you pick up a truck?'

'Fucking wild, mate!'

'Actually,' Kai tried to explain to his friends, 'Dad didn't lift up the truck, he lifted a tree branch.' But they were no longer listening; Jezza was handing out more sausages, Hudson and Cooper passed a vape between them, and Marley was wandering towards the toilet block.

'Um, okay then.' He raised his voice. 'Great to see you. I've gotta go and do some stuff.'

They didn't even hear him.

The pain of everything he was missing in Sydney grew even sharper the following day when his freckly-faced, ginger-haired cousins tumbled out of Uncle Nick's car. Mabel was slurping a Macca's thickshake. Every Friday after school, Kai and his mates would get a Big Mac meal from Warriewood McDonald's. It was the hang: all the plans were hatched there, from a swim at the beach to party nights. And it was where he and Hudson collected cash and discreetly passed over little plastic bags. They'd become pretty popular. But it wasn't like he and Hudson were actual dealers; they just helped out their friends. And it meant he could buy stuff like Xbox games and a new wetsuit. Mum and Simmo found out he'd been taking drugs when Hudson got rushed to hospital back in December, and they'd gone ballistic. Hudson's parents had grounded him for a few months but his life was back to normal now.

'Kaiiiiiiiiii!' Eloise ran towards him, her long wavy hair flying out behind.

Mabel followed carefully, cradling her thickshake; she could be precious and whiny. The two of them were a similar age to his half-sisters, similar in lots of ways, except Daisy and Willow did Nippers and surfing while Eloise and Mabel did ballet lessons. He hadn't expected to miss his little sisters as much as he did. They always wanted his attention and he'd tell them to get lost; Mum and Simmo must have been loving how calm it was at home this term.

'We haven't seen you foreveeeeeeer!' Eloise clasped her arms around his waist, and he reached down and hugged her back. He wished Daisy and Willow were here too. The four girls hardly ever saw each other. Last year for his birthday, Sheridan organised afternoon tea at her house. Daisy had wandered into Eloise's bedroom, taken out the iPad and the dolls and the books. She'd come downstairs sobbing. 'I want another family too. Kai has extra cousins. Why can't I?' He didn't know if an extra family was good or bad . . . it just was.

And now his cousins were begging for his attention. Mabel had finished slurping her drink and was tugging on his left hand. 'Did you see I lost a tooth?'

'Wow, look at that!' He admired her gappy smile. 'Did the tooth fairy come?'

'Yup. She left me two dollars. I bought a Wizz Fizz.'

Eloise tugged his right hand. 'Can you take us to the creek?'

'Can you build a fire?'

'Can we play hide-and-seek?'

Pretending to be overwhelmed by their questions, he collapsed to the ground. The girls giggled and sat on top of him. Tickling them was his way of escaping. They screamed in delight.

'Say hello to Uncle Lachy first,' Kai suggested, 'then we'll play hide-and-seek.'

They disappeared inside. In her excitement, Mabel had dropped her thickshake cup on the ground. Kai picked it up and sniffed the remnants—mmm, the smell of civilisation. The nearest Macca's was more than an hour away, in Cooma.

'They're certainly happy to see you,' Nick said. 'I guess it was a boring car trip with me.'

When they shook hands, Kai found himself at eye level with his uncle. Nick was shorter than Dad, though his curly blond hair gave him a few extra centimetres in height.

'I'm almost as tall as you!' Kai couldn't believe it. He didn't have the usual people to compare himself against; Hudson had always been the tallest.

'Almost a man.' Nick nodded seriously.

Nah, he didn't feel like a man.

'How are you enjoying life down here?' Nick asked.

'Yeah, great. I'm seeing some mates tonight.'

Dad had agreed to a bonfire with the boys, which was how Kai had sold it. If he could get Nick to drive him there, that might be even better. He'd just started asking about a lift when Dad came out of the back door and strode towards them.

'Hey, Rattlesnake.' Dad grabbed Nick in a kind of wrestling move and almost knocked him over.

'Cut it out, Coyote; you might be faster but I'm heavier.' Nick ruffled Dad's hair and the two of them laughed.

Their nicknames, Rattlesnake and Coyote, sounded all wrong out here; they'd got them at an American summer camp where they'd first met, the only Aussies working there. Almost twenty years later Dad and Nick were still best mates. Kai had only been away from Sydney for a term and his mates were already losing interest in him. Out of sight, out of mind.

But tonight was an opportunity to make new friends. Tarni had given him directions and a reminder to bring the gear.

Kai played hide-and-seek outside with the girls for ages. He kept an eye on his watch and brought them into the lounge room when it was time for him to shower. They complained about him finishing their fun, so he took out the box of Trouble from the games cupboard. Minutes later, they were hammering the pop-up dice and laughing again. In his bedroom, he debated which shirt to wear. Pink? The girls would like it but the boys would laugh. Dark green? Probably didn't matter. It'd be cold and he'd wear a hoodie.

After choosing the green shirt, he crept back into the empty lounge room. Eloise and Mabel were now in the kitchen with their parents. If they heard him, they'd come running, so he eased open the doors of the cupboard as quietly as possible. When he'd got the box of Trouble earlier, he'd repositioned the Philadelphia puzzle on top of the pile. Glamma and Granddad had loved playing games and doing jigsaw puzzles. Glamma always received a new puzzle for Christmas. She'd lay the pieces out on the coffee table and family members would help her for five minutes until they were sick of it.

Pulling the Philadelphia puzzle box onto the floor, he decided to give out all the pills tonight—that was how he'd make friends, by sharing freely. If he cut them in half, there would be sixteen. Sixteen new mates. Hopefully he could get to Sydney in the holidays so Hudson could replenish his supply. He knelt in front of the puzzle box, his body blocking the sight of it from anyone who might enter the room, and took off the lid. A thousand pieces of Independence Hall, a kaleidoscope of colours.

But no white envelope underneath containing a plastic bag of pink-and-blue pills.

He scrabbled through the box with both hands, running the jigsaw pieces through his fingers.

Shit—where was it?

Glancing into the cupboard, he spotted the edge of a white envelope between two boxes. Phew. But when he had it in his hands, he saw Dad's handwriting on the envelope: BLUE PUZZLE PIECE. And inside was one puzzle piece.

So where the hell was his stash?

Had Dad discovered it after all?

Kai shoved the boxes back into the cupboard, his gut knotting in fear. The fact that Dad had found it and said nothing could only mean one thing—he was waiting to tell Mum when she got home.

And then she would turn him in to the police.

10

LACHY

SINCE HE'D ARRIVED, NICK HADN'T STOPPED RIBBING HIM ABOUT THE local hero headline. Jesus, Lachy wished he'd shut up. The more Nick and Sheridan went on, the more he felt like a fraud. Now they were at the kitchen bench and Nick was waving the newspaper in the air.

'Check this out, girls,' he said. 'Uncle Lachy is front-page news.'

Eloise took the paper, spread it out on the table and began reading slowly. 'Local hero in windstorm.' She smiled up at him. 'Lachy Wilson risked his own life in last night's windstorm to rescue Dal— How do you say this word?'

'Dalgety. It's a tiny village not far from here.' He inched the newspaper from her grip and redirected the conversation. 'Did you know Dalgety was originally chosen as the spot for our national capital? We could've been living near all the politicians.'

'But there's no city.' Mabel frowned. 'Where's Parliament House?'

'They build the buildings, dummy.' Eloise rolled her eyes at her younger sister.

Eloise, the know-it-all. He couldn't remember Sheridan being like that to him as an older sister; he'd just been desperate to do all the stuff she could do.

'When Canberra was chosen as the capital, it only had a few farm buildings and a river,' he explained. 'They designed a city with a lake in the middle.'

'True?' Mabel stared at him, wide-eyed. When he nodded, she grinned. 'I'm going to design a city when I grow up with a park on every corner. I want seesaws and slippery dips.'

The last time he'd driven through Canberra, more new suburbs had replaced natural ecosystems. Of course, it wasn't just the national capital, development marched on everywhere. But what sort of world would these girls inherit? A scorched, parched landscape with only the hardiest plants and animals remaining. Global heating was speeding up while sections of Australia acted like its resources were infinite. He couldn't bear to think about it.

'You'd be an excellent city designer.' Nick bent to kiss Mabel's hair before turning to Lachy. 'Hey, Coyote, let's take a quick walk on the ridge before it gets dark.'

Out on the track, Lachy tried to distinguish the line where the mountains met the sky. Grey and overcast with the waning light, the clouds and peaks were blurring into one another. A few of the summits had disappeared. Blurry, that was him; he didn't know who he was anymore.

Beside him, Nick lifted his knees and jogged on the spot. 'We should go for a run in the morning,' he said.

'Nah, not with this cut on my arm.' He spoke again before Nick had a chance to start on the hero jibes. 'You been running regularly? You'll lap me!'

Stockier than him and with stronger thighs, Nick had always been faster. If he'd seen Fred Whyte's truck, he would've done the same; the only difference was that Nick would have remembered rescuing the man. He was a proper grown-up: older and wiser, able to control himself.

'No time for running, I'm flat out at work. Still going to the gym twice a week, though—otherwise I'd have a heart attack from the stress.' Nick stopped the high knees and stretched his arms to the heavens. 'This space! So good to be here. Our house is bursting at the seams.'

'Move down here. Join us in the tree change.'

'Yeah, you're living the dream.' Nick sighed. 'But my work isn't as flexible as yours.'

Hah—hiding out here was definitely not living the dream. He wanted to tell his best mate about work, but Nick would discuss it with Sheridan, and she'd demand details and draw up a plan to fix it. There was no fixing it.

'I've missed you, mate.' He thumped Nick on the shoulder. 'Lots of space down here but my closest friend is Ronnie.'

Nick snorted. 'Only geographically, I hope. But you're used to this remote living.'

'I was always with a team overseas.' None of his colleagues had fallen apart like him. 'Now I can go days without seeing anyone other than Kai.'

'Lucky you're on all those Zoom meetings.'

He had to get off the topic of work. And he didn't want to go down the path of Nick and Sheridan's too-small house. At one point, Nick had raised the question of selling Mimosa Hideout so they could afford to buy a bigger place. Thankfully, Sheridan was as vehement in her answer as Lachy: they both wanted to keep the property as long as possible. Mimosa now held all their family memories, with their childhood home in Dural sold.

What he really wanted to talk about was Juliet.

'I . . . um . . . did a DNA test recently,' he started.

'What for?' Nick stopped walking and turned to face him. 'Don't tell me Kai's not actually your son after you've paid all that child support?'

Strange for Nick to jump to that conclusion. When Amber had fallen pregnant accidentally, they'd been infatuated with each other.

'Nothing to do with Kai.' He sucked in a lungful of cool air. 'I met this girl, Juliet, in America last September. After flying in from Kenya, I went to head office, then had a big night. It's a bit hazy.'

That was an understatement—the entire night was a blank. He'd been with his boss, Henrik, but Lachy couldn't ask him about it. Automatically he touched his tattoo, a branding which connected them. He really should read his work emails; there would be something about bloody Henrik. His blackout that night was Henrik's fault too.

'So you had a big night and met a girl?' Nick prompted him.

'Yeah, she was a lot younger than I realised. Maybe twenty-ish.'

Nick made a clucking noise with his tongue. 'Jesus, mate.'

'I know, I know.' His cheeks burnt. 'I didn't think we had sex . . . but then she asked me to do a DNA test because she's pregnant.'

'Oh, shit.'

'I did the test, of course.' He stared at the clouds, the lower part had turned a dusky pink with the setting sun. 'But I can't cope with a new baby in this world. What kind of future will it have? The whole thing has sent me into a spin.'

Nick grabbed his sore wrist and pain shot along his arm. 'Why did she get you to do a DNA test?'

'To confirm paternity.' He shrugged. 'I had to upload the results to a website. She said it was easier because I'm here and she's in the States. But now she's ghosted me. She won't answer my emails. Does that mean it's not my baby? I'm so confused.'

'Lachy, did you look into DNA testing?'

'I just did what she asked.' He'd already been depressed after Kenya and the thought of bringing a new baby into this overheating, overcrowded, fucked-up planet had sent him spiralling. Taking the test and sending it off had been enough of an effort—he hadn't researched anything.

'The thing is . . .' Nick took a breath. 'The thing is you don't normally do a DNA test for an unborn baby. You have to do a blood test.'

'That doesn't make sense.' He tried to think it through. 'We only met in September, and she asked me for the test months ago. The baby wouldn't have been born yet.'

'I think you've being scammed, mate.' Nick picked up a stick from the ground, avoiding eye contact. 'She must want your DNA for some other reason.'

'But what reason?'

His question remained unanswered and fear fluttered in his stomach. What had he done with Juliet? He couldn't remember having sex, couldn't remember anything. Like the first blackout with Tiffany and the last one with Fred Whyte, the night with Juliet was a blank. Just hours before he met her, he'd decided to give up on the world—his anger had seeped into despondency. Bloody hell, he'd driven with Kai, with Tiffany. Had he driven somewhere with Juliet too? Crashed her car? Hit a pedestrian? Drink driving was against all his principles. And this was the dread that ran through his veins: had he acted out of character with Juliet? With Tiffany? On any other blackout nights?

He'd always been too ashamed to discuss Tiffany but Nick's memories might help him understand how he'd behaved; hopefully he could then figure out if the same had happened with Juliet and why she'd asked for his DNA. He phrased the question tentatively while Nick dragged the stick through the dirt.

'What do you remember about that party at summer camp when Tiffany left?'

'Summer camp? Huh? What does that have to do with your DNA?'

'Nothing. I just . . . It's the first time I got shit-faced. The night with Juliet was the last time. Reckon I drink more in the States.'

'We certainly drank a lot at that party.' Nick snorted. 'We can blame it on Britt and the rum she stole from her parents. It was all chill at the beginning with s'mores and ghost stories by the campfire near the lake. Although Conrad was being a dick and kept doing jump scares.'

That part had stayed in Lachy's memory. He'd burnt his mouth on a flaming marshmallow. They went for a swim in their underwear and the girls were giggly and silly. Conrad made a move on Tiffany but she ignored him. She was dancing on the sand, fussing about the cold water. Lachy grabbed her and carried her into the lake; she was screaming and laughing and clinging to him. Really clinging to him. Even though he found her annoying, the sensation of her bare skin turned him on, his drunken desire overriding his true feelings. That worried him: he couldn't trust his drunk self. He didn't remember anything after the lake.

'Do you know why Tiffany wanted to leave in such a hurry that night?'

'You drove her to Deadwood Creek Road,' Nick said. 'I assume she told you.'

'No, she didn't.' He sighed. 'And I shouldn't have taken her.'

'Well, she was pretty insistent and she'd already packed a bag. Anyway, you were the only one who could drive. You were sober at that point.'

So he had appeared sober. Nick would be horrified to learn about the blackouts, the drink driving, the memory loss. Lachy only knew because Conrad had accosted him the next morning: *I can't believe you drove off with her in my pick-up truck. You should have made her stay at camp. She's the hottest one here. Was her friend waiting at the bridge on Deadwood Creek Road? Was it a guy?* Lachy had given a garbled answer, wondering how he could piece the evening back together. Conrad had been shitty for weeks and Tiffany cut contact with everyone.

'Later that night, I was drunk. Do you think . . .' Lachy didn't want to ask Nick but he needed to rule this option in or out for Juliet's DNA request. 'Do you think I forced Tiffany into having sex?'

'Nah, you're not that type of guy.' Nick was using the stick to draw shapes in an ant hill, destroying it. 'I don't know what happened later but Tiffany always got what she wanted. She wanted to get out of camp and made you drive her.'

He appreciated Nick's loyalty, but it wasn't that simple. The next morning he'd discovered scratches on his arms and a red welt on his cheek. Had Tiffany clawed him with her fingernails and slapped him across the face? Maybe everything he did was out of character in a blackout state. Carnal lust over reason every time. Was that why he couldn't commit to a long-term relationship? Too scared of his unknown side.

'I'll email Juliet again and resolve it all.' Lachy focused on the darkening shapes of the mountains, beyond blurry now. 'With my DNA on the system, I keep getting messages from third and fourth cousins in America. One of them was excited to find me. He said my grandfather cut himself off from the rest of the family when he went super religious.'

'All the family secrets will come out.' Nick laughed. 'But seriously, are you sure the person emailing you is Juliet? The whole thing sounds dodgy. Can you call her?'

They hadn't swapped email addresses or phone numbers so Lachy didn't even know how she'd tracked him down. Her email was short and to the point: *I'm pregnant and I think you're the father. Please can you do a DNA test and tick the box to share the results with me. Here's a link to the company I'm using.* When he tried to picture her face, he could only see her startling green eyes. They'd reminded him of Tiffany's eyes; at camp, she'd boasted of a high school boyfriend writing a poem about her 'emerald orbs'.

But Nick could be right. All he'd had from Juliet was an email with no surname. Lachy had willingly sent off his DNA and it might be a total scam. He was a fool for not asking more questions.

'Don't worry, I'll figure it out.' He hoped he sounded confident. 'Enough about me. How's work? You said you were stressed.'

'Crazy busy like it always is in April.' Nick spoke faster, clearly relieved to be on more solid ground. 'Just finished the third quarter. Do you need me to do your tax return?'

'I already did it.' He didn't want Nick to see last year's salary because this year's would look totally different. He'd had three weeks of paid sick leave and now he was on a combination of holiday and long service leave at half-pay. Shit, he had to contact work or find a new job. He needed an income, particularly if Juliet's baby was his . . . The thought came automatically, he'd been worrying about it for months. But there might be no baby, it might not even be Juliet, it might be a scam.

'You've done your own tax?' Nick was asking. 'I'm impressed. By the way, I've got some papers that need your signature. We've finally sorted out your dad's super.'

'Thanks, mate. Appreciate it.'

Nick's accounting firm had taken on their parents' finances after Ralph's death—a real help, because Dad had set up a complicated self-managed superannuation fund that neither Lachy nor Sheridan understood.

He squatted down and reshaped the little mounds of earth that Nick had messed up around the ant nest. Perfect circles of nature, they were amazing. This place, it nurtured his soul. The landscape, the wildlife and the huge sky which implied a world of infinite possibilities. He was supremely grateful to his dad for renovating the old stockman's hut, giving him somewhere to hide from the world.

A world marked by these terrifying voids in his memory.

11

SHERIDAN

FROM THE KITCHEN WINDOW, SHERIDAN COULD SEE NICK AND LACHY out on the ridge near the boulders. A pink ribbon of cloud hung above the mountains. They'd have to come in soon because Nick had offered to drive Kai to his friend's farm.

Kai had entertained the girls with hide-and-seek for hours. Such a good-hearted kid. She wondered how he was feeling about not seeing his mum for three months, but she understood Amber's anger. He'd needed a good kick up the bum. Amber had wanted to get him away from his school group—his friend Hudson in particular. And despite Sheridan's argument that drugs were everywhere, even in the country, the move appeared to have worked; Lachy had reported back to Amber that there had been no incidents of drug-taking. While she wouldn't have been surprised if Kai and Lachy's relationship had changed as a result of their new living arrangements, it hadn't. The boy still adored his father.

If Lachy was here at the end of the year, they could celebrate Christmas at Mimosa like they used to as kids: with a real tree, turkey and all the trimmings, and a swim in the creek later in the afternoon. Last Christmas, Sheridan had invited everyone to her house—lunch on the deck because they couldn't fit into their tiny dining room. Cousin Matthew from Philadelphia had been the guest of honour. In the midst of a divorce, he'd decided to avoid the difficulties of Christmas Day at home by visiting his relatives down under.

The girls were finishing their hot cross buns, a very late afternoon tea. Running through the list in her head, Sheridan realised she hadn't made their beds.

'You can watch TV after you wash your hands,' she told her daughters. 'I'll be unpacking in your bedroom.'

She opened the wardrobe next to the bed and placed the girls' clothing into the drawers. As she rummaged for sheets on the shelves above, a stack of linen dropped out and a piece of A4 paper fluttered to the floor. Unfolding it, she read the typed words.

The Montgomery County Medical Examiner has provided additional information which police hope will assist in identifying a pregnant woman killed on Deadwood Creek Road, fifty miles from Philadelphia. The woman is estimated to be eighteen years old and five foot, five inches tall.

The hit-and-run occurred on a quiet country road in an area with small farms and houses on large blocks. A local resident noticed a pick-up truck speeding off. 'Everyone knows everyone here,' the resident said. 'We're a close-knit community and we help one another. This is a very unusual and tragic situation.'

State Trooper Kurt Haigh implored the public to help: 'Somewhere, a family is waiting for their daughter to come home. They're wondering what has happened to her. Please help us to identify this woman.'

The item must have been copied from the internet into a Word document and printed out—it had no headline, no newspaper title, no date. Why would Lachy hide this in the wardrobe? Putting the paper back on the shelf, she made a mental note to ask her brother about it tonight.

When the back door slammed with the men's return, she called out for Nick to help her. They worked as a team, smoothing the sheets, stuffing pillows into cases and fluffing the doonas.

'Okay, I'd better get Kai to his mate's place,' Nick said. 'Can you save me an Oreo from the Easter slice?'

'If I can sneak it past Eloise.' She smiled.

He gave her a quick kiss on the lips and hurried off to chauffeur Kai.

Lachy drifted into the kitchen as she was laying out the ingredients for the slice: Tiny Teddy biscuits, choc chips, M&Ms, Oreos, marshmallows and mini Easter eggs. The girls sat on the stools at the bench, their eyes focused on the brightly coloured packages.

'How long does it cook for?' Lachy asked, taking a few M&Ms from the open packet and popping them into his mouth.

'No cooking!' Mabel shouted. 'It has to go in the fridge for the whole night.' Although she'd been told moments ago that she wasn't allowed any M&Ms yet, Sheridan saw her little hand dart towards the packet and sneak a fistful. Her own mother had made Sheridan wait but when bubbly, bouncy Lachy came along, he was given everything he wanted.

'Eloise, pass me a wooden spoon,' Lachy instructed. 'And one for Mabel too.'

A minor request but it annoyed her. Sheridan made a point of never asking Eloise to look after her little sister; she didn't want her oldest daughter to have the same sense of responsibility that she felt for Lachy. Of course, she loved her brother and would do anything for him, but it was a burden. And then, while Lachy was working overseas, she'd felt the same responsibility for Kai. Her friends said she needed to 'break the habit' of worrying about Lachy, as if her brother were a glass of wine or chocolate bar. But Gloria had been asking her to keep an eye on her brother since she was three; she could hardly break a 'habit' like that overnight.

Besides, she loved Lachy. And she loved the characteristics he'd inherited from Mum. Most of Sheridan's DNA had come from their dad: reliable, hard-working, loyal, sensible . . . some might even say boring.

Eloise had hopped down from her stool and she was dancing around the kitchen, twirling from the bench to the sink to the oven. In answer to Lachy's request, she took a wooden spoon from the utensil drawer and threw it at his head. Luckily he was quick enough to catch it. The next spoon flew near Mabel but missed, thudding to the floor. Then Eloise began tossing all of the utensils in the air—the spatula, the old-fashioned egg-beater, the corkscrew, the cheese grater, the knives. Oh God, the knives. They clattered to the floor as Eloise let out a high-pitched laugh.

'What the hell are you doing?' Sheridan rushed over to her.

'Baking, making, baking, making. I'm having *fun!*' She sang the words, laughed, and then repeated her little jingle. 'Baking, making, baking, making. I'm having *fun!*'

Her bare feet pirouetted between the knives. As Sheridan crouched to pick up the sharp blades, a knee connected with her head. A shock but not too painful.

'Oops. Sorry, Mummy!' That high-pitched laugh again. 'Baking, making, baking, making. I'm having *fun!*'

Sheridan stared at her daughter. Was this a sugar high? Had she been sneaking M&Ms too? Or had she found the Easter eggs and eaten them? Sheridan put the knives in the sink, crouched down again and held her daughter by her shoulders. Stared into her face. Her pupils were big black circles.

A noise made her turn. Mabel's whole body was shaking. Her feet slammed against the edge of the bench, her arm knocked a mixing bowl off the counter splattering condensed milk into the air. Then she was falling from the stool towards the hard wooden floor.

Lachy sprung forward and caught her just in time.

For a moment, Sheridan froze, immobilised by fear. Then she was at her daughter's side. 'Mabel, are you all right?' She touched the girl's cheek. 'Can you hear me?'

Lachy carried her to the lounge room and laid her on the rug, where Mabel's small body jerked uncontrollably again, her eyes rolling back in her head.

Sheridan watched in terror. She'd lost the ability to think. To speak. What was she supposed to do?

The convulsions stopped and Sheridan reached out, but Lachy gently held her back. He rolled Mabel into the recovery position, checked her mouth, felt her pulse, ran his fingers over her forehead.

'We need to call triple zero,' he said softly. 'And Ronnie. It'll be quicker if she drives us to the hospital. She knows the back roads.'

Mabel lay motionless between them, eyes closed, face red.

'Get your mobile,' he urged. 'Make those calls.'

Walking seemed impossible, her steps back to the kitchen leaden. She should be running, flying. Her mobile sat on the benchtop, near the scattered ingredients. Eloise twirled around and around, waving a tea towel in the air; she hadn't even noticed her sister collapsing.

'Baking, making, baking, making. I'm having *fun!*'

12

LACHY

BOUNCING ALONG IN THE BACK SEAT OF THE TRUCK, LACHY PEERED AT his young niece and prayed to God—any god: *Please don't let her die*. Mabel had stopped twitching and slowly come back to consciousness but now she was listless and confused. Sheridan held her daughter in her lap, stroking her hair, whispering soothing words. Eloise sat in the middle seat, commenting on everything she could see in the falling darkness: a windmill, a crooked tree, a farmhouse lit up against the indigo sky.

The emergency operator had said they should get Mabel to Cooma hospital as quickly as possible. Ronnie hadn't hesitated when they'd asked her to drive, even though she hated leaving the farm.

Sheridan, always the competent one, had floundered at the sight of her daughter. The seizures had the opposite effect on Lachy, snapping him out of his lethargy into emergency mode. In Kenya, they'd been setting up a desal unit at a remote school when a young girl had collapsed onto the classroom floor, her body jerking and twisting just like Mabel. Their LandCruiser was the only vehicle capable of driving two hours to the nearest hospital so while his colleague took the wheel, Lachy attended to the girl, Nyanjera, in the back. He gave her a rehydration sachet, but she vomited it up, all over him. His concern about infectious diseases had him using their precious water to wash it off.

Now he reached over and felt Mabel's forehead. Still so hot.

'Keep cooling her down,' he told Sheridan. 'Put the washer on her chest.'

In the ten minutes it had taken for Ronnie to arrive at the cabin, he'd filled water bottles so they could keep the washer wet and Mabel hydrated.

'It's probably just an infection.' He sounded more certain than he felt. 'A high fever can cause the brain to react. She'll be fine.'

If he kept repeating the words, surely they'd come true. Despite their efforts in Kenya, the five-year-old hadn't been fine. An hour in, Nyanjera had stopped breathing. They'd laid her by the side of the dry, potholed road and done CPR, without success. Later, her death was attributed to cholera; she'd become another statistic of this preventable disease. If only the vaccine program had made it to her area; if only they'd finished their water purification system for the school. He'd seen death before but this one was up close and personal. Perhaps it had made him more vulnerable to what happened later.

Eloise squirmed against him, poking a sharp elbow into his sore arm. He uttered a soft *ooft* and tried to manoeuvre her into a more comfortable position.

'Look at the moon!' She pointed out the window, poking him again.

The huge disc had emerged above the mountains, brightening the sky. Of course, Easter was around the full moon.

Swinging her hands in the air, Eloise began singing. '*Hey diddle diddle, the cat and the fiddle, the cow jumped over the moon. The little dog laughed to see such fun and the cat ran away with the spoon.*'

Sheridan shushed her. 'Be quiet. Mabel is sleeping.'

Sleeping or unconscious?

Eloise stopped singing. She turned to Lachy and asked, 'Why does the cat have a spoon?'

'It's not the cat,' Ronnie interjected from the driver's seat. 'It's the dish. The dish ran away with the spoon.'

'Yes, that makes more sense.' She sang the rhyme again, softly this time.

None of it made sense to Lachy. The song, the seizures, the emergency dash. This couldn't be happening again. Reaching over, he held his hand above Mabel's nose; her warm breath fluttered into his palm. He exhaled himself: a long, drawn-out sigh. At least Cooma hospital wasn't two hours away. Only fifty minutes, maybe even quicker via the back roads.

A large black shape flapped across the windscreen and the truck braked suddenly. He knew Ronnie would be watching out for eagles and foxes scavenging the roadside, kangaroos hopping into their path and any other creature that might prevent them from getting to the hospital in time.

He checked his watch: nearly seven o'clock. It seemed like hours since Mabel had fallen from her stool, every second elongated into a minute. He wouldn't have been surprised if it were midnight.

Focused on Mabel, they'd forgotten to call Nick immediately. And now their truck was in and out of mobile range. Lachy had sent a text: *Meet us at Cooma hospital. Mabel is sick.*

He couldn't tell if it had been delivered or not; they'd find out once they were on the highway.

As Ronnie drove, the moon acted as a beacon, lighting the way for them. He trusted her to get them there safely. She was the right person for an emergency. Except that as they lifted the girls into the back, she'd hissed at him, 'I told you an ill wind was blowing.'

Sheridan had overheard and staggered as if struck.

'Everything will be fine,' he'd assured her. 'Honestly, there's no ill wind. Ronnie's just being . . . well, you know, Ronnie. The doctors will give Mabel antibiotics for an infection then she'll be all better.'

Infection: he kept repeating the word. It was something concrete, a medical issue which could be diagnosed and solved.

But if it wasn't?

And what about Eloise's euphoria. Earlier, when he'd asked if she felt sick too, Eloise had shouted: 'I feel AMAZING!' Now she was singing again.

Mabel kicked out suddenly, her foot hitting the back of the driver's seat. He hadn't accounted for the possibility of an accident caused by the sick passenger.

'Oh God!' Sheridan sobbed. 'She's going to have another fit.'

Please don't make us stop. Lachy addressed his plea to the moon. *I can't handle another sick child by the roadside, miles from anywhere. Doing CPR on an unknown child was hard enough; I can't perform it on my own niece.*

'How long till we get to the hospital?'

'We'll be on the main road soon,' Ronnie said. 'From there, less than twenty minutes.'

Through the window, he spotted a tiny glow: animal eyes reflected in the headlights. Once they hit the highway, Ronnie could gun the motor and they'd shoot down the straight road to Cooma. Any Easter traffic would be going in the opposite direction, on the way to Kosciuszko National Park. Think about the road, the truck, the route. Silence those other thoughts.

'Thanks for driving us, Ronnie,' he said. 'I know you don't like going into town.'

'I bought a new water tank last time I was there. Must be eight months ago. I wanted to catch all that rain from La Niña.' She made a tutting sound. 'The weather bureau said it would last another year, but I don't believe them. Even with their computers. They got it all wrong with the bushfires.'

'Uh-huh,' he muttered. He was keen to be distracted, but recalling the ecological disaster made his heart ache. The fires had scorched the mountains, ravaging the natural bush, destroying the wildlife. Thankfully their little valley had been spared but so much of Australia had burnt, with estimates of a billion animals killed.

'Did you see there was a cyclone in eastern Africa?' Ronnie's voice went up a pitch. 'Landslides in Brazil and flooding in Thailand. Mother Earth is angry; she's trying to get rid of us.'

He'd been avoiding the news as much as possible, blocking out the horror that had sent him tumbling into a dark place. Fuck, why was she talking about this now? At least Mabel had settled down without having another convulsion.

'Let's sing a different song, Eloise,' he suggested. Her vitality could ward off the blackness. 'How about "Old MacDonald Had a Farm"?'

'I'm not a baby,' she huffed. 'I wanna sing Taylor Swift!'

Eloise shouted the chorus to 'Shake It Off', wiggling her whole body. He jerked sideways to avoid being struck again. Should he shush her or embrace this as a better distraction than Ronnie's list of disasters?

'An ill wind is blowing,' he could hear the older woman chanting beneath Eloise's gleeful singing. 'Burning and flooding and earthquake and cyclones and disease and shootings and war. The end is coming and we've brought it upon ourselves.'

Lachy glanced at Sheridan to see if she'd heard; she appeared oblivious, laying the washer on Mabel's chest, whispering in her ear.

'Ronnie, please . . . Do you want to sing "Shake It Off" with us?'

The truck slowed, and for a moment he worried that she'd order them out of the vehicle; that she'd decided Mabel's life wasn't worth saving in this end-of-times, catastrophic world. Suddenly the truck turned right. They were on the highway. Ronnie pumped the accelerator, and they sped along the smooth tarmac. Cars streaked past them on the other side of the road and the lights of farmhouses flashed briefly from the paddocks.

Ronnie gave a rat-a-tat-tat on the steering wheel. 'I don't know that song but I can play the drums in time to your singing, Eloise.'

Mabel hadn't had a convulsion in the truck, which might indicate her brain was calming down. Or did it mean the opposite? His first-aid training had taught him how to manage the immediate seizure, not what came next. He couldn't bear much more of this, but his nieces needed him; his sister was in shock.

Eloise screeched another few lines of the song and it dislodged something in his brain. The memory overwhelmed him;

he was inside it, breathing it, feeling it: the rasping cries of the vultures overhead, the dried-up creek, the heat, the sense of despair and desolation. And a whole family wailing. His niece's screeching entwined with their guttural howls and amplified his underlying fear: *Did I do something to cause this, something I don't remember?*

13

KAI

UNTIL AUNTY SHERIDAN FLEW INTO THE EMERGENCY WAITING ROOM with Mabel in her arms, Kai was pissed off, not worried. Nick had dropped him at the party and returned exactly five minutes later. For half of that short time, he'd chatted with Tarni, who'd smiled and flicked her long dark hair.

'Did you bring the pingers?' she asked, with a cheeky grin. 'I haven't had a good time in sooooo long.'

'We'll have fun tonight!' he said, delaying the moment he'd have to disappoint her. Was Tarni interested in him or the drugs he'd promised? He couldn't believe that after all these months of hiding them successfully from Dad, the bag had disappeared. If Mum and Simmo knew, he'd be stuck here forever—they'd never let him come home.

He was still trying to figure out how to break the bad news when he'd spotted Nick weaving between the kids from school, his bright blue jumper a beacon among the black hoodies and puffer jackets. Embarrassed, he rushed to intercept him.

'We need to get to Cooma hospital,' Nick had said.

Kai didn't understand why he had to miss the party but Nick was so agitated that he wouldn't listen to his suggestion about staying there. On the drive to hospital, they'd rung Sheridan's mobile at least ten times. Mostly, the calls didn't go through. One time, Dad answered and they caught a few sentences before it cut out. 'Mabel had a seizure of some kind. We don't know what's wrong with her.'

And now here she was, barely moving in her mother's arms.

Unlike Eloise. When she saw Nick in the waiting room, she sprinted towards him.

'Daddy! Did you see the moon? It was ginormous. I *love* the moon!'

Nick hugged her and then handed her over to Kai.

'You stay here with your cousin,' he said. 'I'm going inside with Mummy and Mabel.'

And then Nick was racing along with Sheridan, his arms wrapped around both of them.

Dad collapsed into the plastic seat beside Kai and put his head in his hands. Kai couldn't ask how bad it was, not with Eloise bouncing between them. What the hell was happening?

'Do you need a coffee, Dad?' he offered.

'No, I'm right.' His father sniffed. 'We should get Eloise seen by a doctor too. Come on.'

At the emergency desk, Dad talked in circles and stumbled over his words. Grey and exhausted, more confused than he'd been on Tuesday night. The expression on the nurse's face turned from grumpy to grumpier.

'Take her into the triage room.' She pointed to a separate cubicle. 'They'll check her vitals.'

As Dad led Eloise off, Kai hung behind and whispered to her, 'Can you check my dad too? He cut his arm and he's having memory issues.'

'Did this happen at the same time as your cousins got sick?'

'No, it was the other night.'

'Tell him to make an appointment with his doctor.' She waved him away from the desk. 'We're overstretched here.'

Jeez, he'd only been trying to help. Kai shut his mouth, afraid he'd make everything worse.

He didn't know if he was supposed to follow them into the triage room, but Dad beckoned him inside as a male nurse began chatting to Eloise. Why couldn't Nick have just left him at the party? No-one needed him here. At least, he'd managed to avoid telling Tarni that he didn't have the gear. Hopefully he'd be invited to the next gathering and have sorted out a supply by then. He imagined hosting his own party by the creek. A huge bonfire with the big rocks pushed into place as seats. Sausages and bread, slabs of beer, and pingers all round to put everyone in a good mood.

Mum and Simmo didn't understand—normally the pills were safe, and everyone enjoyed the buzz. It was the best drug, the most social, the happiest. Hudson and the other guy ending up in hospital was a freak occurrence.

The nurse, a big man with a shaved head, was a giant next to Eloise. He was listening to her chest. 'Heart rate elevated,' he said.

It had been scary that night but the next day, Hudson had boasted, 'Don't you know I'm immortal?' He'd taken another pill a few weeks later. In the meantime, Mum and Simmo ranted about the dangers. 'You don't know what's in them. Those tablets are made with fillers like bleach, and they add other drugs like ketamine and PMA. You could've died.' The school counsellor tried another tack. 'All sorts of chemicals affect individuals in different ways. It doesn't have to be a so-called bad batch to cause a life-threatening reaction.' But Hudson's supplier, Faz, assured them that he only bought from a reliable source, and they trusted him.

Eloise pulled her jumper back on and demanded water.

The nurse handed her a plastic cup and asked, 'Did you eat anything unusual this afternoon?'

'My dad wouldn't let us have Easter eggs.'

'I guess that's because it's not Easter yet.' The giant chortled. 'Did you eat something else?'

'We had Macca's on the way from Sydney. I chose a Happy Meal. Chicken nuggets with sweet-and-sour sauce.'

Kai would kill for a Big Mac right now. Maybe they could get one later, on the way back from the hospital. He zoned out as Eloise chatted away.

'I had boring biscuits in the car. I wanted choc chip but Mum had packed the wheat ones. Then two apples. When we got to the cabin, we had hot cross buns for afternoon tea. Then some lollies we found in the games cupboard. They were yucky. I had a tiny bit but Mabel ate a whole one. And then she sneaked some M&Ms when we were cooking but I didn't get any. Can I have dinner now?'

The mention of the games cupboard made Kai focus on his young cousin—her flushed face, her clammy forehead, her legs kicking against the chair. This was bad. Very, very bad. He felt sweat breaking out on his own skin.

'Their grandmother was the only one who kept sweets in the games cupboard and she hasn't been in the house for a year.' Dad told the nurse. 'Could old lollies make them sick?'

The giant raised his bushy eyebrows. 'Unlikely. Lollies are mostly sugar.'

He should tell Dad right now. Tell the gigantic nurse, tell the doctors. But he'd be arrested on the spot and marched down to the police station; he'd end up in Cooma jail next to the museum. Just like Grug had said.

'I'm starving!' Eloise moaned.

Shit, shit, shit.

'Dad, I need to—' Kai couldn't even finish his sentence.

'Food would be good.' The giant turned to him. 'Please can you go to the front desk and ask the nurse for cheese sandwiches from the fridge. Grab an apple juice too.'

Kai did as he was told, his heart hammering with every step. He argued with himself as he collected the food. The girls stole the pingers. It was their fault. They were old enough to know better. Mabel had always been greedy; she took lollies that weren't hers.

No, this was his fault.

Either way, he had to tell Dad.

When he brought the food back to them, Eloise was giggling with the giant. She seemed fine but what about Mabel?

'Dad, there's something . . . I think—' Fear sucked his words away.

Instead of listening, Dad was pulling out his credit card. 'Get a black tea and a muesli bar from the machine and take it to Ronnie? She's in her truck in the car park. She won't come inside the hospital.'

'But Dad—'

'Just do it, Kai.' Dad shoved the card into his hand. 'And a coffee for me on the way back.'

Dad's eyes were red and he looked like he might cry.

Again Kai left the cubicle without saying anything. When he poured the hot water for Ronnie's tea, his hands were shaking so much he scalded his thumb. What if Mabel didn't recover? He'd definitely go to jail. Fuck, why wouldn't Dad hear him out? He left the hospital foyer carrying the cup in both hands to stop it from spilling. As he walked from the bright lights of the Emergency entrance into inky darkness, he tried to prac-tise what he would say to Dad. But he was finding it hard to even form the words in his own head. Maybe he was jumping to conclusions and the tablets had nothing to do with Mabel being sick.

Staring around the small car park, he searched for Ronnie's truck. Above him, the all-seeing moon traced his steps. Watching him like a judge. It knew what he had done.

14

SHERIDAN

WIPING AWAY ANOTHER TEAR, SHERIDAN STARED AT HER TINY GIRL ON the white hospital bed, unmoving. Like a doll. Like Betty. A doctor and two nurses huddled around the bed, prodding her.

In the truck on the way to Cooma, Sheridan had been shocked into numbness, but when Nick had thrown his arms around her, terror roared into her throat and almost made her throw up. Now, it flooded through every pore. She watched the doctor's face for clues. *Oh God, Mabel is going to die. She's dying. Oh God. Any second now, she'll be dead.*

'Sit down.' Nick eased her into a chair and gently pushed her head between her knees. 'Breathe, Sheridan, breathe.'

Visualise a positive outcome, she told herself, as if she were talking to a client. *Skip the difficult part and imagine the achievement at the end.* She pictured a cemetery. White flowers. A grave next to her father's. No, no, no. Scattering ashes into the ocean. No!

Nick's hand pressed against her back.

Mabel is going to die. She had convulsions. A bacterial infection in the brain. She's dying. Meningococcal. A deadly disease. Meningitis. She's gone.

'Hush now,' he whispered. 'It'll be okay.'

Three medical staff were crowded around their daughter on the bed. *Three!* She wanted to scream at Nick: *It's not going to be okay!*

'We're just putting in a cannula,' one of the medics said. 'We'll give her some fluids and antibiotics. That will help straight away.'

'But what's wrong with her?'

'At the moment, she's very hot and we need to cool her down.'

That was hardly an answer.

'Have you seen this before?' Sheridan demanded. 'What's happening to her body?'

Nick put a hand over hers. Stroked her back again. 'Let them do their job. Let them look after Mabel.'

'Children can react quickly to an infection,' the doctor explained calmly. 'But we'll bring her temperature down, and the paediatrician will be in shortly.'

Paediatrician.

'Sheridan, breathe with me.' Nick put his hands on either side of her head, forcing her to focus on him. They'd flipped roles: she was usually the one to de-escalate a situation, the diplomat, the fixer. She barely recognised her husband; she certainly hadn't recognised her brother in the lounge room, taking control of the situation.

'Remember the time Kai swallowed a five-cent piece?' Nick's voice was low and insistent. 'The doctors sorted that out. And remember when Eloise got her foot stuck in the escalator? She was fine. And when your dad was thrown off his horse, he was fine too.'

Kai. Eloise. Dad. None of them had resembled Mabel, barely moving on the white sheet. And there was one name neither of them could mention—their son.

✕

Back in the waiting room, Sheridan hugged Eloise tightly and kissed her forehead.

'Have a good sleep, honey,' she whispered. 'Uncle Lachy will take you home now and we'll see you in the morning. Love you lots and lots.'

Eloise had been thoroughly checked over and given the all-clear. Her earlier manic energy had fizzled out and she kept asking when she could go to bed.

'Did you find Kai?' Sheridan asked her brother.

'Yep. I thought he'd disappeared off to Macca's but he was by the truck with Ronnie.'

Ronnie had waited for two hours in the car park and was now taking Lachy, Kai and Eloise home to Mimosa.

'Love you to the moon and back.' Eloise yawned. 'Tell Mabel about the big moon. I think she was asleep.'

'I will. Hopefully she'll see it tomorrow night.'

Sheridan didn't know if the big moon was a good omen or a bad one. What would Ronnie say? After Eloise and the others had left, she walked outside to breathe the cool night air and gaze at the silver orb. The doctors had taken blood and run all sorts of tests. Mabel had been conscious on and off, which must be a good sign. But even when she was awake briefly, she hadn't needed to wee, so they couldn't do a urine test. Sheridan tried to follow the doctors' discussion but so much of it had been incomprehensible. CAT scans. Lumbar puncture. Cerebrospinal fluid. Pneumococcal. Bacterial. Viral. Pneumonia. Tachycardia. Trigeminy. Hyperthermia. She didn't know what diagnoses they were considering and what they'd ruled out. They promised to explain once they had some results. The medical jargon had worked as a sedative on her brain, quelling her terror.

Nick had spoken to his parents over a crackling line across the country to the top end of Western Australia. Their campervan was parked near a waterfall in the Kimberley. He shouldn't have rung them—they couldn't do anything from over there, apart from fret—but she understood the urge; she longed to call her own father. He'd work through the situation rationally and take away her fear.

The nurses had told her to go for a break in the fresh air, but it was hard to stay outside. What if Mabel needed her? She returned to the waiting area, where Nick had made cups of tea for them both.

'I've never seen Lachy in an emergency before,' she said, collapsing into the plastic chair next to him. 'Well, apart from when he saved Kai at the birthday party, but none of us really saw that happening. Tonight, he was just like Dad. Calm, focused, clear-headed. Maybe he deals with emergencies overseas all the time.'

'Well, if he does, he certainly keeps it quiet.' Nick handed her the disposable cup. 'Like the rescue on Tuesday night. He didn't want to discuss it at all.'

'The humble hero.'

'Yeah.' Nick took a sip of his tea. 'It's a good example for Kai.'

'They seem to be happy living together.' She suddenly remembered that Kai was supposed to be at a mate's house. 'Why did you pick him up from the sleepover?'

'It wasn't a sleepover; it was a party.'

'Really? He isn't allowed to go to parties.' She kept up her end of the conversation, but her thoughts were with Mabel. Gazing around the small waiting room, she hoped desperately that this country hospital had adequate resources to save their little girl. Rural health was always in the news: staffing shortages, lack of supplies, unnecessary deaths.

'Do you think he lied—'

Nick stopped speaking as the paediatrician appeared through the swinging doors. The doctor was neither smiling nor frowning; his face gave nothing away.

15

LACHY

UNTIL THEY WALKED INTO THE KITCHEN, LACHY HAD FORGOTTEN ABOUT the Easter slice. Here, the moment of Mabel's seizure had been frozen in time: a stool overturned, a mixing bowl half full, condensed milk splattered across the floor, chocolate chips dotting the benchtop like flies. He groaned as Eloise reached for some chocolate.

'No sweets now,' he said. 'I'll make you Vegemite toast. Kai, can you take her into the lounge room and pop on the TV while I get it ready?'

He started clearing up, but Ronnie stopped him.

'I'll do that. You feed Eloise.'

'You've done so much already, Ronnie.' She'd waited for hours outside the hospital. 'Go home and have dinner. The dogs will be wondering where you are.'

'They'll survive.' She unearthed the dishcloth from the bowls in the sink and began wiping flour off the benchtop. 'Your mum and dad would want me to make sure you're all right.'

Perhaps she was keen to stick around for news on Mabel or to decompress after the last few hours. That would be fine as long as she didn't start on any end-of-the-world stuff.

From the lounge room came the low drone of the television, the kids chatting and the sound of cupboards closing. Kai had barely said a word in the last hour; he must be in a state of shock. Was he checking for any remaining lollies now? The nurse had said old lollies were unlikely to affect them, though, so what the hell had caused Mabel's seizures?

After Eloise had eaten the toast, Lachy bundled her into bed. Tucking the doona around her shoulders, he kissed her goodnight as her eyes were closing. She was totally wiped out by the evening's events. Yawning himself, he tried to recall Kai at this age but no memories came—had he been working over-seas for a long period? He listened to Eloise's soft breaths, took one last look at her and left the room. His adrenaline response from earlier had given way to a bone-aching weariness and his thoughts were a jumbled mess.

In the kitchen, Ronnie had finished cleaning up and she'd cooked supper: three plates piled with bacon, eggs, baked beans and fried bread, just like Dad used to make for Sunday break-fast. Fitting—it felt like a whole night had passed since the mad dash to hospital.

'Thanks, Ronnie.' He noticed the bacon on his plate but didn't comment. 'You've really gone above and beyond tonight.'

They didn't move into the dining room but sat on stools at the kitchen bench, as if it were breakfast, and kept talking around the fear. Sheridan hadn't rung with an update. He wondered if Kai had spoken to his mum—she'd make him feel better.

'Did you call Amber?' he asked Kai. 'Or do you want to wait until . . .'

'They're in Sumatra,' Kai said with a shrug. 'Out of phone range.'

What was with the shrug? Was Kai blasé because his best mate had gone to hospital and returned with no lasting effects? Maybe Lachy had been too casual about the drugs; he should have ramped up his response, like Amber and Simmo. Had Kai interpreted it as a sign of indestructibility? Lachy felt the opposite: anything bad that could happen *would* happen.

'Did you find the lollies in the games cupboard?'

Kai's head shot up. 'No, nothing there.'

His voice sounded shaky.

'Do the doctors know what's wrong with her?' Ronnie asked.

'Not yet. They ran a lot of tests. I hope the results don't take too long.' Lachy forked his bacon across to Kai's plate; his son always appreciated an extra serve. 'The public holiday might slow it down. Sheridan said some tests had to be sent to pathology in Canberra.'

Kai hadn't taken a single bite of his food. Normally he wolfed it down. Lachy studied his son's face: his cheeks had lost their ruddiness and his eyes were bloodshot. In the hospital car park, Kai had whispered, 'I need to talk to you, Dad.' But with Eloise between them, he'd snapped, 'Later,' and forgotten about it.

Kai dropped his cutlery and pushed his seat back.

'What's wrong?' Lachy asked.

'I think I'm gonna be sick.' He bolted from the room. Was he suffering the effects of alcohol? Had he arrived at the bonfire and drunk fast, in the same style as his father? He wasn't stumbling or slurring, but Lachy knew firsthand that if you could hold your liquor, you didn't necessarily appear intoxicated.

'It might be imported food products,' Ronnie said. 'They could be poisoning us. Now Kai's sick too. It can't be your water because you're not on the town supply. Unless it's in the air. One of our enemies flying over with an insecticide—'

'*Stop!* Please, Ronnie, just stop.' He didn't need this shit right now. 'I'm so grateful for everything you've done but I just can't . . .' He shook his head.

'You believe in the goodness of the world, Lachy, that's your problem. Too optimistic, like your mum. Beautiful woman. She wouldn't listen to me either. Gloria preferred the rose-tinted version.'

He used to be optimistic, but now he agreed with Ronnie about their falling-apart world. However, he would not follow her down the rabbit holes of conspiracy theories. A conversation about Mum would be preferable to a poisoning plot.

'Mum did see the best in things,' he agreed. 'Excuse me, I have to check on Kai.' Hopefully, she'd get the hint and disappear.

The bathroom and Kai's bedroom were empty. Lachy found his son curled up on the leather sofa in the lounge room. Sitting down beside him, he rested a hand on his back.

'How are you feeling, mate?' he asked. 'Did you throw up?'

Kai gave a slight nod.

'Is it something you ate or the stress of tonight?' Hesitating, he wondered how to continue without upsetting their equilibrium. 'Or did you have a drink at Ethan's place?'

'I didn't drink anything.' Kai snapped at the question. 'I was only there for five minutes then Uncle Nick came back.'

'Good.' Amber would have been furious with him. 'So is it the stress?'

'Dad, I'm scared . . .'

'I know, mate, but Eloise is fine and Mabel . . . it's probably an infection and the doctors will make her all better.' Please God, let it be true.

'Have you looked in the games cupboard lately?' Kai asked.

Blinking twice, he focused on the cabinet under the window. He remembered finding a puzzle piece when he was vacuuming on Tuesday afternoon. No, that must have been Wednesday. Tuesday was the blank afternoon. Had he left something in there on Tuesday and forgotten about it? A bottle of whisky or sleeping tablets or painkillers?

'I put a puzzle piece back the other day.'

What if something he'd done in blackout mode had harmed the girls? For fuck's sake, he couldn't remember saving Fred Whyte and injuring his arm. Self-loathing flared, hot and accusatory.

Kai unfurled his legs and leant back against the couch. 'Did you see anything else in there?'

A pointed question. Kai must know what he'd done in those missing hours. Lachy would never forgive himself if his actions had led to Mabel's sickness.

He stood quickly, as if he could run away from his thoughts. 'I have to check on Eloise.'

In the kids' bedroom, she was sitting up, playing on Sheridan's iPad—so engrossed in a game, she didn't even react as he entered.

'Come on, El, it's time for sleep.'

'Not tired.' She set her mouth in a stubborn line.

'Finish the game and I'll sit with you for a bit.' He nestled beside his niece, and brushed her wayward hair from her face.

When the iPad was off, he started crooning the first song that came to mind, a nursery rhyme Gloria had sung when they were young. *'In a cavern, in a canyon, excavating for a mine . . .'* As he came to the chorus, he realised his mistake. *'You are lost and gone forever, dreadful sorry, Clementine.'*

He began humming the tune instead. Jesus, why had Mum sung them to sleep with this tragic tale? He'd never considered the words before. It ended on a cheery note for the singer though:

How I missed her, how I missed her,
How I missed my Clementine,
Till I kissed her little sister,
And forgot my Clementine.

One sister had died and he'd taken up with the other.

Sheridan still hadn't called with any news.

✕

Returning to the lounge room, with Eloise finally asleep, he hoped that Ronnie had left. At the sight of her on the couch with Kai, flipping through photo albums, he groaned inwardly.

'I was showing Kai some of your mum's old parties,' she said. 'She organised our family reunion and managed to please everyone. I've got eight siblings and heaps of cousins and they were all happy.'

'Mmm.' Did Ronnie feel an obligation to Mum—was that why she wouldn't leave?

'I made you peppermint tea.' She pointed to a cup on the mantelpiece. 'And I found this brochure about DNA testing there. Did you read the page on siblings? *People say you share half*

109

your DNA with your sibling but it's not really that straightforward.
While siblings inherit their genes from the same parents, they don't
inherit the same part of DNA. That's so true. I'm nothing like
my brothers and sisters.'

The DNA brochures: they'd set him off on the memory
blackout. Ronnie and Kai were both watching him, waiting for
an explanation.

'We really need to get some sleep, Ronnie. Thanks again.'
He took the photo album from her and put it back on the book-
shelf. He suddenly recalled Sunday's invitation. 'I'm not sure if
we'll be doing Easter lunch. I'll let you know.'

'Can you call me when you hear how Mabel is going?'

'Of course.' Feeling guilty for his irritation, he gave her a
hug. None of this was her fault. She'd been the local hero today.
He'd probably caused the emergency.

'You know, you look just like your mum, and Sheridan has
lots of your dad's features.' She hugged him back hard. 'Family
was always number one for Gloria.'

Ronnie must think he was concerned about his genetic background. He didn't have the energy to set her straight; he just
wanted to crawl into bed and close his eyes. His brain needed
to rest. For once, he craved oblivion. Not for one second had he
worried about any family secrets. Ronnie was right: he looked
exactly like Mum and his sister looked exactly like Dad.

His phone buzzed in his pocket. It was Sheridan.

16

ELIZABETH, 1968

'THIS IS ELIZABETH,' THE NURSE TOLD CAPTAIN DELBERT. 'SHE'S HELPING with your meal tonight.' Turning to me she said, 'You'll find the captain is a talkative fella. He likes to tell everyone how he lost his legs in the war.'

The patients I'd met so far in the Soldiers' Home had been unable to speak. I'd spooned orange mush into the first man's mouth; the nurse told me to hum a hymn as I fed him. The second man couldn't sit up and we had to roll him into a new position to prevent bedsores. I prayed for every patient and thanked them for their service to America and to God.

'You're a pretty gal, Elizabeth. I'd have combed my hair if I knew you were coming.' Captain Delbert laughed and stroked his bald head. 'What's on the menu today?'

'Meatloaf, mashed potato and peas,' I announced, as if I'd cooked it myself.

As the nurse was leaving the room, she issued him a warning: 'Please give her the clean version of your tale, Captain. She's very young.'

The captain winked at me and called out, 'She's on the cusp.'

On the cusp. That was exactly how I felt: neither young nor old. Mother considered me ready to marry while Father was still giving me a whupping for talking to boys. Maybe in a year's time I would be as certain about the world as Gloria.

'You can call me Betty,' I told Captain Delbert as I cut up his meal. 'And I'm seventeen.'

'A perfect age, sweetheart.' He took a mouthful of meatloaf and gravy. 'Let me tell you how I came to leave my legs in the middle of Italy . . .'

We had a few war veterans in our church community, but they didn't talk about their experiences. Nor did Father. All I knew was that he'd wanted to join as a chaplain and ended up fighting.

'We were trying to take Rome, but we couldn't get through the Winter Line. Week after week we were firing away but not gaining any ground.'

'That must have been difficult.' I couldn't imagine living in the trenches. Some of the soldiers had been seventeen, just like me.

'Hard work, sweetheart. It's why we needed a break. Three of us had gone to a nearby village. We met some lovely ladies, and I shall remember Giulia until my dying breath. Please don't tell my wife I said that.' He smirked. 'I admit we had too much grappa afterwards, strong stuff. We couldn't find our way back and ventured into dangerous territory. That was when we were hit. I took the brunt of it. The other two were fine, joking that I'd made the most of my last minutes on earth.'

My mouth hung open and I shut it quickly. Was old Captain Delbert really telling me that he'd lain with a woman just before he lost his legs? Not knowing how to respond, I thrust a forkful of mash into his mouth. Suddenly he was coughing and spluttering, waving his hands.

'Help! Someone help!' I yelled through the doorway. 'Captain Delbert is choking.'

A man came flying into the room. He stepped around me, pushed Delbert forward and thumped his back with both fists. A mess of food spurted from his mouth, dripped down his shirt and onto the tray table.

'I'm so sorry,' I apologised as I cleaned him up.

'My own fault, sweetheart.' The captain managed. 'I shocked you.'

Our saviour gave him a severe look: 'You were telling her about Giulia, weren't you?'

'Doc, I gave her the clean version.' Captain Delbert coughed again. 'Could I have some water, please?'

The doctor and I reached for the water at the same time, our fingers touching. It was only then that I took notice of his face. The same blue eyes as Robert Redford, the same chiselled jaw.

'I'm Dr Charlie Stanbury. I help out every Wednesday. I haven't seen you before.'

'Aren't you too young to be a doctor?' I blurted and then quickly apologised. 'Sorry, Dr Stanbury, that was a little rude.'

'It's all right, I am still young.' He chuckled. 'I'm in my final year of training. Please call me Charlie. And you are?'

My heart had been racing from the choking incident; now it continued a fast beat from my proximity to this handsome doctor.

'Her name's Betty,' Captain Delbert answered for me. 'She's seventeen and she's an absolute doll when she's not trying to kill me. These beautiful young women—deadlier than the Krauts. They'll be the death of me yet.'

A hot flush rose to my face.

'Go easy on her, Captain, or this beautiful woman won't return next week.' Charlie grinned. 'And I'm sure we'd like to see her again.'

I just stared at him. Father had meant this shift at the Soldiers' Home as a punishment, but I would come here every Wednesday evening willingly if it meant I could see Charlie.

✖

Walt, the building supervisor, was supposed to drive me home when I'd finished serving the evening meal. He was a cousin of one of our church members. When I went to meet him at the back entrance by the car park, however, I found Charlie waiting instead.

'Walt had to leave early,' he said. 'I promised to get you home safely.'

'I live over in Leeville in Berks County,' I told him. 'It's a long way.'

'Even more important that I drive you then.'

We walked to the car in silence, and I wondered if Father would consider this acceptable. Charlie was a responsible doctor but also young and attractive. I would be spending forty minutes in a car with him.

He opened the door of his Ford Mustang for me, and I knew I'd have to ask him to let me out down the lane from our house. Father said these cars were too flashy. A sensible man did not buy a Mustang.

Charlie switched on the car radio as we accelerated onto the main road. I didn't recognise the song.

'Do you like The Beatles?' he asked.

'The Beatles are . . .' My whole body was hot, so close to him in the cabin, this car and the words of this song, 'All You Need Is Love'. I knew I was about to commit a sin. 'The Beatles are great.'

He talked about his medical training and asked about my plans after school. I did not mention that arrangements were being made for my marriage.

'I'd like to see the world,' I said. 'Maybe travel to Australia.'

'Why Australia?' His voice was rich and luscious like maple syrup; nothing like the boys on the bus.

'They loved our president when he went to visit.' It wasn't much of a reason, but I couldn't admit the truth to him: I wanted freedom, far beyond the reach of my father and his church.

'Australia is looking for doctors.'

Oh my gosh, was Charlie suggesting that he come with me or merely making conversation? I wished we could drive forever in this cocoon, but we were nearly home.

'Would you mind parking near that farm gate? I'll walk the rest of the way.' I paused. 'My father is very . . . strict. It's best if he doesn't see your car.'

I worried that I might have offended him, but he was smiling.

'The Mustang is always getting me in trouble. I bet your dad is envious and wants one just like it.'

Covetousness was one of the seven deadly sins. The idea of Father being envious of a car made me giggle.

'Betty, you have the most delightful giggle.'

Father always instructed me to stop—he said life was not to be laughed at—but in the kitchen, when he wasn't around, Mother told me the sound was joyful and infectious. When Charlie commented on it, I giggled again: nervously this time.

At the farm gate, he stopped the car and turned towards me. His shoulder brushed against mine; it was the smallest touch but it sent an electric current coursing through me.

'See you next Wednesday,' he said.

I had the strongest feeling that Charlie was part of my future.

17

SHERIDAN

SHERIDAN SAT MOTIONLESS IN THE PASSENGER SEAT AS NICK PARKED the car outside the cabin. The late-afternoon sun shimmered, casting a golden glow over the rocks and the mountain range. A few clouds were tinged with oranges and pinks, a contrast to the blue sky. She squeezed her eyes shut and opened them again. In the hospital, under the fluorescent lights, she'd lost all sense of time. Surely it should be sunrise now, not sunset. Mum said Easter Saturday was also known as Bright Saturday, and here the colours of the landscape were almost too garish for her fatigued, hyperaware state.

As she opened the car door, Eloise rushed from the cabin, carrying a silver tray that glinted in the sunshine.

'We made the slice, Mum!'

She'd forgotten about preparing the Easter slice. A shiver rippled down her neck with the memory of Mabel falling off the stool.

'Well done, darling.' She wrapped Eloise in her arms, careful not to upset the tray.

'Can Mabel have some now?'

'Let's get her inside first.' Nick was lifting Mabel out of the car, draping her over his shoulder. 'It might be better to wait until tomorrow. Your sister's tummy is still a bit sore.'

And her arms, her legs, her head, her heart. It had taken hours and hours for the doctors to get her temperature down. Such a terrifying night—made more frightening because they couldn't find any cause. Nothing had shown up on the scans and they were still waiting for pathology results to come back from the lab in Canberra. 'Will it happen again?' Sheridan asked as they were getting ready to discharge Mabel. 'What if she has convulsions as soon as we get home?' In the hospital car park, she'd been trying to convince Nick they should stay in a nearby hotel—Mimosa Hideout was too far from medical care—when Mabel had spoken up: 'I wanna go to the cabin. I wanna see Eloise and Kai and Uncle Lachy.'

And here they all were, coming out to greet her.

'How's my brave little niece?' Lachy kissed her forehead. 'Are you feeling better? Ready for the Easter Bunny tomorrow?'

Sheridan had blanked out the chaos of yesterday evening, but Lachy's cheery chatter reminded her of his strength. Slinging an arm around his waist, she whispered, 'Thank you.'

Kai hung back, much more aloof than when Nick and the girls had arrived from Sydney on Friday. Had the hours in emergency brought flashbacks of his friend's overdose? Beckoning him over, she hugged him tight for a long time.

'Thanks for coming to the hospital and looking after Eloise last night.'

'Is Mabel going to be all right?' His voice went high at the end of the question.

'The doctors think so.' She sighed. 'They said we could come home.'

'Good.' He broke out of her hug and began walking back to the cabin.

He waved to Mabel from a distance but didn't approach her. She smiled at him, a flash of happiness on her pale face. Dark circles rimmed her red eyes. In the middle of the night, Sheridan had whispered her deepest fears to Nick. *What if she has brain damage? What if it's a tumour? What if she dies?* They'd both cried until exhaustion had Nick nodding off in the chair beside the hospital bed. Sheridan hadn't slept.

Still in Nick's arms, Mabel began squirming to get down. She slithered to the ground to investigate the tray in her sister's hands.

'Yum!' she said. 'I want a piece with M&Ms on top.'

'It looks delicious.' Sheridan brushed away her tears. 'You carry it into the kitchen, Eloise, and we'll cut it up.'

An appetite for Easter slice must be a good sign of recovery.

Lachy had cooked a chicken and vegetable casserole, one of their mother's old recipes. It reminded her of Gloria's cuddles, snuggling up in bed together on a cold, rainy night. Mum didn't read from books but invented stories or shared memories from her own childhood. Tales of dancing in the church hall, learning to play the ukulele, fishing in streams. She made it sound idyllic. Later, they found out the truth was somewhat different.

Sheridan hoped this Easter wouldn't destroy her girls' childhoods, that it would be a passing moment in an otherwise happy-enough youth; a moment like Kai's third birthday, which had turned into a Wilson family story. Of course, that would only happen if her daughter recovered. They wouldn't be telling the birthday anecdote if Kai had remained underwater for longer.

Kai had barely spoken over dinner, but he'd been so helpful: laying the table, clearing up, packing the dishwasher. With him and Lachy doing all the chores, she'd had time to sit with Mabel and Eloise and play Trouble. The girls loved bashing the plastic pop-up centrepiece and the game had become louder and louder. Trouble had been in that cupboard since she and Lachy were children, a staple of their early years. Despite it being a game of chance, Lachy always won. He was a lucky bastard. Tonight, without him in the game, Mabel snagged the first round and Eloise the second. Now they were bathed, fed and asleep, and she was yawning herself.

'You should go to bed,' Nick said.

'Good idea.' She stifled another yawn. 'Are you sure you'll be okay in the single bed?'

They were splitting up: Sheridan and Mabel in the double room, Nick and Eloise in the kids' room. She wanted Mabel beside her, where she could check her breathing and temperature without getting out of bed. Nick was too tall for the single bed, his feet would dangle over the end, but he wasn't complaining. He'd been such a rock at the hospital, unlike with their son. Back then, he'd shut himself off from her. He'd thrown himself into work, leaving Sheridan to grieve with her parents and her best friend. She still wondered if Nick had suffered some kind of breakdown. While she insisted on commemorating Toby's birthday each year, they'd never really been able to talk about his death. But their marriage had survived, and Nick was a good father to the girls. Last night, he'd stepped up in every way possible.

'I'll be fine.' He kissed her. 'Get some sleep.'

'Love you so much.'

She waved goodnight to Lachy and Kai, who were on the couch watching television. They'd both been so thoughtful. She'd tell Amber how well Kai was doing here.

Tomorrow evening, they'd have the bonfire and chat properly. She'd figure out why Kai had begged her to drive down to Mimosa early, and ask Lachy about that newspaper article in the wardrobe. Did he know the girl who had been run over?

She was changing into her pyjamas when Mabel grunted in bed and pointed at the chair in the corner.

'Mummy, can you move Betty? She's scaring me.'

That creepy doll. She'd put it on the top shelf of the wardrobe with the door closed. As she lifted Betty, something fell from her skirt. Sheridan reached down and picked up a plastic bag. She frowned at it.

'I just have to switch on the lamp, darling,' she told Mabel. 'I can't quite see.'

In the glare of the light, she stared at the bag of pills—pink-and-blue with smiley faces on them.

'I'm sorry, Mummy,' Mabel piped up. 'We shouldn't have eaten the lollies. Eloise hid them there so we wouldn't get in trouble.'

'You ate these yesterday?'

'They tasted yucky. Eloise said they were old.' Mabel bit down on her lip. 'Is that what made me sick?'

The terror that had been coursing through her body for the past twenty-four hours twisted into a searing rage. She froze for a moment as the truth sank in. Her hands shook and the pills bounced against each other, their smiley faces mocking her.

Grabbing Betty by the neck, she flew down the hallway to the lounge room. Three heads snapped towards her, startled by her furious entry. She fixed her gaze on just one of them. How could he have endangered his cousins?

'You idiot!' she screamed at Kai, hitting him in the chest with the doll. 'You're still doing it down here. Your bloody drugs!' She held the pill packet high in the air.

'What are they?' Lachy stood up and tried to take the doll from her, but she wouldn't let it go.

She smashed Betty against Kai's shoulder. 'He left his pills lying around and the girls thought they were lollies. That's why Mabel had a seizure. He could have killed them!'

Her brother was as irresponsible as his son. Why hadn't he checked the house before her girls had arrived?

Kai curled up in his chair, his knees protecting his middle, his arms protecting his head. She slapped the doll against his back. He moaned and the noise inflamed her—this boy didn't know the meaning of pain.

'Eloise told the nurse she'd eaten a lolly from the games cupboard,' Lachy said, his forehead creased in confusion. 'I thought it was one of Mum's old sweets.'

'For God's sake, why didn't you tell us?'

'I assumed the nurse would mention it.' His eyes flicked between her and Kai.

'Did you know, Kai?' she demanded. 'Last night at the hospital—did you know?'

'I don't . . . I tried . . .' he stammered, his head still covered by his arms. 'I wasn't sure if Dad . . .'

He was lying.

He knew and he'd said nothing.

'You poisoned your cousins!' she shouted, whacking him with the doll so hard that Betty broke in two. Her legs dangled on the side of the chair for a few seconds, then flopped onto the floor. The other half swung from Sheridan's trembling hand.

'Get him out of this house.'

When neither of them moved, she roared, 'Both of you: GET OUT NOW!'

18

KAI

KAI WOKE TO A WET TONGUE LAPPING HIS CHEEK. WHAT THE HELL? He half sat up and Ronnie's dog took that as an invitation to jump on the couch beside him. Its mouth was dangerously close to his face again. He shoved the kelpie back onto the floor. 'Go away.'

Almost like Aunty Sheridan had screamed at them last night: GET OUT!

In the car to Ronnie's place, Dad had been stunned, then baffled, then enraged.

'I thought it was my fault,' he said. 'That I'd done something.'

Kai gritted his teeth. As if Dad, Mr Local frigging Hero, would ever harm anyone. 'I'm really sorry. I didn't mean to hurt them.'

'But why did you have the drugs?' Dad shook his head. 'I trusted you.'

The queasiness had rolled in his stomach again but there was nothing left to vomit. When he'd arrived at Mimosa in January, he'd promised himself that his dad would be proud of him, that he could be a better son for his cool father. And now he'd stuffed it all up.

'Please don't tell Mum and Simmo,' he'd whispered.

That was when Dad really lost it.

'Mabel could have *died*! We don't know if she has organ damage.'

Kai had doubled over in the car seat, his gut cramping, the same words on repeat in his mind: *Let her be okay.*

'I tried to tell you at the hospital but—'

'Well, you didn't try hard enough. Don't you DARE blame anyone else.'

He kind of blamed Eloise and Mabel for eating the pills, they weren't toddlers. It was Sheridan's fault too; she was so strict about lollies that Mabel would sneak them at every opportunity. And Dad's fault twice over—the pingers were in that cupboard because Dad was likely to search his bedroom, *and* he wouldn't listen when they were in the triage cubicle. Kai had tried to confess his suspicions at least three more times after that, in the hospital foyer, in the car park and in Ronnie's truck on the way home. Dad ignored him every time. Last night, when Sheridan had rung to say they'd got Mabel's temperature down and she seemed to be stabilising, he'd decided the doctors had sorted her out and there was no point saying anything.

If only the girls had arrived a day later, Kai would've had a blast at the party, shared the pingers and made new friends. And his cousin wouldn't have been in hospital.

The dog jumped onto the couch again and sniffed his face. His iPhone said 6.57 am. Too early for Easter Sunday, but the dog wanted to play or eat or poo.

Kai pulled on his jacket and crept out the back door with the kelpie. His warm breath made puffs of white in the cold air. Four other dogs rushed from the wooden shed to greet him, with Ronnie following. Her old grey duffel coat flapped as she moved; the purple beanie on her head was a shock of colour against the neutral landscape.

'Ah, there you are.' She addressed the dog, not him.

'Happy Easter,' he said, hoping she'd calmed down overnight. Dad had told her everything and her anger had almost matched Sheridan's.

'Right. Yes. Happy Easter.' Patting the dog, she kept her eyes on the animal. 'I hope the Easter Bunny has arrived for the girls. Lachy was going to do that.'

'I have eggs for them too.' He'd wanted to spoil his own sisters as well. Last week, he'd asked Mum to buy them chocolate from him. Oh God, Mum. She was going to murder him. In the meantime, he needed to make it up to Mabel. 'I'll give the Easter eggs to the girls at lunch.'

'Lunch is cancelled,' Ronnie said. 'I'll figure out something here. I've got lots of veggies and some tins.'

He didn't know what to do with this sick feeling about Mabel and his total panic about what lay ahead. He'd been banished again; an apology to Aunty Sheridan and Uncle Nick wasn't going to cut it. Late last night, when he couldn't sleep, he'd found a spot in the kitchen with some mobile reception and scrolled through his phone. All his Sydney mates were at parties or away on holidays: laughing, drinking, having fun. None of them had nearly killed their little cousin.

Stupid coward. Why hadn't he just blurted it out at the hospital? All those drug videos at school encouraged them to speak up: *If your friend is unwell, call your parents or an ambulance. Their life is more important than you getting in trouble.* Staring at the moon above the hospital, he'd come up with other possibilities—maybe it wasn't the pingers, maybe Dad had confiscated them, or they'd slipped out of the puzzle box and through a crack in the cupboard. But he'd known he was lying to himself.

The biggest dog circled him, then squatted to produce a steaming pile of turds. One, two, three. The smell hit Kai full force; it was what he deserved. Gagging, he raced to a bush and heaved. Only a trickle of bile came out.

He wished Mum were here to make him feel better.

But she wouldn't—she'd never forgive him.

No-one would.

><

Instead of sitting down to a lamb roast, they ate corned beef from a tin with mashed potato and pumpkin. Although he still felt queasy, he ate Dad's share of corned beef as well. All that vomiting had emptied his stomach.

Ronnie apologised for the meal. 'I wasn't expecting guests.'

From the look of her place, she never expected guests. The dogs had the run of the house and fur covered most surfaces. Ronnie spoke to them like children: *Boxer and Clover, come over and have some food. Muriel, stop teasing Snowball, he doesn't like it. Napoleon, darling, don't be afraid of our visitors.*

There was no chocolate, no Easter egg hunt.

'Easter Sunday is also known as Resurrection Sunday,' Ronnie said as she poured orange cordial into his glass.

Was that a dig at him? He was supposed to have resurrected himself into a new person by moving down here. Well, Ronnie barely even went to the shops—she had no idea how hard it was to make friends, to go to high school in that tiny town.

✕

After lunch, Ronnie took them out to her veggie patch.

'I need help lifting these planks into place.' She gestured to a stack of wooden beams.

When they'd finished shifting the planks around each garden bed, Ronnie had another job, then another; all the heavy lifting that required more than one person. Grunting with the effort, he realised the amount of work needed for this farm, too much work. She proudly explained how the place was self-sufficient; she even had a generator in case the electricity went down.

'Did you grow up on a farm?' he asked.

'Yes, like your great-grandad and your granddad. But not here in the Monaro.'

'Where was your parents' property?'

'Somewhere else.'

Why did she have to be so cagey? He was just making conversation.

✕

Later, when they went inside for afternoon tea, Dad mentioned that he'd rung Sheridan. 'They're all doing okay,' he reported. 'Mabel is feeling a lot better.'

Thank God. He considered texting his aunt so she could give his eggs to the girls but decided against it. Ronnie wouldn't want them here for long; surely they'd be back at Mimosa by tomorrow.

His phone buzzed and he jumped, surprised to have coverage. Imagine if it were Hudson saying he was coming to visit or Tarni inviting him out next week. During the party, she'd messaged:

Where did you go? He sent a short reply: *Family emergency.* They hadn't communicated again. Were Tarni and the others pissed off that he hadn't brought the pingers? He'd failed everyone, in every possible way.

The caller ID read *Mum.* Oh no. She'd go ballistic about everything, including the fact that she had to ring him from her once-in-a-decade, overseas holiday.

She didn't even wait for him to say hello. 'Oh my God, Kai, I don't understand how you could possibly . . .'

He braced himself for the onslaught, but instead she broke down. Shit, he'd never made her cry before.

'I'm so sorry, Mum, I really am.' He swallowed his own sobs. 'I didn't mean to. It was an accident.'

'Those gorgeous girls. They could've been . . .' Mum's crying stopped abruptly. Had the phone cut out? She was on an island somewhere in Indonesia. He heard a rustling sound and then his stepfather came on.

'Kai, we cannot tell you how disappointed we are in your behaviour. You've let down your whole family.' Simmo sounded like an old-fashioned headmaster. 'Those drugs could have killed Mabel.'

He mumbled, 'I know.' Poor Mabel. Thank God, she was okay.

'Sheridan said the hospital rang with the results this afternoon and they confirmed traces of MDMA,' he continued. 'They have to report it to the police and the child protection agency. There will be an investigation.'

Police. Investigation. Child protection. Shit, he was going to Cooma jail for sure. Or did they put fifteen-year-olds in juvie? Either way, he wouldn't survive. Would his mates visit him in jail or would everyone pretend he no longer existed? He thought he might puke again.

'Listen to me,' his stepfather demanded. 'Do you understand the damage you've caused?'

More frantic swallowing before he could answer. 'Yes,' he whispered.

'Your mother is so . . .' Simmo seemed to be struggling for the right word. 'We can't change our flights. We're on frequent flyer points and it's complicated. Can you put Lachy on?'

'He's in the garden,' Kai said. 'The reception doesn't work out there.'

Simmo huffed. 'Tell him to call me.'

They weren't going to blame Dad, were they?

'Dad didn't know I had the drugs and I haven't been using them down here.' He needed to explain. 'I'd hidden them—'

'Too late for excuses, Kai. The damage is done.' Simmo ended the call without saying goodbye.

The girls just found them. It was an accident. Even if he'd managed to say that on the phone, Simmo wouldn't care. And now the police were coming for him.

Everyone hated him and he was going to jail. No-one wanted him around, but how was he supposed to leave this nowhere place? He couldn't drive, couldn't walk. For once, he wished it weren't holidays. The school bus delivered him right to the centre of town. From there, he could catch a train to Sydney. The house in Narrabeen was empty, with Mum and Simmo away and his sisters with their grandparents. Last year, Kai had hidden a spare key under the ledge of the front porch. The thought of being back home, in his own bed with his own things made him feel slightly better.

He had to get out of here.

19

SHERIDAN

SHERIDAN HAD PLANNED TO WAKE EVERY HOUR TO CHECK ON MABEL, but she'd slept like the dead from three am. Opening her eyes to daylight, she felt a small hand prodding her.

'Mummy, are you awake? I'm hungry.'

Yesterday, despite the roast lamb and her favourite crispy roast potatoes, Mabel had hardly eaten.

'Morning, darling.' She hugged her gently. 'Let's get some brekkie then. Any headaches or any pains?'

'Nope.' Mabel wriggled out of her grasp. 'Your breath smells yucky.'

'Sorry.' The brutal honesty of kids. 'How many fingers am I holding up?'

'Four.'

'Who's your teacher?'

'Miss Nixon. She's going on holiday to see the gorillas in Africa!'

She should introduce Miss Nixon and Lachy next term—they were both interested in travelling the world. The thought came before she could censor it.

For so long, she'd automatically considered her brother's welfare. Even when she was putting away the leftovers from lunch yesterday, she suggested Nick take some down to Lachy and Kai, but he cut her off before she finished talking: 'NO!'

She'd always considered her nephew's welfare too. All the playdates, the sleepovers, the holidays; Kai had almost become a stepson rather than a nephew. The rage coursed through her again, disorientating in its ferocity.

For so long, she'd been caring for her brother and his son. Not anymore.

After the kids were in bed last night, Nick had squeezed her tight and said, 'Mabel will be okay.'

Was he giving reassurance or asking for it? She couldn't tell. At the hospital, he'd been the strong one, but since then their roles kept switching back and forth—hopefully they wouldn't both collapse at the same moment. Her fear had been bubbling under the surface as she watched Mabel pick at her meal, as she asked questions to test her memory and her brain function.

'We could take her for a check-up as soon as we get home,' Nick suggested. 'There's that neurologist in St Leonards.'

The neurologist who had assessed Gloria. It was unfathomable that her daughter should have to see the same specialist as her mother.

Once Sheridan had the test results, she'd googled MDMA and ecstasy overdoses. She read of children being lured by the bright colours and cute stamps of their parents' drugs. One child had taken them to school and shared them with friends in the playground, assuming they were lollies. Most of the research talked about immediate management in hospital, but that meant recognising it as a drug overdose and responding accordingly.

Other kids hadn't recovered: a five-year-old and a twelve-year-old. And then there were the parties and music festivals where young people died in Australia, England, all over the world.

Drugs were the reason that Kai had been sent to live down here. Why hadn't Lachy realised he was still using them? That was his one job. Perhaps Amber had sent Kai away because she was concerned about the effect on her daughters.

The girls were allowed to eat Coco Pops over Easter, as a special holiday treat. Sheridan noted that Mabel finished a whole bowl.

Eloise looked up from her own breakfast. 'Is Kai coming back today? We have to do the bonfire.'

Another Wilson family tradition they'd missed yesterday.

'We'll do it by ourselves,' Sheridan said. 'It'll be great fun!'

Mabel burst into tears. 'You're wrecking everything.'

'You were mean to Kai,' Eloise grumbled. 'You yelled at him so loud.'

She could hear her own mother telling her to pull the family back together: *Don't you dare create a family rift, Sheridan.* Which would be hypocritical, considering Gloria had basically run away from home. *Not from home,* Mum would correct her on the rare occasion they discussed it. *From my father and his church.*

If Mabel seemed fine, they'd leave tomorrow morning and Lachy and Kai could return to the cabin. They'd skip the week in Jindabyne and go home to Sydney, organise a follow-up appointment, and keep an eye on Mabel. Fortunately, Royal North Shore Hospital was less than ten minutes from their house. There wouldn't be another terrifying trip in Ronnie's truck through the dark, twisty roads of the high country.

✕

In the afternoon, they built a fire, toasted marshmallows and made damper, but Mabel still complained: 'It's not the same without Kai and Uncle Lachy.' Kai would have told silly ghost stories by the fire. Lachy always helped them toast the perfect marshmallow. The girls sniped at each other, argued over the length of their toasting sticks, cried when their marshmallows dropped off and melted in the flames. The damper was too hot, the golden syrup too sticky, the ground too hard, the wind too cold, the fire too small. Sheridan gathered her girls into a cuddle, but they pushed her away.

'Can we see Kai before we go?' Mabel asked.

'Why can't they sleep in their own beds?' Eloise demanded.

'You're ex-clu-ding them, Mummy.' Mabel's small fist hit her in the thigh. 'At school, we're not allowed to exclude anyone. It's not kind.'

Even if she explained, the girls wouldn't understand; they'd say they found the 'lollies' and it wasn't Kai's fault. But they wouldn't be seeing their uncle or cousin any time soon. Who knew if they'd be speaking again by Thanksgiving, the next tradition on the Wilson calendar.

The girls went inside to watch *101 Dalmatians*; she'd check on them again in a few minutes, but right now, she needed some time out. Sitting by the fire, she sipped her mulled wine, another of her mother's traditions. With Lachy elsewhere, she'd decided not to make it, but while she'd been playing with the girls, Nick had simmered it on the stove, following Gloria's recipe. Bless him. The smell of it conjured the happiness of bonfires past: Lachy strumming his guitar, Mum singing and dancing in the orange glow, Dad poking foil-wrapped potatoes into the coals, and a much-younger Nick kissing her sneakily while they collected wood.

As the spiced red wine warmed her, she stared at the flames, still shaken by how close they'd come to tragedy. The doctor who had called with Mabel's results explained it was mandatory to report the drug poisoning. A risk assessment would be undertaken. When Kai was interviewed, would he be charged?

Nick offered her a refill of wine from the thermos, but she declined. She needed to stay alert for Mabel. She heard Cruella de Vil's rant drifting from the television inside: *I don't care how you kill the little beasts, but do it, and do it now.*

'I'm not sure I can ever forgive Kai,' she said. 'Or Lachy.'

'You don't have to.' He massaged the knots in her shoulders.

'I thought things were going well down here.' Her agitation was rising again and she took the last sip of her wine. 'But Lachy didn't even realise he had the drugs.'

'He'll probably argue you can't stop teenagers doing what they want, but that was the whole point of Kai being here—' Nick paused. 'He should've been on top of it.'

'It's Mum's parenting all over again.' The expectations placed on Sheridan were a zillion percent higher than those put on her brother. 'She let Lachy get away with everything.'

'And we do too.'

Surely she'd misheard him. 'What?'

'Lachy's my best mate, but we've helped him and his son for too long. Now we need to hold them to account. They almost killed Mabel.'

Conflicting emotions jangled inside her. Lachy's work on water projects saved lives while she and Nick did office jobs.

She'd loved having a baby nephew and spending time with Kai. Last year, though, it had felt too much. With the girls, her own business, Nick working all hours and Mum in the nursing home, Kai was one obligation too many.

When Kai was a toddler, she'd imagined him and their first baby as great friends. She could still recall her joy at her eighteen-week ultrasound: a boy! They told Kai he'd have a new playmate called Toby. 'You'll have so much fun together.' It would be the same age gap as her and Lachy; two little boys, almost brothers, kicking a ball, digging in the sandpit. They'd go on holidays together, play in the snow at Mimosa Hideout, ride horses with their grandfather, have dress-ups and parties with their grandmother. Then, at twenty-four weeks, the specialist said the baby had three defects in his heart and pronounced the pregnancy incompatible with life. On a sunny spring day, full of blooming buds and renewal, she'd laboured to deliver her son. Tiny Toby. They'd scattered his ashes off the headland where Nick had proposed. Their families had been with them, holding their hands, tossing flowers into the sea, crying. Lachy sent his love from somewhere in the Pacific. For months afterwards, every time she cuddled Kai, she'd had to steel herself against the pain. Sometimes she imagined Toby playing alongside him. It took years for her to fall pregnant again. And while she was ecstatic to give birth to a very healthy Eloise, she knew the relationship between her daughter and Kai would never be the same as the one she'd imagined for the two boys.

Lost in her grief, she didn't answer Nick.

'Lachy didn't have to work overseas all the time,' he said. 'Look at him now, consulting from here. That doesn't require so much travel. He could've found a different job.'

Then her brother wouldn't have been who he was.

'Um, I don't know.'

'You're doing it right now.' He poked at the flames. 'You're excusing him.'

'But we need someone to make a difference in the world while we live in comfort and pay our taxes.' She gave a half-laugh.

'Are you kidding me? You're making a difference to so many people. You've been helping with Kai forever. You sorted out everything after your dad died and you've been looking after your mum for almost two years. I'm taking care of the finances. But where's Lachy for the medical appointments and the weekly crises? He finally comes home and hides down here.'

Whoa. Nick had clearly had enough of her family. Leaning over, she kissed him hard on the lips. 'I appreciate everything you've been doing.'

'I'd do anything for you.' He took a deep breath then went back to his tirade. 'Did you know some woman in the States told Lachy that she might be pregnant with his baby?'

For God's sake, Lachy was totally irresponsible with his one-night stands. As far as she knew, he hadn't had a proper girlfriend for six years.

'A baby? Really?' She sighed. 'We should welcome it into the family but after this weekend, I just can't . . .'

'It's weird, though.' Nick sipped on his mulled wine. 'She asked for a DNA test, but you can't check the paternity of a foetus like that. It has to be a blood test.'

Sheridan didn't know enough about paternity testing to add anything useful, and perhaps Nick didn't either. Why else would someone want Lachy's DNA? Friends had done the online DNA kits and, for the amount of information that came back, it seemed like a waste of money. She knew her ancestry: Dad's side was descended from Irish convicts transported to Australia in the 1840s, presumably the girls' red hair had come from them; Mum's family were American, probably with a bit of German from the Pennsylvania Dutch settlers.

She'd seen a brochure on the mantelpiece last night: *Who do you resemble more, your father or your mother?* It made her wonder about her own girls: Eloise had Sheridan's practical approach but where did Mabel get her sensitive side? She'd kept reading: *Every child inherits half of their DNA from their mother and half from the father. Technically, though, because the X chromosome is a different size, and due to mitochondrial DNA, we all inherit just a little bit more from our mothers.* She should tell Ronnie: it was a scientific fact that mothers did more than their fair share in the world.

And some fathers were frigging irresponsible; there might be another child inheriting Lachy's irresponsible genes.

After their whingey, whiny day, she expected her girls to grumble about bedtime, but they both went off easily. Later, crawling into bed with Mabel, she too went straight to sleep—only for them both to be woken in the middle of the night by her phone.

'Mummy?'

'It's all right, darling,' she whispered. 'Go back to sleep.'

She took the mobile out into the kitchen, answering it on the way. The caller had an American accent. Was it one of her relatives from Pennsylvania?

'Hello, can you hear me?' A female voice she didn't recognise.

'Yes.'

'Am I speaking with Sheridan Brandt? You're next of kin—' The blood drained from her head to her toes. The woman must be calling about Mum. Why did it have to happen when she was five hours away from the nursing home?

She held on to the kitchen bench for support. 'Gloria Wilson is my mother.'

'No, this isn't about your mother.' The woman paused. 'I'm so sorry. I've woken you, haven't I? I got the time difference wrong. You didn't catch my introduction?'

Sheridan released the breath she'd been holding. 'No, I must have missed it. I was trying not to wake the rest of the family.'

'I'm Naomi Chidozie and I'm calling from Global Social Solutions in Washington DC. You're listed as next-of-kin for your brother, Lachlan Wilson. He hasn't been in contact with head office for months and we need to speak with him about some allegations.'

20

LACHY

AT MIDNIGHT, A BARKING DOG ROUSED LACHY FROM SLEEP. WHEN THE yapping stopped, he tried to settle down again but his thoughts jumped from one dilemma to the next. Would Mabel recover fully? Would Kai be charged? Could Amber stop him from seeing his son?

Lying there, he wished for a book or his laptop—anything to distract him. He pulled open the drawer of the bedside table, hoping to find a novel or an old magazine. The moon lit up the room and he could see a mess of odds and ends inside the drawer, along with an old guidebook to Russia. As he lifted it out, he realised it was entangled with a thick blue ribbon. Not just a ribbon; a heavy gold medal with *Australia* engraved on the front. Jesus, had Ronnie been awarded an Order of Australia?

The guidebook was in German so he couldn't read it. The photos provided a brief distraction for five minutes until his mind began to replay his phone conversation with Amber and Simmo and the implicit subtext: *You're not fit to be a father.* And they were right. In addition to the drug episode, Tuesday night still haunted him.

He gave up any pretence of looking at the Russia guidebook and placed it back in the drawer. Stretching out on the bed, he stared at the ceiling, his thoughts jumping from missing Mum and Dad to eco-grief to moving here. Living at Mimosa was supposed to bring back that sense of security he'd had as a kid. But instead of reassuring him, it had reinforced how much had changed.

Or maybe he'd changed. At the beginning of last year, he'd felt his anxiety growing. There was no defining moment, just an accumulation of the effects of climate change on his work. Half a billion people faced constant water shortages. For another four billion, water was scarce for part of the year. Insane numbers of lives. Reports of more droughts and bushfires and floods and heatwaves across the globe had intensified his ecological distress. He'd done all the right things, talked to his colleagues, joined some online forums and read up on strategies to overcome climate anxiety. And it had been helping . . . until the last month in Kenya . . . until DC . . . until Juliet requested a DNA test.

Since then, his brain had gone into overdrive and hadn't stopped spinning.

Except during the blackouts.

After that first time at summer camp, he'd freaked out. It had taken him a little while to learn how to pace his drinks and stop it happening again. By the time he started work, he had it under control. The only times it seemed unavoidable were the nights he'd fly back from an aid project into the land of plenty. Before the Dalgety pub, it had happened in Australia twice, at uni. Sheridan had been there but he'd never told her; she'd be appalled about his memory loss.

Oh God, Sheridan. How could they move on from this? They'd never had a proper falling-out before. Only minor arguments about her overstepping boundaries; heated discussions about the best care for Mum; or him working overseas at a 'crucial' time.

His sister was capable of holding a grudge. And in this case, it was absolutely justified.

But he needed Sheridan. And Nick too, of course. They were his safe haven of acceptance, his memories. He couldn't lose them.

✕✕

He must have dozed off eventually, as the clattering of the screen door woke him: Ronnie going out to feed the dogs, the chickens and the goats. As he dressed in yesterday's clothes, he decided he would go back to the cabin before lunch. Sheridan wanted him to wait until her family had left, but they needed to see each other now, otherwise the distance would grow. Kai should apologise today, face to face.

In the kitchen, Ronnie was pouring tea from a pot while porridge bubbled in a saucepan on the stove.

'Thanks for having us,' he said. 'We'll get out of your hair today.'

A relieved grunt from Ronnie.

'And thanks for making porridge. It reminds me of Dad—he'd serve it every Saturday morning in winter. I'll wake Kai so he can have it hot.'

'Leave him to sleep.' She took out two bowls from the cupboard. 'He'll need his energy.'

Ronnie was right; his son would need strength for the firing squad of Sheridan and Nick. He had thought that Kai would feel secure enough to confide in him about the drugs; it hurt that he hadn't.

'Before you leave, could you help me with one last job?' Ronnie asked. 'A falling branch knocked the lid off the trough in the bottom paddock. That ill wind did damage everywhere.'

><

After they'd fixed the trough and checked the horses, they returned to the farmhouse. Kai was still sleeping. Ronnie shook her head in disapproval. 'I didn't mean he should stay in bed all morning.'

'I'll wake him up,' Lachy said, trying to tamp down his irritation.

At fifteen years old, Lachy had been up early every morning, feeding the horses, helping Mum out with her events on weekends, and working Thursday nights at the local fruit store. He'd placed hardly any expectations on Kai, and yet the boy couldn't even get out of bed. So what if he was shattered after all the physical work on the farm? It was disrespectful to Ronnie.

Kai had been sleeping on a couch in the small sitting room near the back entrance; he would have heard them go out earlier. Lachy knocked on the sitting room door and waited for an answer.

Nothing.

'Kai, time to get up,' he called.

Not even a grumble.

As he turned the doorhandle, his whole body tensed. *We all just blamed him, accused him of nearly killing his cousin. That's a lot for a teenager to handle; he must have been terrified. Why didn't we arrange for him to see a counsellor straight away?* Lachy had meant to give him a hug last night. *I have to tell him how much we all love him. Please, please don't let it be too late.*

The sleeping bag was folded, the pillows stacked on top, but there was no sign of Kai.

Stepping forward, Lachy noticed a sheet of paper on the coffee table. With shaking hands, he picked it up.

Dear Dad,
I've let you all down. Please tell Aunty Sheridan, I never
meant to hurt anyone. I'm going away to give everyone
a break. Don't look for me. I'm not worth it.
Kai

21

ELIZABETH, 1968

FOR THE PAST SIX WEEKS, I'D VOLUNTEERED AT THE SOLDIERS' HOME every Wednesday and enjoyed the pleasure of Charlie's company, especially on the way home. Thankfully, Father never heard about the change in driving arrangements although Walt, the building supervisor, wasn't happy. He kept sidling up to me in the kitchen, offering me a ride in his truck. His dark hair was slicked back and, whenever he saw me approaching, he'd take a comb from his pocket and run it through the sides. One night, he invited me to a dance, even though he was twice my age. Walt gave me the creeps and I was so relieved to be going home with Charlie instead.

Charlie told me about the first death he'd witnessed, a twenty-eight-year-old injured in a factory accident. 'He had everything ahead of him,' Charlie said. 'It made me realise how precious our time is on earth. I want to live life now.' His words echoed exactly how I felt, and we began sharing our dreams. I'd never talked like this with anyone, apart from Gloria. She still didn't know about Charlie—he was my special secret.

And this week, I would be seeing him twice. He'd invited me to a fair in Pottstown on Saturday afternoon. I told my parents that a doctor at the Soldiers' Home required additional assistance on the weekend. Even while I was apologising to God for the lie, I was looking forward to it. Pottstown was in Montgomery County, the same as the Soldiers' Home and far enough away that I was unlikely to see any of the church community. I had assumed Charlie was taking me to the fair where ladies in Regency dress served a chicken salad luncheon and raised money for the historical society. I felt Father would not object to such an outing, except that Charlie was not from our church.

When Charlie steered the Mustang into a makeshift parking lot in a field, I spotted a Ferris wheel in the distance and realised my mistake. This was no historical country fair but a travelling carnival. Now I had to beg God's forgiveness for attending a place where all types of sins were committed.

As we weaved through the crowds, Charlie took my hand. 'I don't want to lose you.'

He was more handsome than ever in the afternoon sun. I knew it was wrong to compare him to others but I couldn't help it. Charlie was more attractive, more sensitive, more knowledgeable. Being around him made my world bigger.

'Let's start with the speedway.' He indicated the small cars going around a circular track.

My senses overwhelmed by the sights and sounds, I was happy to follow his lead. When I admitted that I'd never been to such a place before, that Father would never allow it, he held out his arms like the showman we'd just strolled past. 'I'll be your guide and unveil the wonders of the travelling carnival to your amazed eyes!'

As we arranged ourselves inside the tiny car on the speedway, our thighs pressed together. I felt myself blushing, which only made me heat up more.

'Let's pretend we're driving to Australia?' He smiled at me. 'Yesterday I saw a classified ad in the medical journal about a position in the city of Brisbane. It feels like . . .'

And now, he was the one blushing.

'It feels like what?' I prompted him.

'Our destiny.'

><

All through the afternoon, my body remained aquiver with the excitement of the new: Charlie, of course, but also the thrilling rides, the sideshow alley with its raucous patter and fun games. Men drank at the bar, showgirls flaunted their décolletage, hippies lounged on the grass passing around cigarettes that smelt different from ordinary tobacco.

'Marijuana,' Charlie explained.

'No!' I gasped. 'Why are they being so indiscreet?'

'It's the new age. Young people are breaking free from their parents' traditions.'

What must he think of me, with my talk of Father's strict rules? Desperate to show him that I could be free too, I stood on tiptoes and kissed his cheek. A bold move. I had to shut my eyes while I did it.

'Thank you for bringing me here,' I said.

He answered with his own kiss, pulling my body against his, lightly pressing his lips to mine. Dizzy with delight and shock, I couldn't breathe. God worked in mysterious ways—my punishment for talking to the bad boys on the bus had led me to the man of my dreams.

'You are the most gorgeous girl.' His intense blue eyes fixed on my face. 'You bring light and laughter wherever you go.'

At the top of the Ferris wheel, he asked if he could kiss me properly. His lips sent shockwaves through my body, the swaying carriage adding to my butterflies. *Thank you, God, for creating him and for bringing us together.*

Afterwards we strolled down sideshow alley; I averted my eyes as we passed the exotic show with a line of men, young and old. Charlie spotted a game of knock 'em down cans and promised to win a prize for me.

'I've got great hand–eye coordination,' he boasted.

I giggled at his cockiness even as I repressed a shiver. Pride, the deadliest of all sins and the root of all evil. It was the original sin, committed by Satan when he wouldn't recognise God as the Almighty.

Charlie gestured to the dolls and teddies hanging behind the pyramids of tin cans. 'What takes your fancy, Betty?'

The prettiest doll was the largest one, almost the size of a toddler. 'How about her?'

'You've got good taste, miss, but expensive,' said the man running the stall. 'That row cost double.'

'Anything for my girl.' Charlie handed over a dime and took the balls.

My girl.

I held my breath as he lined up his throw. The first ball knocked down the entire pyramid; the same happened with his second ball, and the third.

'You'd make a good surgeon with skills like that,' I said.

'Maybe I'll specialise as a surgeon in Australia.' He held the doll in front of me and jiggled her in a little dance. She was prettier than any doll I'd ever seen, with wide-open eyes and a lovely smile on her leather face. The red ribbons in her plaits matched her red polka dot dress, and she wore white socks and red shoes.

'She's adorable,' I cried, hugging her against my chest.

'What should we name her?' His arm was around my waist, his hand on the doll's hair. I could picture our future in Australia: Charlie the surgeon with me, his charming wife, and our daughter.

22

LACHY

LACHY DROVE TO MIMOSA, HOPING BY SOME MIRACLE THAT HIS SON had walked home. But there was no sign of him. Sheridan was in the kitchen packing the dishwasher while Nick and the girls played out on the ridge.

When he told her about Kai going missing, she was unimpressed.

'Oh for God's sake, these self-centred teenagers think it's all about them. I've got enough to deal with at the moment.' She stomped across the kitchen, put the milk in the fridge and slammed the door. 'Does he have a location app on his phone?'

'Amber is all for trust and honesty. She doesn't believe in tracking people.'

'Hudson might be able to find him on Snap Maps,' she suggested. 'Call his friends, ask them where he's gone.'

'I don't . . .'

'You don't know who his friends are.' She rolled her eyes. 'Such an involved father.'

The sarcasm cut deep. Her attitude echoed the implicit message from Amber: *You're a crap father—you don't even know him.* He'd tried to be a good dad by moving down here, but he'd been too distracted by his own issues.

Unlike Nick. The perfect father, building a cubbyhouse with his girls under the clump of snow gums out on the ridge.

'I don't think Kai has any friends here,' he said. 'That sleepover the other night was the first time he's been out.'

'When Nick went to pick him up, he said there were sixty kids on the farm.' She pursed her lips. 'It wasn't a sleepover, it was a party.'

So Kai had lied to him, and Lachy hadn't double-checked with Ethan's folks. Another parenting fail.

'I'll call Hudson.' He took a breath. 'What about the police?'

'Sure. They'll be keen to talk to him after he endangered my daughter's life and put her in hospital.'

The nebulous dread that had been drifting through him formed into a lump in his throat. He swallowed and clenched his jaw. His brain had stopped working, he couldn't figure out the first step to finding his son.

Sheridan sighed and sat down on a stool. 'Sorry for being a bitch.' She put her elbows on the counter and held her head in her hands. 'I just can't deal with Kai running away. I'm exhausted. I was awake all night worrying.'

Earlier, rushing into the cabin, he hadn't looked at her properly—now he noticed the dark circles under her eyes, the pale cheeks, the cracked lips.

He made a cup of tea for her and put a hot cross bun in the toaster. Food was their dad's answer to any problem. But this time, the problems were all Lachy's fault, and he couldn't solve them. Thank God, the girls were in good form, back to their usual selves. He couldn't bear thinking of the alternative.

'Kai is devastated about it all. I'm scared he'll . . . do something to himself.' Saliva filled his mouth; it couldn't get past that lump in his throat. 'His note said: *Don't look for me. I'm not worth it.*'

'He won't harm himself.' She shook her head so emphatically that her thick hair bounced. 'He's hiding from the mess he created. That's his usual style. I'll send him a text saying the girls are fine.'

Lachy was about to ask if she could go one step further—say she accepted it was an accident and Kai was forgiven—when she began speaking again.

'You're part of the reason I was awake all night.'

'I'm fine. You don't need to worry about me.'

'Everyone is worrying about you, Lachy.' She placed her mug on the benchtop and eyeballed him. 'An HR woman from your work called me. You're not answering their emails or phone calls. Apparently, you're on extended leave.'

'Oh, shit. I'm sorry.' If he'd discussed this with her months ago, she would have been supportive; now she'd just think he was negligent and irresponsible. And he was. But he was also demoralised and heavy-hearted. And angry. That bloody organisation had done nothing.

'What's going on?'

'Let's talk about it later. We have to find Kai.' He busied himself locating Hudson's number on his phone.

'He'll be okay. This is how he responds to difficult situations. By refusing to face them.' She paused. 'A bit like you right now. Your HR woman wouldn't tell me anything. I've been imagining horrendous scenarios all night.'

'I really don't want—'

'Did you know Kai rang me to come down early because he was concerned about you? It's affecting him too.'

'I . . . uh . . . hadn't . . .'

The screaming seemed to fill the whole kitchen; his body tensed and he instinctively put his hands over his ears. Sheridan watched him quizzically. She couldn't hear it; he carried the sound within him.

'What's happening?' she asked. 'You look like you're in pain.'

Relentless, excruciating pain: she was also in pain, Kai too, and the whole fucking planet. But if he told her, she'd interpret it as another of his failures. A shitty father *and* a pathetic man.

She was studying him, her face creased in concern. 'You're scaring me, Lachy. Do I need to call triple zero again?'

'No, no.' The last thing he wanted was to worry her. 'The pain's not . . . physical. It's in here.' He lay a palm across the crown of his head, as if he could soothe the agony inside.

'I'm seriously freaking out now.' She grabbed his other wrist. 'Please just talk to me.'

It would hurt him to tell her about it, but could it also help? Maybe speaking of it would get the screaming out of his head. He was still deciding when she squeezed his arm and pleaded with him again: 'Tell me'. His big sister, his biggest supporter, Sheridan was always in his corner; she might judge him but that wouldn't stop her from helping him.

'It's . . . um . . . I've seen so many tragedies, but this one . . .' He started slowly. On the one hand, there was the cumulative effect of death: five-year-old Nyanjera dying by the roadside, undernourished babies and vulnerable grandparents collapsing from disease, neighbours killing for water, the devastating impact of drought on the whole community. And on the other hand, the betrayal of his trust and the sense that he was somehow accountable—he should have prevented this particular tragedy.

They'd been working in north-eastern Kenya, near the Somali border where the rivers had dried up, the crops were gone and much of the livestock dead. The women and children were walking miles every day in search of puddles of water, while the men took the remaining goats and camels to find scraps of vegetation. Lachy's team had provided water filters so the community could safely drink the muddy sludge the women carried home. In the meantime, they were drilling a series of bore holes and setting up desalination units to purify the groundwater.

'Do you remember me talking about my boss, Henrik?'

'Yeah, the German guy.' Sheridan nodded. 'You joked that you'd been with him for five years, longer than any girlfriend. You said he taught you so much.'

Henrik, his mentor, his mate. After their third project, on a big night out in DC, they'd got matching tattoos, a circle of water around their biceps. The next morning, Lachy had wondered aloud about the bandage on his arm. He'd admitted to Henrik that the entire evening was a blank. Lachy liked the tattoo, but these days, it was a constant reminder of his boss.

'Henrik was great . . . and then he wasn't.'

'What did he do?'

Looking back, Lachy assumed there must have been a pattern he'd missed. Like him, Henrik was single with an ex-partner and kids back home. During their trips, they'd both had flings with fellow aid workers, double dates with expats and fun nights with women in DC. Out in the field, their role was to help vulnerable communities but Henrik had been doing the opposite.

'We'd put solar-powered desal units in this community, then we had to go back a few months later to check on them.' He closed his eyes against the memory. 'A teenage girl approached us. She told us she was pregnant, that Henrik was the father and he'd promised her money and marriage.'

The girl was weeping, her parents yelling in their tribal language. Henrik answered in Swahili. *Nini? Unanitania?* He'd kept uttering in disbelief. *What? Are you kidding me?*

'Culturally, it was a huge problem for the girl to be pregnant and unmarried,' he explained to Sheridan. 'A real predicament, especially in the drought. The family had six children; they couldn't feed another. The girl needed a husband. Henrik said it was a ridiculous accusation, that they were trying to exploit him for money. I believed him. They could just as easily have accused me. Foreigners are always being asked for cash or encouraged to take a wife.'

The politics of working in Kenya were tricky, with the ongoing effects of colonisation on the economy and capitalism on the climate. Lachy was no white saviour—he just wanted to use his skills where he could make the most impact. Installing water systems and training locals in remote areas showed immediate, meaningful results.

'Did Henrik give them money?' Sheridan asked.

'No. We had to check the units before it got dark, so we promised to see them in the evening. But just as we were finishing, these awful screams ripped through the air. Down by the dried-up river, we found the girl's family with her body. She'd tied a rope to a tree . . .'

'Oh my God.' Sheridan blinked in shock. 'That's horrendous. How old was she?'

'Fifteen.' The same age as Kai. 'Her name was Zahra.'

'And did you find out if Henrik was responsible?'

'He kept denying it. Henrik had his pick of sophisticated ladies in Nairobi. I couldn't imagine he'd choose a young country girl out in this dusty place. He insisted she'd used him as a scapegoat for her shame.' Lachy massaged his temples. 'But she'd been so desperate that she'd taken her own life. It didn't make sense to me.'

If Lachy hadn't been so quick to defend his boss, if he'd listened properly to what the girl was saying, Zahra would be alive. Over the next month, he'd held off notifying head office, even though her suicide had unhinged him. But when they were back in Nairobi at the hotel, he spotted Henrik kissing a young girl and pulling her into his room. She was wearing a bracelet that Henrik had bought at the market that morning as a gift for his daughter. For the next few days, Lachy spied on his boss. He watched two other young girls enter his hotel room.

'It was sickening. I wrote up what I'd seen and delivered it to the HR department when I returned to head office. The operations director was called into my meeting and he said that Henrik was our best project manager in water and had important German contacts. He wanted more concrete evidence to support my accusations, but I didn't have any.'

Concrete evidence was almost impossible, especially from remote, north-eastern Kenya. Zahra's father might corroborate Lachy's report but there were language and cultural barriers to overcome. All of the team, local and international, would side with Henrik—he was a great boss to them. And despite their policies, GSS wouldn't act without more evidence. Lachy knew how long an investigation could take; they'd just spent two years trying to prosecute a contractor who had stolen aid funds meant for solar hardware. Lachy had put so much time into the investigation and it wasn't resolved satisfactorily. The contractor never returned the money and continued to work for other firms.

Disillusioned by the director's priorities and overwhelmed by the impossibility of getting more evidence, Lachy had walked away. He knew it was wrong—guilt ate at him—but he'd felt betrayed by everyone.

'Is Henrik still in the field?'

'Yes. He has all the right connections in Kenya, in America and Germany.' Lachy shook his head. 'Henrik went to uni in DC. He was in college with half the senior management team.'

Sheridan leant closer; he could almost see the cogs turning in her brain. 'You have to keep fighting. It's not fair that the whistleblower leaves and the wrongdoer stays. Henrik is a paedophile preying on vulnerable girls. You need to go to America and talk to them.'

'No, Sheridan, you don't understand.' This was more than a job; it was his whole life. He'd been with Henrik day and night, working, eating, sleeping, travelling together. They'd relied on each other in extreme circumstances. When a Somalian rebel had pulled a gun on them, Henrik had talked him down, got them both out of the situation safely. Lachy had trusted him completely. Just like GSS continued to trust in him. 'I can't work for a company that doesn't stick to its child protection policies. I tried but they won't listen.'

'Come on, Lachy.' She persisted. 'It's not like you to give up.'

'I know but right now I'm burnt out. Done.' He picked up his phone again. 'And I have to find my son.'

He understood Sheridan's distress at the thought of what damage Henrik might still be causing, but Lachy had already lost that fight. The agonising screams reverberated in his mind.

Zahra had considered herself a shameful burden and could see only one solution.

He was terrified his son might feel the same way.

23

KAI

KAI HAD SPENT THE WHOLE NIGHT AWAKE, TERRIFIED. ALONE IN THE shearing shed, he'd pulled the top of the sleeping bag over his eyes to protect his head from mice and rats and redback spiders. The floorboards were infused with sheep shit, the scent wafting into his nostrils whichever way he turned. The corrugated-iron roof creaked as if someone were walking across it. The air outside was pierced by screeching—owls hunting or possums fighting. He hadn't asked Tarni about snakes: would they be slithering around at this time of year? The nocturnal fears just piled onto his fears about Mabel and his own future. To distract himself, he'd begun an alphabetic listing of countries: Afghanistan, Albania, Algeria, Andorra, Angola, Antigua and Barbuda . . . He felt the whisper of a touch against his face and repressed a scream. Had the spiders made it inside his sleeping bag? His country listing changed into a chant: *By tomorrow evening, I'll be back in Sydney. Tomorrow night, I'll be sleeping in my own bed.*

Tarni and her brother Max had picked him up at midnight a kilometre from Ronnie's house. He was sure the rumble of the engine would wake Ronnie and Dad; hardly any cars came down

159

that road and sound echoed around the valley. But he'd made it out with just one dog yapping. When Tarni had agreed to help and hide him in her family's shearing shed, he'd imagined she would stay with him, talking until the early hours and watching the sun rise together. But she'd rushed inside to her bedroom, not wanting to alert her parents. Max showed Kai to the shed, handed him a sleeping bag and warned him to watch out for the rats; that was when Kai had started freaking about the nocturnal wildlife.

But what did one sleepless night matter? Tomorrow morning he'd hitch a ride from Warabina into Cooma, and from there he'd get the train to Sydney. He imagined the look on Hudson's face when he casually turned up at Macca's. Chuckling to himself, he'd switched off his location on Snap Maps so he could surprise his friends.

✕✕

But things didn't go according to plan the next morning. A bunch of sheep had escaped into the wrong paddock, and Tarni and Max had to round them up and bring them back before Max could give him a lift into town.

'You'll have to hide out here till lunchtime,' Tarni said, as she delivered an apple.

Around midday, she popped in with a peanut butter sandwich.

'Sorry, Dad needs our help fixing the fence. The stupid sheep snapped some wires. Max reckons he can take you into town around four.'

At four thirty, she walked in with a packet of chips.

'Dad has made Max drive him over to the Pengillys' place. He reckons they've got a couple of our missing sheep.' She slumped onto the sleeping bag beside him, narrowly missing his phone. As she went to move it, she must have noticed the screen.

'There's like a hundred missed calls from your dad,' she said. 'Do you think you should tell him you're okay?'

'Nah. He doesn't want to see me.' He offered her some chips to end the conversation. She didn't know about his cousins going to hospital and he planned to keep it that way; he'd told her that he needed to escape from a family drama.

She moved closer to him, her leg brushing his. He'd kissed two girls so far and the second one had said his kissing was too sloppy. How could he make sure it was perfect for Tarni?

They heard the sound of a car parking alongside the shed.

'That must be Max.' Tarni stood to open the big metal door. 'Do you still want that lift to town? It's getting pretty late to make the bus from Cooma. And I don't know what time the last train goes from Canberra to Sydney. Maybe you should stay here another night?'

'Why don't you come with me?' He grabbed her fingers, gently pulling her back down to the sleeping bag. 'There's no-one at my house. We can stay there, and party on the beach with my mates.'

Close beside him, she smiled and put a hand on his thigh. 'I'd love to, but Dad would kill me. I've got a list of jobs to do around the farm over the holidays.'

The imprint of her hand burnt into his jeans and heated his whole body. Yes, she definitely liked him. He leant towards her but was startled by voices outside the shed.

'Are you in there, Tarni?'

It wasn't Max.

'Shhh,' Tarni hissed. 'That's Mum. But I don't know who's with her.'

Please, not the police. Not here, in front of Tarni.

He stared across the wooden floorboards to the pens and the chutes where the sheep entered. Could he escape down the ramp? But that would just take him into the yards. He could hide at the bottom while Tarni covered for him.

Legs trembling, Kai took a few steps towards the chute. Were there rats down there? He wasn't moving fast enough; light began filling the shed as the huge metal door screeched open.

24

LACHY

LACHY RANG HUDSON AND ASKED IF HE COULD LOOK UP KAI'S LOCATION on Snap Maps.

'He's turned it off,' he said. 'Probably wouldn't matter anyway; the reception down there is crap.'

Hudson didn't know the names of any of Kai's local friends, apart from Grug.

'But he's not a mate. Grug's the school bully.'

Was Kai being bullied at Warabina High? It added another level of urgency to the search. And another level of guilt—Lachy should have known what was happening at school.

Nick gave him directions to the farm where he'd dropped Kai for the party on Friday night. Thankfully, Ethan was more helpful than Hudson, and more concerned.

'I'll give you a list of schoolmates and their addresses.' Ethan stopped to think. 'Kai wasn't here for long but he spent the whole time talking to Tarni. You could try her place.'

Tarni's mother, Mrs Ritchie, had never heard of a school friend called Kai, but she had noticed both of her children disappearing into the shearing shed at odd times during the day. She took Lachy out to check. The noise of the shed door opening, metal on metal, sent an involuntary shiver through his body, and he prayed again that Kai was safe.

At the sight of his son, tears blurred his vision. Thank God, this wasn't going to end the same way as the Kenyan nightmare. He pulled Kai into a bone-crunching hug. Despite Sheridan's reassurances that his son would be fine, he hadn't quite believed it until this moment.

'I've been so worried about you.' He sniffed back a sob. 'We all have.'

He could feel Kai wriggling with embarrassment but he didn't care. His son was alive.

'I'm sorry,' Mrs Ritchie said. 'I had no idea he was here.'

'Don't blame Tarni,' Kai said. 'It was my fault.'

Kai was taking the blame but he wasn't apologising. Lachy's relief flared to anger.

'Say sorry to Mrs Ritchie,' he ordered, aware that he was treating his son like a five-year-old.

'Sorry.' Kai gave a nervous shrug and rolled his eyes at the girl.

'Well, I'm just pleased we found you,' Mrs Ritchie said. 'It's scary when kids go missing. Do you want to come inside for a cuppa?'

'That's very kind but we need to get home. My sister's packing up to leave for Sydney and she's desperate for news about Kai.'

In the ute, Lachy managed to suppress his anger and rekindle his gratitude for Kai's safe return. Zahra hadn't been able to see any future; he had to make sure his son could picture a way forward.

'You've had a lot to deal with lately,' he said gently. 'How about I organise some counselling sessions for you?'

Kai screwed up his nose. 'A counsellor will just say I'm bad.'

'That's not what counsellors do. They help you understand your behaviour, process what's happened and give you strategies to cope.' He realised his own hypocrisy. So far, he'd refused counselling: he didn't want to talk about Kenya and he couldn't see the future for himself. 'Tomorrow, I'll take you to a counsellor in Cooma and we can get Macca's afterwards. You can eat as much meat as you want.'

Kai smiled. 'Wow, Dad, you must've been really worried.'

That smile would disappear when he learnt the address of their other appointment in Cooma.

✕

Sheridan and Nick gave Kai a quick hug and then the girls enveloped him.

'We've got Easter eggs for you,' Eloise said.

'We love you,' Mabel shrieked with delight. 'But you're very naughty because—'

Lachy held his breath waiting for her to finish. *Because you had illegal drugs . . . because you nearly killed me . . . because the police want to speak with you.*

'Because running away is very bad. Mummy says we shouldn't run away from problems.'

'You made a mistake,' Sheridan said to Kai. 'But it's all about how you behave after that mistake.'

God, she could have been talking directly to Lachy. He'd run from country to country to country. Little Miss Perfect Sheridan never needed to run away because she never made a mistake.

Eloise and Mabel begged to stay another night and have a bonfire with Kai. After much nagging, Sheridan agreed, and

Kai helped the girls find long sticks to toast their marshmallows. Mabel was telling Kai about *101 Dalmatians*. 'Pongo and Perdita have to save their puppies from Cruella de Vil. She kidnapped them to make fur coats.' Listening to her chatter gave Lachy a double shot of relief. Maybe, just maybe, they could all come out of this weekend intact.

Staring into the flames, he pictured his parents here with them. Mum would be pouring mulled wine 'to warm up the insides'—Gloria had a naughty streak herself, which he presumed was a reaction to her strict upbringing. She rarely mentioned her childhood but she said her biggest sin was looking at library books when she was only supposed to read the Bible. How would her family have managed the wayward, drug-taking Kai? With a heavy hand, he suspected. They hadn't experienced the swinging sixties: Mum wasn't allowed to listen to pop music or see a film or go on a date. 'God was supposed to be our saviour, but it was a friendly Aussie called Ralph who saved me.' At this, she'd plant a huge kiss on Dad's cheek.

Lachy didn't often think about his mother's bolt for freedom. Who would she have married if she hadn't left Pennsylvania? Who would Lachy be now? A pastor in the Good News Church, like his grandfather, probably. A morally upright thirty-seven-year-old with a regular job, a supportive wife and a law-abiding teenager. In that alternate reality, he never would have drunk whisky, had blackouts and questioned his own actions. And his son never would have touched drugs.

'Can you come inside and help me with dinner?' Sheridan's question cut through his musings. 'Nick, keep an eye on the girls.'

He followed her into the kitchen, wishing she hadn't been so open about the fact that she didn't trust Kai to look out for his cousins. 'What do you want me to do?' he asked.

'I want you to go to Washington DC and sort out this situation with your head office.' She put her hand on his back. 'You can't keep running away from it.'

Bloody hell, she sounded just like Mabel talking to Kai. So she had been thinking of him in that conversation.

'I'll sort it out when I'm ready.' He gritted his teeth to stop himself from snapping at her interference. 'I told you, I'm exhausted.'

'But this isn't just affecting you. What about the other girls Henrik might be abusing?'

As if he didn't think about that every day.

'What about Kai?' she continued. 'You have to be on the ball. No-one wants to see him falling apart after this . . . episode.'

He wished he could say: *Leave me alone, keep your nose out of my business.* But Mabel's accidental overdose had proved that his problems affected her family as well. He didn't articulate his next thought either: *You're absolutely right.*

'My managers would prefer that I just resign.'

'Of course they would. It's easier for them. But that doesn't make it right.'

'I can't fly to DC.' He couldn't drive to the shops; how could he get on a plane to the States? 'I'll organise a Zoom meeting.'

'A video call?' She snorted. 'That's not going to cut it. They'll pretend to listen and do nothing. It's too easy to brush you off that way. You need to be there, in person. Show them you're serious. Refuse to leave the office until they take the next step against Henrik. You know what happened last time.'

A two-year corruption investigation which ended in stalemate, so much effort for nothing. Lachy understood what GSS would require legally and he didn't have the energy to go through it again. If only he could send Sheridan in his place, she'd keep arguing until she won.

'I'll just have to do a series of Zoom meetings to get the message across,' he said. 'I can't leave Kai here by himself and Amber's away.'

'Take him with you. He can meet all the relatives. You might even be there at the right time for Theresa and Leonard's wedding anniversary party.'

'That's next month. I've already told them I can't come.'

'Well, you can celebrate with them early. Anyway, it would be good for Kai to get an education about the world.' She raised an eyebrow. 'Show him the drug addicts and homeless camps. Scare the hell out of him.'

Jesus, she had an answer for everything. Kai had never been to America, and yes, those things would shock him. They might even make him understand how lucky he was. But honestly, neither of them would be getting on a plane.

'Okay, okay, I promise to think about it.' He moved the conversation to another topic. 'What will we have for dinner?'

As usual, his sister could see straight through him. Ignoring his question, she took his arm and marched him down the corridor to the far bedroom. She gestured for him to sit on the bed while she rummaged around in the cupboard. He could see the remains of Betty on the chair; Mum would be horrified.

'While you're in America, you can also find the girl who asked you to do the DNA test.' She was on tiptoes with her back to him, trying to reach something on the top shelf. 'I want to know if there'll be another baby in the family.'

Of course Nick had told her. Had they sat in this bedroom discussing all the ways he'd stuffed up? 'Well, Juliet has ghosted me. She won't answer my emails. Anyway, Nick reckons it could be a scam.'

'So you need to find out. Can you track her down on Instagram or Facebook?'

'I don't have her surname.' He winced as he spoke, knowing it would make her think worse of him. 'It isn't on her email address.'

That night in DC, he hadn't even planned to go out but Henrik insisted. His friend had no idea that he'd spent the previous two hours in a meeting with the HR department and the operations director lodging a formal complaint about his predatory behaviour. Not wanting to arouse suspicion, Lachy had agreed to go to the bar.

He remembered a girl with striking green eyes smiling at him from the next table. They began talking because she was wearing a brightly coloured necklace similar to the Masai tribal style. What he didn't remember: going to her apartment, having sex and leaving. The next morning, he'd woken in his hotel room panicking about his blank memory and what he might have said to Henrik. Had he told him about the complaint? Called him a paedophile? Insisted he should be locked up in jail?

The next day, GSS had requested another meeting but Lachy couldn't face it; they clearly weren't going to fire their golden boy and he couldn't recall the conversations with Henrik from the night before. He'd fled the country, telling work that his mother was sick and he needed a month's leave. Then, later, he used Kai as a reason for remaining in Australia. Henrik had messaged twice about the latest project; nothing in his tone indicated he knew of the report. Lachy had been so worried about his work situation that he'd forgotten Juliet. Her email had come out of the blue.

'You should take responsibility and find her.' Sheridan pulled a piece of paper from the cupboard and waved it at him. 'And tell me: is this related somehow?'

She handed the paper to him. It was a printout of a newspaper report detailing the death of an unidentified pregnant woman on Deadwood Creek Road, fifty miles from Philadelphia. With a rising sense of unease, he read:

> State Trooper Kurt Haigh implored the public to help: 'Somewhere, a family is waiting for their daughter to come home. They're wondering what has happened to her. Please help us identify this woman.'

Deadwood Creek Road. Apparently he'd driven Tiffany there from camp; that was what Conrad had told him the next day. Was this article about her? No, she hadn't been pregnant.

Sheridan was watching him closely, waiting for his explanation. But he had none.

'Where did this come from?' he asked. 'Why was it in the cupboard?'

'I don't know. I found it when I was making the beds and I assumed it was yours.'

It had no date on it, no newspaper masthead. Did he print it while he was in a blackout state and been so shocked that he'd hidden it from himself?

'If you haven't heard from Juliet, do you think . . .' She didn't finish her sentence.

Juliet had been killed in a hit-and-run? That was a leap. He ran another theory in his head. He'd been driving with Juliet in the car and they'd hit someone else; she remembered the accident and he did not. But why would she want his DNA? Anyway, Deadwood Creek Road was a few hours from Washington DC.

'That road is near the summer camp where Nick and I worked.'

'Yes, I googled it last night. It's notorious for deaths. There was one in the 1960s, another eighteen years ago when you were at camp. And a more recent one in September last year.'

Eighteen years ago, Tiffany had asked him to drop her off there in the middle of the night. A friend was supposed to collect her. Had he waited for the friend? Had he left her there in the dark alone? Or had he . . . had he done something to her? She'd fought back, slapped him, scratched him. The evidence had been on his own body. Fucking hell, he had no idea. He'd never heard from her again. But if something had happened to Tiffany, the police would have come to the camp and interviewed them.

The piece of paper shook in his hands. Sheridan said there had also been a death in September—the last time he'd been in the States. What was his subconscious trying to tell him with this printout?

His sister was waiting for him to speak but he couldn't even think.

'Go to America,' she said when the silence had dragged on too long. 'Talk to your work and then find Juliet. I've looked at some flights for next week and I'll email you the links. Kai will need to get an ESTA visa. I've told Naomi Chidozie from HR that you'll be coming in person for a meeting. Aunt Theresa and the rest of the family can't wait to see you.'

Unbelievable.

She'd railroaded him, practically booked the trip.

Before he flew out, he'd have to sit down at his laptop and go through all of the emails about his allegations against Henrik, his leave, his future . . . or lack of future at GSS. He'd probably had an email to say he was fired. It was too much; he'd have to do it in short bursts.

'Umm.' He tried for one last excuse not to leave the country. 'We'll have to see what happens tomorrow first.'

He didn't know which option frightened him more: flying back to America or the police interviewing Kai.

25

SHERIDAN

SHERIDAN HEAVED A SIGH OF RELIEF AS HER BROTHER LEFT THE bedroom. Thank God he'd agreed to her plan. He just didn't understand what was good for him; honestly, he was her most difficult client—made more difficult by the fact he didn't realise he *was* a client.

As always, her first instinct had been to protect her little brother. But then she'd pictured Mabel in the hospital, pale, unresponsive. It was time for Lachy to step up.

Last September, when he'd come back from Kenya, she knew something was wrong but he wouldn't explain.

'I can't do this anymore,' he'd said.

She assumed he meant the travel and the jet lag—the opposite of her domesticity.

'We should swap lives,' she'd replied, only half-joking. The thought of getting on a plane and leaving all the demands behind filled her with absolute joy. Lachy had no idea about her life; although his world always made her feel inadequate.

'I'm serious. I'm going to stay here.'

Soon after, when Amber asked for his help with Kai, his homecoming had seemed fortuitous. Now it all made sense though: he'd run away from his problems and was hiding out in Mimosa. But he had a duty to protect those young girls from Henrik. He had a duty to Juliet.

Sheridan was about to take drinks out to the bonfire when her mobile rang. Lydia. The nursing home night manager never called to deliver good news.

Lydia got straight to the point. 'Your mother has been quite agitated over the weekend. We had a small Easter service in the common room and after that, we had to give her sedatives. If you're returning tomorrow, are you able to pop in?'

She shouldn't have left Gloria alone over the holidays. And telling her that they were coming to Mimosa had probably made it worse. Poor Mum. This whole Easter break had been one disaster after another. If Kai hadn't gone missing, they'd be in Sydney already.

'Yes, I can be there tomorrow afternoon.'

It wasn't so long ago that her parents had been fit and active. Walking in the alps, cross-country skiing, horseriding, even camping on an overnight walk along the Bundian Way. Dad's death had been a shock to them all: a heart attack while bushwalking. Mum deteriorated rapidly after that, and Sheridan had found herself in the sandwich generation, crushed between crises of young and old.

'Your mother keeps asking about Betty,' Lydia said.

'That's her old doll,' Sheridan explained. 'I was planning to bring her back with me, but . . . I'll see what I can do.'

She'd have to scour the internet and find a replacement.

Betty, like the rest of them, was broken.

26

ELIZABETH, 1968

CHARLIE WAS NOW TAKING ME ON AN EXCURSION EVERY SATURDAY afternoon; he wanted to delight me with new experiences. My parents assumed I was providing extra assistance at the Soldiers' Home each week—the same lie I'd told the first time.

We went into Philadelphia and caught a trolley to Lit Brothers. I'd never been in the city before and never inside a department store. Mother and Gloria would have been amazed by the hats in the millinery section and by the dresses. Instead of sewing another outfit in the same yellow material for Constance's wedding, Mother could have bought a ready-made gown in light blue with a scalloped white lace overlay.

Charlie led me to the jewellery cabinets. 'My darling, I want to buy you a ring.'

Oh my gosh. My heart thumped with excitement while my stomach churned. Father would never approve a marriage with this wonderful man. If only I could convince him to join our church.

Charlie pointed to a silver band with an emerald setting; it was the ring I would have chosen for myself. The sales assistant opened the cabinet with a huge smile and handed it to him. He slid it onto my finger. My ring finger.

'I want to be with you forever,' he whispered. 'Once I finish my training, we can go anywhere you like. That practice in Australia has a job opening, if that's what you want.'

The ring fit my finger perfectly. It felt so right; *he* felt so right. Flinging my arms around his neck, I decided that I would leave it in God's hands. Maybe God could help Father understand our love.

When we left the department store and stepped onto the sidewalk, the emerald sparkled in the sunlight. I'd have to hide it in the potting shed, alongside my doll. That would be easy— but how could I hide my happiness?

'My father . . .' I didn't know how to have this conversation. 'Would you consider coming to our church next week?'

'I have Sunday rounds at Montgomery General for another four months. But after that, I'd be happy to join you. Does your father always give the sermon?'

'Usually.' I imagined Charlie listening to a lecture on the evils of pop music; he played those songs in his Mustang all the time. 'He is very concerned about . . . about the changes in society.'

'So am I,' Charlie said. 'Those assassinations really shook the country. We need to move forward together. Abolish racial segregation in favour of a free America.'

We'd been walking towards the trolley, and I had to stop. Stand still and take a breath. God had spoken to me, through Charlie, in a way I hadn't expected. I suddenly realised that Father was a hypocrite, railing against pop music while ignoring the real social troubles.

The thunderbolt took the gloss off my happiness; I didn't have to conceal my joy after all. At home that night, as we were finishing dinner, I asked the question.

'Father, the Bible teaches us to be loving and kind to our neighbours, to the unfortunate and the poor, so why are we not doing more in the fight against segregation?'

There was a shocked silence. Gloria widened her eyes at me.

'Elizabeth, this is not something that should concern you,' Father replied sternly. 'Where did you hear of such things, anyway? Have you been visiting the library?' He folded his napkin and laid it beside his dinner plate. 'Reading newspapers and listening to the radio? You know that is forbidden.'

'No. I was just talking to'—I couldn't think of an acceptable person quickly enough—'a cleaning lady in the Soldiers' Home.'

'Perhaps I was wrong to send you there.'

'I promise not to speak with her again.' I couldn't give up Charlie on Wednesday nights. 'I'm sorry, Father, for questioning things outside of my understanding.'

My apology wasn't enough. I would receive a whupping later.

The only way to safeguard my secret was to become the most dutiful daughter. Suppressing my questions, I turned myself into a carbon copy of my sister. Gloria had changed from a fun, adventurous teenager into a devoted worshipper; so would I.

'You've been listening attentively in youth group,' Gloria said. 'I must be doing a good job for the Lord. You're learning from me.'

Acting like my older sister bought me more freedom. As long

as I completed my chores and gave thanks to God, Mother did not ask where I was going afterwards.

Charlie took me to see *Romeo and Juliet* at the drive-in. My first ever proper film. Utterly romantic! Leonard Whiting was so handsome as Romeo and Miss Olivia Hussey, perfectly beautiful for Juliet. And there, in the passion pit, I discovered the true meaning of desire. He kissed me until my body was aflame, but he respected my virtue.

'The first time has to be special for you, my love.'

We couldn't go back to his room because he was living in hospital quarters. He promised to plan a romantic evening.

And when it finally happened, it *was* perfect. One Wednesday, after the residents in the Soldiers' Home had been settled for the night, Charlie whisked me into a consulting room and locked the door. He'd brought a quilt and cushions, a bottle of wine and a plate of cheese. As he undid my buttons, my skin tingled with excitement . . . and fear.

Could I really go through with this sin?

'I'm not sure.' Shame heated my cheeks.

'My darling, I'll be so careful.' Kind as always, but he'd misunderstood my hesitation.

'No, it's not that . . . this is against God . . .'

He sat back and held my face in his hands. 'Sweet Betty, our love is forever. The ring is a sign of my commitment. If you want to wait until we're married, we can wait.'

Of course he understood about my father, my faith.

'Thank you.' Now it was my turn to show my gratitude. I kissed his face, his throat, his chest. I'd slipped on my ring and now he clutched my hands in his. We were betrothed to each other. As our desire grew, I felt the solidity of my engagement ring. We were in love; we would marry next year. How could it be a sin if we consummated it now? Surely this would make our love even stronger.

I had never been closer to another person. Afterwards, I thanked God for this magical moment. It infused me with love, not just for Charlie but for everyone—my family, my friends, my church community, the librarian, the bus driver, the nurses, the veterans. Everyone! An intense love of the world and each creature within it.

At home, as I readied myself for bed, Gloria commented on my radiance. Oh, how I wanted to tell her about the transcendent moment of giving myself to Charlie. We'd been warned of the corruption of our morals, but it had been nothing like that. Charlie had shown me an entirely different way of seeing, as if I'd stepped out from behind a heavy curtain.

Instead, I said, 'God is magnificent and I am grateful.'

'You should ask Father if you can become a youth leader too. You've taken all of the lessons to heart and God is speaking to you. At last!' Gloria smiled. 'I thought there was no hope when you were reading those subversive books and talking to the bad boys on the bus.'

'Don't worry, Gloria, I've put all that behind me.' Soon enough, I would be a married woman. 'Although I still think we should become missionaries in Australia.'

If Gloria came with us to the faraway land, it would make me the happiest bride on earth.

The only blot on my overwhelming happiness was Walt, the building supervisor at the Soldiers' Home. The more I tried to avoid him, the more he sought me out. He gave me Hershey's milk chocolate bars and single red roses; he invited me on a variety of dates—to a picnic, a dance, even the drive-in. The thought of being in the cab of his pick-up truck, all alone with him, made me shiver. 'I can only see boys from my church,' I said. He seemed to take that as a challenge.

His persistence was scaring me. Eventually I'd confided in Charlie and he offered to speak with Walt, but I feared that the look of love on Charlie's face would reveal our secret in an instant.

And Walt would react badly: he'd be angry with me. He'd tell his cousin and the news would get back to Father.

27

KAI

AT MACCA'S, KAI ORDERED A BURGER, CHOCOLATE THICKSHAKE, FRIES, nuggets and hash browns while Dad had a single cup of coffee.

'What do you think about a trip to America?' Dad asked.

'If you have to go back to work, I can go to Narrabeen next term.' He said it casually, as if moving home wasn't his most desperate desire.

'I meant for us both.' His father grinned. 'Sheridan thinks it would be good for you to meet all the relatives. And I'd love having you with me.'

'That would be awesome!' His aunt wanted him out of sight. But he could deal with that for a trip to the States. And it would mean missing school—another few weeks without Grug and his gang.

'Great, I'll start getting it sorted.'

After lunch, Dad took him to the counsellor's office. Kai assumed it would be some lame middle-aged lady who would echo everyone else's disappointment and make him feel even shittier, but it was a guy, younger than Dad, who asked him about school and mates. He found himself sharing his biggest worry: *My old friends will forget me and I don't fit in down here. I'll have no-one and I won't belong anywhere.* The counsellor didn't mention the drugs and Kai was surprised when their fifty minutes were up. He booked in for a second visit.

His sense of relief didn't last long though.

'We've got another appointment,' Dad said, parking the car outside Cooma Police Station.

Kai's stomach churned with the junk food that Dad had used to soften him up. For a moment he considered bolting, but he'd already proven useless at running away. Useless at life.

A lanky police officer with black hair introduced himself as Sergeant Stuart Ayling. He smiled but Kai wasn't fooled. They followed the sergeant into an interview room. Kai perched on the hard chair and put his hands under his thighs. His guts were churning so much he thought he might throw up.

'Can you talk me through how you came to be in possession of ecstasy tablets?'

Sergeant Ayling had a soft voice and freckles on his knuckles. He looked more like Kai's old maths teacher than a police officer. But if Kai mentioned any names, he could never go back to his old high school, never joke with that maths teacher in the playground at lunchtime.

'I got them from some guy at a party in Sydney.' He bit down on the inside of his cheek. 'An older guy. He hangs around the parties. No-one knows his name.'

'Are you a regular user?'

'No,' he lied. 'I've only tried it twice.'

'And why did you have the pills in the cabin?'

'They were left over. I'd forgotten they were even there.'

The sergeant raised his eyebrows. Dad had told him to tell the truth—well, this was a version of the truth. But what if they asked Tarni or Ethan? They knew he'd been planning to bring pingers to the party last Friday.

'It's different in Warabina,' Kai said. 'I haven't been to any parties.'

'We don't want drugs from the city here.' Sergeant Ayling shook his head. 'Did you give the pills to your cousins?'

'No! Of course not.' He couldn't stop the rush of tears. 'They're kids. I'd never do that. I hid them in the games cupboard and they found them. They thought they were lollies. I was so scared for Mabel.'

'Do you understand the dangers of ecstasy and illegal drugs?'

'Yes. I'll never touch them again.' Tears and snot dribbled down his face. Dad passed him a tissue and he blew his nose. 'I'm sorry. I know I shouldn't have had them.'

His babbled apology didn't seem to make any difference to Sergeant Ayling, who was writing something on a form.

'Where are the pills now?'

He had no idea but Dad answered. 'My sister disposed of them. I think she crushed them up and put them into the bin.'

'Right, so we have no physical evidence remaining?'

'I guess not,' Dad agreed.

'You endangered the lives of your cousins, Kai. We're considering whether to caution you or charge you. There will also be an assessment by child protection services. Mr Wilson, do you believe there is a risk of this happening again? Are the girls in danger?'

'No,' Dad said. 'My sister and I feel there's no risk.'

That wasn't true; Sheridan didn't trust him. Waiting to hear the outcome, he kept gnawing on the fleshy part of his cheek.

'This is your first offence, so we're not going to charge you'—Kai's spirits leapt, but the sergeant hadn't finished—'*yet*. We'll need to investigate further.'

'Thank you, Sergeant,' Dad said. 'I have to go to America for work and I wanted to take Kai with me. Is it possible for him to come? We'll be away for less than two weeks.'

'I'll check with my superintendent.'

Until the very last minute, Kai wasn't sure if he'd be allowed to leave the country. Eventually the approval came, and with it, a date for his next appointment at the police station. He had to return in four weeks' time. A metallic taste filled his mouth; he'd bitten so hard on the inside of his cheek that he'd drawn blood.

The last time he'd flown with Dad had been to Thailand for a beach holiday when he was ten. So much fun. They'd snorkelled, trekked in the jungle and eaten street food. This trip felt like the opposite of fun. His dad seemed super tense.

'You can stay with Aunt Theresa while I do work stuff,' Dad said. 'And you'll meet your second cousins. There's no-one exactly your age, but Uncle Ernest's grandson Aidan is twenty-one, and he's keen to hang out.'

It sounded like Dad wanted him babysat the whole time. At least he'd been kind, ever since Kai had bawled in the police interview.

When they went home to Narrabeen to collect his passport, Kai managed to see Hudson for a total of fifteen minutes. He told him what had gone down with Mabel and the police.

'What a fuck-up,' Hudson muttered.

Kai didn't know if his mate was referring to the situation or to himself.

Mum and Simmo were still in Indonesia and he could feel their disappointment all the way from there. They'd both lectured him again about his irresponsible behaviour and Mum had cried down the phone again. When Dad told her that the child protection services would be getting in touch with them as well, she'd cried even more. The house felt strange without anyone there, and his bedroom was like a guest room. Daisy had been using his desk for craft and Mum had left a washing basket of clean sheets on his bed. The photos on the fridge were the only sign that his family was missing their fuck-up of a son.

When they dropped in at the nursing home, Glamma didn't even recognise him. Dad tried to explain that Kai was her grandson but she still couldn't understand. *Don't worry about it*, he wanted to say. *No-one wants to be related to me. I'm not worth knowing.*

He was shitting himself that he wouldn't be allowed to board the plane for some reason, that the sniffer dogs would smell a trace of drugs in his bag from January, but they made it through security without a problem.

As they flew hours and hours over the Pacific, Dad gave him a whole history lesson without drawing breath. The name Philadelphia came from two Greek words meaning 'love' and 'brother'; its founder, William Penn, had wanted to create a harmonious city which welcomed people from different religions and different races. That was how it came to be called the city of brotherly love. Once upon a time, Philly had been the most important city in America: the Declaration of Independence had been signed there, and the Constitution; they'd started the anti-slavery movement and . . . Kai zoned out.

He was more excited by the prospect of an overseas trip with two extra weeks of holidays from school. He'd only just escaped being arrested, and who knew what the police would decide when he returned to the station next month? If he was going to be sent to juvie when he got home, then he'd better live life to the fullest in America. After all, it was the land of the free and home of the brave.

That was a good motto to follow. Brave and free.

PART TWO
REMEMBERING

DNA:Match

Tracing your past through DNA

Your DNA helps you trace your biological ancestry. Some of our clients have been shocked to discover they were not genetically related to their parents or other family members. We have counselling resources in place to assist in these situations.

Remember that your genetic information does not change the love already given to you by your existing family.

Be aware that a DNA test may result in more questions than answers.

28

LACHY

THE SIGHT OF ARMED POLICE AT PHILLY AIRPORT MADE HIS HEAD SPIN. Lachy shouldn't have let his big sister push him into this. Aside from his work issues, he was freaking out about the DNA test. Why had Juliet asked for it? 'Find her,' Sheridan had said. 'Face up to your responsibilities.' But what was he responsible for, exactly? He'd sent another email saying he was flying to the States but Juliet hadn't replied, yet again. It didn't help that he'd read an article on the plane about the magic of DNA solving criminal cases across America. A detective was quoted as saying, *'If you've committed a crime, we'll find you. There will be no getting away with it.'*

What if he *had* committed a crime? As he walked past another group of armed police, the possibility of ending up in jail felt starkly real.

On an intellectual level, he knew Sheridan was right—the only way to move on with his life was to resolve all of this, but it required more bravery than he possessed. He'd decided to start with the easiest option, and do something he should've done long ago: get in contact with Tiffany and talk to her about that night at camp. If he'd behaved appropriately then, he could assume that he'd behaved respectfully every other time. Sheridan would say that was a dumb theory and he was procrastinating about Juliet. That might be true but she didn't know how he'd driven Tiffany to Deadwood Creek Road in a pick-up truck.

'What was Tiffany's last name?' he'd asked Nick before they left. 'Where did she live?'

Nick thought about it for a minute then shook his head. 'Can't remember. I think her home town was a couple of hours from camp.'

Aunt Theresa had mentioned that Camp Happiness was having an open day and she wanted to take them to look around. Hopefully there would be a record of Tiffany's surname and her old address.

✕✕

In the arrivals hall, he spotted Matthew right away.

'Stylish threads, mate!' His cousin was wearing tartan pants and a black shirt. 'You're a total hipster. This post-divorce fashion is kicking arse.'

'I've overdressed for you. It's hot as hell outside.' Matthew laughed. 'Great to see you too, bro.'

Matthew pulled him into a bear hug. He was the closest blood relative Lachy had to a brother. Mum's family was full of girls: Gloria with her two sisters, then she and Ernest both had girls, and then along came Sheridan's girls. It would be good for Kai to meet the two boys: Ernest's grandson Aidan and Matthew's son Carson.

'The kids can't wait to see you,' Matthew told Kai. 'I'm picking them up on the other side of Philly so we'll go past a few sites, but Destiny really wants to show you the penitentiary while you're here. It's a museum of an old jail. Very spooky!'

Lachy exchanged a look with his son, neither of them keen for a prison visit.

Once they collected the children, they would be driving to Leeville, sixty miles west of Philly, over in Berks County. Aunt Theresa had stayed in the house where she'd grown up; in fact, all of his American relatives lived within a two-hour radius of their childhood home. His mother had been the only one to leave.

Their route into the city took them along the river, past factories and fast-food joints, with skyscrapers rising ahead of them, shimmering in the heat. Kai was taking photos on his phone, commenting about Burger King and laughing at the traffic 'on the wrong side of the road'. As they came into the centre, Matthew pointed out the sites.

Suddenly Lachy felt close to his mother. She'd always been vague about why she'd left Pennsylvania, and only returned to the country of her birth after her parents had died. While he didn't know the circumstances, he understood the same desperation, the same flight response.

He'd been running away from America, just like his mother.

Entering Aunt Theresa's house, he was greeted like a long-lost son. Even the dog, a nervous little poodle, seemed to remember him from his visit the year before.

'Welcome home!' Theresa said. Really, she was addressing Matthew and his kids, Destiny and Carson, but this house did feel like Lachy's American home—a place full of family and love on the other side of the world. He'd stayed here as a kid, then before and after summer camp, and on various trips since. Whenever he flew in for meetings at head office, he always found time for a few nights here; it was only two and a half hours from DC.

Despite her mauve-tinted hair, Theresa reminded him of Gloria. She had the same curve of the nose, the same smile, the same mannerisms. She was shorter, younger and plumper, but when he hugged her, it felt a lot like hugging his mother. Uncle Leonard had aged in the last six months, and his hair had receded, leaving an expanse of bare scalp on top. They were all getting older, just like Mum.

Blinking away his tears, he introduced Kai.

'You're a big boy!' Theresa embraced him while Uncle Leonard slapped his back. 'The last time we saw you was at Sheridan and Nick's wedding. You were just a toddler and you fell asleep in my lap.'

Kai smiled awkwardly. He was saved from responding by Destiny.

'I wanna show you Dad's old bedroom. He's got a Rubik's cube.'

'And we've got bikes in the garage,' Carson interjected. 'Pop gave me a red one for my birthday.'

The kids disappeared down the corridor with the poodle following them and Destiny talking nonstop. Theresa sat the adults in the lounge room and poured iced tea from the old sunflower jug that brought back instant memories of past visits.

His aunt flapped a hand across her face. 'Too hot. Sorry about this weather.'

'Not something you can control, love,' Leonard said, offering around peanut butter cookies.

Lachy bit down his automatic response: *Climate change is something we can control.* The hottest day in May for forty years, that was the main news story as they'd driven up from Philly. In the car, he'd googled global temperatures. The Copernicus services noted a heatwave in south-western Europe and above-average temperatures in Siberia, India, Central Asia, southern USA and Antarctica.

'A storm is supposed to break tonight,' Theresa said, then asked after Mum and the rest of his family. He told her how Sheridan had spent Easter at Mimosa, omitting the emergency trip to hospital.

'How's my handsome fella, Nick?'

At summer camp, whenever Aunt Theresa had invited Lachy for a meal, Nick would tag along. She'd met him before Sheridan had ever laid eyes on him, and had been thrilled about the two of them getting together.

'Nick's great.' He wondered what else to say. Not the truth: Kai nearly killed their daughter, they hate us, they've sent us away.

In bed, his brain foggy with jet lag, he thought about Tiffany. He'd got along with all of the camp counsellors, except for her. She was an entitled, judgemental princess. Usually he made friends easily, so the intensity of his dislike shocked him, and he'd done everything he could to hide it, going out of his way to be chatty and helpful. And then the party and her sudden disappearance—he hated himself for driving that night, for whatever had happened.

Why was an article about a hit-and-run on Deadwood Creek Road hidden in the cupboard at Mimosa? He must have printed it out that Tuesday afternoon in his blackout state. But why? Bloody hell, he couldn't trust his own actions. This was partly why he'd been so reluctant to push the allegations against Henrik. What if he were just as bad?

Unable to sleep with these swirling thoughts, he picked up his phone and searched online for State Trooper Kurt Haigh and Deadwood Creek Road. No results. Next he googled Juliet and DC and the bar where they'd met. He put her email address into the browser to see if anything came up. Nothing.

Two girls with green eyes and no surnames. Had one of them died on Deadwood Creek Road?

Finally he typed in 'Deadwood Creek Road death'. After scrolling through links relating to the town of Deadwood in South Dakota, he found a short news article. Different from the one in the cupboard at home.

> Norristown police are investigating the death of a young woman found underneath the bridge on Deadwood Creek Road. The body was discovered on Sunday morning by local teenagers. Both the identity of the woman and the cause of death are currently unknown. Her age is estimated between 18 and 35 years old. On her ankle was a tattoo of the word BELIEVE. Police ask anyone who knows the woman's identity or has information relating to her death to contact Norristown police department.

The body had been discovered in September the day after he'd met Juliet. There couldn't possibly be any link to him. Unless he'd driven Juliet from DC to Pennsylvania that night . . . back to where he'd left Tiffany. No, that was batshit crazy. And the unidentified woman wasn't Juliet because she'd emailed him. But, as Nick said, it was just an email address, how could he be sure it was her?

Trembling, Lachy pulled the duvet up to his chin, as if he could ward off his preposterous jet-lagged thoughts.

The entrance to the summer camp was still the same: two stone pillars topped by a triangle of wooden planks with the name painted in white letters: CAMP HAPPINESS. He'd had his first lessons in life working here after he'd left school.

Tall trees lined the driveway, blocking out the sunshine. The car skidded on the dirt track as they went around a corner. It had been a white-knuckle experience the entire forty minutes from Leeville. In the back seat, Kai gave a small yelp.

'Oops, sorry,' Aunt Theresa snickered. She slowed down. 'Look through that gap and you can see where Constance and Melvin lived.'

Constance was her mother's cousin. Melvin had been the camp caretaker but they'd left before Lachy arrived. Their cottage was part of the old farm, built before the camp existed.

'Leonard is Melvin's youngest brother,' Theresa explained to Kai. 'The first time we ever danced together was at Constance and Melvin's wedding.'

'And look at you now, celebrating fifty years of marriage!' Lachy said. 'You'll have to show us some photos of you both back then. And I'd love to see what Mum looked like too.'

'Oh no. Gloria wasn't there. She ran away a month before. Our father was very upset.'

The main part of the camp hadn't changed but there were more activities on offer, including something he'd never heard of, a gaga pit. They left Aunt Theresa chatting to the new caretaker and joined a tour of the grounds.

'That's where I lived.' Lachy pointed to one of fifteen identical cabins. 'Falcon Force.'

'You lived in the same cabin as the kids?'

'Yep. And we all had camp nicknames. A few kids gave themselves the weirdest names.'

'That's right. You were Coyote and Nick was Rattlesnake.'

They continued down to the lake: a huge expanse, surrounded by trees and dotted with little sandy beaches. A few kids were already swimming, cooling off. As he watched, Lachy realised he'd carried a secret fantasy here with him—that seeing the lake would bring back the memory of the night. Everything looked the same but different. A stone path ran through the forest where he'd been with Tiffany that night, the bushes and trees no longer thick and tangled but open and airy. He was flooded with memories: the fear of kayaking with children who couldn't swim; the boy who threatened them with a knife; kids asking what language they spoke in Australia; making iced tea; singing songs every day.

But no memories of being in the forest with Tiffany, borrowing the truck, driving her to the bridge on Deadwood Creek Road.

At last, the tour brought them to the main hall with the dining room, games area and stage. The side table had moved to a different wall but a guest book sat on it, the same as in his day. When he started looking through it, the camp director walked over and asked if she could help.

'I was a camp counsellor here about eighteen years ago,' he said. 'We had a guest book that all the staff signed. I wanted to show it to my son.'

'Amazeballs! Have you written on our Facebook site for our centenary anniversary?' She turned to Kai. 'Will you join us as a camp counsellor too? We love Aussies!'

'Umm . . . I'm only fifteen. What age do you have to be?'

Lachy couldn't imagine Kai at camp; his son would roll his eyes at every cheesy American moment. He interrupted them, 'Well, it'd be great for him to see the history of Aussie counsellors. Do you still have the old guest books?'

'Of course. History's important to us. A hundred years! Can you believe it?'

The camp director—the name on her badge said MAMA CHIPMUNK—led them to a cupboard at the back of the dining room. As Lachy watched her squat down and sort through books on a shelf, a memory came back to him.

Tiffany sitting cross-legged on the floor here, whispering with Britt. He'd noticed them on his way to get the first-aid kit to soothe a kid's insect bite. Somehow Tiffany managed to avoid all the difficult, dirty moments with the campers, she didn't apply sticking plasters to wounds. Her speciality was teaching dance and she practically refused to do anything else.

'I'm late.' He'd overheard her saying to Britt.

She was always late, that was part of her princess style.

Britt had squealed, 'Omigod, you're gonna be a mama!'

Jesus, had he not taken that in at the time? Tiffany thought she might be pregnant.

Mama Chipmunk brought out a red book and handed it to him. 'This one should cover your summer.'

He flipped the pages, searching for the right year. Each camp counsellor had written a message when they arrived and another before leaving.

'I think this is our group.' He scanned the top lines. 'Yes, here's Nick's message: *It's awesome to be in the great US of A! Can't wait to have fun, HOORAY!*'

He scanned the entries below and there was Tiffany's: *I hope we bring happiness to our campers every day. And what a great team—local counsellors and Aussie boys and me! I aim to be crowned Queen Happiness by the end of summer.*

Queen Happiness—hah! She was only ever happy when she got her own way.

'Here's your entry, Dad.' Kai read it aloud. '*Happy Dayz! Cheers to summer days by Lake Hopper! We're going to have the best time, kayaking and sailing!* That's lame.'

'But we did have a great time.' Apart from whatever had happened with Tiffany. His farewell comment said: *Best mates forever. I'll never forget you all.* He'd stayed in touch with just one person: Nick.

'Did Tiffany get crowned Queen Happiness?' Kai asked. 'There's no farewell comment from her.'

'No, she wasn't that happy after all.' Lachy closed the guest book and placed it back in the cupboard. He'd found what he was looking for, and more: her full name and a memory. Tiffany Jones. No wonder he'd forgotten her surname, it was such a common one.

And she might have been pregnant the night he left her at Deadwood Creek Road.

29

SHERIDAN

'HI, MUM. HOW ARE YOU TODAY?' SHERIDAN SAT ON THE EDGE OF THE
bed and kissed her mother's cheek.

'Theresa, why aren't you in the kitchen peeling potatoes?'
Mum stiffened against the pillow. 'Father won't want you in
the good room with your dirty hands. Did you wash them?'

Today, she was Mum's younger sister. If only Gloria were
properly present, she'd lean against her shoulder and tell her
everything. They'd cry together. And even though Mum would
defend Lachy and Kai, Sheridan would walk away feeling lighter.
Later, she might even be able to see the situation from Lachy's
perspective.

'Oh, Mum, I wish you could . . . I don't know if I can ever
forgive them . . .' She clamped her lips shut. No point speaking
like that; it wouldn't achieve anything.

Mum turned her face away. 'What I did was unforgivable.
I can't even ask God for mercy. You shouldn't forgive me.'

Sheridan berated herself for saying anything; her words had
stirred up a bad memory.

'Of course I forgive you,' she said soothingly.

'Well, you shouldn't, even though we're sisters.'

Sisters, brothers, nephews, nieces . . . would she ever be able to forgive her brother and her nephew, even though Mabel had been declared perfectly healthy at the follow-up appointment? The doctor said child protection services would be coming to interview them, although he'd written in the notes that the cousins didn't live together so it might be a while before the busy social workers contacted them.

Even though she knew she wasn't to blame, Sheridan was mortified at the prospect of being interrogated by a social worker. Her head ached with the stress of it. Between school holiday activities, she'd frantically tidied the house and admonished the girls for making a mess with their craft supplies. And then she wondered if art and craft showed an engaged family life, and whether she should leave it out. It didn't seem right to her: Kai was to blame, but now her parenting would be judged. Amid the worrying and the cleaning, she hugged the girls fifty times a day.

Soft pressure on her fingers; Mum was squeezing her hand.

'You're a wily one, Theresa. You always wanted what your sisters had. You took Leonard, even though he was never interested in you.'

And now a jab in her side. Her mother was elbowing her— or, rather, elbowing her little sister Theresa. Time to go before Mum became more agitated. She wouldn't tell her that Lachy and Kai were in America with Theresa right now, nor that she felt a bit better having them on the other side of the world.

'Family, hey?' she said to Mum as she got to her feet. 'Can't live with them, can't live without them.'

The chatty carer, Kasanita, entered the room as she was leaving. They were lucky that she'd been looking after Mum for the past six months; so many other carers had come and gone.

'Did you bring Betty?' Kasanita asked. 'Your mother talks about the doll like it's part of herself. She's very attached. It can be good therapy to have a doll, helps with the agitation.'

'I'm . . . working on it.'

Betty remained at Mimosa Hideout, in pieces.

Their house was in chaos—clothes strewn across the sofa, shoes in the dining room, cut-up green paper all over the carpet. She'd only been gone two hours. God, they needed a bigger place with a separate rumpus room where toys could be contained. As she stormed down the hallway, pink feathers swirled in her wake.

'Hands up!' Eloise appeared from behind the kitchen bench brandishing a cardboard tube. She wore an eye patch and had a green paper hat on her head. 'You've been caught by Pirate One-Eye and you have to walk the plank.'

'Fine. I'll walk the plank and Daddy can clean up.'

Nick and Mabel jumped out from the laundry also wearing pirate hats. Nick must have heard her snarky comment but he didn't react.

'Tie her up! Tie her up!' They wrapped string around her. 'Now, walk the plank!'

She wanted to be part of their game but her headache throbbed harder with their chants. And there was so much to be done. Muesli bar wrappers and yoghurt containers dotted the kitchen counter. And five empty cups. A social worker could arrive any time; Saturday would be the right day to catch a family interacting together.

She glared at Nick. 'Why didn't you put the cups in the dishwasher?'

'We've been sailing out on the wild seas.' He held up his cardboard sword. 'Plundering and capturing other ships. Ahoy there!'

The three of them raised their swords together.

Yanking at the string around her waist, she swore in her head and tried not to explode.

'I'm having a shower and I want this house tidy by the time I get out.'

Silence. Nick didn't even apologise. She grabbed a packet of painkillers from the top cupboard and turned to leave the kitchen. Mabel's words followed her out.

'You're no fun, Mummy.'

The shower calmed her slightly. Why couldn't the child protection services just hurry up, so she could stop stressing about it? If any of her friends knew, they would freak out too. Or laugh at the irony of Sheridan and Nick Brandt being investigated for their parenting. Rachel would tell her to chill-the-hell-down, remind her that she hadn't done anything wrong. Even though it felt like she'd been negligent in keeping her daughters safe.

Nick came into the bedroom and handed her a cup of coffee. 'The pirates have cleaned up,' he announced.

'Thank you.' The smell of the coffee filled her nostrils. Ah, that should help her headache. 'I'm sorry for ruining the game . . .'

'It's going to be fine.' He rubbed at his cheek where one of the girls had drawn a jagged scar. She hoped they hadn't used permanent markers. 'Mabel and Eloise are happy and healthy. That's the most important thing.'

She couldn't get past that image of Mabel in the hospital bed. 'But it's a whole load of stuff at the same time. Mum, Lachy's work, the DNA thing . . . He texted that he's going to summer camp. What's he doing there? He doesn't have time for trips down Memory Lane—he's meant to be meeting the HR person at head office.'

'He's going to Camp Happiness?' A frown flashed across Nick's face. He knew something, Sheridan realised, but before she could ask, Eloise sprang through the doorway, her cardboard sword in one hand and the green paper hat on her head.

'There's a lady at the door.'

In the lounge room, with the social worker perched on the couch, Sheridan tried to guess at the woman's assessment of their house. Had Carmel noticed the bits of green paper and feathers scattered over the carpet? Did she interpret that as a dirty house or as parents who played with their kids? While Sheridan showered, Nick had done a superficial job of tidying: the girls' jumpers were piled on one chair and a pair of shoes lay under another.

Carmel accepted Eloise's invitation to visit her bedroom. What sort of state was it in? Tagging along behind the girls, Sheridan held her breath as Eloise opened the door. Not too bad. She'd been doing a clean and tidy every morning but it only took minutes for the girls to make a mess again.

'We don't just have pirate dress-ups,' Eloise was saying. 'We have a whole dressing-up box! Superman. Peter Pan. Princesses. Fairies.' She pulled costumes from the box as evidence.

'Do you have a favourite?' Carmel asked.

'I like this wig.' Whipping off her pirate hat, Eloise plonked the red wig over her hair. 'It was Glamma's. She made parties!'

'I like that wig very much too.' Carmel grinned and dimples appeared in her cheeks. The social worker must have been around sixty, but she had hot pink glasses and matching pink hair.

'You're not as old as my grandma,' Mabel said. 'She's sick all the time.'

'Sorry to hear that.'

'Actually, she's been in a nursing home for eighteen months,' Sheridan said, aiming to reassure Carmel this wasn't a recent trauma for the girls. Oh God, would Carmel start asking questions about their grandmother? The girls only went to the nursing home occasionally these days; she had to bribe them—they disliked the smell and Glamma's confusing chatter.

'Granddad died. Gran and Grandpa B live in Cherrybrook.' Mabel accounted for all the grandparents. 'But they're driving a caravan now in Western Australia. They had a cat called Possum. But he was a cat, not a possum. So silly!'

Eventually the girls tired of their guest and the adults moved to the dining room, with tea and biscuits.

'Your daughters seem to have recovered from the incident,' Carmel said. 'Are they suffering any ongoing effects?'

'No, thankfully.' Sheridan blinked away tears. 'But we're keeping a close eye on them.'

'Do they understand what happened?'

She said, 'No,' at the same time as Nick said, 'Yes.'

Despite being so worried about this interview, she hadn't thought to discuss any possible questions and answers with her husband.

'So what do they think happened?'

This time Nick got in first.

'They think they ate some of their grandma's old lollies that were out of date and that made them sick.' Nick cleared his throat slightly. 'But they realise their cousin is to blame because we made him leave the house and he wasn't allowed back for Easter Sunday.'

'Did you know your nephew had ecstasy tablets?'

Carmel's probing gaze settled first on her, then Nick. While she wanted Kai to acknowledge the seriousness of what he'd done, she didn't want him charged and to have a criminal record.

'Kai had some problems with drugs here in Sydney.' Nick sounded so calm. 'It's why he was sent to live down there. But Lachy has never been a full-time father before. And I think that's the problem here. He should have been aware that Kai had brought drugs into the cabin. He's the one at fault.'

Wow, he'd dropped Lachy right in it. She covered her mouth with her hand to stop herself from gasping. This was the child protection agency he was speaking to; they could take Kai away from his father. Deep down, she might have had the same thought, but she would never have voiced it to Carmel, not in a million years.

Look after your little brother. Make sure he's okay. Protect him.

She hadn't realised she'd have to protect Lachy from his best friend.

✕

Sheridan pushed the doona off her legs; the red wine had made her sweaty. She'd gone to bed early, hoping to be asleep by the time Nick came in, but here he was, unbuttoning his jeans, throwing his jumper on the chair in the corner. She hadn't wanted to challenge him in front of the girls this evening, but now she didn't hold back.

'Why did you do that?' she demanded. 'Why did you say Lachy wasn't a competent father?'

Nick knew Lachy almost as well as she did; he was practically a Wilson! He'd met all their American relatives while working at summer camp; he'd helped look after Kai as a toddler; he'd spent holidays with Mum and Dad.

'I just told her what happened . . .' He hesitated. 'Maybe it came out a bit bluntly.'

'Too right it did. You said he's to blame.'

'Well, Lachy *is* at fault.' He pulled on his pyjamas and got into bed. 'You said you wanted him to feel the consequences.'

'*Kai*, not Lachy.' Was he pretending to be obtuse? 'My brother understands the consequences. He's one of your best friends. How could you do that to him?' She was almost shouting now. 'What if Kai gets charged? Ends up in juvenile detention?'

'Stop being melodramatic.'

'It happens! Kids get taken away. And their lives turn out worse, not better. Mum would be furious with you. She always said I had to look after Lachy and Kai.'

'No. You don't.' His mouth was set in a hard line. 'You're busy enough looking after the girls and Gloria. It's time for Lachy to take responsibility for himself and his son.'

Even so, they were family who worked stuff out together. They didn't tell a social worker that Lachy had been a crap dad for fifteen years.

'You shouldn't have—'

'Shh, you'll wake the girls. This bloody house is too small and too cold.' He yanked the doona up and turned on his side, facing the wall. 'I'm going to sleep. I've got a breakfast meeting tomorrow.'

Rolling away from him, she tugged back her half of the doona. What had got into him? In the hospital and at Mimosa, they'd acted as a team, but now he was withdrawing from her. Just as he had after Toby's death. She wondered what the hell was going on inside his head.

30

KAI

BY THE TIME THEY REACHED THE HOUSE OF DAD'S COUSIN, KAI HAD vowed never to get in a car with Great-Aunt Theresa ever again. They'd narrowly missed a head-on collision with a sedan, then a huge Jeep had almost rear-ended them when Theresa slowed right down to listen to a radio report about the Casanova Killer.

'He murdered two girls in eastern Pennsylvania,' Theresa said. 'The police have been trying to catch him for years. But now they've had a breakthrough with new DNA techniques, and they're sure to get him. They think he's linked to other deaths.'

Dad had been glued to his phone since they left Camp Happiness; he might not have even noticed the near misses and he didn't seem to be listening now.

'Why's he called Casanova?' Kai asked.

'He's a romantic. He placed roses on his victims.'

That was revolting, not romantic.

When the news item finished, Theresa accelerated to normal speed, but then she nearly swiped a pole on the verge. Dad should tell Uncle Leonard that she was too old to drive. Kai didn't want to die today—not when he was finally able to breathe for the first time in what felt like forever.

It was great to be here, away from his fear and failure. No school, no Grug, no teachers, no accusing looks from his aunt. Though in some ways, it didn't feel so very far from Warabina. Philadelphia had been a buzzing city but now they were in the countryside. When he thought of the States, he'd imagined New York, Chicago and LA, skyscrapers and cool bars, basketball, baseball and rock concerts. He hadn't imagined paddocks. Of course, they weren't called paddocks here. Green fields with barns and white fences. It was picturesque, different from the scrubland around Warabina but, still, countryside.

'You'll have great fun with Aidan,' Theresa said.

He hoped so. His twenty-one-year-old cousin had an Insta grid of skateboarding tricks, guitars and band shots. But Kai was nervous about being with complete strangers for two days while Dad went to Washington DC. Though he and Aidan weren't exactly strangers, were they? Just relatives who had never met before.

Dad had given him the lowdown. 'You'll be staying at my cousin Celeste's house. Her husband is in the army and away a lot. Aidan is their only son. They're a religious family. My uncle Ernest is a pastor; he followed my grandfather into the church. So be on your best behaviour.' A strict, religious family—the only reason Dad would let Kai out of his sight. 'Don't do anything illegal here, Kai,' he'd warned. 'You'll end up in jail.'

Luckily Dad hadn't seen Aidan's Instagram profile; it looked like he had a lot of good times. They'd been messaging this morning and Aidan had mentioned a get-together with mates.

If they were all into skating and bands, there might be booze, maybe drugs.

After driving through a small town with American flags everywhere, they'd pulled up outside a modern, two-storey home on a quiet street. The house looked nice, but the garden was overgrown.

'Tell Aidan he should be mowing the lawn while his father's away,' Theresa said. 'You guys go in. I need to call Leonard and remind him to have lunch. We normally eat together.'

The tall, skinny guy at the door matched the online pictures. Black ripped jeans, black t-shirt, black earring. Kai's bravado faltered. What if Aidan thought he was just a kid and didn't want to hang out with him?

Aidan fist-bumped him then Dad, who didn't know what to do with his hand.

'Great to meetcha,' Aidan said, running his fingers through his black hair; maybe he was nervous too.

'I haven't seen you since you were about Kai's age,' Dad told him.

'I've grown a bit.' Aidan chuckled. 'I'm big enough to look after Kai for a few days. Mum will be home later tonight, and Pa might drop over.'

Dad seemed to want to come in, but Aidan blocked the doorway.

'Okay then,' Dad said. 'Say thanks to Celeste for me and tell her we'll catch up when I'm back. She's got my number if she needs me.'

Please don't embarrass me and tell me to be a good boy. Kai sidestepped his dad's hug by slinging his backpack over his shoulder. 'Good luck with your meeting, Dad. See you in a few days.'

Before Dad could say anything else, Aidan was pulling him inside and closing the door.

'Some of the guys are already in the basement.' Aidan led him down the stairs. 'Mum won't be home for a coupla hours. Let's get partying.'

As Aidan introduced his mates, Kai rubbed his hands on his blue Billabong board shorts and wished he'd worn jeans. One guy was sprawled on the couch with a guitar in his lap; two girls were playing foosball; another guy lined up in front of the dartboard and almost hit the bullseye. The rest were lounging around chatting. He felt ten years younger than them, not six. They all wore similar clothes to Aidan: black jeans, black t-shirts with a few chains. Grunge or punk, Kai didn't know. The girl with the ripped stockings, denim miniskirt and black boots could have stepped out of a nineties music video.

Aidan handed him a can of root beer from the fridge. This basement was kitted out perfectly. Parties down here would be amazing. It was below street level so you could crank up the music and with no windows, you could make it dark any time. Kai stared at the ceiling—yep, strips of lights. Aidan and his friends must party hard.

Balanced on the arm of a couch, Kai surreptitiously tried to read the label on the root beer. Alcoholic or not? The drinking age was really old here.

'Haven't you had root beer before?' Aidan asked.

He'd been caught looking at the label.

'Um, no. We don't really drink it back home.' His cheeks flamed red; he couldn't ask if it was alcoholic. 'Does it taste more like ginger beer or real beer?'

'Sweeter.' Aidan nodded. 'Have a taste. See what you think.'

That didn't answer his question. He tipped the can and took a sip. Sugary and minty. A bit like mouthwash. He forced himself to swallow. Yuck.

Aidan was watching him, waiting for his verdict.

'Yeah, it's . . . ah . . . different from anything we've got in Oz.'

Unlike Matthew's daughter, Destiny, who had a thousand questions about Australia, Aidan and his friends didn't seem particularly interested, but they were still waiting for him to say something.

'We've got the major soft drinks. You know, Coke, Fanta, Sprite . . .' As the stupid words came out of his stupid mouth, he wanted to crawl behind the couch and hide.

'Soft drink?' One of the girls at the foosball table, Natalie, laughed. Her big silver earrings jangled with the movement. 'You mean soda.'

'Right. Yeah. Soda.'

Did that mean root beer wasn't soda, that it *was* alcoholic? He felt like a dumb kid; Aidan's gang was too cool, too American. He'd just keep his mouth shut and smile.

'Soda,' Natalie repeated. 'Don't worry, we'll teach you the right words to fit in. How long are you staying?'

'I . . . um . . .' Did she mean today or tonight? Or the whole trip?

'He'll fit in just fine.' Aidan slapped him on the shoulder. 'And he's here long enough to come to the party tonight.'

Aidan was taking him to a party! He didn't think of him as a kid too young to hang with them. They'd definitely have booze and maybe pingers. Shit, what if they offered him some? He wanted them to think he was cool too, but he'd go to jail if he got caught.

'But first, let's take him to the Dairy Bar.' Aidan stood up.

A bar? How the hell could he get into a bar? He didn't look anywhere near old enough. Ignoring the butterflies in his tummy, Kai smiled and followed his cousin and mates to the car.

><

They drove past farms with fields full of cows. Perhaps the bar was in a big old barn on someone's farm, a real country and western pub. But Aidan and his friends wouldn't go to a place like that, not in their black punk outfits. Kai was squashed in the back seat with Natalie in the middle, her torn stocking against his bare leg. Every time she laughed, which was often, she threw her head back and her earrings jangled. With her sassy outfit and cropped bleached hair, she was so exotic that he couldn't speak to her; he'd say the wrong thing.

'Here we are.' Natalie pointed out of the window.

The car slowed to a stop. A huge fibreglass black-and-white cow stood beneath a sign decorated with ice-cream cones. DAIRY BAR. Dairy, like milk. A milk bar. Thank God he hadn't said anything about alcohol and asked for a fake ID.

'Let's have a round first,' Aidan said. 'You any good at minigolf, Kai? You gonna beat us all?'

'I've played a bit.' Kai didn't say that he *loved* putt-putt golf, always thrashed his friends. For three birthdays in a row, he'd insisted on a party at the Treasure Island putt-putt place near his house. Then he'd grown up and it all seemed so lame.

This minigolf course was anything but lame. There were bridges, windmills, waterfalls, a replica of the Empire State Building, rollercoasters, the Sphinx, that rock with the carved faces of the American presidents. He did okay on the first hole.

He lined up for the second and watched the ball sail over a wooden bridge, through a windmill and straight in.

'And my Aussie cousin Kai is on the board,' Aidan boomed like a sports reporter. 'The first hole in one for the day. Great job!'

All Aidan's friends congratulated him. Natalie gave him an ironic high five.

Overconfident, Kai botched the next hole. The special glow faded instantly.

'Do you know the capital city of Australia?' he quizzed them as they passed the carving of the American president. Oh no, why had he said that? Such a dork.

'Sydney!' Natalie yelled.

'Nup, Canberra,' Aidan corrected her. 'Am I right?'

Kai nodded and his cousin gave him a fist bump.

'Hey, did your dad tell you that I'm taking you sightseeing with the other cousins in Philly tomorrow?'

'Great.' Philadelphia was a proper city, not like these small towns where his relatives lived.

They moved on to the next hole. It had a huge waterfall gushing through it.

'I was wondering if you could help me solve a family mystery?' Aidan asked. 'There's always been this secrecy about why your grandma moved to Australia. Do you know anything?'

'I thought she had an argument with her father and didn't want to be in the church anymore.'

'Yeah, but Gloria left suddenly, a month before a big family wedding. And she was only eighteen. I'm doing a history major and one of my projects is the development of our church community from a sociocultural perspective. I tried to include the family history, but Pa won't talk about that side of it.'

214

'He's a pastor, isn't he? He must've been angry about Gloria leaving the church.' Kai collected his ball from the hole and wrote down his result: four, not too bad.

'It's more than that. Pa won't talk about his childhood at all.' Aidan paused as he finished his round and noted his score. 'All he says is that our great-grandfather, Abraham Dunstan, was a man of his time. He believed religion was the moral fabric holding America together.'

Moral fabric. Aunt Sheridan would say Kai needed some of that. But no-one here knew about the drugs, he could be a different person. He lined up the next shot, his last chance, focused on the Sphinx, and swung. Yes! Another hole in one!

'And Kai does it again,' Aidan announced. 'Reckon you'll be top of the rankings today.'

Inside the Dairy Bar, they tallied up their scores. Kai beamed at his result—third in their group. The guys congratulated him, Natalie gave him another high five, and Aidan took out his wallet. It had a silver chain, old-school punk style.

'I'll buy you an ice cream,' he said. 'Best in the county. Made fresh every day. What do you want?'

The board above the counter listed more than forty flavours. Boston cream pie. Oreo. Cotton candy. Teaberry. Pumpkin. Who ate pumpkin ice cream? He chose the next thing that caught his eye: 'Chocolate marshmallow.'

It tasted pretty good. He took a photo of the ice-cream flavours and sent it to Tarni.

This was an excellent afternoon, and they still had the party to come. Aidan was totally chill. Kai would definitely help him find out why Glamma had left America.

ᕽᕽ

Back in the car, he was sitting beside Natalie again, and this time he managed to chat with her. Although when she asked about his favourite band, his mind went blank. Glancing out the window for inspiration, he made up a name as they crossed a small bridge.

'Fat Creek. It's an Aussie group. Indie. Super sick.'

'Fat Creek.' She gave her big laugh. 'Interesting name. Can I hear one of their songs?'

'Oh, I haven't . . . got any on my phone.'

'I'll google them.' She started tapping on her mobile. 'There must be something on YouTube or Spotify.'

Why did she have to be so fascinated? He dug himself in deeper.

'They've only just started recording.' The lies tumbled out, one after another. 'I've seen them live. They don't have anything up yet.'

Every band had some kind of online presence; she wouldn't believe his excuse. Isaac, the guy in the front passenger seat, turned to eyeball him. Had he caught on?

'See that bridge we just crossed?' He nodded at the road behind them. 'They reckon three people were killed around here and their ghosts haunt the place 'cos their murders have never been solved. One of them might have been a victim of the Casanova Killer.'

'My great-aunt was just telling me about him.'

'He left a rose on each of his victims.'

Aidan waved a hand to stop the conversation—did his cousin think he was squeamish? Before he could reassure him that he wasn't, Natalie spoke up.

'It's gonna be great tonight. We've got a hundred coming. And the ice cream helped my throat. I'll be fine to sing.'

'Well, that's a relief,' Aidan said. 'I couldn't do it.'

If he'd known she was a singer, Kai never would have made up a band called Fat Creek. It sounded like Aidan played too. No wonder they were so epic. A band and a hundred people meant a huge party, definitely drugs and booze. During the minigolf, he'd given himself a lecture: *You can't take drugs in America. Mabel almost died. You'll be arrested. Mum will be so upset. Dad will say you haven't learnt anything. And Aunt Sheridan will disown you.*

But what would he do if Natalie offered him something?

Aidan interrupted his thoughts. 'So, Kai, will you help me solve the mystery?'

'Sure.' He didn't know if Aidan was referring to the serial killer or his grandmother but either way, he was good for it.

'The one time Pa talked about Gloria leaving, he got teary and said it changed their lives. It's what made him become a pastor. He said it was a life-defining moment.'

A life-defining moment.

Kai was only fifteen and he'd had two life-defining moments in the past six months. One had got him kicked out of home in Sydney, the second had him interviewed by the police, then packed off to America.

'Maybe Gloria didn't plan to leave,' he said. 'Maybe her father threw her out.'

31

ELIZABETH, 1968

I'D HAD TO PUT CHARLIE OFF THIS SATURDAY BECAUSE WE WERE HAVING a picnic lunch with Constance and Melvin. All morning, Mother, Gloria and I worked in the kitchen making ham-and-cheese roll-ups, devilled eggs and banana chiffon cake. Father had cut a posy of his special roses for the happy couple. I yearned to celebrate my engagement too. But in another month, Charlie would be finished his Sunday hospital rounds and I could introduce him to my family at church. That was the best way to approach it, I'd decided. Did I dare to dream that, one day, Father would conduct the ceremony to bind us together in holy matrimony?

So far, I'd kept our secret from everyone, even Gloria, but I couldn't wait to share the news with her. She and Charlie would get along well; they were both clever, kind and caring.

'What time are we leaving?' Theresa bounced into the kitchen. When Gloria and I were married, my little sister would have to step up with the domestic duties and help Mother.

'Soon,' Mother said. 'Tell Ernest and Virginia to use the bathroom.'

We were going to the Schuylkill River to have a walk first, then the picnic. Melvin's brother Leonard would probably challenge me and all the youngsters to a running race—he always made everyone laugh.

When I went to the bedroom to change into my pink skirt, I found Gloria curled under her quilt.

'What's wrong?'

'My monthlies just arrived.' She sighed. 'I've got terrible cramps. I'll have to stay in bed.'

'Shame.' I sat down beside her. 'You'll miss the fun and my delicious cake.'

'It's okay, I don't feel like eating.' Gloria winced. 'Did you suffer the curse last week? I didn't see you do any washing.'

Preoccupied with Charlie and my deceptions, I hadn't taken much notice of the date. Normally Gloria and I had our monthlies at the same time.

Mother called from the kitchen and I rushed out to help her.

For the entire afternoon, during the walk and the picnic, I could barely concentrate on the conversation around me. Counting back, I realised this was the third month I'd missed. The bright sunshine reflected my joy: Charlie's baby was growing inside me. I had imagined we'd have time together before children, but it didn't matter that we'd catapulted into our future. We would just have to marry quickly.

This secret now felt too big to contain. Surely all of the family at the picnic could see the happiness radiating from me. My hands kept fluttering around my tummy.

Our child. An expression of our love. I couldn't wait to tell Charlie on Wednesday.

XX

That evening, Gloria and I knelt for our prayers before bed. Usually, we spoke silently to the Lord but tonight, she beseeched him aloud reciting a verse from Hebrews: 'For the word of God is living and active, sharper than any two-edged sword, piercing to the division of soul and of spirit, of joints and of marrow, and discerning the thoughts and intentions of the heart. Lord, you can see inside Betty's heart. Please give her the guidance she needs in this situation.'

Gloria knew! She must have worked it out when she realised I hadn't had my monthlies. At last I could tell her about Charlie and our love.

'I have the most wonderful news,' I began.

'You have committed an abhorrent sin.' She put her head in her hands. 'You haven't bled for months. Is it a boy from the bus? Teenage boys can't control their urges. It's up to you to cool their flame, not ignite it. I thought you'd been following my lead, but all this time you've been sinning.'

'It's not a sin when you're engaged. It's the most incredible feeling in the world.'

'You can't be engaged. Father hasn't approved it.' Tears ran down her cheeks. 'You're a slattern, Elizabeth. You've offended God, you've failed yourself, you've disgraced our family.'

'No, I love him. We're going to be married.' She didn't understand. This was not my ruination; it was my future.

'Clearly he's not in our community. Will he join our church?'

'Yes. He's a fine, upstanding man. When you meet him, you'll love him too.' I smiled at her, willing her to see the truth. 'After we're married, we're planning to go to Australia. Will you come with us? It'll be an adventure!'

She did not return my smile. 'Betty, you've always lived in a dream world. Can't you see this affects us all? Father is head of our church. His position will be compromised. As will my role as a youth leader. It taints the whole family. Your sin brings shame on us.'

My love for Charlie was pure and sublime, the opposite of shameful. Gloria couldn't see past Father's narrow interpretations of the world. She needed to have her eyes opened as mine had been.

'We'll tell Father first thing in the morning,' she said.

'Please give me a few days. This is a surprise to me too. I didn't realise until you said your monthlies had come.'

Gloria pursed her lips. 'We need to sort out this mess quickly.'

If only she could understand this wasn't a mess.

'Don't tell Father yet. I'm begging you.'

'I will not lie for you, Betty.'

This time last year, she would have done anything for me but Father becoming head of our church had changed her so much. I wanted our old relationship back.

'Do you remember when I took that whupping for you?' Saying this was a risk, it might infuriate her more. 'You'd secretly joined the debating club. I said it was my fault that we were hours late home from school that day so you could stay on the team.'

She was silent for a minute, then she sighed and looked at me properly. 'You have until Tuesday afternoon. I can't go to youth group and counsel others when my own sister has committed such a sin.'

⋊⋉

The only words Gloria spoke to me over the next two days were instructions for prayer. 'You must ask God for forgiveness.' Instead, I prayed she would come to Australia with us and find her own happiness there, away from Father's oppressive rules. The excitement of my secret kept me strong, but the minutes still dragged until Monday afternoon, when I could make a detour after school to the hospital in the next county.

I'd never been to Montgomery General before, and I had no idea how to find the residential dormitories. A friendly fellow pointed me in the right direction. As I walked through the grounds, I practised my speech for Charlie: 'I know we didn't mean this to happen right now, but it must be our destiny.' His ring was on my finger and I twirled it nervously. It seemed tighter; perhaps I'd put on weight already, my body expanding for our baby. Were there any other signs? I didn't know what it meant to be pregnant, only that the monthlies stopped.

I was walking up the path to the dormitory building when a nurse stepped out from inside. 'Hello,' she said. 'Can I help you?'

'I'm looking for Dr Charles Stanbury,' I said. 'Do you know which room is his?'

'Doctors don't live in this dormitory, only nurses.' The middle-aged woman put her hands on her hips and looked me up and down. 'What's your name?'

Something about her open appraisal made me uncomfortable. Reluctant to reveal my own name, I gave my sister's instead. 'I'm Gloria. I'm . . . a relative from Philadelphia.'

'Well, Gloria, your family must be very proud of Dr Stanbury. He's so good with his patients. I predict that he'll become a fine surgeon.' Her disapproving expression had softened into a broad smile. 'But dear girl, I'm sorry to say you've been sent here by mistake. None of the doctors reside at the hospital. Dr Stanbury lives in New Hanover with his wife.'

32

SHERIDAN

SHERIDAN WATCHED RONNIE SAUNTER ALONG THE HALLWAY OF MUM'S nursing home. Wearing a flannelette shirt, jeans and riding boots, with a big duffel bag slung over her shoulder, she looked completely out of place. Even her stride was wrong, too long and loping for the city.

'I saw my brother,' Ronnie said in greeting; he was the reason for her visit to Sydney. 'He's a picture of health! Not at death's door, like he told me. Reckon he'll outlive us all.'

'That's good to hear,' Sheridan replied. 'Hopefully Mum will recognise you, but it depends on the day.'

Gloria was perched on a chair in the residents' lounge, a queen at her own party, throwing her head back and laughing with a male resident.

'My darlings!' she called out when she caught sight of them. 'This is Ernie. You know I have a brother called Ernest. He's far too serious to shorten it to Ernie, though. And you are . . . you are Ronnie!'

Mum gave her a huge hug. When the man shuffled off, Ronnie took his seat.

'I've brought you a present,' Ronnie said, reaching down and unzipping her bag. 'It's your old doll from the farm.'

Sheridan had searched online for a replacement but had no luck, so she'd asked Ronnie to bring Betty to Sydney with the aim of locating a doll hospital. Mum wouldn't want to see Betty in her ripped-apart state. As Ronnie began pulling the doll's torso from the bag, Sheridan put her hands out.

'Wait . . .'

Miraculously, Betty's body did not stop at the waist; the legs had been reattached. Wow! It seemed that Ronnie had stitched up the doll herself. Impressive mending. Sheridan gave her a grateful look.

'Betty!' Mum snatched the doll and cradled it against her chest. 'Sweet Betty.'

'Your doll is almost as old as us,' Ronnie said. 'Where did she come from?'

'She's mine.' Mum stroked the doll's plaits. 'Do you think I'm a good Gloria or a better Betty?'

Jesus. What a question. Had Mum totally lost it?

But Ronnie was unperturbed. 'They both sound fine to me. We could merge them together and call you Glotty,' she joked. 'How about that?'

'Glotty.' Mum gave her trademark giggle. 'Imagine if I'd introduced myself to Ralph as Glotty. He never would've married me. You know, he saved me from my own family.' She retold the story of how Dad had been working on a horse stud nearby. She'd been sent there one rainy afternoon to collect apples, a donation for the poor. 'As soon as I met Ralph Wilson, I knew it was a sign,' she said. 'God approved of the match with a horse trainer from Australia, but Father didn't. We had to keep it a secret.'

This was a new twist. Had she left America in order to elope with an 'unsuitable' husband?

Ronnie started talking about Dad's horses and Mum had no trouble keeping up with the conversation. In a rush of gratitude, Sheridan invited Ronnie to come to lunch at her house later. If only Ronnie could visit every week; Mum needed to see more old friends. Without her siblings in Australia, Mum had no-one to reminisce with about her earlier years, the years which she now recalled the best. Sheridan's own childhood was gradually being erased from her mother's mind.

When she and Ronnie readied themselves to leave, Mum clutched Betty tightly.

'You're not taking her.'

'It's okay, Mum. Betty is staying here with you.'

'I can never forgive Father. As long as we both shall live.'

Sheridan wondered whether to remind Mum that her father had died decades ago. She was still deciding when Ronnie spoke.

'Quite right,' she said. 'Forgiveness is overrated.'

In his last message, Lachy had asked his sister to pull out Nick's old photos of summer camp; he wanted a picture of a counsellor called Tiffany. She'd sent a huffy message back: *Why don't you ask Nick to do it?* It seemed he had but Nick hadn't replied. Her husband had stopped speaking to her brother.

Nick had been distant with her too. When she'd asked if he was stressed, he'd snarled, 'I'm worried about any long-term effects on Mabel's brain. Of course I'm bloody stressed!'

With the kids back at school, she'd been expecting to have the house to herself for a couple of hours but Nick was working from home today. Well, she hoped he felt guilty when he saw her sorting through the cupboard trying to find his old photo album when she should be working herself. The hall cupboard was crammed full of boxes and plastic tubs. For a moment, she imagined a proper storage space: a huge walk-in cupboard with deep shelves where she could hide all their junk. This morning, she'd seen a listing in Cherrybrook, a modern four-bedroom house in the same suburb as Nick's parents. But she was reluctant to leave Willoughby. She loved the village atmosphere, and everything was within fifteen minutes: the girls' school, Mum's nursing home, the shops and restaurants of Chatswood, Nick's office in North Sydney. She and Nick had bought their Federation cottage before they'd had kids and it had been perfect.

At last she found the box containing the summer camp album. Nick's mum had put it together during her scrapbooking phase, and every page had captions and dates. Sheridan opened it at random and saw the youthful faces of Nick and Lachy. For both of them, it had been their first solo trip overseas. After meeting at camp, they'd travelled around the States together, north to Canada and then over to Europe. A boys' own adventure. Maybe these old photos would remind Nick of his long friendship with Lachy.

She returned to the kitchen, brandishing the album, to find he'd made them each a cup of coffee.

'Here's your album from camp,' she said. 'Look how young you were!'

She turned the pages, feeling a pang of envy at the fun they'd had: kayaking on the lake, basketball games, campfires, all sorts of activities with kids and other camp counsellors. Mum and Dad hadn't suggested she take a gap year; she'd gone straight from school to university.

An attractive dark-haired girl appeared in photo after photo.

'Is that Tiffany?' She pointed at a picture of a girl in a red bikini by the lake. 'What happened to her?'

'She went home early.'

'Did you meet up with her after camp?' The boys were always looking for a free night's accommodation.

'No.' He ran a finger over the plastic photo protector. 'Lachy had a thing for her, though.'

'Really?' She stared at the photo more closely. Pale skin. Dark hair. Prissy. Not Lachy's type; he preferred outdoorsy girls. 'How come I've never heard that before?'

Nick shrugged. 'It was nothing serious. Anyway, once he was back home he started seeing Amber straight away.'

'Did you both like her?' He'd touched the photo in an adoring kind of way. 'Did you argue over her?'

'Nup. I've gotta get back to my laptop.' He picked up his coffee and walked off.

She shook her head and glanced at the photo again. Her mother-in-law had captioned it: Tiffany Jones. Sheridan took pictures of the photos and texted them to Lachy. It was time for her to get back to work herself; she only had ninety minutes before Ronnie was due for lunch. As she went to put the album back in the box, she noticed envelopes of loose photos: the ones that hadn't made the cut for presentation. Telling herself she was tidying up, definitely not snooping, she flicked through them. Sure enough they were all unremarkable—except for one: an out-of-focus shot of a woman standing by a bridge in the countryside with a guy. Was that Tiffany Jones with Lachy? No, not Lachy. The image was blurry but it looked more like Nick. And Tiffany seemed to be holding something in front of herself . . . a jumper or a coat. No, that wasn't it.

She studied the picture closely.

Nick's arm was around Tiffany's waist and he appeared to be glowing with pride. Sheridan had seen that look before; there were similar photos in her own albums. Nick and Tiffany beamed like a couple in love, looking forward to the birth of their baby.

And yet, it couldn't have been long after this that she'd first met Nick at a pub in Newtown, a week after he and Lachy had arrived home from their overseas trip. When they were introduced, she expected to like Nick as her brother's friend; she hadn't expected a spark to zap between them. The following Saturday, they'd gone on a date without telling Lachy, and they'd been together ever since. Seventeen years now. Sheridan had been totally open about her past boyfriends, three in total, all short-term. Nick had told her about his girlfriends in high school and two in first-year uni.

He hadn't mentioned Tiffany.

She could hear Nick on a teleconference; now was not the time to ask him about it. She carried the photo to her work satchel and slipped it into a pocket where it wouldn't accidentally be discovered.

Opening her laptop, she got to work herself, speaking to clients, but she was so preoccupied she could barely hold up her end of the conversation. Luckily, Brendan had achieved his next goal of networking with local tourism operators and all she had to do was congratulate him. Dom required more of her input but, working on autopilot, she suggested he make a list of six goals for his first six months living in Sydney. Her other new client, Tammy, was at a conference in America so she didn't have to check in with her. As usual, Heidi took the most energy; she complained about her subordinates and how they couldn't be trusted. Urging her to come up with some action points, Sheridan wondered about the concept of trust. The foundation of every relationship. For Heidi, this issue of trust was more likely to be about herself than her team.

Trust. Sheridan trusted her husband but during her sessions, her mind kept churning: *Why has Nick never mentioned Tiffany? Were they just friends? Did Lachy take the photo? He's the one trying to find her, after all. Is Lachy the father?*

The doorbell snapped her out of the overthinking cycle. Lunch with Ronnie would be a welcome distraction.

'I need some water.' Ronnie had never been to their house before but she dashed past her to the kitchen. 'I can't deal with this city. It's giving me the heebie-jeebies. Too many cars. Not enough trees.' She took a glass from the draining rack and filled it from the tap, gulped half then sank into a chair. 'I'd forgotten that town water tastes like chemicals.' She grimaced with the next sip. 'It's probably doing terrible things to your kids' brains.'

Sheridan flicked the switch on the kettle, wishing that Ronnie hadn't referred to her children's brains. 'Thank you for visiting Mum. It really perked her up. Will you have time to drop in again before you go home?'

'I was worried about seeing her but she's the same old Gloria. I'll go tomorrow morning.'

'That would be wonderful.' She meant it. Having someone else to entertain Mum helped share the load. It was what her brother should have been doing.

Nick came out when lunch was ready. As she served up the quiche and salad, she glanced at him—he seemed so self-contained, closed off from her.

Ronnie took her plate of food and sat at the head of their dining table. 'Sheridan, I didn't want to discuss this earlier in front of Gloria, so I'm glad you asked me to lunch. The other day, a real estate agent came to see me.'

'Are you planning to sell?' She couldn't imagine Ronnie living anywhere else.

'Hopefully I'll die in my back paddock, my bones will dis-integrate into the earth and no-one will notice.' Ronnie gave a chuckle. 'Nope, not my property. The agent said he'd been doing an appraisal of Mimosa Hideout.'

What? Lachy couldn't sell without her permission. They had joint power of attorney over Mum's affairs. Mimosa was part of the family, the place of holidays and celebrations. Apart from the last disastrous Easter. Was this a knee-jerk reaction from Lachy? Sell the place to move on from the memory of his son poisoning her daughters?

'I don't care what the agent says, we're not selling.' Anger made her voice louder than she intended. 'Lachy shouldn't have called him.'

Silence filled the dining room. Ronnie was staring intently at Nick. Eventually they spoke over the top of each other.

'—going to tell her?'

'—just an appraisal.'

For a moment, she couldn't think straight. *Nick* had ordered the appraisal? Without consulting her? There must be a reasonable explanation, but she couldn't imagine what it would be. Just like she couldn't imagine why he'd never mentioned Tiffany Jones and her pregnancy over the past seventeen years.

One thing was clear, though: Ronnie was here on a mission to dissuade them from selling.

'You pretended to be Lachy.' Ronnie jabbed a finger in his direction. 'You told the agent your mother wanted to sell.'

'Don't worry, we're not selling,' Nick said smoothly. 'I needed an appraisal to work out how much it's worth so we can increase our mortgage. We're looking for a bigger house in Sydney.'

It was a reasonable explanation but they always discussed financial decisions together.

Ronnie shook her head. 'The agent won't be happy about being tricked. He was excited about a new property coming on to the market. There's not much movement around there.'

'It wasn't a trick. I simply asked for an appraisal.'

Sheridan's thoughts seesawed from reassurance to fear: *Nick is doing his best for our family. No, he's lying, something is going on.*

She broke into the discussion. 'Did you tell Lachy?'

'There was no need.' Nick's calm explanations kept on coming. 'It's about our borrowing capacity. Mimosa will be staying in the family.'

In *my* family, she wanted to say. Panic flooded through her. She didn't want to discuss this in front of Ronnie but she had to know. Standing up abruptly, she fetched her work satchel and pulled the photo from the pocket. She placed it on the table in front of him. He'd been scraping up the last of his salad, but when he saw the photo, his fork fell from his hand and clattered against the plate.

'In the photos from camp, I found this one of Tiffany Jones,' she said. 'Is it . . . Is it . . .'

Is it Lachy's or yours? The sentence stuck in her throat.

'Tiffany was a complicated girl. She didn't like being at camp. It wasn't really her thing.' He was weighing up each word. 'Lachy said he was trying to track her down, but I told him it would be better to leave the past behind.'

Nick picked up his plate, put it in the dishwasher and headed for the door. 'Good to see you, Ronnie. I've got to get back to work.'

Sheridan stared after him.

Trust. Distrust. Her instinct was right, she knew from the way he spoke, the way he'd addressed his comments to the floor, the way he'd left the room.

Whether it was about Tiffany Jones or the appraisal for Mimosa, her husband was definitely hiding something.

33

KAI

THE CAR WAS STOPPED AT A TRAFFIC LIGHT WHEN NATALIE LEANT across him, her body so close that Kai could smell her orangey perfume. She opened the window and called out to a girl on the street, 'Hey, Vivien! You coming tonight?' The girl yelled back and he turned to look at her: she was eighteen or nineteen and had a crown of red curly hair. The colour matched Mabel's exactly. His stomach cramped, like it had at Mimosa that night. For the first time, it hit him fully. Mabel might never have reached this girl's age because of him.

When they pulled up behind a massive community hall, Kai knew the evening would be going off. This wasn't a simple house party; Aidan, Natalie and their band were playing a proper gig. Epic! But did that mean drugs were more likely to be around? He wanted to be one of the gang, wanted to go along with whatever they did, but the shock of seeing that red-headed girl on the street . . . No drugs for him, not anymore, not ever. Hudson would tell him to live it up in America. His best mate had been the first one to try the pills and then he'd started buying them to share with friends. With that thought came another scary realisation: Hudson could have died at the party that night.

The band clambered from the car and began hauling bags and equipment from the trunk.

'Can you carry my guitar?' Natalie asked, handing him a black case.

'Sure.' Kai slung it over his shoulder, and hoped he looked as cool as the rest of them.

While he'd never dress in a punk rock outfit himself, he appreciated their style. It took guts to dress differently. No-one would do it in Warabina for fear of being targeted by Grug and his mates. That macho bully would bloody love America, with its gridiron games and guns and huge SUVs. He'd fit right in. Presumably there were tons of Grug clones at the local high school. Maybe later, when they were chilling, he could get some tips from Aidan on how to deal with him.

Following Aidan into the hall, he saw microphones and a drum kit already positioned on the stage. In the corner trestle tables were draped with cloths—that must be the bar. A professional set-up.

'What time is it kicking off?' he asked.

'People usually arrive about six o'clock.' Aidan carried the amp up the steps.

'So it's a regular thing?'

'Yeah, once a week.' When Aidan had finished plugging cords into a power board, he beckoned for Kai to join him. 'Can you bring Nat's guitar up here?'

Hurrying up the stairs to the stage, he handed over the instrument. They must be a pretty good band to have a gig every week. Behind them on the wall, a huge screen suddenly lit up, the white light blinding them.

'Hey, Isaac, can you turn it off or put on the intro?' Aidan shielded his eyes as he spoke. 'We can't see anything when it's like that.'

'Sorry!' said a disembodied voice.

The white light gave way to soft greens and blues. A disco-ball effect. Aidan yelled his thanks and started moving cords around the stage.

'How can I help?' Kai asked.

'Could you do the drinks with Leilani? She always needs an extra pair of hands.'

Heading towards the trestles in the corner, he walked taller— his older cousin trusted him to do the bar. About twenty people were moving around the hall, shifting chairs, carrying boxes and plastic tubs. He couldn't see Natalie among them; maybe she'd gone to change. She was going to be awesome on stage. She had a presence, charisma.

Leilani put him to work, unpacking paper cups and placing them on the tables. Dressed in a leopard-skin jumpsuit, Leilani had her own unique style, different from Natalie, but she owned it in the same confident way. As he helped set up, he wondered if they were making a sneaky alcoholic punch. He could only see soda bottles, no cans of beer nor vodka mixers.

'What do you do in Australia for fun?' Leilani asked.

'Umm . . .' As he searched for an appropriate answer, a screeching noise erupted from a speaker. Glancing up, he noticed an image projected on the big screen. Blue words on a green background: *Music is the rhythm of God's love for us*. It must be from an earlier booking . . . but Aidan had just asked

Isaac to put on the intro. No, that couldn't be right. These guys were way too hip to be playing at a Christian meeting.

Leilani was looking at him, still waiting for an answer.

'I surf.' Not lately though. There was no beach in Mimosa. He played video games most of the time. 'What about you?'

'Well, I love our worship group.' She nodded towards the stage. 'It's such a great night. Sometimes we go hiking together on weekends too. I love music and Nat is teaching me the guitar. I'm not very good. Yet. But one day, you'll see me up there, singing about God's love.'

This gig wasn't gonna be what he'd imagined.

Not. At. All.

✕✕

The hall had filled with young people—more than the hundred they'd expected. When the band took to the stage, the crowd roared. Nat's husky vocals streamed through the speakers, electrifying them all. It was like being at a proper rock concert, the punters dancing and chanting the chorus. While he didn't know any of the words, his body buzzed with the drumbeat, the strum of the bass guitar and Nat's soulful melody. He'd never known you could be cool *and* Christian.

'Come and dance!' Leilani yelled, dragging him by the arm into the scrum.

Red with embarrassment, he stood awkwardly opposite her. Dancing wasn't his thing, but he didn't have much choice— Leilani held his arms, jerking them in time to her movements. He attempted to copy her steps, wiggling his hips. If Hudson were here, he'd be laughing at him, but Kai was with strangers and he could dance however he liked. The fact that he knew the band, that he'd spent the afternoon with Natalie, helped to loosen him up. He could feel the music inside him. Eventually Leilani let go of his arms and he continued rocking it to the beat.

For half an hour, the band played and they danced. Everyone was smiling and singing, their positive energy ricocheting around the hall. He'd never experienced anything like it. Could he ever achieve this level of happiness? Aunty Sheridan would say he didn't deserve it, but wasn't God supposed to forgive people? Natalie was singing something like 'I was lost and now I'm found'. Maybe he could be found?

The tempo ramped up with the next song, Nat's lyrics raw and intense, Aidan's back-up vocals almost a shout. The crowd went ballistic, screaming, swinging their arms, pumping fists. Kai jumped up and down with them, the beat taking over his whole body. Two guys next to him were going for gold, their hands in the air, bouncing like they were on pogo sticks. As he moved closer to jump along with them, he copped an elbow in the head. With the crowd swirling before his eyes, he collapsed to the floor.

He'd blacked out briefly. When he opened his eyes again, two young women were kneeling beside him and an old man stood above. They helped him to an office at the back of the hall and settled him into an old leather armchair.

'How do you feel, Kai?' asked Leilani, who'd followed them.

'I'm okay,' he mumbled, wishing he could disappear. What would Natalie and Aidan think if they knew he'd fainted? Totally feeble. He hoped they hadn't seen the commotion from the stage.

'This is the first-aid team.' Leilani gestured towards the others. 'They'll look after you. I'll check in on you later.'

She left and the old guy stepped forward. 'Hello . . . Kai, is it? I'm Dr Charlie Stanbury. I'm just going to feel your head.'

Even though his touch was soft, Kai flinched with the pain.

'Sorry, that's going to be a big bump,' the doctor said. 'Can you tell me what day it is?'

'Thursday?' he guessed. 'I'm not concussed, just jet-lagged. I've only been here a few days.'

One of the women passed him a mug of water while Dr Stanbury pulled a small torch out of an old medical bag.

'Is that an Australian accent? I travelled down under once and we went to the outback.'

'I'm from Sydney.' It was too complicated to explain about Warabina. 'My grandmother grew up here, and my cousin Aidan is in the band.'

Dr Stanbury shone the torch into his eyes then asked him to recite the months of the year backwards from December. That was hard, but he managed it.

'Are you feeling dizzy?' the doctor asked.

'Nah, I'm good.' It wasn't quite true; everything was a bit fuzzy.

'I think you should rest here for a while and sip on that water. Is that okay by you?'

He nodded, happy to hang in this quiet room, away from the music and crazy dancers. Looking around, he noticed a cross on the wall and cabinets full of old books.

'Girls, why don't you go back out and keep an eye on things? I'll stay with Kai.'

The young women left the room and Kai, feeling tired and muddled, leant back in the chair and closed his eyes.

'Kai, I'll need you to stay awake in case of concussion,' Dr Stanbury said. 'Open your eyes and tell me about your grandmother. Was she born around here? When did she emigrate to Australia?'

Kai tried to dredge up what he knew about Glamma's past. 'Um, her name's Gloria and she grew up in Leeville, a tiny town on the way to Reading.' He yawned. 'It's over in Berks County. Her father was a pastor.'

There was a silence, and Kai thought the doctor hadn't been listening, but then he asked, 'And can you recall Gloria's maiden name?'

'Wilson,' he answered automatically and then realised that was her married name. For a moment he couldn't think properly, his brain foggy, but then he remembered it was the same as Great-Uncle Ernest's name. 'No, not Wilson. It's Dunstan.'

'Dunstan,' the doctor echoed. 'Gloria Dunstan . . . hmm . . . Dunstan.'

Kai had assumed the old doctor was mentally fit but now he sounded unhinged, repeating the name. Dr Stanbury's eyes filled with tears and he stared upwards to stop them from falling. Had he known Glamma in the olden days? Been her boyfriend? Kai's head, as if exacerbated by this strange reaction, began to throb.

'Am I allowed to take a painkiller?'

Dr Stanbury seemed to shake himself back to the present. He took a tissue from his pocket, dabbed at his eyes then blew his nose loudly.

'Of course. I've run out of Advil but I have some more in the car.' He picked up his bag and walked towards the door. 'Stay awake and I'll be back in a few minutes.'

Kai waited and waited, but the doctor never returned. Was he too upset about something that had happened in the past or was there another medical drama out on the dance floor? It would be a relief to know Kai wasn't the only one. He stared out at the sky through the high window. A church spire soared upwards. When they'd parked the car, he hadn't even noticed it—he'd been so sure about what type of gig this was. Now he realised the community hall was part of a church campus. They must hold large services here.

Even though it was after seven thirty, the sun hadn't finished setting. At home it would be dark by this time. And cold in Warabina. He didn't want to go back there. Tarni was the only good thing about Warabina High. She'd replied to his message about the ice-cream flavours: *Pumpkin ice cream? Disgusting!!!!!!*

Looking at his phone made him dizzier. He tried phoning Dad, but there was no answer. God, his head hurt. When would the doctor come back with the painkillers? The thought of going outside to find him and hearing that loud music was too much. Yawning, Kai wondered if he did have a concussion. Dr Stanbury had said he shouldn't fall asleep; he needed to focus on something.

He wandered over to the bookcases. Two shelves held thick leather-bound journals, like the spell books from the Harry Potter movies. He took one out and glanced at the fancy handwriting inside: a list of births, marriages and funerals at the church. Would Glamma's birth be in there? He estimated the date by remembering the year of her seventieth birthday party and plonked himself at the desk. Leafing through the pages, he eventually found her name: *Gloria Dunstan, female, baby, baptised.* There she was, in black and white. He needed another task to keep himself alert; he'd look for Great-Aunt Theresa and Great-Uncle Ernest too. And Virginia, who had already died. Sad that the youngest sibling had died first.

Twenty minutes later, the music stopped. Finally, he could leave this church office and get some painkillers and go to bed. It didn't matter if Natalie and Aidan thought he was a dork; his head hurt too much now for him to care. He'd just got to his feet when the door opened and Aidan appeared.

'I heard you got whacked in the head,' his cousin said. 'You okay?'

'I'm fine.' He tried to summon his earlier enthusiasm. 'You guys were amazing out there. You should audition on *American Idol*. And Nat's singing was incredible.'

'Thanks.' Aidan's face lit up. 'She's certainly the star. Were you all right in here by yourself?'

'Yeah. I was looking through the old books.' He tapped the relevant volume. 'This one lists the baptism dates of our grandparents and their siblings.'

Aidan took the book and opened it. 'I haven't seen these before.'

'Look, there's Gloria's name and Theresa and Ernest.' Standing beside him, Kai flicked through the pages to show him. 'And there's another Dunstan listed as well. Did they have a cousin called Elizabeth?'

'Not that Pa has mentioned.' Aidan read the baptism information out loud. 'Huh. She has the same parents as them. Did they have a sister who died as a baby?'

'I dunno. Glamma has never talked about anyone called Elizabeth.'

'I'll ask Pa.' Aidan closed the book and put it back on the shelf. 'The rest of the band is staying for a while but I'll take you home. Are you good to go?'

'Yep. Have you got any headache tablets?'

'There are some in the first-aid kit behind the drinks table. We can get them on the way out.'

He was relieved that Aidan was treating him normally, not like a toddler who had hurt himself in the ball pit.

'Dr Stanbury was supposed to bring me some Advil from his car,' he said, 'but he disappeared and never came back.'

34

LACHY

LACHY HEARD THE PING OF HIS PHONE AFTER MIDNIGHT, DRAGGING him from sleep. Hopefully Kai was all right. They'd spoken earlier and Kai said he had mild concussion but was fine to stay with Celeste and Aidan.

In the dark, Lachy stared at the screen. The message was from Sheridan: fifteen pictures of Tiffany at summer camp. Numerous shots in her red bikini; too attractive for her own good, treating everyone as if they were beneath her. When he'd googled Tiffany Jones, hundreds of entries had popped up. Was she any of those women or had she died on Deadwood Creek Road decades ago? Feeling sick at what he may uncover, he'd narrowed the search to Pennsylvania and found an address for a Jones in Tremont, Schuylkill County. Tremont was familiar, she must have mentioned it at camp. Could they be her parents? There was no phone number listed, though. He'd have to turn up on their doorstep in two days' time.

Unannounced and unprepared.

What would he say to her parents if she were dead?

Wide awake now, he texted his thanks to Sheridan then lay on his back, flicking through the photos again. A new message appeared, from Nick this time. His mate had been silent over the past ten days, not responding to any of Lachy's texts.

Why are you asking for photos of Tiffany? Don't go there.

Fuck, Nick knew something and was warning him off. If he could just find out what, then he'd stop looking for her and focus on Juliet. If he was brave enough for the truth. He forced himself to type out a message and send it before he changed his mind: *Can we talk about her? Are you free now?*

Lachy waited an hour for a reply, but none came, and eventually he drifted into a chaotic dream. Tiffany was screaming his name from underneath the bridge on Deadwood Creek Road. Instead of helping her, he sprinted off as fast as he could. A pick-up truck approached with Nick behind the wheel; it didn't slow but accelerated towards him. The bonnet clipped his hip and sent him flying down the embankment.

He woke before he landed in the grass: his pulse still racing with the shock of being hit by the truck; the image of Nick glaring at him through the windscreen imprinted on his mind. The dream was so vivid that he automatically felt along his thigh to check he wasn't hurt. Then he lay awake, staring at the ceiling until dawn brought stripes of dark mauve into the bedroom.

'Lachy, phone for you,' Uncle Leonard yelled from outside the bathroom.

'Who is it?' He finished rinsing off the shaving cream and patted his face dry; he needed to look his best for this meeting with Naomi at head office.

'A man.'

If Theresa had answered the call, she'd have the person's life story before handing it over to him. Who would possibly ring him on this landline? Opening the bathroom door, he took the receiver from Leonard and carried it to the kitchen.

'Lachy Wilson speaking.'

'This is Lieutenant Blade Davis from Pennsylvania State Police. Lachlan, we'd like you to come in for a chat. Your DNA has come up in connection with a case—'

DNA. Juliet. How could he defend himself when he couldn't remember what he'd done? He'd end up in an American prison for life.

His palm around the phone was slick with sweat and his head spun with a dozen different questions; he blurted out the first, interrupting the police officer. 'How did you get this number?'

'You put this address on your customs declaration when you flew into the US.'

His legs began trembling and he leant against the fridge for support. Bloody Sheridan! He should never have flown here. His name must have been on some watch list which triggered an alert.

'I . . . uh . . .' The ability to speak deserted him, along with his grasp on the phone. It fell from his sweaty hand and clattered to the floor. He bent to retrieve it, but when he put it to his ear it had reverted to a dial tone. Shit, he'd hung up on the police officer.

He was still holding the receiver when Leonard entered the kitchen. 'Everything all right?'

'Yep.' He struggled to think of an excuse. 'It was . . . an old friend from camp . . . playing a stupid prank. If you get a call from someone pretending to be a police officer, just hang up.'

'Still acting like kids, huh?' Leonard chuckled. 'Will you boys ever grow up?'

Was Blade Davis calling about something he'd done to Tiffany when he was practically a kid, or about Juliet, who was little more than a teenager herself? Would the police turn up to arrest him here? He had to leave this house, this state.

He wouldn't do the grown-up thing and call the police back; he was going to do exactly as Leonard said: act like a kid—and run.

The lesser of two evils, Lachy thought as he stood outside the head office of Global Social Solutions. The meeting he'd been avoiding for months was now a better prospect than a chat with the Pennsylvania State Police. He'd fled from Aunt Theresa's house and, exactly like a suspect on the run, paid cash for a train ticket to DC.

The storm that had been threatening broke while he was on the train; a wild wind whipping branches, leaves and sticks, tossing them alongside the tracks. The rainwater didn't collect into puddles, though, it had been sucked into the hot, thirsty earth. Now it was a pleasant twenty-five degrees compared to yesterday's thirty-five—or ninety-five, as they measured it here, which sounded even hotter. On the train trip, he'd googled Blade Davis. Blade. Such an outlandish name for a police officer that he half-believed someone was playing a prank on him: Aidan and Kai making mischief or perhaps Nick getting back at him in a bizarre way. But no: his phone displayed a photo of Lieutenant Blade Davis, head of criminal investigations, dressed in full uniform, fifty-something, muscular, Black, with a shaved head and full beard.

Definitely not a prank. And Lachy wasn't a kid anymore; he couldn't run away forever.

He would sort out his work situation today, then return to Celeste's place, pick up Kai and take him to Theresa's house. Tomorrow he'd contact Blade Davis. Hopefully he hadn't made the situation worse for himself by disappearing like this.

Your DNA has come up in connection with a case . . . It must relate to Juliet. She was the one who had asked for his DNA. He'd been planning to find her somehow, but that seemed foolish now, when he had no idea what had happened. In the cab from Union Station, as they'd driven along Tenth, he'd shut his eyes at the sight of the FBI headquarters, annoyed the cabbie had taken that particular route. By the time they reached the neighbourhood of Foggy Bottom, he was distracting himself with the streetscape: the irony of men sleeping rough outside the International Monetary Fund. In a small park near George Washington University, students strolled past a tent encampment with the residents' washing hanging on a chain-link fence.

Sheridan had been right, this homeless crisis would have shocked Kai. But an even greater shock would be seeing his dad in police custody. He'd have to tell him what was going on—but not yet. Instead, he texted his son a photo of the university: *Hope you're having fun. What's the capital of America? Ha ha. Guess where I am? Love you.* It was the best he could do at the moment.

Shaking his head, he focused on the steps leading up to the GSS office block and the fountain flowing at the entrance. He thought of his tattoo, the sacredness of water, and his former mate, Henrik. Head office didn't care about the sacredness of human life.

248

As he walked into reception, he nodded to the security guard and plastered on a smile. It was time to climb out of his dark pit of hopelessness and despair; time to stand tall and do the right thing.

The receptionist handed him a plastic visitor's pass and told him to take a seat. *I'm not a visitor,* he wanted to say. *I'm still on the payroll.* He didn't expect to wait long because this meeting had been scheduled a fortnight ago. But the minutes ticked over. Leafing through the company magazine, he came across a profile of the north-eastern desal project in Kenya with quotes from 'global water expert' Henrik Bergmann. Bloody hell. He dropped the magazine back onto the coffee table.

Before he'd left Mimosa, he tried to prepare for this meeting as much as he could in his dispirited state. The red circle showing 5,387 unread emails in his inbox almost had him logging out again. But he knew some of those were company-wide messages, industry updates and newsletters. He'd tried to sort them into subject areas: Henrik, leave conditions, pay arrangements, work issues. The emails relating to his allegations against Henrik requested additional evidence of criminal behaviour. Just like the operations director had said when he'd provided the report. That depressed him so much he closed the laptop. The next day, he managed to read three emails about his salary; it seemed they hadn't fired him yet. At the airport, he tackled a few more but the wi-fi was slow. And when he clicked on an attachment, it was encrypted. He needed a password. Had he been locked out of the system? It was all too hard and he'd given up. Hopefully he had read enough to get him through this meeting.

Finally, Naomi Chidozie appeared, greeting him with a brisk handshake.

'We've been so worried about you, Lachlan.' She stared at him intently and he wondered what she was hoping to find in his face—a reason to sack him, no doubt.

'Sorry . . .' He pushed his damp hair off his forehead. Still sweating. 'Sorry, I've been difficult to contact.'

'Let's go up to the meeting room.' As she led him towards the elevator, he caught sight of their reflections: Naomi's electric blue skirt and jacket, the epitome of professional chic; him in a crushed white shirt with chinos, his hair longer than usual, his face glistening red. Sadly, he looked better than he felt. He wished Sheridan were with him: she spoke the same language as the HR people.

Naomi took him to the sixth-floor meeting room, with its view of the Potomac River, sparkling greeny-brown today. She poured him both water and coffee and gestured for him to take a chair. After she'd sat down opposite him at the huge board-room table, she lined up a folder, laptop, phone, notebook and pen in front of her, almost like a shield. He had nothing.

'Do you mind if I record our meeting?' she asked, fiddling with her phone.

His default was to agree, but not today; not with the thought of Lieutenant Blade Davis on his tail.

'I'd rather you didn't,' he said. 'Before we discuss my work situation, I'd like to ask about the complaint I lodged in regard to Henrik Bergmann. Has it progressed?'

'Actually—' She paused. 'I was wondering if you wanted a legal representative with you in this meeting?'

Her words sent a hot flush through his body. 'Why would I need that?'

'We've sent you many emails.' She tapped her shiny pink nails against her computer, as if indicating the numerous messages. 'You must have read them.'

Shit, he should have gone through them one by one. What was in the other emails he hadn't got to that indicated a need for legal advice?

'Uh . . . I didn't keep up with my emails.' He considered lying about internet access but chose the truth. 'I needed a break from thinking about work. I wasn't in a good place.'

'I'm not surprised.' She pushed a report across the sleek mahogany tabletop. 'We're still awaiting your response about the incident in Nairobi. It was noted that you may suffer from memory loss but that cannot excuse your actions.'

Flicking through the report, phrases jumped out at him. *Drinking to excess. Taking advantage of an underage girl in the hotel. Conduct violating GSS policy. Unable to cope in the field.*

It was *his* name in the report, not Henrik's.

Lachlan Wilson had been accused of child sexual exploitation and abuse.

Fuck, no. He'd never do that. Even with the question mark of a memory blackout, that wasn't him. He knew it to his core. That bastard. Henrik had turned the tables on him, using his knowledge of Lachy's blackouts.

Twelve years he'd given to this company, the past five years working with Henrik—and this was how they repaid his loyalty: assuming the worst of him, accepting this fabricated charge.

'This is absolutely false.' He managed to keep his voice just below a shout as he thrust the file back across the table. 'It's in retaliation to the report I wrote about Henrik. What's happened with that?'

Naomi slid the document inside her folder. 'Both sets of allegations are being investigated,' she said. 'However, this is not a counter-complaint. Henrik's report was lodged prior to yours.'

Unbelievable! Henrik must have guessed he'd make a complaint and got his in first. Lachy now knew one thing for sure: Henrik was guilty and fighting for his career and freedom.

'I can give you some contacts who will vouch for my integrity,' he said. 'Local contractors and government officials.' As he began thinking of names, he realised Henrik would already have spoken to them; a small bribe went a long way in difficult conditions. And it would be hard to find people to condemn Henrik. He'd been so discreet that even Lachy, his closest mate, hadn't known about his deplorable actions.

Naomi, who hadn't bothered responding to his offer of character references, took another document from her folder and passed it across the table to him.

'There's a second allegation about you in DC with another young woman. The police have been in touch.'

He stared at her with his mouth open. Juliet.

Sheridan would tell him to stay calm, answer the questions truthfully. Do not bolt from the meeting, do not head straight to the nearest bar, do not slug three whiskies in a row. His mind churned. Henrik must have plied him with drinks that night, hoping to send him into an alcoholic blackout—a place from which it would be impossible to defend himself. Henrik was the only person who knew about his memory blanks. His best mate for so many years had shafted him. Lachy would go to jail for a crime he didn't commit and Henrik would walk free.

He closed his mouth, forced himself to think.

'This is a smokescreen. Henrik made up all of this to protect himself.' He steepled his fingers over his nose, trying to find a way forward. 'Henrik is the real issue. He practically killed Zahra himself. He's taking advantage of vulnerable, underage girls in desperate circumstances. His actions are abhorrent and against our company's guiding principles.'

'The DC case has nothing to do with Henrik Bergmann.' Naomi's pen was poised to take notes. 'You've been obstructive in both of these investigations against you.'

Oh God, they'd been investigating him, not Henrik. He did need a lawyer. Glancing at his watch, he calculated the time in Australia, four in the morning—he couldn't ring Sheridan for her advice. Matthew might know someone in Philadelphia who could help.

'I'm sorry. I haven't been deliberately difficult. I just didn't read my emails.' He'd be polite and pleasant until he could get legal advice. 'I went on leave because of Henrik, and because this company did not take my report seriously. I felt let down on all sides.'

'GSS takes every report seriously,' Naomi snapped. 'You were asked to provide concrete evidence.'

'Yes, but the operations director knows how difficult it is to get evidence,' he argued. 'He doesn't want to lose his top water engineer.'

Unlike him, Henrik had played his hand to perfection, with his concrete evidence: photos of Lachy in a Nairobi bar talking to a young woman and a fabricated statement from her. She must have been a waitress.

Jesus, he was cornered. GSS had been too busy investigating him to even look into Henrik. And he'd assisted by blithely giving Juliet his DNA. What the hell had he done?

Lachy had only come back to DC in September to file the report against his boss. He should have taken a break on Lamu Island, then flown home straight from Nairobi. He never would have met Juliet, and the police wouldn't have a sample of his DNA. Alternatively, he should have acted faster, reported his boss immediately, cut all ties and not hesitated because of their friendship. He should have stayed at work, pestering GSS until the company acted. Ensured they upheld their child protection policies.

Naomi scowled at him. 'As this is a criminal matter, you will need to speak with the police.'

Criminal? What the hell? He hadn't done anything! Well, not in Kenya; he wasn't so sure about Juliet. His thoughts whirled, searching for the words that would put an end to this sham. But before he could speak, there was a knock at the door. The security guard he'd smiled at downstairs led a uniformed officer into the room. He stared at her badge—it featured an image of the White House. Behind her was a man in a suit who did not resemble Lieutenant Blade Davis. Bloody hell, Lachy had fled Pennsylvania this morning to avoid the state troopers, and his HR manager had delivered him directly to the Metropolitan Police.

'Lachlan, you'll understand that I had to notify the police of our meeting today,' she said. 'They've been asking about you for some time.'

Good God. He was trying to protect other girls from Henrik; now he was the one being crucified.

'Thank you, Naomi. We'll take it from here.' The man in the suit escorted her and the security guard to the door. After they'd left, the female officer stood against it, assessing him. Did they think he was going to make a run for it?

'Hello, Lachlan,' the man said, sitting down at the boardroom table opposite him, and pulling out a recording device. 'I'm Lieutenant Ignacio from the Sexual Assault Unit and we'd like to ask you some questions.'

35

ELIZABETH, 1968

DR STANBURY LIVES IN NEW HANOVER WITH HIS WIFE.

He couldn't possibly have a wife. He planned to marry me and take me to Australia. The nurse must have confused him with another physician. I walked back to the main part of the hospital and spoke to the receptionist. She repeated what the nurse had already said: 'There are no doctors' residences here.' Charlie worked at two different locations, so perhaps I'd muddled it up. When I asked about the other hospital, the receptionist said it had no residential quarters.

I begged Gloria to give me more time before telling Father. On Wednesday night, I was sure, my fiancé would explain the misunderstanding. My fiancé. We were engaged, like Constance and Melvin. Just because our engagement was secret didn't mean it wasn't real. Gloria's stony face crumpled when I asked for the delay.

'Why aren't you ashamed and begging God's forgiveness?' she sobbed. 'How can you be smiling?'

'Because I'm in love.'

Our love was stronger than Father's censure, stronger than Gloria's disapproval. Our love would bring this baby into the world.

'It's not love, it's hormones. We discussed it in youth group.' She blew her nose into an embroidered handkerchief. 'Your hormones trick you into sin.'

'There's no trick. This is the most beautiful feeling in the world.' I spun around in a circle. 'It's like The Beatles song, "All You Need Is Love".'

'You shouldn't be listening to The Beatles. Those bands encourage deviant behaviour. That's why you've fallen into sin. And now this boy is corrupting your soul, and hormones are affecting your brain.'

He wasn't a boy; Charlie was a grown man who had chosen to spend the rest of his life with me.

><

On Wednesday evening, after I'd helped the veterans with their dinner, I found Charlie waiting for me in our usual spot— the consulting room where we had consummated our love. He pulled my body against his, wrapped his arms around me and kissed me deeply. Soon, we would be married and we could be together like this every night.

He disentangled himself and held me at arm's length. 'Did you come to the hospital?' he asked. 'A nurse said a girl called Gloria was asking for me. Was it you or your sister?'

So the nurse hadn't mistaken Charlie for another doctor; she'd passed the message on to him. There must be a simple explanation.

'I was nervous and gave Gloria's name instead. But I came to find you because I needed to tell you something.' I paused. 'Where *do* you live, Charlie?'

'At the other hospital. You mixed them up.'

His lodgings didn't really matter—soon we'd be living together. I took his hands and held them over my tummy, our fingers entwined around my engagement ring.

After a deep breath, I announced the joyful news: 'We're having a baby.'

'*What?*' He snatched his hands away. 'It's too soon; I haven't finished my medical training. I can't look after you properly.' He stared at my belly, his face pale. 'It's early days. Maybe you'll have a miscarriage.'

'Charlie, no! I realise the timing isn't good, but this is *our baby*. A sign of our love.'

He was shaking his head, muttering to himself. 'I've heard about terminations. Could I perform one here?'

I knew it was the shock talking, but still it pierced my heart. Inside my head, I reassured our baby: *Daddy loves you; he's confused. Everything will be fine.* And now, I had to tell him that.

Standing in front of him, I touched his cheek and made him look at me. 'Listen, I have a plan. We can get married in a few weeks. You'll finish your training and we'll take the ship to Australia. When the baby comes, no-one there will know it was conceived out of wedlock.'

For once, I was the grown-up, taking charge, telling him how to proceed. Our six-year age difference had disappeared with my impending motherhood. I prayed he would see the sense in what I was saying and be able to feel the joy.

'I love you so much, Betty. You are the light in my life.' God had heard my prayer: he understood. 'But there's something you need to know . . .' He led me to the bed, sat us down, side by side. 'My parents made me marry a girl last year. The daughter of my father's business partner. It was an arrangement between our families. He paid for my training so I could become a doctor.'

I couldn't breathe; there wasn't enough air in the room.

'It's a business arrangement,' he repeated. 'Not a love match.'

The nurse had been telling the truth. *Dr Stanbury lives in New Hanover with his wife.* And my sister was right. I had committed the worst sin. I was Jezebel, the wickedest woman in the Bible.

My disbelief was giving way to fear. Tears dripped down my cheeks. 'What will become of me?'

I hadn't realised I'd spoken aloud until he answered.

'You're my one true love,' he assured me. 'You're my future.'

'But I can't be . . . you already have a wife.'

'I don't love her. I love *you*.'

Charlie held me in his arms but this time, I felt no comfort. I'd prayed to God for guidance about Charlie but He'd abandoned me because I had disobeyed His teachings.

'My parents will turn me out of the house.' I was sobbing, just like Gloria had on Saturday when she'd understood the danger. 'I'll be banished from my church, shunned by my family and friends.'

'You've always said our love is big enough to overcome any obstacle. I'll work something out. Please,' he begged, 'don't tell anyone yet. Give me time to make some plans. Think of our future in Australia.'

XX

I spent half the night pleading with Gloria to stay quiet for another week, but she refused. Before breakfast the next morning, she asked Father to meet us in the garden for a private discussion. There she announced my condition. Father went deathly quiet, which was more frightening than if he'd ranted and raved. Then finally he asked the name of the boy.

'I'd rather not say.' My body trembled as I defied him, but I had promised Charlie. 'Not just yet. He's making some plans for us . . .'

Father locked me in the potting shed by the henhouse while he decided my fate. Too bewildered and terrified to resist, part of me knew that I deserved punishment. *Charlie has a wife.* Every time I said it to myself, it was with the same sense of shock. I assumed Father would keep me in the shed for the afternoon but day turned to night, and one day rolled into the next, until a whole week had passed. Gloria escorted me to the toilet, and brought me meals and a Bible to read. Other than that, I only had my doll for company.

Gloria said no-one else knew I was there. Father had told Mother, my siblings and my school teachers that I'd been sent away in an emergency to nanny for a family whose own mother had suddenly died. To stop anyone from approaching the shed, Father said he'd spilt pesticide and they mustn't go near it.

For the first few days, I curled up on the blanket Gloria had given me and cried. Rain drummed on the roof, echoing my heartbreak and my tears. How could Charlie have courted me while he was married? Did he really love me and not his wife?

She must be older than me, and richer. What if she wanted to have children? How could we ever be together?

I didn't care about being locked inside the shed; my future outside had evaporated.

Then one morning, the rain stopped. Sun streamed in the tiny window and I could hear birds chirping again. I studied the beautiful doll he'd won for me at Pottstown fair and remembered how he'd talked about our destiny that day. We were destined to be together; our love was stronger than this. I told God we were meant to be husband and wife. And I knew it would happen.

Every day Gloria instructed me to pray for forgiveness, and every day she tried to guess the man's name.

'Why won't you tell me?' she asked. 'Then we could talk to Mother about a double wedding with Constance and Melvin.'

I remained resolute, even though I was desperate to speak with Charlie and find out his plans. While I was locked in here, it was impossible to get a message to him.

'It must be Leonard,' Gloria decided. 'He likes you a lot. But there's no need for secrecy. Father will be angry that you've sinned, however he'll accept Leonard as your husband.'

Leonard was a real gentleman; he'd never kiss another girl if he were already married. I scolded myself for being disloyal to Charlie; the situation was more complicated than that. His parents were similar to mine, old-fashioned. They'd arranged a marriage, just like my parents were arranging husbands for me and Gloria. His parents had done it for business interests while mine were focused on growing our church community.

'I've worked it out,' Gloria said. This time she sounded certain. 'It's the man who drives you back from the Soldiers' Home. Walt. He's the father.'

'Ugh.' I gave an involuntary shiver. 'Absolutely not.'

One day, she came with surprising news. 'Theresa and Leonard have pledged themselves to each other.'

'No, she's too young,' I argued. 'She's supposed to wait until you and I are married.'

Typical Theresa. Only fourteen but desperate to catch up to us. Father shouldn't be considering her marriage before ours, but Theresa had a way of getting what she wanted. Maybe Father thought announcing good news would distract the community's attention from my absence. I couldn't repress a feeling of chagrin, though; I'd been thinking that if Charlie couldn't figure out a way to leave his wife, then maybe Leonard would save me. Theresa's scheming meant there was no possibility of that now.

If Theresa were locked in the shed, she would have screamed until it fell down around her. She was petrified of spiders and hated the dark but none of that bothered me. I wanted to move my body so I'd do one hundred star jumps after breakfast. When Gloria took me to the outhouse, I'd skip and run across the grass.

One afternoon, Gloria slipped a library book called *My Family and Other Animals* under the gap at the bottom of the shed door.

'Do you know what Father is planning?' I asked her.

'You've dishonoured him and God, and you're making it worse by refusing to reveal the boy's name.' At least she was chatting to me and bringing food and books. 'He will come and see you soon. You may be sent to a home for unwed girls.'

'And what about Mother?'

'She thinks you're in Ohio, nannying. Father doesn't want to burden her with your shame.'

Mother would love Charlie as a son-in-law. If only I could ask Gloria to help me escape but she was too focused on impressing Father with her devotion. And I wanted to give Charlie enough time to wrap up his affairs. Hopefully he was applying for a divorce, contacting the Australian medical practice to confirm a job, sorting out his funds. It would all be very difficult for him but I was happy to wait patiently in the shed. I read my book and wrote poetry and talked to my baby. It was almost as if I were in a dark womb myself, about to be re-born into a new life. My one issue was getting a passport. Would Mother sign the papers for me?

'There's no shame,' I said. 'We're in love and I'm not giving up the baby.'

Gloria sighed. 'Betty, you don't understand what a precarious position you're in. You have no money, no husband and a baby on the way. If you can't marry this man, your life will be ruined.'

'We're going to work it out,' I insisted.

'There must be a reason why you won't say his name,' Gloria said. 'Please tell me he's not married already.'

I'd thought she'd never guess, but my shocked silence confirmed her worst fear.

'Elizabeth! How could you?'

'Please don't be angry, dear sister. It's complicated. He didn't want to marry her. They don't love each other. He loves me. We're going to be together with our baby.'

'If he truly loved you, he would have done the honourable thing and stayed away. He's selfish and sinful and so are you.'

Gloria thumped the wooden door. 'You've been reading too many love stories. This is real life. You'll never be together.'

She was wrong. I tried to make her understand, but Gloria wouldn't listen.

'Father wanted to give you a whupping and beat the baby out of you, but I convinced him not to. Now I realise it's the most appropriate punishment for your terrible sin.'

Gloria was my only supporter; I couldn't lose her. For the last few days, I'd dreamed of a house in Australia, living on a farm with my husband, my baby and my sister. Away from Father, Gloria would revert to her old self—fun and kind with an open heart and open mind.

But keeping her onside required more deception. Another lie for which I'd have to beg forgiveness.

'I do deserve God's judgement,' I said. 'Not a whupping from Father, though. I've been praying all these nights in here alone and I can recognise the wisdom in what you're saying. I'll do whatever you advise. Please help me.'

'I've been asking for God's guidance,' she said. 'Yesterday I found a leaflet in the library. It listed a concoction of herbs to bring on bleeding. It's another sin against God. But perhaps it's the best way. After this, you must dedicate your life to the church.'

'Thank you, Gloria. I'll do exactly as you say.'

In fact, I would do the opposite; I would protect Charlie and my baby with my own life. But if I pretended to eat the herbs, pretended they worked, I would be able to leave the potting shed and find Charlie. It had been ten days. He would've made arrangements by now. And he'd be frantic with worry about me missing a Wednesday evening at the Soldiers' Home.

Sitting on the floor in the dark, I cradled the doll against my chest, just as I would cradle my baby one day, and sang her a lullaby:

Star of Faith the dark adorning,
All through the night;
Leads us fearless toward the morning,
All through the night.
Though our hearts be wrapped in sorrow,
From the home of dawn we borrow,
Promise of a glad tomorrow,
All through the night.

Tomorrow will be a good day, I promised my baby. I will pretend to take the herbs, leave this shed and find Charlie.

36

SHERIDAN

THIS MORNING SHERIDAN HAD DRIVEN THE GIRLS TO SCHOOL, WALKED them into the playground and hugged them hard. 'Love you to the moon and beyond,' she whispered. They didn't give her a backward glance, skipping off to join their friends. In the car she sat for a few minutes, letting the tears fall. The emotional rollercoaster she'd boarded at Easter continued to twist and lurch. And now that she and Nick were barely communicating, her fierce love for her daughters was everything.

They hadn't heard from the child protection services again; she didn't know if that was a good sign or not. She'd missed a couple of calls from Amber and avoided calling back. Had the social worker interviewed her already?

Driving away from school, Sheridan had to stop at the pedestrian crossing for a woman with a pram. She remembered the shock of devotion she'd felt when she'd first laid eyes on Kai as a squishy ball of pink in the hospital room. At the time, she'd been excited about the new baby nephew but preoccupied by her final-year uni exams; she hadn't been prepared for the deep protective instinct that emerged and her vow to keep him connected to the Wilson family. Over these past few weeks, though, she'd wondered if her girls would have been better off without him in their lives.

Family, connections, genes. And the photo of pregnant Tiffany. She'd decided that if Tiffany had had a baby, it must be Lachy's. He was so casual about hook-ups and birth control: there was Amber's accidental pregnancy and the woman in Washington DC asking for a paternity test. In all likelihood, Tiffany's baby was his too. After a few glasses of cabernet last night, she'd gone down a DNA rabbit hole online and come across something called 'the murder gene'.

Is murder in your DNA?
A decade ago, there was much excitement about a 'murder gene' and its implication that we could analyse DNA to determine which individuals were more likely to kill. A study of Finnish prisoners found that most of the inmates serving time for violent crimes carried the genes known as MAO-A and CDH13, while other prisoners incarcerated for minor crimes did not.

More recently, researchers looking at MAO-A, dubbed the 'warrior gene', have come back to the issue of nature versus nurture. About twenty percent of the population has the warrior gene. If you are brought up with love and kindness, nurture may counteract it. However, if you experience childhood abuse, then the effects of the warrior gene will be heightened, and you are more likely to become a violent individual, possibly even a murderer.

She'd never really thought about the genetic strands that linked them all. As far as she knew, no-one in the family was violent but there was definitely a trait of irresponsible reck-lessness that Kai had inherited from Lachy. Did that come down Mum's side of the family with her sense of carefree fun? But Mum's parents sounded exceedingly puritanical, the opposite of her.

Sheridan gave herself a mental shake and concentrated on the road. She needed to get to work and focus on her clients.

At home she managed a couple of hours of coaching and phone calls before hopping back in the car. Today she was doing an in-person for a change, meeting Dom at a pub in Kirribilli for lunch. She whizzed down the eight-lane freeway towards the Harbour Bridge and took the slip lane to Kirribilli, not far from Nick's accountancy firm in North Sydney. Dom had suggested they meet at the Kirribilli Hotel, the sort of place young people went after work. She recalled drunken Friday nights there many, many years ago.

It took her longer than she expected to find a parking spot, and she was feeling flustered by the time she reached the pub. Being late was against her principles. She spotted a young man at a corner table, busy on a laptop, his head down. Ah, that must be him.

She hurried over. 'Sorry, it was impossible to park but it's lovely to meet you, Dom.'

'You've got the wrong person.' The man didn't even bother looking up from his laptop.

She surveyed the restaurant and bar area: older couples, a group of women, a table of work colleagues. None of them matched her mental image of Dom. She'd meant to google his photo before coming today but had been too distracted. Her training had stressed the value of phone calls over video meetings: clients could focus better with less visual stimulation; they couldn't check your body language for approval; and you could have reflective silences. Phone calls also helped counter any unconscious bias on the part of the coach.

They'd spent enough hours talking that Sheridan felt she knew Dom.

Out in the courtyard, a younger crowd perched on high stools. One boy was sitting by himself, nursing a schooner and staring at his mobile. In jeans and a navy collared shirt, he was slightly better dressed than the others but clearly too young to be Dom—almost too young to be drinking in the pub.

She dug into her bag to find her phone. Maybe she'd come to the wrong place or Dom was running later than her. As she was unlocking the screen, she noticed the navy-shirted boy had stood up and was striding towards her.

'Sheridan,' he said, 'nice to meet you.'

The voice was Dom's but from a distance, he'd looked younger—eighteen, a backpacker, rather than a twenty-two-year-old business graduate. Dropping her phone into her bag, she took him in properly.

'D—'

His name caught in her throat. The decades disappeared and she was in third-year uni again, in the pub at Newtown. This boy. No, she must be imagining it. But the cut of his jaw, the slope of his nose, the flop of strawberry blond hair . . . he looked exactly like her husband when she'd first laid eyes on him all those years ago.

'Dom,' he finished for her and held out his hand.

She choked on her confusion. Who was he? And what was he doing here? In this moment? At this business lunch? In this pub? In her life?

'I'm sorry if I've shocked you.' He took back his hand, which had been hanging between them, unshaken. 'It's wonderful to meet you. I have so many questions, and I'm hoping you can help.'

He had the same hair, the same thick lips. A dead ringer of Nick at that age. But his accent was American. Did he actually have a job here in Australia or was that all a ruse?

Her head spun.

'I didn't want to do it this way,' Dom said with an apologetic smile. 'Can we just sit down and talk?'

Sheridan found her words at last. 'Why did you trick me? Become my client? Say you were from Canada? Why didn't you just get in contact with . . . my husband?'

He gestured towards a table but she didn't want to sit down with him. He'd been lying to her for weeks. How much personal information had she shared? She recalled their last conversation; he'd tried to get her to talk about her own life. *Does your family go to the beach much? Does your husband surf?* He'd been mining her for details of his biological father.

She'd ring Nick and make him deal with this situation. Why should she have to sort out something that had nothing to do with her? If only Nick had told her the truth, then she'd know how to proceed.

'Please,' he begged when she didn't move. 'Please sit down and I'll get you a drink. I really need to talk to you.'

His face, so familiar, and yet he was a stranger. But one thing was clear: Dom was very determined to see his biological father.

She shuffled forward towards a stool. 'Gin and tonic.'

That would give her a few minutes to order her thoughts and ring Nick. This boy had an Italian name, Dominic Marciano. Nothing like all-American Tiffany Jones. She assumed Tiffany must be his mother.

A vision materialised: Dom sitting at their breakfast table, joking with his *half-sisters*.

Dom returned with her drink before she'd even taken out her phone. She took a large gulp, swirling the alcohol around her mouth. And when that mouthful had gone, she took two more swigs.

'Why did you contact me and not my husband?'

'I found out where he worked and emailed him but he didn't answer.' Dom fidgeted on his stool. 'In February, I finally heard back from him. He said, *You have your family and I have mine. Do not upset the balance.*'

Do not upset the balance. It was exactly the sort of thing Nick would say. As if he could control everyone's life and everything that happened around them.

'And you lied to become my client to get close to him.'

'I'm really sorry. I was desperate.' Dom sniffed. 'I just wanted to meet him. It's strange to discover that I'm half-Aussie, instead of half-Italian. I'm staying at a youth hostel in Bondi and learning how to surf. Then I'm going to travel around. Down to the snow and up to the reef. Maybe go to Uluru.'

He seemed genuine: he needed to know where he was from. Did he want more than that?

'Who paid for your coaching sessions?'

The invoices she sent had been paid promptly. He could hardly cry poor if he could afford regular life-coaching sessions.

'I told Dad that you were a job counselling agency and he agreed to pay.' He screwed up his face. 'He doesn't know about Nick . . . I don't want him to disown me. He brought me up. He's still my dad.'

So complicated. Dom wanted to meet his biological father *and* keep his family intact. But was that too much to ask?

She wouldn't ignore him like Nick; she would do what she could. Her husband owed this boy something. 'Hold on a moment,' she said. She pulled her phone from her bag and tapped out a text: *Can you meet for lunch at Kirribilli Hotel? I need to discuss something with you. I'm here already.*

The answer was immediate: *Sure. Give me fifteen minutes.*

Reliable Nick. She'd always been able to count on him. But what did that mean now?

In Kai's early years, they'd taken him for playdates and sleepovers, and every so often Nick complained about Lachy's casual approach to parenting. She'd kiss Nick and tell him what an amazing dad he would be when they were ready to have kids. And yet he'd already had a child.

She gnawed at her thumbnail. How would Nick react when he saw his son? Would it have been better to go home and discuss it with him tonight? She imagined the two of them in the kitchen after the girls were in bed, Nick weaving another lie about the photo of Tiffany and her baby, implicating Lachy.

In front of Dom, she'd find out the truth.

37

LACHY

SEXUAL ASSAULT UNIT? LACHY STARED AT THE DETECTIVE, UNABLE TO hide his fear. If this was about the false allegation in Kenya, all he could do was assert his innocence; Henrik had used his knowledge of Lachy's blackouts to bolster his claim. But if this was about the night with Juliet, there was no way to defend himself—his memory was blank.

'We'd like to discuss your movements on the fifteenth of September last year,' Lieutenant Ignacio said. 'What time did you meet Juliet Kinsley at the Vesper Bar?'

Ignacio had a round face and a Cheshire grin that was way too friendly; Lachy bet he was super quick and super smart, ready to pounce on any misstep. The uniformed police officer continued to stand by the door, her face expressionless, her eyes on Lachy.

'I . . . uh. Maybe seven o'clock.' He tried to picture Juliet and came up with a vague impression of her features—those vivid green eyes, the tribal necklace, possibly a pixie haircut.

'Would you mind providing a DNA sample?' Ignacio kept smiling encouragingly.

'I already did.' Lachy swallowed hard. 'Juliet asked me to give my DNA for a paternity test. Because I was in Australia, she told me to put it on the DNA:Match database.'

'We'd like to cross-check that it was actually your sample.'

Jesus, Nick had been right. Juliet had requested it for some other reason, definitely not a paternity test. But wait, the police hadn't cautioned him, they hadn't arrested him—did that mean his DNA test exonerated him?

'It was absolutely my own saliva, and I may provide another sample—' he hesitated '—once I understand what's happening. I assume Juliet's not pregnant.'

Ignacio shook his head. 'As you weren't in the States, she was trying to find another way to get evidence.'

No baby—that was some relief. He wouldn't be bringing a newborn into a world facing catastrophic climate change. All those months he'd spent worrying about the possibility and it hadn't even been real. Unless the other reason was more concerning.

'Evidence for what?'

'Her roommate was sexually assaulted that night.' Ignacio studied him as he spoke. 'She'd been blindfolded and couldn't identify her attacker. Juliet assumed it was you.'

Lachy's whole body began shaking. The fear that had festered inside him for months spread outwards as an uncontrollable tremor. He had no memory of Juliet's apartment. No memory of her flatmate.

'That's a charge of first-degree sexual assault,' Ignacio pronounced. 'We've been in touch with the Australian Federal Police for your details but everything runs slowly in cross-border investigations.'

Surely he hadn't committed such a sickening act. So traumatic for the poor woman. Shit, had he been in the apartment at the same time, sleeping through the attack? The lieutenant was waiting for him to say something but Lachy couldn't order his thoughts.

'The DNA you provided didn't match the forensic evidence,' Ignacio continued. 'However, Juliet said you gave it so easily that we wondered if you'd swapped in someone else's sample. We'd like to check.'

Thank God, thank God, thank God. This must be why Lieutenant Blade Davis had called him this morning.

'My DNA shows I'm not a suspect.' He put his relief into words, breathing out slowly. The trembling in his body finally stilled. 'Yes, I can give another sample.'

'Good, we'll do that now.' Ignacio took a kit from his bag and began unwrapping the plastic packaging. 'When you met Juliet at the bar, you were with a friend. Who was he?'

'Henrik Bergmann. He's not my friend.' Lachy wanted to make that very clear. 'He works here too at Global Social Solutions. He's my direct supervisor.'

'Is he in this building now?'

'No, he's on a project in Kenya.' How much should he say? Were they aware of Henrik's accusations against him?

'Do you know when he'll return to DC?'

'There's an annual meeting at head office next month. He usually attends it.' Lachy would not be there. By then, he'd either have resigned or been sacked . . . or been arrested. 'Why are you interested in Henrik?'

Ignacio answered the question with one of his own: 'Can you tell us what time Henrik left Juliet's apartment?'

He didn't even know if Henrik had come to the apartment, couldn't remember being there himself. All these years of hiding his shame had brought him here. He was a coward who should have talked to a doctor or a counsellor.

'I need to . . . explain something.' Ignacio would assume he was lying, but he had to get it out into the open. 'When I drink too fast, I have alcoholic blackouts. I appear to behave completely normally, but my brain doesn't lay down memories. I had a blackout that night. I remember meeting Juliet at the bar and waking up the next morning in my hotel room, but nothing in between.'

A tiny snort of disbelief came from the police officer guarding the door.

The lieutenant eyed him suspiciously. 'Seriously?'

'I can't be a witness.' Admitting it didn't feel good but at least now he could be totally honest. 'But I can tell you whatever you need to know about Henrik. I'll tell you what he's been doing in Kenya.'

If Henrik had committed this crime, he would be caught through DNA evidence. He wouldn't be able to charm his way out this time.

Lachy swabbed the inside of his cheek while Ignacio wrote the paperwork for the sample and took his contact details.

'It's interesting how a DNA sample taken in one investigation can provide a breakthrough in a completely unrelated case,' the lieutenant said.

What the hell was he talking about? Lachy had a sudden urge to snatch the swab back.

'Lieutenant Davis from Norristown is keen to speak with you. He said you hung up on him this morning.'

Shit, he'd thought this investigation had covered everything off.

'I didn't mean to.' Lachy could feel the fear spreading again. 'I dropped the phone when I was rushing to catch the train here. Do you know . . . uh . . . why Lieutenant Davis wants to talk to me?' He cringed at his own stumbling and mumbling; he sounded guilty just asking the question.

'He'll tell you all about it. He's working on a cold case.' Ignacio gave his stupid, encouraging smile. 'Can you get yourself there this afternoon? I'll take you to Union Station.'

Lachy hesitated. 'The train takes three hours. Won't it be too late for today?'

'Hurry up and I'll get you on the fast train.'

He had no choice but to follow Lieutenant Ignacio and his offsider down the hallway, into the elevator and out of the front entrance. The humiliation of being led from GSS by a detective and a uniformed officer overrode his concern for a few minutes. But then sitting in the back seat of a cop car, he felt like a criminal. The officer parked outside the station and Ignacio walked him all the way to the platform. As he was shaking Lachy's hand, the train arrived.

'I'll be in touch,' Ignacio said. 'But call me if you remember anything else about that night.'

Lieutenant Ignacio didn't understand, he would never remember.

On the train, Lachy leant back in the seat and closed his eyes. Juliet wasn't dead, she wasn't pregnant, and Lachy hadn't driven her to Deadwood Creek in the middle of the night. But now he was headed back to that area. The news article about the September death had mentioned Norristown Police Department. Clearly, he wasn't under arrest or Ignacio would have organised a police transfer. But how the hell was his DNA connected?

At Philadelphia, he had to change trains for the line to Norristown. He considered leaving the station instead, and catching a cab to Matthew's design studio. Having a drink with his cousin and debriefing about Henrik's betrayal. Putting off Lieutenant Blade Davis for another day.

Really, he just wanted his parents: Mum to hug him and Dad to sort it all out. Pathetic. What would Sheridan do? She'd show up, ask questions, face her responsibilities, do her duties. Right, so would he. If he could get through that shit show with Naomi and Ignacio at GSS, he could get through the next meeting with Lieutenant Davis.

Ignacio had said it was about a cold case. Something from the past. It could only be summer camp and Tiffany Jones.

38

KAI

THIS MORNING WHEN HE'D WOKEN, KAI'S HEAD HAD STILL BEEN throbbing slightly. After more tablets, the pain disappeared, and it only hurt when he touched the lump on his temple. Aidan had driven them into Philly—much less terrifying than a ride with Great-Aunt Theresa—and they'd met up with Destiny and Carson for a cousins sightseeing day.

Again Destiny fired off a barrage of questions. *Why don't we have your animals here? Why is your hair so shaggy?* Her frizzy black hair was the same as her mother's, and her bright orange top featured a cartoon of the sun. Destiny was certainly a sunny kid with bags of confidence. His Aussie cousins and sisters wouldn't talk to a strange teenager like this, even if they were related.

First, they took him to Independence Hall. It looked exactly the same as the picture on the front of Glamma's jigsaw puzzle—his hiding spot for the pingers. While he didn't need a reminder of that terrible night, entering the building hardened his commitment. No more drugs. Ever. Destiny led them into the room where the Declaration of Independence had been signed, and then Carson had to show him the Liberty Bell. 'It hasn't been rung since 1846, but its message is equality and freedom.' The Americans really went on about their freedom.

At the next historical site, Kai saw the opposite of freedom. With its stone walls, turrets and towers, the building resembled a gothic castle from *Game of Thrones*. But Eastern State Penitentiary was a prison.

Destiny's class had come here on an excursion. 'So good! You'll love it too.'

He didn't want to think about his school excursion to the Cooma jail museum.

Carson overtook Destiny and rushed them along to Al Capone's cell. The prison walls had chunks out of them, paint and plaster were peeling off in strips, and the windows had no glass. It was practically a ruin. Aidan read aloud from a brochure they'd been handed at the ticket office: '*The world's first penitentiary was designed to strike fear in the prisoners' hearts and inspire penitence and regret.*'

Penitence and regret, Kai had both of those.

'The penitentiary was all about solitary confinement,' Aidan continued. 'They believed that if prisoners were left alone to reflect on their crimes, they would feel remorse.'

'I wanna show you the hole.' Destiny tugged at his hand.

As if solitary confinement wasn't bad enough, the prison also had the 'hole' Destiny had mentioned: four underground isolation cells. The ceiling was low and the walls were lined with water pipes. It smelt dank and musty. Kai's head began to spin. The old pipes seemed to be moving, writhing like snakes, ready to wrap him in a stranglehold. What would happen at his next police appointment in Cooma? In the crowd at the concert last night, he'd spotted Vivien, the girl with Mabel's red hair. She'd been dancing with a group of friends, her face radiant with laughter. Watching her, he'd made a promise to Mabel and his entire family: *I will never put anyone at risk like that again.*

He couldn't breathe inside this place. Reeling around, he barged past Destiny, knocking her over. As he ran down the corridor towards the courtyard, trying to gulp in fresh air, he heard a high-pitched scream.

He'd hurt her. Another stuff-up. He'd already broken his promise from last night.

Halfway along the corridor, he stopped. Turned around and sprinted back.

Destiny lay on the ground, her arm crushed beneath her. *Please don't let it be broken.* Aidan was beside her, helping her into a sitting position.

'I'm so sorry.' Kai squatted down. 'Which bit hurts the most?'

'My wrist.' She was cradling it against her chest.

Last night when Kai was hit in the head, Dr Stanbury and the first-aid girls had been so helpful to him. He didn't have their medical knowledge but he could follow their lead in kindness.

'Can you stretch out your fingers?' he asked. 'Can you make a fist?'

She did it all without grimacing in pain.

'I don't think it's broken,' Aidan said. 'Let's get you up.'

They lifted Destiny to her feet.

She looked at Kai. 'I'm okay,' she said. 'The floor's really hard, though. Did you know some prisoners dug an escape tunnel?'

Phew, she was back into tour guide mode.

'Destiny, I'm sorry I knocked you over,' he said. 'I freaked out in that small space. How can I make it up to you?'

She gave her brother a sly look and he nodded; they could read each other's minds.

'Wooder ice,' they shouted together.

Aidan laughed and said he knew a good place. Kai didn't understand where they were going but he was happy to get away from the crumbling prison of penitence and regret.

Ten minutes later he discovered that a wooder ice was a water ice, like a slushie but tastier. He and Destiny chose the same rainbow combo.

'When we come to Australia, will you be our tour guide?' she asked.

'It's a deal.' He shook her hand solemnly. 'I won't knock you over and I'll protect you from redbacks and snakes.'

'Are redbacks like quarterbacks?'

They all laughed. His sisters and cousins would love Destiny and Carson; they should definitely meet one day. And hopefully he would be there when they did, as part of the family and not still shunned for his terrible actions.

39

LACHY

WHEN LACHY HAD WORKED AT THE SUMMER CAMP, THEY'D DRIVEN INTO Norristown a few times for supplies and burgers. He never imagined returning nearly twenty years later for an appointment at the police department.

Lieutenant Blade Davis greeted him with a crushing handshake and led him to an interview room. After they were seated, Lachy babbled an apology for hanging up on him and not calling back.

'Well, Lieutenant Ignacio found you for me . . .' Davis paused and patted a small stack of folders on the desk. 'So, your DNA has been connected to a cold case after you uploaded it to the DNA:Match database.'

His face must have shown confusion because Davis rushed into an explanation.

'You ticked the box allowing police to cross-check your DNA. We've been making some real breakthroughs on unsolved cases using these mass databases.'

Lachy had been in such a state doing the DNA test, he'd probably agreed to everything. But the whole reason for the test had been a ruse. He hadn't harmed Juliet, he prayed that it was the same for Tiffany despite the scratches he'd found on his arms the next morning. Even so, he worried that Lieutenant Davis would say: *Your DNA has been linked to an historic sexual assault of Tiffany Jones at Camp Happiness.*

Instead, Davis asked, 'Have you heard of the Casanova Killer? I don't like that term myself, but the media loves a nickname.'

Taken aback, Lachy nodded. Since they'd arrived in Philly, he'd seen snippets of news stories about the case. When it came on the car radio, Aunt Theresa had turned up the volume and shouted, 'They'd better get him!' He'd been too distracted to follow the story.

'We've linked him to the homicides of four young women so far, but we're investigating others. He positioned each girl as if she were asleep, clutching a bunch of roses to her chest. The psychologist on the case says he was playing out a fantasy of marrying them.'

Lachy stared at him, his blood pounding in his head. Fuck, was the lieutenant implying he was linked with a serial killer? Had Tiffany been the unidentified girl at Deadwood Creek Road? His rational brain tried to make sense of it. No, they would have arrested him.

'Sorry, I'm jumping the gun.' Davis opened the top folder. 'I might be completely wrong about that connection. Let's start at the beginning. We've been working on cold cases with an organisation called the DNA Project. Your DNA came up in the system with a match.'

'Match with what?' Lachy's throat was so dry his voice came out as a rasp.

'A young woman found on Deadwood Creek Road. We believe she was murdered.'

Shit, he shouldn't have come in willingly, he should have found a lawyer first. He disliked Tiffany but he couldn't have killed her unless he'd run over her by accident.

'Normally these DNA matches require a lot of forensic genealogy work, but yours was close.' Davis rubbed his beard. 'The good news is that your DNA has helped us identify a previously unidentified victim.'

Huh? His DNA was linked to the *victim*? All the air left Lachy's lungs in a rush.

Davis handed him a plastic sleeve with yellowed newspaper clippings. Lachy recognised the top one as the same article Sheridan had found in the wardrobe. It was dated 1968. Nothing to do with Tiffany. A cold case from before he was born. Thank God. He turned to the next clipping.

Police investigators have determined that the fatal accident near Camp Happiness was deliberate and they have labelled the girl's death a homicide. She still has not been identified. The victim was wearing a silver engagement ring with a green stone, and investigators have dubbed her 'Emerald Doe'.

Trooper Kurt Haigh said, 'Emerald Doe was pregnant. She may have seen a doctor or nurse. We ask any medical professionals to look closely at the police sketch.'

The area where Emerald was found is a small, tranquil, semi-rural community. A local resident, Iris Stanbury, said the community was devastated. 'This is her last resting place and we've all taken on the responsibility of helping to find her family. It's absolutely tragic that this young woman's life has been cut short.'

Investigators are working with the nearby summer camp to compile a list of all people in residence at the time of Emerald's murder. An eyewitness reported seeing a pick-up truck speeding towards the camp.

'Emerald Doe . . . who is she?'

'Your aunt. Elizabeth, the second daughter of Abraham and Rosemary Dunstan. She was a year younger than your mother. Her birth is registered but there's no record of her after 1968. No driver's licence, no marriage certificate, no social security number. And no death certificate.'

Lachy shook his head. 'I've never heard of her. Has my DNA been mixed up somehow?'

'There's no mix-up. She's definitely your aunt.'

Had she run away from their father too? Were they even aware that Elizabeth was dead? He had so many questions for Mum, hopefully she could answer some of them.

'I only know about Mum's two sisters and brother,' he told Davis. 'The youngest, Virginia, died a few years ago. Theresa and Ernest are still in Berks County. But if there was another sister, why wouldn't they talk about her?'

'All sorts of reasons. Families are complicated.' Davis passed him an old police sketch. 'I've been working on the Emerald Doe case for about ten years. When your DNA came up in the system as a familial match, we were excited. Unidentified cases are the most difficult because we have no timeline, no connections, few leads to follow. But now we know her name.'

Lachy stared at the black-and-white sketch: a woman with high cheekbones, long hair and a middle part. So generic, she could have been anyone.

'If she was run over, why do you think it was homicide?'

'Her injuries were inconsistent with an accident, but police made assumptions at the time based on information from a bystander. Then the coroner was incompetent with the autopsy, even though she was pregnant and had been whipped.'

Who would whip a pregnant girl?

'I'm assuming that my mum's religious family wouldn't have been happy about a teenage pregnancy,' Lachy said. 'Their father was the pastor of a church. It was a bit cult-ish. You were excommunicated if you broke the rules. That's why my mum ran away to Australia.'

And now the pieces were falling into place. Aunt Theresa had complained about Mum leaving just before a cousin's wedding; around the same time Betty had died.

'Excommunicated,' Davis repeated. 'That might explain why no-one came forward to identify her.'

'Why do you think her death could be linked to the Casanova Killer?'

'He was operating in Pennsylvania in the seventies. We believe he would offer a ride to a young woman, drive her to a remote picnic area and give her a sedative with vodka. He must have looked respectable as there were no signs of a struggle. The tablets were Quaaludes, prescribed for depression and insomnia, but they were also used as a party drug. When washed down with alcohol, however, they could kill.'

Lachy shuddered and pushed away the image of Mabel unconscious.

'Did Elizabeth have this drug in her system?'

'We don't know because the autopsy was perfunctory. But she fits a similar profile to the other girls. We suspect he tried to charm her into his car but she realised the danger. Maybe it was his first attempt. We're working a few different angles.'

A secret aunt, possibly the victim of a serial killer. It was too much after the meetings at GSS. Could he politely leave the police station and crawl into a bed somewhere?

'I need to get back to my son. Is it all right if—'

'I'll drive you.' Davis tidied his folders and stood up. 'We were in the process of contacting your uncle through his church when your name appeared on airport arrivals. Can we meet up with your aunt and uncle? I'd like to bring Elizabeth home to her family.'

Lachy didn't know if the family wanted Elizabeth 'home' as Lieutenant Davis put it. They'd removed all traces of her existence.

40

SHERIDAN

SHERIDAN GULPED HER SECOND GIN AND TONIC, LISTENING TO STORIES about Dom's life while watching the door. Any minute now, Nick would step from the bar into the courtyard where they were sitting. She wished she could turn back time, like that old Cher song. First, she would un-send the text to her husband. Confronting him like this was a mistake; he never reacted well to surprises, even good ones. She'd organised a surprise party for his thirtieth birthday and it had taken him an hour to get over the shock of seeing all his friends, family and work colleagues in the same room. She wanted to turn time right back. Not just the past fifteen minutes, not just eight years to his thirtieth birthday, but back to summer camp, to when Nick met Tiffany. *Don't have sex with her*, she'd shout into the ear of her future husband.

If Nick had held on to this secret for their entire relationship, what else hadn't he told her?

This wasn't the man she thought she knew; the Nick she knew was a great dad, a good husband, a considerate son-in-law. Everything he did was for his family: *I'm working hard to earn*

289

money for a bigger house for you and the girls. Yes, they needed a bigger house, but not at the risk of losing Mimosa Hideout. Yesterday, she'd rung the real estate agent in Warabina and told him that they weren't selling. She wanted to contribute more towards a new house but it wasn't that simple. Nick kept suggesting she hike up her fees and find more corporate clients, but people didn't understand the value of life coaching and they certainly didn't want to pay a professional rate. At school drop-off last week, a mum had asked for six sessions at half-price because she was on maternity leave and looking to change careers. Sheridan had agreed, feeling for her: life and career goals often changed after children. At least that mum was a real client, unlike the boy sitting in front of her.

Nick appeared in the entrance. Framed by the wooden doorway, the lights from the bar gave him a halo, his curly hair almost shimmering at the ends—the very picture of Cupid, an angel. Spotting her, he strode over.

'What's happened?' he asked, anxious eyes fixed on her face. 'Are the girls okay?'

She gestured across the table. 'I'd like you to meet Dom.' Unsure how to describe him, she hesitated. 'He's your . . . he's . . . he's from America. He's Tiffany's son.'

Nick spun around to see the boy, one hand gripping the back of her high stool. She felt the stool tip as he staggered slightly. After righting himself, he glared at her.

'Jesus Christ, Sheridan. Why would . . . ?' His anger ricocheted around them. 'How did he find you?'

Dom stood up. 'I've wanted to meet you ever since my mom told me the truth. I thought if I came to Sydney we could get to know each other.'

Nick refused to glance in his direction. 'Your mother was lying. I didn't answer your messages because I'm not your father.'

'But I look just like you.' Dom crumpled onto his stool and rubbed a hand over his mouth.

Bloody hell, she shouldn't have surprised Nick like this.

'Why don't you give us a moment, Dom?' she suggested. 'Go to the bar and order another drink or some food or something.'

'You'll be here when I come back?'

'I'll be here.' She wasn't sure about Nick.

After he'd left, Nick sank onto the stool opposite and Sheridan explained how she'd met the boy.

Nick ran a hand over his face. 'Tiffany was so . . .' He shook his head. 'First, she said the baby was mine and I was all in. I wanted to be part of his life. Then she left camp and cut contact with me. When she was about five months pregnant, she called me to come and visit. That photo you saw was taken then. But a week later, she said he wasn't mine after all, and I didn't hear from her for a few years. Just before our wedding, she messaged to say her husband was leaving her and she needed money and I was definitely the father. By that time, I didn't believe a word. I thought she was making up another story to get what she wanted.'

'You needed proof,' Sheridan said. It wasn't an accusation; she understood how his logical brain worked.

'Not at the beginning. I'd never met anyone like Tiffany. She took life by the horns.' His cheeks burnt red. 'I was just a kid myself but I was up for doing the parent thing if she wanted.'

'For God's sake, Nick. Why didn't you tell me?' She'd stayed calm, partly in shock, but she couldn't be polite anymore. 'Why the hell was it a great big secret?'

'At camp, Tiffany begged me not to say anything. Later, I found out she had a boyfriend back home while she was sleeping with me and flirting with every male camp counsellor. I didn't realise she was deciding who was the better prospect for fatherhood: me or her high school boyfriend. When she said the baby wasn't mine, I was gutted but also relieved. I got on with travelling and then I met you.'

'But in that first year, we told each other everything.' They used to go down to the park at Blues Point after the pub, lie on the grass and gaze at the bridge and the lights reflecting on the harbour. They shared their most intimate stories.

'I was embarrassed.' He hung his head. 'I'd fallen hard for her and I thought we had something real. But I'd been played.'

He kept making excuses for his deception but it didn't lessen her hurt. She'd opened up to him, bared her history, warts and all. If he'd told her back then, she would have leapt to his defence, and labelled Tiffany a liar and a schemer. Now she just wanted to call *him* a liar.

'Did you tell Lachy?'

'I thought she might've told him in the truck the night she left camp. She was angry with me. I ordered her to stop drinking because of the baby. Instead she had another rum and demanded Lachy drive her to meet a friend. But Lachy didn't seem to know about the pregnancy. And it hurt to talk about her so I avoided it.' He picked up her glass and took a slug. 'I'd finally got over her, met you, proposed, and then she contacted me again. I was like a toy to her. She was cruel. And now, all these years later, her son comes looking for me. She'll want me to pay for his university education, no doubt. But I'm not getting involved. I'm not letting her win.'

All Sheridan could think about was their first baby. Toby. Even then, while they'd been farewelling him, Nick already had a son. Now, every word he uttered stoked her fury. Fury at Tiffany, at her husband, at Dom for having lived when their own son hadn't. No, she told herself; that wasn't fair. Dom was the only innocent party in this mess.

'It isn't a game, Nick.' She leant backwards and crossed her arms. 'No-one's winning or losing. This is Dom's life. He's searching for answers.'

'Well, I don't have any answers for him. It's nothing to do with me.'

The sight of him feeling sorry for himself without a thought for his son disgusted her. Where was the Nick she knew? She wanted to shout at him: *Why did you think you had to manage this problem alone? What does this say about our relationship?* But any moment now, Dom would return.

'He's the spitting image of you when we first met.' She softened her tone. 'You can't blame him for his mother's behaviour. He's just a boy. Talk to him.'

She had no idea what the addition of this young man would mean for their family and how it would affect their girls, but she couldn't let her husband turn him away. Of course it would bring up difficult feelings for all of them; of course it would be complicated; but maybe it could also be a positive thing.

Dom was walking towards them, a tray of drinks shaking in his hands.

'I didn't know what to . . . what you'd like,' he stammered. 'The bartender told me to get Four Pines. If you don't like it, I can go back and choose something else.'

She waited to see Nick's response. Would he say he had to leave for a work meeting?

'Thank you.' He took the beer glass. 'Great choice. So, Dom, why don't you tell me about yourself?'

'I'm the eldest of four kids.' Dom ran his fingers through his strawberry-blond hair. God, he even had the same mannerisms as Nick. 'I'd always assumed Dad was my father, even though my siblings are miniature versions of him and I'm not.'

Nick nodded, encouraging him to continue.

'My parents have been dating since senior year. He's laidback but she's dramatic. Dad moved out last year and Mum was angry that we had to downsize to a duplex. While we were packing, she handed me some letters and said: *Maybe your real dad is nicer than your stepdad.*'

'Ouch,' Sheridan said. 'That must have been a real shock.'

'Yeah, it was. But I didn't understand because the first letters were really nice and you wanted to be part of my life, Nick, but in the last letter, you told my mum to leave you alone.'

As Nick started to explain, she watched him closely. He'd better bloody do the right thing by this boy.

She'd just sent her brother to the other side of the world to sort out his life and now theirs was falling apart.

If Nick had kept this secret for so long, what else hadn't he told her?

41

ELIZABETH, 1968

LAST NIGHT, I'D BEEN FILLED WITH HOPE, BUT IT WAS TRICKLING AWAY with the rising sun. Gloria wouldn't help me now that she knew I'd lain with a married man. And I feared Father's anger—there was no way to appease it. During the dark hours, I'd wondered how to get a message to Charlie. I couldn't trust Theresa or Ernest; they'd only tell our parents. Virginia was too young to help. In the notebook Gloria had given me, I'd written a few lines: *Please save me. I'm locked in the potting shed and I'm scared Father will harm me.*

Gloria came early with my breakfast and a concoction of herbs.

'Eat it,' she ordered. 'It will make the baby go away. Your baby is tainted by your own sin.'

The smell of herbs filled the shed and brought a shame I hadn't felt before. A sob burbled in my throat. I tried to suppress it but more came. And more. I couldn't quieten them. They echoed off the ceiling and the walls. This baby, our baby, was pure and beautiful. But I couldn't keep it without Charlie.

'It's for the best,' Gloria insisted. 'I've told Father everything. He's taking you away tonight. Eat the herbs.'

My heart shattered and, with it, any last shred of hope. If I swallowed the herbs, maybe Father would see it as a sign of contrition. I put a spoonful in my mouth. Minty, bitter. It made me gag. Gloria watched me from the doorway. She was weeping too.

'You need to eat it all,' she said.

'I'm sorry, Gloria. Thanks for trying to find a solution. I've let you down.'

'Wherever you go, send me a letter with your address.' She hugged me briefly and I clung to her, but she pushed me away. 'I'll keep praying for you.'

'Wait.' I handed her my doll. 'Please look after her for me until I see you again. Keep her safe. She's special.'

I broke down completely on the last word. My baby was special. I had betrayed it by swallowing the herbs. I had betrayed my church, my family, myself.

Gloria accepted the doll with an irritated sigh. 'How am I supposed to hide her inside the house? Father will take her to church for the young families.'

'Put her on the high shelf with our sanitary belts. No-one will look up there.'

After she'd gone, I wrote a note and tucked it inside *My Family and Other Animals*. Gloria would find it when she returned the book to the library.

To my dearest sister Gloria,
Thank you for your kindness and concern. I hope you will
know true love as I have with C. Our love crosses all boun-
daries and elevates us to a higher plane.

One day, we will all be together. Maybe in Australia!
Love,
Betty

I wrote another note at sunset, praying that it wouldn't need to be delivered.

But after it was dark, Father came for me.

42

LACHY

BEFORE THEY LEFT THE POLICE STATION, LACHY RANG UNCLE ERNEST and asked him to meet at Theresa's house. He said the boys were already there after sightseeing in Philly earlier today, and Theresa had put them to work cleaning out the shed. Lachy decided not to mention that he was bringing a police detective.

As they accelerated along the Benjamin Franklin Highway, Lachy remembered his first trip to America when he was five years old. Frost blanketed the fields and he called it a white Christmas. Had Mum been missing Elizabeth as they opened presents in the old family home? Estranged from both of her parents, Gloria had been away for over twenty years; she hadn't even returned for their funerals.

Her father, Abraham, must have held so much power over the family and the church community for them to have erased Elizabeth's existence so completely. Five siblings had grown up together and one was wiped from their collective memories.

When Lachy introduced Lieutenant Davis to his aunt and uncles, he watched their reactions; they shared a mournful expression and he knew they guessed this was about their missing sister. They sat in Theresa's lounge room with the family photos on the sideboard, and once again, Lachy was aware of the erasure. Not a single picture of Elizabeth. Through the window, he could see into the backyard where Kai and Aidan were busy taking garden equipment and boxes from the old potting shed. On his arrival at the house, Lachy had told them the policeman was here to discuss Elizabeth, a missing family member. Aidan's response had surprised him: 'We saw her name in the church register yesterday. It listed her baptism date.'

As soon as Lieutenant Davis began outlining the story of Emerald Doe, Theresa burst into tears.

'I always prayed Betty would come back.' She took a tissue from her pocket and wiped her nose. 'We stayed in this house in case she turned up one day. After Father died, I searched for her but it was too late, I couldn't find any trace of her.'

Betty. They'd shortened Elizabeth to Betty. The name of the doll in Mum's bedroom. Was that how Mum had coped—by carrying the memory of her sister around as a doll? He wished he could ask her. And this was the reason Theresa and Leonard had never sold up and bought a newer house in town.

But if Sheridan disappeared, he wouldn't stop searching. 'Why didn't you try to find her at the time?'

'Father told us she'd been sent to Ohio to work as a nanny. We didn't even know she was missing. Later, we were forbidden from saying her name.' Theresa dabbed at her eyes. 'Father said she'd disgraced herself in Ohio and was no longer a member of our community.'

'Did any of the family know about the unidentified woman on Deadwood Creek Road?' Davis asked. 'There was a police sketch in the newspaper.'

'Newspapers were banned in our community. And Father didn't tell us that she was pregnant until a year later. We believed everything he said.' Uncle Ernest's cheeks flushed. 'He ruled with an iron fist and whipped us into submission.'

Whipped. 'Could the marks on Betty's thighs have come from her father rather than an unknown assailant?' Lachy asked.

Theresa and Ernest nodded slowly.

On the drive from Norristown, Lieutenant Davis had shared a few facts with him. The majority of homicide victims died at the hands of someone they knew; a third of female victims were killed by a direct family member. Gloria must have suspected that the unidentified victim on Deadwood Creek Road was Betty. She was the one who had copied the newspaper article from the web and printed it out. Perhaps she believed their father was responsible.

'Father didn't want her found.' Theresa stifled a sob. 'Betty betrayed our church community and the Lord.'

He couldn't stand this sanctimonious bullshit.

'Your father was a self-righteous tyrant,' he fumed. 'Betty was just a teenager, not much older than Kai. Everyone should have helped her, like they supported me when Amber fell pregnant. Mum didn't condemn us for having a baby out of wedlock.'

A heavy silence hung in the room. He'd gone too far but he'd been thinking about all of it—himself, Kai at Easter, Zahra in Kenya. Pushing people away in times of need made everything so much worse.

'It was a different era,' Ernest said. 'Unwed mothers were judged harshly.'

Lieutenant Davis broke the uncomfortable moment. 'Can

you tell me about Betty? What was she like? I've been trying to find out her real name for ten years.'

'Always cheerful. Everyone loved her. She had the sweetest giggle.' Theresa let out a whimper. 'We should have done more for her.'

'Her disappearance changed our lives,' Ernest added. 'Gloria, who had been so devout, abandoned the church and never spoke to Father again. Instead, I was the one who became a pastor. Mother put on a bright mask during the day, but we'd hear her crying at night. The doctor prescribed sedatives and she kept taking them for years.'

Davis broke in: 'Do you know which sedatives she used?'

'It started with Q,' Theresa said. 'I remember because it was an unusual word.'

'Quaaludes?'

'Yes, that was it. I think Mother became addicted to them.'

It was the sedative the Casanova Killer had used. Lachy studied Davis for a reaction, but the lieutenant had a poker face.

'What about Abraham?' Davis asked. 'Did his behaviour change?'

'He'd been a teetotaller, but after Betty left he began drinking,' Ernest recalled. 'On Sunday mornings he'd quote Proverbs to warn about the evils of wine: *It bites like a serpent and stings like a viper. Your eyes will see strange things, and your heart will utter perverse things.* Then at night he'd get so drunk Mother and I would have to help him to bed. He never remembered it the next day.'

Lachy fell back in his seat. His grandfather had experienced alcoholic blackouts too. It was in his genes. And now Lieutenant Davis suspected Abraham Dunstan was the Casanova Killer.

Davis kept probing: 'Did your Father travel around Montgomery County a lot?'

'He was out and about every day serving the Lord,' Ernest said. 'He visited communities in other counties too. After Betty and Gloria left, he became a bit manic, determined not to lose another member of his flock to sin.'

Lieutenant Davis had stood up and was staring into the backyard. 'Nice rosebushes. Were they here when you were growing up?'

'Yes, although those ones have been propagated from an older bush. Father was passionate about his roses. At every wedding he conducted, he gave a posy to the bride and groom.' Theresa smiled at her husband. 'I've still got a dried rose from ours, fifty years ago. The posy represented God. Marriage is a commitment between two people with God in the centre.'

'Do you mind if I take a cutting?' Davis asked.

'Of course,' Theresa said. 'Should I get that for you now?'

Lieutenant Davis didn't answer her but wrote something in his notebook and moved on to his next question. 'Did you or your father know any of these women in the 1960s and 1970s?' He read a list of names: 'Doris Devlin, Olive Ferguson, Maria Mancini, Bonnie Cunningham.'

'Olive Ferguson,' Uncle Leonard repeated. 'Wasn't she a nurse at Reading Hospital?'

'Doris Devlin rings a bell.' Ernest massaged his forehead. 'I need to get the old grey matter working. It's so long ago.'

Aunt Theresa put a hand over her heart. 'I recognise those names. They're all victims of the Casanova Killer,' she gasped. 'Dear God, do you think Betty was murdered by him as well?'

'The roses.' Ernest leapfrogged to the next conclusion. 'You're not implying that our father . . . He would never break the sixth commandment.'

'You have got to be kidding!' Theresa clutched her chest; she looked like she might have a heart attack. 'Our father, the Casanova Killer? Absolutely not.'

For his family's sake, Lachy hoped the lieutenant was on the wrong track.

'I'm not implying anything,' Davis said. 'We've only just determined Elizabeth's identity and that gives us a lot more insight into her death. Can you remember the last time you saw her?'

'No.' Theresa took a deep breath. One hand still rested over her heart. 'A few months ago on the phone, Gloria said, *She's gone and it's my fault. I told Father she was having an affair with a married man.* I assumed she was speaking of Betty but it was a confused conversation. You can't blame Father. He wouldn't!'

She's gone. It's all my fault. Mum had been repeating those words in the nursing home.

'Did anyone meet the married man?' Davis asked.

'We didn't know anything about it. We thought she was in Ohio. I can't believe she was found in the next county.' Ernest made the sign of the cross. 'God forgive us. We've all done wrong by Betty. I'll start planning a memorial service for our poor, lost sister.'

'I'd like that.' Theresa reached over and touched his knee, a sign of comfort, of thanks, of family.

Watching them, Lachy knew he had to fix things with his own sister; this friction in their relationship made it even more difficult to cope with the craziness of the world.

At that moment, Kai and Aidan came banging in through the back door, carrying a rusty metal box.

'We found this underneath a plank in the shed.' Kai cradled it like treasure. 'It's got old photos and stuff. We thought you might want to see if there are any of Elizabeth.'

'Don't put that box on the good carpet,' Aunt Theresa snapped. 'Leonard, get an old sheet.'

Christ on a bike, she was more concerned about the carpet than her murdered sister.

After some fuss, a sheet was laid down and Kai placed the box on top and opened it. Theresa pulled out a handful of loose black-and-white photos. Children lined up in order of size. Images of two older girls, Mum and Betty. A few pictures of Betty by herself.

'Oh my Lord, we're all so young. I'd forgotten what Betty looked like.'

The girl in the photos didn't really resemble the police sketch. No wonder she hadn't been identified.

Ernest was flipping through a notebook, its pages so brittle they crackled with each turn. 'Love poems,' he announced. 'Addressed to an unnamed man and their baby. Heartbreaking.'

Kai picked up a novel with a blue cover and the title *My Family and Other Animals*. He smirked at Lachy, who returned the look, delighting in their shared sense of humour. When they returned to Australia, he'd focus on reconnecting his immediate family.

'There's a note inside from Betty to Gloria.' Kai said. He read it aloud. '*I hope you will know true love as I have with C . . . One day, we will all be together. Maybe in Australia!*'

Australia? Had Betty planned to go there too?

'At least we have an initial. It's a start,' Lieutenant Davis said after examining the note. 'Any idea who "C" might be, Theresa?'

She shook her head. 'Betty was always in trouble for speaking to boys on the bus. I didn't know them. And when Father talked about her sin, we assumed it was a man in Ohio.'

Kai was flipping through the book when he stopped suddenly. 'Here's another note.'

It was folded in half and had a name and address written on one side: *Dr Charles Stanbury, Montgomery Hospital*. Lieutenant Davis took the note from Kai and opened it carefully. In beautiful cursive, Betty had written: *I'm scared of what Father will do to me.*

'The doctor who helped me yesterday when I fainted at the concert was called Charlie Stanbury,' Kai blurted. 'He was really old. Could it be the same guy?'

Stanbury. Lachy frowned. He'd seen that surname recently.

'Iris Stanbury was quoted in a newspaper article,' he recalled. 'Betty died near their house and she was scared of her father.'

Was the Casanova Killer's first victim his own daughter? Not a sick murderer fantasising about being with these girls himself as the police psychologist had theorised, but a twisted church leader 'marrying' them with Christ in death?

Lieutenant Davis asked if he could examine the note and other items back at the station. It felt like Betty was disappearing again, but Theresa and Ernest agreed. Lachy took a few photos on his phone—the pictures weren't great quality, but he could show them to Mum and Sheridan.

When Lachy had finished, Lieutenant Davis gathered up the contents of the trunk and excused himself. The family was left shell-shocked, the empty box still open on the white sheet between them.

'Dad, it's so cool that your DNA was used to identify Betty,' Kai piped up. 'Wouldn't it be amazing if your DNA helped catch a serial killer from fifty-five years ago?'

Not if the serial killer turned out to be his grandfather.

43

SHERIDAN

SHERIDAN WATCHED MUM AS SHE PLAYED ONE OF THE MINDMATE GAMES on the iPad. Elsewhere on the app, there was a section called 'My Life', where Sheridan had uploaded pictures of the family. Should she add a photo of Betty?

She still couldn't believe Betty was a real person—not just a doll, but Mum's sister. The conversation with Lachy had left her rethinking Mum's entire life. When she'd spoken to the counsellor at the nursing home about whether to discuss Betty's death, he suggested she take Gloria for a walk and ease into a conversation about her childhood. If she saw a natural opening she could take it, but she definitely shouldn't dump the news on her.

'Let's go outside, Mum.' She pulled the walker close to her mother. 'It's a sunny day and the birds are singing. We'll just need your jacket.'

'And Betty,' Mum said, placing the doll in the basket of her walker.

'Did you do everything together with Betty?'

Mum nodded as they walked into the garden. 'Have the chickens been fed?'

She didn't know who Mum thought she was now: Betty or Theresa or Ernest or Virginia. The big sister checking on her siblings, keeping them all in line. So different from how she'd behaved as a parent.

'Yes, the chickens are all fed.'

Mum had always refused to have a chicken coop on their property in Dural, despite Dad's hankering for fresh eggs. *I hate chooks, they remind me of my childhood*, she'd said. Mum also hated roses and everyone knew not to buy them for her.

Sheridan risked a question. 'Is Betty here?'

'No, she's gone.' Her voice quivered. 'And it's all my fault.'

'Betty was your sister who went missing.' She stated the fact that had been hidden for so many years and watched to see how Mum would respond. Perhaps now that Sheridan knew, she could help relieve her distress. 'How was it your fault?'

Mum gripped the handles of the walker so tightly that her knuckles turned white. 'I gave her herbs that caused bleeding . . . When Father found out—' her story came slowly '—he said she had to be delivered to . . . to Satan.'

'So it's Father's fault, not yours.'

Gloria didn't seem to hear her. 'I thought he'd taken her to Philly, to a place where . . . a place for unwanted pregnancies. I waited for her to write. But no message came.'

By the time she'd left for Australia, Mum must have known that Betty was dead, but how? Sheridan didn't dare ask; afraid it would cause more traumatic memories. Maybe they could talk about Betty's life instead.

'Did you know Betty's boyfriend?'

'Only that he was a doctor and his name began with the letter C. A few weeks after Father took Betty away, I tracked him down. I knew he must work at the Soldiers' Home. He said Father had whipped Betty and left her to die. No-one else knew. We cried together. If I hadn't told Father about the affair, none of it would have happened. It's all my fault.'

'Listen, your father was to blame, not you.'

But Mum wouldn't listen; she'd carried this guilt for so many years it was too late to make her understand.

'Charlie said there was so much blood from the whipping and the herbs.' Mum didn't wipe away the tears that dripped down her cheeks. 'The herbs that I gave her. Charlie tried to save her but he couldn't. He was distraught.'

No wonder she'd fled America, blaming herself and fearing her father.

'It's okay, Mum.' Sheridan draped an arm around her waist. 'Everyone's safe now.'

Two sulphur-crested cockatoos screeched in flight above them and landed in a maple tree. An old man shuffled past pushing his walker.

'Are we at the Soldiers' Home?' Mum asked. 'Betty's volunteering here. It's where she met Charlie.'

She couldn't believe that Mum was actually talking about Betty; a secret she'd guarded so closely that maybe Dad hadn't even known.

Another resident was sitting on a bench watching her grandkids perform a TikTok dance. Sheridan really should bring her own girls in again. Mum had been more stable since Ronnie's visit and the delivery of her doll.

'Ronnie sends her love. She's coming back to see you next month.'

'Look at them dancing. Aren't they clever kids?' Mum marvelled. 'You didn't want children, did you, Ronnie? You said you had a termination when you were thirty. After what happened to Betty, I didn't want kids either, but Ralph convinced me.'

'And your children love you very much,' Sheridan told her.

'They only loved me because I was pretending to be someone else.' Mum giggled. 'I couldn't be myself anymore. That person had followed rules blindly, done a terrible thing. But Betty questioned everything. She was adventurous and delighted in the world. I'd betrayed her but she was loyal. My sister and my best friend. I dedicated myself to being her, living the life she wanted in Australia. I even copied her giggle.'

Blinking back her tears, Sheridan stared at the cockatoos. She wished she could make Mum understand that it wasn't her fault. But poor Mum hadn't been able to live with herself.

After dinner, Nick suggested that she relax on the couch while he got the girls ready for bed. He brought her a cup of peppermint tea and her favourite dark chocolate with almonds. She switched on *The Marvelous Mrs. Maisel*. The television show was set in the late 1950s, but it gave her some insight into her mother's upbringing in America when women had so little independence. Or maybe it wasn't so different from Tiffany's situation—pregnant at nineteen, she'd chosen a husband she believed was best able to provide for her baby.

Last night, she and Nick had talked for hours. 'But why didn't you tell me?' she kept asking over and over, as if he might have some other, more satisfactory explanation. And then she'd confessed how much she was hurting. 'I keep thinking of Toby. You have a grown son now, but I don't.'

He'd taken her in his arms and held her tightly. 'I wish with every fibre in my body that Toby was here with us today. Listen, I don't know what relationship I'll have with Dom. But you already know him. You've been coaching him for weeks.'

And it was true: she did know him better, and Dom trusted her.

The girls called for her to kiss them goodnight. Sheridan lay with each of them for a moment and thought about Mum and Betty. Two sisters who had been so connected, and then Mum's love and guilt had pushed her to become Betty. Her girls had their whole lives ahead of them in a society where women could be much more independent.

'You can make your own choices,' she whispered to Eloise.

'Can I stay up all night and eat chocolate in front of the TV with you?'

'When you're an adult.'

'That's so long away.' Eloise sighed and snuggled against her.

'Let's go and visit Glamma on the weekend,' Sheridan said. 'We'll take her that yummy orange cake.'

'And I'll draw her a picture of the bonfire at Mimosa.'

'Great idea. Goodnight, darling.'

In the lounge room, Nick was waiting for her with another cup of tea. His forehead was creased in anguish. Oh God, hadn't they done enough talking last night?

But it wasn't that. 'We have to chat about money,' he said.

'We don't need a new house.' Sheridan sighed. 'Let's stop looking and wait until Eloise is at high school.'

Nick rubbed his fingers over his chin, then half-covered his mouth as he spoke. 'It's not about a new house. Your dad ... he made some mistakes with the superannuation fund.'

'What?' Dad had prided himself on his financial acumen.

'I haven't wanted to tell you. I know you idolised Ralph but he stuffed up. And your mum has been donating thousands of dollars every year to a women's shelter. I guess Betty's story explains that.' He shrugged helplessly. 'I've been trying to fix it, but I can't. There's hardly any money left ... I wasn't getting an appraisal of Mimosa to determine our mortgage limit. It's to make sure we can keep paying the fees for the nursing home.'

Bloody hell. Half of her was grateful that he was doing his best for Gloria, while trying to maintain her belief in Ralph; the other half was furious with him for carrying this burden alone.

'I appreciate what you tried to do.' She reached for his hand. 'But you didn't need to keep everything to yourself. We're in this together. Please talk to me.'

'You had so many other things going on, you were already overwhelmed. I thought I could solve it without worrying you.'

'We can solve it together.' She could sign up more clients. They could draw down on their mortgage. Maybe Lachy could dip into his savings to help out with the fees.

'It felt like my responsibility,' Nick said. 'When I was growing up, Dad always took care of the money.'

'But we're not our parents,' she said. 'We need to make our own way.'

She thought about her mum's parents in America—Lachy said the police were investigating their grandfather as a possible serial killer. And here was Mum in the nursing home, blaming herself. She thought about the links between them all and the article she'd read on the murder gene. *We're not our parents, but we inherit their DNA.*

44

LACHY

AN UNEASE LAY OVER THE HOUSE. AUNT THERESA HAD SAID HOW grateful she was that Lachy's DNA had solved the mystery of her sister's whereabouts, but at the same time she was nervy. The prospect that her father could be a murderer, maybe even a serial killer, made her weep at the dinner table.

'Father was very rigid in his principles and Betty wouldn't follow his rules,' she said. 'But I can't see him . . . hurting her.'

Abraham Dunstan had hurt Betty—that was undeniable. He'd definitely whipped her. He'd made her disappear. His treatment of her made Lachy more determined to be a better father; he couldn't just be a good-time mate, he needed to be a role model. And right now, he was role-modelling how to survive a bad patch.

'A parent should try to do their best for their kids,' he said to Theresa. 'You stood by Matthew even though you disapprove of divorce. You didn't cut him out of your life.' The conversation was his attempt to pave the way for what his DNA had set in motion. He was certain Betty had been killed by her father. And he would prefer not to be with his relatives when that news was announced. The morning after his aunt's tears at the dinner table, he rang American Airlines to change their tickets. As the customer service woman discussed options, he could almost smell the eucalyptus leaves. God, he wanted to be back at Mimosa Hideout with the mountain ranges rising above him.

'The flight that can get us home by Sunday sounds good,' he said. 'What's the cost on changing to that one?'

As she was answering, he looked down at his scribbled notes of dates and times. At the end of each, he'd written the destination SYDNEY in capital letters and underlined it. Tapping the pen against the paper, he pictured them flying over the harbour and arriving at Sydney airport. Shit, he was doing it again. Running away. And he didn't even know if he was allowed to leave.

'Actually . . . I'm sorry.' He sucked in a lungful of air. 'We'll stick with the original flights.'

According to Sheridan, Mum had spent her whole adult life trying to atone for betraying Betty. Perhaps he could get some facts to absolve her. Theresa said that when Mum was younger, she'd been a bossy big sister, like Sheridan. And then she'd fled her family and switched her personality to reflect Betty's, the adventurous second child, like him. Strange that his own personality had been shaped in part by his missing aunt. From this side of the world, he could clearly see the sibling roles: Mum and Betty; him and Sheridan. Since a young age, Sheridan had been thrust into a carer role and never escaped it. He'd been relying on his big sister for too long. She'd done so much; it was time for him to do more.

He hung up from the airline and rang Lieutenant Davis.

'I'm just wondering if you've found further information on my grandfather.'

'We're doing tests to see if your DNA matches any of the forensic evidence from the other crime scenes,' Davis explained. 'That will give us a conclusive answer.'

Abraham Dunstan could never have imagined that his future grandson's genes had the potential to incriminate him for multiple murders.

Davis continued with his update. 'We spoke with Charlie Stanbury yesterday and he gave us another possible lead. The building supervisor at the Soldiers' Home was obsessed with Betty and he drove a pick-up truck. He also has a police record. We're tracking him down.'

A pick-up truck was seen speeding away on Deadwood Creek Road. Lachy hadn't asked what type of car his grandfather owned. Aunt Theresa would be relieved to know there was another suspect.

'Did Charlie remember much about Betty?' Lachy asked. 'I assume the baby was his.'

'No, he said he'd only met her once at the Soldiers' Home. That's why he didn't recognise her at the accident site. The poems and letters seem to have been a teenage infatuation.'

'Really?' Lachy frowned. 'Did you believe him?'

'Apart from the letters, we couldn't find evidence to the contrary but we're still looking into it. In the meantime, Iris Stanbury wants you to go visit. She took a keen interest in the case early on and did a lot of publicity to try and identify Betty.' Lieutenant Davis sighed. 'Obviously you need to be sensitive. If Dr Stanbury had an affair, presumably his wife doesn't know.'

∞

The Stanburys still lived on Deadwood Creek Road. Lachy tried to picture how it must have looked in the late sixties surrounded by fields or forest, without the three new houses, the nearest neighbour a mile away.

At the front door, they were greeted by Iris. Tall and elegant, with curly brown hair and tortoiseshell glasses. She had to be older than Mum, but looked ten years younger in a stylish navy pantsuit. He and Kai followed her into the lounge room where a platter of egg sandwiches was laid out on the coffee table.

'I'm so relieved Emerald Doe has finally been identified after all this time. The police said she came from a very religious family that barely interacted with the wider community. I guess that explains it.' Iris put a hand on Lachy's forearm. 'It upset me that her parents didn't know she'd died. I'm pleased she has been returned to your family.'

Dr Stanbury entered from the hallway and recognised Kai from the concert.

'How's the head?' he asked. 'You took a fair whack.'

'It hurt a lot but it's better now,' Kai said. 'Thanks for helping me. I remember at the concert, when I mentioned my grandmother's name, you reacted. What a coincidence that you knew Betty!'

When Kai heard that Dr Stanbury had denied the relationship to the police, he'd been annoyed. *You saw those love letters, Dad.* Despite the warning to be sensitive, Kai was on a mission.

'I met her once, that's all.' Dr Stanbury's voice was deep, assured. 'Working as a doctor, I was introduced to many people every week.'

'But she wrote love poems about you.'

'The police showed me.' Dr Stanbury selected a sandwich from the silver tray and took a bite. 'But as I said, I only met her once. We merely chatted while tending to patients. I was embarrassed to see the poems.'

'All the girls fancied him because he was so handsome.' Iris pointed to their wedding photo on the wall. 'He looked just like Robert Redford.'

Dr Stanbury grinned. 'I still do.'

It was true; Lachy could see a resemblance to the actor.

He gazed at the other photos scattered around the room; they showed the Stanburys walking on the Great Wall of China, standing in front of the pyramids, and posing at the base of Uluru. Charlie and Iris had lived well and, unlike Betty, they'd made it to Australia.

'Dr Stanbury, my mother, Gloria, said you spoke to her after the accident. You told her about all the blood.' He didn't need to know Mum had dementia and might have mis-remembered.

'Please call me Charlie. Of course, I spoke to people about the accident but I didn't know the girl's name so I couldn't make the connection with her sister.' Charlie paused. 'Are you telling me your mother knew Betty had died? Why didn't she identify her then?'

Lachy's head spun. Could Mum's memory be trusted at all? Betty had been a teenager and this man a doctor, maybe she'd made up the affair to protect a boy her age from getting into trouble with her father. Was the father of her baby one of the teenage boys from the bus who Theresa had mentioned? The Stanburys didn't have any kids themselves. He needed to think.

'Iris, would I be able to use the bathroom, please?'

As she led him down the hallway, Lachy glanced into the rooms. The first was a study and the second, a sewing room. A display unit with hundreds of dolls stretched across an entire wall.

'Oh, wow!'

'Ah, my doll collection.' Iris smiled. 'I still have Florence from when I was a baby.'

His exclamation had been loud enough to bring Kai and Charlie from the lounge room.

'Where did you get that one?' Kai pointed to a large doll, sitting up on a shelf.

It was the doll that had caused Lachy's outburst. She was exactly the same as Betty, Mum's beloved doll.

'Isn't she sweet?' Iris took her down and handed her to Kai. 'Charlie won her for me at a fair in Pottstown. He was always a great shot.'

'Perfect hand–eye coordination.' Charlie did a little bounce on the balls of his feet. 'I hit the target so many times that the carnie banned me from the stall.'

'What did you do with the other dolls you won?' Kai asked.

Charlie stopped moving. 'I gave them to little girls at the hospital.'

Iris was standing in front of the shelves, adjusting each doll. 'We always wanted kids but it wasn't to be. That's why Charlie still does first aid at events and I help out at the local school. We get to see lots of children.'

'It's very sad that Betty was pregnant when she died. Why do you think she was killed outside your house?' Lachy hadn't meant to be quite so blunt but he was confused.

'I've no idea.' Charlie shrugged.

'If her baby was—' Iris started. She turned from the dolls on the shelves to glare at her husband, crossing her arms over her chest. 'I don't understand, Charlie. I've been trying to help the police identify her for decades and you knew her all along.'

'I told you, I only met her once. I didn't recognise her in the dark with all that blood.'

'You must have a theory,' Lachy insisted.

'Walt, the building manager from the Soldiers' Home, was besotted by her. He knew where I lived. I can only surmise that he left her here.'

'But why?' Iris spoke as if they were the only two in the room. 'Were you having an affair? Is that why you wouldn't let the police take a sample of your DNA?'

'I've always been faithful to you, Iris.' Charlie sounded cross. 'In all of our years of marriage.'

As they bickered back and forth, Lachy considered sneaking into the bathroom and taking a toothbrush for DNA testing. But that probably wasn't legal. And it wouldn't prove anything. Charlie's DNA would be part of the forensic evidence because he'd tried to save Betty's life.

'Just tell me the truth!' Iris was yelling now. 'I heard voices in the driveway that night. You and Betty talking.'

Charlie sighed loudly and collapsed into the chair by the sewing machine. 'You did hear voices,' he groaned with the admission. 'Walt and Betty. They'd tried to get rid of the baby themselves and she was bleeding badly. Abortions were illegal so they couldn't go to hospital. Walt brought her to me for help. But when he realised she was dying, he panicked and sped off. If I'd told the police, I would've been charged for assisting with a termination and lost my career. I was looking after us, Iris.'

320

Lachy stared at him. The doctor had kept Betty's identity a secret to protect his career. And all that time, her family had been missing her, assuming she didn't want to come home to them. What a self-serving mongrel. Betty had written a note worried that her father would kill her, begging a doctor she trusted for help. And Charlie had abandoned her. Just like her boyfriend, Walt.

'For pity's sake, Charlie!' Iris exploded. 'They've been trying to identify that girl for more than fifty years and you knew her all along?'

With Iris ranting, Lachy was able to surreptitiously send a message to Lieutenant Davis suggesting an immediate follow-up visit to the Stanbury house.

So Betty was not a victim of the Casanova Killer but of the religious constraints, social norms and abortion laws of the 1960s. Although for some women, it hadn't improved. He thought of Zahra—different circumstances but similar issues.

Watching Charlie trying to placate his wife, he was reminded of Henrik's denials. The strident explanations of a man who purported to do his best for his community.

He suspected Iris had invited them here because she sensed that Charlie wasn't telling the full story to the police. That he wasn't so innocent after all.

45

ELIZABETH, 1968

WHEN FATHER ESCORTED ME FROM THE POTTING SHED, I BREATHED IN
the cool night air and lifted my face to the dark sky. I thought
he would give me a whupping in the garden but he ordered
me into the car and then drove slowly down the lane and onto
the main road.

'The sexually immoral person sins against his own body,' he
intoned. 'Or do you not know that your body is a temple of the
Holy Spirit within you, whom you have received from God?'

'Corinthians,' I whispered. My dishonourable body began
to tremble. I should have been elated at being away from the
shed, but Father's wrath filled the car. So thick I could almost
taste it. 'Forgive me for I have sinned.'

'You have sinned against God. You have disgraced our church.
You have brought eternal damnation upon yourself.'

Too frightened to ask where he was taking me, I covered
my abdomen with my hands as if I could protect my baby from
his words. After Gloria had left me that morning, I forced
myself to vomit up the herbs, until my stomach was empty.
I prayed to God to keep my baby alive. I had to believe He

was more forgiving than my Father. Perhaps God had heard my prayer because I'd had no bleeding today.

When Father turned onto the track to French Creek State Park, the oak trees towered over us in the gloom and I lost all sense of direction. I wondered if he was taking me into the forest or to the old Hopewell Furnace. Would he re-create the fire of hell for my eternal damnation?

Deep in the woods, he stopped the car and instructed me to get out. The forest pressed around us, ghostly trunks and the rustle of nocturnal creatures. We were far from the main road, nowhere near the furnace. My legs shook with each step, stumbling over tree roots and stones. Beyond the panting of my breath, I could hear a metallic sound—Father unbuckling his belt. The whupping would happen here, away from Mother and Gloria. Here, in the dark, with only the hickory and maple trees as witnesses; here, where it didn't matter if I screamed.

'With whom did you commit this sin?' Father demanded.

Weak rays of moonlight mottled the forest floor and I could see the belt in his hand. I had to stay strong for the baby, for Charlie. The thought of running crossed my mind—was the wilderness a safer option than Father? Paralysed by indecision, I said nothing. The belt came down hard against my legs. Staggering in shock, I wrapped my arms around myself.

'What is his name?' Father repeated.

'I can't say.'

The belt bit into my thighs.

He repeated the question.

Again I refused to answer.

On and on it went.

I will stay strong, I promised my baby. But the blows moved higher. To my back. Flicking around the side of my stomach. Aiming to hurt our unborn child. I slumped to the ground, pulling my knees up to my chest. Tears and mucus dripped from my face into the dirt.

'Stop! Please stop!' I cried. 'His name is Charlie Stanbury.'

During the hour-long trip, I lay curled on the back seat, my thighs and back stinging, my brain foggy with pain. Father made a stop at a church to use their telephone. I imagined him calling the Soldiers' Home and speaking to Walt—the creepy building supervisor would be only too happy to provide Charlie's address. Would Father dump me at the house where Charlie lived with his wife? I hoped so. *Charlie will save us,* I told the baby. He would dress my wounds and comfort me. His wife . . . I couldn't let myself think about his wife. I prayed that Charlie was at home, that Father wouldn't hurt him.

Charlie's place was outside of Hanover township on a long road with no close neighbours. The white, double-storeyed mansion almost glowed in the darkness. Father did not pull into the driveway. He parked on the grass verge and dragged me from the back seat. I struggled to find my footing and fell forward. Instinctively, I rolled to protect my baby.

Father pointed at the house. 'This is where you belong. You are condemned to remain with this man. Do not attempt to contact my family or the church community. You are not welcome in Berks County.'

'Father—'

'Do not call me that. You are no longer my daughter.'

I was still lying on the ground as he drove off. *Everything will be fine, little one.* The throbbing pain made it difficult to think. I had to see Charlie without alerting his wife. How could I do that? I would rest first, I decided; I needed to gather my strength. I dozed on and off, waking in agony whenever I shifted in my sleep.

✖

It must have been near midnight when I heard a car engine thrumming in the distance. As it came closer, it slowed. Headlights swung towards the house, blinding me, but I recognised the silhouette of Charlie's Mustang.

'Holy Mary, Mother of God.' He was crouching beside me in an instant. 'What happened to you? Are you in pain?'

My nod sent an agonising ripple along my spine and lower back.

'I've just come from an emergency at the hospital.' He was reaching inside the car. 'I'll give you a needle for the pain and then we'll get you cleaned up.'

'Charlie, I'm sorry. I kept your name secret for so long but Father wouldn't stop.'

The injection was a tiny pinprick.

'It's morphine,' he said. 'It works fast. You'll feel better soon, my darling.'

He was holding my hand, smiling down at me. After all my day-dreaming in the potting shed, his face was solid and real. Somehow, we would be together. He didn't love his wife, he loved me. And I was carrying his child.

'Father beat me, but I protected our baby,' I whispered.

I expected him to praise me, but instead he rubbed a hand over his forehead as if he were the one in pain.

'You can't have this baby, Betty.' He squeezed my hand too tightly. 'My father went mad and was sent to a mental hospital. He lost us our money, our business, our reputation . . . everything. That's why I married Iris. Her father took over the business. He paid for my education. He bought us this house.'

'We don't need a mansion.' Easing my fingers from his, I put them up to his chin and caressed his jawline. 'We have love. We can live anywhere. Australia will be a land of opportunity for us.'

His eyes flicked towards the big house. Presumably Mrs Stanbury was asleep inside. He took my fingers from his face and placed them over my belly. 'I'm afraid it's not that simple. My grandmother was in an asylum too. Madness runs in the family. My mother made me promise never to have children.'

Our baby was beautifully innocent but Charlie was condemning her, just as Father had done. I had to make him see his mistake.

'But Charlie, you're not insane, you're a wonderful doctor. Our baby will be as kind and clever as you.'

'It has been a hard journey to get past the terrible shame of my father and become a doctor.' He nodded. 'But now I am respected. Acknowledged. People look up to me.'

I reached for him but he shifted away. He was fiddling with something in his medical bag and then rested his hand on my leg. I felt another pinprick.

'What's that?' I asked.

'Some medicine to stop your sores becoming infected. You know I'll always look after you.'

He held me in his arms, the way I would hold my baby when she arrived. I felt myself floating and a sense of joy spread through me, tingling in my fingers and toes. God had come to me at last. He understood our true love. The moon bathed us in its light, the silvery clouds shone, our love lit up the world.

A shaft of light; not the moon but a door opening. Charlie's wife. How would he introduce me? I tried to speak but no words came out. My chest was tight, my eyes closing, my head so drowsy.

'I love you, darling.' Charlie kissed my forehead. 'Godspeed.'

He pushed me away and the stars were spinning above me, around and around. Cradling my belly, I told our baby: *We're safe now, Charlie will look after us.*

My eyes shut and they wouldn't open again, but I could hear voices in the night air.

'What's happening?' a woman asked. 'Is someone out there?'

'A young girl,' Charlie answered her. 'I found her by the roadside.'

'Is she hurt?'

'Yes, badly. I think she was in an accident. I saw a car speeding away . . . a pick-up truck. I tried to help but . . . she was already gone.'

46

LACHY

LACHY HAD BEEN RIGHT. IRIS'S SUSPICIONS WERE RAISED DURING THE initial police chat, and she'd invited them over deliberately to see if her husband would talk more about Betty. After they'd left, she sent Charlie into town on an errand and searched the house from top to bottom. Later, she'd told Lieutenant Davis that during their long marriage, small moments had niggled at her: a woman crying hysterically at the sight of them together in Norristown; an unfamiliar silver earring in the Mustang; inconsistent hospital rosters and irregular absences from home. Her husband had explained them away each time.

However, Charlie couldn't explain away what Iris found in the basement. An old leather medical bag containing Betty's library card, a nurse's fob watch belonging to Olive Ferguson, and a book of poetry inscribed by Doris Devlin, along with a tortoiseshell hair clip and an enamel brooch. Police were making enquiries to determine if the brooch had been worn by Maria Mancini and the hair clip by Bonnie Cunningham.

Iris presumed that her husband had been unfaithful. Not for one moment had she contemplated the possibility of him as the

Casanova Killer. When the police arrived, she was escorted to the hospital in shock while Charlie was taken in for questioning.

Lieutenant Davis phoned Lachy to thank him for his assistance.

'It was your DNA that identified Betty and led us to Charles Stanbury,' he said. 'We've taken a sample from him and the lab will test it against the forensic evidence from the different crime scenes. We'll have those results in a few weeks.'

Charlie exercised his right to silence but the detectives were piecing together his connection to each girl with Iris's help. She'd kept detailed diaries all her life and they listed Charlie's places of work and activities around the time of each murder.

'Betty's murder was different from the others. It was impulsive. He made his other victims more pliable using the Quaalude tablets,' Davis told him. 'But we also found old vials of morphine in the house and we think he gave Betty a fatal dose. He got away with her murder because the troopers believed his medical assessment that the cause of death was injuries from a hit-and-run. And the coroner didn't follow up properly.'

It hadn't been Betty's father but her lover. In her poems and letters, Betty had pledged her future to Charlie. Instead, he'd erased all traces of her and their unborn baby.

The whole family came to Theresa's house to farewell Lachy and Kai. While they were devastated to learn that Betty had been murdered, they were utterly relieved Abraham Dunstan had been cleared.

And now the Dunstans planned to honour their sister.

'I'm sorry we won't be here for Betty's memorial service,' Lachy said.

They were having it the day after Theresa and Leonard's wedding anniversary party.

'We'll be thinking of you all that day, especially your mum.' Theresa looked like she might cry. 'And tell Sheridan to come over sometime. We'd love to meet her girls.'

Sheridan hadn't been to America in so long but it was an expensive trip for four people. Lachy could look after the girls at home while Sheridan and Nick enjoyed a holiday. That could be part of him stepping up and redefining their sibling roles.

'I wish we'd searched for Betty,' Aunt Theresa sniffed. 'I thought she'd stayed away because of Father. Gloria must have suspected she was dead but never told us. I don't know if she was protecting herself or Father.'

Her secrecy had also protected Dr Charlie Stanbury.

'When Betty and Gloria left, it ruptured our family,' Uncle Ernest said. 'It also made us look at the world differently. Virginia ended up becoming a social worker helping families in crisis. And we adopted Celeste from a pregnant teenager in our church community.'

As they said goodbye, Lachy watched Kai hug all of his relatives. There was a change in him. He'd grown up on this trip. No longer a child, Kai was on the cusp of adulthood. How could Abraham Dunstan have disowned his daughter so thoroughly? Whatever Kai did, Lachy would support him and guide him. Thank God, his nieces were fine. Child protection services had visited both Sheridan and Amber, and they wanted to interview Lachy and Kai on their return. Then Kai would face the police again, possibly a magistrate. But they would get through it. Together.

✕

As they were cruising above the Pacific, Kai pointed to their flight path on his screen. 'Look, Dad, we're flying over ocean the whole way. We might see Kiribati but not much else. Those islands are really in the middle of nowhere.'

Kiribati. Years ago, he'd provided advice on a project to improve rainwater harvesting for rural villages on the outer islands, but he'd never actually been there.

'What's the capital?' He fell into their old game.

'Tarawa . . . is that the town or an atoll or both?' Kai magnified the map on the screen to see if it would supply the answer. 'I remember that Kiribati is made up of more than thirty atolls. It's right on the International Date Line and is the only country spread across four different hemispheres.'

'Impressive! We should go there sometime. What do you reckon?'

'Yeah, sure.'

Staring at the map, Lachy recalled those early work trips to the Pacific Islands. They were shorter and easier somehow. While there had been bureaucracy, fewer levels were involved. Maybe that was what he should do: properly resign from the global company with its multilateral projects and funding; and refocus. Set up his own business and connect directly. Bring solar desalination units to communities in and around Australia. A spark of excitement fizzed inside him. They had the technology to help combat climate change; amazing technologies that needed passionate people to put them into place. People like him. He could do that on a small scale. And do it locally so he was around for Kai.

But before Lachy changed companies, he needed to ensure he'd done everything possible to get justice for Zahra and Juliet's room-mate.

When he'd called Lieutenant Ignacio about flying home, the detective had cleared him to go. 'Your new DNA sample was exactly the same as your original one. I can confirm there was no match to the forensic evidence.'

'That's a relief.' Lachy knew the DNA check should've been straightforward but, still, he'd felt nervous about not being able to remember the night.

'But I need you to do something. Your office is not being very helpful.'

Lachy agreed immediately before even hearing the request. Now he composed a message to Henrik:

Hey mate. Sorry about the radio silence. Tough time back home with my mum and son. But I'll be in DC at the same time as you're there for the annual meeting. I'm resigning. While last year was tricky, I still appreciate our time working together. I learnt so much from you. You'll always be the number one expert in desal solar systems. Let's have a farewell drink at the Whisky Bar.

Henrik's ego would reel him in; he'd definitely agree to meet.

47

SHERIDAN

SHERIDAN COULDN'T BELIEVE THE CHANGE IN LACHY. HE WAS A different man from the one she'd seen at Easter: rejuvenated, re-energised, determined. He'd barely stopped talking since they'd picked him up from the airport. Amber had taken Kai to Narrabeen for a few days. After that, Lachy would drive them both back to Mimosa.

'It turns out Charlie killed a medical student when we were at summer camp,' he told Nick. 'That was the other girl on Deadwood Creek Road. He would have been well into his fifties by then. I suspect she was going to his house but he intercepted her before she could meet his wife. She was pregnant too.'

Nick shook his head. 'Unbelievable. I guess contraception wasn't widely available in the sixties, but he should have figured it out by 2004.'

'Actually, an early version of the Pill was available in the sixties,' Lachy said. 'He gave it to Iris every day, prescribed as a tablet for her heart murmur. That's why she never got pregnant. With his affairs, it's like he wanted a baby. He'd achieve the dream and then he'd have to destroy it.'

A shiver ran through Sheridan. If Charlie Stanbury had been caught for Betty's murder, then the others would still be alive. 'What about the most recent death on Deadwood Creek Road?' she asked. 'The one last September?'

'That wasn't him. The coroner re-examined the case and ruled the girl died as a result of misadventure. No connection with Charlie.' Lachy pulled a newspaper from the front pocket of his suitcase. '*The Philadelphia Times* reported his arrest.'

Sheridan took the paper and she and Nick read it together.

A seventy-seven-year-old doctor from Montgomery County has been charged with six counts of first-degree murder. Charles Stanbury allegedly killed his first victim in 1968, four women in the 1970s, and his last in 2004. Investigators were treating these homicides as separate cases until a few years ago. It was only through analysing DNA which had been collected at the crime scenes and stored as evidence that they were able to connect the murders to a single perpetrator. Cold case detectives have discovered Stanbury was in secret relationships with his victims and they were all pregnant. His most recent victim, Gabriela Gutierrez, was on a medical exchange program from Colombia, working at the same hospital as Stanbury in 2004.

His wife is reportedly cooperating with police and prosecutors. She has issued the following statement.

'My heart goes out to the families who lost their precious daughters. Sadly, Charlie charmed me with lies just as he charmed them. It seems he imagined a fantasy world with a young wife and children.'

A breakthrough in the case came when forensic genealogy identified his first victim after fifty-five years. An Australian man had uploaded his DNA to a public genealogy website and police discovered a familial match. They were able to build a family tree and name Elizabeth Dunstan, who had been banished by her family and church due to her pregnancy.

'Your DNA cracked the case! You're a hero,' Sheridan said.

Lachy snorted. 'There's nothing heroic about being tricked into giving my DNA for a rape allegation. Anyway, while I was away I realised that you're the real hero. Thank you for everything you do for our family. I haven't said it enough.'

She was stunned into silence. Definitely a different man from Easter.

Mabel appeared from the kitchen. 'Uncle Lachy, did you bring me a present?'

'I've got presents from your Great-Aunt Theresa. Who likes American candy?'

Eloise flew into the room. 'Me, me, me!'

Lachy opened his suitcase and produced an assortment of colourful sweets.

'Why don't you take them into the kitchen and share them out between you?' Sheridan suggested. For once, she wouldn't make them wait for later.

'Yay!' The two girls ran off with their bounty.

'Theresa wants you and Nick to go over to America,' Lachy said. 'They'd all love to see you. I'll stay in Sydney and look after the girls and Mum.'

'Who are you and what have you done with my brother?' Sheridan joked.

'That's a kind offer,' Nick said what she should have. 'We'll think about it.'

At some point, they would have to discuss money with Lachy, and work out how to keep up with Gloria's nursing home fees. Sheridan had already started looking for a job with a regular salary. Nick had begged her not to abandon her career goals, but her goal shouldn't be dragging her down. She would focus on herself for once and coach herself into a better role. A former colleague worked in leadership development training—that sounded like an interesting area where she could use all of her skills.

'Did you manage to find Tiffany while you were over there?' Nick asked.

'No. I started looking for her, but then the situation with work went pear-shaped and the police wanted to talk to me about the DNA. To be honest, I thought I was going to be arrested.'

'Well, as it happens, I have some news from that quarter . . .' Nick dropped the bombshell about his and Tiffany's child.

Judging from his stunned expression, Lachy didn't know the pair had slept together. He asked the same question Sheridan had: 'Why didn't you tell me?'

'Tiffany made me promise to keep it quiet at camp,' he said. 'And then she turned around and said it wasn't my baby after all.'

Lachy grimaced. 'She was a tricky one. You could never tell when she was lying.'

The exchange made Sheridan feel better; Nick really had been messed about by Tiffany. Of course he would have done the right thing if he'd known.

'Yep, tricky's the word,' Nick agreed. 'Dom said she might fly out here later in the year.'

'So you haven't spoken to her yet?'

Nick shook his head.

'But she's alive?'

That was a strange question from Lachy. Nick must have thought so too because he frowned.

'Of course Tiffany is alive. Why would you think otherwise?'

'Thank God.' Lachy ran his hands through his hair. 'The reason I wanted to contact her was . . . to find out how I behaved at camp that night.' His voice faltered. 'I've never told either of you this before, but I have these alcoholic blackouts when I drink fast. I act normally but I don't remember anything the next day. Usually I keep it under control, but sometimes when I'm stressed, I drop my guard. The very first time I had a blackout was when I drove Tiffany to Deadwood Creek Road.'

Sheridan stared at him as the pieces fell into place: Kai's concern about Lachy's memory at Easter and Lachy's reluctance to discuss the rescue of Fred Whyte, his shock at seeing the story in the paper.

'Wow, that's terrifying,' she said.

'Yes, it's confusing and scary and I'm not going to let it happen again.' He turned to Nick. 'Do you mind if I ring Tiffany? I just want to talk to her about that night. I won't mention you or Dom.'

'If you really feel you have to,' Nick said; his resentment towards Tiffany was still strong.

'Thanks. And I'd like to meet Dom whenever you're ready.'

'That's for another day,' Sheridan said. 'Right now, we're going to visit Mum.'

xx

When Lachy kissed Mum on the cheek, she turned her head away from him.

'Ernest, hurry up and get those potatoes from the garden or you'll be in big trouble.'

'It's us, Sheridan and Lachy.' She tried to bring Mum into the present. 'We're in Australia. Sydney. Near the beach.'

'The beach. Pah. There's no beach near here. Stop trying to trick me.' Facing them again, she grimaced. 'Father will give you a whupping for telling a falsehood. Thou shalt not lie.'

Lachy pulled out his phone and clicked on a photo of Gloria and Betty in the garden.

'Look, this is you from when you were younger.'

Mum put on her glasses and peered at the screen, frowning. Sheridan watched her closely, worried that the old photos would distress her.

Mum went completely still. Then her face creased in a huge smile. 'Oh, Betty, there you are. I thought I'd lost you.'

'We found Betty,' he said.

The photo seemed to crack open her memory; Mum began telling a long story about playing by the Schuylkill River with Betty. 'We had an imaginary afternoon tea party with imaginary friends. Betty called her friend Sheridan because of an Irish girl who had just arrived in her class. And then she kept talking to her imaginary Sheridan for weeks. Gosh, she was a million laughs!'

Whenever Sheridan had asked about her name, Mum said, 'We found it in a baby book. It means searcher and adventurer.' Actually, Mum had found another way to commemorate her sister.

Memory. It worked in such mysterious ways. Lodging certain things in the brain, discarding others. Sometimes protecting us from our worst experiences, sometimes replaying them over and over, sometimes lying to us. Mum's brain would keep deteriorating, leaving only traces of her memories. They should ask Aunt Theresa and Uncle Ernest to come here. The three surviving siblings together, remembering childhood stories. A memorial for Betty with Mum, before it was too late.

48

KAI

KAI'S FIRST WEEK BACK AT WARABINA HIGH SCHOOL WAS COMPLETELY different from last term. Tarni, Bronte and Ethan asked a thousand questions about America and hung out with him at lunchtime. It meant he was protected from Grug's gang.

On Friday afternoon, Mr Suttor pulled the minibus into the entrance of Mimosa Hideout. Kai picked up his backpack and called out: 'Thanks. Have a good weekend.'

'It'll be noisy. The grandkids are coming to stay,' Mr Suttor said. Kai was waiting for him to open the bus door. 'Last one. What's the capital of Vietnam?'

'Too easy. Hanoi.'

He and Mr Suttor had traded stories about America and discussed how tourists used to mistake New York for the capital. Just like Canberra and Sydney. Kai mentioned Dad's game of quizzing him on capital cities and now Mr Suttor had taken it up. At the end of the route, when they were alone on the bus, he'd yell out a country.

'I'll stump you soon,' Mr Suttor laughed. 'Tell your Dad I can't come up the road next week if there's snow.'

'Okay. See ya.' Kai leapt down the stairs, shivered and balled his fists into his pockets.

It would be even colder next week. Winter in the high country was going to be an experience but he planned to make the most of it. Dad had faced a long interview with the child protection services to prove his suitability as a parent and Kai had been interviewed twice: first by a social worker and then the police. He'd admitted he made a bad mistake and told them all that he was sincerely sorry. Sergeant Ayling gave him a formal caution and instructions to attend a drug and alcohol counselling program. Kai wouldn't be charged or locked up in juvenile detention. Embarrassingly, he'd cried again in front of the police officer, this time with relief.

Mum had also cried at the news, and then followed up like the sergeant.

'Promise me you won't take drugs again, Kai. Promise me you'll never have them in your possession.'

'I won't, Mum.' He meant it. 'I'm concentrating on new stuff now, like learning to play the guitar.'

When he'd gone home to Narrabeen after getting off the plane, he'd told his family about Aidan and Nat's band and how they were playing in a youth convention in Florida. He'd shown them a video and Daisy and Willow had danced around the lounge room. Mum and Simmo were surprised to hear that Kai was interested in a Christian music group.

Aidan had taught him a few chords on their last afternoon together in America. Now Dad was giving him lessons on his old guitar. Kai planned to learn Glamma's favourite song, 'All You Need Is Love', and play it for her on his next visit to the nursing home. Mum said he could go up for the June long weekend so he had to learn fast.

His new approach of making the most of things had him helping Dad and Ronnie on their properties, snowboarding, doing more homework, cooking, learning to drive and asking Tarni out after school next Friday.

But where was he supposed to take her? There were no trendy cafes in Warabina, no cinema, no bowling alley, no putt-putt golf. He'd messaged Aidan and Nat for advice and they'd suggested a picnic in the park. Kai wasn't so sure—it'd be cold, and what if Grug and his mates walked by? Aidan had sent another suggestion: *Take her to youth group! It's Ascension this week, that's a feast time. We celebrate Christ being raised to heaven through the clouds.* There was a youth group in Warabina and Kai might check it out sometime, but not for his first date with Tarni.

Could Dad drive them into Cooma? No, he was busy setting up his new business. He'd thrown himself into it. Actually, where was Dad? No sign of the ute barrelling down the track. At least Dad had an excuse: today was his birthday. Kai had cooked him scrambled eggs before school this morning.

Unexpectedly, the ute arrived from the main road. And instead of waiting for Kai to get in, Dad switched off the engine and opened the door.

'Sorry, just had to pop into town,' he said. 'Do you want to drive up the track?'

Every other time Kai had asked, Dad had said not yet.

'Sure.' He threw his backpack in the tray and climbed into the driver's seat. 'As long as you're prepared to die on your birthday.'

'You couldn't be a worse driver than Aunt Theresa.'

They both laughed but his take-off was jerky. Soon he had the car accelerating smoothly. Man, this felt good. Next February, he could apply for his L plates, but learning on the farm first would make it so much easier.

Dad gave him a few pointers, then asked, 'How was your presentation today?'

He'd done an assignment on the use of DNA and forensic genetic genealogy in investigating cold cases in America, focusing on the Casanova Killer of Pennsylvania. Through interviews and DNA testing against other cases, Lieutenant Davis had discovered two more victims. Dr Charlie Stanbury had been charged with killing eight women over three decades. For once, the class was enthralled. 'Dad's DNA helped identify my great-aunt, who was his first victim,' Kai told them. 'And I even met Dr Stanbury twice. The first time, he checked me for concussion.' When Grug raised his hand to ask a question, Kai was sure he'd take the piss, but he didn't.

'If I took a test and my sample was on file, and in thirty years' time my bad-ass son committed a crime and left DNA at the scene, does that mean they could catch him from my DNA? Even though he wasn't born when I gave the sample?'

'I guess so,' Kai said. 'Dad wasn't alive when his Aunt Betty died. The DNA companies have clamped down on privacy, but police can still get a warrant to search the databases in serious cases.'

Kai had enjoyed every minute of that class. And Grug had approached him afterwards to ask: 'How do you get a DNA test?'

'My dad knows all about it,' Kai said. 'He's got these booklets from the testing company. I can bring them in.'

'That'd be good.' Grug nodded. 'My brothers have been ribbing me forever. They reckon I'm adopted but I'm not. I look just like my uncle.'

Dad congratulated Kai on the presentation and then went super serious. 'Talking of DNA, I need to warn you. Some genes make you more likely to be affected by alcohol and drugs. I reckon I've inherited those from my grandfather. When I drink fast, I get memory blackouts. You might have the same response, especially if you mix alcohol and drugs.'

'I told you—I'm not drinking and never doing drugs again.' He figured Dad was exaggerating as a cautionary tale.

Dad shifted uncomfortably in the passenger seat. 'You know how we rescued Fred Whyte? I'd had a couple of drinks that afternoon and . . . umm . . . I can't remember anything that happened between then and the pub.'

'Are you for real?' Kai put his foot on the brake and faced his dad. 'Wow, that's so messed up. You honestly can't remember?'

'Not a thing.'

It explained why Dad had been behaving so strangely that evening.

'That makes me feel . . .' Kai couldn't quite define it: lonely, scared. Between Dad's blackout and Fred's concussion, Kai was the only one with a memory of the dangerous rescue.

'I'm so sorry,' Dad said. 'I'm cutting right back on my drinking. I won't let it happen again.' He put a hand on Kai's shoulder. 'That's a promise to you. I'll be a better father.'

Dad wasn't a superhero after all.

When Kai carefully steered the ute through the gate, he was surprised to see Ronnie's truck and Sheridan's four-wheel drive parked near the cabin. Since they'd come back from America, he'd written a letter of apology to Sheridan, Nick and the girls, but he hadn't seen them.

Entering the house, they found everyone in the kitchen, perched on stools, waiting for Dad.

'Happy birthday!' they chorused. 'We baked you a cake!'

Sheridan danced around the kitchen, pulling out plates and forks and candles. Kai had never seen her like this before. In the excitement of the surprise, she still hadn't said hello to him. He'd given the girls a hug and promised to build a bonfire later. He was relieved to see that Mabel was totally fine.

'Here you go.' Sheridan handed him plates to take into the dining room. Then she looked at him properly. 'Did we say hello? Put those down and come here a sec.'

She enveloped him in a hug so tight, he couldn't breathe for a moment. Then she released him and herded everyone into the dining room, where presents and cards were stacked on the table beside the cake.

After they'd sung 'Happy Birthday' and eaten cake, Dad unwrapped his gifts. Sheridan had given him a book on how to stay positive when faced with the climate catastrophe. It was one of the worst presents Kai had ever seen.

'Is this going to help?' Dad asked.

'Yep.' She grinned. 'Especially when combined with the next one. Quick open it!'

Sheridan had put Dad's presents in cloth bags rather than use wrapping paper. Dad pulled out a map and a printed page. He read aloud from the printout: '*The Bundian Way is a heritage-listed path from Mount Kosciuszko in the high country, known as Targangal, to the sea at Twofold Bay, known as Turemulerrer. This ancient Aboriginal pathway is more than forty thousand years old, even older than the Silk Road. It was important for trading, and connected families and communities.'* He looked up at Sheridan. 'What's this about?'

'They haven't quite finished connecting up the whole path but I thought we could walk some of it next weekend, if you're free. Ronnie can babysit the girls, so it'll be you, me, Nick, Kai and our new friend, Dom.'

Kai wasn't happy about being roped into a bushwalk, especially since he'd planned to see Tarni on Friday night, but he couldn't argue with Aunt Sheridan now that she'd finally forgiven him.

'Fantastic!' Dad grinned. 'Our parents did part of it on horseback and camped under the stars.'

'I remembered that you always wanted to walk it.' Sheridan looked happier than ever. 'All that history.'

Kai didn't know if she meant family history or Indigenous history or both, but it sounded pretty cool. Maybe he'd see if Tarni wanted to come too.

He hadn't given Dad his present yet. He got up and went to his bedroom, returning with two packages: one from him and one from Great-Aunt Theresa. He plonked both on the table in front of his father.

'Here you go, Dad. Happy birthday.'

Dad unwrapped the gift from Theresa first: a red baseball cap with the letter P on it. 'I told her I'm following the Washington Nationals now. She's trying to convert me back to the Phillies.' He laughed.

When he opened Kai's present, Dad did the opposite—he started to cry.

49

LACHY

LACHY CRADLED THE PRESENT IN HIS PALMS AND SNIFFED BACK A TEAR. For the past nine months, he'd been overcome by emotion so many times. Anger, infuriation and outrage. Self-loathing and shame. Shock and fear. Astonishment. Tenderness and gratitude. And now, he was overwhelmed with love for his son.

'Is it bad enough to make you cry?' Kai asked.

'No, it's beautiful.' He inclined his head towards the sideboard. 'Much better than the one I made at fifteen.'

'It's recycled,' Kai explained. 'From an old shearing shed on Ronnie's farm.'

Running his fingers over the photo frame, Lachy felt the knots and the nail holes, the history in the thick grain of the wood. An embodiment of time from when it had grown as a tree and stood in the valley to the life it had seen in the shearing shed. More than a century. Inside the frame, Kai had placed a photo of the two of them taken by the lake at Camp Happiness. He'd written on the card: *I'll be HAPPY to travel anywhere with you, Dad.*

'Get it?' asked Kai. 'Happy as in Camp Happiness. What was their motto again?'

He and Nick recited it together: '*Every day is a happy day at Happiness!*'

'Jinx!' the two girls shouted together.

'Double jinx,' Kai and Sheridan yelled.

Laughter echoed around the room.

'Am I the only one allowed to speak? Is that the rule?' Ronnie asked. 'Well, my birthday present is outside. Come on, everyone.'

As they donned their jackets, Lachy whispered to Nick: 'Are you okay about Dom coming on the Bundian trip? I'm keen to meet him, but only when you're ready.'

'Yeah, I'm ready. And he'll get on well with Kai. Afterwards, he's going skiing with some friends then he's off to Queensland, then Darwin. Travelling around, just like us at that age.'

They hadn't introduced Dom to the girls yet but Nick had told his parents; they'd taken the revelation in their stride and offered Dom a bunk in their caravan if he made it to Broome.

Last week, Lachy had made an excruciating phone call to Tiffany. Once she'd got over her surprise at hearing from him, he explained about his alcoholic blackout at summer camp that night.

'I can't remember any of it and I wanted to apologise if . . . I upset you in any way or, you know . . . hurt you.'

'I'll say you hurt me!' she exclaimed.

Oh shit, what had he done?

'You completely humiliated me,' she groaned.

Lachy winced, steeling himself for the truth of the night.

'Boys considered themselves lucky to be with me but you were the only guy to turn me down. I'd just found out I was pregnant and I wanted one last fling, but you rejected me.

I'd already become unattractive and the pregnancy wasn't even showing! It devastated me.'

'Er . . . I'm sorry,' he said.

'Your loss,' she sniped haughtily.

'And who collected you from the bridge at Deadwood Creek Road that night?'

'My boyfriend. The one I married.' She gave an exasperated sigh. 'Even though you'd rejected me, you were a total gentleman and you wouldn't leave until his car arrived. It was sweet but totally excruciating for me.'

Thank God, he'd still acted like himself in a blackout state. He meant what he'd promised Kai in the ute earlier: he would never drink himself into a blackout state again, no matter how stressed he was. Even when he had to face Henrik. His former friend had agreed to meet up in three weeks' time at their favourite whisky bar in DC. But it wouldn't actually be Lachy sitting across the table from him; Lieutenant Ignacio planned to get a DNA swab and take him in for questioning.

Lachy had emailed Juliet to let her know and finally she'd answered last night: *Thanks for your help. When I asked for your DNA, it was a long shot, I didn't think you'd do it. And then you gave it so quickly, I assumed it must be someone else's so I asked Lieutenant Ignacio if he could check it against their databases. That's when they found the link to the cold case. The Casanova Killer arrest has been all over the news here. It's long overdue justice. Hopefully we can get justice for my friend too.*

And for Zahra. He'd go back to head office, he'd stand up in court, he'd do everything he could to ensure Henrik was made accountable.

✕

As they followed Ronnie to the wood shed, Lachy breathed in the cool mountain air. So good to be back here. Mimosa really felt like home now, not a place to hide from the world.

Ronnie waved at her truck with a magician's flourish. 'Ta-da! Another full load of logs for you. That will keep you going through the winter.'

'Thank you, Ronnie,' he said. 'That's a great gift. But this will be the last time I need it. I'm setting up solar panels and a battery system this week. No more smoke into the atmosphere.'

'You're right. Even though it's the best smell.' Ronnie patted him on the back. 'Could you set it up at my place too?'

'Absolutely.' He looked around the group. 'Okay, who's going to help unload it?'

'We'll all do it,' Sheridan said. 'Come on, girls.'

He was impressed by how well Sheridan and Ronnie were getting along; it was clear something between them had thawed while he'd been away.

'Sheridan has been telling me about your new venture,' Ronnie said. 'If you need to do any lobbying, I've got a few names.'

'Really? Who do you know?' While Ronnie had always shown an interest in his work, he didn't understand how she'd have contacts in government, business or the environmental lobby.

'Lots of people. I set up EarthFight in the 1970s. I assume you've heard of it. We fought for national parks and green spaces. At one point, I even consulted with the government and they gave me an Order of Australia.'

His mouth actually dropped open. When he glanced at Sheridan, her eyebrows were as high as her hairline. In all their guesses, they'd never come close to this.

'Bloody hell, Ronnie. You're a legend!' He clapped her shoulder. 'Why haven't you told us before?'

'Back in the eighties, we were in Europe demonstrating against nuclear power. I had death threats against me. One of our protests turned nasty. I got battered, arrested and ended up in a jail cell with a brain injury.' She sighed. 'I was lucky to survive. I never knew who attacked me—the police or one of the bastards who'd issued the death threats. Afterwards, I changed my name and moved here. But I'm still connected to people online.'

No wonder Ronnie spotted conspiracy theories everywhere.

'Wow. That sounds terrifying.' Sheridan gave Ronnie a quick hug. 'I'm so glad you decided to come here.'

'You must have so many connections,' Lachy said. 'I'd love to chat with you sometime.' Discussing climate issues and water solutions out here in the high country sounded perfect.

'Don't tell anyone I was in EarthFight.' She held up her index finger as a warning. 'Those death threats still stand.'

They made a solemn vow to her and finished stacking the logs in the shed. Ronnie clambered into her truck and leant through the window to farewell them.

'Have a good birthday, mate.' Her gaze shifted from him to the horizon and she sniffed the air. 'Reckon we'll have snow tonight. I can smell it.'

Lachy studied the heavens: grey nimbostratus clouds in the far distance, but above them, the sky was clear. A snowfall was unlikely.

∞

After dinner, Kai took his cousins into the lounge room to watch a movie. Lachy had worried that Sheridan and Nick would never forgive Kai, but they seemed happy for him to spend time with the girls. Lachy finished packing the dishwasher, then offered them another glass of wine. He poured himself a glass of water.

Sheridan was perched on the stool from which Mabel had fallen. He didn't want that particular memory on repeat.

'Has it been hard for you to come back here?' he asked her.

'A little, but the girls have both recovered. That's what I'm focusing on.' She took a sip of her wine. 'Were you serious when you said you'd look after Mum and the girls while we went to America?'

'Utterly serious.'

A look passed between her and Nick; they must have been discussing it.

'We can't afford America but we'd love a weekend away at Lake Crackenback for our wedding anniversary. We'll go bushwalking and we'll visit the boutique distillery that my client, Brendan, set up.'

'Sounds fun!' He was pleased for them, even if their destination was only an hour from here. 'Let me know when you have a date and we'll lock it in.'

'Thanks.' Nick got up from his stool. 'I'll start the bath and bed routine.'

Lachy suggested to Sheridan that they go out to the ridge and look at the stars. It was something they used to do after dinner with Dad. At the back door, they rugged up in their coats again and he borrowed Kai's beanie. The night air tasted cold and fresh; it reminded him of the snowmelt in the creek. Kai's third birthday party. Maybe they could have his sixteenth down there: a bonfire with some mates from school. Even one or two friends from Sydney. Kai seemed to have accepted he'd be staying at Mimosa for the rest of the school year.

Part way along the ridge, Sheridan switched off her torch and they were encased in darkness. No moon. But his eyes adjusted. The Milky Way stretched across the sky, a swathe of tiny lights. The bushmen of the Kalahari desert called it the backbone of night and believed it held up the darkness, that it stopped fragments of blackness from falling down around us.

Lachy held his arms out and turned slowly in a circle, staring up at the universe. The blackness inside himself was dissolving with each step he took in developing his business and spending time with Kai. And watching Kai's new approach to life was reminding him of how it felt to view the world with optimism.

The Kalahari bushmen also believed the Milky Way contained the spirits of the dead. Was Zahra up there? And Betty? Twice in the past ten months, Lachy's universe had tipped on its axis and he'd tumbled from one unrecognisable place to another. Now, though, he was home. He trusted in himself and he'd keep aiming for honesty. No more family secrets, no more guilt and shame.

'I hope we have stars like this next weekend when we're doing the walk,' Sheridan said. 'Dom will be amazed.'

As she spoke, Lachy glanced to the south. The sky was darkening with shadows, huge clouds drifting their way. Maybe it would snow.

'Wouldn't it be magical,' he said, 'if the kids woke up to a white wonderland?'

They could pull the toboggans from the shed and spend the morning careening down the hill. Kai and the girls would have a ball, just like he and Sheridan did when they were young. The memory was so clear that it could have been last week: the two of them perched on toboggans at the top of the slope, Mum and Dad standing at their backs, ready to push. The joy in that moment of take-off, the rush of air, the feeling of weightlessness.

He slung an arm around his sister.

'The kids could go tobogganing,' she said, as if reading his mind. 'Remember how we used to do that?'

'I remember how you screamed all the way down the hill.'

'It made me go faster. I always won.'

'Not every time. I beat you at least twenty times.'

'Only once.' She elbowed him, indignant. 'And that was because Mum said I had to let you win.'

'No way!' He didn't remember that.

'Yep. I was always stronger and faster.'

'Well, I bet I could beat you now,' he said.

She laughed. 'You're on! Let's hope it snows all night.'

Tomorrow, they'd get out the toboggans, and their kids would experience the same exhilaration as they had.

The next generation. Making their own imperfect memories. Together.

ACKNOWLEDGEMENTS

BOOKS AND STORYTELLING ARE IN MY DNA. MY GREAT-GREAT UNCLES founded the famous Foyles Bookshop in England. My great-grandfather, Walter Booth, was a pioneer in British film and directed the very first adaptation of *A Christmas Carol*. During lockdown, my mum wrote a history of her family, and I kept thinking about connections between past and present. My grandmothers both come from big families and I'm the second youngest of five children, so I've always been fascinated by birth order and the relationships between siblings, parents and extended family. I've dedicated this book to my siblings, Fiona, Icara, Hamish and Shelalagh, who are all inspiring in their own ways.

We grew up on a farm in central west New South Wales during a drought and we were always thinking about water. When I started writing this book, the Horn of Africa was suffering its worst drought in recorded history while on the east coast of Australia, we were experiencing torrential rain. The town of Lismore was devastated by catastrophic flooding and, as part of a fundraiser for its recovery, I auctioned off a name in this novel. Fiona Taylor, writer, bookclubber, podcaster and all-round supporter of Australian authors, won the bid. Her husband, Brendan Taylor, will find himself as a character in these pages setting up a boutique distillery.

This book required research on a range of topics including child welfare, life coaching, aid work, water projects, mental health, eco-grief, climate change technologies, dementia, DNA, pathology and police procedures. I appreciate everyone who took time to answer my questions, in particular: Davina Park, Karen Dixon, Sam Chaffey, John Nell, Laura Prickett, Kerryn Mayne, Jessica Dettmann, Kate Dean, Amy Johnson, my brother and sisters. (Cheers to Katherine Collette and Joanna Nell for putting me in touch with the right people.)

There are all different types of families, and I love my book family! After releasing *The Good Teacher* during the pandemic, it was absolutely joyful to go to bookshops and libraries for *The Liars* and meet with readers and booksellers. Many thanks to you all, and to Laura and Bec from Allen & Unwin for organising my tour.

The fabulous team at Allen & Unwin are with me every step of the way from editing the manuscript to promoting the book. My wonderful publisher, Annette Barlow, and expert editors, Christa Munns and Ali Lavau, provided suggestions to help me create the best version of *The Last Trace*. To Matt Hoy, Mary-Jayne House and the sales team, thank you for taking my books out into the world and into the hands of booksellers.

Numerous friends and family read the manuscript at various stages. Christina Chipman and Ber Carroll, I always appreciate your insights and support. Thanks to Ashley Kalagian Blunt, Theresa Miller, Nicole Davis, Caz Hardie, Sha McGovern,

Angus Chaffey, Jeremy Nicholson and Krishaa Tulsiani for your helpful feedback. My fellow graduates from the UTS Master's program also read a few early chapters: Cameron Stewart, Zoe Downing, India Hopper and Louise Sinclair. It was serendipitous to be invited on a writing retreat in Monaro country as the book is partly set in the Snowy Mountains. Cheers to Trisha Dixon for having us at beautiful Bobundara, and to my fab fellow retreaters, Ashley Kalagian Blunt, Anna Downes, Rob McDonald and Josh Pomare.

Many thanks to my super-agent, Alex Adsett and her team. A shout-out to the Aussie writing community who are so supportive of each other, and special thanks to the Not So Solitary Scribes for the Friday chats.

To my closest family: Jamie, I'm appreciative of your endless support and incredible cooking all the time, but especially when I'm in editing mode and need to keep my head in the story. Tia and Jeremy, thanks for answering questions about teenagers and for being my biggest cheerleaders. Here's to you two getting all the best bits of our DNA and a cleaner planet.

HIGH RISK

Climbing to Extinction

HIGH RISK

Climbing to Extinction

Brian Hall

Foreword by
Joe Simpson

SANDSTONE PRESS

First published in Great Britain in 2022 by
Sandstone Press Ltd
PO Box 41
Muir of Ord
IV6 7YX
Scotland

www.sandstonepress.com

Editor: Robert Davidson

ISBN: 978-1-913207-82-3
ISBNe: 978-1-913207-83-0

Sandstone Press is committed to a sustainable future.
This book is made from Forest Stewardship Council ® certified paper.

Cover design by Ryder Design
Typeset by Iolaire, Newtonmore
Printed and bound by CPI Group (UK) Ltd, Croydon, CR0 4YY

For Louise

and in memory of:

Sam Cochrane
John Syrett
Alex MacIntyre
Mike Geddes
John Whittle
Roger Baxter-Jones
Georges Bettembourg
Pete Thexton
Joe Tasker
Paul Nunn
Alan Rouse

and too many more.

'Are you oblivious to the sufferings of birth, old age, sickness and death? There is no guarantee that you will survive, even past this very day! The time has come for you to develop perseverance in your practice. For, at this singular opportunity, you could attain the everlasting bliss of nirvāna. So now is certainly not the time to sit idly, but, starting with the reflection on death, you should bring your practice to completion!

'The moments of our life are not expendable, And the possible circumstances of death are beyond imagination. If you do not achieve undaunted confident security now, what point is there in your being alive, O living creature?'

Padmasambhava, *The Tibetan Book of the Dead*

CONTENTS

LIST OF ILLUSTRATIONS

BLACK AND WHITE

1. Introduction: Brian Hall in the Yorkshire Dales, 1976. (John Sheard)
2. Al Rouse after soloing *The Boldest*, 1969. (Leo Dickinson)
3. Sam Cochrane recovering after the car accident in 1971. (Cochrane family)
4. John Syrett at the base of Malham Cove in the early '70s. (Mike Mortimer)
5. Alex MacIntyre getting ready to climb *Cave Route*, Goredale, winter '72. (John Powell)
6. Mike Geddes, Piraňa Club meet, 1975. (John Sheard)
7. John Whittle relaxing while filming *Touching the Void* in Peru, 2002.
8. Roger Baxter-Jones on the walk in to Jannu, 1978.
9. Mélanie (aged eight) and Roger in Chamonix in 1983. (Christine Baxter-Jones)
10. Rab Carrington on the Jannu expedition, 1978.
11. Georges Bettembourg at Kanchenjunga Base Camp, 1979. (Doug Scott)
12. Pete Thexton at a Bhuddist monastery on the way to Everest, winter 1980.
13. Joe Tasker at Everest Base Camp, winter 1981.
14. Paul Nunn on Everest, winter 1981.
15. Alex MacIntyre at Leeds, early 70s. (Mike Mortimer)
16. Andy Parkin and Brian Hall bivouac on The Ogre II, 1982. (Paul Nunn)
17. Al Rouse in his tent during the last days of the K2 expedition, 1986. (Jim Curran)
18. Afterword: Fixed ropes on the Abruzzi Ridge of K2.

COLOUR PLATES

1. The author on a Piraňa meet in Yorkshire in 1975. (John Sheard)
2. Sam Cochrane on *Main Wall*, Gimmer Crag, the English Lake District in 1968.
3. John Syrett on *Early Riser* (E5 6a), Earl Crag, Yorkshire. (Bernard Newman)
4. John Syrett making the first ascent of *Joker's Wall* (E4 6a), solo, 1971. (John Stainforth)
5. John Syrett belays the author on *Midnight Cowboy*, Malham Cove, 1972. (Bernard Newman)
6. Tim Rhodes, Roger Martin, and Alex MacIntyre outside the Glen Nevis caravan (John Powell)
7. Al Rouse on *Erabus* (E3 5c), Tremadoc 1969. (Leo Dickinson)
8. Roger Baxter-Jones with the author and John Moore in the summit bivouac hut on the Badile, the Swiss Alps (John Stainforth)
9. Early '70s, Al Rouse and Choe Brooks at Snell's Field campsite in Chamonix. (Steve Arsenault)
10. Al Rouse below Mike Geddes on the *Croz Spur* in the Alpine winter of 1976.
11. Mike Geddes settles into his hammock on a winter ascent of Pointe du Domino, Mont Blanc Range.
12. The author climbing *Geddes's Gully*, Scotland, 1986. (Al Rouse)
13. Anglo-French Meet in Scotland with (l – r) Nick Donnelly, Alex MacIntyre, René Ghilini, Jean-Marc Boivin, Dominique Julien, Rainier Munsch, and Jean-Frank Charlet.
14. Alex MacIntyre on South Face of Agujo Nevada 3 (first ascent), 1979. (John Porter)
15. John Whittle and Dick Renshaw at Holyhead after cycling from Bangor to climb at Gogarth, mid-70s. (John Sheard)
16. Rab Carrington, the Burgess Twins, Al Rouse, Sue, Christine, John Whittle, Daphne, and the author in Rio Gallegos, Southern Argentina.

FOREWORD

There is a lot of death in Brian Hall's book *High Risk*, but it is far from a grim read. There is also great joy in these pages. It is a wonderful portrait of a generation achieving great things in a very particular style. Brimful of excitement, ambition and fun, it is peopled by remarkable characters living constantly on the edge of disaster. Brian Hall has done them a great service, although he left me filled with nostalgia and an uneasy sense of loss, wondering whether it was all worth it.

The attrition was truly appalling. It has been said that the cream of British mountaineering was wiped out in the eighties and, having lived through that period, I can attest to that. In his introduction, as lucid a credo as I have ever read, he outlines the devastation on K2 in terms of sheer numbers. He also suggests, correctly in my view, that his generation pushed the boat of risk out further than others, before or since, in pursuit of a purity of style that, in fact, changed everything.

To present this fact may have been Brian's primary intention but *High Risk* is much more than an examination of death statistics. It is about characters, experiences, friendships, and paths through life. It tells the story of an extraordinary group of mountaineers in the golden age of alpine style climbing in the Greater Ranges, when mountaineering radically changed, moving away from big beast, siege expeditions to answer Reinhold Messner's clarion call for lightweight, small team, climbing.

Doug Scott stepped away willingly, as did Chris Bonington, but it was the next generation that really forced the routes. Pete

Boardman, Joe Tasker, Alex MacIntyre, Brian Hall, Rab Carrington, Roger-Baxter Jones, Georges Bettembourg and Al Rouse made iconic ascents on Kanchenjunga, Nuptse, Jannu, K2, and the West Ridge of Everest. The list of ascents, failures, epics and amazing adventures goes on and on.

It was a free-wheeling anarchic lifestyle of obsession, ambition, damaged relationships (and minds), hard partying and hard climbing, and my generation, a decade later, tumbled happily in its wake. My hopes and ambitions crashed and burned on my very first trip, but many others carried on, eventually reining back on altitude in favour of hard technical ascents in the six thousand to seven thousand metre range. Here, Mick Fowler and Paul Ramsden carried the banner with a list of incredible first ascents.

Each chapter in *High Risk* acts as a standalone memorial to one of eleven climbers, but the book's back-and-forth in time provides a wonderful insight into the way that generation lived and died. Brian, thankfully, survived, to gift us this lyrical, heartfelt commemoration of a mountaineering era and the climbers who changed their sport.

I've known Brian for nearly forty years: partied with him, worked with him, and attended too many wakes with him. When I first came to Sheffield at the beginning of the eighties he, along with Al Rouse, Paul Nunn and Rab Carrington, were inspirational mountaineers whose ascents I'd followed avidly. Suddenly I found myself drinking with them in Sheffield pubs. There was a huge inclusivity in this climbing scene. At any party Paul Nunn could be found in deep conversation, dispensing wisdom to young rock stars like Andy Pollitt, Ben Moon or Jerry Moffatt, with Don Whillans in a corner, teaching Johnny Dawes hard lessons in etiquette.

There was no sense of separation, of arrogance or superiority. There were no generational boundaries, and advice was freely given. More information and vital contacts could be garnered in one night than could ever be gained from the Alpine Club library. Simon Yates and I did exactly that, gleaning all we needed from Rab, Al and Brian who pointed us in the direction of Siula Grande.

'Watch out for the rock fall, it was bad,' Rab warned. Off we went and the rest is history.

The loss of Paul Nunn stunned me. I think many of us made the mistake of thinking he was indestructible. Quite a few of us quietly braced ourselves when others departed, knowing the probability of some not returning was high, but never with Paul. He had been everywhere, done everything and seemed to know everything. His wily, shrewd judgements made him the safest of climbers, but he and Geoff Tier were overwhelmed by a massive icefall while descending from the summit of Haromosh II. At the age of fifty-two, halfway through his stint as President of the British Mountaineering Council, he was gone. If Paul could be wiped out so easily, any of us could.

Reading Brian's account, I was astonished by his young age, as he seemed to have lived forever. Later in the book I was equally astonished to learn that his great friend and mentor, Tom Patey, was only thirty-eight when he died. Both these men packed so much into their years it seemed that they had been around for lifetimes.

Everyone had plans, expeditions organised, trips on the go. There was a constant churn of people setting off and returning, but sometimes not returning. We lived in a febrile atmosphere, full of nervous excitement, buzzing with energy. Pushing boundaries in the Himalayas and the Karakoram, we thought we could do anything. We were immortal, awash with youthful arrogance. This insane confidence was inherited from Brian's generation, who had shown the way. Off we went to the mountains, but we also went to an awful lot of memorial services.

Each generation pushes on to new heights, advances in equipment raising technical standards year on year. Protection on ice climbs in their heyday was dubious at best, when to place three ice screws on a fifty metre frozen waterfall required the energy to power a small city. Climbers today could happily put in ten. Heightened fitness, training and psychology all play their part and today the leading climbers put up ascents thought impossible barely a decade ago.

The 1970 British Annapurna South Face expedition was the first

Himalayan climb to take a deliberately difficult route up the face of an eight thousand metre mountain. After fifty-eight days Don Whillans and Dougal Haston reached the summit of Annapurna I which, at 8,091 metres, is the highest peak in the Annapurna massif. It was a massive advance in Himalayan climbing, as was the South West Face of Everest expedition five years later. Chris Bonington led the team, using advanced climbing techniques to put fixed ropes up the steep South Face. Apart from all else, such expeditions were difficult to finance.

By the 1980s though, speed and lightweight tactics had blown away the era of heavyweight siege expeditions. In 1986 Swiss climbers Erhard Loretan and Jean Troillet, climbed through the night, alone, up and down Everest's North Face in an astounding forty-three hours. The next generation went even further with the young Swiss alpinist Ueli Steck soloing the South Face of Annapurna in 2013, completed in only twenty-eight hours. Brian Hall's generation, the climbers so fondly remembered in this book, built the bridge between the old and the new.

As his narrative draws to a close Brian assesses the attraction of risk to the young, and how it diminishes with advancing age and increased responsibility. However, his accounting of such psychological factors as post-traumatic stress disorder is even more illuminating and worth the price of this book on its own, as is his assessment of the circularity of physical and technical improvement with increased risk-taking. The risks don't reduce the more experienced you become. The fitter, faster and more skilled elite mountaineers simply become higher level risk takers. It was, and remains, a vicious circle in which the benefits that greater fitness and skillsets create may, at any time, be overwhelmed by objective dangers such as avalanches, crevasses, falling rocks and storms.

Mountaineering has always been a risky proposition and for the reasons given above is unlikely to change. However, Brian Hall's *High Risk* gives the clearest sense of the how and the why of this dangerous lifestyle and shows how his generation changed high-altitude mountaineering enormously but at a heinous price. It is a fascinating and poignant account of tumultuous times. As

Syd Marty, the Canadian mountain poet, wrote in his poem 'Abbot':

> *Men fall off mountains because*
> *They have no business being there*
> *That's why they go, that's why they die*

Joe Simpson
2022

Brian Hall in the Yorkshire Dales, 1976.

INTRODUCTION
What Happened to All my Friends?

Imagine putting one bullet into a six-shot revolver, spinning the chamber and putting the cold steel barrel on your temple. Breathe slowly and think your last thoughts and then, if you're both brave and stupid, pull the trigger. You have a one in six chance of killing yourself.

During a dozen expeditions to the Himalayas between 1976 and 1986, I tied on a rope with twenty-four individuals of whom seven were killed in the mountains. A further four died of natural causes or by their own hand. In simple terms, I had roughly the same chance of dying while mountaineering as I would have had playing Russian Roulette. As to why I continued climbing, death after death, I hope this account will answer that question.[1]

The three million soldiers who fought at the Somme in 1915, the bloodiest battle in history, suffered the terrible death rate of one in ten. British Bomber Command lost 44.4 per cent of its aircrew flying missions in the Second World War. Of the sixty-eight members of the English Fell and Rock-Climbing Group who fought in the First World War, nineteen did not come back and many more were injured or maimed for life. However, those brave soldiers, sailors and airmen had little choice.

The death toll in the 1980s on each of the world's fourteen highest peaks makes uncomfortable reading. For every three climbers who reached the avalanche-prone summit of Annapurna, one died. On the precipitous slopes of K2, it was approximately one

1. To calculate the statistics, a population of forty-two climbers were involved because some people came on several of the expeditions. Seven died in the mountains, with one of those deaths occurring after 1986.

in four. On Everest, one in seven. Mountains do not judge. We are not at war with them and, when we reach their summits, we have not conquered them. Their challenge is in our minds, and the risk is of our own making. If high-altitude mountaineering was a mainstream sport, it would surely be banned or heavily regulated.

Trawling the Himalayan Database,[2] I became convinced that proportionately more of my generation of mountaineers died during the '70s and '80s than in the decades before and after.[3] I wrote this book, at least partly, to understand why we suffered so many deaths proportionally. Were we a one-off blip on the graph of life or part of a cyclical pattern? More than likely it was a combination of factors including the style in which we climbed, what we climbed, our attitude and possible addiction to risk, our level of fitness and the amount of time we devoted to it. No doubt, some were simply terrible examples of bad luck.

A few years back, I gazed out of my upstairs office windowpane at a typical October day in the English Peak District. Gritstone walled fields spread across the hills. Flocks of sheep grazed peacefully. On the moorlands above, the heather had lost its purple bloom.

I picked a photographic slide from a box marked ''70's Various' and slotted it into our digital scanner. An electronic clunk followed, and a whirring noise, before my computer screen slowly came to life and revealed an image. It was a group of mates from way back, all long-haired and wearing multicoloured flowered shirts and outrageously flared jeans. Slugging beer from pint glasses, suspiciously large cigarettes between their fingers, they could have been at a fancy dress party.

Another slide revealed a young man with a beard and long blond hair sprouting from beneath a top hat, standing one-legged on a pile of ropes while putting his boots on. It was me, and I was

2. The Himalayan Database (Himalayas by Numbers) is founded on the meticulous records kept over four decades by the late Kathmandu based journalist, Elizabeth Hawley.

3. Figures in the Database for Members on Nepalese peaks over 6000 metres climbing above Base Camp (not hired staff) 1950–1989: 12,480 / 324 deaths at 2.6 %. 1990 – 2019: 41,945 / 418 deaths at 1 %.

transported back to my coming of age in the post-hippie and punk era, part of a bunch of free-spirited and like-minded guys whose only aim in life was to go to remote places and climb. Always broke, we drank, partied, and played music too loud. We slept on floors and hitch-hiked everywhere. Most of us were students but we wanted this laid-back lifestyle to continue rather than to ever settle down to a proper job.

'Cup of tea?' came a shout from Louise, my wife.

'I'll be down in a minute,' but I was already thinking that it might be time to remember my eleven friends who are no longer alive. To put their stories down in writing before my recollections disappear. Who were they, and why they were so important to me, and to the history of mountaineering?

We are better at remembering the retelling of our experiences. Each time we talk about an event, we solidify that retelling as the memory itself.[4] All those nights I spent in bars, chatting and reminiscing about past days, have no doubt resulted in a heavily edited memory. While researching this book, I've enjoyed a fantastic and revealing journey when talking to my contemporaries, delving into old diaries and looking at photographs. In writing it, I have tried to let the story tell itself.

As a youth, I avidly read about the exploits of famous mountaineers such as Chris Bonington, Riccardo Cassin and Walter Bonatti. Stories of surviving lightning storms while hanging off vertical walls above immense glaciers or stepping triumphantly onto a summit after many days of struggle. These paladins of the climbing world were gods to me, and their routes were unattainable dreams.

When visiting the Alps for the first time in 1970, I gained an inkling of what they had endured. I was just nineteen when I pitched my tent on a clean and peaceful campsite in the Bregaglia, in southern Switzerland. The following day, accompanied by John Stainforth, my Leeds University climbing partner, we left the manicured green valley, walking through conifers to the edge of an alabaster coloured glacier to sleep under a huge boulder. As the dawn sun rose, we climbed up crisp snow, ice axes in hand, the

4. Corinne Seals, Applied Linguistics, Victoria University, Wellington, NZ, Stuff N.Z. Feb 2021).

view changing with every step. This was what we had come for, to reach a high summit, and it seemed remarkably simple, logical and enjoyable. The weather was perfect, nothing bad had happened, and I became hooked on alpine climbing.

After more routes, another friend from the University climbing club arrived, Roger Baxter-Jones (RBJ). He suggested we do a route together.

'How about the North East Face of the Badile?'

'The Cassin route?'

'Yep. It's one of the six classic North Faces of the Alps.'

Stainforth agreed before I had a chance to say no. I spent a sleepless night, but we climbed the twenty-two pitch climb graded *Très Difficile* in five hours, much faster than guidebook time, and straight after drove to Chamonix to meet up with more friends. I pitched my tent next to my mate and fellow student Alan (Al) Rouse, who sat idly amongst bottles from last night's party. Mick Jagger's voice blared from his cassette player, and the smell of weed drifted in the air. Ice axes and ropes lay ignored, but ready for the next climb. I looked around at the close-knit community and recognised the faces of famous climbers from photographs in magazines.

'How about climbing the Dru?' RBJ suggested.

'Isn't that hard?' I replied, looking at the thousand-metre needle piercing the sky above the campsite.

'It is, but let's try the Bonatti Pillar. It's the best route on the mountain.'

'You must be joking . . .'

He wasn't, and the next day I toiled my way up to the Charpoua refuge, feeling out of my depth. We were preparing our bivouac among some nearby boulders when the warden shouted. 'Come, sleep inside.'

'We have no money.'

'You climb Bonatti? C'est libre.'

It took three days up and down, bivouacing on tiny ledges, and an intense lightning storm drenched us on the glacier as we descended. I learnt a lot that season, particularly about the oxymoron of enjoyable danger.

At that time, in 1970, the British magazine *Mountain* was full of news from the Himalayas. *A team led by Chris Bonington reached the summit of Annapurna I (8,091 metres) after climbing the massive South Face.* The expedition included nine of Britain's best mountaineers, a base camp manager, a doctor and a four-person film crew together with six high-altitude Sherpa porters. Three hundred and eighty porters carried tons of gear to Base Camp, with 5,500 metres of rope for fixing, forty cylinders of oxygen and six breathing sets. Here was a scale and complexity that I could hardly grasp, with a level of costs that requires commercial sponsorship.

It was apparent from the article that the lead climbers slowly pushed the route out over some of the most challenging climbing ever done at altitude. Ropes were fixed between six camps that were provisioned so the team could survive on the face. It was structured as a logistical pyramid and planned with military precision. The siege continued for fifty-eight days until Don Whillans and Dougal Haston reached the summit, but tragedy struck as the team evacuated the mountain. A serac collapsed, killing Ian Clough, further fuelling the newspapers, which treated the expedition as a triumph of British skill and bravery. I began to understand the big difference between Alpine and Himalayan climbing.

That autumn, back from the Alps, the Leeds climbing club members were enjoying rock climbing on the local cliffs. The dedicated climbers were becoming stronger and more skilled by training on the University's unique climbing wall, which enabled success on new ascents while eliminating the need for artificial aids like pitons and bolts. Using aids makes a climb easier and safer and the outcome more certain, but reduces the level of adventure. We viewed such ascents as inferior and done in a poorer style – even as cheating.

For us, the style by which we climbed was becoming more important than reaching the top, even though, at that time, the concept of style was hardly considered in the Alps and Greater Ranges [5]. For example, on our ascent of the Dru, we had pulled on every peg available to help with speed and efficiency. In the Himalayas,

5. The Greater Ranges comprise the high mountain ranges of Asia, including the Himalayas, Karakoram, Hindu Kush, Pamirs, Tien Shan. However, some people also include the Andes, Rockies and the Alaskan mountains in this definition.

heavyweight expeditions used all manner of aids such as fixed ropes, supplementary oxygen and high-altitude porters.

A groundbreaking article, written by American Lito Tejada-Flores called 'Games Climbers Play' (Sierra Club Journal *Ascent 1967*), illuminated the different styles by dividing climbing into a series of games of escalating risk and complexity. He described the *bouldering* game and worked his way through various *rock* and *ice*-climbing games before reaching the *alpine* game. By the time I read this I had played all these games, and understood that a three-metre boulder was safer and needed a lot less equipment and organisation than, say, a long rock or ice route on Ben Nevis. Bigger and more serious again were the alpine routes, with crevassed glacial approaches, vicious storms and remote summits. The further and higher we went into the mountains, the more the activity's complexity increased, with a corresponding rise in the number of things that could go wrong.

I was intrigued by the top two games on the list, where Tejada-Flores compared the *heavyweight (or traditional) expedition* game to the *super alpine* game. These last two games describe the style used when climbing in the Greater Ranges. I could easily understand how Bonington's undertaking on Annapurna was categorised as heavyweight expedition style, but was interested to read that the style I had used during that first season in the Alps was now being seen in the Greater Ranges. This would obviously make expeditions easier to organise and save money.

Climbing and mountaineering differ from other sports in that there are no rules or referees, just a series of styles and ethics overseen by consensus. Honesty is key. At its heart, climbing is a culture rather than a competition.

Reinhold Messner, the most globally renowned mountaineer of that time and the first to climb Everest without supplementary oxygen, gave a succinct explanation. 'Climbing and mountaineering have never been sports. They are adventures with a level of danger and an uncertain outcome.' As the climbing style moves from the rock faces to the high mountains, there is an increase in the level of risk. Very few people die while climbing at the indoor gym, whereas there is a significant death toll in the Himalaya.

Fast forward to today, and the aim of most elite climbers is to make an ascent in the best style, using only the minimum of aids. Solo climbing is the purest and most dangerous style, reserved for a few individuals prepared to risk an ascent made alone, usually without a rope for protection. Predictably solo climbing has a high death rate.

Anatoli Boukreev, the acclaimed Kazakhstani mountaineer, echoed this ideal in his book *Above the Clouds*. 'Mountains are not stadiums where I satisfy my ambition to achieve; they are the cathedrals where I practice my religion.' Tragically his style was no defence, and Boukreev died in an avalanche on Annapurna in the winter of 1997.

The heavyweight expedition style served mountaineering well, with a tidal wave of first ascents from 1950 with the French ascent of Annapurna, the first of the eight thousand-metre summits to be scaled. By 1964 all fourteen of the world's eight thousand-metre peaks had been climbed, including Everest by the British in 1953 and K2 by the Italians a year later. In 1975, a watershed between the demise of heavyweight style and the rise of alpine style was established when Chris Bonington led the successful bid to climb Everest's South West Face. This expedition was on an even grander scale than his Annapurna effort five years earlier.

One of the summiteers, Pete Boardman, observed, 'For a mountaineer, surely a Bonington expedition is one of the last great imperial experiences life can offer.'

Nevertheless, these big, traditional expeditions were not immune to accidents. Most famously, Mallory and Irvine on the British Everest expedition in 1924, and the tragedy on Nanga Parbat in 1937 when nine Sherpas and seven Germans were engulfed in a single avalanche. More recent examples include the infamous Everest tragedy in 1996 when eight died in a vicious storm, albeit on a guided ascent (described in Jon Krakauer's book *Into Thin Air*), and the 2008 K2 debacle when eleven perished because an ice cliff avalanched and wiped out their fixed ropes.

In my office, I opened a cardboard box lying in the corner. It was labelled 'Expeditions' and inside, packed tightly together, was a stack of files, each marked with an expedition dating from 1976 to 1986. When I began leafing through the papers, diaries and photos, memories flooded back from Jannu, Nuptse, Everest, K2 and more. With our passion and drive we attempted to raise the standards of climbing in the United Kingdom, before transferring our skills to the longer climbs of the Alps, which in turn would give us the confidence to progress to the Andes and Himalayas. Following that path, we hoped to change high-altitude mountaineering from heavyweight expeditions to alpine style ascents.

Looking through those notes from my first trips to the Himalayas, I remembered how the older guard of expedition climbers formed a virtually impenetrable clique. Hence, as a new generation of alpinists, we had to go our own way. Staring at a picture with a bold red line drawn up the blank face of a distant snowy peak, my mind went back to a dimly lit room in Sheffield where we pored over images of the Himalayas, paper and pen at the ready, planning and dreaming of our next crazy objectives. We were having the time of our lives, and climbing was all we lived for.

In the mid-'70s, this adoption of the alpine style in the Greater Ranges was nothing less than a revolution. Speed and nimbleness over difficult ground opened new possibilities on the steep virgin walls of high peaks. As part of this new breed of mountaineers, I convinced myself that alpine was safer because the zones of avalanches and stone fall had to be negotiated just once and less time would be spent at high altitude. The bare numbers were persuasive. For example, two alpine style climbers on a seven-day ascent were exposed to fourteen climber-days of the mountain's dangers, while ten people on a heavyweight expedition over thirty days were exposed for three hundred climber-days.

We rejected the use of oxygen bottles and fixed ropes on ethical grounds, which in any case were too heavy to carry in a single push. Fast and light was our mantra, and ascents could and had to be made in days rather than weeks as the weight of food and fuel that could be carried was limited. However, the term lightweight was a misnomer as most alpine climbers carried cripplingly heavy loads, even when the overall expedition was classed as small scale.

Because rescue was virtually impossible, ascents required a high measure of commitment, and typically the team would stick together in success or failure, significantly heightening the experience of the adventure. Small expeditions also had a much lower environmental impact than large expeditions which, sadly, often left their fixed ropes in place and abandoned their camps, littering the slopes.

Voytek Kurtyka, the Polish sage of this style, wrote, 'It became clear to me that alpine style is a higher form of the mountaineering art, not only in its sporting aspect but also in human terms because through it you can experience the mountain world more intimately and deeply.'

Despite the growing popularity of alpine style, we accepted that heavyweight *style* had some advantages with a slow ascent allowing more time for altitude acclimatisation. It also permitted one group to rest or recuperate while another party pushed the route further up the mountain. In addition, the support of fixed ropes and the shelter of camps helped in poor weather and provided an escape route at the end of the expedition or in emergencies. Using supplementary oxygen is a considerable benefit above eight thousand metres but this can only be carried within the structure of a heavyweight expedition. To ensure success, it continues to be used on commercially guided expeditions, where long queues of bottle carrying climbers can be seen near the summit of Everest.

From my office filing cabinet, I selected a blue folder marked 'Magazine Articles' and pulled out a faded photocopy of an obituary, then another, and another. Throughout the '70s, our alpine style ascents in the Greater Ranges had been successful and mostly without tragedy. Sadly, by the early '80s, accidents started to happen with concerning frequency, demonstrating that our approach was not as safe as we had thought. So many of my friends had died, most in the mountains.

A line jumped out at me: *the generation that climbed themselves to extinction*. That was my generation, and I was one of the survivors. Forty years later, at home on that autumn day, I questioned: 'Why did we face the risks of mountaineering?'

Answering this could be key to understanding the deaths of

many of my friends. In the arrogance of our youth, buoyed and perhaps blinded by our triumphs, we had no sense of our own mortality. Ignoring the warning signs with a flippant, *it will never happen to me*. Genetically programmed to take risks, we had a sense of invincibility. One thing was clear, we were intoxicated and addicted to the feeling of going into the danger zone and coming out unscathed. That was at the heart of why we kept climbing. The mountains gave us no choice.

Staring at the moorland outside my office window, I remembered the words of my mate, Al Rouse, aged nineteen, after soloing a challenging rock climb called *The Boldest*, where the slightest slip would have plunged him to his death. 'Fifteen minutes on the Thin Red Line is worth an awful lot of ordinary living.'

Mountaineering did not pass through this period in isolation. The 1970s was a time of rapid change in society, when it became acceptable to live the alternative life of a climber rather than have a normal job and family routine. I was raised in a post-war world of turmoil when prosperity was growing. Car ownership was increasing, and the Jumbo jet heralded the start of foreign travel for the masses. Students, and youth in general, gained power, and the long-neglected equality of the sexes became a priority. Anti-Vietnam War demonstrations and race unrest spread across the Atlantic to Paris and the rest of Europe. Music tastes changed from the Beatles and the Stones to Pink Floyd, the Sex Pistols, and Disco. Beer and marijuana were supplemented by wine and pills. These cultural changes encouraged a pattern of anarchistic behaviour and counterculture tastes.

Not surprisingly, climbing changed too. The glue of climbing clubs whose members shared transport and hut accommodation began to dissolve, and climbers operated more independently. Before the mid-'70s, visiting the Greater Ranges was a complex process, and when expeditions ventured to India and Nepal travel was overland or by sea. Additionally, social and economic changes made it possible to climb globally, with geopolitics opening the borders to China and other mountain areas. In 1980 I could work for four months, save my earnings, jump on a plane with three mates and climb in the Himalayas.

Alpine style climbing fitted perfectly into this new world.

Before one asks why we took such high risks, perhaps the question should be why we started in the first place. I can only answer for myself. Attracted by the landscape of the Lake District near my home town of Kendal, I enjoyed the beauty and peace of walking amongst the hills and lakes with a group of school friends. The mountain tops were clothed in snow and ice in winter, so I had to learn how to use crampons and an ice axe. Before I knew it, I was using a rope to climb an icy gully and, soon after, I attempted my first rock climb. Hooked by the excitement, I swapped track running and kicking a ball around for the esoteric pastime of climbing, intrigued by the mental and physical challenges. I never made a conscious decision to climb.

Entering my 70th year, I wonder if anything unites the eleven climbers portrayed in this book. Indeed, do their life stories do anything to explain why we risked our lives? I like to think we were part of a unique movement whose collective achievements encapsulate the spirit of that time. A generation who, all too often, drove themselves until the ultimate price was paid.

This is no history lesson. Instead, it is a joyous and sometimes sad account of adventures with my friends and how we changed the style of climbing together.

My risk-taking days as a high-level mountaineer are long gone and, with older eyes, I look back on many of our actions as idiotic and unjustifiable. But viewing those pictures and unpacking those old boxes in my office took me back to an exhilarating and happy part of my life. It was a significant time in climbing and mountaineering, and my dazzling and outrageously talented companions deserve to be remembered. They left a legacy on which many of today's climbs are forged.

Before I share the wonderful adventures I had with my friends, I must first reflect on why my time as a high-altitude mountaineer came to an end.

© Leo Dickinson

Al Rouse after soloing *The Boldest*, 1969.

1

THE TIGER AND THE LAMB
Return to K2

After a long day's walk along the Goodwin Austin glacier, under the majestic 'Shining Wall' of the West Face of Gasherbrum 4, past the giant mass of the 8,051 metre Broad Peak we finally arrived at K2 Base Camp. It was Monday, 17th July 2000; a day still etched in my memory. The Base Camp was a sprawling village of small tents on the grey moraine-covered glacier. Above them, the vast ramparts of K2, the second-highest mountain in the world at 8,611 metres, christened the Savage Mountain, rose with menace.

Our small team, here to make a documentary film, started unpacking the bags when a familiar figure appeared out of a nearby, large, drab and torn canvas kitchen tent. Tall, skinny, with a mop of unkempt hair, Voytek Kurtyka, the Polish mountaineer, stared at me through intense steel-blue eyes.

'Ah, Brian, good to see you. It's been a long time.'

Then his posture changed. Instead of his usual direct manner, he looked at his boots, obviously uncomfortable. Finally, he raised his head, 'Brian ... Brian, we found your friend Alan Rouse yesterday.'

I suddenly felt weak and tasted bile in the back of my throat. I just stared back, and there was an embarrassing silence, which Voytek finally interrupted in his Eastern European matter-of-fact manner: 'We found him in avalanche debris on the way to Advance Base Camp. He must have been washed down from above the 'bottleneck'.'

Tears filled my eyes as I thought back to '86 when I had last been with my close friend Al. I was already on my way home from the expedition, with an injured knee, when he made the first British ascent of the mountain tragically disappearing in a storm as he descended from the summit.

'We buried him . . . but I think you must identify him. Perhaps tomorrow.'

Voytek broke my silent stare.

'We will dig him up in the morning.'

The acetazolomide (Diamox) pills I took to aid altitude acclimatisation also helped me get to sleep that night. Previously the side effects had been vivid and entertaining dreams, but tonight I had nightmares. Soon I was on a rollercoaster of torment; half-awake, half-asleep. A skull, half-covered in skin. Al's eyes. Oh no. They were bulging behind his black horn-rimmed glasses. Why are they bizarrely askew on his tattered nose? The skull again and again. I never saw the rest of his body, just this grotesque head. It kept repeating in a neverending loop. I tossed and turned in a cold sweat all night and woke up feeling spent. My head hurt, my face was puffed with altitude-induced oedema[1] and my mouth felt like sandpaper.

After a cup of sweet tea, I was just about capable of taking the short walk over to visit Voytek. But part of me was re-living this recurring horror. What would I see when we exhumed the body?

K2 had a reputation as the most challenging eight thousand metre peak to climb due to its steep, rocky slopes and the frequency of bad weather. Voytek, widely regarded as one of the world's top mountaineers, had not climbed it yet, and was driven by an obsession to complete a new route on the East Face, which would become his 'masterpiece on the planet'. I had met him first in his home country, Poland, back in the '80s and our paths had crossed on several occasions since. This season he was giving K2 one more try, with married Japanese climbers Taeko and Yasushi Yamanoi. I opened the flap of their kitchen tent and let my eyes adjust to the half-light. There before me was an orderly and relaxed base camp breakfast scene. Steam poured from a blackened kettle spout,

---

1. Oedema is a condition characterised by an excess of watery fluid collecting in the cavities or tissues of the body. Typically the symptoms of high-altitude sickness are life-threatening when it occurs in the lungs [Pulmonary] or brain [Cerebral].

balanced on a large paraffin stove in the middle of the icy floor. Immediately I was offered porridge and tea. I gratefully accepted, though my mind was still in a daze, as I sat down on a battered camping chair next to Voytek.

I tried to think logically. Al's death had been years ago, but I still thought about him all the time. Now all the sad memories overwhelmed me. Whether it was pride or simply embarrassment, I could not confide my confused mental crisis. Sipping tea with Voytek, Yasushi and Taeko as though nothing had happened seemed to increase my anxiety. Was Alan Rouse just another name on a long list of mountaineers who had died on the Savage Mountain? For them it was just the start of another day at Base Camp, whereas for me, the news was devastating. I first met Al in 1969, and we had travelled the world's mountains together till his death. He had been my closest friend.

It was Voytek who finally brought me back to reality: 'Should we go?'

'I suppose so.' I whispered.

'Should I take a picture?' the thought guiltily entered my mind, but I then realised I had left my camera in the tent. I had not considered any of the practicalities. Should I take something back to Al's partner, Deborah, and his family? Would people think it insensitive? As a mountaineer, I was not prepared for this situation.

We stood up, and Voytek waved dismissively to a small pile of dirty clothes and climbing gear in the corner of the tent.

'We found all that on the body.'

I took a step back. But I had to look. Slowly I sifted through torn clothing. I did not recognise anything as Al's. Then under the clothes, I spotted a large red expedition rucksack in remarkably good condition. I pensively noted the label 'Berghaus'. They were one of our sponsors back in 1986, and we had worked closely with the company designing a range of gear for our expedition.

'It must be Al.' I thought.

I looked again. The pack did not look quite right. I had helped design our 'Cyclops Expedition Pack', and surely it wasn't this model? I supposed that during the confusion of the horrendous epic of '86 that had taken so many lives, packs could have been swapped between climbers and it could nonetheless be Al lying in the new grave dug into the glacial moraine.

I opened the zip lid, and a box of matches fell out. I was about to put them back when curiosity overtook, and I carefully examined the box. On it was printed the date of manufacture; 1994. I showed this to Voytek, and our eyes met. We both knew immediately; the body was not Al's. The evidence proved that the climber who wore the rucksack must have died after the manufacture of the matches. Possibly it had been carried by one of the unfortunate three Ukrainian or five Spanish climbers who died during horrendous storms in '94 or '95.

I was on an emotional rollercoaster. Soon I felt more at ease as I realised that I had avoided the gruesome exhumation. But another thought struck me; this was a body of a climber just like me. Someone who had arrived at Base Camp excited, full of life and anticipation of climbing K2, yet a tragic accident had destroyed their dreams. Somewhere in a house in Spain or Ukraine on a mantelpiece would be a picture of a climber on top of a peak, and every day his proud wife, children, mum or dad would glance at the image and remember.

Tick. Tick. Tick. Tick, the massive, wobbling, fan on the ceiling only made the heat more unbearable. Three weeks earlier we had just arrived in Islamabad, and for the last three hours we had been in a meeting inside a Pakistani government office. The usually affable film producer, Mick, was sitting lathered in sweat with his shirt glued to his stocky frame. His pale face was glistening with beads of perspiration running from his receding hairline and down his high forehead. He had lost his patience. We had reached an impasse; they did not want us to film on K2. Sat opposite behind a large desk slouched the overweight Pakistani bureaucrat, with his jet-black, greased hair and weasel eyes he looked like a B list actor who played the henchman of a mafia boss.

'Let us meet tomorrow, and we can have another look at your proposal,' he announced curtly while closing the file. An indication that the meeting was at an end.

'What time should we come back?' sighed Mick.

Keith, the third member of our team, was first to stand up. Tall and wiry, dressed in shorts, sandals and tee-shirt, his dress code was at odds to the crisp white shirt of our officious host.

At the beginning of July 2000, I flew into Islamabad, accompanied by film producer Mick Conefrey together with my long-time friend and cameraman Keith Partridge. My role was providing safety and logistics while they filmed for a TV programme on K2 as part of a BBC2 series called *Mountain Men*. It was fourteen years since I was last in Pakistan as a member of a British expedition to K2. Sadly thirteen climbers died in different incidents that season of '86, including my close friend Al Rouse. Even before we reached the high Karakoram mountains, I was uneasy about returning as my last visit had ended so badly.

It was my fourth visit to Pakistan, and I was well aware of the endless bureaucracy necessary to gain a permit to visit the mountains. As K2 was close to the Indian and Chinese border, the Pakistanis were sensitive about people going there, particularly film crews from the BBC! Granting permission was aggravated by the high altitude conflict being waged on the Siachen Glacier between India and Pakistan. A war that started in 1984 and which still rumbles on today with both countries having a strong military presence on the mountain borders. Finally, on day three, Mick's negotiating skills endured, and we set off on the two-week journey to Base Camp.

Bad weather cancelled our flight from Islamabad to Skardu, so we squeezed into a minibus, piled high with camera and camping kit, for a rough two-day ride up the Karakoram Highway, through the region that was later to become the home of terrorist Osama Bin Laden. We stopped for a couple of days in the cool mountain air of Skardu, the Baltistan capital that is the gateway to the Karakoram mountains. The town sits in a broad fertile green valley formed by the Indus whose lazy, inky waters snake past the eighth-century fort. The haphazard streets were lined with white-walled Balti cafes and half-finished, breeze-block offices with iron rebar sprouting out of badly poured concrete. Corrugated iron and telephone wires prevailed while shocking green willow and poplar clung to the sides of polluted, litter-strewn irrigation ditches. It felt like a border town; though firmly Islam it was sprinkled with the salt of Tibetan Buddhists and the pepper of Kashmiri Sikhs.

As we drove to the roadhead in two battered open-top jeeps, we passed small villages that clung to the arid slopes. Apricot and almond groves surrounded the flat-roofed houses, creating a vivid emerald oasis irrigated by channels of cold water fed from the high glaciers. Eventually, we entered the gigantic Braldu Gorge framed by bare ochre-coloured cliffs, its deep channel riven by the foaming milk waters of the river. In years past the only passage through was via a narrow and dangerous path precariously cut next to the torrent. Since my last visit, a dirt road had been bulldozed precariously on the steep slopes high above the canyon. As I looked down at a sheer drop of five hundred metres from the back of the jeep, I wished I was on the footpath way below! I was primed and ready to jump out of the jeep as our wide-eyed driver wrestled with the steering wheel, narrowly avoiding the crumbling road edge as he manoeuvred across landslides partially blocking the road.

We spent the night below the small community of Askole. It was the last habitation before the mountains, and as it was at the limits of the crop and fruit tree growth, the inhabitants must have had a hard life surviving on their subsistence living. The local women, backs bent double, worked in groups, scything the rye in the small patchwork fields while their snotty-nosed kids dressed in tatters played happily around their feet. Men sat watching, smoking and idly chatting the day away.

Mohammed, the leader of the Balti porters, shouted and cajoled his fifteen locally recruited men with a one-toothed happy smile. He was dressed traditionally, in a shabby, earth-coloured shalwar kameez long shirt and baggy trousers. A Nating wool hat sat atop his swarthy face, skin creased like old leather. On his feet were a pair of shabby Converse baseball shoes, worn without socks and unsuitable for the ice and snow ahead. Wearing similar rags to their leader, these sturdy porters carried well over twenty-five kilos in hessian sacks slung on their backs, held by shoulder cutting thin hemp cord, trying to earn a pittance for their family.

We set off walking through Askole. A maze of narrow trodden earth paths wound between crude buildings made of stone, wattle and daub. Half of each house was underground, designed for months of cold winter solitude, and the whole place looked like an archaeological dig. Grain and apricots dried on colourful cloths on the low flat roofs. Women scurried into hiding behind veils, and wide eyes watched through small dark windows.

Gaining height, we left the fields behind and walked along small tracks through scrub and grass-covered glacial moraine. On the third afternoon, we arrived at Paiju and rested a day to acclimatise before the harsh icy barren glacier. It was a completely different place to the first time I passed through in 1980 when it was a pleasure to relax next to the small brook that fed the lush island of green-leaved trees and sweet-smelling grass. I was dismayed, as now there were only eroded terraces of sandy earth littered with abandoned charcoal fires, plastic bags and used toilet paper. It had become a squalid place due to overuse by trekking groups and climbing expeditions. We had only ourselves to blame, and it was the reason why the indigenous wildlife such as the ibex, bear and snow leopard struggled to survive.

I was looking forward to staying at Urdukas, our next stop. It was one of the most breathtaking campsites in the world, situated on a small verdant envelope above the lateral moraine wall of the Baltoro Glacier. Opposite rose a pronounced silhouette of jagged peaks, the Trango Towers, like the turrets of a giant's castle, sheer and bold, the highest rock wall in the world. Drenched in early evening light the surrounding snow was painted the colour of fresh butter.

Since my last visit, the military had placed a camp nearby. An evening breeze carried a pungent air of mule and human ordure heavily laden with overexcited flies. In an earlier era, the granite boulders by the camp had been a serene place, the playground of climbing icons Walter Bonatti and Don Whillans. I walked behind the boulders to find an easy way to the top, to gain a better view, but gave up when a human cesspit confronted me. Our porters started bedding down for the night in the damp, squalid caves under the boulders. I was ashamed to watch these groups of hardy folk, huddling around small fires made with twigs they had carried from Paiju, more like animals than men. Small rough woven, brown wool blankets were their only warmth. They were making dough balls of gritty flour, which they rolled flat to create chapatis cooked on a simple metal plate. A battered pan blackened by a lifetime of fires heated a weak vegetable broth. This was their dinner for the night – for every night.

'Hee-Haw . . . Hee-Haw'. The mountain silence was punctured by the nearby braying of pack donkeys as we arrived at Concordia, a remarkable confluence of glaciers. Their plaintive call came from the dishevelled military camp used as a staging post for carrying supplies to the battlefront. A small group of hollow-cheeked, malnourished young Pakistani squaddies huddled together outside a canvas tent; their heads bowed with high-altitude headaches. Were they dreaming of hot Punjab nights? Soon they would slog four days through the deep snow, up to the Conway Saddle, to fire on the Indian soldiers below. No doubt aware that frostbite, avalanches, bad weather and altitude-related illness had killed thousands of their comrades rather than enemy bullets! All this suffering while fighting an unknown war for an icy border that only politicians cared about?

At sunset, the clouds parted, revealing our first view of the distant and familiar outline of K2 in all its glory. Slowly the surrounding mountains changed, chameleon-like before our eyes. White to blue to yellow to orange then red. This raw evening theatre never ceased to amaze, but seeing K2 brought back memories and I had no appetite for dinner that evening. Later, in my tent, I had a splitting headache, and I could not sleep. I was tormented by the 1986 disaster, my mind full of questions with no answers. Somewhere on that lofty summit lay Al, entombed in ice, or so I thought?

Climbing in the Greater Ranges had given me so many good memories and close friends, and it still defined my life, but now the dangers seemed to outweigh the joy.

'Do I really want to be here?' I questioned.

It was mid-morning on the second day at Base Camp, and I was more relaxed knowing the mystery body that Voytek had discovered was not Al. Mightily relieved not to exhume the corpse, I left Voytek's kitchen tent and strolled back to our small camp. I joined

Keith and Mick who were busy getting their camera gear ready.

'Can you help me carry the tripod and camera gear?' Keith asked.

'Sure. Where are we going?'

'The Gilkey Memorial.'

I had forgotten we were doing this, and it was not exactly the most uplifting thing to do after trying to identify the dead climber's possessions earlier that morning.

The air was loud with the sound of ravens as we scrambled up a rocky promontory to the memorial, a mile away from Base Camp. Originally it was built as a memorial for Art Gilkey who died on the unsuccessful 1953 American expedition. In a heroic rescue attempt he was being lowered, after suffering an altitude-induced thrombosis of the leg, when an avalanche hit and swept him away. The memorial, was a large boulder obelisk, now shared with plaques and engraved tin mess plates commemorating all those who had died on K2's unforgiving slopes. These included epitaphs for friends: Nick Estcourt, who died in 1978, Al Rouse and Julie Tullis, in 1986, and Alison Hargreaves, in 1995. A tinkling sound of memorabilia moving gently in the breeze provided a haunting soundtrack to this sombre place.

Had I not found the box of matches I would be here with a spade and ice axe to re-bury Al. The practicalities were so removed from reality that I cannot comprehend how I could have coped with the exhumation. In a trance, flashes of the dream return; the skull, the eye and the horn-rimmed glasses. The images haunted me, but with a shiver, I came back to reality and noticed Keith filming. Although not religious, I felt affronted. It was a private place. Detached and withdrawn, I read Alison's epitaph.

Alison Jane Hargreaves 17th February 1962–13th August 1995

In what distant deeps or skies
Burnt the fire of thine eyes?
On what wings dare she aspire
What the hand dare seize the fire.

W Blake

Everest 13.5.85   K2 13.8.95

The 1995 American / British K2 Expedition

While Keith continued filming, I looked up 4,000 metres towards the top of the mountain hidden by boiling dark clouds. Then lower to the vast talons of black rocks scarfed with snow stretching to the rubble moraine of the Godwin-Austen Glacier speckled with the colourful dots of orange and yellow Base Camp tents. It would be no place for humanity up there today, yet Al, Nick, Allison and Julie were still resting up there, somewhere in their icy tombs.

The temperature plummeted as the sun disappeared behind storm clouds. We scrambled down the mound and inadvertently strayed from the path into a necropolis of rocks. It was a cold and grisly place as winter winds had uncovered body parts and we could occasionally glimpse a ripped climbing suit or an old boot. A sickly sweet putrid smell of the dead filled the air.

We had only planned to be at Base Camp for three days. For me, that was too long; I was consumed with unhappy memories and wanted to get out of this miserable place. But Mick wanted to get to Camp 1 and film at the foot of the Abruzzi Spur, the original ascent route of the Italians in 1954. So the next day we set off early, in menacing weather, over the glacier that skirts under the vast South Face. It was not a place to linger due to the threat of avalanches, and with trepidation, we quickly picked our way over snow and ice blocks that had fallen from high on K2.

Over to the right, in the snow, we noticed an unfamiliar dark shape, and when we investigated, our worst fears were realised. It was a body; more a torso with no legs, one arm and no head. What clothing remained was tattered and torn roughly woven cloth, the type our Balti porters wore. The skin was desiccated and tanned like thin hide pulled over the rib cage. We guessed we were looking at the remains of a local high-altitude porter who had died many years ago, higher up the mountain and who had recently been washed down by an avalanche. We decided to leave the body and when we got back to Base Camp tell the local high-altitude porters about our discovery. Without much conviction we carried on towards Camp 1 and filmed as much we could before cloud enveloped the slopes.

The next day we left Base Camp to start the long journey home. As I walked down the glacier, silently immersed in my thoughts, each step took me further from my life-defining passion of high mountain climbing. I smiled when I took my last step off the ice; overwhelmed by the first whiff of rich earth and grass, familiar, like a forgotten friend. The valley stretched below cloaked in green.

I realised that since Al's death in '86 I had been in denial, but these last few grim days on K2 had been a catharsis and confirmed that my risk-taking days in the high mountains were over. For the last fourteen years, I had lived in limbo, and a large part of me had wanted to quit high-altitude mountaineering. I was no longer a risk taker but could not admit it to myself. At home, I felt inspired and keen to continue, but as soon as I reached the high Himalayan peaks, my anguish began. Ironically, I still enjoyed climbing more than ever in the Alps as a mountain guide, visiting exotic locations working on film safety and sports climbing on sunny cliffs. As I strode off the Baltoro Glacier, my defining moment had arrived, and I remembered William Blake's words.

Did he who made the Lamb make thee?

Sam Cochrane recovering after
the car accident in 1971.

2

CHANCE OR FATE?

Simon Cochrane

For some time, I had been trying to meet up with Simon (Sam), my school friend and first climbing partner. Through my lax behaviour, I had lost contact with him. I must admit to a certain trepidation reconnecting, out of the blue, but found it fulfilling and cathartic after the first moves, swapping tales and remembering all those things the brain has hidden away in mysterious parts of the cranium. Eventually, Sam and I put together concrete plans to get together. He and his wife Carol would be staying at a holiday cottage in the Peak District, only a few miles from my wife, Louise, and I. With great anticipation, we planned a weekend to catch up on all those lost years. On 22nd August 2014, the Friday before the reunion, an email arrived from Carol.

Brian

There is no easy way to say this, but Sam died suddenly yesterday. I know no more at this point but wanted to let you know.

Carol

Sam was sitting in a chair after coming back from a run; a heart attack killed him instantly. Head in hands, I started to cry. At first, I felt guilty about all the missing years when we lost contact. We had a good time together, and there is no point in dwelling on what we might and could have done. When it's my turn to go, I hope it will be as fast and straightforward.

In the autumn of '69, I arrived at Leeds University with my best friend, Sam Cochrane. He was taller than me, six foot with a mane of blond hair, a pale complexion, bright blue eyes and a wicked sense of humour. We had grown up together and sat in the same lessons at

Kendal Grammar School. Our friendship allowed me to get away from my middle-class home life, which was an emotional trial, continually arguing with my domineering and bigoted father. Dad ran his own small organ building business and had an outlook from a past generation. Ruling our household with an iron fist, he verbally abused both my lovely mother Kathleen, and me. He succeeded in destroying my self-confidence, even forbidding me, as a teenager, to see girls! I understand now that my parents must have been trauma-tised by the war, making them cautious, frugal and overprotective of their children. Whenever possible, I escaped to Sam's house, where we spent hours listening to the Beach Boys, the Stones and the Beatles.

We were both sixteen when we were introduced to climbing by our maths teacher, Geoff Causey. Soon we were obsessed, and whenever we had free time, we would visit the crags. One sunny, early summer's day in the English Lake District, we attempted our first route independent of Mr Causey. An early morning bus took us from Kendal to Ambleside; from there we hitched the remaining fifteen kilometres to the Langdale valley.

Sam got the guide book out at the roadhead. 'I think the quickest way to the cliff is up the Band, that grassy buttress on the left.'

'I'll carry the rope.' We'd been saving months' of pocket money to buy our new, prized red rope.

Two hours later we arrived at the toe of a rambling pillar of rock interspersed with small ledges of grass and bilberry bushes.

'Do you think it starts here?' Sam asked, sweat dripping from his brow, and the guidebook open at the page describing '*Bowfell Buttress Climb*: a classic long mountain route, 350 feet climbed in seven rope lengths (pitches)'.

'I'm not sure. It all looks the same to me,' I replied nervously, still a novice at translating guidebook descriptions to the actual rock face.

'It looks steeper than I thought,' Sam voiced in concern.

Eventually, Sam led off up an open groove and into a chimney.

'I'm safe,' he shouted down from a large ledge, and I climbed to join him below the most challenging part of the climb, the crux.

'Who's going to lead the difficult crack,' I asked, concerned that neither of us were proficient at placing the borrowed slings and homemade 'nuts' to protect and make the climb safer.

'It's your turn to lead . . . you go,' encouraged Sam.

The rock was worn and polished from years of wear from climbers' boots. It looked slippery, but I felt confident, dressed for the part in my Hawkins walking boots, brown corduroy britches and checked wool shirt. As I got higher, the rope attached to my hemp waistline snaked down to Sam way below. A fall would have had severe consequences.

I am a climber now, I thought, feeling a powerful inner confidence, that as a boy, I had never felt before.

A few more pitches and we were scrambling to the top full of pride and joy.

Soon we bought our own climbing paraphernalia: rock slippers, helmet, nuts and slings and harness. Steadily we progressed to enjoying harder climbs, and imperceptibly it gave us belief in our independence as we grew into adulthood.

We made plans for our first holiday alone, and travelled to Scotland in a train with carriages divided into compartments pulled by a steam engine.

'You will be careful?' my worried mother asked. 'Here are some sandwiches for the journey.'

The campsite by the sea, in Glen Brittle on the island of Skye, was perfect and the imposing Black Cuillin range above felt like the highest mountains in the world. On our last day, we sat atop a lofty pinnacle called the Cioch. It was nine in the evening, and the sun was still in the west, an orange orb hanging over an oily sea. We were in heaven, and had both fallen in love with the mountains.

We left home at eighteen to the new soundtracks of Santana, Bowie and Hendrix. The news was dominated by the Cold War and the Prague Spring uprising, which triggered the first buds of change from behind the Iron Curtain. Martin Luther King and Robert Kennedy were assassinated, and the Americans were still embroiled in the Vietnam War with the recent launch of the Tet Offensive and the 'draft'. The British army was deployed in Northern Ireland and turned a problem into a crisis. And soon, half a million people would descend on a small village called Woodstock, to create what would become the mother of all music festivals.

Sam was more intelligent than me and could have gone to any

university he wanted. He chose Leeds. I was not a particularly
academic person, more practical and interested in sport. I got
average grades at school but by pure coincidence the only university
that would accept me for my chosen subject, Geography, was Leeds.
As soon as we arrived, we joined the Leeds University Union
Climbing Club (LUUCC). But Sam took academic life more seriously than me, and I saw him less and less on the climbing meets.
In that autumn of '69, I had no idea that the LUUCC would have
such a profound effect on my life. Little did I know that during
those first outings on the local Yorkshire crags, I was climbing with
a group of contemporaries who would change the face of British
(and world) mountaineering. The majority of my friends who I
remember in the pages of this book I met through that club.

The post-Second World War years had not been kind to Leeds,
the once-proud Yorkshire industrial conurbation of just under half
a million people. Victorian entrepreneurs founded a fine city on the
textile industry, which was now in irreversible decline, facing cheap
foreign competition. The university was a beacon of progress
surrounded by the once bustling and thriving red-bricked terraced
streets that had sadly fallen into decay; shabby, run down, covered
in grime from the coal smoke of the Industrial Revolution.

Even though I had a host of new climbing friends, I still kept in
contact with Sam. At the end of our second term at university, we
planned a trip to Cornwall for a short Easter climbing holiday.
Another club member, John Bassford, joined us; he could borrow
his dad's almost new Austin Cambridge car.

We arrived on the Cornwall coast in the dark and pitched our
tents in some confusion. Next day Sam, John and I climbed on the
warm granite sea cliff of Bosigran, then gulped down a campsite
meal before driving to the Gurnard's Head pub. The low ceilinged
Cornish bar was full of cigarette smoke, banter and loud music. A
group of locals hotly contested a raucous game of darts in the
corner.

'Another beer?' shouted Sam.

'No, I've had enough' . . . Sam waited . . . 'Oh go on just one
more,' I yelled above the noise.

Returning from the pub, the headlights of an oncoming car

blinded us as we rounded a corner. It was inevitable. At nineteen, we were reckless, and we had drunk far too much. John tried to swerve, but the road was narrow, bordered with large granite block walls typical of that part of the country. We hit the wall going too fast. There was a screech of crumpling steel. In 1970 cars had no seat belts and the impact catapulted me forward from the back seat, over the front seat. I don't remember much. I was in a swirling world of semi-consciousness, half out of the front windscreen with Sam trapped underneath me. Ominously there was no sound.

Flashing orange neon lights and the muffled echo of a siren was all I remembered as I went in and out of consciousness in the back of the ambulance. I woke in a bed, not knowing where I was. My head felt as though it had been cleaved with an axe.

Sam was in the next bed to me in Penzance hospital. His face bandaged like an Egyptian mummy. I probably did not look much better. The doctor reported that glass had slashed his face and seriously damaged one of his eyes. He had broken bones, but they would mend. Bassford had come off lightly with only bruised ribs from the steering wheel, which fortunately cushioned the impact. He had been discharged and came to visit us. Now he would have the embarrassing job of contacting our parents, to explain how and why their sons were lying in a hospital, and telling his father that he no longer had a car.

I had suffered a concussion, two black eyes and a sore, whiplashed neck. Thankfully I was discharged after a couple of days. Guilt-ridden at having pushed Sam through the windscreen, I caught the train back to my parents in Kendal. Sam was in a bad way, spending a lengthy spell in hospital and losing part of his vision in one eye. His face would remain criss-crossed with scars. He also suffered emotionally, with a change in his relaxed personality, losing his confidence and humour. His condition was so debilitated that he had to take a year out of university.

Nevertheless, we escaped with our lives. The RAC (Royal Automobile Club) calculated that 25 per cent of all deaths for the age we were at the time (fifteen to nineteen years old), each year, are caused by traffic accidents. Additionally, overall, men are three times as likely to die from a road accident in comparison to women. It was apparent that Sam was not only physically injured but had suffered mentally. Ten years later, in 1980, the medical profession defined post-traumatic stress disorder (PTSD). Research showed it most commonly affects soldiers. However, after serious accidents, anyone could suffer from this illness, including a quarter of all road accident victims. Symptoms include involuntary intrusive thoughts of the traumatic event, concentration deficits, sleep disturbance, irritability, and avoidance of risky activities that remind them of the trauma. Over the years, I have recognised these symptoms in both myself and others affected by mountaineering accidents. In 1984 I was hit by ice and knocked unconscious high on the Himalayan peak of Chamlang. I narrowly escaped with my life thanks to my companions who lowered me down the mountain for four days. In 1992 I was involved in an accident on the icy slopes of Mont Blanc du Tacul in the French Alps. One of my three clients tripped, pulling the other two off and with their combined weight, I was powerless to arrest the fall. We tumbled 350 metres down the slope, and the taut rope catapulted me over a crevasse. The clients were OK, but I hurt my neck. After both accidents, mental anguish, probably PTS, was more long-lasting than the physical injuries, and I did not climb for some time afterwards.

Through discussions with Geoff Powter, the highly accomplished Canadian mountaineer and psychologist, he explained the differences between PTS and the more serious disorder, PTSD and how we can relate these conditions to mountaineering accidents.

'We should be profoundly affected in this way. The (climbing) accidents are our chance to understand better the rules of the games we play and their consequences, which we don't always have when playing the games ourselves. We can too easily convince ourselves that we are safe, that it "wouldn't happen to me", but these are not always the most grounded truths. Sometimes we survive by the skin of our teeth, and by virtue of luck rather than by skill or good reason.

'So, when something traumatic happens, we recalibrate, sometimes so much, that it starts to seem insensible to go back out again. Perhaps that's good, clear thinking rather than disordered thinking.

'For example, not wanting to climb after your best friend dies climbing is not disordered, and could be diagnosed as PTS.

However, not being able to leave your house and go to work because of a contagious fear of any kind of death is technically what a PTSD diagnosis requires.'

Sam recovered from most of his injuries, though the accident impaired his sight in one eye, but I suspected he was mentally scarred for many years, probably by PTSD. With time he started to recover from his trauma. After University he and close friends Dick Crofts and Nigel Abbott decided they needed 'some serious adventures in serious places' and set off to cross Iceland on foot. Dick remembers, 'Sam really relaxed into post exam euphoria and on the trip, he was very happy. Nigel recalled their next trip to Morocco, 'We had what I would call a good *boys*' trip' from the Sahara to the high Atlas with lots of challenges produced by cheap overnight bus journeys, the remoteness of where we went, medical issues and of course the general need for student style economy as per that age!'

He never climbed again. After university, he married Carol and raised two daughters. He worked for the Coal Board, and when the pits closed, he became a school teacher in Leeds. We met only a couple of times during the intervening years, but I understood that he fully recovered from the car accident. We made a pact that on our 50th birthdays we would return to the Lake District and revisit our first climb on Bowfell Buttress. Our plans fell apart, so we vowed to do it on our 60th. I was busy working, and again we failed to meet. I was bewildered by how callous I could be; drifting apart from my best mates.

As boys, we had lived parallel lives. In youth, our climbing abilities were average, as was our appetite for adventure and risk. Over the next dozen years, I became a high-level mountaineer able to face elevated levels of apparent danger, and Sam appeared to be a contented and happy family man. I believe much of life is based on chance, or is it fate? Consider the space–time continuum of mathematicians, where the three dimensions of space and the one dimension of time give an incomprehensible, ever changing number of opportunities for us to make seemingly inconsequential decisions or take actions that will alter the outcome of future events.

I often wondered what would have happened if I, not he, had got into the front seat of that car in Cornwall.

John Syrett at the base of Malham Cove
in the early '70s.

3

SHOOTING STAR
John Syrett

Each October Leeds University students held a week of fundraising events for charities, called the *Rag*, which generally meant a lot of fun and parties. The *Rag* committee asked the climbing club (LUUCC) to organise a stunt. It would be fair to say this did not go as planned. The idea for the club's contribution to the *Rag* was to scale the two impressive spires on Leeds Civic Hall and hoist the large Leeds *Rag* 1970 banner between them.

Our clandestine operation started well. Four members of the climbing club, John Stainforth, John Syrett, Chas Macquarie and me, together with a non-climbing *Rag* committee member, were dropped off in a dark back alley at the bottom of the outer wall. Syrett climbed up a desperately slippery drainpipe to the third-floor roof, from which the two towers projected. He then dropped a rope to help the rest of us follow. The night almost ended prematurely when the chap from the *Rag* ran out of energy near the top of the rope. With his grip about to fail, Syrett heroically managed to grab him by the collar and with immense strength yank him onto our ledge, thereby rescuing him from a fatal fall. We were dressed in black and looked every bit like burglars. Inside our packs were crowbars (to create handholds by prising open the lightning conductors), ropes, pulleys, knives and the banner. Syrett and I were given the role of climbing the two towers while the other pair belayed and organised the ropes to hoist the banner. It was 2.00 a.m. on Saturday, and everything had been going to plan when someone must have seen us and phoned the cops.

John and I were part way up the towers, about twenty-five metres above the ground. Then a voice distorted by a megaphone split the silent night.

'POLICE! Stop and come down immediately or we'll send the dogs up.'

I looked down and saw a constable's head poking out of a window, helmet slightly askew. He was trying to manhandle a rather excitable Alsatian dog out of a third-story window onto a sloping slate roof. I could see the poor animal did not fancy the prospect at all. On the road below a fire engine screeched to a halt behind three police cars. Two piercing spotlights, which looked like they were last used in the wartime blitz, illuminated Syrett and me. We'd been busted.

The police must have assumed we were robbing the city jewels. The first wave of cops were confused by the situation, but soon someone of more intelligence had arrived and realised that dogs (nor the average policeman) had little experience of climbing, so they started to extend the ladder from the fire engine. With little chance of escape, we abandoned the stunt and surrendered.

We were ushered through a window, handcuffed and pushed down a grand, curved staircase with a gauntlet of police standing to attention along the bannister. At the bottom stood an elderly gentleman, the Lord Mayor, looking slightly out of place in a paisley dressing gown. Beside him was the smartly uniformed Chief Constable. The Chief turned to the Mayor and gruffly demanded, 'What do you want to do with these . . .' He paused a second before spitting out the loathsome word, 'STUDENTS?'

The erudite, and luckily for us, good-natured Mayor replied with a slight stutter, 'Let's just say . . . thi-this was an unfortunate s-s-stunt that went wrong.'

When I arrived at Leeds in 1969, I made many new friends, especially within the University climbing club. The 'two' Johns were my frequent companions on the Yorkshire cliffs.

John Syrett came to the University the year before me. He was born near Dartford but had lived with his parents in Newcastle upon Tyne since the age of twelve. As far as I could tell, he had never climbed before arriving at University. He was of average height, athletic build, a bush of black curly hair and haunting dark brown eyes, reflecting a sensitive yet somehow distant character. A shyness about his demeanour that strangers mistook for arrogance made him difficult to get to know. Syrett appeared to have only one set of clothes: flared jeans, brown suede desert boots, and a white shirt, which he wore every day, winter or summer, in the pub and on the crag. Wherever he went on foot was a race, at the pace of an Olympic speed walker.

John Stainforth started at Leeds at the same time as me. He had come from a South of England public school, and at first, I felt like a country bumpkin in his presence, having being brought up in a northern country town. He was very much a scientist: precise, punctual and steady. He spoke in long sentences without appearing to take a breath. A thatch of uncontrollable brown hair had to be continually pushed out of his eyes. Stainforth was already a much more experienced climber than I, as he had been to Switzerland where his parents had hired a guide to introduce him to alpine climbing around Zermatt. When he was seventeen he and his twin brother, Gordon, attempted the *Fiva* route on the Troll Wall in Romsdal, Norway, the highest rock wall in Europe. The one-day climb turned into a four-day epic, and they almost died. His survival gave him an air of confidence, of being older and wiser than me. Most important, he owned a yellow Mini, which would be our transport for the next few years.

My other close mates were five fellow geography students with whom I rented an old three-storey red-bricked terrace house. Like much of the student accommodation, it was on a rundown street in the Hyde Park area. It had been cheaply renovated with wallpaper already peeling from the walls, sink drains that leaked and windows that would not shut. The back of the house overlooked a Chinese takeaway whose extractor fan churned out sickly fumes day and night, which gave me a long-lasting aversion to Oriental cuisine. But we had our independence, and it became home for the next four years.

Life verged on poverty, subsisting on a student grant. There was one gas fire in the front room which we huddled around in midwinter, often wearing hats, gloves and outdoor jackets. Cooking was not our forte, and we used the cheapest ingredients, preparing mundane potato, rice or pasta dishes with a smattering of ketchup for flavour. Dirty dishes were piled high in the kitchen, which smelled of stale food and burnt fat. Slugs and snails paid nightly visits to our Lino floor, on which a fridge, devoid of food, cultivated green mould. There was no cash to feed the electricity meter for the hot water immersion tank. So it was only on special occasions that I endured a bath in cold water made more bearable by adding a kettle of boiling water. We mostly wore the same clothes each day, as clean clothes were a low priority, although we did visit the launderette once a month. Unsurprisingly our girlfriends refused to visit the house.

My roommate was Nick Parry, also a climber, who came from the Wirral, near Liverpool. He introduced me to his climbing partner, Al Rouse. We were all eighteen, but Al was still living at home, preparing for his Cambridge University entrance exams in maths. He was so intelligent he hardly needed to study, so he spent a lot of time visiting Nick in Leeds. Nick eventually lost interest in climbing, so Al began climbing with me. He was tall, skinny and broad-shouldered, with long brown hair, often tied with a bandana, which failed to stop hair flopping across his black horn-rimmed glasses. Even on hot days, Al wore an old red down jacket and ridiculously flared jeans with an incongruously neat silk cravat around his neck. It was the start of a close friendship, and he became the central figure in my life for the next fifteen years.

On Friday evenings, a group of LUUCC members met at the Fenton pub. Syrett, Stainforth and me, with two other close climbing friends, Bernard Newman and John Porter, lounged on the tattered burgundy, beer-stained seats at the back of the bar sipping our drinks. Midway through the evening, Al arrived after a five-hour hitch from Cambridge, where he had just gained entrance. He carried a large rucksack full of climbing gear and a rope over his shoulder. As usual, the conversation turned to climbing, with Syrett recounting his unconventional tale of how he started climbing. 'I came out of a martial arts class in the gym and walked down this strange corridor behind the squash courts. On the wall were pieces of rock sticking out of the brickwork, and holes chiselled at random in the mortar. I wondered what on earth is this?'

After taking a large swig of beer, he continued. 'A couple of days later I was walking down the same corridor, and I stopped and started to touch the wall. I was curious. Then this older guy came up to me and introduced himself. It was Don Robinson, a lecturer at the University, who explained he had built this "climbing wall" in 1964. He encouraged me to give it a try. So I did, and I've been hooked ever since.'

On bad weather weekends we spent our time sat in the pub, with most Saturday nights at a rock concert in the Union refectory. On Sunday we gathered at the climbing wall, invariably with hangovers that hindered our enthusiasm for climbing.

Coincidentally, we heard later about Robinson's reaction to the success of his indoor wall. 'I was indebted to Syrett because he was "proof of concept". He had never climbed before, yet after training on the wall, he went out and climbed on gritstone crags to a very high standard right from the start.'

An entirely new genre of climbing evolved from this chance meeting when Syrett's natural talent combined with Robinson's innovative thinking. Although climbers had been practising on outdoor walls and buildings since Victorian times, the Leeds indoor wall was regarded as the first in the world specifically designed for the purpose. By chance, Syrett had set a new paradigm in climbing. By modern standards it was primitive. It was little more than five metres high with a hard concrete floor and stretched to around twenty metres in length. It was used for 'bouldering', with no ropes, training to gain strength and improve technique. Over time many new indoor walls were built to a similar design, and soon their popularity turned into a revolution. Today it is the typical way to enter into the sport. Their use has evolved into an enjoyable and popular genre of climbing, to such an extent that indoor walls staged Olympic competitions, almost sixty years after Robinson's first wall.

Soon Syrett became obsessed with the wall and spent hours inventing new and ingenious problems using specific sequences of holds. Many of Syrett's problems were so demanding that nobody could repeat his feats. Within a year he became its master. He admitted, 'I go there most days; usually I'm the only one there'.

The wall, free to use for students and the public alike, became a social meeting point for Yorkshire climbers, particularly in winter when the crags were wet and daylight short. Typically, on a Tuesday evening, it was crowded, with a cacophony of shouts and instructions.

Put your foot there ... no a bit higher.
Where are you climbing on Saturday?
Can I have a lift to Almscliffe?
I've got an old rope for sale.

Syrett soon became integrated into the local climbing scene, even though he was hampered by glandular fever in his first year and he rarely ventured outdoors to climb. He had natural flexibility; his double-jointed limbs allowed him to make outrageous gymnastic moves. Undoubtedly, practising yoga, a regime seldom used at the time, enhanced his range of movement. At parties, he was always the best dancer, and he would duly amaze us with his incredible gyrations under a broomstick doubling as a limbo bar.

Al Rouse had a very different introduction to climbing. More conventionally, he started outdoors, following a traditional template of hillwalking, then rock and ice climbing, which eventually were a rite of passage for alpinism and expeditions to the Himalayas. As a schoolboy he visited a small, seven metre high, sandstone outcrop called the Breck almost daily, as it was a few minutes' walk from his family home in the Wirral. Just like Syrett's obsessive routine indoors, Al would typically be alone, bouldering unroped for fun and to hone his finger strength. At that time, the abilities of Rouse and Syrett were well ahead of the rest of the climbers at Leeds.

There was always a keen rivalry when these two got together. One particular piece of rock consumed our attention at Brimham Rocks, fifty-five kilometres north of Leeds. Regularly we squeezed into Stainforth's Mini, drove to the rocks, and stood and gazed at a large boulder with an unclimbed overhanging wall of perfect gritstone; a rough sandstone found in the Pennine spine of England. We christened it *Joker's Wall*. Stainforth and I eventually managed the start; however, the real battle was eight metres up, where gaining a small ledge required putting a foot in a horizontal crack by your ear then rocking up. This acrobatic move thwarted us at every attempt. Time, and time again, Syrett tried but failed, landing cat-like on the ground, a fall that would have hospitalised lesser mortals. It became a pilgrimage for Al to hitch the 270 kilometres from Cambridge to join us in battle. And some people say there is no competition in climbing! We spent days on the *Joker's Wall*, where finally, the gymnastic prowess of Syrett won over Rouse's steel fingers.

The *Joker* was vanquished and has now been graded E3 6a. The climbing grading system is mind-numbingly complicated, with many countries having different systems. The highest graded UK rock climbing in 1970 was Extreme, but with the increasing standards, it was decided to subdivide this grade using E and a number to represent an escalating difficulty. Back then, E3 was about as hard as it got. This grade expressed the overall difficulty (including the danger and length of the climb). A second number with an a, b, or c suffix was added after the grade for technical difficulty. The hardest at this time was 6b. Boulder problems and short climbs, usually ascended without a rope, were just given the technical grade. To add to the confusion alpine and ice climbing both have their different grading systems.

Music was the other important part of our lives. At University, we often had the opportunity to see bands play live. One eagerly awaited concert was the Who, as their rip-roaring mod-rock had established them at Woodstock six months earlier, as one of the world's best live bands.

'Al, do you want a ticket to the Who concert? Stainforth and Syrett will be there and keen to climb over the weekend. See ya, Brian.' I wrote and posted a cryptic letter to Rouse and waited for his reply.

The Who concert was something special at the exorbitant ticket price of 11s 6d, equating to £10 or $13 US in today's money! A beer was 1 shilling. The concert was a three-hour sensual assault of pulsating cacophonous heart-pumping music. At the crescendo, the audience was a unified mass of writhing, dancing, clapping and shouting. We came out both drunk and stoned, drenched in sweat, ears ringing and on an emotional high. *Live at Leeds* was soon released, widely regarded as the Best Live Rock Album in the world.

Over that winter of 1969–70, the Saturday night concerts were a ritual, and we were privileged to attend a list of pop royalty of which The Who were just one of the acts.

October 4	Fleetwood Mac
October 11	Moody Blues
October 30	Deep Purple
November 8	T-Rex
November 22	Free
January 17	Joe Cocker
January 24	Led Zeppelin
January 31	Ten Years After
February 7	Small Faces
February 14	The Who
February 28	Pink Floyd

At the time, arguably the hardest route on any gritstone outcrop was *Wall of Horrors* (E3 6a), Alan Austin's 1961 test piece on Almscliffe, Yorkshire. It had gained a fearsome reputation with only one repeat ascent. On a cold and windswept day in November '70, Syrett climbed the route. It was a marvellous achievement and confirmed his transition, in just two years, from a specialist at indoor climbing to one of the most talented climbers of the age. Uncharacteristically he rappelled down to inspect the route, which he later admitted was, 'an evil act'. Usually, his integrity at not using aid nor practising and inspecting climbs was a breath of fresh air.

Later Syrett wrote, 'I'm up. I've done Wall of Horrors. It will never be like this again (and it wasn't). Such a high is unrepeatable, approached perhaps, but never again reached'.

Syrett had a powerful effect on women. His mysterious personality, and a relaxed, can't be bothered attitude, seemed to attract the opposite sex like a magnet. They flocked to him and craved his attention. An athletic physique and a mass of black curly hair made him even more desirable. He often juggled several relationships simultaneously, yet he rarely talked about his girlfriends or introduced them to his climbing friends. Compartmentalising his life was a trait that ran through most of his actions, and he rarely mixed climbing and his affairs.

Jan Brownsort, a student at nearby Bradford University, had a brief relationship with him and she remembers: 'We met in the Fenton pub and immediately I was attracted to him. A deep, thoughtful person; intense, serious and enclosed, not that much fun but it did not make him any less attractive, just different. An unusual and slightly worrying person who showed signs of mental anguish. Perhaps even slightly paranoid.'

Only once did Syrett open up to me about his love life. We were climbing at Ilkley and he seemed anxious and impatient, as though he was on 'speed', running from one climb to another but with little satisfaction of the outcome.

'Sorry, Brian I'm a bit stressed. I've just split up with Chrissie.' he finally admitted.

While hitching home, he opened up. 'She started talking about holidays and what we should do at Christmas!'

'I wish I was so lucky!' I replied, though realising he was becoming frustrated at being continually chased. I could see his attraction to women was becoming a curse, leading to cynicism at his girlfriend's well-meaning intentions, which consequentially gave him guilt and mental anguish. He was a realist and emotionally he could not commit, splitting with one woman after another. A few months later, this led to tragedy.

Stainforth went round to his flat, 'I found him crying, distraught and emotionally in bits. Syrett had recently parted from his latest girlfriend. She felt so rejected and distressed that she travelled to Switzerland where she died climbing the Matterhorn. Syrett was convinced she took her own life.'

His sister Pol explained, 'Our mother had a guilt complex, and our father was a perfectionist. John inherited both these traits, and he felt responsible for her death, especially as he had introduced her to climbing'.

Syrett graduated in the summer of 1972, with a degree in Applied Mineral Sciences, but remained in Leeds, taking various temporary jobs. The next twelve months became his 'golden year' when his ability and fitness peaked. He climbed every moment he could, pioneering new routes on the local gritstone crags, most at the highest standard of the day. Historically, climbing standards rose gradually, but Syrett made a quantum leap that redefined the whole period.

Every summer the Leeds cabal would migrate to the Alps. On Syrett's one and only visit he failed on his first route, packed his bags and went home. Usually, he would push himself physically and mentally to the limit. Evidently Alpine climbing did not suit him, disliking the lack of control over objective dangers such as rockfall, unstable snow conditions and lightning.

He had an appetite to repeat all the desperate climbs first pioneered by Joe Brown and Don Whillans, two of Britain's most celebrated climbers. Ascents, which defined gritstone climbing. One day at Chatsworth, in the Peak District, I followed him up Sentinel and Emerald Cracks, both difficult E3 climbs. On the latter, he found it so straightforward he could not be bothered to protect it with runners. He heel hooked, sat on his heels and rocked over, using body positions not generally used in that age. Syrett was a genius, a magician who defied the laws of gravity. With undefinable flair, he floated upwards while I scrabbled and scraped. Annoyingly, he climbed so effortlessly, leading many of the era's test pieces with ease. One day, he burst into Stainforth's bedroom after succeeding on *Our Father*, one of the hardest routes in the country, enthusing: 'You've got to do it, John, it's so easy!'

The limestone cliffs of Malham Cove were one of our favourite climbing grounds and Syrett and I had spotted a blank, unclimbed wall high on the right wing, near a cave. Our attempt to climb the wall almost ended in disaster. I was perched on a ledge with one hundred metres of space below me as Syrett climbed above. Unusually, and totally out of character, he started to show off high above the void. Finding the climb too strenuous he hung, resting from a nut he had placed for protection, then flipped himself upside down. Suddenly there was a piercing scream. The nut came out, and Syrett hurtled headfirst into space. Belaying, with the rope around my waist (the usual way at the time), I was yanked off the ledge as I held the fall and we both hung precariously in space, high above the valley floor. It was dark before we untangled the ropes, got back to the ground and retreated to Leeds. The next day, with prior knowledge of the difficulties, Syrett cruised the climb. I struggled to follow. We christened the route *Midnight Cowboy* (E3 5c).

Almscliffe was Syrett's favourite crag. Locals said it looked like a castle, visitors described it as a wart, perched on a gentle mound above the rolling Yorkshire farmland between Leeds and Harrogate. In the book *Extreme Rock*, he described the day before climbing one of Almscliffe's finest new routes *Big Greenie* (graded E3 6a). It was May '73, and John was at his peak, living and dreaming of climbing night and day.

'I was suffering from a wasted summer in the Alps, and a winter season in the Fenton pub and I realised I had some catching up to do. Nonetheless, life was good; riding the crest of a wave. A milder obsession grew. Psyching up the previous evening with Lou Reed, pacing in the streets...'

He then described the following day's ascent, 'The sun shone, it was a classic golden evening on the crag. On to the foot of *Big Greenie* and up. It all went so very easily. All that fuss and worry! Two beautiful little finger holes are at staggered heights above the pocket, and another on the rounded edge above. Then a hand jam over the top, to welcome you home, very satisfying. The moves get harder the higher you go.'

That year 'Hot' Henry Barber, America's top rock climber, visited Leeds and discovered a like-minded companion in Syrett. They climbed together at Almscliff and afterwards had a riotous evening of fun at a Halloween party. Their approach to climbing and enjoying life was identical: alcohol, loud music and adventurous on-sight climbing. Barber joked with ironic truth in an article for the LUUCC journal, 'The English have hooked another poor soul into their debauched and lethargic scene.' Adding, 'Three cheers for Pasquill, Syrett, Littlejohn. Evans and others like them. The new era has begun.'

Confidence in his ability was probably Syrett's biggest strength, and he would often solo climbs at the limit of his talent. With a body seemingly fashioned from rubber, this natural suppleness gave him the ability to jump from great heights, landing unharmed, without the safety of a cushioned bouldering mat, which are used today. This strategy backfired on occasions, especially when he broke his ankle falling from the top of *Black Wall Eliminate* at Almscliffe.

A year later, in May '74, more disaster struck at a party held by fellow student, John Porter, at his well-to-do uncle's house in the Lake District. The night was in full alcoholic swing with most of the Leeds clan dancing wildly. I have a blurred recollection of the party getting dangerously out of hand, with a lot of embarrassingly juvenile behaviour, typical of drunk young men. In search of more drink, a small group, including Syrett, pillaged the fine wines stored in the cellar. They found a can of lobster which Syrett stupidly tried to open with a serrated kitchen knife. The blade slipped and cut deep into the tendons of his hand. This severe injury was to have a profound effect on his life. Worried that it would impair his finger strength, he started to think that he would never climb at the same high standard again. Climbing was a considerable part of his identity and armour. At twenty-four, the injury left him vulnerable to his doubts and worries.

Bernard Newman, one of his close friends at Leeds, wrote in *Mountain* magazine, 'Perhaps this was the moment Syrett began to die. Unable to channel his vital energies into the activities at which he excelled.'

The last time I climbed with John was in 1974 when he came to stay with me in Bangor, where I had moved to study Ecology at the University. He had applied to join the renowned outdoor education course at the college and came to have a look around. We had a great day on the cliffs of Tremadog, but his injured fingers were annoying him. He never did return to Bangor. Instead, despite his wounds, he travelled to California that summer to climb on Yosemite's granite walls. It was difficult to comprehend how he had such a successful time with the injured fingers. Many of Syrett's friends thought the hand injury had destroyed his climbing ability. Tim Rhodes, a close friend of his, had a different point of view. 'I don't think the injury particularly impaired his physical ability, but his approach to what he was doing was different. He had lost his motivation.'

Eleven years later, in June 1985, Syrett turned up unannounced, on Friday evening, at climber, Pete Livesey's house, in the picturesque village of Malham in the Yorkshire Dales. Livesey was regarded as the top British climber of the day, applying Syrett's training philosophy and a professional athlete's dedication. They had been one time rivals on rock; more recently they'd got to know each other on more amicable terms. Syrett was carrying a rucksack containing two bottles of whisky. They got drunk and talked through the night. In the early hours, Syrett departed.

On Saturday night, two Scottish climbers were sleeping in a cave precipitously positioned at the top of Malham Cove, next to our climb *Midnight Cowboy*. They reported hearing someone arrive in the middle of the night who must have scrambled to the Cove's top, then into the cave. There was no sign of anyone when they awoke in the morning. Eighty metres below Syrett's body lay prostrate and lifeless in the stream that issued from the cliff's base.

Did he accidentally slip or was his fall planned?

Livesey was one of the first on the scene and was convinced Syrett took his own life, as a note was attached to his body, though he never showed it to anyone. Livesey died of cancer in 1998, keeping strangely silent about that dreadful weekend. Pol, Syrett's sister, came to the same conclusion, as at the inquest, Syrett's housemate, Derek Underwood, revealed that a few days before his death he made his last will, and said he was going to throw himself off a cliff somewhere. A few days after the fatal incident, Underwood received a letter headed 'To be opened in the event of my death.' Enclosed was Syrett's door key.

At the inquest the Coroner, Dr Jacobs said, 'There was considerable evidence to indicate Mr Syrett had been depressed and was brooding about death. But it was all circumstantial, and there was no direct account of how he actually met his death. All we know is that he fell from a cliff, but the circumstances remain a mystery.' He returned an open verdict.

Bernard Newman wrote in an obituary for *Mountain* magazine,

'Syrett's cruelly short life was shaped by a series of definite irrevo-
cable decisions, as was his climbing, as was the manner of his death;
not a cry for help of some lonely soul, but a bold statement, a
premeditated decision to choose his own time and place.'

There is no evidence to suggest that mental illness and suicide
within the adventure sports community is any different to the
population as a whole. Sadly there has always been a stigma which
conceals depression and emotional anguish from public view. What
does that mean in the context of thirty-four-year-old Syrett's death?
Looking at the recent figures from the UK Office for National
Statistics highlights a number of interesting facts. 96 per cent of
mortalities are medical with the highest causes being heart failure,
dementia and stroke. The remaining 4 per cent is split:

> Falls and other accidental injuries (including sports) 2.16 per cent
> Suicide (and injury or poisoning of undetermined intent) 0.84 per cent
> Transport 0.52 per cent
> Complications in care 0.4 per cent
> Assault 0.08 per cent.

For males in their early thirties, the figures are dramatically
different due to a much lower chance of dying from medical conditions. I was astounded to find that suicide, in the UK, was the leading
cause of death for males and females aged twenty to thirty-four
years. Yet males had over three times the number of deaths from
suicide compared with females. In 2018 they accounted for 27.1 per
cent of all male deaths for those aged twenty to thirty-four years!

What had happened to Syrett since we last climbed together on his
visit to Bangor all those years ago? Then he was full of enthusiasm
as he chatted with excitement about his forthcoming trip to
Yosemite. His sister Pol and many of his friends have tried to piece
together how his life unfolded.

By the winter of 1974–5, Syrett's fingers were sufficiently healed
to allow him to climb regularly. Much of the winter he was based
at a caravan, in Glen Nevis, Scotland. It was rented by American
climber Roger Martin, who was a friend of John Porter. That

winter the cramped and steamy hovel became home for many of the Leeds team who escaped the student life to ice climb. While they frenetically climbed, Syrett was happy to wander the snow-covered hills enjoying the solitude, though there was a suspicion that he climbed more than he admitted! Inconveniently his stay was punctuated every fortnight by mad, long-distance hitch-hiking forays to and from Leeds to sign on the *dole;* the unemployment cash handout from the government which required a visit to your 'home town' employment office to claim.

Tim Rhodes and Syrett worked together for the geological survey in the spring. In their spare time they climbed regularly in the Lancashire gritstone quarries, Wales and the Peak District. By then, three operations on Syrett's fingers had sufficiently healed the injury for him to stroll up challenging climbs such as *Fingerlicker (E4), Silly Arete (E3), Citadel (E5)* and *Ramshaw Crack (E4).*

'The finger injury was not as seminal as some people suggest' said Rhodes, 'But it was probably a psychological trigger.'

He had lost his magic touch and moved from world-class to being just one of many good climbers around at that time.

His sister observed, 'My brother enjoyed excelling. When his climbing standard dropped, he was frustrated, and he never found a substitute for climbing'.

Syrett's life had changed, developing a deep restlessness that he could not satisfy, accompanied by bitterness towards some of his close friends, who he thought should have taken him to hospital after the accident.

He was the epitome of a shooting star never to return to his glory days. Whether the accident triggered a physical or a mental reaction was debatable. The result was real, and he lost his drive to operate at the highest level. In a modern era, he may have been diagnosed with post- traumatic stress, similar in some ways to the car accident that had affected Sam Cochrane, and changed his perspective on risk. It seemed a recurring theme that victims questioned and changed their direction in life after an accident, violent incident or mental anguish.

He spent much of the mid-seventies in Leeds working long nights at petrol stations and stacking shelves in supermarkets.

'Increasingly, he liked to be alone.' Rhodes recalled, then added, 'It was almost as though he had an air of self-persecution and showed signs of obsessive-compulsive disorder (OCD). He developed a bizarre habit of carrying a rucksack full of bus timetables, just in case he got stuck whilst hitching.'

With a certain inevitability, he became a bystander to the rock-climbing advancements. Becoming resentful and intensely frustrated at missing out on much of the new developments in the sport. Young athletes were training at higher levels of intensity. In particular, his climbing contemporary, Pete Livesey, drove standards upwards with ascents such as *Wellington Crack*, (1973 E4 6a) at Ilkley and *Right Wall* (1974 E5 6a) in Llanberis Pass. Although a rival, Livesey admired Syrett, describing him as an 'iconoclast' and suggesting that history showed Syrett as the best and most natural gritstone rock climber of the time. With a mixture of purity of style and boldness, he laid the foundation for a new high standard climbing era. Unfortunately, his talent evaporated, then wasted as a new wave of gifted climbers including Ron Fawcett, John Allen, and Jerry Moffatt took the grades to the stratospheric level (at the time) of E7 and 8a.

With a sense of going back to his roots, Syrett decided to return to his home town of Newcastle upon Tyne in 1978. Lesley Cooke, his girlfriend, a sports psychologist at the city's University suggested he retrain as a physiotherapist. Everyone was surprised by his uncharacteristic commitment when they got engaged in February, and started looking for a house to buy. Predictably, after a couple of weeks, they cancelled the marriage and put the house purchasing on hold.

I heard through the grapevine that Syrett enjoyed revisiting his nostalgic childhood haunts in the Northumbrian countryside. He revelled in the simplicity and ease of cycling as a means of transport and keeping fit, often pedalling for hours to remote crags to enjoy climbing alone, no longer seeking recognition from his peers. His confidence and humour improved as he rediscovered some of his boldness and skill, climbing regularly with poet and artist Richard Kidd. His adventurous spirit was rekindled, then backfired, when a ten-metre fall from *The Tube* at Back Bowden

Doors in Northumberland, ended with him in a hospital with a broken hip. There was no sign that he was drinking more than he had in the past; yes, enjoying a good night in the bar or a can of beer when he climbed, but nothing one would regard as excessive.

He wrote frequent letters to his mum and dad in Dartford, less so to his sister Pol, who emigrated to New Zealand. He visited his parents virtually every Christmas. There was very little money in his pocket, nor did he own a car, house or any luxury possessions: he didn't seem to need them. His sister remembers as a boy he collected cactus plants. In Newcastle, his obsessive tendencies resurfaced. He rarely threw anything usable away, developing a particular interest in old books, maps, bicycles, clock parts, and old clay chimney pots. John Given, a close friend, described Syrett's rented bed-sit, as having the appearance of a bicycle repair shop with a huge church clock mechanism on the floor, which he was trying to reconstruct.

After finishing his Newcastle studies he remained close friends with fellow student, Elaine McMaster. He could not find suitable work within the National Health Service and took a job labouring on the North Sea oil rigs. His work timetable was in shifts of two weeks on and two weeks off. Whilst on the rigs, no alcohol was allowed. The isolation seemed to suit his disposition, and he became an avid reader. However, during downtime, back in Newcastle, friends reported a marked increase in Syrett's alcohol consumption and were worried by his withdrawn, apathetic behaviour and mood swings.

In '83 I happened to be working in Newcastle. By chance, I walked into the Lonsdale Hotel in Jesmond and saw Syrett. At first glance, he looked no different: slim, a full head of curly black hair and a white sleeveless shirt. I was so pleased to see him, but he did not recognise me. Dismayed by his reaction, I sat next to him and tried to chat, but he seemed not to understand my conversation. He was a mess. His speech was slurred, a cigarette limply hung from his lips, beer and food stained the front of his white shirt.

Even though I understood little of the complex mental health and addiction problems, I could see he was in a downward spiral.

His deteriorating condition seemed to go hand-in-hand with alcoholism. Looking back, it was clear he was standing on the edge of sanity and needed professional support. But sadly I was one of the many friends who abandoned him. I had lost contact with John Syrett, just like I had disappeared from Sam Cochrane's life. I felt troubled that I had been so involved with my own life that I had no time for old friends.

Later that year, in September, there was an accident on the oil rig that was fundamental in Syrett's life. He was working a motorised winch that lifted a work colleague twenty metres to the top of the drill head in a Bosun's Chair. The winch malfunctioned, and the wire cable snapped, killing his workmate. Syrett was devastated and blamed himself. His fellow workers exonerated him of blame, but he was inconsolable, leaving the oil rigs for good. In Newcastle he gradually retreated further into solitude, drink and depression. The next months must have been a road to perdition as he waited for the results from the inquest investigating the accident.

Nine months after the rig accident and a couple of days before the inquest results, he hitch-hiked down to Malham to see Pete Livesey.

The day after his death, the official inquest on the oil rig accident reached its conclusion, absolving Syrett of all blame.

His sister Pol conjectured, 'My feeling is that the oil rig accident was the trigger, but that John was not destined to make old bones. Perhaps it was his life that was the tragedy. I think there was a negative side to his personality, and he used alcohol to alleviate his depression. My overall feeling is that life didn't live up to his expectations, even as a child, he was idealistic. I think that we all feel guilty about what we might have done to prevent the tragedy of John's death.'

John Syrett has become a cult figure in British climbing folklore. But why?

Yes, he climbed a few new routes, though he was only at the top of the game for five years. He excelled on Yorkshire gritstone, but he did not have anywhere near the same impact in other areas or rock types. Born out of the camaraderie of Leeds, his legacy was more inspirational; introducing a training ethic on indoor walls and purity of traditional style climbing on outdoor cliffs, which remains a beacon for future generations.

'Syrett was a genius, one of that rare breed of athletes whose performance makes a total mockery of the efforts of others. It was a pure joy to watch him move across the face of steep rock.' Bernard Newman wrote fondly in his obituary.

John Syrett's life was an enigma, his death even more so. He died aged thirty-four. An utterly committed climber, remembered as a loveable, perplexing and complex character, with the sensitivity of an artist rather than the brawn of an athlete.

Perhaps all great talents have a dark side.

Alex MacIntyre getting ready to climb
Cave Route, Goredale, winter '72.

4

METAMORPHOSIS
Alex MacIntyre (Part 1)

By 1976, many of my friends from Leeds University were now living for climbing. In particular, Alex MacIntyre was planning his next alpine season, habitually poring over photographs, diligently researching future objectives. His next ambition was one of the biggest challenges in the French Alps, the unclimbed central couloir on the Grandes Jorasses, which had been attempted by the leading climbers of the day, Dougal Haston, Chris Bonington, Mick Burke and Bev Clark in January 1972. Ignoring standard alpine climbing practices they fixed ropes over a seventeen-day siege, citing the high level of difficulty and freezing temperatures as justification for the use of heavy-handed expedition tactics. Regardless of strategy, the couloir repelled their efforts and gained its reputation as *a line too cold for ethics.*

Based in Chamonix, the summer season started well for Alex. Partnered by Tim 'Bush' Rhodes and Willie Todd, he climbed a new route (which they christened *Petit Mac*), to the left of the couloir. Realising that ice conditions were excellent, Alex attempted the couloir with Gordon Smith, a Scot and one of the best young alpinists of that time. It turned out to be suicidal and they retreated.

In Alex's article 'Cold Comfort', he describes the stone fall that stopped them, the fear of which was to haunt him throughout his life. 'I was like prey in the jaws of a monster – the stones – about the size of average dustbins, I'd say. It was a veritable avalanche of rubbish that bounced and leapt, ricocheted and crashed, and all so close, oh so close. How close? Nine inches in three thousand feet close ... (we were) like ants going the wrong way up a bowling alley.' They dodged them all though, and Alex got ready for another attempt in August, when he returned for a re-match, this time with one of his regular climbing partners, Nick Colton, whom he described as 'an aristocrat from Longsight, Manchester,[1] and one of the scruffiest people on God's earth.'

Colton was clear about their motives. 'Both aged twenty-two, we saw ourselves as the new kids on the block, taking things to a new level and, in the process, upstaging the older generation with what we perceived as their outmoded methods of doing major new routes.'

From his earlier experience, Alex knew they had to be *fast and light* to run the fearful gauntlet of the rockfall, so they started in the evening and climbed the lower slopes in darkness when the night cold held the stones in place.

Colton described the start, 'Our head torches didn't reach far into the darkness, but they did pick out what looked like the start of an ever-steepening Scottish-style ice runnel ahead. Our hands held state-of-the-art *Terrordactyl* ice axes. Alex swore by them and ably and efficiently led the steep ice pitches up the first runnel, without any fuss. I tackled the face above. It was all very dusty and crumbly. I was climbing above Alex. As I reached leftwards, a handhold disintegrated. Without warning, I was off! Flying directly past Alex, I took a big fall.'

With no runners, Colton's full weight came straight onto Alex's waist belay, but they were fortunate, and a poor belay peg saved them from disaster. They pressed on, climbing five relentless pitches on a mix of rock and ice, before heading diagonally rightwards onto bare rock devoid of cracks. With no belays for safety, they were forced to climb simultaneously. Colton remembers, 'We were both exhausted and struggling hard to maintain concentration to avoid any slip-ups that would have terrible consequences.'

Higher, Colton knocked off a dinner-plate sized rock, watching in horror as it hit Alex. 'He howled until the pain subsided, and then we continued'.

Throughout the afternoon, they overcame difficult and nerve-wracking climbing which resulted in more falls. It was 6.00p.m. and getting dark when, with relief, they saw the summit cornice.

1. An area with high levels of poverty deprivation and crime.

Nightfall forced a bivouac through long freezing hours sitting on a small icy ledge and, next day, they reached the top without further incident to complete one of the most historic climbs in modern alpinism.

Four years earlier, starting my last year at Leeds, I was sitting in the Students Union having lunch with a group of mates from the LUUCC when a youth with a huge mop of black curly hair approached.

'I'm Alex . . . Alex MacIntyre. Is this where the climbers meet?'

'It is,' John Syrett replied.

'Someone's here most lunchtimes,' Bernard Newman, the club's arbitrary secretary, added.

'Have you got a car?' I asked, wheels being the most important asset of anyone new to the club.

'No.' Alex answered, confirming our suspicion that he was as destitute as the rest of us.

He was dishevelled and of average height, but made taller by his hair. Stubble suggested a lazy habit of rarely shaving. He wore a black leather motorcycle jacket loosely on his shoulders, regulation patched flared jeans and dirty pumps, which perfected the unkempt look. We christened him *Dirty Alex*.

I didn't see him again for a month, neither at the climbing wall nor at any of the club meets until, unexpectedly, we bumped into each other at a party, a male affair in a small smoky kitchen with lots of canned beer and loud music that made conversation virtually impossible. Through the noise, we arranged to go climbing the next day at Almscliffe, a nearby gritstone cliff, and he agreed to pick me up on his newly acquired motorbike.

Well past midday, he arrived on a noisy, old, blue 250cc machine wearing the same black leather jacket and clothes as when we first met. I got the impression they were permanently grafted to his body and that he climbed, ate, attended lectures and slept in them. Obviously, he was not a man who changed to go out.

He appeared to be very proud of his newly purchased bike but, as we lurched down Woodhouse Road, we narrowly missed a bus and drove over a pedestrian crossing full of people. Suddenly, on the outskirts of Leeds, there was an ominous metallic clunking sound, and the engine spluttered to a halt with a pungent reek of burnt oil. Alex twisted round, 'What do you think's wrong?'

'Haven't a clue,' I replied, having never owned a bike. We sat by the roadside in silence until, eventually, I asked how long he had been climbing. There was no reply, and I thought he was annoyed with the bike or perhaps shy.

'Do you climb a lot?' he finally asked.

'More and more.'

'Where?' Alex was subtly questioning me before revealing himself. His shrewd eyes seemed to reflect an inquisitive brain.

'I had a great time in the Alps this summer, but now mainly around Leeds on the grit or limestone.'

'Who do you climb with?'

'It depends on transport. There are so many good climbers here it's easy to find partners.'

He told me that he began climbing when he was in the sixth form at Watford Grammar school and joined the London Mountaineering Club. He seemed to have done a lot of climbing with them and had even hitched to Snowdonia a few times whilst still at school. I began to realise he was confident and independent for his age, and highly intelligent. He had been offered a place at Cambridge University but turned it down in favour of Leeds because of the reputation of the climbing club. Now here he was, at the start of his first term studying geography and economics. In contrast, I felt like an old-timer with only one year left at the University. 'Should we see if the bike starts?' I suggested sceptically.

It kick-started the second go so, with a big smirk on Alex's face and clouds of blue smoke billowing from the exhaust, we spluttered into the countryside.

At Almscliffe, I started up one of the classic medium difficulty routes called *Z climb*, which I'd done before. When it was Alex's turn, I was surprised at how slow and clumsy he was and how difficult he found the moves. I had anticipated a better rock climber. We finished at sunset and headed back to the bike where he aggressively stamped on the kick-start. The bike wouldn't start, and soon it was dark. He stared indignantly at me as though it was my fault.

'Better get the thumb out,' he said. We made it back before last orders in the Fenton, our local pub in Leeds. I never saw the bike again.

Alex started University at the same time as John (Did) Powell, and they became close friends, climbing and socialising together. Did's short stature and pale, fresh-faced complexion made him appear younger than his age. With his blond hair folded tidily in one sweep above his round, metal-rimmed glasses he always wore a smile. His status was high as he owned one of the few vehicles in the club, a beaten-up blue Ford Thames van which was regularly crammed with people speeding to a climb, to drink at a country pub or visit a late-night curry house.

One late autumn evening, a group of us were drinking as usual in the Fenton pub with Alex relaxed on a grubby and cigarette-burnt, velvet seat. Next to him sat Did, his accomplice, with a wide alcoholic grin on his face. 'We've spotted a new climb on the Lecture Theatre,' Alex announced.

Nighttime building climbing was all the rage at that time, so, at closing time, Alex donned his grubby black leather jacket and Did followed in a threadbare sports jacket, clean white shirt and crepe-soled Hush Puppies. It was a straightforward climb up an external lift structure ending at the eleventh floor, where a glass roof sloped upwards to meet a vertical concrete wall. The flimsy glass sheets looked dangerous, so they carefully padded up with hands and feet on the metal strips either side of the glass. Next, they were faced with a sheer concrete wall where, luckily, the builders had left finger-sized holes big enough to aid their progress. A second wall looked insurmountable, but a protruding metal hook provided the key. Taking off his leather trouser belt, Did climbed onto Alex's shoulders, deftly lassoed the hook and, with a quick pull, they were on the top.

Bernard Newman and his girlfriend Val attempted the climb a week later but disaster struck crossing the glass roof when Val disappeared with a sharp squeal in a cascade of glass. Bernard found her on the level below with a broken wrist and bruised hip, having narrowly avoided falling down the stairwell. Bernard cut

his finger badly trying to find a window for their escape and bled
everywhere before deciding to climb back out to raise the alarm at
the campus security office who phoned for an ambulance. Val
spent a night in hospital but luckily they escaped action from the
university, though the story did make the *Daily Mirror*.

Each winter, the club arranged ice-climbing excursions to
Scotland. There was a good forecast for the first trip of 1973, and
the minibus was crammed with a mix of old and new hands,
constantly drinking canned beer. The talk on the journey was full
of bravado, but only a few hungover bodies stirred from the motley
selection of tents the following day. Eventually, John Syrett and I
plodded off on the two-hour walk to Coire Ardair of Creag
Meagaidh, a large cliff dripping in snow and ice. Alex and Did,
who were strangers to the winter group, eventually caught up.

'Can we join you?', wheezed Did, being slightly asthmatic, his
large round glasses misted in the cold.

'What route are you going to do?' Syrett asked

'We're not sure . . . perhaps *Centre Post*,' Alex replied, puzzling
how to re-attach his ice axe to his rucksack.

'What ice routes have you done before?' I asked.

'This is our first time,' replied Did, wrestling with his gaiters,
which he had put on the wrong way round.

'You'll find *Centre Post* pretty straightforward. It's a classic
gully. I did it last year,' Syrett said.

'Where is it?' Alex asked, with his ice axe hopefully secured.

'Follow us. We're climbing nearby.'

Alex and Did had done a lot of rock climbing together but had
only read books on how to climb ice. They chose *Centre Post*
because, from the pictures in the guidebook, the big gully looked
suitable for their ability but, as soon as they set off, the air filled
with expletives.

Alex's untidy cramponing technique had ripped his new over-
trousers. When the gully steepened, Did stopped and watched as he
arrived with them shredded from the knees down. Infuriated, he
tore them off and threw them to the wind. After that, they dithered
over how to make a secure ice axe belay. From there, Alex climbed
to the start of the ice. Did soon realised that Alex wasn't sure what

to do, as he took ages to cut a step and almost dropped his ice axe in the process. Finally, he said indignantly, 'You have a go.'

It was then Did's turn, 'I laboured to cut steps, trying to remember what the book had said. It was exhausting work – it felt much steeper than it looked from below. Eventually, we had to admit defeat, realising we had no idea how to climb the ice.'

They retreated down the gully, somewhat depressed by their own incompetence. Next day John Eames, one of the club's more experienced ice climbers, volunteered to join them.

The weather was poor but they persisted, walking through driving rain, which turned to heavy snow at the bottom of the climb. Eames led but soon came down looking concerned. 'If this snow keeps up, the cornices will avalanche'.

'What's a cornice?' Alex asked.

There was a long pause while Eames's brain pulsed. *What am I doing here with these two plonkers?* he thought.

They decided to retreat, but there was a rumble and the inevitable happened. Thousands of tons of snow thundered past, catching and pulling their ropes but narrowly missing the trio. The long drive south gave plenty of time for reflection on a lucky escape and their first weekend of ice climbing.

Next summer, Alex's first visit to the European Alps did not fare much better. He joined John Porter, with whom he had climbed sporadically since they met in 1972. Porter had dark hair, a healthy tan, and was of medium build. Born in the USA from Anglo-American parents, he had arrived in 1967 having chosen British nationality to escape the Vietnam War. In a strange country with few possessions and no friends, he enrolled in English literature at Leeds University. A natural storyteller with a sharp ironic humour he had bouts of romantic volatility and pessimism, neither of which got in the way of his remarkable climbing drive. He was a perfect foil to Alex, who was optimistic, logical and perverse. In the following years, they became close friends as well as climbing partners. Porter remembers their first alpine climb.

'It was a shambles. Alex lost his boots, so he rented a pair and accidentally chose different sizes. We set off well before dawn to climb the South Face of the Fou, with him inevitably hobbling, got disorientated in the dark and ended up on a different peak, the East Face of the Lepiney. I had to drag him up; he was inept and totally out of his depth.'

At the top, they were caught in a dramatic storm of hail and wind, with lightning flashing all around. With ice axes humming, and hair standing on end with static, they were in considerable danger. However, they found shelter in the nick of time and endured a miserable night in the cold. When they finally got down, Alex vowed never to climb again but, of course, he did, and the next year returned to the Alps with Did. They completed a series of challenging climbs, notably the Bonatti Pillar on the Aiguille du Dru, their new competence informed by their previous failures.

In the early 1970s, under the guidance of Edward Heath's Conservative government, Britain's economy was in a desperate state. The Three-Day Week was introduced to conserve electricity in the face of the coal miners' strikes resulting in a grim winter of frequent power cuts, no heating and reading by candlelight. We could not afford a television or phone and fuel was in short supply, severely restricting our travel and access to climbs and, I am ashamed to admit, a survival strategy we adopted was the *cinema scam*. With electricity frequently cut in the early evening the resulting blackout occurred just as the local Hyde Park cinema began its show. The disappointed audience exited and, as they left, got their tickets refunded. Alex and I developed a scheme where we sprinted from our homes to the cinema to mingle with the crowd and claim our bogus entrance money of a shilling (five new pence), enough for a beer or a bag of chips. Desperate times.

I lost contact with Alex for a year and only later learnt that he'd become disillusioned with his studies and left University. Fortunately, his father had connections with shipping and secured him a return passage on an oil tanker to Morocco and a hippie lifestyle. In the autumn he returned to Leeds and switched courses to study Law. His intellect, combined with charm, wit and logic, gave him a knack for persuading the most obstinate characters to change their minds, a skill that boded well for a career as a barrister.

While at University, Alex preferred to cultivate his *Dirty Alex* image, keeping his studies and family background to himself. In truth, he grew up in a contented middle-class family. His parents, Jean and Hamish, were from Scotland before moving to Hertfordshire where they brought up Alex and his younger sister Libby. They were strong Catholics, and in Alex's early adolescence, sent him to a strict Jesuit boarding school, which he said put him off religion for life but gave him a trait of toughness and a strict work ethic. Despite climbing regularly and a chaotic student life-style, he gained a First Class honours degree, a rare feat in the Law department at Leeds.

Meanwhile, within the climbing club, a tragedy had occurred. The bodywork on Did's van finally collapsed. A solution was found when Alex discovered a similar wreck with a knackered engine. Did (the oily handed mechanic), aided by Alex (better at crashing cars than putting them together), swapped the engines and, hey presto, the club had transport again.

During this student period, he became close friends with John Syrett, and spent many hours drinking with him in the back bar of the Fenton. With their looks and hair, they could easily have been brothers. They often climbed together though Alex, a less talented rock climber, would generally just hold John's rope. They also had a similar taste in women, having an open relationship with the same girl, Jan Brownsort, who remembers Alex with fondness.

'He was exciting and, yes, beautiful. We were typical, randy students with a very strong mutual attraction, but our relationship was casual and sporadic; he could sleep with almost any woman he liked, he was a successful alpha male, and knew it.' Then, adding, 'Alex could be soft and caring, or he could become cruel and hurtful. You never knew if he would be nice that day. Maybe he liked to have this power over people; for sure, he needed to prove something.'

She vividly recalled when coming out of the pub, 'We were amazed to see a stack of whisky boxes piled high outside the local supermarket. So naturally, Alex and John loaded a box into a supermarket trolley. We wheeled it across to the bus stop, onto the bus and back to the flat to drink all twelve bottles. A week later, we staggered into daylight with alcohol poisoning.'

In an argument with Jan centred around middle-class-ness, Alex refused to accept that he was a member of that comfortable class. 'But you are!' she challenged.

'No, I'm not,' he snapped back, which Jan thought was mere contrariness. He was looking for a fight.

Asked whether she thought Alex wanted to be a working-class hero, she replied, 'No, he wanted to be a posh barrister.'

In February of 1975, one of John Porter's American climbing buddies, Roger Martin, arrived. We suspected he came more for the beer and nightlife than the climbing, but he rented a beaten-up static caravan parked in Glen Nevis, conveniently placed under Ben Nevis. It was no fun making the long hitch to get there, but soon the Leeds climbers arrived, packed together in squalid conditions: unwashed bodies, damp smelling sleeping bags, dirty pots, empty bottles and bags of rotting rubbish. Roger was the leading light and, that winter, made stunning solo ascents of two of Britain's most difficult ice climbs: *Point Five* and *Zero Gully*. His success being partly enabled by revolutionary new ice axes.

What a difference these new climbing tools made. For hundreds of years, the humble ice axe was the symbolic identifier of an alpinist. The design, a simple wooden shaft with a straight metal pick and an adze, had hardly changed since 1865 when Whymper ascended the Matterhorn, until, around 1970, two leading climbers revolutionised the design. An American, Yvon Chouinard, curved the pick so it held more securely in the ice. Soon after, a Scot, Hamish MacInnes, produced a short metal *ice tool* featuring a radically angled downward pointing pick which he called the 'Terrordactyl'. Along with improved designs in crampons, ice-climbing techniques were transformed, which stimulated a rapid rise in standards.

Alex arrived at the caravan, the proud owner of a new pair of MacInnes *Terrordactyls* and Chouinard crampons. Since his first foray on ice, he had become more proficient, though we still regarded his ability to be run-of-the-mill. Then, unexpectedly, one day, he decided to solo, without the security of a rope, an icefall called the *Curtain*. He had never attempted anything so difficult, and several fellow climbers watched in horror as he scraped and scratched his way up the climb in a very unconvincing manner. Nobody could have foreseen what occurred a few days later, when he left the caravan alone and soloed the much harder and longer *Point Five* and *Zero Gullies*, repeating Roger's earlier feat. For sure, the latest gear helped, but even the slightest mistake was unthinkable. We were astounded, marvelling at how he had gained enough confidence to make such a leap of faith? Did he think Roger had laid down a challenge? Whatever the reason, it was the birth of a new persona, brave and totally committed. On that day, Alex crossed his Rubicon, taking a giant step towards becoming a world-class mountaineer.

Back in Leeds, Alex couch surfed, never paying rent, preferring to keep his money for climbing trips, eventually moving in with his new girlfriend, a feisty Welsh student called Gwyneth with her long waves of blonde hair and a sharp temper. She and Alex were a passionate couple but hopelessly incompatible as both were single-minded and refused to participate in domestic duties.

The volatile relationship lasted on and off for the next four years, continually interrupted by Alex's long spells away in the mountains.

In the early summer of 1975, sitting under a tattered polythene extension to my tent in Chamonix, France, I watched raindrops splash into puddles forming between a group of stolen white plastic cafe chairs circling a burnt-out hearth. On a good day, you could see the snowy dome of Mont Blanc and the pointed granite spires of the Aiguilles, but that day the clouds hung low in the surrounding pine woods. Empty bottles and food waste lay on the grass. A big white van, which I had not seen before, drove between the tents onto Snell's campsite, the free-to-use field that was the summer home for British alpinists. With engine revving and wheels spinning it tried to gain traction on the muddy ground until, out of the front door jumped *Dirty Alex*, with a broad grin on his face and the dishevelled look that fitted his epithet and out of the back fell five mates in similar disrepair. They had pooled their money to buy the van to make their annual pilgrimage to the Alps.

The long drive had obviously been well lubricated. The lads were staggering around with sore heads looking for spare places to pitch their tents, only just settling when the Gendarmes raided the campground and closed it down as a health hazard. To the bystander, it looked more like a refugee camp than a holiday venue. Unquestionably unhygienic, it had just a solitary water tap and no toilet, obliging climbers to piss where they wanted and defecate in the nearby river Arve. We migrated to the nearby Biolley campsite, which was still a hovel but at least had a toilet.

These Chamonix campsites had become the spiritual home of British alpinism, very much as Camp 4, in Yosemite, had for the American climbing community. Antisocial behaviour was the norm, and dinner regularly came as the fruits of petty crime. Bodies lay around on foam mats, sunbathing half-naked, smoking weed, and drinking from litre beer bottles or glasses of the cheapest *vin ordinaire*. Lazy groups chatted about their recent and upcoming climbs while waiting for the next spell of *beau temps*, and climbing became more of a counterculture than an arena for athletic prowess.

Until now, Alex had climbed within the sphere of our friends at Leeds. There was a strong bond of camaraderie amongst the group but, of course, there was competition as well, where success and failure were met with mocking praise or merciless piss-taking. That season, Alex broke away to join top British alpinists, Al and Aid Burgess (the Twins) and Paul 'Tut' Braithwaite. This trio were ten years older and more experienced than Alex. In particular, Tut was exceptionally strong as he was in training for Chris Bonington's expedition to the South West Face of Everest that autumn. The Yorkshire born identical twins were blond-haired giants of the climbing world and were also fighting-fit after success on a string of alpine test pieces. Alex was now climbing with the elite.

They planned an ascent on the North East Face of the Grand Pilier d'Angle on the Italian side of Mont Blanc, a climb of formidable reputation that had not been repeated since its first ascent in 1962 by Walter Bonatti and Cosimo Zapelli.

The Italian Bonatti was regarded by many as the greatest alpinist of all time and said of the climb, 'The mixed terrain of the face was, without doubt, the most sombre, the most savage and the most dangerous of any that I have ever encountered in the Alps.'

The foursome succeeded without incident and another alpine season was over.

Alex's next season in the Alps was even more successful with the aforementioned ascent of the unclimbed central couloir on the Grandes Jorasses with Nick Colton. In the three years since his first disastrous Scottish climb, he had undergone a remarkable metamorphosis from an average to an exceptional climber. His ambitions and character had also changed dramatically over the four years I had known him.

Jan, his ex-girlfriend, observed, 'When younger, he played on his squalid lifestyle, wanting to be accepted by mates he admired for their downright roughness. I think he outgrew that phase and wanted to be acknowledged as one of the elite: intellectually, financially and, more importantly, a world-class climber.'

He now looked over the horizon to the high peaks of the Greater Ranges: the Hindu Kush, Karakoram, Himalaya and the Andes. Anything was possible.

Mike Geddes, Piraña Club meet, 1975.

5

A SCOT ON ICE

Mike Geddes

A loud knock on the door echoed around the house in Leeds. Even though I was expecting visitors, the violence of the rat-a-tat-tat surprised me. Pushing aside piles of unwashed plates scattered on the kitchen table, I found a place to rest my mug of tea, stood up and walked a few strides down the dark corridor and opened the front door. A stranger stood there dressed in a well travelled, ankle-length grey, greatcoat with a pair of heavy mountaineering boots protruding from its bottom hem. Fag in mouth, his soft skinned face was framed by long black hair with a badly cut fringe across his forehead.

'I'm Mike, most call me Jimmie.' A beige scarf was wrapped neatly round his neck, giving him an incongruous look of elegance.

'Come in, how was the hitch?'

'No so bad,' he answered in a gentler than expected Scottish brogue.

I let him in, struggling to manoeuvre his companion, a huge brown canvas rucksack, through the door.

'Sorry about the light, the bulb went a few weeks back.'

'Bloody hell it's cold in here, it's warmer outside,' he complained, as he took off his worn coat, revealing a lean frame, a little taller than my average height.

'Is Rouse here yet?'

'No sign of him,' I replied.

Aye . . . we both left the doss in Cambridge together but I got the first lift. The weather was foul, raining most of the way up.' He pushed his chin forward, and a tight-lipped grin spread across his face. A strange mannerism of pleasure that I would get to know well.

'Come through and have a brew. Put your sack upstairs, you can sleep on my bedroom floor. First door on the left.'

That late afternoon in February 1971 was my first meeting with Mike Geddes and the start of a close friendship. He shared a room with Al Rouse at Cambridge University. Although Al was a much better rock climber, he spoke with great respect of Mike's extraordinary enthusiasm for the Scottish hills and his superior mountaineering skills. By the age of seventeen Mike was the youngest person to ascend all the Scottish peaks over 3,000 feet called the Munros of which there were 282, plus an extra 227 tops or ancillary summits. A remarkable feat of dedication, independence and endurance for someone so young. During their student years it became a habit for Mike and Al to escape the academic claustrophobia of Cambridge to taste the more vibrant party life at Leeds University, often extending their break to join me and other Leeds climbers travelling to the Scottish Highlands.

It was getting dark and there was still no sign of Al.

'Let's get some chips and then go round to the Royal Park for a pint. Al could be a while yet, he always seems to be late!' I suggested.

Just in time for last orders Al arrived, and the following day we set off for Scotland, all squeezing into a heavily laden minibus we'd hired for the long journey north. For Mike these excursions were more like pilgrimages; his whole life seemed to revolve around the snow-clad Scottish hills. This required a degree of masochism, especially for Mike and Al, whose journey usually took two days each way, all to enjoy a few hours of frigid climbing in the short, winter days and often in atrocious weather.

These long weekends blur into a chaotic memory of several winters of epic climbs and arduous hitches. We were following in the footsteps of generations who had been hooked by the rich legacy of Scottish ice climbing. This distinct branch of climbing had achieved a worldwide reputation and had become a valuable way for climbers to gain experience for the higher mountains of the Alps and Himalayas. Since the late 1800s the prominent snow and ice gullies and buttresses on the major cliffs had been climbed. In February of 1960 a remarkable achievement occurred, etched in the folklore of climbing, when two talented Scots, Jimmy Marshall and Robin Smith, completed six first ascents on Ben Nevis in a week. They also made the second ascent of the intimidating *Point Five Gully*. At that time such feats were only possible by laboriously cutting steps up steep snow and ice, as each climber used only one traditional ice axe, and crampons without front points.

Much of the activity took place on the 'Ben', as it is affectionately known. Standing proudly on the west coast of Scotland, the view from the summit after a climb was breathtaking, surrounded by the silhouetted summits of the Highlands. In the distance the Atlantic Ocean stretched far into the setting sun. At 1,345 metres the highest mountain in Britain, snow clung to its rocky slopes all winter long. The south and west slopes of the mountain could be ascended with relative ease, whereas the north side was steep and foreboding, holding the biggest and best collection of ice climbs in the country.

It was on the Ben in March 1971, that Mike's talents first made headlines in the climbing press. On one of his sorties from Cambridge, he succeeded on ascents of the hardest routes at that time, including: *Point Five Gully* and *Smith's Route*. Later in April he took another step forward when he pioneered a new ice line on the steep 300 metre Indicator Wall and called it *Hadrian's Wall Direct*, giving it a grade of V, the most difficult of the day.

'Well, ice climbing's easier now,' wrote Mike modestly in a magazine article, referring to his pioneering use of front point crampons and two curved-pick ice tools. He used the ice axes for direct aid by wielding the picks above his head into the ice, hanging off them and then pulling up on the embedded tools. Thanks to his conversion to the new equipment he has been credited as a key figure in the development of modern ice climbing. Though, strangely, nobody could figure out why he was so good. He certainly did not train, nor did he learn his skills from anyone. The only explanation was raw talent.

The last climb of the Marshall/Smith Ben Nevis 1960 odyssey, and perhaps the most significant, was *Orion Direct*, a feat so advanced that it still had not been repeated twelve years later. In February of 1972, Mike and Al planned to make the elusive second ascent, which by then had become one of the most coveted prizes in British mountaineering.

They made their way up the boggy path of the Allt a'Mullin valley, on the way to the North Face of the Ben. At the snowline they arrived at the sombre Scottish Mountaineering Club (SMC) hut; its stone walls merged into the landscape so well that many people missed it completely in bad weather whiteouts. They had not booked a space to sleep as they had recently been banned from staying in the hut for not paying their dues on a previous visit. On arrival they met with some rancour from local SMC members before they managed to squeeze into a bunk. Above the hut hung the five hundred metre Orion Face, pale with snow and blue with ice, its northerly aspect shadowed from the sun all winter long. The *Direct* followed a cunning line, akin to an alpine route, first following ribs and runnels to the central snow-basin, christened *The Spider,* then tenuously traversing to reach dribbling ice, a feature called *The Fly*, before finishing up on glistening snow-plastered vertical rock to reach the summit.

'Don't come back,' bellowed a disgruntled SMC member as Mike and Al slammed the hut door at 5.00 a.m.

'We stumbled ... all excited and thinking about the aura of the route ... on the steep snow beneath the North Face, lamps bobbing in the clear cold dark, us gazing at the route, gazing at the stars, the hut going down, the dawn coming up,' Mike later wrote.

Higher, they were in a quandary as to which direction the climb took.

'Hey Mike,' Al shouted as he traversed round a steep corner. 'The way's clear to the basin.'

Mike charged up to Al and continued in soft snow, to a stance in the very eye of *The Spider.* They moved quickly up the snowfields with the vertical drop growing below and the clouds swirling around them. Mike led a superb diagonal pitch up *The Fly* and described Al's struggle to follow.

'The gloom came down in hissing spindrift to curse Rouse's glasses, but through he came ... over the last bulge, the pick of his axe woefully mangled, if not right angled. He battered away at some deceptive grooves like a woodpecker with a bent beak.'

By fluke they discovered that their route up the final tower corresponded perfectly to Marshall's original description, '. . . a trouser-filling traverse was made on to the right wall, along a short ledge, then a frightening move, leaning out on an undercut ice-hold, to cut holds round on to the slab wall of a parallel groove.'

Al was by now groaning and panting as impending nightfall and clouds of spindrift obscured his bespectacled sight. His badly damaged ice axe provided no purchase as Mike unceremoniously hauled him up the final pitches

They had succeeded on *Orion Direct* despite the handicap of carrying heavy rucksacks full of all their weekend gear, an eccentric strategy, which enabled them to rush down the tourist track on the west side of the mountain, from where they started their long hitch back to Cambridge well after midnight. Two weeks later the pair repeated the tiresome journey north, and completed the second ascent of another Marshall test piece, *Minus 2 Gully*, cementing their status as two of the leading ice climbers of the day. Although Mike wrote several excellent articles for climbing magazines, despite his growing status, he never courted publicity or financial gain from public lectures or sponsorship deals. He quietly got on with his own climbing agenda without the fanfare of some of his contemporaries.

That spring of 1972 I decided to visit Mike and Al in Cambridge. It took me most of the day to hitch from Leeds but by early evening I had arrived at their flat, with just enough time to smoke a few joints and drink a can or two of beer to get into the mood for a Roxy Music concert. In the pub afterwards, full of high spirits, we joined a small group of University climbers who suggested a nocturnal tour of some of the building climbs.

At Leeds we had become adept at urban climbing, partly under the influence of Al and Mike whenever they visited. Because of the paucity of climbing around Cambridge, generations of climbers had ventured onto the city's structures, usually late at night and invariably inebriated. It felt like a rebellious thing to do and the practice dated back centuries, with one of the first notable climbs being made by Lord Byron with his ascent of the Great Court Fountain in 1806. The British mountaineer and poet Geoffrey Winthrop Young documented all the activity in his book published in 1899, *The Roof-Climber's Guide to Trinity*, written in part as a parody of an alpine guidebook. It describes the practice as, 'cat burglary, but without the robberies'. A second publication, *The Night Climbers of Cambridge*, in 1937, has been credited with inspiring the modern generation of night climbers. Records suggest that nobody had died but quite a few students had been caught by police and dismissed from the University.

Our night excursion followed this long tradition and started with a routine church steeple climb after which we crept past the Porter's lodge and started climbing an ancient building. Mike claimed it was the Vice Chancellor's residence and it had a reputation of both difficulty and objective danger. On the surface, Mike was an introverted, dour Scot who spoke rarely and kept his opinions to himself. When in the company of friends he came to life, showing a deep character with an enthusiasm for 'having a laugh'. Hot or cold, he was rarely lukewarm. He loved the subterfuge and jeopardy of this escapade, where a fall would involve serious injury, and if caught, there was a risk of prosecution. While Mike was hand traversing a bedroom window ledge, the ancient diamond glass pane was flung open unexpectedly. He almost lost his grip and with surprise, looked up, finding himself eye to eye with a venerable, grey haired gentleman. They stared at each other for an eternity until the elder whispered, 'Boy ... if you must do such reckless jaunts please do so quietly!'

Chastised we skulked away into the darkness arriving back at the flat full of chatter and laughter.

'What are you going to do when the term finishes?' I asked Mike, as we sat in a smoky bar. He rubbed his stubbly chin, pausing to think and picked up his glass of beer.

'I don't know ... I've no job so I'll probably go to the Alps and see what crops up when I get back. What about you?' he replied in his laconic way before taking a long swig from his glass.

'I've applied for a few jobs. One as a marine hydrologist and another to train as a geography teacher.' I added.

'You don't sound enthusiastic!'

'No, but I've got an interview for a Master's degree course in ecology.'

'Where?'

'Bangor, North Wales.'

'Mm . . . that'll be good for the climbing.'

We sat looking at our drinks and in silence Mike rummaged around in his pockets for a cigarette.

'Bloody hell I've run out already . . . A packet of Number 6,' Mike asked the barman.

We sat in silence, Mike not prone to idle chit-chat.

'I don't know what to do about Christine,' he eventually confided.

Mike had a lovely girlfriend, a student and an active outdoor person, but not really a climber.

'I know what you mean. I have been thinking a lot about Jane.'

For about a year I had been seeing Jane, a law student who lived just around the corner from me in Leeds. She was unhappy with me disappearing every weekend to the crags. She had no interest in climbing.

It was good to chat with Mike over our similar problems. We silently finished our drinks.

The last few years had felt like a fantasy. My imminent departure into the real world was now throwing my mind into confusion. Mike, like an echo of myself, wanted the happy-go-lucky student years to go on forever, so he could just keep climbing without responsibilities. The doors to a normal life were open but we couldn't handle the commitment. Society had given us an education and deep down we felt guilty at not using it wisely. We thought the joy of climbing was important, a higher calling, something that life should revolve around. Justified by this arrogant notion I convinced myself that I was a better climber than teacher, hydrologist or ecologist.

Back in Leeds one night, towards the end of my last term, Jane and I were slowly walking home, along an empty street, hand-in-hand, after a night out in the city centre. I suddenly stopped and silently stared at my reflection in a shop window.

'I don't know how to say this . . . but I want to finish with you,'

I blurted out, followed by all that had been on my mind for the last month, as tears were streaming down my cheeks. Jane was speechless, her big, beautiful eyes clouded. She brushed her long brown hair from her face and flung her arms round my shoulders, held me tight and started to shake uncontrollably.

'Why? . . . Why are you doing this? I thought we were happy?' She sobbed into my ear.

I hugged her hard knowing my unexpected decision had really hurt her. I felt awful and regretted not discussing it properly and letting her know my feelings in a gentler way. I had been a complete bastard but I knew from my bar room conversation with Mike that I had to do something. My limp excuse for our split was that I knew Jane's focus was to turn her law degree into a good job and settle down, whereas my plans were vague but mostly centred around climbing. We had been growing apart for some time but were still in a loving relationship. I could see no other way of resolving the dilemma other than separating.

To compound my troubles I was having difficulty explaining to my parents my future plans. They were upset that I had not sorted out any employment and preferred to go climbing.

'Grow up and get a proper job at a bank,' my dad suggested.

'You will be careful?' my mum implored. Not really knowing how the climbing lifestyle worked and perhaps not wanting to know! Neither of my parents appreciated the immense satisfaction I got from the sport. I had been an only child since the age of twelve when my younger brother Stephen died at just eight from a congenital heart condition. Devastated, my parents' total devotion to my sibling was now transferred to me. From having my freedom as a boy, my teens were the reverse as they became ultra protective and drowned me with their love. This resulted in an opposite reaction in my behaviour; a desire for independence.

With no long-term plans I left Leeds with a heavy heart and headed for the Alps to climb for the summer season of 1973. There I met Mike and Al at the campsite in Chamonix. I soon found out that Mike had split with his girlfriend Christine.

One evening we were in our usual drinking hole, the Bar National. Maurice the overweight, jovial owner was perched on his stool behind the counter. He swept back the remaining few strands of his greasy hair, his red-veined nose a sign of his bar-owners' profession and ordered his incongruously angelic daughter to serve us another beer. Mike and Al had just come down from making the second ascent of the difficult *Zapelli/Bertone* route on Mont Maudit, an outlier of Mont Blanc. Rain was drumming on the windows as an evening storm spread across the mountains, signalling a few days of rest and drinking.

'Do you fancy coming to South America this autumn?' Al asked me unexpectedly, adding, 'Mike and I are putting together a team to climb the West Face of Fitz Roy in Patagonia.'

'Yeh ... of course ... if I can get the money together,' I answered enthusiastically. Grateful for this simple solution to the problem of what the hell I was going to do next.

'I've managed to arrange a temporary supply teaching job, perhaps you could get one?' Mike suggested.

How I raised the money would be far from simple, as unemployment was rife in Britain at that time.

'Another beer?' Mike shouted, then the night degenerated into drunken bullshit.

The impetus to take the next step and go on an expedition to a far off land was partly driven by the vacuum that the impending departure from university had created. There was no leader amongst us, rather, we were feeding off each other's energy, where the desire for adventure was stimulated by group dynamics. Equally, none of us would have started the escalating ladder of risk without the camaraderie. Yet incredibly, in our group of high achieving climbers, all in our early twenties, I cannot remember a single conversation where risk of injury or death was openly discussed. That wasn't until much later when the deaths began.

At noon next day the rain was still drumming on the canvas of my tent when I heard a shout and poked my head out of the doorway.

'Brian, I've got a letter for you.' A friend who had just driven out from Britain handed the mail to me.

I opened the envelope; it was a letter from Bangor University offering me a prized place on their post graduate ecology Master's degree course. I was stunned and confused; now I had to reconsider. Fitz Roy or Bangor, climbing or academics? I wandered around the campsite for a while debating which way I should go, realising it was an important, life-changing decision. Eventually I convinced myself that if I went to Bangor as a student, I would still have plenty of time to climb and it would delay my 'normal life' while I studied a subject I loved. Out of turmoil came another compromise! I would now have to break the news to Mike and Al.

That autumn I was incredibly envious to learn that they had somehow raised the money for the trip to attempt Fitz Roy. Cash was short and their journey was an expedition in itself. They were joined by Rab Carrington, John Barker and Pete Minx on the flight to Florida to meet American, Jim Donini. From there they flew to Barranquilla in Columbia and using local buses and trains they headed south through Equador, Peru and Bolivia to Argentina. Over a week and eight thousand kilometres later they arrived in Buenos Aires. Unfortunately, they discovered that their equipment, which they had shipped in advance, had been impounded by customs.

Revealing news came in a rare letter from Mike.

Brian,

How's life in Bangor going? Have you found a new woman yet? There's not much climbing going on down here! We're still in BA, waiting for our gear, which is somewhere in the docks. We are now called 'The Dirty Dozen' since the team from the Torre Egger Patagonia expedition arrived. The bloke we are staying with is called Edourdo. He's a rich plastic surgeon with a big house, who used to be a climber. Al has fallen in love with his daughter called Gabriella and I've shacked up with the wife of a local climber, which is a bit awkward. Eduardo and his mate, Hector, take us boozing every night and sometimes we end up in these amazing tango clubs. Its really hot and humid and we went to a swimming pool party where someone started shooting a gun. All hell broke loose and two of us ended up in a cell overnight. On another night Minx got so drunk he lost all his clothes and ran out of the bar naked. The police found him huddled on a street corner and brought him back to the doss at 5 am.

Hope we get our gear soon and go to the hills.

Aye, Mike.

Every day I dreamt of South America. I could not stop thinking enviously about all their wild adventures, yearning to escape normality, to travel and see the world. On the positive side, life in Bangor was better than expected. The studies and getting to know a new group of friends was rewarding and exciting. I had found a great little cottage to live in and started climbing with John Whittle, a philosophy student a couple of years older than me. Over the following years John would become one of my closest friends, a soulmate who was pivotal in many of my future climbs and adventures. The sliding doors of life! If I had gone to South America, what a different future I would have had.

I received another letter from Mike with less optimistic undertones. It explained that their gear took another month to arrive. By then Barker and Donini had gone home. The debauched life in BA had put paid to their fitness and together with the notoriously bad weather of Patagonia, they failed miserably to climb anything significant. They had run out of money and had to eke out an existence in their remote beech forest base camp. With some guilt I sat at my desk in Bangor relieved. Hearing of their misfortune vindicated my decision to stay.

On returning to Britain Mike came to see me in Bangor. He seemed dejected and frustrated at the way his first expedition had turned out. Explaining that he had come home alone, feeling cast adrift, that the world had somehow stood still. He was no further forward in his life nor his climbing, wondering what to do next. Meanwhile Al had gone to work as a climbing guide in California. Rab Carrington remained in Buenos Aires learning how to make sleeping bags with Hector, a skill that laid the foundation for Rab to eventually establish his own successful outdoor clothing business.

During my time at Bangor I only saw Mike that one time. I was getting used to his disappearing act. Luckily, my post graduate course allowed a lot of flexibility and I regularly climbed on the rock of North Wales. In the winter of 1974–75 I climbed in the Mont Blanc range with my new climbing partner John Whittle, a season which will be recounted later and all part of the overlapping kaleidoscope of events. Next summer, out of the blue, I got a postcard from Scotland. Mike obviously felt envious of missing out on the good times we had the previous winter.

11th October 1975
Brian,
    Do you fancy climbing in the Alps this coming winter?

Aye Mike

Mike and I arrived in Chamonix in January 1976. It was a natural progression for Mike to attempt Alpine routes in winter. It had become the cutting edge of the sport; the next level of difficulty, in terms of length and seriousness. Reading reports about the accidents and deaths, it was clear we had moved into an area of higher risk, a specialist game for only the most skilled and experienced climbers. After last winter with John Whittle I was confident of my climbing skills but I recognised I still had a lot to learn about the perils of avalanches and surviving days of freezing conditions. Mike was new to the game, his first Alpine winter.

'I need to learn like a beginner and start with some easier shorter climbs,' I remember, as he acknowledged his lack of experience.

We discussed at length our strategy for each climb mindful of an epic a few years back, which highlighted the dangers. Top French alpinist René Desmaison was the master of this masochistic branch of mountaineering with many first winter ascents to his name. He was prepared to suffer and in 1971 he attempted to pioneer a difficult winter route to the left of the *Walker Spur* on the Grandes Jorasses with Serge Gousseault, a young aspirant guide. It turned into a two-week battle for survival as stone fall cut both of their ropes and Gousseault developed frostbite and suffered from exposure. They could not continue and when rescue finally came,

Gousseault had been dead for three days. Reflecting on the price to be paid for success on extreme alpine routes Desmaison wrote, 'It is for such moments of triumph as this, that the mountains exact their pitiless toll. Logic asks "why?" But the question itself is meaningless. Only the passion and the agony are real.'

Of course this was French romanticism, as death for his partner, Gousseault, was the greater reality, the ultimate sacrifice!

Our plan was to make the first winter ascent of the Rebuffat route on the North Face of Pointe du Domino, a summit on the headwall at the end of the Argentière glacier. We took a cable car crammed with hordes of brightly dressed recreational skiers before snowshoeing, heavily laden, across the glacier, arriving late in the afternoon at the sparse winter quarters of the alpine refuge. Soup, dehydrated potatoes and a slice of cheese was our banquet that night.

By dawn next day we were well on our way to the head of the glacier. On our left and right the snow-clad spires of the Courtes, Droites, Triolet and Dolent turned from steel grey to lavender, then orange-yellow as the sun's rays escaped from the eastern horizon. Our lungs heaved with effort, clouds of breath evaporated in the icy air as our snowshoes crunched into virgin snow. Silent in our own thoughts. How small and insignificant we were in the greater scheme of things, yet we had our sights on something important to ourselves. A few mates knew our plan but in reality we were alone, unknown, unannounced and with no audience. What crazy challenges we invented, what selfish risks we took. And for what? Only our own satisfaction.

By late afternoon next day we were halfway up the climb with the light fading fast. All around were sheer rock walls with no ledge to sleep. The only solution was to fix our micro-thin, nylon, prototype hammock on the vertical face. Hanging, squashed together, neither of us could sleep.

'I wish I had been good at tennis or golf,' I said. 'It would be nice to make a living somewhere warm.'

'Aye perhaps ... but that's just soft, there's no challenge or hardship.'

'But you'd make some money and might meet a girl,' I observed.

I looked at the Milky Way slashed across the darkness. It was −25°C. Just the two of us, hung uncomfortably together, each like a small foetus, almost invisible on a remote precipitous wall 350 metres above the glacier, twenty kilometres from the nearest habitation.

'Why the hell do we do this?' I questioned.

'If you've gotta ask man, you're nevva gunna know,' Mike retorted in a bad American accent.

'What the hell are you talking about?' I snapped back at Mike's uncharacteristic ramblings.

'That's what Louis Armstrong said about jazz,' he explained.

'Aye but I expect he spent every night in a warm bed,' I replied enviously.

Our hammock provided no comfort for sleep and in the dark pre-dawn we started to dismantle our bivouac, preparing for the day ahead in pools of head torch light. It took two hours of contortion: putting on our boots, stuffing sleeping bags away and melting snow to make tea. Finally ready we tethered our rucksacks, full of our overnight gear, to a piton hammered into a crack. We planned to leave them there while we climbed, hoping to reach the summit then return the same way by rappelling back down our ascent route. It was a relief to start climbing, after the cramped conditions in our hammock, and liberated from carrying our heavy packs, we moved quickly.

Mike was a magician when ice climbing. He was not a natural rock climber but on snow and ice I knew nobody better. With customary panache he floated up the committing, insecure and dangerous climbing on the wall above the bivouac site, while I fought and bludgeoned to make progress. The artist versus the navvy! He didn't talk much when climbing. In fact his long spells of silence annoyed me on occasions.

What are you thinking about? I felt like shouting.

Even in the valley and on social occasions he was a very quiet, slightly dozy person who needed alcohol to become animated and loosen his vocal cords, though that's not to say he did not show his feelings at times. When I joined him astride the summit block late in the afternoon, there he was, with the grin of a Cheshire cat, dragging deeply, with satisfaction, on a cigarette. Slowly blowing smoke upwards like a cowboy in an old Marlborough advert.

After our success on the Domino we needed to rest in the valley, to let the mind forget the suffering and give our bruised and battered bodies time to heal. Chamonix, at the heart of the ski season, was a party town in full swing but we were impatient to get back in the hills. Soon we started planning a much bigger under-taking, the *Croz Spur* on the massive 1,100 metre North Wall of the Grandes Jorasses. It was less publicised than the Eiger even though the early ascents had been equally epic. It had only just had its first winter ascent in 1971 by two talented Frenchmen, Jean-Claude Marmier and Georges Nominé.

I had tried to make the second winter ascent of the *Croz*, the season before, in 1975, with my close friend from Leeds, Roger Baxter-Jones (RBJ). In those early days of British involvement with alpine winter ascents it felt very serious, just the two of us on such a big and remote route. On the glacier approach Roger took a huge fall down a cathedral sized crevasse. I almost joined him in the icy tomb as he dragged me, sliding like a rag doll on skates, to the very edge, while he plummeted into the bowels of the glacier. Luckily I managed to hold his fall and we continued our climb in a more cautious manner. Next day, bad weather halted progress and we had to retreat. Mindful of what happened the previous year I suggested to Mike that we invite our friends Rab Carrington and Al Rouse, who were back again that winter in Chamonix, to make up a foursome for our attempt on the *Croz*. There would be safety in numbers on the crevassed approach and their skills would improve our chances of success.

The twenty kilometres approach to the Leschaux refuge, where we would spend our first night, near the base of the Jorasses, was best done on skis. Unfortunately none of us could ski! Thankfully Roger came to our rescue; he was working as a ski instructor that year and was friendly with a group of girls who were excellent skiers and wanted some excitement away from their routine chalet-girl jobs. They would ski down with all our gear while the four of us walked down on snowshoes, unladen, to save energy for the climb. Plans were finalised and we agreed to meet them at 9.00a.m. next morning at the bottom cable car station.

We were sorting our climbing gear the evening before when, unexpectedly we got an invite to a birthday party. In a rush to get to the festivities we stuffed the gear into the bedroom wardrobe in a big pile ready to pack first thing next morning. Needless to say the celebration involved far too much beer and very little sleep. Although Mike had the air of a loner, a quiet private person, alcohol had transformed him into a party animal who was dancing like a dervish on a table while singing and shouting incoherently. In the early hours Rab collapsed on his bed in a coma and sometime later that night he needed to go to the toilet. He mistook the wardrobe door for the toilet entrance and defecated all over our climbing gear. In the morning our plans were thrown further into confusion as Mike was nowhere to be seen. Regardless, we hastily stuffed the gear into rucksacks and rushed to meet Roger and the girls who were on time and expectantly waiting at the base of the Aiguille du Midi cable car station.

'What's that awful smell?' one of the chalet girls shrieked.

They were not at all impressed by the odour emanating from the loads, compounded by Al who was bent double in the gutter puking up his breakfast. Just as we started to board the cable car we saw Mike stumbling towards us, mountaineering boots unlaced, carrying a bulging, ungainly rucksack with most of his gear hastily hung on its outside, looking like a hillbilly after a night on homemade spirit. A local French girl followed closely behind armed with a large brown paper bag full of baguettes. As they barged through a group of skiers, everyone turned to stare at the flippant couple, seeing that they were comically covered from head to foot in white powder.

'Where have you been?' I asked, aghast.

'With Anita, her dad owns the boulangerie down the road . . . I've got some bread for breakfast,' Mike explained

'Ah . . . but why are you covered in flour?' I interrupted.

'Well . . . you see we ended up sleeping in the flour store last night,' he admitted with a sheepish grin.

By the state of them I do not think there was much sleeping involved.

At the top of the cable car it was so cold that every breath burnt the nostrils. The clear atmosphere gave us confidence that the weather was set for *beau temps*. Roger and the girls shouldered the packs and merrily set off skiing, confidently slaloming through the powder snow until they were tiny dots in the distance.

'I think I will learn to ski,' Mike commented as he watched them disappear out of sight.

We followed at a sedate pace; the sudden rise in altitude in the cable car had not been beneficial for our hangovers. An hour later I looked back and saw that Al was not moving. He was slumped, retching into the snow. The floundering trace of our snowshoe steps did not indicate a confident athletic march to the mountains. Eventually we found our rucksacks in a pile where Roger and the girls had left them hours earlier. By now even Al could walk in a straight line as we carried our loads into the small, deserted mountain hut perched on the moraine above the glacier.

In the bitter dawn we took turns to blunder through the waist-deep snow on the glacier, passing the spot where Roger had taken his fall the year before. Eventually, a precarious snow bridge allowed us to tentatively cross a cavernous crevasse to reach a right slanting snow gully, which indicated the start of the climb.

'What the fuck's this?' Mike exclaimed in disgust as he paid out the rope, on which every few metres was a reminder of Rab's diarrhoea.

When we arrived at the top of the gully it was already getting dark so we flattened the snow at a convenient notch and got ready for the long night.

'I don't like the look of those high clouds,' Mike observed while he unpacked his thin foam mat and sleeping bag.

'The forecast in the newspaper said it was going to be good for three days,' I replied as I wriggled my legs into my bulky down sleeping bag.

'Let's see what the weather brings in the morning,' Mike said sceptically as a cold north wind started to blow.

'I'm parched. How's the brew going?' Al asked impatiently as he tried to prize ice from his frozen beard.

'Bloody useless. The stove's been on an hour and the water's still not warm,' Rab snapped back.

'Forget the tea. I just need liquid,' croaked Al.

'Pass the packet of soup. This water is getting warm,' Mike who was in charge of the second gas stove added stoically.

'That's not enough to feed a sparrow,' I complained. 'Where's the chocolate?'

'Here . . . one piece each,' Rab ordered.

I spent all night dreaming of fish 'n chips and apple pie.

Next morning the sky was steel grey, brooding with heavily laden snow clouds, a foreboding ceiling, which seemed low enough to touch. We were in a world of no colour, a black and white atmosphere unique to the big Alpine north faces with the evils of a winter storm threatening.

'Let's carry on. It could be a minor weather front which will soon pass,' Rab urged.

'I'm not sure,' I said, as cloud ominously started to envelop the 4,208 metre summit of the Jorasses.

Progress was slow as our crampons and ice axe picks scraped on the ice covered rock and heavily gloved hands searched for holds. Our heavy, twenty kilo loads severely hindered any gymnastic moves. Worst of all the mid-winter *black* ice was our nightmare. Different from the normal 'skating rink' ice, it had been so polished and hardened by cold and wind to be barely penetrable by our crampons and picks. By late afternoon we were desperately searching for a place to sleep, anything, even a half metre ledge to sit out the night. Each feature was a false hope. Soon darkness came with the abruptness and menace of a guillotine.

At last our weak head torch beams picked out a small buttress of rock protruding out of the ice, which gave some shelter and we managed to place a secure rock piton to hang from. Laboriously we hacked at the almost impenetrable *black* ice to make a narrow, foot wide ledge to perch on. A spider's web of ropes connected the piton with a couple of insecure ice screws, from which we slung our rucksacks to form mini-seats. We struggled to make some lukewarm soup and tea, fearful of dropping our gear into the dark void below. Still wearing our boots and harnesses we each battled to get into our sleeping bags. We pulled them up and over our heads, like tortoises in their shells, to give some sense of warmth. It was the start of an interminable and miserable night where sleep was impossible and the makeshift rucksack seats provided no comfort, cutting off all feeling to the legs.

'For fuck's sake,' the quiet voice of Mike huddled in darkness next to me shook me out of my torpor. It had started to snow.

As the snowfall increased we were exposed to the spindrift cascading down from the slopes above. It built up in piles over our heads, the weight pushed at our backs and threatened to sweep us off our perch. At any time we feared the big one, an avalanche that would wipe us off the face, like a row of four pigeons on a wire waiting to be shot. The cold snow got everywhere and crept inside our sleeping bag where precious body heat melted it. With no sleep the night seemed endless. Our plight was dire and it was a relief when a vague hint of twilight signalled the end of our ordeal. The only sound was the whoosh of avalanches gushing down the couloirs on either side of us.

'I think the snow's stopped,' Al's muffled voice announced.

'Can we get the stove on to make a brew?' Mike asked.

'No chance,' was Rab's reply.

I peered out of sleep-deprived eyes into a thick mist. We had to get down.

It took over two hours to get ready to descend. Every task had to be done wearing our thick, clumsy woollen mitts. Frostbite was only minutes away if we took them off. The last act before descending was to take out our main anchor, the secure piton which we had trusted, hanging in space from its metal eye all night. Mike took a swipe with his hammer to loosen it.

'Fuck me!' he exclaimed as it snapped in half, the intense cold had embrittled the metal causing it to break.

With no more than a knowing glance, perhaps a hidden realisation of what could have been our fate, Mike started to rappel down the route. It took all day to descend to the hut and then the following day to Chamonix. Our brutal alpine winter was over for that year.

As soon as we got back to Britain, in late February, Mike, packed his bags and got a flight to Warsaw for a six-week trip to the Polish Tatra, as a member of an exchange organised between the Polish Mountain Association and the British Mountaineering

Council (BMC). Mike was joined by an elite team: John Porter the Anglo-American climber who was part of the Leeds team, Adrian and Alan Burgess – 'the Twins' – down to earth Yorkshiremen who were amongst the strongest alpinists of the day, and Pete Boardman, the new National Officer of the BMC who had reached the summit of Everest the year before as part of Chris Bonington's legendary South West Face expedition.

Mike was fascinated by life behind the Iron Curtain in Poland. The communist rule imposed by their overlords, the Soviet Union, restricted travel abroad and its people lived on the breadline, devoid of luxuries. Yet the climbing community was strong, vibrant and friendly. They were a driving force in world mountaineering and the five Brits were entertained and hosted in the homes of the top Polish mountaineers.

The climbing highlight of their visit was a multi-day traverse of the ridge between the main peaks of the Polish Tatra, high above Lake Morskie Oko, for which the Poles left their guests to climb by themselves. The British team progressed quickly, without ropes, on the initial slopes covered in deep powder snow, but soon the terrain became more complex and technical. Pete ploughed on ahead at a blistering pace alone and was soon out of sight, while the rest followed in his tracks, eventually to be stopped by a rock tower. There was no sign of Pete, though they could see his steps in the snow traversing the dangerous section. Mike looked at the difficulties ahead, weighing up the situation while lighting a fag.

'What's got into him?' he asked John.

'I've been wondering that myself Mike. You know, I think maybe he's still coming down from the summit of Everest.'

'That's it, you're right. He's still a mad bastard in his head. He's climbing like a demon.'

Sensibly Mike, John and the Twins uncoiled their ropes and tied in, then tentatively climbed round the impasse, where a fall without the safety of their ropes would have led to certain death.

Mike and John were bemused by Pete's behaviour. Was it foolhardy or a product of supreme confidence resulting from his recent narrow escape from the summit of Everest, when a ferocious storm had engulfed the mountain. The inner debate on risk analysis is so personal and many factors come into play including: external conditions, personal mindset, fitness, group dynamics, competition and heuristics. Mike, John and the Twins were concerned over the dangers on that ridge in the Tatra, whereas Pete's perception was obviously different. It foreshadowed Pete's death in 1982, the only one of the group visiting Poland who was to die in the mountains. The sad part was that those friends, those talented individuals who pushed the limits the furthest were often the ones who paid the ultimate price. We all recognised that taking risks was an integral part of elite mountaineering; the dilemma was not the pursuit of success but what motivated our quest.

When Mike returned back to Britain I met him socially on many occasions. Our lives were not all about climbing and we did our fair share of partying. I don't remember who came up with the name Piraña Club but it was an apt title for our loose group of around twenty mates who tried to destroy our minds with alcohol and drugs in the mid-1970s. This was a time when both of us were pressing the self-destruct button too often for our own health. Mike would turn up unannounced, an internal radar pointing him to one of our sporadic meeting places in the Yorkshire Dales, the Derbyshire Peak District or Snowdonia in North Wales with the excuse to go climbing or caving. Rarely did any physical activity take place on these gatherings but on one memorable occasion in Yorkshire, the expert cavers of the group took Mike and I down *Swinsto* into the Kingsdale Master Cave underground system. It was an enjoyable wet grovel and after emerging, we gatecrashed a local dance at the Hill Inn. As soon as the party started he was there, flamboyantly dancing, po-going and spitting to the punk music of the day. After a few drinks had been spilt the locals took exception to the Pirañas and an almighty fight broke out. Mike and I were the least aggressive people of the bunch but as we were wearing top hats, we seemed to attract attention and were roundly beaten up. We woke up next morning as snow fell, freezing, hungover, battered and bruised, Mike squatting in a telephone box, me nearby, huddled in a lidded container of road grit.

Mike disappeared from my life again and it was not until much later that I heard the sad story of his struggles. He moved from London, where he had a temporary teaching job, to Edinburgh. Living what appeared to be a solitary life, he began taking drugs, particularly magic mushrooms. Sliding into a dark underworld, his life fell apart and he started having psychotic episodes. His parents and brother were extremely concerned for his mental health. It was unclear how he came back to life but he started to recover. The catalyst was perhaps his move from the city to near his beloved hills, to Fort William, where he rented a room in a terraced council house with fellow climber Noel Williams ... and started climbing again.

'He came to Fort William with an incredibly wild reputation. I wasn't sure whether to take him on as a lodger but I only saw the exact opposite, all the time he stayed with me. He was quiet, kept the place clean and I never saw him smoke or get drunk,' Noel remembers.

It was long overdue when I arranged to climb with Mike again in December of 1977 in Fort William. A Highland town in a beautiful setting, on the shores of Loch Linnhe, nestling below Ben Nevis. It was an ideal base to go climbing and walking in the surrounding hills. Sadly it was in the depths of depression with shops boarded up, the distillery closed and the fishing industry all but finished. The only employment still available was in the hydro-powered aluminium smelter or the large pulp mill.

On meeting up with Mike I found, to my surprise, that he had started a regular, 'proper' job at the pulp mill as a chemical engineer. To add to the changing circumstances he had met a girl at work called Helen. Soon after Christmas, the sun came out and revealed the hills in all their glory, covered in snow with good climbing conditions. Mike was on holiday from his work and was keen to climb.

And so it was that I found myself slogging through new snow, following Mike, to the base of the Indicator Wall, high on the Ben. He had insisted on a mid-morning start, which would inevitably lead to his preferred finish in the dark.

'Should we have a wee brew?' Mike in no hurry, gave me a thin-lipped smile, searched the depths of his old rucksack and produced a battered flask. With quiet contentment he sipped the coffee, peering at the snow-covered rock above.

'Have you given up fags?' He hadn't had his usual smoke before the climb. He ignored me and took another mouthful of coffee.

'It looks a bit bare of ice,' I observed in a worried tone.

'Och it'll be OK,' was Mike's confident reply, now ready to climb.

He set off with his usual composure, diagonally left on a rock slab covered with the thinnest smear of ice I had ever seen anyone climb.

'Watch the rope!' I squawked as I followed, teetering across the diagonal traverse, from which, if I fell I would take a huge triple 'H' pendulum (heaven, hell or hospital) and I would crash into the ground to the left. My ice tools were of little use on the veneer of ice, so the appropriate technique seemed to be to balance across solely on the very tips of my crampon front points, skidding and scraping on the two millimetres of verglas. Mike had lost none of his skill and made it look so easy. Luckily it was by far the hardest pitch and we romped and hollered our way to the top. Predictably we finished in the darkness that always appeared to be Mike's way! We called the route *Sickle* because of the curving line it followed.

That winter continued to be memorable for Mike as he broke through the barriers of difficulty by pioneering three of the earliest grade VI climbs on Ben Nevis: *Galactic Hitchhiker, Albatross* and *Route 2*. His enthusiasm and unrivalled knowledge gave him a unique edge for discovering new winter climbs. With a visionary approach he moved from the natural snow and ice lines to the steeper, thinly iced rock faces, heralding a new wave of development in Scottish ice climbing.

Mike and Helen moved into a house of their own and their relationship blossomed. She was obviously a strong, settling influence and although he climbed regularly in Scotland he rarely ventured further afield. Helen was active in the hills as well but during their time in Fort William they became perplexed at how Scottish mountaineering was totally male dominated. In 1979 they founded 'The Alternatives' (*An Gearanach Mountaineering Club*), a mixed gender group offering an alternative to the patriarchal Junior

Mountain Club of Scotland. Further afield they became avid supporters of causes they believed in such as Friends of the Earth and Amnesty International.

I wonder why we drifted apart? Was climbing the glue that kept our friendship together? We had an intense emotional bond and closeness through shared experiences, yet when Mike forged a new life with Helen we drifted apart. It happened with my first climbing partner, Sam Cochrane, then John Syrett and now Mike. It seemed to be a common theme, my inability to maintain long-term friendships.

They married in 1980 and soon afterward Mike's employers suggested a move to their Aberdeen factory on the east coast of Scotland. Although he was happy there, engrossed in the culture and traditions of Scotland, Mike withdrew from the climbing scene and concentrated on using his extensive knowledge exploring the hills often staying in remote bothies. I thought this strange at the time but I soon found out the bad news. He had developed oesophageal cancer. It started in 1983 when he began having difficulty swallowing and by the end of that year he underwent a traumatic operation. With strength and support from Helen he confronted the disease with a complete change in lifestyle, and the recovery went well … at first. He gave up his job and moved to the Cairngorms, where, with an incredibly positive attitude, they bought a house and started a business in computing consultancy, along with providing bed and breakfast holiday accommodation that specialised in vegetarian cuisine. With orthodox medicine failing they explored alternative therapies and became strict vegetarians. There was hope and he never became downcast as he started to explore the hills again, often alone. On one of his last excursions in his cherished Scottish hills, during Easter 1985, he joined a meet of his SMC friends and despite being weakened by his illness, had a gloriously day on the NE Ridge of Aonach Beag. Soon after his health deteriorated.

We will never know whether it was his love of the odd cigarette, alcohol or bad luck? I was surprised by the depth of my grief. He was the first of my friends to become terminally ill. Subconsciously, I was prepared for a character like Alex MacIntyre not to come back from the mountains, where there was a degree of self-determination as to the level of risk one was prepared to take. Whereas fate was cruel to Mike and I felt cheated that someone so close had disappeared that soon from my life. I expected to be sitting in a pub with him, swapping yarns when we were well past our prime. Mike was different from most of my friends, with no crazy ambitions, never pushy, he had a truly original mind and an incredible affinity for the mountains.

He died of cancer in 1985, aged thirty-four.

One winter weekend in February, a few months after Mike's death, Al Rouse and I took the long drive from Sheffield to the Highlands and bivouacked in a lay-by just outside Ullapool in north-west Scotland. As usual Al was asleep in an instant. I tossed and turned, shivering as I stared at the clear February starlit sky with a hint of the aurora borealis to the west. Sleep would not come as I pondered the strange circumstances that had brought us to this remote corner of Britain.

After Mike's funeral, Helen had given Al a bequest, in the form of a cryptic code, NH 273 863, which turned out to be a grid reference of a remote Scottish location. Evidently a year previously, Mike, using his unrivalled knowledge of the Highlands, was walking alone near Ullapool, in the hills behind Seanne Bhraigh, at the head of Gleann a'Chadha Dheirg, when he found a large, unclimbed north facing cliff. The note indicated he had been especially impressed by the 300 metre gully splitting the highest part of the face. His strength on the wane, he died without climbing on his virgin cliff and we were determined to make the climb in his honour.

Still dark, Al and I headed along the path to Beinn Dearg. We then made our way up a broad ridge on the hillside to the left. As we gained height the dawn broke purple over the snowy tundra. I soon became aware of an almost religious aura; we were on a pilgrimage to Mike's Highland Mecca.

It was a complicated approach, over a high plateau, through a hidden valley and under small cliffs dripping with smears of ice. Even though it was a long slog through the deep snow time passed

quickly as Al and I talked randomly of the good times we'd had
with Mike. An intimate requiem of parties in Leeds and
Cambridge ... drunken caving in Yorkshire ... long days on the
Ben ... winter attempts on the *Croz Spur* ... red wine, big steaks
and tango dancing at 5.00a.m. in Buenos Aires. Eventually our
compass led us to the base of the cliff where Mike's compelling
gully line could be seen slashing through the precipitous hoary
walls above. How climbers, particularly the canny Scots, had not
climbed here before was a mystery, though the fact that it had no
name, was not a peak and was so remote, goes some way towards
answering that question.

The first pitch and the snow slope above turned out to be relatively easy but then the action started as the dark walls closed in
around us and the ground steepened. Here the climbing became
more anxious, with ice thick enough to climb but too thin to protect
with ice screws. An ominous umbrella of ice overhung the whole
top section of the gully. The icicles hanging out of reach looked
impossible to scale, having not formed completely, yet strangely we
felt there was no question of failure. Both fired with emotion we
began climbing with confidence. We were blocked by a rock wall
but to our left a vague ramp wove through the balustrade of icicles,
allowing an escape to easier ground. The elegant crux produced a
fitting climax to the day.

The early northern night was soon upon us and we hastily stuffed
our stiffly frozen, snow-covered gear into our packs and in the
gloom found our windblown walk-in tracks. The snow was crisp
and our way was lit by pools of yellow head torch light as we
walked quickly, in complete silence. All was routine at first but
soon I started to get a peculiar feeling, a tension, a strange compulsion to look behind into the hollow darkness from where we had
come. The feeling persisted but of course when I looked back there
was nothing, though this did not satisfy my curiosity or quell the
strange unknown. I looked back again and again. The calling got
stronger. I wasn't frightened, instead; I was smiling; I had an inner
glow. Happy, yet sad.

The final steep descent below the snow line of heather and
tussock grass jolted me back to reality. It was already nine o'clock

and we should have been in the bar at the Alpine Climbing Group (ACG) annual dinner in the Kingshouse pub. These nights of beer, bullshit and mayhem were one of the highlights of the social calendar. We were already late and the piss-up would be in full swing. We would have to drive like crazy to arrive in Glencoe before midnight.

I had kept my feelings to myself all the way back, yet as we reached the car Al turned and said, 'Did you feel something strange on the way down?'

In the ethereal moonlight we both gazed up the slope at the ridge line. I just smiled and knew that Mike had been one step behind us all day.

John Whittle relaxing while filming
Touching the Void in Peru, 2002.

6

THE SILVER FOX
John Whittle

My old Morris Minor car, packed with all my worldly possessions, slowly motored past the small harbour of Bangor, a small cathedral city perched above the sea channel separating the Welsh mainland from the island of Anglesey. A warm September breeze blew off the Menai Strait sands, carrying the smell of seaweed and the squawk of gulls. I arrived at my student lodgings, unloaded the car, lay on my bed, and stared at the ceiling. I was all alone. I had moved from the frenetic industrial city of Leeds, where most of my friends lived, to study for a Master's degree in ecology at Bangor University.

In the evening, I walked into a busy pub, which I had been told was the student climbers' meeting place. Sat around a table was a group of people loudly chatting. One guy with scraggly brown hair that fell onto his broad shoulders, was entertaining the group. 'I reached up for a hold . . . the rope . . . then I fell off!' I had found the climbers. And on that evening in 1973, I also met the raconteur, John Whittle, for the first time. We soon became friends and started climbing together.

He grew up on the outskirts of Manchester and was a couple of years older than me. Built for climbing, he was a powerful guy of medium height. Hair and beard masked a face which always smiled, a guise which I soon discovered betrayed a helter-skelter life of financial and relationship turmoil.

During one of our early conversations, he mentioned his frustrations and disappointment with academic life.

'I was interested in my philosophy course, but I hated all the studying. It was stupid, but I failed my final exams,' John admitted with a hint of embarrassment. The day before his last exam, he went climbing with his friend Doc O'Brien. On the way home, they stopped by at an end of term party. He assured Doc that he'd only have a quick beer. Predictably, under the influence of a few drinks, John stayed all night, and in the morning, had to go straight from there to sit the exam. By then, fatigue had caught up with him, so he decided to lay his head on the desk for a short while. He awoke suddenly, with twenty minutes to go before the end of the exam.

Initially, I was more impressed by John's adventurous spirit than his climbing. He was a great storyteller, and I was enthralled as he recounted a recent expedition to Arctic Norway. With a group of friends he bought a forty-foot schooner, and with minimal experience sailed across the North Sea. On the voyage out, they were lucky to survive a Force 9 gale that all but wrecked them, and when returning, they were becalmed, ran out of drinking water, and they had to survive on the juice from canned peas. Their objective was an ascent of Norway's national mountain, the granite obelisk of Stetind. They succeed by a fifty-three pitch, 2,000 metre new route on North-West Spur, which was almost a sideshow to their sailing escapade. It showed maturity and confidence beyond his years. I soon realised this was typical of John's quest for daring and intrepid ventures, where the sea and the mountains were his natural colosseum.

After a year, I finished my studies and in the autumn of 1974 moved into Treborth, John's rented ramshackle farmhouse in North Wales. I was given a stained mattress behind the piano in the disused front room, sleeping next to John's mongrel dog, *Hardd* (meaning Beautiful in Welsh). John had recently bought the old instrument from the nearby village and transported it in an open-back Landrover with two friends' help. As they drove through Bangor town centre, John gave a recital to the amused pedestrians. He played boogie-woogie, the limit of his repertoire. The farm became home to a small group of climbers, an artist, a musician and a Dutch boat builder. John welcomed any free-thinking mavericks who enjoyed the company and could keep talking deep into the night. It had a feel of a commune where there was always room for visitors to sleep on the floor. A bonus was the outbuildings, an ideal playground for climbers, giving a venue for finger strength training by traversing back and forth on the rough stone walls. We paid for our food and drink by working part-time at a friend's fish farm. It also gave me just enough cash to run a beat-up car, which transported us for happy days of climbing on the North Wales cliffs.

John had just finished with his girlfriend, Kay, but otherwise, I am unsure what persuaded us to move our ambitions from a happy and tranquil farmhouse to the rigours of high-level mountaineering. John and I were contently climbing at a similar standard, and although we thought ourselves as competent at our sport, we were a long way from the highest level. Almost by fate, we were caught in an upward vortex, gaining experience, ability and fulfilment with a group of like-minded friends. In the years ahead, a whole series of opportunities seemed to appear by accident rather than design, and a collective energy would take us far beyond our individual dreams and aspirations.

Unexpectedly one day, Al Rouse appeared on my doorstep, having just flown back from guiding in California. The following balmy day we climbed at Gogarth, a sea cliff on Anglesey, where my direction took one of those unexpected turns. High above the blue, grey water, I struggled to follow a particularly steep climb called *Wonderwall*. At the top, as we coiled the ropes, Al revealed his outlandish plan. 'How do you fancy a winter in the Alps?'

'How the hell am I going to afford that? It'll be too cold to camp!' I replied incredulously.

I've found an apartment in Argentière which, if we take it for the whole season is really cheap.'

'How cheap?' I interrupted.

'Not as much as you would think. I've asked Rab and he's keen and will come back from Buenos Aires. Unfortunately, Mike can't make it. But if you and John Whittle come, the rent will be split four ways.'

'OK, I'll ask John ... Pity about Mike.'

In mid-December 1974, John and I arrived by train to Argentière, a French village in the upper Chamonix valley, below the slopes of Mont Blanc. It was our first winter climbing season in the Alps, and the plan was to stay for three months to learn how to climb in the harsh conditions. Up until then, we thought alpine winter climbing was the reserve of the most talented continental climbers.

One of the most significant differences between summer and winter was the effort it took to approach the climbs. The local French climbers negotiated the waist-deep snow on skis, but they had been slaloming down the slopes from childhood. We were novice skiers, so it was sensible and easier to use snowshoes. But John had this romantic idea of skiing and had carted a pair of 210 centimetre cable binding skis from Britain on the train, and he was intent on using them. The testing ground was the Brevent ski area above Chamonix. Al, Rab and I had our snowshoes fitted and were ready to go within five minutes. Half an hour later, John was still struggling to fit the complicated ski bindings and skins. Eventually, we set off, but immediately, John's skis fell off. We carried on without him and waited higher up. An hour later, he arrived, rather frustrated and exhausted.

On the descent, the three of us wearing snowshoes ran ungainly, but speedily downhill. Meanwhile, John tried his first ski turn. His fall started slowly, but as one ski went at ninety degrees to the other, it was inevitable.

There was a cry of 'Aah... Oh!' Then came a display of the splits, for those lucky enough to witness the incident, performed with unbelievable speed and agility. Undoubtedly the weight of the twenty-kilo pack forced the legs to do the otherwise impossible 180-degree contortion. Unfortunately (for John) the impressive gymnastic manoeuvre rapidly degenerated into a painful explosion of legs, skis and poles. One ski, with a mind of its own, then glided arrow-like down the hill, never to be seen again. Next day John bought a pair of snowshoes.

After Christmas, the blue skies tempted us away from our alcoholic life in the valley.

'What should we do for our first route?' John asked one evening as we relaxed over a beer. We decided on the Aiguille L'M as we thought it was a short route with simple access, and we should easily return in time for the New Year's Eve festivities. The gear

was packed, yet even for this relatively minor objective, our rucksacks were monstrously heavy. On the first day, we waded through
waist-deep snow and only reached the tree line by nightfall.

We bivouacked, but our stove malfunctioned, and with just luke-
warm soup in our bellies we had a restless night. Then we overslept.
The usual summer approach was avalanche prone, so we decided
to follow a saw-toothed ridge through more deep snow. We could
see it snaked directly to the base of the Aiguille L'M, but it looked
a long way. It was already going dark!

'We're going to have to get up a lot earlier and get going at first
light,' John suggested.

Even with dawn starts, it was still another two days before we
finally arrived at the bottom of the route. Leaving our packs at the
base, we found the rock bare of snow, and we were up and rappelled
down the climb in half a day; the same length of time it would take
in summer. It was the approach that had cost us the time, and we
missed New Year's Eve.

Arriving back at the apartment, our friends treated our farcical
four-day foray with derision. But in truth, our incompetence was
a valuable lesson in what not to do. It was particularly embarrassing as James Boulton and Dave Robinson, friends from Bangor,
who were staying in our apartment, made the first winter ascent
of the Droites North Face over the same period. With a similar
level of experience to us, they had made an outstanding climb of
one of the most challenging routes in the Alps. We were envious of
their success, though amazed by their tenacity and adventurous
spirit.

Disappointment at missing the New Year festivities was
adequately compensated when the SW Face of Everest expedition
members, including Chris Bonington and Dougal Haston, arrived
in Chamonix for a 'training camp'. We held a party at our apartment in their honour, which turned out to be an all-night drunken
success. Although most of the team were a generation older, many
were good friends, particularly Doug Scott, Nick Estcourt, Tut
Braithwaite and Martin Boysen. With youth's arrogance, we
thought that our generation was at the cutting edge, breaking
through to a new level of difficulty. So we were surprised when we

found out that Haston and Bonington, whom we thought were 'past it', had just come down, fresh from a challenging new route on the Aiguille du Triolet. Dougal had a reputation of being an enigmatic Scot, but John Whittle spent most of the evening in deep conversation with him. They became friends, and over the winter, they occasionally met to have deep and private discussions on what John termed 'our adventures in philosophy'.

After the enlightening time on the Aiguille L'M, our approach to winter climbing evolved. On the next foray, we made the first winter ascent of the Boccalatte Pillar on Mont Blanc du Tacul and the Lagarde Couloir on Les Droites. Meanwhile, Rab and Al succeeded on the Gervasutti Pillar, then they made a seminal ascent, at the highest level of difficulty, by climbing the North Face of the Aiguille des Pélerins. While on these climbs we were surprised by helicopters buzzing above us, and even more amazed when we saw aerial photos of our ascents on the local newspaper's front page. Inconsequential to us at the time, but looking back I suppose the media thought we had joined the world of the elite continental alpinists.

In early February John and I abandoned any plans to climb as the weather forecast was terrible for a week. We decided to visit an ex-girlfriend of John's who was working in a hostel for young adults in Florence. After leaving Argentière, our journey came to a halt in Milan. The rain fell as the gloomy day drew to a close and water spray followed every car that sped past, ignoring our hitching thumbs. A miserable night in the nearby tin bus shelter beckoned. Then, to our surprise, a big, comfortable Mercedes car screeched to a halt in the lay-by, and we thankfully bundled our rucksacks and soaking bodies into the warm, smoky interior.

'Florence?' John asked the driver.

'Si . . . Si,' the driver nodded, a cigarette poking out of the side of his mouth, his wide eyes, behind wire-rimmed glasses dilated by too many espressos. Impatient to get going, he accelerated the limo into the foggy darkness.

Next morning we eventually found the address of the hostel. John's friend was a lovely, petite woman with long wavy black hair and dark, intense eyes. Although English, she was bilingual and soon asked the staff to give us breakfast.

'You two need a shower,' she ordered rather than suggested, adding, 'There's a municipal shower just down the street.'

At the shabby red-bricked *Bagno Comunale* we paid our lira and were given a towel and a small bar of soap. Neither John nor I spoke any Italian so grunts, and sign language found us in the changing room amongst a group of loudly chattering Italians. John started to strip off, and suddenly everyone went quiet.

'Oh Mio Dio!' a shriek broke the silence.

Staring in amazement, the Italians rapidly put on their clothes and scrambled to the exit. I looked round to see John, with a sheepish grin on his face, standing semi-naked, his muscle-bound chest bare, dressed only in a pair of women's pink tights.

'What the fuck's that?' I looked in horror.

'I've been wearing them under my jeans to keep warm.'

'Not the tights; what's that big stain around your crotch?'

'I don't know, but it hurts like hell when I have a piss.'

Four days later, back in our flat in Argentière, I developed the same symptoms as John. The inquest started immediately. Every night, our debauched, carefree life alternated between the Savoy Bar and El Rancho. Over beers, we had fun with a small group of British and French alpinists, Canadian ice hockey players, and a team of ski bums. Lara was a beautiful blonde-haired Dutch skier, and over the season both Roger Baxter-Jones and I had relationships with her. Then, late one night, we saw a very drunk John Whittle and Lara merrily sliding down the icy road. She was the link, and it was no surprise to find that Roger had recently visited the doctor's.

Although the weather was now perfect for climbing our priority was to get medical treatment. There was a strong smell of surgical spirit as an elderly, bald doctor, dressed in a white cotton gown opened the surgery door and ushered us into his treatment room.

After some comical finger-pointing and a pidgin French session, a knowing grin crossed his face.

'Take off your trousers,' he politely suggested in broken English.

John and I stood, side by side, as he examined us, pushing and prodding with his gloved hand.

'Gonorrhoea,' he whispered.

We looked at each other with guilty smirks.

'One injection of penicillin now and one in five days.'

'But we are setting off to climb the North Face of the Dru tomorrow,' John complained.

The doctor looked up from his large syringe with raised eyebrows.

'You are alpinists? The Dru In winter, that is *formidable*, you must be very careful.'

As we left, he called after us.

'Bon chance. If you succeed, I will have champagne in the fridge.'

Nobody had repeated the North Face in winter since the first winter ascent, over twenty years earlier. The spectacular granite pillar of the Aiguille du Dru (3,754 metres) was our favourite peak, standing proudly like a sentinel over the Chamonix valley. We had both climbed routes on its granite walls in summer, so we were familiar with the mountain. However, in winter conditions, the rock would be cloaked with snow and ice, daylight hours were shorter, and our heavy packs of gear would slow us down. For us, it would be a significant step forward.

We had an unforgivably late start as we were drinking late into the night and had failed to pack our gear until the morning. Conveniently the infrastructure of cable cars in the Alps facilitates much easier access into the mountains than nature would usually allow. Even with a late morning start, we anticipated we would reach the base of our climb well before nightfall.

'Fancy a coffee before we catch the lift?' John suggested; the inviting smell from a cafe at the bottom of the cable car was too strong to ignore.

'Sure. It will be our last taste of luxury for a few days.'

Finishing our coffee, we battled through a frenzy of brightly coloured skiers onto the Grandes Montets cable car. At the top the skiers went left, we went right, and soon we were alone. To reach the base of the Dru was a two-hour approach, simply down the Couloir Rectiligne, before crossing the crevassed glacier under the Pic Sans Nom and Aiguille Verte. A route we thought was straightforward and benign.

Before we crossed the glacier, we paused to rope-up for safety.

Suddenly there was an almighty whip-crack noise, followed by a thunderous rumble.

'What the hell's that!' John shouted in panic.

Looking up, we saw a gigantic ice serac at the top of the Verte collapse. In what seemed like slow motion, it cascaded down the face.

'Watch out! It's going to hit us,' I yelled and dived to the ground, wrapping arms around my head; a futile gesture, as the whole basin in front of us was obscured with airborne powder snow and the deafening roar of the avalanche.

All went quiet as a frozen white mist settled.

'I thought seracs didn't fall in winter?' said John.

'Like hell, that's right across our access route.'

A dusting of fine white ice crystals covered our hair and beards. The path of the avalanche had just missed us. Slowly the light from an eerie haloed sun pierced the mist, and the hills returned to normal, as though nothing had happened.

'It's a good job we stopped for that coffee,' I said.

'For sure, you should never rush,' John observed, a mantra that he strictly followed all his life.

Feeling very insignificant we set off across the glacier at an ungainly gallop, our cheap wooden snowshoes forcing a gait more akin to lame carthorses than racing equines. With bursting lungs, we crossed the avalanche debris. Crevasses thwarted our progress as we jumped across one and crawled over another via an unstable snow bridge.

'Are we out of danger yet?' a breathless John pleaded.

The sun was already setting as we finally reached safety under the towering Dru. Hastily we climbed to our planned bivouac site on a snow terrace above, and dug out a flat area on the snow-covered ledges, big enough for us to lie.

'What do you want for dinner?' I asked as our homemade gas tower stove roared to life, melting snow.

'I think I'll have the steak followed by the crème brûlée,' John ordered, knowing full well that we only ever ate soup mixed with potato powder and slices of cheese, washed down with mint tea. A rationed piece of chocolate was our only luxury.

When I closed my eyes, I was in a nightmare, tumbling in a mael-strom of car-sized blocks of snow. Buried, I couldn't breathe, and I awoke with a gasp from my snow tomb ordeal.

'Oh, I'm so stiff,' John croaked as he switched on his head torch.

'What's the time?' I asked, manoeuvring the stove from the depths of my sleeping bag where it had been all night, keeping warm to ensure it worked efficiently for the morning brew.

'Five. Time to get up.' It was still dark, the coldest part of the day. A naked moon the size of a dinner plate and the colour of bone hung above the horizon. 'Did you sleep?'

'Like a log,' said John, as he lit his first roll-up of the day. I decided to keep quiet about my restless night.

The first signs of light were painting the sky as we finished dressing. We each wore thermal underwear, a homemade one-piece fleece suit, a pair of canvas builders' salopettes and an Army and Navy Store cotton anorak (at that time, in the mid-'70s, waterproof and breathable Gore-Tex fabric had not been invented). Woollen mitts and silk liner gloves protected our hands, and wool balaclavas covered our heads. Our double layered footwear was protected by homemade gaiters permanently stapled to the welts. With some discomfort, we kept the boots warm overnight by squeezing them inside the sleeping bag, companion to the stove.

That day's climbing was hard but superb. We followed a line of ice-clogged chimneys and cracks up the wall towards the promi-nent and gigantic Cyclops eye of snow called *The Niche*. Ahead was the crux of the climb, the imposing Lambert crack.

'Your turn to lead,' John said, smiling as he laboriously took off his rucksack, sat on it and wiped his dripping nose, picking icicles from his beard then carefully rolling a cigarette.

My crampons scraped and teetered as I made the first moves on to the verglassed granite. It was a desperate fight, and soon I was exhausted, needing a rest to warm my frozen hands and catch my breath.

'Below!' I howled, as I dislodged a brick-sized chunk of ice, which whistled directly for John's helmet. He ducked at the last second, and it missed by a whisker.

'Hey, that was a bit close,' John shouted.

'Sorry.'

'Get a bloody move on; I'm freezing down here!' as he lit another roll-up.

With energy to spare, John followed the pitch, then led to a bivouac at the bottom of the Niche.

Sitting, with legs in our sleeping bags, we enviously watched the last of the sun caress the snow on the far side of the valley. High on our North Face, there was no warmth, and the light was second-hand, cold and grey.

'Have you read the *Tractatus* by Wittgenstein?' John suddenly asked while tending the stove.

'No, I can't say I have. What's it about?'

'It's a bit complicated, but it tries to identify the relationship between language and reality and to define the limits of science.'

'Can you pass me a tea bag?' I asked as I tried to figure out what he had just said. His attempt at a conversation about philosophy had fallen on deaf ears!

Drifting off to sleep, we looked down into the valley, as if from an aircraft window, the occasional lights of cars tracing red and white lines along the road, in silence far below.

The next day the route slowly unfolded. There was no chatter, and already halfway up, everything was perfect: the weather, the equipment, and our implicit understanding. The rock above the *Niche* was free of ice, much like summer conditions, except that it was much, much colder. Frozen hands required warming, an excru-ciating process involving stuffing them inside the layers of clothing next to the body and massaging the fingers. As the warmth returned, there was the agony of 'hot aches', which brought out howls of pain, before climbing could continue.

'Almost there,' I smiled at John as we burst out into the sun.

I spoke too soon. I was relaxed and climbing confidently above John when a foothold broke. In desperation, my hands clawed at the rock, but immediately my heavy sack turned me upside down. I screamed past John in a blur and mercifully crashed to a juddering stop below him. Skilfully he had managed to hold the rope. I was uninjured, and for the second time on the climb, our luck was with us.

The weather was still perfect as we reached the summit. Together, yet alone we hugged each other and witnessed an unforgettable panoramic vista of the snow-covered Mont Blanc range turning pink then blue in the crepuscular evening rays. The night was bitter, the coldest I had experienced. The following day the deep snow descent was uneventful, tiring and tedious, but gravity helped and by early afternoon we were amongst the skiers, then the warmth and the fresh coffee of the valley.

Next day we visited the doctor. 'Bravo! I read of your success in the local newspaper this morning.' A wide grin filled his round face.

'First, the injection.' He carefully administered the antibiotic, and apparently we were cured. He opened the fridge and pulled out a bottle. 'Now we shall drink champagne.'

The Dru was our final climb and the pinnacle of our successful season. Though we did not know it at the time, these ascents gave our group the knowledge and confidence to attempt greater challenges in the Andes and Himalayas over the next ten years. With a twinge of sadness, we carried our heavy bags, one last time to catch the train from Chamonix station back to the UK.

A few months later, in the summer of '75, we were back in Chamonix. We had just got down from the Petites Jorasses, where we encountered eight parties on the same route.

'We need to get away from the crowds,' a disillusioned John lamented.

'It's not like winter,' I replied.

'We need to go somewhere remote and silent,' John suggested.

'There's so much litter, and the huts are crammed full,' I sadly concurred.

Soon after we narrowly survived being hit by a salvo of stones dislodged by a party above us, on the North East Spur of the Droites. When we returned to the valley, we took down our tents and went home to earn some money to fund our dream of an adventure somewhere in the mountains further afield.

One evening that autumn, I was playing darts in the Moon, a climbers' pub in Derbyshire, and I got talking to Alan and Adrian Burgess.

'Come and stay in Chester with us, there are loads of teaching jobs in Ellesmere Port,' Aid encouraged.

'Aye, the schools are so rough nobody wants to work there,' Al, his brother, added.

Alan and Adrian Burgess (aka the Twins) were two giants of British mountaineering. They were identical and by reputation even their girlfriends, Christine and Daphne, had trouble distinguishing them! Over six foot, broad-shouldered, long blond hair and not an ounce of fat on their muscle-bound bodies they would have fitted perfectly into a Viking raiding party. They came from Holmfirth, Yorkshire and had a no-nonsense approach to life. They liked beer, women and especially fighting. A couple of years older and more experienced than me, they had a rack of difficult alpine ascents and an overland trip to the Himalayas under their belt. They were on top of their game having just come back from an alpine ascent of the gruelling *Cassin Spur* on McKinley in Alaska.

Together with Rab Carrington and Alan Rouse, they were plotting a crazy idea of an expedition to South America, lasting eight months. They invited John and me to join the ambitious project. To go, I needed cash. However work opportunities had dried up in North Wales, so I reluctantly left the commune in Treborth. Over the next year, I followed the Twins' advice and worked on and off as a temporary teacher with disruptive kids. I hated teaching, but it was a means to an end. Somehow John scraped and saved his six hundred pounds by working on a fish farm, and bizarrely set up a one-person Punch and Judy show at Llandudno, the North Wales seaside resort. By the beginning of November, we had just enough savings to buy one-way air tickets and cash to tour South America.

The Twins' partners would join the team. Daphne was a fiery blonde, dwarfed by her giant boyfriend, Al. The dark-locked Christine, a French girl who spoke alluring Franco-English with an incongruously broad Yorkshire accent, accompanied Aid. Vivacious ginger-haired Sue, the partner of Rab, was the ninth member of the party. None of the women climbed, but they loved the mountains, and they were well attuned to our annoying habits. All three were equally strong-minded, adding a welcome female perspective to the adventure as well as keeping our immature male exuberance in check.

On 11th November 1976, we flew into Buenos Aires and made our way to the house of the Argentinian *andinista*, Hector Vietes. On their South American expedition, two years previously, Rab and Al had become friends with Hector, with Rab staying on, to work in his small business making down clothing and sleeping bags. Hector was a shortish, swarthy guy with long black hair, centre-parted with an overgrown beard hiding a smiling face, a cigarette always hanging loosely from his mouth. Nobody ever saw him eat, though by day he sipped *maté* through a *bombilla* straw poking out of a hand-held gourd, by night he sipped a bottomless glass of red wine. Hector was incredibly hospitable and sociable and was well connected to the middle-class *inteligencia*, the beautiful people of Buenos Aires. At a party, on the first night, John and I fell in love with all the beautiful Argentinian women, and the next three days were a drunken haze of alcohol and all-night tango clubs.

With Hector's connections, we managed to get a cheap flight to Patagonia rather than taking the tiresome, multi-day overland route. We landed at a windswept Rio Gallegos to a less than friendly welcome. An officious military junta governed Argentina, and there were already rumblings of their claim for Las Malvinas, what Britain called the Falkland Islands. The airport doubled as a military base and the staging post to any possible fighting on the Islands. Jostling through the airport terminal, we got an uneasy feeling that Brits were unwelcome. As we walked out of the building, two jeeps, mounted with machine guns and a lorry carrying a dozen soldiers screeched to a halt in front of us. With a lot of intimidating rifle-butt pushing and shoving, it became apparent that we had to line up against the wall of a nearby building, legs apart and hands in the air, while a dozen guns pointed at us.

'Pasaporte,' was the curt order from their commander.

'A dónde vas,' he barked his next demand.

Rab, our Spanish speaker, cleared his throat, 'El Parque Nacional Los Glaciares . . . Chaltén.'

1 The author on a Piraňa meet in Yorkshire in 1975. (John Sheard).
2 Sam Cochrane on *Main Wall*, Gimmer Crag, the English Lake District in 1968.

3 John Syrett on *Early Riser* (E5 6a), Earl Crag, Yorkshire. (Bernard Newman).
4 John Syrett making the first ascent of *Joker's Wall* (E4 6a), solo, 1971. (John Stainforth).

5 John Syrett belays the author on *Midnight Cowboy*, Malham Cove, 1972. (Bernard Newman).
6 Tim Rhodes, Roger Martin, and Alex MacIntyre outside the Glen Nevis caravan (John Powell).
7 Al Rouse on *Erabus* (E3 5c), Tremadoc 1969. (Leo Dickinson).

8 Roger Baxter-Jones with the author and John Moore in the summit bivouac hut on the Badile, the Swiss Alps (John Stainforth).

9 Early '70s, Al Rouse and Choe Brooks at Snell's Field campsite in Chamonix. (Steve Arsenault).

10 Al Rouse below Mike Geddes on the *Croz Spur* in the Alpine winter of 1976.

11 Mike Geddes settles into his hammock on a winter ascent of Pointe du Domino, Mont Blanc Range.
12 The author climbing *Geddes's Gully*, Scotland, 1986. (Al Rouse).
13 Anglo-French Meet in Scotland with (L–R) Nick Donnelly, Alex MacIntyre, René Ghilini, Jean-Marc Boivin, Dominique Julien, Rainier Munsch, and Jean-Frank Charlet.

14 Alex MacIntyre on South Face of Agujo Nevada 3 (first ascent), 1979. (John Porter).
15 John Whittle and Dick Renshaw at Holyhead after cycling from Bangor to climb at Gogarth, mid-70s. (John Sheard).
16 Rab Carrington, the Burgess Twins, Al Rouse, Sue, Christine, John Whittle, Daphne, and the author in Rio Gallegos, Southern Argentina.

15

16

17 Cerro Torre, Torre Egger, and Cerro Standhardt, Patagonia.
18 Base Camp in the Patagonia woods; Al Rouse with John Whittle and Rab Carrington.
19 John Whittle traversing steep snow on Standhardt with Fitz Roy behind.

20 John Whittle on difficult mixed climbing on the final summit attempt on Standhardt.
21 The author was turned back, ten metres from the summit of Standhardt, by a furious storm (John Whittle).
22 Jannu. The ascent followed the ridge on the right (Dave Binns).

21

22

23 Roger Baxter-Jones contemplates Jannu's Tête du Butoir at 6500 metres.
24 Roger Baxter-Jones nearing Jannu's summit with the snow plateau of *The Throne* below.
25 The author with Roger Baxter-Jones bivouacing at 7,000 metres on Jannu. (Al Rouse).

'Abra su bolso.'

We slowly lowered our arms and undid our rucksacks as the soldiers moved closer, to peer inside; guns cocked at the ready.

'Por qué estás aquí?' This time his question was more conciliatory.

'Andinistas,' Rab forced a smile, directly at the commander. He was trying to win him over even though his shock of unruly black hair and bushy beard gave him the look of Che Guevara.

With their show of strength, the soldiers seemed satisfied with our purpose and surprisingly waved us on our way. Hector had arranged for us to stay at a local climber's house. Moving around with all our belongings for an eight-month stay in South America was hard work, and the word taxi had not been coined in this edge-of-the-world town, even if we could have afforded such a luxury. So it was with some relief that we found Pedro Korchenevsky's address was not too long a walk from the airport. He was much older than we expected, and his hunched back and aged physique, indicated he had not climbed for a long time. He was also distinctly eccentric; his job was rewinding electric motors with copper wire, but his passion was penguins. A large sign above his shed, which he called home, read *Pingüino Eléctrico*. Inside, the walls were covered with pictures of penguins, and the floor littered with comical stuffed birds. He showed us to our room for the night, a window-less bunker with a cold concrete floor. He asked if we wanted a drink.

'Cerveza?' John proudly asked, using his only word of Spanish.

'No yo no tengo,' Pedro croaked, and proceeded to get an old lemonade bottle down from a shelf. He rummaged in a drawer and found a selection of dirty glasses, most chipped, and started wiping them with an oily rag he found on his workbench. He lifted the bottle carefully to look at three strange layers of liquid, unlike anything any of us had ever seen in a bar room beverage.

'What's that?' John exclaimed, still dreaming of an ice-cold beer.

Pedro seemed to understand John's question.

'Esta bebida es abogado.' He proudly shook the contents and opened the cork with a slight pop. Then carefully poured this lumpy syrup, the colour and consistency of snot, into our glasses.

There was no rush to pick up the drinks, but Pedro raised his glass for a toast, which meant we could not refuse. Always eager for a drink, John was the first to take a swig. As soon as it passed his lips, there was regret; he gasped, his face turned red, then he bent double and started retching and coughing. It later turned out that Pedro was famous for his Advocaat, made from his own distilled alcohol and penguin eggs. A small sip revealed it tasted like liquefied kippers mixed with methylated spirit.

Despite his weird habits, Pedro was incredibly helpful and gave us his old pick-up truck to shop for three months' of food and then organised a lift for us on a construction truck to the roadhead in the National Park. He even offered us a bottle of his Advocaat! There was room for all nine of us, plus gear and food in the open back of the large, light blue Chevrolet truck. For hour after hour, we passed through the monotonous arid Patagonian steppe, the home of the gaucho and their sheep; a land formed in the rain shadow east of the mountains. Nearing the end of our journey, we sped along the banks of the vast turquoise-coloured Lake Viedma with a long plume of dust in our wake.

'Look . . . Look,' Al Burgess suddenly shouted, pointing down the ruler-straight, bumpy, dirt road.

'Fitz Roy, and there's Cerro Torre on the left,' an excited John replied.

The lorry pulled to a halt at the roadhead before a small bridge over a foaming river. A short distance away was the only habitable building, the park warden's house, from which came a man on a brush polished skinny horse, moving slowly towards us at an easy trot. He wore a wide-brimmed black hat, a *chiripa* girding his waist, a drab woollen poncho, and long, accordion-pleated *bombacha* trousers, gathered at the ankles and covering the tops of high black leather boots. A silver-handled knife shone prominently at his side, and his whip and an old rifle hung loosely off his ornate saddle.

'Hola qué tal?' The park warden greeted us suspiciously.

'Buenas tardes. Bien, y Usted,' Rab replied.

The rest of us looked on in ignorance as Rab chatted with our host. There was much gesticulating, and eventually a smile; then a laugh indicated we were welcome.[1]

The mountain range is named after its dominant and highest peak, Fitz Roy. A mountain often called by its local name, Chaltén, meaning smoking mountain after the plume of cloud that billows from its summit. Fitz Roy was climbed first by Lionel Terray and Guido Magnone who were members of a French expedition in 1952. When we arrived, its summit had been reached no more than ten times, always by heavyweight expeditions. An alpine style ascent of the original route was the Burgess twins' priority, and a new route on the west face, the main objective for Al and Rab.

At 3,405 metres it is not a high peak and climbers attempting its golden granite walls do not have to contend with altitude-related conditions. Instead, they have to battle with the worst weather in the world. Situated on the narrow tail of South America it is exposed to the westerly winds of the Roaring Forties that blow across the Southern Pacific, picking up speed and moisture. The air mass is cooled as it crosses the Patagonian Icecap before abruptly rising over the Fitz Roy massif. The rapid changes in the air mass are measured in hours, and intense storms descend without warning. Wind speeds of 150 km/hour are typical, accelerating even higher as they are funnelled by the mountain features. Humid air is forced to rise over the mountains, plastering the vertical walls in rime ice and crowning the summits with unbelievable giant snow mushrooms. In the mountain valleys, torrential precipitation creates luxuriant temperate rain forests.

On the opposite side of the glacial valley to Fitz Roy, and over-looking the ice cap are the Torres, often regarded as the most impressive and beautiful group of peaks in the world. The highest is Cerro Torre, at 3,128 metres, which is an unbelievable spire of granite and ice, providing the ultimate difficulty in mountain-eering. This challenge is not because of its height, rather its 1,250

1. By 2020 this area had morphed into the village of El Chaltén having around 2,000 inhabitants, featuring hostels, shops and restaurants, with a regular bus service to the outside world. Most climbers stay here rather than at base camps in the woods, as they can access the internet to get sophisticated long-term weather forecasting to plan their climbs.

metre sheer rock and ice walls, which are some of the tallest on the planet. The first ascent was claimed by Italian Cesare Maestri in 1959, maintaining that he and his partner, Toni Egger, reached the summit. Tragically Egger was swept to his death by an avalanche while they were descending. Their ascent line looked implausible, and with no other witnesses, the climbing world's most intriguing controversy surrounded the event, and most climbers accused Maestri of lying.

To vanquish his detractors, Maestri went back to Cerro Torre in 1970 and made a new route on the South East Face using rock-bolts fixed with the aid of a gas-powered compressor drill. Leading mountaineer, Reinhold Messner, called this style 'the murder of the impossible' in his 1971 article in *Mountain* magazine, complaining that using so many bolts for artificial aid was unethical, enabling anything to be climbed.

The first undisputed summiteers were the Lecco Spiders in 1974. Led by Casimiro Ferrari, the Italians climbed the peak from the remote west, ice-cap side. The majority of subsequent attempts of this desirable peak have been by Maestri's 'Compressor Route' by climbers who used Maestri bolts to claim their ascent. Then in 2012, American Hayden Kennedy and Canadian Jason Kruk made the first 'fair-means' ascent of the route and removed most of the bolts.

The other two prominent peaks of the Torres are the slightly lower Torre Egger and Cerro Standhardt. The year before we arrived, in February 1976, John Bragg, Jim Donini and Jay Wilson from the United States, took two months to climb Torre Egger in an ascent prolonged by poor weather. That left Standhardt unclimbed. For John and I this became the focus for much of our stay in Patagonia.

We spent several days portering heavy loads for a month's stay at our first Base Camp in the Eléctrico valley in the north of the range, at a dilapidated corrugated tin farm hut called Piedra del Fraile. The early December weather seemed to follow a pattern of one-day good followed by a three-day storm. With careful management, this allowed us to climb a few smaller peaks.

Over Christmas, the weather deteriorated, and it rained

biblically for five days. The river broke its banks, and floods stranded us. Depressed by the conditions Al, Rab, Sue, John and I moved over to the Torre valley, a long day's walk through the stunted beech woods, bent and twisted by the wind, teeming with birdlife. Bright red-headed Magellanic Woodpeckers, with no fear of humans, would sit on a branch a metre away, while we sat for a drink and snack. In the fast-moving rivers, the lovely Torrent Ducks and their tiny ducklings played in the frigid rapids.

Our new Base Camp was in the enchanted woods next to the Rio Fitz Roy, which drained from the Laguna Torre, less than an hour from the snout of the glacier. We immediately started to build a kitchen shelter. We had brought a saw, axe and sheets of polythene. Soon a wooden frame was constructed in the shape of a large tent and covered in poly. At one end stood a stone hearth for a wood fire, with a chimney made from tin cans wired together. A large square box was partially filled with sand and used as an oven for bread and pizza. Deadwood was gathered for our fire, which was kept burning day and night. During the continuous rain, we would carve things out of wood, cook, read and play chess or card games.

In many ways, it was utopian heaven, but we had two problems. The first was the bloody awful weather, and the second was the paucity of food. We could do very little about the wind and rain, but the food issue was of our own making. Partly because we had no money we had not bought enough, or more correctly, we had erred towards quantity, not quality. We had a lot of rice, flour (though we bought forty kilos of cornflour by mistake!), porridge oats, dried beans and pasta. There were no fresh vegetables apart from onions (which soon rotted), nor did we have any fresh fruit. Back in Britain, John and I were accustomed to a diet of beer and chips, so this was a disaster. We had no alcohol and no potatoes. Of course, being British, we had enough tea to last a year. Thankfully a few tins of goodies such as carrots, peas, tomato puree, dulce de leche and peaches supplemented our subsistence diet. Who knows what the meagre diet would do to our supposed athletic performance?

As Al and Rab had been here two years ago, they assured us that the sheep would provide plenty of meat.

'There are sheep everywhere, and as long as the gauchos don't catch you, it's easy to rustle them,' Al assured us when we arrived.

'But I haven't seen any sheep,' John complained.

'I was going to break the bad news,' Rab interjected, adding, 'Unfortunately, they are all being sheared at the estancia. They won't be around here for another month.'

'What . . . no meat?' John was aghast.

Climbing seemed like a distant memory as days turned into weeks of rain drumming on the polythene roof of our shelter. During short breaks in the storms, we managed the occasional half-day forays up the Torre glacier. Mostly we looked into turbulent clouds, which hid our dreams of success and failure. Occasionally we glimpsed tantalising ridges and snow-clad summits, but we were resigned to waiting for the weather to change.

On a red cord, hanging from a branch of wood in our kitchen, dangled a Thommen altimeter. Every time we passed this pocket-watch sized Swiss instrument, we would examine it, in case its single pointing hand indicated a drop in altitude, meaning a rise in pressure and an improvement in the weather. It had become the centre of our attention, creating a weird habit, akin to addiction. The slightest drop in the wind, a temporary break in the rain or a lone star shining through the cloudy night sky and we would crowd around what had become our oracle. We even took turns getting up in the middle of the night, to squint, bleary-eyed through torchlight at the damn machine, hoping for a break in the weather. We were getting restless, it was 23rd January, and we had not climbed for a month!

'Get up!' A shout from Rab stirred me unexpectedly in the pitch black of night.

'John!' I elbowed the snoring body lying next to me in our small cotton tent.

'The pressure's rising.' Rab's enthusiastic voice was a call to action.

By the time John and I made the short walk to the kitchen shelter, Rab and Al were in full packing mode and already dressed for climbing.

'Are you sure?' John peered at the Thommen as rain accompanied the silence.

'Aye . . . we've got nothing better to do.' Rab blew vigorously at the embers to get the kettle boiling.

It was dark when Al and Rab left the shelter carrying their bulky packs for an attempt on Quatro Dedos, an unclimbed peak of around 2,200 metres which they hoped to succeed by a lightning-fast, single-day ascent.

'What do you think?' John asked after they had left.

'We'd look stupid if it turns out good . . . we have to try,' I said with more enthusiasm than I felt.

We left the camp as the first calls of birdsong played to a grey and cloudy dawn. It was time to try Standhardt, our main objective.

It took all day to approach our mountain. Scrabbling through the maze of huge boulders and moraine, a lottery as to which stone was secure and which would topple and cast you in a heap on the ground. The glacier surface turned to snow just as the clouds parted and the sky became blue. The sun rose, as did the temperature. The steep glacier sloping up to the Col to the right of Standhardt looked trivial, but we grossly underestimated its size. The snow from weeks of storms was thigh deep, and the blazing sun turned it into the consistency of porridge. Two days earlier, the weather had been appalling, and now the incongruous intense heat sapped our energy.

Why do I do this? Wait weeks for good weather then go through purgatory, I thought, sweating up the interminable slope.

It was nightfall before we reached a bergschrund below the col where we could shelter for the night.

We ate our breakfast to an eerie melody, a whistling noise that changed octaves seemingly at random. The weather was perfect on our east, lee side of the mountain, and crisp frozen snow took us rapidly to the col where a huge chockstone was wedged in the gap. There, the strange noise was deafening. Formed under the stone was a large hole through which a vicious west wind was being funnelled, and like the reed of a massive organ pipe, it played its haunting fugue. It was impossible to stand in the gap as the gale had too much power, forcing us to don our goggles. The hole was a doorway to another world, the most fantastic vista of the ice cap spread out to the western horizon, and out of sight, sixty-five kilometres away, would be the Chilean fiords and the Southern Pacific Ocean. Looking in awe, we saw a desolate white moonscape with an alien sky of lenticular clouds shaped like flying saucers, tadpoles, flat caps or whatever you wanted to imagine. This one panorama, this one sublime view made us feel so small. Despite the howling gale, we had found our 'silent' place.

'We need to get out of this wind,' John suggested with some urgency.

'It should be sheltered on the ramp across the East Face,' I replied as I quickly prepared to lead across hoary rock slabs, which would eventually lead to the prominent snow ramp that slashed across this side of the mountain.

John remembered this stretch of climbing in an article he wrote for the magazine *Crags* #1:

> Brian set off, and it was quite an effort just to watch him, and the rope slowly move. It meant turning my face into the wind, exposed to the relentless onslaught of horizontally driven ice particles which poured through the gap.
>
> When I started to climb, my crampons kept searching for adhesion on the iced rock. With my head recoiled into the collar-bone, my movement upwards was more reminiscent of a rusty piece of automata than that of a human being. I reached Brian, whose face appeared red-raw with the incessant ice-particle bombardment. It wasn't a place to linger, so I set out to tension across the granite slabs on the left.

Eventually, we reached a tongue of snow, the start of the ramp proper, and much easier climbing. We were now sheltered from the wind but had another problem. The sun was melting large sections of honeycombed ice that had been plastered by recent storms on the walls above. We were in the firing line and had to dodge the blitz of ice that cascaded down. We pondered below an overhanging chimney festooned with ice and loose rock. Jim Donini, John Bragg, Ben Campbell-Kelly and Brian Wyvill had attempted to climb this way two years ago. It was in our plan that we would also try this line, but it oozed with evil. With reluctance, we started up the chimney. Partway up, John described his plight.

> No obvious technique seemed possible to negotiate this steep, loose and featureless section of the chimney. All the pitons I placed acted as levers, prizing out blocks from their fastenings, and my endeavours often sent these blocks hurtling down onto Brian, who stood braced and incarcerated in the narrowest point of the chimney chute. I remember one large block cascading down, tracing an inevitable path towards him. I winced in anticipation as I saw it land squarely in the middle of Brian's huddled form and there it stopped, a 5-kilo block having fallen 20 metres, sitting motionless on the top of his rucksack: a near thing.
>
> (Higher) I inserted a piton, which to my dismay entered a little too easily, but it would give me a couple of feet I needed to finish the pitch and reach easier ground. I hung on it, and in a split-second, I saw it move. The next moment was a blur of rapid descent accompanied by the clatter of scraping ironmongery and various gurgling exclamations. Ten metres lower I came to rest, dazed and unsure whether I was injured. I checked myself for damage, but I was unhurt except for a few minor abrasions. Below, Brian's only wish was that he should be released from the pillory he'd been chained to for the last four hours, and whether it was up or down didn't seem to matter. I was in favour of retreat, so we rappelled the 100 metres to the bottom of the chimney.

It was mid-afternoon, and the skies were still blue.

'What should we do?' I asked John, somewhat dispirited from the claustrophobic nightmare of the chimney.

'We can't go down and waste this spell of good weather, we may not get another chance.' John surprised me with his enthusiasm.

We sat for a while and had a bite to eat. Looking around, we could not see any way of breaching the wall above other than by the chimney we had just failed to climb.

'Come on, let's carry along the ramp and see what's around the corner, on the South Face.' John got up and readied to climb.

We had scanned the mountain with binoculars from the valley during brief clearings of cloud in the past weeks. So we knew there was a slim possibility that the south face could be climbed but had also noticed the enormous summit mushroom threatening those foolish enough to venture there. With that in mind, we continued for seven rope lengths and found an eyrie on the edge of the South Face where we bivouacked.

The morning promised a good day, and we crossed steep icy slopes above a sickening void plunging straight down to the glacier far below. Directly opposite was an utterly jaw-dropping view of the summit of Egger; a colossal totem pole of pink-red granite garlanded with vertical snow and dazzling chandeliers of ice. Behind, the big daddy of Cerro Torre hung like a spectre, hewn by Michelangelo's feral ghost. We were treading into a hallowed place, the Vatican of climbing.

As we climbed, the haunting wind started to roar louder, ever-present tinnitus that fried the nerves, reminding us of our temporary existence in this wild world of giants. Luckily we were still sheltered from the wind's wrath.

'Brian . . . look what's happening.' I was so immersed in my climbing I had not noticed the weather.

'Look at Fitz Roy,' John shouted above the howling gale.

Within minutes Fitz Roy's summit, on the other side of the valley, was being engulfed by a battalion of grey spaceship clouds.

'I think we should retreat,' John suggested in an urgent tone.

'No, let's carry on. We have the experience and equipment,' I replied.

> A direct conflict. I decided not to put any more pressure on Brian but hoped after this pitch when I took the lead; his consequent immobility would allow the damp and disquiet to awaken his prudence. I spent ten minutes battling above, saying nothing but convinced that his request for our retreat was imminent. Fortunately, it was.

Within the space of minutes, my confidence had evaporated. The wind direction had changed, and we were in a whiteout, engulfed in clouds. We were being buffeted from side to side by the hurricane strength gale, like being punched by an invisible boxer. My mind struggled to cope. I had been stupid to ignore John's request and the obvious signs of the impending Armageddon. With only two ropes between us, the 1,500-metre descent loomed as the largest demand ever placed on our climbing lives.

The first rappel was awkward as our ascent line had been diagonal. I half-pendulumed, half- climbed, managing to reach a ledge where John joined me. The situation was quickly deteriorating as supercooled moisture in the wind-driven cloud was caking our clothing and beards in ice, and our frozen ropes were rapidly becoming unmanageable.

> We attempted to separate the two ropes so they would run freely, but they were fused together. This was just the kind of thing every climber dreads. When everything was deteriorating, weather, strength and equipment, to have one's ropes rendered unusable is all but the last straw. To survive, we had to retrieve them by swinging out to the left with one of the ends in an attempt to break the weld. Luckily they separated, and we managed to haul them down. Our remaining rappels back to our bivouac site were made shorter and more cautiously.

We spent the rest of the day down climbing and rappelling, mindful that it was imperative to keep the ropes as short as possible as they whipped uncontrollably in the wind. When we eventually reached the col, it was impossible to stand upright. To ensure the vortex did not blow us off our feet, we crawled like crabs across the icy slope. Thankful for the miracle of deliverance, we collapsed into the same bergschrund bivouac we used two days earlier. We had nothing to eat but sugar, which we mixed with the snow for some nutrition. Back at Base Camp, we slept for two days. Rab and Al's tactics had been more successful than ours, albeit on a much smaller peak. They had climbed Quatro Dedos in a day.

It rained for the next three weeks, and camp life revolved around food. Above our camp, in an ablation valley at the side of the Torre glacier were the remnants of a deserted Italian Base Camp. On several occasions, we walked up there to plunder pieces of camp material that would be useful to enhance our basic living. They had left it in a sorry state with garbage strewn all over the otherwise pristine landscape. With plenty of spare time, John suggested a visit to tidy the place and bury the rubbish.

'Look at this,' John shouted, as he frantically tore apart a half-buried cardboard box.

'It's tins of food,' I said, joining his excitement.

'Are you sure, what do you think is in them?' The tarnished tins had lost their labels.

We loaded them into our rucksack and carried them down.

'What have you two boys found?' Sue asked.

'Food!' Immediately, Al and Rab gathered round, keen to examine our bounty.

'There's a label on this one,' Al noticed.

'*Mondongo en Salmuera*. What the hell's that?' John already had the can opener in his hands, salivating at the thought of some Italian delicacy.

'Oh my God!' exclaimed John as he revealed the contents, 'Its bloody tripe, I can't eat that!'

One day we were festering as usual: John and Al played chess, Rab and Sue baked bread, while I read.

'Baaah, Baaah, Bah.' A new sound drifted in on the wind, and we looked up in unison. The sheep were back!

With some hesitation, we sharpened our knives and set off hunting, with dreams of lamb chops. There was a degree of uncertainty about whether or not we should be rustling the impoverished gaucho's flock. But Al justified our actions saying we would be stealing from the wealthy estancia owners.

Three days later, we still had not caught our prey. How could they be so fast and elusive? Eventually, Rab threw a stone, which by pure fluke hit a poor lamb on the head. Confused, it ran into an old wire fence, where it got trapped. Having lived at Treborth farm for the last five years, John volunteered to slaughter the sad beast. He expertly tied its back legs together and hung it on a tree branch. He'd clearly been keeping quiet about his talents! At this point 'Larry the Lamb' started bleating pitifully.

'Baaah, Baaaah Bah.' Its big eyes stared at John's knife.

'Brian, do you want to have a go?' the plaintive cries seemed to have put John off his murderous intent. I politely declined, as did Al and Rab. The first of John's stabs were not from the 'Dummies Guide to Butchery'. He missed the neck and didn't even draw blood, but it must have hurt as the petrified creature started to writhe, twisting in pain and fear. I was beginning to think our enforced vegetarian diet was a good idea.

'What if I knock it out with a stone, then it will be easier to kill,' John suggested.

'Go on then,' I replied, not feeling any enthusiasm for the next stage in the murder.

Eventually, the animal died, but the following part of the process was equally gruesome.

'I killed it; somebody else can gut it.' John insisted.

Like most of the population, I usually bought meat wrapped and pre-packed from a shop and was ignorant about butchering a sheep. I'd prepared a fish, but a lamb was a whole new gruesome experience, I felt sick and almost fainted as its intestines poured out of the carcass onto the bloodstained ground.

Regardless of the bloodthirsty hunt, that evening, squeezed around our small table, we contentedly devoured our first fresh meat for months; lamb al asador.

At last, the altimeter indicated another rise in pressure, and we set off on our next foray on Standhardt. We climbed to the col and across the ledge and ramp in a single day. Optimistically, the next day we left our bivouac gear behind at the top of the ramp, at the edge of the south face. Our strategy was to carry nothing and make a run for the summit before any incoming storm could stop us. After ten wild pitches up the face, using mixed climbing and some direct aid, we were two rope lengths from the summit, confident of success. But ominously the clouds were descending on Fitz Roy and Cerro Torre; our window of opportunity was rapidly closing.

We now started to climb the honeycomb ice that draped down from the summit. The only way to negotiate this stuff was to kick away until the snow had consolidated under your weight, then punch and slash arms into the crystalline mass, Karate-style, and ease up gently. Brian led through to the summit. Well above me he pulled himself over a crest of snow, only to be knocked flat by the full force of the wind. The gear on his harness was being blown vertically, and his arms were blowing wildly about him so that Brian had to embrace himself, pinching his anorak with his hands to bring them under control. He crawled to a point a few metres below the summit mushroom.

I was pinned insecurely to the slope, being beaten senseless by the wind. John was belayed to the last rocks below me, his hoarse cries lost to the gale while, all around was unconsolidated snow. Just above I could see a V notch in the mushroom. Could I make it? Would I be able to dig through the crown of snow? I forced myself to breathe and think. No, the storm had beaten us. Now success was going to be measured by survival. Our last descent was a dress rehearsal of what was to come. This time we were much higher on the mountain and the storm far stronger. We used every piece of knowledge and all our experience on that descent. We lived because we had to, survived because we knew how, but above all, luck was with us.

At Base Camp, we found that Al, Rab and the Twins all had similar tales of failure and survival on Fitz Roy. It was a shared experience in Patagonia, one of the earth's most beautiful yet desolate corners.

Soon after, Yosemite veteran climber Jim Bridwell visited our camp. We described our attempt and claimed the first ascent of Standhardt, but we knew full well we had not finished the job and had failed to reach the summit. With Jim came an unexpected delivery of mail. It bore sad news. Our friends from Bangor, Dave Robinson and James Boulton, who had made such a remarkable ascent of the Droites the previous winter, had just succeeded on the equally demanding North Face of the Matterhorn. Tragically they fell to their deaths on the descent. To make the news worse, the letter also carried word that Dougal Haston had been buried in an avalanche while off-piste skiing above his home in Leysin. John was distraught. He knew Dave and James much better than me, and Dougal had become a soulmate during our winter in Argentière.

'I'm going home, this life is not what I want.' John sat cross-legged, with head in hands and started to sob.

'John, you can't go. Just think about it for a few days.' I tried to persuade him to change his mind.

'I'm thinking about it too much. It's just not worth it,' John blurted.

John wandered around camp in silent bewilderment, somehow lost in another place. Although not physically injured, it seemed as though a spear had pierced his heart. There was no discussion or analysis; our camp fell strangely silent. I needed to marshal my thoughts, but emotion defied logic, and my mind was in conflict. Like a fatal car accident, I put myself in the driver's seat and relived the carnage. We were in the same situation as Dave, James and Dougal, just in a different mountain range. I asked myself if the reverse were true, and they heard of our demise, would they give up mountaineering? I doubted they would, having invested so much in their chosen lifestyle. I felt very detached from the real world, living in that cabin in the woods; our Shangri-la, our adventure, our 'silent' place. If John left what would I do? Eventually, my mind defaulted to doing nothing, and I decided to stay and see what transpired, hoping that time would heal the wounds. For sure thoughts of returning to Standhardt's defiant walls were forgotten. Next day John walked out of Base Camp.

The snow-encrusted cap of Standhardt frustrated climbers for the next eleven years. Finally in January 1988 Jim Bridwell, together with fellow Americans, Jay Smith and Greg Smith followed 'our' ramp on the East Face. But before turning the corner onto the south face, they discovered a steep thin chimney choked with ice (one hundred metres left of the chimney we failed to ascend). Climbing at the highest standard they eventually reached the summit.

By chance, an American climber, Mike Weiss, walked into camp. I got on well with him, and we left to weave our way north, travelling by boat through the Chilean fiords and then attempted the highest peak in South America, Aconcagua. My time in South America lasted a further four months, joining up with Jim Bridwell on a new route in Bolivia and finishing with a multi-day epic on Huascaran in Peru with the Burgess twins.

When I got back to the UK from South America in 1977, I headed to North Wales to visit John. In his local pub, we chatted about Patagonia, and then he confided. 'I've given up mountaineering.'

'Oh . . . perhaps you'll change your mind in time.'

'I don't think so. For too long climbing has defined my life, ahead of everything else. There are a lot of other opportunities.'

We sat quietly drinking; then John broke the silence. 'I've met a girl called Chris. We're getting married.'

'Congratulations,' I replied, thinking that he seemed a different person, less happy-go-lucky, more normal.

'She's pregnant; I'm going to be a dad.'

With no hard feelings, I wished him well, seeing he was reconciled to stop mountaineering.

I didn't see much of John for the next few years. He was busy with tumultuous family life; helping to bring up his daughter Jess, splitting with his first wife, then moving in with the new love of his life, Caroline. They settled down and had two children: a daughter, Lhotse and a son, Cho. Though still managing to rock climb, he spent most of his days working on construction sites as a plasterer. He soon tired of building work and had a yen to revisit his nautical days by investing in an old wreck of a boat called 'Fyburg Lass' with his close friend John Coppock, Caroline's brother. Together, in this leaking rusty tub, they fished in the Menai Straits, ignoring the regulations and quotas, struggling to make a pittance in 'under the counter' wild salmon, which they accidentally caught in their nets.

It was not until the late '80s that I started to see more of John. Initially, I was surprised when I found out that he had come back to the mountains. Like me, he had qualified as an International Mountain Guide, and on occasions, we bumped into each other in Scotland and the Alps. On his Guides winter training course, there was a horrendous incident on Ben Nevis. Fellow guide and friend Richard Peart was with him that day. 'A guy stumbled into the CIC mountain hut shouting for help. An avalanche had swept six climbers off Castle Gully. We spent an awful day rescuing the climbers and digging out two bodies.' This experience undoubtedly gave John a meticulous attitude to guiding safety.

It was a constant juggling act for him to balance family life with mountain guiding. He adored his children, though I think the pressure of broken relationships and providing for his family exposed his fragile side. Deep down, he was a free spirit who did not want to be shackled. Emotionally he was at peace in the mountains; they gave him a sense of direction and purpose. And a place to escape from the stresses of everyday life.

Jess his eldest daughter has fantastic childhood memories of that time. 'Dad spent quite a bit of time working away when I was little. But we spent summers camping together in the Alps. Dad was often tired from being on the hill, but we were all together, and we did fun things on his days off. As I grew up, we always stayed in touch. And when we visited Chamonix in winter Dad, taught us all how to ski.'

By the early '90s John and I had become expert skiers, and we spent the winters, often working together, guiding off-piste skiing and touring. One evening in the Argentière Refuge above Chamonix, we were overnighting with our separate groups of ski clients.

'You seem to be enjoying the mountains again?' I idly commented over a glass of red wine.

'Loving it! But guiding is different from hardcore climbing. It's more in control,' he replied.

'Its work . . . good work in a place we love.' I ordered another carafe of wine as John fashioned a roll-up between his strong fingers.

'Did you know I've split with Caroline?'

'No, I didn't. I'm sorry about that.'

'It's all very emotional, and I've got nowhere to live. All my money goes on maintenance for the kids.' He sighed sadly and downed another glass of wine.

'I'm setting up a guiding company. Do you fancy working with me?' I asked.

John joined my newly formed business, Mountain Experience, based in Chamonix. He soon found his niche teaching beginners and taking less ambitious climbers on modest alpine climbs. Without fail, he gave everyone a good time, and they loved his tales of misadventure. I learnt a lot about guiding from John. Mostly that people came to us, not with ambitions to climb challenging peaks, but for company. To have an adventure outside their busy routine lives and experience the solace of the Alps.

For the next twenty years, John was my close companion. He rented a small ground floor apartment in Argentière, and slowly his guiding work gave him an income to enjoy life again. The old John was back; away from the flatlands that dimmed his spirit. Our guiding work slowly morphed into providing safety, rigging and logistics for film companies working in the mountains. We set up a company with five other friends, called High Exposure, and worked on dozens of productions. It was a riot of world travel with exciting challenges on every continent. John was always a favourite with the female film crew and actresses. In the evening, he would be in the corner of the bar intently and patiently listening, absorbing their angst like a sponge, then telling them tales and making them laugh.

On one occasion, high above Courmayeur, on the slopes of Mont Blanc, we were helping to film the opening sequence of *Alien vs Predator*. John was coordinating the action where one of the female Hollywood stars had to climb over a cornice. She had been particularly surly during the previous week, and John's attempts to win her over had no effect.

Suddenly she broke down in tears and yelled, 'I can't do this! I need to go to the bathroom.'

In the real world, this would be a normal request. But in the film world, and on this particular occasion, there were thirty crew, four actors and a hovering helicopter all on standby. She seemed distraught.

'Can I help?' John asked sympathetically.

She stared at John. 'Fuck off. How can YOU help?'

'We all have the same problem,' John patiently explained, adding, 'When you come up here, the cold and the altitude make you want to go more often, it's only natural.'

'For the last fucking week, I've wanted the fucking bathroom all the time. It's embarrassing! And the nearest bathroom is forty-five fucking minutes away in the godforsaken, freezing cable car station!'

'Look, this is what we do; we make a place away from prying eyes where we can go. I'll make a place for you.'

'What, outside . . . in the snow!' she looked at John as though he was deranged.

'Yes,' said John, carrying a snow shovel and disappeared for five minutes behind a snowdrift.

'Just go over there and don't fall in the hole.' John pointed, and then got on the radio to the 1st AD. 'We'll be another ten minutes. We just have to sort out some safety issues.'

'Copy that.'

Soon the actress appeared with a huge grin on her face. She'd had the first wild pee of her life, and John was her best friend for the rest of the filming.

Probably the most rewarding film we worked on together was *Touching the Void*. The film crew shot part of the footage in the Cordillera Huayhuash of Peru, on the actual mountain, Siula Grande, where Simon Yates and Joe Simpson narrowly survived a horrific accident. John ensured Joe's safety while re-creating the action across heavily crevassed terrain, but soon the mental stresses and strains endured by both Joe and Simon, because of returning to the place of their epic, started to tell. Simon, in a foul mood, fell out with the director Kevin Macdonald. The situation deteriorated and a heated argument degenerated into a scuffle. John, with his mild manner, defused the incident by mediating between the aggrieved parties, but Simon refused to have anything more to do with filming. Joe, who showed post-traumatic stress symptoms, continued to advise and aid the production.

After Peru the plan had always been to recreate much of the action in locations in the Alps using actors with the help of our expertise. Macdonald used the dialogues from the interviews he had shot with Joe and Simon before the disagreement, to narrate the film. Despite the turmoil the film was a triumph, winning the Best British film in the 2004 BAFTA awards.

Sadly, as age took its toll, John's life descended into chaos. His friends were convinced he was not clinically depressed, more likely just another of his familiar emotional yo-yos. It was perplexing that he had endured the storms of Patagonia, yet found everyday life impossible to navigate. Approaching sixty, he seemed to be going through a crisis of identity and self-confidence. He was lax in keeping up with the annual training required to maintain his guides qualification and failed to pay the third-party liability insurance. As a result, he lost his status as a mountain guide. Legally he could no longer work as a guide on film productions, and his income disappeared, together with the motivation to keep fit. His girth expanded as he climbed less. An unhealthy diet, together with drinking too much and smoking, accelerated his demise. The dependable geniality evaporated as melancholy took hold. Eventually, he was forced to leave his home in France, not welcome anymore, when he failed to repay his debts to his former friends.

By 2010 John was back in North Wales and his humour improved, at least in public. He made a renaissance when he started producing his own films: especially *Quest for the Sublime*, which was set in 1791, when William Wordsworth, hailed as one of the founders of English Romanticism and Naturalism, travelled to North Wales, and made a night ascent of Snowdon, the highest mountain in Wales. This climb took on such importance for the poet that he recounted it in his famous work *The Prelude*. The introductory narration by John was, in many ways, a mirror of his own life.

William Wordsworth, like most young people, liked his walks peppered by danger and drama. For him and many of the romantics, he actively sought out the high places. The places that promised adventure and uncertainty. Mountains for him were the temples of the sublime; beauty with a scary twist.

His son Cho played William, and his daughter Lhotse portrayed Dorothy, Wordsworth's wife. He was very proud of his offspring, and it seemed he was making up for his absent fatherhood in their youth.

Jess fondly remembers, 'Dad certainly wasn't perfect, but he was good company, fun to be around and loving so we would forgive everything else! He would take my daughter to the climbing wall, which she loved, and he would carry her in his backpack when she got tired, up in the hills when she was little. He was very proud when he took her right to the top of Tryfan when she was four, and I remember him saying she was like a mountain goat!'

Then tragedy struck in early 2012 when Cho lost his long fight against leukaemia. In a haunting film tribute to his beloved son, John shows Cho skiing joyously under the Dru in Chamonix, entertaining crowds with card tricks while he worked as a magician on Chester's streets and playing the young Wordsworth on Snowdon.

He made a handful of other films to critical approval, all on themes reflecting his emotional relationship with the mountain landscape. Unfortunately, they were financial disasters as he spent every last penny on camera equipment and editing computers.

The last time we met was at a Bangor University Climbing Club reunion in 2015. With a glass of beer and a whisky chaser on the table, he was laughing, joking and telling tales; the raconteur of old.

Doc O'Brien, his long time friend, pulled me to one side.

'I'm worried about John; he's drinking and smoking a lot. I don't know how he exists.'

'Where is he living?' I asked.

'He's moving around, sleeping on different people's floors, he's got no money.'

Behind the bravado, John's life was spiralling out of control.

Next day I organised to climb with John, meeting first for a fry-up breakfast at Pete's Eats cafe in Llanberis. John was in the same clothes as the previous night and reeked of booze. While walking up to the cliff in the slate quarries, high above Lyn Padarn, we idly chatted. I looked around and realised I was talking to myself. Fifty metres back John was bent double, coughing and wheezing. When it came time to climb, he could barely get off the ground. I had to pull him up the whole route.

'I'm sorry, Brian, I've lost my fitness,' he sighed and looked skyward with a tear in his eye.

'You'll get it back.' I gave him an embarrassed hug and was shocked how big he felt.

'Can I help in any way?'

'No, I'm fine.'

It was apparent to his friends that John was far from fine, but he was too proud to accept help. He got considerable satisfaction from his film making, but I could see he was fundamentally unhappy. Strangely he seemed lonely, even though he had numerous friends. Age and lack of fitness now restricted his access to mountains, a place that had been his escape, his happy place. I could only speculate that alcohol had now become his crutch.

In February 2017, John and his good friend, Dai Lampard were working on a documentary of the famous British climber Joe Brown near the Welsh village of Llanberis. With the filming successfully finished, they retired to the Vaynol Arms at 5.00p.m. for a drink. It turned out to be a brilliant night of ale and stories, with a host of friends John had not seen for a long time. Shortly after midnight, they were last to leave the pub. It was a beautiful clear, starry night as they made their merry way back to Dai's house. Walking along a path by the nearby river, John unexpectedly sat down saying, 'Just give me a minute.'

Dai could see that John was unwell. With no mobile phone reception, he rushed to his house and raised the alarm. When Dai returned back with blankets John was still conscious. Shortly after the paramedics arrived he went into cardiac failure. They could do nothing, and sadly he passed away. The post mortem indicated a massive heart attack.

I like to remember him on a night in 1999 when, we had just finished shooting a BBC series called *Wild Climbs*, on the sandstone towers of the Czech Republic, with top British climbers Andy Cave and Leo Houlding. All day John had been skilfully rigging safety ropes for the cameraman. Later, at our low-key wrap party, it was 4.00a.m. and Euro-techno music blasted out of the speakers inside a small town nightclub. He was on the dance floor spinning in a trance with three beautiful blonde women dressed in high heels and very short skirts, half his age. Strobes flashed, and the fluorescent lights highlighted his long grey hair and the litre glass of gin and tonic he balanced in his hand, turning them both into a vivid turquoise blue colour. His timing was perfect, and the whole nightclub watched and clapped to the rhythm of his dancing. Over the mic, the DJ announced, 'Aaaaa-and the next tune is for you . . . the Silver Fox.'

Roger Baxter-Jones on the walk in to
Jannu, 1978.

7

HIMALAYAN VIRGINS
Roger Baxter-Jones

I was relaxing at home when the phone rang. My good friend Jan Brownsort was speaking from Chamonix. 'I've got some bad news. Roger has been killed.' My heart sank, and a great emptiness opened where once had lived a friend.

On 8th July 1985, Roger Baxter-Jones and his American friend and regular client, John Ryder, left the Argentière mountain refuge. It was 2.00a.m. when they fitted their crampons. Opposite were the ghostly profiles of the Verte, Droite, Courte and Triolet on which some of the most majestic routes in the Alps climbed their icy walls.

Roger planned to guide John up the classic North Face of the Aiguille de Triolet. The dangers on this climb were obvious. Ice cliffs would occasionally fall, although that night's bitterly low temperatures ensured the ice was well frozen, giving ideal conditions for a safe and speedy ascent. Following normal practice they climbed in the dark, with their way illuminated only by the moon and pools of head torch light, planning to reach the summit as dawn broke the horizon. Partway up the face a serac collapsed and Roger, his client and two nearby Austrians were swept down the face. One Austrian survived. Fate changed a great day's climbing, robbing the world of one of its finest mountaineers. It was a classic *Mort du Guide*.

Roger knew that mountain guiding was a dangerous calling, but now his bountiful life was over. He was in the oblivion of the dead, and all his family and friends were the losers. I grieved selfishly and resented his loss. No more time to enjoy the company of such a vibrant, energetic and happy friend.

What if you had set off ten minutes earlier, I thought. *Or later? You stupid bloody idiot, why did you go and get killed?* My mind spun with questions, but I could find no answers other than that his luck ran out.

At that fateful moment, life also changed for his wife Christine and ten-year-old step-daughter, Mélanie. I cannot imagine how difficult it must have been for Christine, especially telling Mélanie the dark news. The young girl had grown close to Roger and given her blessing for Mum's mountaineering boyfriend to enter their home.

Roger arrived at Leeds University in 1968 to study English. When I arrived, a year later, he was already an established member of the climbing club. Born in 1950, he was brought up in London with his older sister, Penelope, by their mother, Pip, who worked at Harrods. Their father was killed in an industrial accident when Roger was ten. He never talked about his adolescence, but I gathered that he was a member of the North London Mountaineering Club, though it was not until University that he started climbing seriously.

Most of Leeds Climbing Club members were Northerners who mocked his posh southern accent, which he took as a compliment. Over the next ten years we climbed together regularly and, at first, he was my mentor, being a year older and with big-city confidence. To most people he was known as RBJ, but to me he was simply Roger. With his casual and offhand manner, he seemed oblivious of everyday complications. He had a clean-shaven freckled complexion and was taller than average with a muscular body. An unkempt mane of strawberry blond hair gave him the aura of a lion in its prime and, just like the big cat, he lazed around most days. He tended not to leave his bedroom until midday, only then to idly browse on pastries, smoke dope and drink beer or red wine.

Then, without warning, he would spring into life, transforming into a diligent health-freak, getting up at dawn to engage in periods of volcanic activity, when climbing or skiing overtook everything else. Between these lifestyle yo-yos, he would mysteriously disappear for months at a time. Asked about his private life, he would give his characteristic offhand shrug of debonair arrogance and flash his infectious smile, which at the slightest excuse turned into a joyous laugh. Blessed with formidable stamina and endless optimism, he was a powerhouse who would become one of the best mountaineers of the day.

Although a good rock climber, he lacked the virtuoso talent of some of the other climbers in the club, nor did he train on the indoor wall. Instead, using his abundant energy and smart research, he would devise all manner of crazy projects and every time I climbed with him we had a memorable adventure. One such scheme was to climb every one of the hundred or more routes at Malham Cove in the Yorkshire Dales. I was swept away by his enthusiasm and joined him on *The Macabre (E3)* and *The Right Wing Girdle (E2)*, the last two climbs to complete his project. Another unique feat of skill and strength was his climb out of the gigantic vertical shaft of Gaping Gill, at ninety-eight metres deep the largest underground chamber open to the surface in Britain.

It was in the Alps that he excelled. On my first visit in 1971, John Stainforth and I joined Roger and his climbing partner John Moore on our first big alpine climb when we raced up the Cassin route on the Badile. We then moved from Switzerland to Chamonix, where Roger suggested that we join him and Nigel Helliwell on the famous *Bonatti Pillar* on the Aiguille du Dru. This arduous and long climb was a rite of passage for any aspiring alpinist. Tragically, it provided our first experience of a fatality in the mountains.

There are two ways to reach the bottom of the Pillar, and we elected to approach from a side ridge, the *Flamme de Pierre*, and abseil into the dangerous couloir where the climb started. A separate British party began on the same day, but chose to ascend directly up the couloir. While we were abseiling, there was an almighty explosion of rockfall, the ground shuddered, and the couloir became thick with cascading debris. An awful cordite odour filled the air. Slowly, the dust cleared to reveal two bodies, like puppets tangled in their string, prostrate on the rock-strewn snow far below.

Could they still be alive? How could we help them? With rockfall ricocheting around the couloir it would have been suicidal to descend. Our dilemma was solved when a helicopter arrived and we watched, dumbfounded, as it hovered over the bodies while a rescuer was lowered on a thin thread of wire.

'Should we carry on?' I whispered.

'We can't do anything about it,' said Roger, in a somewhat detached tone.

Climbing in silence, I struggled to understand how he could be so matter-of-fact after such a horrific incident. Like me, he must have been in shock and turmoil, so I concluded that it was just his way of reacting to the tragedy. A day later, when we reached the top, it was as if the incident had never happened. My conscious brain had forgotten what it did not want to understand.

After studying, Roger took up the transitory life of an odd-job builder in Sheffield, along with guiding in the Alps. Through the '70s, he excelled with a long list of significant ascents in both summer and winter, the zenith being on the imposing North Face of the Grandes Jorasses where he completed two of the hardest routes in the Alps: the long-awaited second ascent of the Whymper Spur Direct with Nick Colton, followed by a winter ascent of the Walker Spur with Tut Braithwaite.

After helping the British Mountaineering Club host some of France's top alpinists on a UK based climbing meet, he became impressed by the French lifestyle and the prowess of their climbers, and increasingly spent time there, living much of the year in Chamonix. This cosmopolitan town was then (and still is) the world centre of alpinism, a cauldron of new ideas within mountain sports. Eventually, he made the town his home and, in the autumn of 1983, married a local girl, Christine Comte, becoming stepfather to her daughter Mélanie. Roger gained French nationality, and became ever more continental in attitudes, tastes and language. He became the first British guide accepted into the Compagnie des Guides de Chamonix (a unique accolade, as it is such an elite organisation), and would have had his official inauguration at the *fête des guides* on 15th August, five weeks after his death.

As a top professional, Roger was proud to guide difficult routes, which he did within a considerable safety margin, and it was plain to see that guiding regularly on the peaks above his home enhanced his fitness and judgement. However, even the best of us are mortal and must respect the environment's different moods. Sombre headstones line the cemeteries of both Chamonix and Zermatt, commemorating famous and talented Alpine guides lost over the years.

Adapting to an environment is a trait of all living things. For mountaineers, this is enhanced by exposure to conditions such as low temperatures and lack of oxygen at high altitude. However, it is mental fortitude gained from regular exposure to risk that counts especially as, whatever we do, avalanches will sweep down, rocks will fall, and storms will engulf the peaks. I believe that the most successful mountaineers are those who adapt best to risk but, unfortunately this does not bestow immortality. Mountains have no regard for humanity.

Tragedy is a reasonably expected outcome in dangerous environments and will keep happening. This does not fit well with the risk managed world of today. Sadly, as in Roger's accident, regardless of what strategies mountaineers devise, humans have little control over what happens in the mountains, other than staying away, altering our timing, or changing our path. Risk is an inevitable consequence of mountaineering.

'There is no real "control", just temporary, humble coexistence with an infinitely complicated environment,' Will Gadd, the talented Canadian mountaineer, posted on Facebook in October 2020. 'The basis for surviving is not control, but understanding: of the environment, yourself and life. Letting my guard down because I felt in control is where it has usually come up to bite me.'

In January 1978, soon after Roger settled in Chamonix I visited him and soon learnt that he had recently skied down the long glacial Vallée Blanche to the Aiguille des Grands Charmoz where he made the first winter solo ascent of its North Face. Incredibly, he covered this huge there-and-back distance and elevation all within the same day in an achievement well ahead of its time.

His enthusiasm for skiing began in Leeds while he was instructing on the artificial dry ski slope. Like many of the continental climbers, he realised the importance of skis to move efficiently about the mountains. Next day I asked if he could help with my skiing technique.

'Point your skis down the fall line,' he shouted. I knew the theory but, in practice, every time I pointed downhill I started going too fast, and would crash in the deep snow.

'Feel your bodyweight pushing through your feet, and don't clench your toes,' he explained. 'Visualise yourself as a car. Steer with your legs and feet and keep your upper body still and in balance.' He elegantly slalomed down the slope, his body shape perfect, dressed in a pink one-piece suit. I followed like a comic snowman in threadbare, baggy climbing clothes. A tractor that, predictably, crashed after two turns, compared to Roger's Ferrari.

That winter he simply climbed faster and more efficiently than me, and was better attuned to the mountains he lived beneath. I had a lot of catching up to do but by then Roger, like me, was looking at the next level: the Greater Ranges.

Al Rouse, Rab Carrington and I returned from South America keen to find new challenges. When researching objectives in the Himalaya for 1978 it seemed only natural that Roger would join the party. By chance, Al read an account of Frank Smythe's 1930 travels in the remote north-east corner of Nepal, close to the borders of Tibet and Sikkim and a particular mountain caught his eye. Described by Smythe as *one of the most appalling rock peaks in the world.* This was Jannu, a tormented mass of ice-blue ridges rising to a pair of distinctive shoulders, which gave the mountain its Hindu name: Kumbhakarna, the shoulders of Kama, the mighty warrior. Above rose an imposing granite head, topped by the lofty, 7,710 metres snow-capped summit.

In the 1950s, the French were eager to attempt Jannu, following their first ascent of Makalu, at 8,481, the fifth highest peak on the planet. Lucien Devies, President of the Fédération de la Montagne and its Himalaya Committee, wrote:

'It seemed to us that the time had come, as in the Alps earlier, to turn towards greater difficulty rather than tackle one of the remaining 8,000'ers. Now our thoughts turned to Jannu, a huge and imposing fortress, which combines problems of intensely diffi-cult climbing, sustained over an enormous height differential, with those of high altitude itself.' After several attempts, in 1962 a team of ten led by Lionel Terray succeeded.

Accompanied by a cameraman, a doctor and two scientists, they employed four hundred porters to carry twelve tons of equipment to Base Camp. On the mountain they were supported by thirty high-altitude Sherpas who fixed over three kilometres of rope to supply six high camps. Using supplementary oxygen, they won through after a six-week struggle by forging an extraordinarily long and arduous route up the south-west side from the Yamatari Glacier.

Using similar heavyweight tactics, Jannu had received two more ascents. In 1974 a Japanese expedition repeated the French route, then in 1976, another Japanese party climbed the extremely difficult North Face.

We gained permission to attempt a new route on the unclimbed East Face in the autumn, post-monsoon season. We would climb the only way we knew, alpine style, in one push, using no high-altitude porters, no fixed camps, no fixed ropes and no supplementary oxygen, just as we had climbed in the Alps, Patagonia and the Andes.

Our first question was: how to get there? Some of our older friends had been on expeditions to Nepal, as well as Afghanistan, Pakistan and India, having bought dilapidated old vans and taken the 'hippie trail'. The story of our mates, Dick Renshaw and Joe Tasker, in '75, driving to India in a beat-up Ford Escort van, was almost as legendary as their incredible ascent of Dunagiri. It was no surprise that, in the '70s, these overland drives took weeks and often appeared to be the most adventurous part of the trip, certainly with the delays and mishaps. In our geopolitical climate of today, to even contemplate such a journey would be foolhardy.

We chose to fly, which was seen by our contemporaries as a revolutionary concept. It certainly took the lion's share of our budget, and all the equipment had to be crammed into eight rucksacks. A contact in Air India organised a few extra bags but, even so, we sweltered on the plane in high-altitude double boots and climbing clothing with carabiners, pitons and gas cylinders stuffed into our pockets.

Kathmandu was all we had dreamt about. Disorientated by jetlag, soaked to the skin by monsoon rain, Roger and I found a bar where we smoked a joint and drank chang, the local beer made by pouring hot water through fermented millet. Too excited to sleep, we walked the exotic night streets in a daze, and laughed our way around the markets in Freak Street, Thamel, Durbar Square, Asan and Indra Chowk. The night ended hilariously when we made fools of ourselves watching Peter Sellers in *The Pink Panther* at the British Embassy club.

There were few cars, and most of the streets were made of clay, which turned to mud in the torrential downpours. Bicycles weaved between Hindus dressed in white and shaven-headed Buddhists in purple. In the back alleys lay the darkest depths of human misery: beggars in rags, children naked and covered in mud, piles of rubbish and fetid human waste. Monkeys squabbled on the domes of hidden white stupas, which were draped in colourful flags. The bazaar hung thick with the scent of perfumed balms and fragrant spices. Down a narrow alley, the meat stalls displayed slaughtered ox carcasses, swarming with flies, and the overpowering muggy odour of sweet intestines.

The next day we started assembling everything needed for two months in the mountains. We had never done anything like this before, so we enlisted The Sherpa Co-operative, a trekking company which specialised in expeditions. For a ridiculously cheap fee they provided us with a sirdar (the Head Sherpa who organises the porters and guides the expedition to base camp) called Padaam Rai and a cook, Kusang Sherpa.

'I arrived down at the Bazaar with Kusang and drifted around in the back streets buying umbrellas, pots and pans, jerry cans, rope and so on,' Roger wrote in a letter to Sarah, his girlfriend at that time. 'I seem to have quickly got in-tune with the city; slow and easy . . . a big laugh solves many problems here. We eat at a Tibetan or Chindian restaurant each night . . . good food. Then we get stoned and walk or cycle the streets . . . there's a lot of music in this city, and amazing scenes occur all the time . . . I love it!'

Meanwhile, Rab and Al met endlessly with that hydra of bureaucracy, the Ministry of Tourism, in a long-winded process confirming our permission to climb Jannu. Finally, we met Mr. Ghale, our government Liaison Officer (LO), who would accompany the expedition, ensuring we remained within the labyrinth of rules and regulations.

Our severe shortage of cash meant we had to adopt the local lifestyle so, when the time came to travel to Dharan Bazaar, we caught the regular bus with our twenty-four sack loads. The driver was not amused, and only after a certain amount of persuasion allowed us to tie our loads on top of the bus amongst bags of clothing, a massive box of vegetables, a cage full of mangy chickens and a large dead pig with its legs pointing skyward.

The vehicle looked more like a Hindu temple on wheels than a bus, adorned as it was with gaudy yellow and red paintings of weird animals and serpents depicting Hindu gods. Flashing, multicoloured lights hung on wires above the windows, and the front bumper was an array of what could best be described as searchlights. There was no tread on the tyres, and wire and cloth poked from their patched sidewalls. People stood in the aisles, and a dozen lay on the roof. Nevertheless, you get to know the people and a country a lot better by using public transport.

Eventually, with a loud blast of the horn, we lurched forward, the radio blaring out a tinny wail, a soundtrack that must be specially recorded for Asian bus journeys. The driver took the first corner at what was to become his trademark high speed and, due to the gross overloading, we leant alarmingly to one side, tyres squealing, and almost toppled over. Inside was mayhem but, in reality, it was an ordinary, everyday bus journey in Nepal, where death by bus-crash is common. Newspaper headlines would often herald 'Tragedy! 103 people perish as bus plunges down a ravine.'

This bus journey began the deterioration of our relationship with Liaison Officer Mr Ghale. A short weasel-faced man with slicked, black hair and the start of a round belly, he had heard of rich western expeditions with fantastic gear and food, and the life of luxury that an LO could expect. Instead, he got us, and was sandwiched on a seat for two between a pair of jovial and rather plump local ladies dressed in bright pink. From that point we had nothing but trouble from him.

The trip should have taken a day but, after six pothole bumping hours, with the suspension bottoming out, the back axle then snapped and the bus had to be unloaded. Some remarkable repair work ensued with hammers and greasy rags, raucous shouting, a host of novel suggestions, and frantically waving arms. We huddled in blankets around makeshift fires with the other passengers, while a pack of local dogs circled on the edge of darkness, howling for food scraps. Even at night, the Terai, the Nepalese lowland plains, were oppressively hot and humid.

'Sahibs, here is your dinner.' Our cook, Kusang handed us enamel bowls. 'I am sorry but I have nothing to cook with. This meal has been made by my friends over there.' He pointed at our fellow passengers. With little enthusiasm, we quietly ate a luke-warm broth of dahl, mixed with lumps of gristle and bone covered in globules of ghee, helped down with burnt chapatis made from flour and road grit.

'Mosquitoes!' Roger's pale skin attracted them in swarms.

'A bidi might help. The locals smoke them,' I suggested.

'I can think of something better.' Roger rolled a huge joint, and soon we were laughing at the comical start to our expedition.

A day late, the bus limped into the sauna-like heat and torrential rain of Dharan. The thermometer in our first aid kit showed 40°C at nine o'clock in the morning. To save money, we planned to sleep rough. Noticing that most of the wood and straw buildings were on stilts, we rolled out our sleeping mats under a friendly merchant's shop, from whom we had just bought extra supplies of oats and rice. Though littered with dirty refuse and smelling of urine, it was sheltered from the monsoon rain.

'No, Mr Roger, you cannot sleep under there,' Kusang exclaimed.

'It looks fine to me, and it's dry,' Roger replied.

'Ah, Mr Roger, it is full of rats at night, and they attract the king cobra. It is most dangerous.'

We changed our minds and took a room in a cheap hotel. Meanwhile, Padaam hired thirty-one porters, each of whom was to carry a regulation thirty-kilo load (though some strong porters carried double or triple loads for extra pay) in wicker baskets slung from their forehead by a rope tump-line. On our first visit to Asia we entertained an unfounded distrust of the locals, and carried much of our vital gear ourselves, shouldering rucksacks just as heavy, but it was soon obvious that the burden was too great for bodies unused to such weight. Although we aimed to climb the mountain in alpine style, we understood our reliance on a team of porters to carry supplies to our Base Camp. The next day, we started our long approach march.

The first hill out of Dharan was a killer. Setting off late, under a wicked sun, weighed down by our heavy loads, we were unfit from months of organising and overindulgence. We laboured all day, up hairpin after hairpin, on a serpentine path that wriggled through terraced paddy fields with farmers knee-deep in mud and dressed only in cotton loincloths, tending their crops. In other fields, oxen strained to pull ploughs. Long columns of wiry, barefooted porters passed by, bowed under baskets of produce. This thoroughfare of human porterage was the arterial trade route for a vast area of rural Nepal.

On the second day, our problems began with Roger walking uncharacteristically slowly.

'Are you okay?' I asked, as he staggered towards me, neck bent and sweat dripping from his nose.

'No. I feel awful.' He took a large draft from my water bottle and started retching. 'It's that meal we had when the bus broke down.'

Rummaging around in my first aid kit, I gave him some pills. 'I'll get a porter to carry your pack.'

When we arrived at camp he collapsed on the ground, moaning in semi-delirium. Worried that he was seriously ill, we got him into a bed in a villager's house. 'Do you think we should send someone down for a doctor?' Al asked.

'I think we have more drugs in our medical kit than they have in Dharan,' I replied.

'Perhaps it's the sun?' Rab added.

Next day Roger was no better. 'We can't stop here with all the porters,' Rab said.

'Roger can't go anywhere today,' I insisted.

'Okay, I'll go ahead with Padaam and the porters. You, Al and Kusang stay with Roger,' Rab said. 'If he doesn't improve, we'll need to get medical help somehow.'

Roger was barely conscious that day, but managed to sip at a homemade rehydration drink of water, salt, and sugar. He seemed to be burning, but without sweat and a deathly, white pallor, suggesting that he was suffering from life-threatening heat stroke. That evening, as we were formulating a plan to find a doctor, he woke up. 'Where am I?' he whispered. Thankfully, recovery was rapid. As we walked, we left behind the rich terraced fields of crops and prosperous villages. Ahead lay stony potato fields and grazing yaks tended by people at the limit of survival.

The team reunited a couple of days later at Dhobhan and, from there, in more invigorating air, followed an undulating ridge between the rivers Arun and Tamur like a giant's arm stretched out to the north-east to hold the snowy peaks on the distant horizon. Our path hung above misty valleys, and it felt a little like walking through a Japanese painting. One early morning, we had the first view of our Hindu deity, the head and shoulders of Karma – Jannu jutting majestically above a wooded ridge. It was an electric moment, appreciating this wonderful peak and realising the enormity of our task.

'The nights are very atmospheric. We bed-down on earth floors, in the shacks of local families, animals downstairs and living space above. Sit around in the half-light, smoke a joint, and watch the fire and the people,' wrote Roger. 'It's delightful – often difficult to tell whether you are stoned or not. One night we heard children singing in a room behind a grill. A girl came close, so she was inches from our heads. Here we were sat in our sleeping bags, a choir behind, a fire in front, a beautiful place – a place to get lost in.'

At Taplejung, we had a rest day, changed our porters for hardier local hill people and, when we found the local chang house, consumed more than was good for us. Ghale, our Liaison Officer, thought we were irresponsible and could hardly speak for anger. Apoplectic with rage, he said, 'This expedition is a disgrace. I order it to stop. We must turn round and go back to Kathmandu.'

Eventually, we reached a compromise. Ghale would stay with a fellow police officer in Taplejung. He hated the effort of walking and, even more, of camping in the mountains. By staying in this remote mountain village, he would save face with his superiors and we would not have to listen to his moaning.

On the four-day walk to Yamphodin we encountered many obstacles including the monsoon, which arrived with a vengeance, soaking us from dawn till dusk. The route through the rain forest was barely visible, and we crossed numerous brown foaming streams by balancing on bridges fashioned from slippery logs and hemp rope. Through it all, we slept with the porters in caves and cowsheds to preserve our base camp tents.

With the drenching rain came the leeches and, despite soaking our socks in salt and disinfectant, we suffered. Roger in particular fared terribly, on some days accumulating thirty leeches on each foot. If we didn't pick them off before sleeping, they would find their way into crotches, ears, eyelids and armpits, to gorge themselves to the size of sausages.

When the rain subsided, we got glimpses of distant snow-covered peaks through small windows in the mist. Ridge upon ridge stretching to the north, a fresco of rolling waves on a turbulent ocean. In brief spells of sunshine, we enjoyed striding through the riot of green flora, with butterflies big as birds, a cheeky red panda perched on a branch and giant Himalaya vultures soaring high above.

Unfortunately, Roger rolled his ankle while descending a steep path. 'It gave three sharp cracks, and I almost cried, thinking the expedition was over for me.' he wrote. 'Nothing holds this team up, so a porter took my sack, Rab cut me a stick, and off I hobbled. I would set out first in the morning and arrive last at night. It is only the cynicism of the others and the magic of this place that have prevented a slide into self-pity.'

He walked painfully slowly and, on one incredibly long day, lost his way in a confusion of small paths in a rhododendron forest. We sent out a search party, but failed to find him until he staggered into camp well after midnight.

As we gained height the leeches disappeared, but it became colder, the incessant rain turned to sleet and we questioned our sanity. Our plan was to arrive at Base Camp by the end of September to ensure we had the maximum opportunity to climb in the good weather of post-monsoon. In November, bitter winter winds would ravage the summits.

At Ramshey, the last place marked on the map, at the side of the Yalung Glacier, we passed a group of nomadic Tibetan yak herders living frugally in a yurt. It was the only habitation or people we had seen in the last four days, and we had no idea how important this dignified family would be to the outcome of our expedition.

As we gained height, heavy snowfall halted our progress. Our porters wore only basic footwear and clothing so, with no shelter for the night, we erected our five two-person tents and tried to fit thirty-seven people inside. Each man was given a square of poly-thene for cover, but this was inadequate in the storm. Although most found some form of protection, it was a night for survival rather than comfort. Roger, Al, Rab and I, squashed together in one tent, gradually accepting that we were in a difficult situation. It had become apparent that our sirdar, Padaam, and most of the porters had never been to this uninhabited region and as a result we had underestimated the harsh terrain. In good weather we would have been fine, in the storm we were woefully under-resourced.

'What's all that shouting about?' Roger sat up, wakened by a kerfuffle outside. There was a distinct smell of burning as we got out of the tent to face the blizzard and a scene of chaos. The strongest porters had commandeered the tents, which bulged like giant orange eggs, leaving the weakest to huddle miserably outside, almost like a waddle of frozen penguins. To keep warm, the porters inside had lit fires. We shouted at the porters inside to put out their fires and tried to reassure the porters outside. Fortunately, the soaked cotton fabric did not catch light and little damage occurred, but the welfare of the porters was compromised as were relations between them. It was our fault. We should have prepared for the worst rather than subjecting our hard working and loyal men to such distress.

The next morning the campsite was a sorry sight: a quagmire of slush, mud and porters shivering uncontrollably while suffering from altitude headaches. We had little option but to pay most of them off and let them descend as quickly as possible, retaining a few volunteers to ferry loads on the final day's walk up the glacier to our Base Camp.

After eighteen days, on 15th September, we reached our home for the next month, a fine place situated at 4,800 metres on a small grassy haven, a hundred metres above the glacier. In the short breaks in otherwise incessant snowfall, we had a grandstand view of our objective, the enormous unclimbed East Face of Jannu, with the giant mass of Kangchenjunga, the third highest mountain in the world, dominating the head of the glacier.

'We have built a kitchen out of stones, turf and polythene. And are engaged in the vital task of lazing around, festering, eating and sleeping for a couple of days,' wrote Roger. 'The ankle is much stronger now, and in a couple of days, we will try an acclimatisation climb. Everyone is on good form. Rab, in particular, is amazing; he does three times as much work and eats three times as much as anyone, claiming it's his Scottish pedigree. This trip is becoming timeless; I seem to be losing all concept of civilisation as we zero-in on the task of climbing Jannu.'

By 21st of September we were ready to make a reconnaissance on the East Face. The key would be to reach the small, hanging Tso Glacier at the base of the face. Over two days, we circumnavigated a rock wall threatened by dangerous ice cliffs. Conditions were appalling as we grappled with slimy rock covered in melting snow, waterfalls and wet sods of vegetation. The risk was significant and, with the weather still poor, we retreated to Base Camp. Immediately an almighty row broke out.

'This was not what I travelled halfway around the world for,' Roger shouted.

Rab interrupted. 'We knew it was going to be hard. We can't give up this easily.'

'Look guys, that was our first look at the face,' Al said. 'Next time we need to try a different line.'

'It's obvious that any route on the east side is going to be extremely difficult, long and above all dangerous,' Roger countered.

'When the good weather comes, we will probably only have the resources and strength for one major attempt,' I said, occupying the middle ground. The argument carried on well into the night, and only finished when Roger lost his voice.

The next morning an acrimonious atmosphere hung over camp, and we split into two parties with widely different views. It was no surprise that Al and Rab were of one mind. They had formed a close climbing partnership, travelling the world, always climbing the same way: a rope of two making fast ascents with little gear and even less food. Their list of achievements in the Alps and South America was peerless, and they had not gained such success by arguing. In truth, it was Al who had the idea of a route on the East Face of Jannu.

'Al had a drive and determination to become the "best" climber in the world,' Rab wrote in an article for *Vertical* magazine, published much later. 'With this vision, he had neither geographical boundaries nor constraints in his thinking about what was possible. For Al to be able to achieve his goal, he needed a partner. I was the Sancho Panza to his Don Quixote. The person to do the mundane work while he continued dreaming.'

Socially, Rab and Al were close friends, but we were outsiders to their partnership in climbing terms. There would be no compromise when it came to climbing plans; we would have to adapt to their style and strategy. On Jannu, that meant attempting the primary objective. Roger and I went for a walk to try and decide what to do.

'We're not much of a team, are we?' Roger complained.

'Rab and Al have been climbing together for a long time. I don't think they know how to climb as a four.'

'Al's so pushy, he believes he's always right.' Roger scratched his unruly mop of ginger hair, which had not seen soap or water for a month.

'He's a mathematician and sees things in black and white; he'll argue all night and still won't let you win.'

Roger was adamant. 'I'm not going on the East Face again; we'll get killed.'

'So, do we split into two teams and do our own thing?'

'I think we should walk around to the other side of the mountain and have a look at the south-west side,' Roger suggested.

'To repeat the original French route?'

'Yes.'

'Do you know the way?'

'No, but we'll find a route.' A big Cheshire cat grin filled his face.

Al and Rab were drinking tea when we got back to our small kitchen tent. After an embarrassing silence, Roger explained our plan.

'Do what you like,' was Al's curt reply.

The next day Roger and I left for a week-long reconnaissance trek around the south side of Jannu. There were no tracks marked on our hand-drawn map, but it looked like we would have to descend all the way down to the yak herding family at Ramshey. Snowy weather forced us to spend two nights in their company.

'Strange nights, exchanging food and watching them sing while churning milk,' Roger wrote to Sarah. 'I am turning into a kind of machine in this strange place, faced with this ridiculous objective, and only the mountain world seems to have weight; perhaps that's why we come here. I have some delightful fantasies while tramping these stony paths – maybe they could be made real?'

Leaving the yurt, we climbed over a desolate 5,000-metre pass, the Lapsong La, hoping it would take us to the opposite side of the mountain and the start of the French route. A hard day's walk took us to the Yamatari Glacier, at the approximate site of the 1962 French Base Camp where we gazed upwards, transfixed by what lay before us. Our challenge would be to navigate a way through the maze of hanging glaciers and icefalls that twisted between long contorted snow ridges, eventually to reach the *Throne*, the high snow field nestling below the rocky summit tower.

While we were away, Al and Rab concluded that the best chance of success on the East Face was to follow a line further right than our first abortive attempt. This would lead to the virgin col between Jannu and Kangbachen. From there a long ridge rose to the summit. Having decided on this plan, they established an Advanced Base below the route and made a reconnaissance of the lower rock slabs.

We had become a strange sort of expedition; two pairs of fiercely independent climbers acting together only through the compulsion of circumstances and only after interminable discussions.

At the beginning of October both pairs returned to Base, where the atmosphere changed dramatically. It was as though our separate forays had lifted a great weight from our shoulders. I think the pressure of planning, then the travelling and the walk-in had got on top of us. We had all gone for a walk about and come back refreshed. The task in front of us was daunting and to succeed we had to stick together, though both teams were still keen on their own idea.

Sense prevailed, and we worked out a compromise which, in retro-spect, resulted in the ideal formula: to acclimatise and climb the mountain in alpine style.

The immediate strategy was to try the route that Al and Rab had reconnoitred. If we failed on the first attempt we would have just enough time to go round the mountain and attempt the French route, but we were running low on food and fuel. Moreover, although the monsoon was over, and the sky was blue, the further we moved into autumn the winds would surely increase and the temperatures plummet.

As the dawn sun slowly slid down Jannu on 3rd October, we left Base Camp and headed up the glacier. Our kit was as light as possible, cutting edge for the day, but primitive compared to modern times. Our leather double boots weighed five kilos a pair, twice the weight of current high altitude boots. Before Gore-Tex our outer garments were made from sweaty, polyurethane coated nylon. Woollen mitts and balaclava, together with fleece and down jackets, kept us warm. There was no room in our rucksacks for tents. Instead, we carried a flimsy, nylon bivouac shelter.

Over the next four days, we climbed granite slabs, unstable snow flutings, long icy couloirs and finally, a steep unstable snow slope to reach the North East col of Jannu at approximately 6,500 metres. It felt like a victory, being the first people to reach this wild and wonderful place. Over our shoulder were the endless snow slopes leading to the lofty summits of Kangbachen, Yalung Kang, and Kangchenjunga and, in profile, the impressive North Face of Jannu, the largest and steepest mountain wall I had ever seen. In the distance, we could identify Makalu, Lhotse and Everest. Above us was our intended route, an astonishing arête of whipped meringues and mushrooms of soft snow leading to the East Summit of Jannu.

We all enjoyed those four days; challenging climbing, compan-ionship and the fantastic atmosphere of being in such a remote and beautiful place without another expedition anywhere near. This was why we came. It was why we climbed, and it was a pity it had to end. The weather was perfect and we all felt strong, though a little tired from the altitude. We estimated the route ahead would need many days of sustained effort. With only three days of food and fuel left, dare we carry on? Probably not. Our courage evaporated; it was pointless and foolhardy, as the chances of success were small and the risks too high.

Since our expedition, there have been ten unsuccessful attempts on the east side of Jannu. The closest to success was in 2020 when two Russians, Sergey Nilov and Dmitry Golovchenko spent three weeks on the face, reaching the skyline ridge where poor weather thwarted their summit bid. Nor has anyone repeated our climb to the North East col, and attempted the continuation ridge to Jannu East.

Back at Base Camp, we knew time was running out and the only possibility of reaching the summit was to attempt the French route on the far side of the mountain. 'It's vital we set off tomorrow,' Roger insisted, knowing we only had ten days before the porters arrived and our departure from Base Camp.

'We need more rest,' I implored. The last attempt had taken a lot out of me.

'Let's pack today and see how we feel in the morning,' Al said, 'but we need to have lighter packs than last time.'

'Leave the bivouac tent behind. We'll sleep out in the open, just in our sleeping bags.' Roger was already sorting the gear. 'One, nine millimetre rope for each party and an ice stake each – a few slings but no rock gear.'

Rab started cutting labels off his clothing, including his underpants. Such actions are now called 'marginal gains'.

We planned to follow the route that Roger and I had taken on our reconnaissance, asking Padaam, our sirdar, to carry a load to Ramshey, and once there to ask the yak herders to give us a lift over the Lapsong La. This would enable us to take a bit more food and fuel to the start of the climb.

Still undernourished after our last foray, we gorged on bowls of rice to replenish our energy levels. Unfortunately, we had little food left at camp, only rice, dhal, tea, sugar and milk powder and only enough specialist hill food for five days: Nepalese soup powder and dried potatoes, Chinese noodles, English fudge and mint cake, Tang drink powder plus tea, milk powder and sugar. If that menu can be called specialist!

The next day we were back inside the yak herders' yurt, where our friends welcomed us with a bowl of Po Cha yak butter tea. The extended family was a dozen or more, relaxing around a central open fire, its smoke lazily floating out of a blackened hole in the roof. They were dressed in grease-polished sheepskin robes, fringed with fur. The women wore skirts with multicoloured woven aprons. The men, baggy trousers and long, brightly woven boots with a sturdy leather base. The women plaited their hair into two long braids. The men coiled theirs into long, shining black braids on the tops of their heads. Both men and women proudly wore necklaces and earrings of turquoise and orange coral. I imagine it was a scene that had not changed since medieval times.

We thanked the family for their hospitality and left with two young, short of stature Tibetans who shouldered our heavy loads with ease, donning their fur hats and whistling their pack of vicious-looking dogs to accompany us. Even with help, our sacks were monstrously heavy. When we arrived at the south-west side of the mountain we waved goodbye to our two Tibetan friends.

Setting off from the glacier at dawn on 17th October, we were a team again but none of us had attempted such an intimidating mountain, rising 3,000 metres within eleven kilometres. Rab and Al insisted on the pairs making independent ascents, operating as two completely self-sufficient teams, whereas Roger and I thought this a rather eccentric style and felt it would have been safer and faster for one person to lead with the others following as a unit.

Above our first bivouac the real problems started. Over the next two days we climbed the most dangerous and challenging snow that any of us had encountered. It was impossible to grade this type of purgatory, but it was at our limit with the weight of our sacks hindering progress. The irony of alpine style being lightweight! We had to carry so much gear to climb the mountain in one push that I started to question our ethics and whether we would have been better stocking a series of camps in the old way.

A long, complicated snow ridge led to a giant alabaster gendarme named the *Tête du Butoir* by the French team. Progress was only possible under or over huge cornices, like battling a series of frozen *Great Waves of Kanagawa*. With no safety belays, the snow was deep and bottomless and gave way unpredictably. An ungainly swimming action usually proved the only way to make headway.

Sixteen years before, Lionel Terray had described their tactics at a similar height in his book, *At Grips with Jannu*. Using fixed ropes, their Sherpas had carried up tree trunks to build a bridge, allowing them to cross the crevasse which held up their advance. Seven tons of equipment went to camp three, which included a dozen tents and a cook tent which had to be stocked with food and bottles of oxygen before they felt sure they could continue with sufficient safety.

Our next day started badly. I was leading when the snow gave way under me in a mini-avalanche, leaving me wedged in a crevasse. Luckily, Roger was able to arrest the fall and haul me out. While I got my breath back, Al and Rab forged slowly on, over a series of tortuous cauliflowers of snow the consistency of dune sand.

'I'm not enjoying this,' shouted Al as he tried to gain purchase with his feet. The more he kicked the more the snow gave way, undercutting his body and increasing the angle.

'It's awful,' Rab said, then shouted, 'I think we need to have a chat about continuing.'

'Let's carry on till this evening and then decide,' interrupted Roger. 'Let me have a go.'

We were now under a feature described by the French as the *Tête de la Dentelle* – Head of Lace. A romantic name for a ship's prow of fluted snow, which was beautiful to look at, but improbable to climb.

Are we mad – how are we going to get down? I thought.

Looking back at this hiatus, Rab wrote, 'On Jannu, there were four of us. Safety in numbers? However, our strategy was to climb as two completely separate teams of two. I believe, should there have only been Al and me on the route, we would have retreated. However, peer pressure kept us going on. So much for safety in numbers?'

Roger came down from his Sisyphean struggle, and Rab took the lead, thrashing as a man possessed. He went up – then slid back down. There followed a set of Glaswegian expletives that would make a docker blush and off he went again. It was an appalling struggle, and all he succeeded in doing was to dig a crater in a slope the consistency of frozen feathers, with little upward movement. He confronted us, sweat dripping from his nose. 'I wouldn't climb on Ben Nevis in these conditions, let alone pay thousands of pounds and waste three months coming out here.'

'We're putting a noose around our necks if we carry on. We won't be able to get down,' Al responded.

'It could easily avalanche. Let's go down,' I said, adding, 'What do you think, Roger?' But Roger was not there; our rope was snaking around a buttress.

From out of sight came a yell, 'I've found some firm snow.' He had discovered an avalanche runnel scoured of soft snow and, with ruthless determination, led to the top of the *Dentelle*. From there, it was straightforward terrain to the snow plateau of the *Throne*.

We bivouacked on a flat area but a bitter wind picked up spindrift and made our life a misery. With no tent for shelter and little remaining energy, we constructed windbreaks out of blocks of snow and settled down, sitting in our sleeping bags with our two stoves cradled precariously in our laps.

'There's no gas left in the canister.' Roger frantically shook his stove.

I stared in disbelief.

'Ours is the same,' said Rab.

This was serious. Each pair had set off with six kilos of food and three gas canisters. We had used one canister on the lower bivouacs and were onto our second, which should have been at least half full. Inspection revealed the rubber sealing washer between the canister and the burner had frozen hard and dislodged within the rucksack, allowing the gas to escape. We only had one canister left each. After all our efforts, would this mechanical failure abort our climb? We had a poor meal with too little to drink.

It was a perfect starry night, but with an increase of cloud in the valleys way below. If the weather turned bad and the visibility deteriorated, we could easily lose the route and stray into suicidal ground. Even a trivial accident could be catastrophic. We were at our limit with no margin for error and zero chance of rescue. I hardly slept for worrying.

Crossing the *Throne* next day was a slog. It looked flat, but was steadily uphill, with deep snow and a crust that broke through with every step. It looked no distance to the bottom of the summit tower, but getting there took a whole joyless day of punishing labour. It was such a strange feeling to be on easy ground but so totally committed that I had an uncomfortable feeling we were heading into a trap.

From our recollections, the French had climbed the ridge line at the edge of the *Throne*, then kept to the right-hand skyline of the summit headwall, before following a long, difficult arête to the top. We planned a shortcut and headed for a bergschrund nearer the centre of the headwall, where a steep snow couloir broke through the granite ramparts directly to the top.

With parched throats and bouts of rasping coughs, we gratefully found shelter in the bergschrund, but there was little prospect of sleep. Tomorrow would be the culmination of all our plans, the day that mattered. At midnight we started the stove and put on our boots. Leaving our packs of gear in the bergschrund we hoped to climb quickly to the summit, 700 metres above, and descend in the same day. Going light was the only way we would cover all that ground, but it was a gamble that could easily fail. We each stuffed a couple of bars of fudge in our pockets and, at 3.00a.m., started to climb. A half-moon crisply illuminated the surrounding walls; the scene was like a black and white film negative. As we set off, each person's world was a pool of head torchlight and his private hopes and fears for the day ahead. A frigid wind whistled but, surprisingly, the snow was firm *névé*, the best we had encountered on the whole mountain. It was steep but straightforward, and our crampons and ice axes bit into it with satisfying ease.

'Roger, I'm going to have to stop! Everything's double,' I cried, looking at a bizarre reflection of myself.

Concerned by my state, Roger came to my side. 'Have a rest, take some deep breaths. It's probably the altitude.'

'It's really weird. I feel spaced out,' my words seemed to come from someone over my shoulder. 'I think I'll have to go down. You catch up with the other two. Oh, I feel dizzy.'

'Just relax.'

'Where am I?' an echo cried in a confused dreamland. Just as suddenly as my psychosis arrived, it disappeared. I was half-conscious, but now fully alive. We thought using bottled oxygen was cheating, but how I now wished for a few puffs of the gas.

With only the ink-blue infinity of the stratosphere above, we hoped it would get warmer as the sun rose. Instead, the wind increased and conditions deteriorated. We passed a tricky mixed section of climbing which had me panting hard, prompting another wave of psychosis and a shadow of self-doubt. By now, Rab and Al were a hundred metres above us. Flashes of agony in my calf muscles from constant front-point cramponing suggested we should rest, but Rab and Al forged ahead like men possessed. Their enthusiasm was infectious and, by the time we reached the skyline ridge, everyone was climbing strongly. The final knife-edged arête was like a tightrope in the sky and led to the summit, which we reached at 11.30a.m. on 21st October.

That morning I had gone from confusion to clarity, pain to fulfilment, doubt to certainty, insanity to lucidity, the full gamut of emotions within high-altitude mountaineering. I looked down on the glaciers far below, but there was no time to reflect on our success, so, after taking a photo of the stupendous view we downclimbed in a hurry. It was imperative that we reach our bivouac site before nightfall and, at 4.00p.m., we crawled into our bergschrund crib, exhausted after thirteen hours of continuous effort.

The downward drive to the glacier over the next two days was made unexpectedly easier by our partially consolidated ascent footsteps. Nevertheless, there was neither rest nor margin for error in our exhausted, semi-hallucinogenic state. Fuel and food had run out at our highest bivouac, so our bodies were running on hope and adrenaline. Eating handfuls of snow skinned our tongues and barely quenched our thirst, and we viewed the anvil-shaped black clouds boiling in the lowlands with acute apprehension. Would they rise to entertain us later in the day? We combined ropes, for the only time on the whole journey, for the abseils, but soon used our four snow stakes. It was with serious reluctance that we had to rely on insecure mounds of powder snow as bollard anchors for the rest of the descent.

We attacked the first pool of glacial meltwater like wild animals, lubricating our tormented throats and slaking our raging thirst. Our bodies responded to the gritty, cold liquid as if transfused with a magical elixir. The air was cool, not cold, smelling pungently of earth and grass and it was silent apart from the babbling of a glacial brook and the swish of wind over a rocky knoll. We were alive!

One day merged into the next of painfully slow staggering towards the mirage of the Lapsong La, during which our attempts at chewing the dry leaves of alpine plants were futile and gave us no nourishment. Drained of all energy, each step became a trial of strength. The absurdity was comical, we had succeeded in the climb but were in real danger of not surviving the walk back home.

'Surely we must be getting near?' Roger sighed, as he lay prostrate on the ground.

'What did you say?' I had fallen into a deep exhausted sleep next to him. Rab and Al were in no better shape. I forced my aching body upright and stared, hollow-eyed, at Roger, who had started to stagger away from me like a befuddled mannequin. The curtains of darkness were closing at the end of the fourth day without food. An hour lasted a minute, but that minute was an eternity.

'What's that noise?' Roger asked.

'I can't hear anything,' I replied.

'There it is again,' he insisted.

Now we all heard it – the sound of barking – the Tibetan yak herders' dogs.

Reaching Base Camp utterly spent, we hugged the beaming Padaam and Kusang. They were packing up camp as they were living off scraps and had given up hope of seeing us alive. We had been on the move for seventeen of the last eighteen days. They prepared rice for us, the only food left in the camp, which we devoured bowl after bowl, then dozed and slept and slept some more. It was another five days before we reached a village and the promise of something tasty.

'I've lost fifteen kilos,' Roger shouted, as he weighed his emaciated shell. Other than weight loss and exhaustion we were all uninjured and in remarkably good health. I had taken on the earthy, burnt wood smell of the local people, and felt that I was one of them now. In my first shower for over two months, standing in a daydream, the water pouring over my hair felt like spring rain on a parched desert.

My long-lasting memory is of an out-of-this-world delirious happiness as we walked back to the real world, brought on by starvation and the euphoria of having made a bold ascent with my three best mates. I feel privileged to have had such an experience and survived. On reflection, it was the highpoint of my mountaineering life. The climb gave me enlightenment and an enduring bond with Roger. A feeling of brotherly love I cannot express more openly. Our souls became one.

Our high altitude mountaineering careers had started with a bang, and soon we were plotting more expeditions, but our plans failed to coincide and we went our separate ways. For Roger, the trip to Nepal had sparked an interest in Buddhism and yoga, and he developed an even more relaxed perspective on life than during his University days. He left Sheffield and moved to London to live with his girlfriend, Sarah, and together they adopted an alternative philosophy, taking up the theories of sports performance under the umbrella of the *Inner Game*, which they applied to teaching skiing. This revolutionary technique was first developed for tennis by Tim Gallway. It takes place within the player's mind and is played against such obstacles as fear, self-doubt, lapses in focus, and limiting concepts or assumptions.

He was back in Nepal in 1980, climbing Kangchungtse (7,678 metres) with Doug Scott and Georges Bettembourg and coming within a whisker of climbing the South East Ridge of Makalu (8,481 metres). He hinted at the expedition's flavour in one of his letters home.

'This is a magic place – fifteen days from a road and out in time. We take it very easy, climb for as long as we have good breath, smoke a little number then sleep well. We were accompanied to Base Camp by a Buddhist Swami looking for a cave. It was too cold for him, so he gave us all a piggyback around camp and left. Georges was disappointed; he wanted to be taught how to walk on top of powder snow without sinking in! Near the camp is a big boulder with Buddhist inscriptions. Behind are prayer flags and a little shrine where a juniper fire burns when we go on the hill.

There's much dream talk with the 'fourth member' of the expedition, Carl Gustaf Jung (the Swiss psychologist) and our route will be decided by the I Ching.'

Despite the metaphysical aura around this trip, his desire to climb was not satisfied and, at the end of the expedition, he made an audacious solo attempt on the original route of Makalu, narrowly failing to reach the summit in what would have been the first British ascent of the fifth highest mountain in the world. When he returned he split with Sarah and moved to Chamonix where he later met Christine.

Two years on, he made a remarkable ascent of Shisha Pangma (8,013 metres) with Doug Scott and Alex McIntyre. The expedition planning was fraught with financial problems and Roger observed with some irony, 'On Doug Scott trips, you only know you're going when the plane takes off, not before.'

Tibet had only just opened to modern mountaineering, and Roger wrote to Christine about their journey. 'It is very bleak and yaks emerge from the dust cloud that follows our truck. Yesterday we visited Tashi Lumpo, the monastery of the Panchen Lama. One doorway concealed a room where seventy or so monks were chanting. It stopped me dead. All the romantic tales of mysterious Tibet were contained in that room. The centre was illuminated by a shaft of sunlight coming from above, the space largely filled with silk hangings and twisted wooden pillars holding the roof. On padded benches sat the monks, cross-legged dressed in dirty saffron wool robes with high collars, nodding back and forward as they chanted, led by a monk at the entrance to a shrine containing a buddha. His voice seemed to come from his stomach. The monks seemed to regard us with disinterest.'

Their ascent of Shisha Pangma South Face has gone down in the annals of mountaineering as one of the most significant in the Himalayas. Never had such a large, unknown face been climbed using such a pure pioneering spirit.

Nearing the summit, as Roger recalled, 'Himalayan climbing is about putting one foot in front of another and breathing while doing so. Keep doing this, and you will make it. The mind spins off into protracted fantasies, the lone survivor battles to safety. Only when you stop can you look around and see the Himalayas. Here, as nowhere else, the climber sees the immensity of the world – on the earth but not of it, playing games with gravity amongst all that beauty.'

Despite the success, he started to doubt the value of climbing these Himalayan giants. Complaining that the trudge up the interminable slopes of their acclimatisation peak, Nyanang Ri, was purgatory in contrast to the joy of climbing the technical Jorasses North Wall in the Alps the previous winter, he openly admitted his dilemma to Doug and Alex. 'Should I quit?' he wrote, 'Maybe after the planned ascent of K2 next year, maybe even after Shisha Pangma itself?'

Regardless of his misgivings, he joined Scott on another of his multi-peak extravaganzas in 1983. Visiting the Karakoram, he made a rapid ascent of the 8,051 metre Broad Peak with Jean Afanassieff, Andy Parkin, Al Rouse, Steve Sustad and Doug Scott. Two days after their climb, tragedy hit the expedition when our friend Pete Thexton died of altitude sickness on the upper slopes while descending with Greg Child. A sour mood hung over the expedition as they moved to K2 but, soon, with emotions running high, most of the team returned home.

'I miss you more and more – this seems like an unreal half-life here particularly since the accident – its all so false,' Roger wrote to Christine. 'And yet I'm going to stay for as long as possible. I don't quite understand why I want to climb K2 so much but I do, so I will tolerate the bad weather and bad feelings until we climb it or run out of food. Your letters seem to present a more interesting world – so much more life and interest. I think this trip is dull because of our winter together. This trip seems like an interruption. Why did I stop all that to try and climb this silly mountain?'

Roger stayed and made two determined attempts on K2. The first was foiled when Afanassieff became unwell at high altitude. It was a mark of Roger's determination that he then befriended a Basque climber and made a second attempt but, near the summit, a storm hit and the climb was aborted. It would have been the first British and first alpine style ascent of K2 if the mountain gods had been kind and given him one more day of good weather.

For the last few years of their relationship Roger had persisted in asking Christine to marry him until, finally, she agreed, saying, 'If you come back from K2 alive I will marry you.' On his return to Chamonix from the expedition he went straight to the *Mairie* to get the paperwork then took the cable car to Plan de l'Aiguille, where she was working. She saw him coming, waving the forms required to get married.

The last time I saw him was in Chamonix's Bar National in 1984 to make plans for an Alpine climb together. I had just returned from another Doug Scott led expedition to Makalu.

'How was Doug?' Roger asked.

'Good – just the usual organised chaos – you know Doug's mantra as well as me . . . 'I'm not equipped to lead, but I don't want to be led.' I laughed, thinking about Doug's unique leadership style, where democratic Buddhist philosophy runs headlong into his dictatorial opinions on how to climb and what to eat.

'I heard you almost climbed the South East Ridge. That's the second time Doug's failed near the summit,' Roger said.

'I didn't go on the ridge attempt,' I replied. 'I had an accident midway through the expedition which unsettled me.' I was about to explain when Roger interrupted.

'I've decided to give up Himalayan climbing. I've had enough. I'm getting too old, and I don't enjoy it anymore.'

'You're only thirty-four!' I replied, knowing deep down that I shared the same turmoil.

'Alex MacIntyre had been quite clear that he would survive another five years of dangerous face climbing and then take the job of simply "being famous".' Roger smiled as he recalled their conversation on Shisha Pangma. 'Well, I think my time is up.'

'It's madness! I love living in Chamonix with Christine and Mélanie, and I've just finished rebuilding the house. I need to move on,' he added, getting up to order another two beers.

'I would like to live here and guide,' I said as he returned.

'Yep, you get all the fun of the mountains without the slog,' he said, adding with a wry smile, 'I always had the quaint idea that climbing has something to do with pleasure.'

'Cheers,' we raised our glasses and drank our beer.

Mélanie (aged eight) and Roger
in Chamonix in 1983.

EULOGY TO ROGER

Mélanie Baxter-Jones

In the course of researching this book I corresponded or met with several of my lost friends' children, by now fully adult and often with children of their own. All carried their memories within their hearts, and seemed a little torn between protecting their parents' reputations and a necessary honesty on the subject of bereavement.

Mélanie replied with the following letter which, in my view, can be read as a poem, a brief but evocative summation of grief and loss. Now an adult with two children of her own, she remembers her stepdad, Roger, who died in the mountains when she was ten years old.

July 8, 1985 was the date that changed my life
The end of your life.

I've lived so much more since then, three times more.
I am a mother, older than you, with my younger child older than me.
She has finally finished her 10th birthday.
I breathe better, I know she won't have to go through all this.
And I still have a life left to live.
It's all upside down, time is all over the place.

I feel you close to me, and I, closer to you.
I miss you.
I'm no longer a little girl, but the loneliness of missing you is still overwhelming and still there.

So many things we did not have time to share.
Would you have been proud of me?
It's a stupid question and I'll never have the answer.
But it matters so much!

Your arms – your laugh – our readings – your voice.
Your terrible driving, always with eyes on the mountains, not the road.

Your smell when I unpacked your expedition down jacket.
A familiarity deep inside me.
Taking me by surprise, in the pit of my stomach, invading my whole body.
Until an explosion of tears.
It didn't hurt.
Very warm and generous tears.
Generous like you.
That's what disappeared the fastest. Your scent.
I didn't dare close my eyes,
I wasn't strong enough!
Even on hot days, I wanted to sleep in it, in the warm down.
One last kiss, a night protected in your arms while you evaporate forever.
But I put it back in the trunk, for another day,
THE day, when I really need it.
One smell of you – one more.

It turns me upside down,
that you're not here with me!

You carried my toy owl to the top of Shishapangma.
And promised to take a picture for me.
I was so proud, I knew you could not die because you had to bring it back.
I hated expeditions because I was scared.
But loved them as well, 'cause I knew how excited you were, how important it was.

I remember the preparations with everybody together.

The joy, and the never ending stocks of dried banana that have lived longer than you.

A time, where you had no phone for communication and no computers to check the weather forecast,

When we knew someone died, only because a Sherpa ran back to Kathmandu with the news.

All we had, was our love and those little blue airmail letters.

I would dry flowers, draw, write and sprinkle perfume.

As thin as they were, those letters were the fuel which kept me feeling so much ****.

The fragile thread of hope.

After you came back from K2,

After the cramps in the bath, the 'force-feeding' to regain weight, you asked ME if you could marry my mother.

If we could officially become a family.

All the things you said, all our promises, that I too would sign, at the town hall.

I will never forget, we went together to her dad, Monsieur Gerard Comte.

You asked for my mother's hand.

We were together, team work makes dream work.

You were scared!

So you asked me to put on a nice dress, and the special lace socks you bought me.

As special as your posh accent and your very special loud and contagious laughs.

All those little special things made you so special!

Don't worry, I'm fine!

I'm making it up as I go along, for myself.

I don't forget what we said to each other, our promises.

I hold our memories deep within me.

I swear to you that they are a treasure map.

To pass on to my children, Merlin and Ninon.

So that they find you, on their way.

So that they find their own way.

Giving them the keys, so that they can make this recipe for a magical life.

Filled with the fun and energy, that you gave me.

That taught me one of the most important things, to live a full life, to laugh, to dare to live my dreams.

A wonderful guide and Himalayan mountaineer but ALSO an unforgettable dad, loving and caring, we had so much fun. You potato . . . you just came back from K2!

Miss you so-so-so Fucking much, Roger Baxter-Jones!

XXX

Mélanie Baxter-Jones,
Actrice en France

Rab Carrington on the Jannu expedition, 1978.

8

THE SNOW LEOPARD

Alan Rouse and Rab Carrington

A lingering lucid dream of a cat-like prehistoric animal, which was both fearsome and gentle, evaporated as I stirred inside my warm sleeping bag. I moved stiffly, reluctant for my slumbers to end. Only my nose poked out into the bitterly cold, pre-dawn Himalayan air.

The ritual of getting up from the bivouac started. Head out – peer around – were the storm clouds of yesterday shrouding the summits? Secretly I hoped the weather had deteriorated so I could dissolve back into the warmth and continue my dreams, but the sky was aglow with stars.

Rab Carrington was already sitting up, his torch pooling light through the veil of steam rising from our homemade gas tower stove as he boiled water for our first brew. Al Rouse lay motionless a few metres away.

'Good sleep Rab?' I enquired, both to get the day started and to wake Al.

'Brilliant. Water should be ready soon.'

Two days earlier we had left our Base Camp to attempt a new route on Kangtega (6,782 metres) in Nepal's Khumbu Himal. The area's topography was complicated, and the maps poor, so arriving at our second bivouac site had been disorientating. We had climbed a difficult, virgin 800-metre face, and surprisingly reached a glacier that was hidden from below, which we later identified as the Hinku Nup. Our objective rose half a kilometre away: the North East Ridge. If we had pitched our Base Camp in the Hinku Valley we could have avoided our two-day approach climb and walked to the bottom of the ridge.

Cradling a plastic mug of sweet tea, I watched as the copper dawn sky, slashed with purple clouds, revealed the peaks to the north: the elegant spire of Ama Dablam, behind which towered the brooding walls of Nuptse and Lhotse, with the summit of Everest – Chomolungma, Goddess Mother of the World – rising above. To the south the snowy crests of Thamserku and Kasum Kanguru turned golden in the early morning sun. What else the dawn light revealed was something of a surprise . . . footprints.

From a distance the tracks meandered lazily up the glacier, obviously made by a reasonably sized animal. Had the beast arrived at our bivouac searching for food? Prints approached each of our sleeping bags in turn. It must have leaned into each face, smelling our human aroma intermingled with cooking waste and urine-soaked snow, and no doubt been confused by the bird scent of our down filled sleeping bags. On closer inspection, the tracks belonged to an animal with paws. Astonished, we realised our visitor could only have been a snow leopard. The feline ghost had left and sauntered back down the snow-covered moraine. My dream had been more than lucid, it was real.

Our crampons crunched in the frozen snow as we walked across the glacier to the base of the ridge. Ominously the purple dawn clouds turned to black and began to envelop the sky. The weather was rapidly deteriorating, and so was our mood. I had an inkling that something was not right. Before starting the challenging part of the route we were exhausted from two days of effort, compounded by a lack of altitude acclimatisation. We had also used half our food and fuel. Unexpectedly, there was a lot of belligerent chatter between Al and Rab, distanced by long pregnant silences, like the bickering of an old married couple. Finally, after a heated argument over a trivial decision as to which way we should cross a crevasse, Rab, who was in the lead, came to an abrupt stop and turned to Al and me. 'This weather looks bad.'

'It's not looking good,' Al replied.

'This is a waste of time,' Rab said. 'The plan isn't working. It's our third day and we haven't even started the significant part of the route.'

'Let's go back,' I suggested.

We returned to our bivouac, and to the tracks in the snow. With a few hours of insipid sun, they had ablated and doubled in size. They looked like the mirror image of the infamous Yeti tracks photographed by Eric Shipton in 1951.

Al, Rab and I were part of an ambitious, international expedition assembled by Doug Scott, attempting four mountains in the Khumbu region of Nepal, in the autumn of 1979. In total, we had permission to climb Kusum Kanguru (6,369 metres), Kangtega (6,782 metres), Nuptse (7,861 metres]) and Everest (8,848 metres). In addition, the team included Georges Bettembourg from France and Michael Covington from the USA. At Base Camp, wives, girlfriends and children completed the happy family. It was a new and experimental approach, an attempt to climb several mountains in a lightweight, alpine style in a single season, by a 'loose' band of climbers.

For the first part of the expedition, we split into two units. Doug, Georges and Michael went to Kusum Kanguru, while Rab, Al and I tried Kangtega, reasoning that, on lower altitude peaks, two separate, small teams would give better and more intimate alpine style experiences. The post-monsoon, autumn climbing window of good weather only lasts six weeks, so we had to utilise the time efficiently. Although attempting these two lower mountains was significant, they also provided the opportunity to acclimatise for the higher altitude peaks. As such, we had a limited timescale before we had to move onto the two primary objectives: a new route up the North Spur of Nuptse and the first alpine style ascent of Everest.

With little time to spare Al, Rab and I departed Base Camp for our second attempt on Kangtega. Our plan B was a more direct route on the S-shaped North Ridge. Midway through the second day, Al and Rab argued again and it was apparent that they were not getting on well. Climbing under threatening seracs at 6.000 metres they stopped and slumped in the snow.

'I've had enough,' Rab curtly announced.

'It's not working, is it? Let's go back,' Al replied and, without further discussion, abandoned the climb with me following behind. Bewildered by the decision, it seemed to me that I was an inconsequential stranger on the end of their rope.

Rab's partner Sue, who had accompanied us to Base Camp, was surprised to see us return so soon. There seemed to have been a breakdown in communications between Al and Rab. To get away from this rancour, I went for a walk. On returning, Rab and Sue were packing their bags.

'Have I been a problem Rab?' I asked, as a confused bystander to the confrontation.

'No. It's nothing to do with you.' He looked down sadly before adding, 'Everything must come to an end sometime.'

I lay awake that night, upset at what had happened. It now seemed obvious that, since our success on Jannu, Al and Rab had been going in different directions. Al was ambitious and had been planning some very committing projects in the Himalaya. He was also in a weird confrontation with Joe Tasker, Pete Boardman and Alex MacIntyre, posturing over who had the higher status and the better reputation. More simply, who would the future figurehead of UK climbing would be. The next Chris Bonington. For Al this was particularly important, as whoever became top dog would be better positioned to raise sponsorship for future expeditions. Rab, I suspected, had no time for politics and rivalry. He was totally driven and committed once climbing, but I presumed that his long-term relationship with Sue now took precedence.

Later, Rab wrote in *Vertical* magazine in 2008, 'Looking back on that period, Al and I "did bravery" for eight years. That felt like a long time, and my head and circumstances told me to "do bravery" no more! I think I must have used up all my courage in the '70s!'

Their ascents throughout the world had significantly raised the bar of alpine style mountaineering, but that era ended as Rab and Sue walked out of camp for Khumjung and home. Over the next few years they bought a house, had a family and started a business manufacturing sleeping bags. Rab stopped being a professional mountaineer and, a few years later, after a final abortive expedition to the Karakorum, hung up his crampons to concentrate on rock climbing. He then spent his leisure time travelling the world rock climbing and became very good, eventually succeeding on his first, elite graded 8a route at the age of fifty-nine. Rab was an exceptional mountaineer but even the best have their limits.

So, at the age of thirty-four, he stopped alpine climbing, a perfectly respectable retirement age for any top athlete. After all, sporting greats such as racing driver, Stirling Moss, retired at thirty-two, and the boxer, Muhammad Ali, at thirty-nine.

In the same article he explained, after they had climbed three arduous new routes on Rasac West Face, Yurupaja South Face and Rondoy West Face in Peru. 'We believed that we were the best in the world and with that came a feeling of invincibility. Our self-belief was running so high that it must have bordered on madness and yet at the same time, we understood this. I said to Al in all seriousness, "We had better leave now otherwise we will get ourselves killed!"'

It was a very subdued atmosphere as Al and I packed up camp, with neither of us talking about what had happened. On 5th October, the two of us left Kangtega Base Camp with eleven Sherpani porters carrying our loads. Rather than going home, we apprehensively headed for Everest Base Camp and the second phase of our expedition: Nuptse and Everest.

Georges Bettembourg at
Kanchenjunga Base Camp, 1979.

9

SURVIVAL OF THE FITTEST

Georges Bettembourg

High in the Khumbu Valley of Nepal the two factions of our multi-peak expedition had operated separately. Rab Carrington, Al Rouse and I had abandoned our attempt on Kangtega. The others, Doug Scott, Georges Bettembourg and Michael Covington, had completed their climb on Kusum Kanguru and were making the three-day trek to Everest Base Camp, at 5,360 metres. When they arrived at the dry humps and hollows of grey icy moraine that form the site, they pitched a small group of tents and built a small canvas-roofed kitchen tent with stone walls. Their camp was dwarfed by the nearby bases of the German Everest and the Polish Lhotse climbing groups, both making summit bids at the culminations of their respective expeditions.

The morning after arriving, Doug, Georges and Michael easily climbed the Khumbu Icefall with the help of the ropes and ladders fixed by the Germans. The Icefall allows the only entry into the glacial amphitheatre of the Western Cwm, which gave access to the routes on Everest and Lhotse, as well as our projected new route on the North Spur of Nuptse. They laboured through the hot afternoon sun to Everest Camp 2, at 6,400 metres, to inspect the snow conditions. They stayed one night and descended, satisfied that conditions looked excellent.

Unfortunately, Michael contracted a serious stomach bug at the beginning of the trip and the sickness had returned. His expedition was over.

They were discussing what to do in the kitchen tent when one of the Germans burst in, shouting in panic. Evidently Ray Genet and Hannelore Schmatz had got into difficulty while descending from the summit of Everest and been forced to spend the night near the top of the mountain. Close to tears, he explained that Ray's wife, Kathy, had just arrived with their young child, hoping to celebrate her husband's success.

Within the hour, news came through that they had not survived the night. Ray was nicknamed the 'Pirate' and was a Swiss-born, American mountaineer. He had been a guide on Alaska's Denali, and knew Michael Covington well. The day before, the Germans had been celebrating their success. Today, the whole camp was enveloped in sadness. Michael volunteered to accompany the distraught Kathy and child back to Syangboche airstrip.

Meanwhile, life carried on for everyone else on the mountain. With Michael gone, and after a day's rest, Doug and Georges continued their reconnaissance and acclimatisation by climbing to the Lho La Col, part way up the West Ridge of Everest, to inspect the approach to our final ambitious objective: the first alpine style ascent of Everest. While making their way to the Lho La, Georges spotted an old leather boot in the glacial moraine. On closer inspection, a bleached-white ankle bone poked out of the footwear. Carefully, he removed the bone and read, etched on the leather inside, the letters GDX. 'Mon Dieu c'est mon oncle!' he exclaimed.

It was the boot of Gerard Devoussoux, who was a father figure to Georges growing up in Chamonix, until tragically avalanched in 1974 from the West Ridge along with five Sherpas.

After the duo returned to Base Camp the expedition became fragmented with different members scattered throughout the Khumbu Valley. Doug said goodbye to Georges and began the three-day trek down to Namche Bazaar to meet up with his family and Michael. There was going to be a wedding. The year before, while in Nepal on an earlier attempt with Doug on Nuptse, Michael had met and fallen in love with a local girl, Chumjee Sherpani. Despite Michael's illness, the marriage celebrations would last for several days, involving colourful dancing and copious quantities of chang. Georges stayed at Base Camp before heading, all alone, into the Western Cwm for a hugely ambitious, clandestine solo attempt on Everest.

Over on Kangtega, Al Rouse, Rab Carrington, Rab's non-climbing wife, Sue, and I had been in a world of our own, cut off from any news of our team mates on Kusum Kanguru but, after the discord between Al and Rab, we had abandoned our attempt and packed up. After sadly waving goodbye to Rab and Sue, Al and I began the trek to Everest Base Camp, where we planned to meet Doug, Georges and Michael. On the way, we were surprised to meet Doug, alone, tucking into a lunch of dal bhat at a scruffy teahouse in Lobuche, on his way down the valley.

Doug was thirty-eight, and one of the best mountaineers in the world, a great bear of a man, broad-shouldered and immensely strong, with a presence even bigger than his height. He spoke in measured bursts, often finishing a statement with 'youth', while looking at the ground or with a distant stare through his long brown hair and round John Lennon glasses. Although he was from a beer-drinking, rugby-playing background in Nottingham, he chose the path of becoming a vegetarian with a keen interest in Buddhism. He was a decade older than me, with more mountaineering experience. I particularly liked the way he discussed and debated topics in a refreshing, democratic way, before making decisions. Democratic or not though, he had a knack of getting his own way.

Inside the teahouse Dawa, a wrinkled old Sherpani, knelt on the earth floor, feeding the fire with wood. Her ragged clothes were brightened by a beautiful amber, turquoise, and jade necklace and a brightly striped, wool pangi apron. Doug sat at a crooked table, illuminated by a shaft of smoky light from a small window, which was the only illumination in the room that served as kitchen, dining and a bedroom. He finished eating and over a cup of chi tea explained, 'I'm off down the valley to Namche Bazaar to meet Jan and the kids, Martha and Rosie, and attend Michael and Chumjee's wedding. Where's Rab?'

'Rab and I fell out on Kangtega and he's on his way home,' Al replied, adding, 'You might catch up with him in Namche.'

'Where's Georges?' I asked.

'Left him up at Base Camp . . . youth.'

Al was keen to be updated on the climbing news. 'What happened on Kusum Kanguru?'

Doug described their stunning climb with typical understatement, 'Kusum is a beautiful mountain, and I was amazed it had never been climbed before. We did it in three days. Fast and light.'

'Was it hard?'

'Dangerous rather than hard, youth. The snow was in poor condition. The descent was the worst, with difficult route finding. As the peak was not too high it was ideal for acclimatisation. We got to the top ten days ago.' He corrected himself. 'Georges and I did. Unfortunately, Michael became ill.'

'Is he any better?' Al asked.

Doug stood up, stooping slightly to avoid the low ceiling, and replied, 'He's still got a bug and can't climb. With Rab leaving we are down to a team of four for the rest of the trip.'

As he walked out of the tea house he turned, 'Must go, youth. I'll be at Base Camp with the missus and kids in a few days.'

Outside the tea house, the sun was setting as a cold wind whipped up a dust storm at this desolate last habitation before Everest Base Camp. Inside, Dawa asked in broken English. '*Chi ... Chang ... Rakshi?*'

'Chang,' Al replied, and I agreed it was time for some alcohol.

'*Sutnu ...* can we sleep here?' I asked hopefully. It was too late to reach Base Camp.

'*Las,*' she affirmed, before gesturing with her hand to her mouth. 'Eat?'

'*Dhanyabaad,*' I thanked her, and she went into the corner to fill a battered, soot-blacked pan with water. We sat in silence until it got dark and Dawa's shaking hands lit an old paraffin lantern that threw a dim, flickering, golden glow over the walls. 'I'm sorry about you and Rab,' I said to Al.

'It was going to happen sometime.' Our food arrived: a cracked bowl full of rice, a tin plate of chapattis, with a meagre portion of dhal. Al sipped at his chang and sighed, 'I'm confused. What's happened to this trip?'

'I know. We were meant to be climbing and here we are abandoned. Michael is getting married and Doug is at his wedding. There's not much chance of seeing them for a week.'

'And it looks like Michael's not well enough to climb.'

I changed the subject. 'What do you think of Doug's kids coming to Base Camp?'

'It could be odd. Martha is only six and Rosie is a baby.'

'At least we will get to Everest Base Camp tomorrow and meet up with Georges. Perhaps we can start climbing as a three. When Doug arrives, we can work out a plan for Nuptse and Everest.'

'Yes', Al agreed. 'Chaos. Typical Doug.'

Next day, Al and I arrived at our team's Base Camp to find only Ang Phurba, our sirdar, and Nima, the cook. Ang Phurba rummaged in his pocket and handed me a crumpled piece of paper. With astonishment I read the short cryptic note scribbled in pencil by Georges. 'Gone to climb Everest.'

This galvanised Al who said, 'I'm worried that our altitude acclimatisation is a long way behind Georges and Doug's.' They already had several sorties on Everest under their belts, and reached the summit of Kusum Kanguru. He started sorting his gear. 'Let's pack and leave early tomorrow. If we go up to Everest's Camp 2 we will be able to carry a load of food and camp gear for Nuptse and have a look at the route, as well as getting acclimatised.'

The following dawn, we set off up the jumbled and dangerous Khumbu Icefall, labouring through the intense, reflected heat of the Western Cwm. We reached Camp 2 late in the afternoon and pitched our diminutive tent, which was hardly big enough to squeeze inside. That evening, before sleeping, I unzipped its entrance and stuck my head out to look at the starlit, silver mountains.

'Come and have a look,' I said. 'The air is so clear.'

'Uh', was the uninterested grunt from inside.

The mountains dwarfed our small shelter and the strange, celestial aura gave me a peculiar out-of-this-world feeling. I felt so small and insignificant, yet still part of the Gaia. Where was Georges? Somewhere high above us, on Everest. I had not yet met him, but was already impressed by his spirit and enthusiasm. Closing the zip I buried myself in my sleeping bag but had hardly closed my eyes when Al woke me, coughing and retching.

'I've a really bad headache,' he slurred. It was four in the morning, dark and freezing. Half out of my sleeping bag, I realised the gravity of the situation, and helped him get dressed. He was too weak to shoulder his pack.

Carrying only emergency gear, we left the tent, food and stove for our return in a few days, assuming Al recovered. Supporting him, with his arm over my shoulder, we were only able to stumble fifty metres before collapsing in the snow with Al's chest heaving, consumed in a bout of coughing. The situation was dire and I feared that if he couldn't get up he might die. However, although he was stricken with altitude sickness, his mind was still full of fight and he would only allow himself a few minutes before lifting his forlorn body and plodding on. 'Let's go man,' he whispered hoarsely.

'We've got all day. Take it slowly and we'll stop before the next crevasse.' I was concerned that his next step might be his last.

Miraculously, by mid-morning, he staggered like a punchdrunk boxer into the abandoned Everest Camp 1 at 6,065 metres, on the upper lip of the Icefall. We had made it halfway down to Base Camp. Al lay in the snow groaning, totally spent but after a long rest and a drink, some colour came back into his face. The 350 metre loss in height proved to be the catalyst for his recovery.

The trail down the Icefall was difficult to follow, but Nima and Ang Pherba spotted us from Base Camp and rushed to help. Exhausted, but safe, we eventually collapsed like two dishevelled hobos and lay on our tattered yellow foam mats next to the kitchen tent.

Later that afternoon, unshaven, smelly and stripped to the waist we warmed our aching bodies in the sun, our gear strewn untidily on the gravel moraine and ice. Al looked more dead than alive. A shout broke our torpor. 'Hello my friends!' A bundle of energy strode into camp. Georges Bettembourg must have followed us down the Icefall. 'Where have you been?' croaked Al, his throat dry and sore.

Georges threw his ice axe down, took off his rucksack, and removed his red cap to reveal a mop of black hair. On his haunches, resting against a boulder, he traced a stick of lip salve across his sun-cracked, bleeding lips. 'I got to the Yellow Band, 7,500 metres.' Nima, our Sherpa cook, handed him a chipped white enamel mug of sweet tea. '*Dhanyabaad,*' he said. 'I've been dreaming of soloing Everest. It was more like walking than climbing, but I got so, so tired with the altitude.' Then with a huge grin, 'But I am happy!'

I had never met Georges, but we got on immediately and, as we chatted, it became apparent that we had many mutual friends and parallel experiences. We were both aged twenty-eight and committed to a life of climbing. It was amazing that I had not bumped into him before.

He was a flamboyant Frenchman, of average height but athletic build with piercing dark eyes that held your attention, a *Chamoniard* who spent the summer guiding, climbing and crystal hunting around Mont Blanc, and in winter based himself in Seattle with his partner, Norma. In the States and Western Canada he operated as a heli-ski guide and ski coach in the Bugaboos, Monashees and Cascade Range. With a traditional, alpine-family heritage, he was related to the renowned guides Georges and Armand Charlet, who pioneered many first ascents in the Alps at the beginning of the twentieth century.

'What have you been doing?' he asked, 'and what happened on Kangtega?'

'We did not have a good time on Kangtega,' Al explained. Georges eyes widened.

'Where's Rab? Is he OK?'

'He's fine. We had an argument, so he and his wife have gone home.' Al's voice was strained with fatigue.

'You and Rab have been climbing together for years. The Alps, South America, Jannu. You're the best team. You can't split up!'

Upset, Al left for his tent, leaving Georges and me to talk into the night, resuming in the morning after I found him sitting cross-legged, barefoot and wearing only bright yellow shorts, taking in the hot, high altitude sun. 'I didn't sleep much last night, thinking over what you said about Rab,' he said. 'I'm writing to Norma. We are going to get married after the expedition. Perhaps you can come to the wedding?'

'Are you going to live in Seattle?'

'I'm trying to sort that out, but the mail runner does not get here for three days and the letter will take weeks to get to America. By the time she replies, the expedition will be finished.' He looked me in the eye, 'Have you been writing to your girlfriend?'

I focused on a small piece of ice protruding through the moraine gravel, embarrassed to admit that I didn't have a girlfriend. 'I was in Peru a lot of the summer, then here. It's difficult to have a steady relationship and be away climbing all the time.'

'I love Norma so much, but I have been away six months this year. Kanchenjunga then here. I worry.'

I picked up a stone and threw it at a distant boulder. 'I like the freedom from work and home. I love the isolation of the mountains.'

'And I enjoy climbing without justification.'

Muscles still aching from yesterday's climbing, I walked slowly to the kitchen tent where high-pitched, Indian singing rose from an oversized cassette player. Nima was diligently washing the breakfast dishes. 'Can I take this?' I asked. He looked disappointed but nodded.

Returning to Georges' tent, I searched through a stuff sack of music cassettes and put on Joy Division's *Unknown Pleasure*. 'Tell me about Kusum Kanguru,' I asked, while I took off my tee-shirt and sprawled on a foam mat.

'I am not sure where to begin,' he said. 'We started climbing before you on Kangtega. I think we were a week ahead, because you trekked in while we flew direct to Lukla.'

'Do you enjoy climbing with Michael and Doug?' I asked.

'I have never climbed with Michael before.'

'Me neither. I know very little about him. We have never met.'

'He's an interesting guy, a real Californian hippie and a musician who played with Simon and Garfunkel and hung out with Joni Mitchell. She wrote the song about him called *Michael from Mountains*.'

'How did Doug meet him?' I asked

'He and Michael climbed in Colorado, before trying Nuptse last year. But the snow conditions were too dangerous,' he said, pausing to listen to the music. 'Can we change the cassette? Put on Neil Young's *Rust Never Sleeps* ... That's better. I've had to listen to Bob Dylan for the last two weeks. Doug plays him non-stop.'

Al made a remarkable recovery and we had a sociable few days while resting before our attempt on Nuptse. Doug arrived back with his wife, Jan, and their two young daughters. To Georges and my strong approval, they were accompanied by two young women, Ariane Giobellina from Leysin in Switzerland, who had been a close friend of Dougal Haston, and Canadian Nena Holguin, the girlfriend of Peter Hillary. Georges and I relaxed amiably, smoked joints, discussed Buddhist philosophy and rambled on about how mountains, high altitude and wilderness in general, heightened our senses. I found his command of English with a heavy French accent beguiling. He declared, 'I have a fatalistic mind which helps me analyse the risk of dying.'

'I'm not a fatalist,' I replied, 'as I think I can make choices which may help keep me alive, though I suppose I am a pragmatist and life and death are part of nature.'

He held his arms out, palms up. 'I am so lucky I have no worries. You have to be ready to die at any time. But I don't want to die, because I live.'

I agreed in part. 'Yes, you need luck in the mountains but, even then, accidents happen. By making good decisions you create your own luck.'

Later that afternoon, he disappeared to his tent to show me a newfound trophy. 'Have a look at this,' he said, proudly handing me his late 'uncle's' boot, the leather sun-bleached almost white, and hard as wood. 'I am going to take it back to his family in Chamonix.' Rather confused, he added, 'Brian, what am I going to do with the bones?'

The boot prompted him into lengthy explanations of his Chamonix family roots. 'After becoming a member of the Compagnie des Guides de Chamonix in 1969, I was keen to travel and try harder climbs, but every time I was knocked back by older climbers who said I was too young and inexperienced. I tried to get on French expeditions to Everest in '74, Nanda Devi in '76, Dhaulagiri and Ama Dablam in '78 and finally with the Americans on K2.' He became animated at this point, 'I was so frustrated by the arrogance, politics and social web in the Chamonix valley I now spend a lot of time in America.'

I thought he had got his frustrations off his chest, but he continued, this time with a smile, 'Finally, in '78, I went on my first expedition to Broad Peak (8,047 metres) with Yannick Seigneur. I loved the simplicity and intimacy of that low-key climb. We climbed it fast and in alpine style, just the two of us. Brian, do you know what my mantra is? No rope, no burden.'

I now understood why Doug was climbing with Georges. He had a rare talent, ideally suited to the Himalayas. He was a master of solo climbing on mid-difficulty terrain at speed.

Six months previously, in the spring of '79, Doug had invited Georges and two top new-generation mountaineers, Joe Tasker and Pete Boardman, to join him on Kangchenjunga, at 8,586 metres the world's third highest peak. Doug was in the process of rethinking his strategy for Himalayan climbs after his experiences on K2 when his close friend, Nick Estcourt, was killed by an avalanche that Doug miraculously survived. He eventually concluded that a complete change of style was required.

Afterwards he wrote, 'I decided not to employ heavy siege tactics on any future climbs, as crossing dangerous ground once was maybe a justifiable risk, but to repeat the crossing many times was foolhardy. I also think siege climbing inherently boring'.

One evening after drinking too much chang, Georges opened his heart to Doug, Al and me about Kangchenjunga. Explaining that he thought the expedition was a success as Doug, Joe and Pete made the third ascent of the mountain by a new route. But he admitted that even though he did not get to the summit, the main reason he did not enjoy the climb was because relations were strained. 'Our intention was to go lightweight, alpine style with no supplementary oxygen or high- altitude porters, but it ended up as a siege when poor weather forced us to use fixed ropes and camps.' Early on, Pete was injured by rock fall and Joe was incapacitated by altitude sickness. This gave them time to rest in the first half of the trip, which gave them extra reserves later. Georges described, 'Doug and I burnt ourselves out forcing the route, and I had to descend before the final push. In the end, with a supreme effort, Doug managed to join Joe and Pete on the summit.'

Georges perhaps revealed more than he had intended. 'For me it was an unhappy expedition. Joe and Pete were cold and had no humour.' Explaining that they did not act like mates. They were serious and would not play games. From their point of view, he was too impulsive. Perhaps a simple case of the stoic Anglo Saxons and the emotional Gaul, but it awoke in him a realisation that the closer to the summit they got, the higher the egos climbed. The climbing had not been for the joy of climbing, but for the glory. He was glad to give his all, but he burnt out doing so. Saying Kangch was hard-core with a lot of suffering and he much preferred the fun he had with Yannick on their pure alpine style ascent of Broad Peak.

Doug joined the conversation, telling us that he later heard via Georges that Pete and Joe had been discussing him behind his back. They thought that he had been slow. Doug agreed there was a lot of truth in what he heard. Nevertheless, it was painful to hear, concluding that it was a state of affairs that occurs between older and younger climbers, feeling that he had been in the way of their ambition, particularly Joe's.

It was becoming obvious that this autumn's multi-peak plan was directly influenced by Doug's experiences over the last couple of years. I believe he'd had his fill of the straightjackets of large scale expeditions such as the South West Face of Everest in '75, and this year's new, liberated approach was in reaction to that orthodox and regimented style. From his recent success on Kangchenjunga, he knew that big mountains could be climbed safely without oxygen.

It was getting late, but Doug enthused, 'What a wonderful feeling to be climbing high without the weight of two oxygen bottles on my back.'

Al agreed and said, 'I want to climb like we did on Jannu and the peaks in South America. Lightweight and in small teams.'

We all had differing opinions on how to execute Doug's plans. In particular, Georges' mind was in conflict between the challenge of Nuptse and what he termed 'the inflated prestige of Everest'. Now the other expeditions had left, he became obsessed with the idea of the first true alpine style ascent of Everest, without Sherpa support or supplementary oxygen. 'Surely, it would be the next step in the mountain's history and are we not in a great position to do this?'

Only a year before, on 8th May 1978, Reinhold Messner and Peter Habeler broke through perceived barriers and amazed the world by their ascent of Everest without supplementary oxygen, albeit within the structure of a large scale expedition.

Georges continued. 'We can take the next step. I want to try Everest first.'

I pointed out, 'At the moment Al and I are not sufficiently acclimatised to go above eight thousand metres.'

He sighed and countered, 'Nuptse will take too much time and energy and after the climb and recovery it will be the end of October. Too late and too cold. The winter jet stream winds will be hitting the summits.'

Doug brought the discussion to an end, 'We need to stick to the plan. First, attempt the technically more difficult new route on Nuptse, then we will be acclimatised for Everest.'

I smiled at how Georges, *le paysan alpin et Guide de Haute Montagne,* had estimated the difficulties after coming down from his solo attempt. 'I couldn't help thinking that it would go easily alpine style. Just plodding up, so easy you could bring your grandmother and your cow. But ... I would not mind climbing Everest with my grandmother and my cow!'

Doug later revealed that he thought Georges had slightly different motives. 'Having not made the summit on Kangchenjunga, he was on the surface outwardly calm. Inwardly, I felt he was nursing wounded pride and was now bent on restoring his self-respect.'

Doug, who had already climbed Everest with Dougal Haston in 1975, got his way. We attempted Nuptse first.

Georges enjoyed life to the full. He liked to laugh, joke, love and play. He was a pleasure and an inspiration to be with. A serial romantic, he seemed to practise his art more than he should have, in hours of deep conversation with Nena. When we joked about it, he got confused about his infatuation but confided that he could not bear the guilt of being unfaithful, even on the other side of the world from his long-time love. I did not know whether to believe him or not, but I fancied her just as much as he did. She was gorgeous and so was Ariane. Women at Base Camp were in a powerful position and at that time were rare gems in the chauvinistic world of mountaineering. They both flirted with us and it was fun, but in the end we were left to fantasise on the improbable.

To help us climb at the limit of our ability and try more difficult climbs in faster times, we had to keep abreast with new developments in mountaineering gear. One piece of kit that we trialled were revolutionary plastic boots. Modified from a ski touring design by Kastinger, they had been worn by Messner and Habeler the year previously. In the past we had used double layered leather boots, a design hardly changed since the first ascent of Everest in 1953. In comparison, the plastic boots were lighter, warmer, and did not freeze solid.

Misgivings about Doug's family were unfounded. In fact, they improved the dynamics of the group. One day a small group of American trekkers arrived at Base Camp, looking exhausted and totally disorientated by the altitude and the environment, although they were delighted to have achieved their goal. 'Gee how old are you?' a rather large Texan man asked Martha as she served them tea.

'Eight', she proudly proclaimed.

'Reeaally . . .' he replied, wide-eyed.

'This is my sister Rosie who is nearly one.' Martha proudly pointed to the baby in the corner of the tent.

'What was that?' The Texan stood up, startled, at the distant crash and growl of an avalanche.

'More?' asked Martha, as she lugged around a heavy kettle of hot, sweet, milky tea, comfortably accustomed to the daily moods of the mountains.

The time came for us to prepare our gear and return to the Cwm. On Sunday 14th October, we had porridge and tea at 4.00a.m. and ascended back into the Icefall. By then the Germans and Poles had left, ending the maintenance of the fixed ropes and ladders. Even in the week since our last visit, the route had deteriorated and returned, more or less, to nature. Ladders had collapsed into gaping holes and fixed ropes snapped under the constant movement of the ice. Avalanches covered much of the track and we often had to forge a new path. It was a dangerous place and we wasted no time in reaching Camp 1 at the start of the Western Cwm.

'My pack's too heavy,' I complained.

'Aye, and it's hot. It's like being in a cauldron,' Al replied, sweat dripping from his nose.

Georges put one vertical finger to his lips before whispering, 'It's so quiet.'

We were surrounded on three sides by stupendous peaks, whose aura stretched high into the ink-blue sky. The ramparts of the South West Face of Everest on the left, Lhotse, a castle dripping in ice, towered at the back of the valley, and the prow of Nuptse, our objective, on our right.

'This deep snow is hard work. It's going to be a long afternoon,' Doug said. He unpacked the stove and melted snow for a brew. The hum of the stove seemed out of place in this hallowed arena.

Sitting on my pack, I had difficulty comprehending where I was. *Alone in the Western Cwm!* Just the four of us, in a place so iconic in the annals of mountaineering that merely sitting here was an experience that penetrated deep into my soul. Hard to believe that we were on the same planet as the rest of humanity. It was one of the most humbling and joyous moments of my life. In subsequent years I have been asked to guide on commercial Everest expeditions but refused lest it dilute a private memory that can only be shared with Doug, Al and Georges.

'Tea, youth.' Doug handed me an orange plastic mug.

'Thanks.' My heart pounded all through my out-of-body experience, a new perspective in which I was very small and irrelevant.

'Time to move,' Doug said.

I shouldered my pack and followed.

At Camp 2, nestling in an avalanche protected zone under the South West Face of Everest, we found our tents and the supplies we had left on our sortie the week before. Here we rested next day, eating, drinking and getting used to the 6,400 metre altitude.

Late in the morning Al rummaged through a pile of abandoned boxes next to our tents. 'Brian and Georges,' he shouted, 'come and have a look. Boxes full of packets of dried potatoes and salami.'

Georges tore one open, 'This one's full of chocolates. What a waste! We could live off this for a month!'

I kicked at a pile of gas cylinders and a wrecked tent. 'More than a waste,' I murmured, more to myself.

We spent a futile hour tidying the abandoned gear, but finally admitted defeat and left it to the winter snow and winds.

During the afternoon I began to feel rough, first a headache and then sickness. Next day I rested, melted water and prepared food while the other three crossed the Cwm to the base of the North Spur of Nuptse, searching for a way through a barrier of seracs and crevasses. On this foray Georges was outstanding, leading the team up an overhanging serac of poor ice. It was a dangerous section as there was little protection to arrest a fall, but it proved to be our key. They left a fixed rope, preparing the way, so we could avoid the difficult ice, enabling fast and safe progress when we returned the next day.

On the 16th, in the half-light of dawn, we retraced the previous day's steps to pass through an eerie landscape of huge ice blocks and deep powder snow that must have avalanched from high above. I was impressed with what the guys had achieved in the face of such obvious danger. Thankfully, their tracks and fixed rope allowed rapid progress into a large snow bowl, which we traversed to the base of a prominent, steep, icy spur, the most obvious feature of our objective. As the slope steepened, we found a line of crevasses forming a bergschrund at 7,150 metres.

'Looks like we're in luck,' shouted Doug, who was in the lead.

The bergschrund narrowed at one end to form a natural ice cave, and soon Doug and Al were filling in the base to make a floor we could sleep on. We carried two aluminium snow-shovels to dig snow caves, a much lighter alternative to a couple of tents.

'This is really good snow to make a cave, I hope it's the same higher up,' Al observed as Georges and I unpacked. We had the two stoves going, melting snow and making instant noodles. 'It's a bit of a gamble, assuming we can dig a cave higher up.'

'It'll be all right, youth.'

'We don't want to bivouac out in the open near the top.' I was not quite convinced but, like bears preparing to hibernate, we settled into our cave within the blue icicled depths of the bergschrund.

To help acclimatisation, we rested all next day. Our only activity was to climb 200 metres of steep and hard *névé* snow to fix the ropes that would speed the following day's ascent. Back at the bivouac we dined frugally on soup mixed with dried potato. None of us liked the new American, freeze-dried hill food, developed ten years earlier for the moon landing, which was beginning to appear on expeditions. The following morning, we climbed to our previous day's high point carrying three days' food. Out of avalanche danger we had a full day of steep ice climbing ahead.

Doug devised our method of ascent; climbing with two, one hundred metre lengths of seven millimetre rope, which were thinner and lighter than usual. A constant dialogue continued on what gear to take. Reducing weight was crucial, but sufficient food, clothing and safety equipment was vital for survival. We shared the lead on these mammoth hundred metre pitches and at every belay left ice screws with strips of orange marker tape to ensure we could locate them on our descent. It also meant that we did not have to carry them up the mountain. After the leader had secured the ropes the rest of the team climbed using Jumar ascenders (a rope-climbing device). Exhausting and tedious as it was, it was still the fastest and most economic way to climb this route. By late afternoon we reached a ledge at 7,620 metres and were relieved to find the snow suitable for digging.

On the summit day, the 19th, we carried little, leaving behind our bivouac gear, sleeping bags, food and stove. Speed was essential. We had to reach the summit and return before dark.

'I think the weather's changing.' Doug looked worried by high clouds as they raced across the tops. A wind was picking up and it had turned noticeably colder. 'If it snows, this slope will avalanche, youth.'

'The snow will hide the markers on the ice screws, which we need for our abseil descent,' I remarked.

'I think the weather will hold. Let's risk it,' Al said.

'As we plan to descend by the same route, we can retreat at any time if conditions deteriorate.' Georges supported Al's view.

It took a couple of hours in the dark and cramped ice cave to get dressed and nibble a handful of muesli and drink a mug of tea but, once outside in the crisp pre-dawn air, we set off in a hurry. A stream of frozen breath, illuminated by our head torches, poured from our mouths as we huffed and puffed. Coughing in fits, the frigid air rasped our throats.

The effort of climbing and gaining height made us hypoxic from the lack of oxygen and our minds started playing tricks. Georges had a recurring fantasy, reciting between gasping breaths, 'We are fleas, we are fleas. Fleas climbing up the scales of prehistoric monster Stegosaurus's back. We are fleas, fleas.'

'Brian what are you doing? Get a move on!' Al shouted.

I was in a world of my own, mesmerised by the massive bulk of Everest hanging as if in touching distance. As the morning wore on my legs felt like jelly and my breathing was laboured, I had burnt myself out by spending too much time in the lead. We reached the col where the first ascent, the Anglo-Nepalese 1961 route arrived from the opposite side of the mountain. With the difficult climbing behind us, we split into two ropes for the short distance up the final summit slope.

Doug was in the lead with Georges as we took the last steps to the summit. The sun shone through a yellow halo and rainbow colours radiated like gigantic soap bubbles. The weather was definitely deteriorating. Mist and cloud raced northwards over the summit into Tibet. It was the end of October and the bitter winter winds were setting in.

Al and I, who were not as well acclimatised, battled to follow. My face was cocooned in the red hood of the down suit and my eyes covered in slightly askew goggles. With their lenses iced up my vision was blurred and out of focus. I clumsily rubbed my frozen beard with a blue mitted hand, breaking the icicles that hung from each nostril. Attempts at conversation were futile.

Georges walked a few paces towards the summit, but stopped just before the top. The whole summit was an overhanging cornice that could collapse at any time. 'We need to get down,' Al gasped in a hoarse whisper. Our tracks were rapidly filling with snow.

'Yes. Down.' My reply was taken by the wind. It was 2.30p.m. with spindrift blowing across the sastrugi snow. I was aware of feeling clumsy and slightly disorientated and, worryingly, I had no feeling in the fingers of one hand, they felt like lumps of wood. The ascent had drained me. I was at my limit and had to get down. With little celebration of our success we started to descend.

The cold orb of an orange sun was setting as the four of us abseiled to the top ice cave after fourteen exhausting hours sustained by only a pint of water and a few energy bars. Frozen to the bone, heads pounding from lack of oxygen and dehydration, we sheltered from the wind and warmed up in our sleeping bags. The small gas tower stove was soon humming for the first of many mugs of tea. Settling for the night we began to smile again, sheltered from the wind and spindrift that battered the slopes outside. Doug poked his head outside. 'It's snowing hard,' he said, worry etched on his face.

In the morning Doug tended the stove again, whilst Al and I were only half-conscious. 'Where's the tea bags?' he asked. The cave was in chaos with four of us squeezed into a space the size of the interior of a small car.

'Georges, that's the worst smell ever,' Al exclaimed in disgust. Squatting over a small hole in the snow, Georges was publicly attending to the most private of human functions. Weather conditions and limited space meant there was no room for normal social distancing.

'Doug, can you have a look at my fingers?' I thrust my right hand in his direction.

'Let me have a look,' said Al, half out of his sleeping bag and leaning away from Georges. 'They look swollen. Could be frostbite. Do they hurt?'

'Yes.' I began to worry until the irrepressible Georges broke the spell, his voice muffled as he was half out of the cave entrance. 'It's a beautiful day!' The overnight snow had not been as serious as we had feared.

Under a cobalt blue sky we whooped and yelled as we abseiled in giant, hundred metre leaps, easily finding the orange tape marking our belay stations. We reached Camp 2 by 3.00p.m. and felt that we could relax, confident that we were safely back down. However, the old adage 'you are not safe until you are all the way down' had never been more true. We lowered our mental guards, thinking the danger was over and we could relax, when energy levels were at their lowest. I'm sure this is the reason why so many mountaineers are killed on the descent. In reality, we were still at 6,400 metres on Everest, and did not foresee the utter terror the following day would bring.

Early next morning we shouldered our heavy packs and made fast time down the Cwm, reaching the top of the Icefall in two hours. Autopilot took over and we descended in a dream until HORROR struck.

Georges and Al stood at the edge of the Khumbu Icefall.

'Can you see the route?' Al asked.

'It's completely gone. Look at those massive ice cliffs. We'll have to go under them, but it's a death trap.' A chaotic scene lay below us, as if a cataclysmic explosion had scattered house-sized ice blocks in every direction, leaving them perched over bottomless, black pits. The bombing of Guernica as an ice sculpture.

We set off under decks of seracs arranged like crazily angled playing cards. If one fell the whole pack would go. Occasional remnants of twisted ladders and frayed ends of fixed ropes protruded, almost apologetically, out of the ice. Nature has its own way and, for some reason, the glacier had become more active, faster flowing, or had changed direction. Perhaps we had angered the mountain deities and this was their retribution? Tibetans call Everest Chomolungma, meaning Goddess Mother of Mountains. Had we annoyed the giant matriarch when we climbed her daughter, Nuptse?

Tentatively, I abseiled into a crevasse with no apparent way out. A deep, blue tomb, it was beautiful but full of menace. What struck me most was the noise: haunting groans, creaks and crashes of ice, whooshes of small avalanches emanating from unknown directions, spraying my bearded face with powder snow. Worse still, the ground moved and shook underfoot.

On one occasion we had to climb back up and over large ice serac cliffs, formed in waves like a frozen rollercoaster. Doug's features were normally a mask of calm, but here he looked visibly worried. Trapped in the guts of the Icefall, by a huge ice pit, we had no way out other than to climb its overhanging, three storey-high walls as they crumbled. Doug set off using our two remaining ice stakes and three ice screws while Georges sat below, holding his rope. With great skill he ascended, but near the top gave a terrified shout. 'This whole face is detached. It's going to collapse!'

Georges squirmed, directly in the firing line; he would surely be crushed beneath hundreds of tons of ice, and Doug would be hurled to the ground like a helpless doll. Al and I, who were ferrying gear, surrendered to the inevitable and moved away. Time stood still. Georges audibly swore that he was going to die. Doug knowing time was short, thrashed and flailed with his ice axe and I am sure he was on the verge of tears as he flopped over the top. He lay still for a long time, his legs sticking out over the drop. Eventually he threw a rope for us to climb and join him. I have never climbed a rope so fast in my life. It was frantic, but this was our Rubicon.

We abandoned most of our possessions, keeping only a rope and a few essential pieces of gear, but didn't care. We had no strength to carry them. Survival was the name of the game and we were fighting for our lives. First Al, then Georges, led down a blind alley. Thwarted, we retraced our steps, crawling on hands and knees through a jumble of ice boulders supported by who knows what. In the next hour they would certainly collapse.

Doug stopped and pointed. 'Look at that enormous crater,' he said, 'it must be a hundred feet deep.' He paused in wonderment. 'It goes right down to the bedrock. I've never seen anything like it.'

We scrambled over more loose blocks, on occasions pulling each other out of crevasses, until we reached the area known as the Eggshell. It presented a gentler slope, but was deceptively dangerous. Our retreat was blocked by a huge crevasse and the only way across was to jump. It was my turn to take the lead. 'Let the rope out fast as I run.' My voice sounded high-pitched and squeaky, as though someone else was talking. It was madness.

I shook the pack off my tired shoulders and walked up and down the 'runway' stamping down the snow with my cramponed boots. At the edge of the crevasse I looked down. The jump looked massive, terrifying, and my only glimmer of hope was that the far side was slightly lower.

'Here goes', I said, more to myself than the other three. Al coughed and tried to say something, but his voice was lost in his parched throat. Doug adjusted his harness and looked the other way, too nervous to watch. Georges sat in the snow, digging in his heels, braced as he held my rope. My life was in the hands of a jovial Frenchman I had only met a couple of weeks back.

I couldn't see their eyes behind their dark glasses. Was their look one of hope or a last farewell? I could no longer put off the inevitable. Someone had to do it. Today, everyone had put their life on the line.

'Georges, give me plenty of slack,' I implored. 'Are you ready?'

'Yes . . . Go,' Georges encouraged.

I ran, ice axe gripped in one hand above my head, stretching for the other side, but . . . horror . . . the edge collapsed and I was falling. Instinctively, I dived forward and swung my axe. It held. There was no feeling of doubt, it was all in the moment and I lay, face pressed into cold snow that seemed strangely refreshing. For what seemed an eternity I was utterly spent.

A committed sadist or a spiteful god must have devised our last obstacle. When we looked down on moving dots of people at Base Camp I wondered, *Are those Doug's children playing?* On a still day, our terrified shouts would have carried to them.

Stretching the full width of the Icefall, we were halted by a huge crevasse, crossed by a single old frayed rope stretched so tight it seemed to be horizontal. When plucked I'm sure it would have played high C. As the lower wall of the crevasse was moving downhill faster than the upper, it had stretched the once eleven millimetre rope to half its original thickness. It would snap soon. Without hesitation and with a wry smile, Georges clipped on his harness, hung under the tightrope and bravely hauled himself hand over hand to the far side. It was a Tyrolean traverse of the utmost strenuosity. Having towed our one remaining rope behind him he used it to pull us across.

On the other side the ground flattened, there were no more crevasses, and we walked across the benign moraine-covered ice to Base Camp. It was difficult to comprehend, but our ordeal was over. Calm and relief welled up in me. An intensely personal moment with the other three as adrenaline from the orgasmic rush of fear subsided. Our team had worked together to get down, and that was how we had stayed sane. Otherwise, our survival that day came down to luck. Doug called it Karma.

I sat with my head in my hands and cried, utterly drained, as people from Base Camp rushed to meet us. Our camp Sherpas, Nima and Ang Pherba, watched wide-eyed as Georges crawled on his knees, holding bits of moraine up in the air with both hands, reciting hoarsely in his mother tongue the full Catholic Hail Mary. Shouting the ending, 'Mother of God, pray for us sinners now and at the hour of our death. Amen'.

A veteran of perhaps fifty Icefall ascents and descents, Doug later reflected, 'I don't think any of us had ever been as scared for so long. For the nine hours it took us to get through the Icefall, we had written ourselves off. We had been through the worst day of our lives.'

Recovering in Base Camp, we discussed our forthcoming attempt on Everest, but after eight intense days on Nuptse we were exhausted. Three of my fingers were black with frostbite and Al had a hacking high-altitude cough. A plume of cloud sped across the summits like smoke from a power station cooling tower. A cold winter wind was blowing from Tibet and the *first* alpine style ascent of Everest would have to wait. I was certainly satisfied and happy with what we had achieved. I could do no more.

Doug's words mirrored my thoughts, '. . . it was a very successful climb. Looking back, perhaps the reason for that was a unity of effort demanded by the situation – four men, out on a climb so far from home, on unknown ground, dwarfed by the highest mountain in the world. No wonder. We had come there more humble than usual, not out to prove anything, not to be the hard man, not to score points and put the other fellow down. It was a better climb for that.'

We packed up Base Camp and went our different ways, and I wore a big grin as I walked down the Khumbu. The experience had been so profound it made life seem joyous, but my happiness was shortlived.

As I walked below the beautiful peak of Ama Dablam, news

filtered out that there had been a terrible accident. It was not only our team that had been climbing alpine style. People from other countries were also risking their lives. Four Kiwis, Peter Hillary, Merv English, Geoff Gabites and Ken Hyslop, who we befriended during a night of chang on the walk-in, back in September, were attempting the first ascent of Ama Dablam's West Face. They had been hit by an avalanche. Hyslop had been killed instantly and the other three were injured and stranded on the face. Reinhold Messner and Oswald Oelz had been climbing on the South Face at the time and responded to the emergency, heroically rescuing the stricken climbers.

Eventually Georges arrived home in Seattle and was devastated to find that Norma had left him. He moved back to France but, much to my regret, we never climbed together again. We kept in touch and I remember his excitement when he described his latest invention, which he christened '*ski-voile*', a technique of ski descending with a small sail or parachute that enabled spectacular jumps over cliffs and seracs. Using this system, he skied down Mont Blanc and, later, Illampu in Bolivia. Today it has become one of the new mountain adventure sports.

In 1980 he was active again in the Himalayas, returning to Broad Peak, then Makalu, where he made the highest ever ski descent from Makalu 2 (7,678 metres). A more significant achievement came in June 1981 when he joined Doug Scott, Greg Child and Rick White on a thirteen-day ascent of extreme difficulty on the massive east pillar of Shivling (6,543 metres) in the Garhwal Himalaya of India.

On one of my many visits to Chamonix he said, 'You must come and see my crystal collection.' I went round to his house and met Martine, his new partner, with whom he had fallen in love after his return from North America. 'This is pink fluorites and the one over there is smoky quartz.' He proudly handed me one of his prizes. They were stunningly beautiful and bigger than I expected.

He was a passionate crystal hunter and, with his cousin Jean-Franck Charlet and friend René Ghilini, explored some of the most inaccessible areas in the Mont Blanc massif. Georges had a growing reputation in this field, having found one of the world's most beautiful pink fluorites. As a young Chamoniard boy, he was intrigued when his father returned from the mountains carrying quartz, and this local tradition became instilled in his bones.

Mountain guides and crystal hunters are inextricably linked to the origins of mountaineering in Chamonix. Two centuries ago, the poorest Alpine farmers would sell crystals to complement the inadequate earnings from their herds. Long before the Golden Age of Alpinism (described as the eleven years between Wills' ascent of the Wetterhorn in 1854 and Whymper's ascent of the Matterhorn in 1865), when *les alpinistes anglais* explored the high peaks and the sport of mountaineering emerged, the French *cristalliers* searched the glaciers and cliffs for gems. In his notebooks, Horace Bénédict de Saussure, the Swiss naturalist, describes the enormous risks taken in search of crystals and it is no coincidence that one of them, Jacques Balmat, in 1786, made the first ascent of Mont Blanc.

The summer of 1983 was hot and dry around Mont Blanc and a combination of rock fall and a paucity of snow revealed hitherto unknown areas of crystals. Georges, Jean-Franck and René instinctively knew where to search. It was hard work climbing, abseiling, chiselling and extracting the amethysts, pink fluorites and tourmalines. Some were monstrously heavy and required specialised lifting tackle to get them back to the valley, and some were valuable enough to finance their expeditions. Rumours abound that explosives had been illegally used, and this may be the explanation for what happened that summer.

On 18th August, Georges and Jean-Franck took two regular clients to the Aiguille Verte to explore a quartz vein near the Contamine spur; a classic climb that is usually relatively safe. In the early evening, their descent took them just short of the glacier below a teetering pillar of granite. Without warning a flake detached and a monstrous rock avalanche engulfed all four men. Jean-Franck survived, but Georges and the two clients died instantly. He was thirty-two.

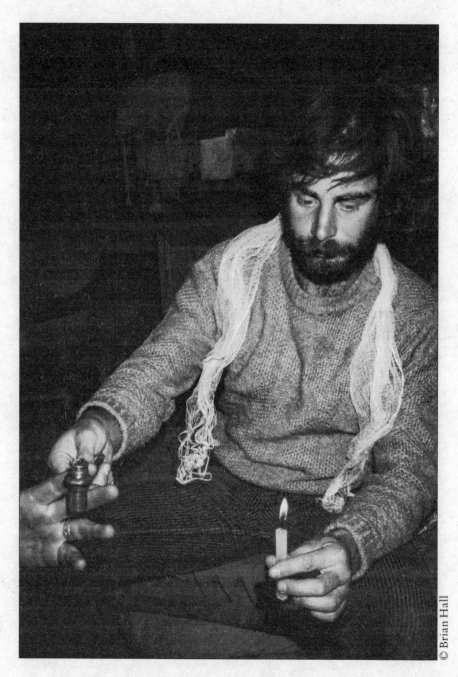

Pete Thexton at a Bhuddist monastery on the
way to Everest, winter 1980.

10

A FRIEND ON EVEREST
Pete Thexton

'How would you describe Pete Thexton?'

'Drop dead gorgeous!' Louise replied, biting her lip. I could see my question had stirred emotions and her reply had seemed flippant.

I was with Pete when I first met Louise, who came with her friend, Gwyneth, to our 'Everest Return Home Party' in 1981. Being the only unattached members of the expedition, we joined the girls to laugh and dance the night away. I was instantly attracted by Louise's feisty attitude, long blonde hair and good looks, but she was already in Pete's arms while Gwyneth only had eyes for me. The festivities ended with allegiances swapping, and I had found my lifetime partner, Louise.

Pete and I met in the mid-'70s, when he travelled from London to North Wales to climb on the sea cliffs at Anglesey and ended the day raving about it over a pint. After that, I occasionally bumped into him on the crags or in climbers' bars. A good looking guy, he was lean, powerful, shorter than average. Deep set, smouldering eyes and high cheeks were framed by a beard and bushy eyebrows, and a head of black hair that fell just short of his shoulders.

'Brian, you should come down to climb on Lundy. It's brilliant rock and there's loads of new routes to do. I'm going in two weeks' time.'

'Sounds great.'

'I'm meant to be at lectures, but I'd much prefer to climb.'

'What are you studying?'

'I'm trying to become a doctor.'

'I should have guessed from the amount you drink!'

Pete's love of sea-cliff climbing came from his strong attachment to this small island in the Bristol Channel and many family holidays when he was younger. He was born in 1953 and brought up in a close London family. His father, Clive, was a Methodist minister. His mother, Robina, a doctor. Mike was his younger brother, and Vicki and Penny were his sisters. He was educated at Kingswood School in Bath, a traditional boarding school founded in 1748 by John Wesley.

Unfortunately, our climbing visit to Lundy never worked out, but I learnt later that he had opened many new climbs, including *Wolfman Jack (E3)* and *Immaculate Slab (HVS)*. Relaxing in his company was easy; he always seemed cheerful and mellow with a lightly sarcastic sense of humour. Regardless of his religious school upbringing, he would typically arrive at the pub with an attractive nurse on his arm, and no trace of Methodist piety.

In the Alps, his battered Morris 1000 Traveller, an estate car with a mock Tudor wooden back, was a familiar sight on Chamonix's Snell's Field campsite. He climbed with a small group of friends, succeeding on challenging routes such as the Walker Spur, on the Grandes Jorasses, and the Dru Couloir. When the weather deteriorated, he would flee the valley to the sun-soaked sea cliffs of the Calanques near Marseille with his car full of compatriots.

In the late '70s he frequently worked long hospital hours in Nottingham, Mansfield and Sheffield but, after qualifying in 1978, I would see him more often in the local climbers' pubs. Knowing that I had been to the Himalaya he enquired in his courteous manner: 'Brian, what are the peak fees in Nepal?' and 'Do you have to give the Liaison Officer mountain clothing?' and 'Can you buy gas for mountain stoves in Delhi?'

I answered the best I could, but was far from an expert.

'My family view me as a maverick,' he said. 'They think I am more interested in climbing than being a doctor.'

'Aren't you?'

'I suppose I am, but I feel a responsibility to use my qualification.'

'My dad tries to make me feel guilty for not using my education,' I said, 'but we don't see eye to eye on much so I try not to worry.'

I got the impression that Pete had a happier relationship with his family, with a generous father and a caring mother. I was out of the country for much of '79 and '80, climbing in Pakistan, Peru and Nepal, so it was not until much later that I heard about his three expeditions, two to India and one to Pakistan.

Meanwhile in Nepal on the multi-peak expedition in 1979, Doug Scott, Al Rouse, Georges Bettembourg and I had permission to climb Everest. However, following our success on Nuptse we were physically and mentally exhausted, and we were forced to abandon the idea. Another chance soon was unlikely as the Nepalese had issued permits to other expeditions. Unexpectedly though, they opened a new booking window, inviting applications for the winter season between 1st December and 31st January. The Poles got the first permit for 1979–80.

In early January 1980, the team of twenty Polish climbers led by Andrzej Zawada arrived at Base Camp. Fighting hurricane-force winds, they set up Camp 4 on the South Col from where, in unbelievably harsh conditions, Leszek Cichy and Krzysztof Wielicki reached the summit on 17th February (after getting an extension to their permit). This success led the Polish climbers to a decade of winter mountaineering in the Himalaya in which they perfected the 'art of suffering',[1] succeeding on the first winter ascents of ten 8,000 metre peaks.

The Poles triumphed because they gathered a team of hardy countrymen familiar with winter climbing in their own mountains. This tight knit group had no need for Sherpas who, at that time, had neither the clothing nor experience to operate in winter. Their group comprised of journeymen climbers who worked tirelessly carrying loads, fixing ropes and establishing camps from which their elite compatriots would reach the summit. They had used supplementary oxygen and concluded it was essential for their success. In preparation for their ascent of Everest they had made several winter reconnaissance expeditions to lower peaks in the Greater Ranges.

Unbeknown to me, Al Rouse applied for the following winter

1. The Art of Suffering , Voytek Kurtyka, *Mountain* Magazine #121 1988

season of 1980–81, but a Japanese team had already negotiated the sole permit for the standard South Col route. Surprisingly, the Nepalese offered Al a permit to climb the much harder West Ridge on a 'take it or leave it' basis. Ambition overwhelmed the practicalities, and he accepted the booking to become *de facto* leader, casually announcing in the pub: 'Brian, we've got permission to climb Everest next winter.'

'Great!' I replied, at the same time wondering what I was letting myself in for.

He raised his glass with a wry smile and a sly sideways glance. 'By the West Ridge, the Yugoslav route via the Lho La, then across to the Hornbein couloir which the Americans climbed.'

This took a moment to sink in. 'Is that possible? It's a really long and difficult route and only been done once.'

'Anything is possible in mountaineering.' He ordered more beer. We drank it. The deal was sealed. My life would have been a lot simpler and safer if I had dared to say no.

Mount Everest – Sagarmāthā – Chomolungma, *Goddess of the Sky – Head in the Great Blue Sky – Holy Mother Peak,* is the highest mountain in the world, measuring 8,848.86 metres, or 29,031.7 feet. Despite the earthquake of 2015, current commercialisation and overcrowding, Everest has a worldwide spiritual and symbolic significance to this day, and in 1953 its summit was untouched.

That year, a British expedition climbing from the Nepalese side reached the summit via the Western Cwm and the South Col, and Tenzing Norgay, a Sherpa, with Edmund Hillary, a New Zealander, were first to stand on the top of the world. Success was a triumph of human endeavour and adventurous spirit akin to reaching the South Pole or the moon. In 1960, a Chinese team succeeded on the North Ridge from Tibet, the route on which Mallory and Irvine vanished in 1924. Most climbers who attempt Everest follow these two routes using fixed ropes, established camps, Sherpa support, and supplementary oxygen.

The more adventurous expeditions, not satisfied with repetition, explored Everest's unclimbed lines. The first with a difference was in 1963, when Jim Whittaker became the first American to climb Everest via the South Col. Three weeks later, fellow Americans from the same expedition, Tom Hornbein and Willi Unsoeld, took an unknown route up the West Ridge, crossing to the North-West Face to ascend a steep and narrow gash now known as the Hornbein Couloir. Reaching the summit in the evening, they made the first traverse of the mountain by descending in the tracks of two other climbers from their team who had just repeated the South Col route.

In 1975 Chris Bonington led the British expedition which climbed the South West Face, making the first ascent by British nationals when Doug Scott, Dougal Haston and Pete Boardman, along with Nepalese Pertemba Sherpa, succeeded on the most difficult route ever climbed at that altitude.

The flood gates opened over the next two decades, with expeditions climbing a whole series of impressive new routes. In 1978, Italian Reinhold Messner and Austrian Peter Habeler became the first to summit without the help of supplemental oxygen. However, this was within the confines of a traditional expedition in which other members did. A Yugoslavian team, in 1979, climbed the vertical rock of the Lho La directly above Base Camp, ascending the long West Ridge direct, to create the most technically challenging route on the mountain. That same year, Messner returned and summited solo, without supplemental oxygen, Sherpas or climbing partners, a spartan ascent by a new route on the northwest side which astounded the mountaineering world and confirmed his position as the best mountaineer of his generation.

The challenge to find new and difficult lines of ascent continued, but when we left for Everest in November 1980 most attempts were still by huge national expeditions repeating the South Col route. Our plan was different, we would begin on the Yugoslav '79 route and finish by following the Hornbein Couloir which the Americans had climbed in '63.

Move forward to 2021 and the summit of Everest has been reached approximately ten thousand times by six thousand individuals (many Sherpas and guides have climbed it numerous times). Of these, only fifteen have been in the winter season, the last being in 1993. Maybe 'the art of suffering' has gone out of fashion? (See Appendix 1 Winter Seasons in Mountaineering.)

We decided on a close-knit team of eight, thinking that two groups of four could alternate between operating on the mountain and rest. This arrangement would give a lightweight feel without adopting the methods of a full-scale, heavyweight expedition. Due to the winter conditions, we compromised around tactics, persuading ourselves that camps and fixed ropes were essential for safety, although we had previously scorned them on our trips to Jannu and Nuptse. Our budget was too small to employ Sherpas to carry supplies and bottles of oxygen, but was Everest possible in winter without oxygen? We would find out.

Despite all this, everyone we invited said yes. The Twins, Alan and Adrian Burgess, had no hesitation. My Leeds mate and regular rock-climbing partner, John Porter, also confirmed, provided he could get three months off work. Paul Nunn, a stalwart of the British expedition scene and one of our drinking partners in Sheffield, immediately said yes. He was older than the rest of the team and, crucially, had a house in which we could store and pack all the gear. Paul was the only one who was married, and goodness knows what his wife Hilary thought as their home was filled with towers of boxes and eight boisterous climbers. We invited Joe Tasker, because of his peerless stature as a mountaineer. I was the sole expedition member to have climbed with Joe, who usually operated within a discrete circle of friends.

Relaxing over a beer, Al Rouse, Paul Nunn and I debated who could fill the final place.

'Why not ask Pete Thexton?' Paul looked at me.

'He's a doctor as well as a strong climber,' Al added.

'I haven't seen him for ages.'

'He's been on an expedition to Thalay Sagar. He went on two trips last year. First to the Tos Glacier in the Indian Kulu with three mates. They climbed ten peaks between 5,500 and 6,500 metres, including three, first ascents,' Paul said. 'He came straight from there to meet me in Pakistan for our trip to Latok 2.'

A silence cloaked the corner of the bar as we remembered the outcome of that trip. Pat Fearnehough became ill on the approach, and Pete stayed behind to care for him. When Pete caught up with the others he gave them grave news. As he and Fearnehough were negotiating the tortuous trail in the Braldu Gorge, a mud sidewall had collapsed, sweeping Fearnehough into the river to his death.

'Pete had only just met Pat and was determined to carry on,' Paul continued. 'Like most good climbers, Pete is driven.'

The reduced team spent two months on the unclimbed West Ridge of Latok 2 in hazardous conditions, but failed to summit.

On Paul's recommendation we invited Pete.

At that time, we were the smallest team ever to attempt Everest, and had the additional handicaps of winter and a miserly budget of fifteen thousand pounds. Joe knew a film production company called Chameleon who put together a crew of three in hope of making a documentary. With the prospect of film publicity, we gained sponsorship from Bass Brewery and New Era, a homeopathic pill manufacturer. We could drown our sorrows and clear our hangovers afterwards! Grants from British mountaineering institutions and a mass of donated equipment and food enabled us to reduce our personal contributions to a barely affordable five hundred pounds.

A jumble of glacier ice and moraine formed the site for our Base Camp, which we would share with both a Japanese expedition climbing Everest by the regular South Col route and an Italian group attempting the first winter ascent of Lhotse, Everest's neighbour and the fourth highest peak in the world. Our arrival on 6th December was shambolic.

'Watch that, yak.' Al shouted. These normally placid beasts had been carrying our loads for the last part of the trek. As their teenage Sherpani handlers were unloading, the animals went berserk.

Pete and two Sherpanis ran after a wayward yak, with its precious load half off its back. Another charged the Japanese camp, destroying a tent with its fearsome horns. The Burgess twins stared in amazement, not knowing whether to laugh or cry.

The Japanese had used eight hundred porters to transport all their supplies, so there was no one available to carry our hundred and fifty loads. Instead, we used a rotating cast of locals although, since they did not want to travel far from their homes, we were constantly paying them off and rehiring. Eventually, we used yaks, but consequently missed days of beautiful weather.

In the first few days, between constructing Base Camp and organising gear, we lay around on our sleeping mats in the sun, resting and acclimatising. 'Your trip to Nuptse sounded amazing,' Pete said.

'The route was incredible, but we had a hard time descending the Khumbu Icefall.' Pete sat speechless as I described our epic. 'What of your adventures in India, that summer of '79?'

'I went with three Americans to try Thalay Sagar in the Gangotri, unclimbed and nearly 7,000 metres.' He had received a phone call out of the blue from Roy Kligfield in the US, whom he had enjoyed climbing with a few years before. 'It was all very last minute which was a problem as I had to resign from the medical practice I worked at.'

'I've never heard of the peak.'

'A fairy tale mountain; steep golden granite with a cap of snow.'

He met the three Americans, Kligfield, John Thackray and Jon Waterman, at Heathrow airport in transit on their way to India. Arriving in June, they set off up the North-West Couloir to join the West Ridge. Near the top, Waterman developed altitude sickness and waited at their last bivouac.

'The three of us continued on ice and rock to a band of crumbly black rock. It looked bloody awful and we questioned whether to continue. I could see the others were wavering so I said: come on it can't be as bad as it looks. Let's get on with it.'

'Was it as bad?'

'Three hundred metres of vertical shale!'

With incredible modesty he described how they reached the virgin summit late on the eighth day, forging a route of great difficulty on a peak that has provided some of the most challenging climbs in the Himalayas in recent years.

Our limited budget and inexperience resulted in a base camp more suited to the warmer pre- or post-monsoon seasons, with our small personal tents grouped around a communal kitchen-dining structure of drystone walls with a tarpaulin roof. The roof almost disappeared into Tibet with the first strong wind and, when the snow came, it collapsed. Modifications involved all manner of ropes and poles to keep it in place, and when the wind whistled through the gaps the flapping canvas drowned all conversation. For the two months that we occupied Base Camp, the daytime temperature did not rise above freezing and was below −10°C at night. Himalayan winter climbing was in its infancy, but we were learning all the time . . . from our mistakes.

In the evening, with no heating and poor lighting from paraffin wick lanterns, we sat on stones or broken camping chairs on the ice and moraine floor, keeping warm in our one-piece downclimbing suits. It was not a place to relax and enjoy a convivial conversation so, as soon as we finished dinner, everyone disappeared to their own tent, to the warmth of their sleeping bags for a twelve-hour stint of reading, headphone music and fitful sleep.

Understandably, our Nepalese staff were not happy. Wan Chup, our cook, and Mingma, his assistant, slept on the kitchen floor. We gave them a tent, but they preferred to sleep next to the warm stoves. Requiring constant attention, the stoves roared twenty-four-hours a day, to melt glacier ice, our only supply of water. We arrived with six high quality Swedish stoves, but soon they were wrecked, by constant use, frozen paraffin wax, and Mingma's well-meaning repairs, so the mail runner was dispatched to Namche Bazaar to buy locally made replacements. These proved to be unreliable and frequently would not light. On one occasion Mingma was seen running from the kitchen, juggling a fireball in his hands. During our stay, we destroyed twenty-two stoves.

Having arrived first, the Japanese had picked the best camping site for their extensive base, centred around a vast, bright orange marquee. Naomi Uemura, their leader, invited us around one evening.

We walked into a different world, entering through an airlock, I imagined similar to going into a space station, that ensured minimal heat loss. Inside was a long table neatly set for twenty people. To the side was a line of discreet curtains, behind which were individual sleeping quarters. We were asked politely to take off our boots before walking on the wooden floor, and were graciously introduced to the Japanese expedition members, several journalists and a television executive. At the centre, a wood-burning stove pumped out so much heat that our Japanese friends could lounge around in tee-shirts. A slight hum came from a bank of Honda generators supplying electricity to light the place, power a cassette player with substantial speakers and run a prototype fax machine in direct contact with Kathmandu, receiving weather forecasts and relaying news back to Japan.

They served us warm sake and food that would have graced an expensive Japanese restaurant. Unused to sake, light-headed, we stumbled back to our deep freezer. From then on, we hardly saw our Liaison Officer, Ram Singh, who had frequent 'meetings' with his Japanese counterpart.

During the early part of December the weather was perfect, and the camp buzzed with optimism for the task ahead. Half the team would climb for a few days then, exhausted by the effort, recover at Base while the other half went onto the mountain. Unfortunately, during the walk-in, most of our team contracted dysentery, which persisted, especially for Paul, Al, Pete and me. This reduced us to load-carrying during the first part of the climb.

I enjoyed Pete's relaxed and quiet company, talking about past experiences and mutual friends. He had the air of a proper English gentleman and, if he had not chosen the medical profession, would have made a good diplomat. We were the most reserved characters on the trip, neither leaders nor followers but quietly going about our own business, rarely shouting or arguing.

'I read in *Mountain* magazine that you had a bit of an epic on Elliot's Downfall in Glencoe,' I said.

'Last March. I was in Scotland but had nobody to climb with until I met a friend of yours, John Given, in the bar. We had a whisky together.'

Next day, Given belayed Pete in dripping cold meltwater as he made steady progress on vertical ice. As he neared the top, there was a huge bang and Given dived for cover. The pillar had detached, shattering into a thousand shards. 'It was bloody desperate, but at the same time comical. I was left hanging on my ice tools just above the fracture line.'

'How high up were you?'

'About fifteen metres. I soloed to the top expecting the remaining ice to collapse at any moment.' Pete smiled and added, 'We were lucky. It could have killed us both!'

Our first objective was to reach the Lho La Col, a short distance to the north, which was guarded by a seven hundred-metre wall frowning above Base Camp. This vertical granite rampart had been climbed by the Yugoslavs the year before and promised to be the most technically difficult part of the ascent. It took us ten days of hard labour to fix a line of ropes to the col, a kilometre wide saddle of snow on the border between Nepal and Tibet. On the Tibetan side, we dug a sizeable four-person snow cave, Camp 1, to provide the springboard for the icy slopes of the West Ridge which stretched 3,000 metres to the summit.

Shortly before Christmas, a steep rock band, part way up the West Ridge, halted our progress. Before Everest I had never climbed with Pete, but we were comfortable in each other's company and well matched in speed. I never had to tell him what to do and he never gave me directions. When recovered from illness, we felt strong enough to take our turn at the front. Our task was to push the climb higher and break through the rock band and was the opportunity Pete and I had been waiting for. To discover if we could cope with the challenging conditions. We left our frosty burrow at first light.

'We must be getting acclimatised,' he said, moving quickly across the Lho La.

'I didn't realise it was going to feel so cold,' I replied. 'My thermometer reads −33°C.'

'Surprise, surprise. It's mid-winter, the coldest time of the year.' Pete smiled. 'Oh, and by the way, we are at 6,500 metres on Everest!'

By late morning we were climbing new ground. I was in the lead while Pete belayed my rope below. To keep warm we wore thick layers of down clothing enveloping our bodies with enormous hoods pulled tightly around our faces. Goggles and a mask protected any bare skin, which otherwise would be frostbitten within minutes. Over a thousand metres lower, I could make out the tiny coloured tents of Base Camp, far removed from life's everyday conveniences and comforts. There, the rest of our team watched this crucial episode of the climb through an enormous camera lens belonging to the film crew.

Higher, on the rock band, Pete took the lead. 'Brian, watch the rope.' He was having problems, forced leftwards as one icy groove after another resisted his attempts.

'Come on Pete, it's freezing down here,' I shouted, thinking to myself that we could have run a marathon in the time it took to climb two hundred metres.

Stamping my feet, I stared idly at the leaden sky while a curtain of grey clouds dropped over the surrounding peaks of Pumori and Gyachung Kang. To my right, the Rongbuk glacier stretched to the barren, bisque-coloured hills of Tibet.

'Climb when ready!' Pete's shout broke my reverie. He had finally reached a ledge and attached himself to pitons hammered into the granite. I followed, eager to move, the action bringing warmth to my frozen toes. 'These winter days are too short. It's already getting dark,' he said.

'One more pitch might get us through the rock band.' It was my turn to lead, and I set off at a canter, crabbing sideways on steel hard ice, but my impatience in the rarefied atmosphere resulted in a spell of breathless coughing. But I was happy. At last, I was doing some 'real' climbing, not working as a porter. I started up an ice gully from where a narrow ledge ran leftwards to a corner, cutting through the overhang. The steeper terrain would have been trivial at sea level, but here it made me hang on my rapidly tiring arms. A few minutes before, I had been climbing confidently. Now, I was terrified at the prospect of falling, but . . . I could not fall. I must not fall. We trusted each other not to fall. 'I'll try and get a peg in,' I shouted.

Thankfully, I found a resting place from which I could look down on Pete, seemingly bored, fidgeting and stamping his feet impatiently. For him, I knew the time would be passing slowly, but the climbing engrossed me completely. I cleared the snow, discovering plenty of holds to pull myself through the overhang. A heave upwards and a swing leftwards landed me on the easy snow slope above.

We had a sense of fulfilment and achievement but, now the difficulties were over, time DID matter. Night was upon us bringing low cloud and windblown snow that, like a lace curtain, obscured the view down to the Lho La and our snow cave haven. Speed was paramount, and abseil followed abseil until we reached the barren expanse of the Lho La. It was now dark, and a storm was brewing. We lost our bearings crossing the featureless ground, following the sweep of our anaemic head torches, like peering through the windscreen on a night drive in the reflected mesmeric wash of horizontal blown snow. Benighted in a winter storm on Everest had never been part of our plan.

'Footprints!' Pete shouted. We had found the gentle rise to the snow cave and soon were inside, sheltered from the howling wind. 'That was too close for comfort,' he explained, already half inside his double sleeping bag.

'My water bottle has frozen solid. I haven't had a drink for six hours,' I said, and I've got a splitting headache. It's probably dehydration.' Pete searched in his medical kit for a packet of pills while I tended the stove, melting snow. Liquids were crucial to our recovery, but it was an hour before a cup of tea slaked our thirst. 'What does your thermometer read?'

'You don't want to know.' An impish smile filled his face. 'Minus eighteen, the temperature of a mortuary deep freezer.'

Amused by the absurdity of the conditions, Pete christened our snow cave Stalingrad. Just as I was about to doze off, there was a loud HUMPH!, like a mortar bomb, that caused my ears to pop.

'What the hell's that!' Pete shouted. HUMPH – HUMPH! 'Perhaps we ARE in Stalingrad.' Pete enjoyed keeping things light during tense situations. He got up and shuffled to the tunnel entrance, moving the rucksacks that protected the hole. 'It's horrendous,' he said. 'It's like sticking your head out of the window of an express train.' HUMPH! A wind gust hit the entrance, and he recoiled, hair and beard covered in snow.

In the morning, a strange blue-grey umbra filled the cave. 'You look terrible,' I said. His puffed-up haggard face, slit eyes, and cold-sore bleeding lips had aged him twenty years.

'I can't say you're an Adonis either!' he croaked. From outside we could hear the muffled whistle of the tempest. We were at the mercy of the first big winter storm of the expedition. 'We can't climb in these conditions, Brian. We need to get back to recover at Base Camp.'

'I agree, we could be stranded for days; anyway, it's Christmas in two days'.'

'And we can't miss Christmas dinner, can we?'

We relied on radio communication, but there was no reception within the snow cave. At rendezvous times, one of us braved the elements in the entrance.

'Camp 1 to Base do you receive? Over.' Pete held the walkie-talkie close to his ear.

'Receiving you, strength five. What's the weather like? Over.' Joe Tasker replied.

'Gorgeous – hot and sunny – over.'

'Seriously?'

'No, there are high winds and snow. We can't do anything here. We're coming down – over.'

'Lots of snow here. Watch out for avalanches – over.'

'Understood. Get the turkey in the oven – out.'

The banter was premature.

Outside, I had difficulty standing in the wind. A fixed rope ran two hundred metres to where the descent proper began, a distance we would usually cover in ten minutes. I clipped onto the line with my *Jumar* rope ascender to pull myself across the slope. Facing into the maelstrom, I could not breathe, so I tried making progress backwards, but lost my footing when the vortex lifted me and blew me over. Dropping to my knees, head low, almost touching the snow, I crawled along the slope, constantly being lifted like a kite. The force of the wind was such that I had never felt before. It was like being battered from side to side by an invisible martial arts opponent. The taut rope sang under tension.

Progress was best achieved with bursts of energy, then a stop. I rushed for three metres before collapsing, panting, face buried within my arms, in a ball, like a hedgehog. The force of the wind reached heightened intensity. Facing away from it, I had difficulty breathing as a vacuum formed in the lee, sucking air from my mouth. Unable to breathe, I panted furiously to overcome this unexpected suffocation. The frigid air in my lungs was like a knife stabbing my chest, and I could not see because my goggles, like my face, were plastered with ice. Panic started to take hold as I reasoned that it was not too late to turn back. Looking behind, I lifted my goggles to squint at the ghostly outline of Pete crouched, like me, fighting the hurricane.

'Go back!' I yelled but the wind took my cries. It seemed a silly place to die, just a few rope lengths from the safety of the cave.

At that point, the rope crossed a two-metre wide crevasse. Usually a feature to avoid, it appeared as my saviour. Still attached to the rope, I launched myself into its depths, plummeting three metres into an eerie calm and, with that, the anxiety disappeared. Hanging on the rope in my crevasse refuge, an embryo on an umbilical cord, I had time to recover and consider my fate. Whether to return to the ice cave or battle on for the rocks.

For what seemed like an eternity, I expected Pete to bundle in beside me, but he did not arrive and I thought he must have retreated to the cave. As the exposed section was nearly at an end I decided to forge ahead, and tentatively poked my head out of the crevasse. The blast hit me with such force I could neither see nor breathe. Ducking down, I took a gulp of air before dashing for the rocks, pulling frantically on the fixed rope with my body at forty-five degrees. I do not remember that final stretch, only the sense of relief as I collapsed in the shelter of the rocks. When Pete arrived, we stared at each other, wide-eyed through ice-glazed goggles, too exhausted to speak.

I had found a new respect for Pete, a high risk-taker disguised as an English family doctor. Together, we had found out how weak and fearful we were against the elements, a test you can only take by exposing yourself to their danger.

Further down we were sheltered from the wind, but the route was now covered, disguised, by a thick white blanket, and what had been easy ground was a nightmare of uncertainty. The fixed ropes, sometimes buried deep in snow, were swollen three times in thickness with ice. All day long we fought our way down, frozen to the core with little food and nothing to drink. Sloughs of snow threatened to turn into avalanches as we slipped and slid, finally stumbling into Base Camp just in time for Christmas.

Pete and I were happy to be among friends again but existence in our Camp was arduous. John oversaw the food, with all manner of problems disturbing his carefully prepared menus. Wan Chup made excellent Nepalese fare, but his talents did not stretch to European cuisine. Our pressure cookers were too small, so we mainly cooked in large open pans. Due to the lower pressure at altitude, the temperature of boiling water was well below a hundred degrees, and foods such as rice or pasta arrived either uncooked or boiled to mush. Even after our meal was prepared, the freezing temperature instantly congealed the food on our plates. Most evenings, Wan Chup cooked his dreaded 'noodly stew', a gruel of mushy vegetables, lentils, Chinese noodles and tins of dubious Nepalese fish or meat.

Worse, we hadn't eradicated the curse of dysentery, probably due to the intestinal parasite Giardia, and I was sorry for Pete who had to put on his doctor's coat to treat the infirm, even though he often needed care himself. 'We need to take action against the bug circulating camp,' he announced one evening. 'Two decades of expeditions have polluted this area, and our weekly delivery of fresh vegetables, I suspect, are fertilised by human waste.'

'There is no way we are going to climb Everest if half the team can't get out of bed at Base Camp,' Al said.

'What do you suggest?'

'Wash our hands, especially after going to the toilet. Clean our mugs, bowls and cutlery, ourselves. I've got pills for anyone who needs them, and we'll treat all the water with iodine because I suspect the low boiling temperature is not killing the bugs.'

'There is another problem,' John added. 'Altitude is destroying our appetites. I prepared food based on eating 4,500 calories a day, but we are eating less than 2,500.'

'On the mountain we use 1,000 calories every hour. I know most of us hate the freeze-dried hill food, but we are wasting away and losing strength,' Pete said.

Another ailment was afflicting the team. At altitude, a simple cough can be a constant irritant. As breathing increases during exertion, the cold, dry air causes a persistent hack, which becomes painful and disturbs sleep. Acute Mountain Sickness (AMS) correctly makes the headlines as the most serious illness at altitude, but our slow rate of ascent ensured that we were all acclimatised. Our reaction to the altitude was limited to headaches, mild sickness and appetite loss rather than more severe forms of AMS. Even so, Base Camp became more like a field hospital than a springboard for an ascent of the highest peak in the world.

One of my roles was organising all the technical equipment and clothing. The most popular items, by far, were the innovative Mountain Equipment down suits which kept us warm in the coldest temperatures. Our hands and feet avoided frostbite by using multi-layered glove systems, plastic boots with foam inners and thick neoprene gaiters. The biggest problem was protecting our faces, for which we had several alternatives. My favourite was a mask used by Canadian runners in winter, and modelled on the single cup of a lady's bra.

As we approached New Year, there were rarely two consecutive days of good weather with which to gain momentum, and a general malaise replaced our initial optimism. Most days, I partnered Pete on the mountain, coming to know him well, enjoying his companionship and humble confidence. Although a small man, and despite illness, his appetite was gargantuan. He became known as the 'Midnight Cowboy' as he lazed around camp in the morning, then set off long after everyone else, and arrived at the high camp as darkness fell.

On 2nd January, we established Camp 2, a thousand metres above the Lho La, where the slopes consisted of hard ice with no prospect of digging a snow cave. We carved out two small tent platforms, but they were exposed to the full brunt of the wind and provided no comfort and little chance of sleep, in the morning, we were exhausted and needed a day's rest. The camp was a staging post to a future and hopefully more agreeable Camp 3 above.

It was again Pete's and my turn to load-carry in support of the lead climbers, and for ten days, we plugged away at consolidating the supplies and the route to Camp 2. Stalingrad was a godsend as we could get ready and have breakfast in its shelter but, once outside, our breath billowed in frozen clouds, and our beards froze with rime ice as we readied for the forty-rope-length climb to Camp 2.

Kick, step, push the ascender up the rope,
Think: a hot cup of tea – a whisky toddy
Pant – stop – rest.
Dream: a warm bed – with a woman in my arms.
Pant – stop – rest.
Repeat a thousand times.
Concentrate on every rope change.
Any mistake could be your last.

I vowed never to go on another expedition that required fixing ropes and supplying camps – so much monotonous, mind-numbing work – so different to the freedom of single push, alpine style mountaineering. *How do Sherpas cope?* I wondered. *I guess they have no choice, what they earn helps their family survive.*

After a long day's effort, Aid, John, Pete and I were ensconced in Camp 2. Pete and I sheltered in a canvas box tent designed by Don Whillans for the high winds of Patagonia. A wretched place, it resembled a coffin, cramped, with no room to cook, and sleep was nigh on impossible as it rattled like a basket of empty tin cans. Condensation on the interior formed hoar frost, which shook off in showers of ice flakes, and we lay wide-eyed in anticipation of its collapse.

On the ledge above, Aid and John huddled in the supposed haven of a 'state-of-the-art' hooped mountain tent. The constant wind snapped the poles, so it was lashed to the slope with all manner of ropes and bungee cords. Torn fabric flapped like a ship's flag in a storm. It looked like it had been sat on by an elephant.

The grey light of dawn heralded relief from the awful night. Pete cradled the stove trying to melt snow until, eventually, he handed me a precious plastic bowl of tea. Suddenly the door ripped open, and the pounding gale inflated the tent like a balloon. All the guy ropes sang and twanged as it tried to take off. (Pete later said, 'That was our best chance of reaching the summit!') In dived John, coated with white frost. 'Help – HELP – our tent's collapsed.'

Unbeknown to Pete and me, the howl of the storm had camouflaged a battle for survival next door. Aid and John had sat up all night, fully clothed, holding the broken tent poles until, at dawn, the hurricane ripped it away. John's mitts went with it, and he fought to fit his crampons with bare hands on the icy slope. In desperation, he dived into our box tent. Half in, he plunged his frozen hands into my bowl, spilling most of the tea. It saved him from frostbite, though he almost fainted with pain from the ensuing 'hot aches'. I gave him my spare mitts and we left the wreckage of Camp 2. It was a tired and bedraggled group that returned to Base that evening.

The storm which destroyed our camp also wreaked havoc with the other expeditions. One of the Japanese climbers had been blown off their fixed ropes and fallen to his death. Several Sherpas were severely frostbitten in the ensuing rescue, one to die later in hospital.

Al Rouse wrote to his girlfriend Hilary, 'The cold is intense and even at Base Camp we often experience −30°C. Everybody is very thin and the cold seems to permeate our bones. Conditions on the mountain are the worst any of us have ever encountered. I think we will be lucky to make the top. On the mountain you cannot spend more than twenty seconds even in thin gloves, after that frostbite starts. It's all because of the constant wind.'

It was always part of the plan to mix who we partnered with, so Pete and Joe started climbing together and, in the next spell of better weather, made a breakthrough by pushing the route to the top of the West Shoulder. Fortuitously, they found a crevasse which they fashioned into an ice cave, finally establishing Camp 3. This cave would provide a platform to stage an attempt on the summit pyramid and greatly improved the morale of the team. It gave shelter from the wind, and was a significant improvement to the Camp 2 tents but, during that first night, the pair found it was an inhospitable place. Cold and draughty with fine spindrift constantly in the air.

'If only we could get a few days of stable weather,' Pete mused.

'Let's hope we can get along the ridge tomorrow and find a site for Camp 4.' Joe replied.

A radio call the following day destroyed their plans. 'Base Camp to Camp 3 – over.' Paul shouted into the radio.

'Receiving – over.'

'We have a medical emergency at Base – over.'

'What's the problem – over.'

'Wan Chup is seriously ill. Stomach pain, vomiting, delirium and excreting blood – over.'

'Understood. I will come down – out.'

Pete usually guarded his innermost feelings, but had already talked about the conflict between doctoring and climbing. Now it was reality – and not just for him. The whole expedition had to change its focus to help Wan Chup. Pete left Camp 3 and descended all day to Base Camp where he diagnosed a perforated ulcer. Luckily, he had two vials of the drug required for treatment. Unluckily, his assistant was the enthusiastic but accident-prone Alan Burgess, who dropped and smashed the first life-saving vial. Fortunately, the second one stabilised our cook's condition, and we made plans to evacuate him.

Pete's supreme effort exacerbated his own uncontrollable cough, and with the constant explosive hacking, he cracked his ribs. From then on, he was severely debilitated yet continued climbing in persistent pain.

With no formal leadership, our plans occasionally became chaotic. An example was when John and Al Rouse set out on a load-carry to Camp 3 and sickness forced Al to abandon his ascent. John continued, anticipating that reinforcements would arrive the next day, but a storm arrived and he had to survive alone for four long days. On the fifth night, he became aware of a faint noise, a shout from the darkness outside. Crawling out into the blizzard, he saw, fifty metres away, the dim light of a head torch. The Midnight Cowboy had arrived. After battling through high winds all day, Pete had become lost and benighted and was in a bad way, holding his cracked ribs, grimacing every time he coughed. John soon had the stove on and made him a brew and a freeze-dried meal.

'Could you make me another one,' Pete croaked. After he finished, he regained his customary, easy-going humour. 'You look terrible,' he said to John the following morning. 'Let me have a listen to your chest.' John coughed and wheezed. 'I think you've got pneumonia. You need to go down.'

Now it was Pete's turn to wait alone at Camp 3. Lower on the mountain, I was concerned but understood that this was not fool-hardiness but characteristic of his solitary confidence and determination.

After a lone foray to the expedition high point, he realised that nobody was coming to support his efforts, and descended. His injured ribs were now seriously affecting him and at Base Camp he joined the growing list of the infirm: John with pneumonia, Al and Paul with Giardia. I had recovered from illness but was exhausted and demoralised and, in truth, wanted to go home. I'd had enough but had invested so much time and energy. All we could hope for was an improvement in the weather.

At the end of January, John was lying in his tent, recovering, waiting to go back up the ropes, when Paul poked his head through the entrance. 'I'm packing up and leaving today,' he said. The sudden announcement took John aback. 'I think you and I should leave. You are not well, and I want to get back in one piece. Someone is going to die if we continue.'

'Let me think about it.'

'Suddenly the dam had burst, and all my thoughts turned to escape from the misery,' John later recalled. 'At the same time, I worried about letting friends down.'

John and Paul walked out of camp, heading home. Meanwhile, Al managed to contact Kathmandu to obtain a two-week extension to our permit. Six of us remained, hoping for an improvement in the weather, but the miracle never happened and, in a fraught radio conversation between camps, we decided to abandon. Despite no summit, the expedition had been an incredible experience. We had climbed to within 1,500 metres of the top without using bottled oxygen or Sherpa support and, despite horrendous conditions, everyone returned home safely, without frostbite and only minor injuries.

After Everest, Pete and I took a break from expedition climbing. Pete pushed his rock-climbing standards to a high level. Travelling to New York in 1981 to visit Roy Kligfield, his Thalay Sagar mate, he took the opportunity to climb in the nearby Shawangunks where, having hooked up with the best local climbers he met Beth Acres who became his girlfriend. Returning to the UK, he returned to medical practice and made enough money as a locum to fund his climbing. He was his old self, super friendly and keen to make plans when we met at social gatherings and climbed together in the Lake District and Derbyshire.

Falling in love with Louise changed everything for me. Having reached thirty I was making that inevitable transition as one gets older, of settling down in a small cottage with a mortgage and then marrying Louise. After five years of expeditions I was in debt and had to start getting serious about earning money. Making a living through my love of mountains was my preference, much to the chagrin of my father.

At this point, opportunities appeared. Although I was not experienced in the retail business, I took the job of manager of the Alpine Sports store in Manchester. I also decided it could be advantageous to become a mountain guide, and enrolled on the training scheme to gain an international qualification. Time and effort were also required in organising the Kendal Mountain Film Festival, which John Porter and I founded on the back of a beer mat in the pub between expeditions. It needed better management as it was expanding to become one of the highlights of the climber's social calendar.

Doug Scott was in the throes of getting an international team together for one of his multi-peak extravaganzas in the summer of 1983. He invited Pete and me, together with fellow Brits, Alan Rouse, Andy Parkin, Roger Baxter-Jones. Accompanying us would be Australian Greg Child, American Steve Sustad and Jean Afanassieff from France. The veteran Don Whillans and Pakistani

Gohar Shah also joined the team. The aim was to climb three peaks: Lobsang Spire, an unclimbed rock pinnacle 5,713metres high; Broad Peak, at 8,047 metres, the twelfth highest mountain on earth, and K2, the second-highest mountain in the world at 8,611 metres, regarded as one of the most demanding mountaineering challenges.

This time I declined, feeling that disappearing for three months on a risky expedition was not a responsible thing to do so soon after marrying Louise.

On Lobsang Spire, Pete partnered with Scott and Child, despite having never climbed with them before. They employed Yosemite-style big wall techniques for the first time in the Greater Ranges, placing pitons, nuts and cams into cracks to aid their way upwards. They slept on porta-ledges, a stretcher-like sleeping platform hung from the vertical rock face and, over six days, set new standards of difficulty in the Greater Ranges. On the last pitch, Child was reduced to hand drilling small holes in the featureless granite to place metal 'skyhooks' on which to pull to complete their ascent. A fall from this extremely challenging pitch would have been catastrophic.

Next was Broad Peak, three days further up the Baltoro Glacier, which, like Lobsang, was regarded as a prelude for K2. But Broad Peak was different. Rather than the technically difficult vertical granite of Lobsang, it presented long, arduous snow slopes and a summit over eight thousand metres high. It required further acclimatisation, which they gained by exploring the surrounding mountains until each person was happy that their body had adapted to the altitude.

The ten members were a strong-willed bunch who had different ideas of how to climb the mountain. This would be fine for alpine ascents in pairs, but not for working as a cohesive group with one goal. The expedition split into five pairs, with Pete and Greg teaming up after forming a strong friendship on Lobsang.

The first two pairs, Parkin with Rouse, and Baxter-Jones with Afanassieff, made an impressively fast ascent over four days. Like the rest of the expedition, they used no supplementary oxygen. On their descent, at 6,400 metres, they met the other three pairs resting at a bivouac. Whillans and Gohar Shah decided they would stay there till the following day, while Pete with Greg continued upwards, reaching the high bivouac at 7,500 metres. They were followed by Scott and Sustad.

On 28th June, by the time Greg and Pete left their bivouac, Scott and Sustad had already reached the col at the start of the summit ridge. Descending from their successful ascent, they met Greg and Pete in the early afternoon, climbing slowly, still only halfway along the final ridge. In the 'death zone' above eight thousand metres, where the hourglass of life runs out fast, it was arduous making progress on the neverending rocky knife-edges overhung by big cornices.

Soon, Greg felt ill. He was familiar with lethargy and pounding headaches at altitude, but that day he was also disorientated. He momentarily blacked out and experienced a strange tingling feeling in his arms and, after discussion, suggested that Pete should go to the summit without him. It was probably only thirty minutes away.

'The idea of turning away from success when it was so close was maddening . . . and Pete's ever-present determination nearly got me going,' wrote Greg later. 'There is a state of mind that sometimes infests climbers in which the end result achieves a significance beyond anything the future may hold.'

'We stay together,' said Pete, and they started to descend, but now Pete began having difficulty breathing, and slowed to a crawl. As Greg started to recover, Pete deteriorated. His lips turned blue, he was near to collapse, and it took a superhuman effort for Greg to cajole, pull, and lower him. The wind picked up, and spindrift covered their ascent tracks. They descended through the col, down the slope in the dark and finally, at 2.00a.m., reached the tent where Whillans and Gohar Shah were sleeping. They attended to Pete, who seemed to be revived by a warm drink. At dawn, he asked for water, but before he could drink, he died. In his last minutes, his lungs gurgled loudly, apparently from pulmonary oedema. Greg tried frantically to revive him. 'But Pete would have none of it. He would only lay there with an expression of sublime rest on his face'.

Greg had done the almost impossible by carrying his partner

halfway down the mountain. They had no resources to move Pete's body, so they zipped up the tent and walked away, leaving him to be buried by the windblown snow. Greg, utterly exhausted at the bottom of the peak, threw his axe on the scree, crying, 'It's not worth it. It's not bloody worth it!'

In his book *Thin Air*, Greg Child gives a harrowing account of the epic and his past expeditions. 'I was intrigued with the notion that I was involved in a 'sport' in which the consequences of a mistake, or just standing in the wrong place at the wrong moment, could be death,' he explained. 'This is not the same as condemning risk, as risk is inherent to climbing; the two are indivisible.' Like me, he has never stopped climbing and, in the few years following the accident, made the coveted second ascent of Gasherbrum IV, a new route on Shivling and summited K2 and Everest.

In 1997 I spent some time with Greg climbing in Vietnam, where he told me that the tragedy stayed with him. Even though they had only just met, like me he had an almost saintly picture of Pete. He said, 'I'd entered this phase of climbing that is dangerous. I know people get killed here. But of course, you don't think it's going to happen to you or the guys you're with.' He summed up by saying, 'It's part of my history and my experience. One of the most powerful things I know. Not only did Pete share his life with me; he shared his death too.'

Personally, I can reflect that my attitude has changed from when I relished near-miss epics and felt a sort of immunity from the effects of losing climbing partners. Greg empathised: 'I know my attitudes towards climbing have changed. I no longer embrace the culture of risk-taking as being integral to the climbing experience.'

From this point, Pete's story takes a bizarre twist. One of which, until recently, I and most of his other climbing friends were unaware. His younger brother, Mike, wanted to visit the foot of Broad Peak as a means of closure. A pilgrimage to a deceased climber's resting place seems to be a way of helping loved ones grieve. In 1986 he left for Pakistan to pay his homage and to read a poem he had written. He quit his job as a lecturer in accountancy and tagged along as Base Camp manager with an expedition organised by Pete's old climbing club at St Mary's Hospital. They would attempt to climb Lobsang Spire in Pete's honour and complete a research project on altitude sickness. From their camp, near the Spire, Mike trekked to the foot of Broad Peak to recite the poem and say his last farewells.

No one could have predicted what would happen on his return journey. On 5th September, at Karachi airport, he boarded Pan Am flight 073 to fly back to Britain. Suddenly five heavily armed Palestinian terrorists, members of the Abu Nidal Organisation, stormed the plane, shooting one passenger and throwing his body out of the aircraft. During the attack, the pilots escaped, fortuitously leaving the plane inoperable. The terrorists collected the passengers' passports, evidently looking for a Christian male, and shouted: 'Michael Thexton!' The bearded, ragged figure of Thexton rose from his seat and went forward, where the hijackers forced him to kneel in the doorway of the plane. At the sharp end of a Kalashnikov, he contemplated his impending death.

'How will the devastation of a second death affect my parents?' he thought, remembering how Greg Child spoke to the family, his parents stoic in the garden as Greg told the tragic story of Broad Peak. His mother said that Pete knew the risks, and it wasn't anyone's negligence that precipitated his altitude sickness. Inevitably, it had left a huge scar on the hearts of all the family.

For unknown reasons, the hijackers lost interest in Mike, ordering him to go and find a seat. Suddenly all hell erupted as automatic gunfire raked the interior of the plane and bombs exploded while the hijackers, indiscriminately and without mercy, threw grenades into the rows of passengers. During the indescribable carnage, the emergency exits were opened, and passengers flooded down the chutes. There were many heroic acts in that smoke-filled inferno, including the bravery of the female flight attendants who remained to marshal the passengers out of the exits. The attack killed twenty people and injured over a hundred of the 380 onboard.

Miraculously Mike survived without injury. Later, in his book,

What Happened to the Hippy Man? – Hijack Hostage Survivor, he wrote, 'You can predict that something unpredictable will happen, but you cannot predict what it will be, or when it will be.' It was the paradox of his brother's mountaineering life.

Joe Tasker at Everest Base Camp, winter 1981.

© Brian Hall

11

OBSESSION?

Joe Tasker

For many people, Everest is the only mountain it makes sense to climb, but should height be a criterion for quality, attraction or for that matter obsession?

All eight of us on the winter expedition of 1980–81 had different reasons for being there and, for sure, getting to the top of the highest point on earth was important. As dedicated mountaineers, I believe most of us wanted to test ourselves physically and mentally at the limits of what we thought possible. Whether we could succeed in the inhospitable winter season without supplementary oxygen was unknown, and that was the attraction. For me, to have tried my utmost and come home was more important than success. For some, that is not enough and the satisfaction of climbing a mountain *must* involve success. There is no better arena than Everest to witness climbers becoming hooked with summit fever, to such an extent that in a hypoxic state, above eight thousand metres, they are willing to risk their lives for their summit goal. From what I saw when I climbed with Joe Tasker, he was one of those people. Perhaps it was why he was so successful? Again, maybe it was why he died?

Our failure on Everest frustrated him, and he went back the following year to attempt one of its last great problems, the unclimbed North East Ridge. It was a small team for such a significant objective. Chris Bonington, the best-known British mountaineer of the day, led, accompanied by a trio of younger climbers: Joe Tasker, Dick Renshaw and Peter Boardman. Dick had been Joe's partner on his early alpine climbs, such as the Eiger, and his first foray to the Himalayas on Dunagiri. In recent years, Joe had joined Pete Boardman to make landmark ascents on Changabang, Kangchenjunga and Kongur Tagh. The lead climbers were supported at Base Camp by two of Chris's closest friends, Charlie Clarke, a highly experienced expedition doctor, and Adrian Gordon, who provided logistical help and managed Base Camp on the Rongbuk Glacier.

After travelling across Tibet they arrived in mid-March 1982, and by early April had established an Advanced Base camp at 6,400 metres. The plan was to employ a hybrid expedition style using fixed ropes and camps, but without bottled oxygen or Sherpa support, a style that Joe and Pete had used on previous expeditions. Bitterly cold winds prevailed as they climbed the lower part of the ridge to just below eight thousand metres. Fixing ropes on the difficult sections, they excavated three ice caves which they stocked with supplies. Although laborious to dig, these caves ensured greater safety than tents in the high winds.

The top cave was situated just below the crucial part of the climb, where three pinnacles blocked the knife-edge crest of snow. They anticipated this would give them some of the most committing and difficult climbing ever attempted at altitude but, if they could traverse the pinnacles, they would reach easier ground where their line would merge with the North Ridge. From here they would follow the route to the summit attempted by the pre-World War II expeditions and the successful Chinese expeditions of 1960 and 1975.

The four reached the first pinnacle on 4th May when Dick experienced a strange tingling down one side of his body. Extremely tired after spending four nights above eight thousand metres and worried by his symptoms, the four thought it prudent to descend. At Base Camp, Charlie diagnosed a mild stroke and recommended that he continue to a much lower altitude. In fact, Dick returned home, where he fully recovered. During their break, Chris decided to remain at Base Camp, concluding that he had gone as far as he could. Aged forty-seven, he felt that he would hold back Pete or Joe.

On 16th May Pete and Joe returned to the third ice cave. The next morning Chris took a radio call from Pete, who sounded full of optimism. Throughout the day, he watched through a telescope as they slowly progressed along the ridge. In the evening, they reached the second pinnacle where they disappeared, out of view, onto the snow on the far side of the ridge. The radio was silent, and Chris assumed that they were looking for shelter or their walkie-talkie had developed a fault.

By the 18th, Chris had grown increasingly worried. He could see the ridge, but Pete and Joe failed to come into sight or respond to radio calls. They were fully committed, knowing that it would be better to continue and join the easier North Ridge than make an arduous retreat the way they had come. Almost certainly, something had gone seriously wrong.

The Base Camp team watched in vain for three days, but Joe and Pete were never seen alive again.

'We had been so close to success, had worked harder, and had been more stretched both physically and mentally than we had ever been before,' Chris later wrote.[1] 'We were totally united in what we were doing, and until the tragedy, it was the happiest expedition any of us had been on.'

What happened? Exhausted, nearing the end of the climb, they must have perished, out of sight on the far side of the ridge. The team at Base were bereft; the expedition was a tight group of friends with a special bond.

Charlie Clarke compared it with the mindset of being at war. 'You know, I felt that we'd been on a bombing raid, and somebody hadn't come back.'

In 1992 a joint Japanese-Kazakh expedition discovered Boardman's body, 'sitting peacefully' near the base of the second pinnacle at 8,200 metres. The body of Tasker is still missing. It is not clear what happened.

In the ten years prior to his disappearance on Everest Joe Tasker had developed into one of the world's most talented mountaineers. Remembering his incredible achievements helps me understand his character.

Born in Hull into a traditional Roman Catholic family in 1948, Joe was Tom and Betty Tasker's second of ten children. They moved to near Middlesbrough, where he spent his early childhood.

1. American Alpine Journal 1983.

Between the ages of thirteen and twenty, he attended Ushaw Jesuit seminary, County Durham, training to be a priest. This education strongly affected the rest of his life, making him very disciplined and extremely hard working. Joe was taller than average, and had a skinny frame with powerful shoulders. He had the look of a modern-day wizard, with high forehead and receding straggly hair and beard. Inquisitive, narrow squinting eyes were surrounded by wrinkles more appropriate on someone older. He was like a hunter, constantly weighing up the world around him.

At the seminary, one of their supper-time readings was 'The Climb up to Hell' by Jack Olsen, which described how the North Face of the Eiger became the most dangerous in the Alps. This book fascinated Joe and sparked his interest in mountaineering. As a Boy Scout he went climbing in the Lake District, and by his mid-teens he displayed a desire to move away from the church. Leaving the seminary, he followed his working-class roots and emptied bins as a dustman, then laboured in a quarry before studying sociology at Manchester University. Here he met Dick Renshaw.

'Someone who accepted without question the hardship entailed and who seemed motivated by a blind drive to climb and climb, without stopping to wonder about the purpose of it all,' Joe wrote in his classic, posthumous book *Savage Arena*.

Joe and Dick graduated from British rock climbing to mountaineering. Over four seasons in the Alps, they formed a strong partnership, where the power of the pair was greater than the sum of its parts. The highlight of those early years was in the summer of 1973 when they took two days to climb the 'holy grail' of Joe's boyhood, the North Face of the Eiger. Their aspirations were similar, and with few arguments and little need to talk, Joe came to admire Dick's asceticism, seemingly unaffected by discomfort, cold or hunger, and his ability to sleep on any uncomfortable mountain ledge.

They then became fascinated by a winter ascent of the Eiger North Face, which had only been achieved three times, and never by a British party. They worked as temporary teachers in the rough area of Moss Side, Manchester in order to raise the money to spend the winter of 1975 in Switzerland.

'We did not want to overcome a mountain with ease. We needed to struggle, needed to be at the edge of what was possible for us, needed an outcome that was uncertain,' Joe wrote.

The Eiger is unique; at the base of its dark and fearsome North Wall are flower meadows in summer and ski pistes in winter. Within an hour of the start of the climb is a mountain railway and the village of Kleine Scheidegg, with hotels, bars and restaurants where tourists can watch through telescopes aimed at the 'crazy' climbers above.

Usually, in summer, the principal danger of climbing the North Face is the incessant stone fall that rakes the face but, in winter, all the stones are frozen in place. The threat is the cold. A winter ascent is a serious prospect and, allowing for the shorter days, can take over a week of constant physical and mental strain.

The nearby mountain railway took them to near the base. Slowed by deep snow, they were only a quarter of the way up after two days and Joe suffered niggling doubts as to the wisdom of their venture. Typically, Dick seemed unperturbed by such self-questioning. Shivering on their second bivouac, a tiny ledge cut from the ice, they looked down at the lights of the village, thinking of the holiday skiers enjoying their evening meals, fine wines and warm showers.

The sky was heavy with grey clouds on the fifth day as they left the aptly named *Death Bivouac*. From that point, there was no retreat. Over the next two days, they climbed the *Ramp*, across the *Traverse of the Gods* into the *White Spider*. By now their fingers were raw and bleeding with the cold, cracked and bruised from constantly hammering their axes into the hard ice. Finally, they climbed the strenuous *Exit Cracks,* reaching the top in darkness as the threatened storm arrived. After a fitful night exposed on the summit, they battled through driving snow to the valley until they arrived at the railway line, where they had to buy tickets. On the approach they had only purchased a one-way journey!

After their epic ascent of the Eiger, it was time to visit the Himalayas in search of a more demanding challenge. They knew nothing about organising such an expedition and felt like amateurs compared to the tightly knit groups of regulars. Eventually, the Indian government gave them permission to attempt Dunagiri, a 7,066-metre mountain that had only been climbed once before.

From a photograph, they identified the unclimbed South East Ridge as a suitable route.

An old Ford Escort van was purchased but, when inspected at a garage, was condemned as unroadworthy. After a few repairs, they trusted in luck that it would manage the ten thousand kilometre 'hippy trail'. At the beginning of August 1975, Dick passed his driving test, and they left for India. The van was grossly overloaded, the back axle leaf springs had completely inverted, and the exhaust pipe grated along the ground. For the journey, Dick had organised a spartan diet of bread with sandwich spread, designed more for survival than enjoyment. Joe soon craved good food and a comfy bed but Dick favoured the frugal life, putting up with any hardship. After three weeks of dirt roads and breakdowns, they drove into Delhi, where officials were reluctant to allow a two-person expedition into the mountains. Two further frustrating weeks were required to navigate Indian bureaucracy.

In the last week of September, they began their six-day trek from Joshimath with ten porters carrying their supplies. Arriving at Base Camp much later than planned, they immediately set off on Dunagiri. Their ascent would be the same vertical height as the Eiger, so they estimated six days' supplies which proved to be woefully inadequate. On the fourth day they were still engrossed in a rock barrier at two-thirds height, but two days later they reached the summit in stunning weather.

Exhausted, they began descending by their ascent route. Without food and no fuel to melt snow, their situation was serious, but they were confident of getting down in a couple of days. However, the weather deteriorated, and two days later they were still only halfway. While Joe was precariously traversing an icy slope his crampons slipped and he fell. An ice piton held the fall but left him dangling from the rope, with a thousand metres of cliff yawning below. After a struggle, he regained the crest of the ridge, and now it was Dick's turn to cross the slope. As he teetered towards Joe, his crampons lost purchase, and he also fell, to be saved by the same ice piton.

In the storm, they had become hypothermic and failed to recognise their slide into irrational behaviour. Joe found a hollow that afforded some shelter, but there was no movement from Dick at the other end of the rope. Joe got into the bivouac tent and immediately fell asleep. Sometime later, in the dark, he woke to find Dick sitting outside, staring into the night.

'I simply thought that I was with a person who was tougher and who had more mental reserves than I would ever have and fell back to sleep.'

At dawn, Joe found Dick sitting in his sleeping bag, half outside the tent, rambling about what they should climb next while looking at his frozen and blackened fingers. They continued to abseil in heavy snowfall. Rummaging in his rucksack, Dick found a boiled sweet and a handful of muesli which they mixed with snow for a meal. It was their tenth night on the mountain.

'A life of ease, a life of luxury, was what I wanted, and I would never put it at risk again,' Joe later wrote.

At the bottom of the ridge, they had a disagreement about which way to go and split up, something usually frowned upon. Finally, on horizontal ground, Joe regretted separating as he crossed a glacier full of hidden crevasses. He found water but, still in delirium, started hallucinating that an American family accompanied him. Above loomed the nearby peak of Changebang, so impressive and beautiful that, in a trance, he took a photograph.

'The long years of self-discipline in the seminary had left me with the knowledge that I could put up with things I did not like . . . I would make it eventually,' he remembered in his book.

Reunited at Base Camp, Dick worried about his frostbitten fingers and left immediately, borrowing money to fly home. Joe's return journey, on the other hand, was long and eventful. When the old Ford broke down in Kabul he took a bus to Istanbul, then finally a train to London carrying fourteen bags.

Back in the UK, Joe was haunted by guilt as Dick's fingers were still in a bad way, with amputations a possibility, but Joe was also captivated by his photo of Changabang and started working out ways it could be climbed, wondering who would be prepared to join him.

Pete Boardman had recently started work at the British Mountaineering Council. Although he was a couple of years younger than Joe, he was already regarded as one of Britain's top mountaineers. They had met in the Alps and, since then, Pete had worked as a climbing instructor and been on expeditions to Alaska and Afghanistan. In 1975 he reached the summit of Everest on Chris Bonington's South West Face expedition. Caged behind a desk, Pete was keen to hear more about Joe's new project. Joe sensed a kindred spirit, and they started planning an audacious two-person expedition. As Joe got to know Pete he realised that, although he was a forceful and determined climber, in everyday life he was conservative, shy and polite, viewing the wilder antics of the climbing community with suspicion.

Joe found being away on expeditions stressful in his personal life, and after Dunagiri split from Muriel, his girlfriend. 'Sometimes the life I was leading seemed empty and pointless without anyone to share it with,' he wrote. ' . . . it had all the trappings of adventure and variety, but I wondered what purpose it all served if it was only for myself.'

In our group, the emotional turmoil created by the risks involved in expedition climbing was plain to see. Initially, our nomadic life-style might have seemed exotic and attractive to our non-climbing girlfriends, but usually they tired of long-distance relationships. It took time to realise that most partners prefer regular company, a comfortable apartment, a car that works, money to spend on a restaurant meal, and to wake up in the morning together, between sheets, rather than in a well-used sleeping bag.

Like me, Joe tried to keep in contact with his parents, knowing that they begrudgingly accepted our dangerous and outlandish way of life. They were proud of our university educations but disappointed that we now laboured on menial jobs to raise money for yet another expedition away from their love and care. I am sure they would have preferred grandchildren over a postcard from a foreign country.

In preparation for Changabang Joe and Pete carefully prepared their equipment, and at one stage Joe tested a prototype hammock by sleeping in it for three nights in the cold storage depot where he worked. In August, they boarded the plane to India, which was the first time Joe had flown. Despite their show of confidence, they were apprehensive about taking on a greater challenge than either had undertaken before.

At Base Camp, the 1,500 metre West Wall of Changabang looked every bit as impressive as Joe remembered. A cold wall, it was shaded from the sun until the afternoon. Progress was by steep mixed climbing on perfect orange-brown granite, streaked with ice and occasional ledges of snow. On one of the crux pitches, Pete inched upwards for hours as Joe stood frozen below.

'It had been absorbed into my subconscious many years before that physical discomfort was a valuable penance, and I sometimes wondered whether our penance and frequent deprival of physical pleasure did indeed benefit our souls and made us better people.'

They had different personalities, and it was not all harmony. On many occasions tempers boiled over, and they argued about trivial incidents and mistakes. They overslept and blamed each other. Pete spilt the tea. Joe had the comfiest place to lie. Bickering and anger were the result of the intense stresses and anxiety. They were getting to know each other.

More food and fuel supplies were required at the wall's midpoint, and they needed a rest from their cold vertical world. Leaving their ropes in place for their return, they descended to Base Camp. A storm on their next attempt stranded them for two miserable nights, squashed in hammocks, unable to cook or melt snow, before being forced off the mountain again. Time became short and they would miss their flights home if they went back on the wall. Friends and family would worry about the lack of contact, and Pete feared losing his job. Nonetheless, they elected to stay. The mountain was everything.

After climbing the ropes to their high point again, they cut a ledge just big enough to lie on and, four days later, reached the top as a bank of cloud enveloped the surrounding mountain, and a storm engulfed them.

After two days of gruelling descent, they got back to Base Camp to find that a nearby expedition was embroiled in tragedy. Four American climbers had fallen to their death on the nearby Dunagiri. The wife of one of the climbers had witnessed the fall and sat at Base Camp, distraught. Joe and Pete wearily climbed to the bodies lying on the lower slopes. It was a shocking scene, but they forced themselves to collect the valuables from the deceased and buried their remains in a crevasse.

Understandably, the accident shocked Joe. He wrote: 'I was certain that I did not want to die, but I knew that the risk in climbing gave it its value.'

For two years, Joe had focused on the Eiger, Dunagiri and Changabang, and been successful on all three. 'In a way, it would have been more reassuring to have failed. Instead, success left me with an uneasy, unsettling questioning about where to go next; something harder, something bigger?'

Joe was on an escalator and, in the next five years, would go on a further seven expeditions: K2, Nuptse, Kangchenjunga, K2, Everest in winter, Kongur, and finally Everest NE Ridge. His insatiable desire for adventure was plain to see but, spending so much time in the danger zone, a high level of risk was inescapable. I think we all had similar feelings. Were we pioneers or fools?

'Where would it lead?' he wrote. 'Was I destined to be forever striving, questioning, unable to find peace of mind and contentment?'

Joe received an invitation from Chris Bonington to go to K2 in 1978, the second-highest mountain in the world, which had only been climbed twice and now offered Joe the experience of a well organised and fully sponsored, traditional style expedition. They would use fixed ropes, six camps and bottled oxygen for the summit push and what a difference it was from his frugal trips to India. Apart from Pete Boardman, the rest of the team were relative strangers to him. The other lead climbers were Chris's friends who had accompanied him on various expeditions over the last decade namely: Nick Estcourt, Doug Scott and Paul 'Tut' Braithwaite.

A week after arriving at Base Camp, Joe and Pete established Camp 2 at 6,500 metres Progress was good until heavy snow pinned the team down. After three days, when the storm abated, Pete and Joe set off to push the route higher. Far below they saw figures moving between Camps 1 and 2, breaking a trail through the deep new snow.

As Joe climbed, he heard the roar of a nearby avalanche, a familiar sound in those high mountains. Above the noise, Pete yelled a warning, and they watched in horror as the slope between the two camps slid, billowing clouds of airborne snow. Minutes earlier, they had watched two figures crossing the slope. Now, they could only see one. Pete and Joe rushed down the ropes and found Doug Scott, distraught, drinking from a water bottle. Beyond was the avalanche scoured slope. Nick Estcourt had been swept away.

Joe was shocked by the suddenness and unreal nature of the event. I had experienced the same when I witnessed two climbers taken by a rock avalanche on the Dru in the Alps, expecting death to entail a struggle, but there was none of that. Only silence. There were so many heart-searching questions with no answers. Doug and Nick had been on the same section of thin fixed rope. Doug was at the edge of the slide, and the rope dragged him into the avalanche.

'I was somersaulting downwards, resigned to my fate when suddenly I came to a stop,' Doug recalled. The rope had snapped, and he had miraculously survived.

Heartbroken, having just witnessed his best friend's death, Chris stood at Camp 1 with tears streaming his face. Mixed feelings arose within the team about the expedition's future. Some argued that Nick would have wanted them to carry on. Others were profoundly affected and unwilling to continue. Joe was in two minds and wrote later. 'Experience did not help to decide how to behave after a death.'

'You're there in a little group, cocooned from the real world,' Paul Braithwaite recalled. 'The real world has gone, it's behind you somewhere. You're with these people trying to climb this climb, face, mountain, peak and you're just totally involved with that scenario. You fully expect, and I fully expected on trips, people to get killed because of the high risk involved.'

Should they continue? Was the risk justifiable? There was no consensus but finally, they decided to abandon the expedition, agreeing that there had to be a total commitment rather than a half-hearted majority. Chris and Doug left immediately to break the news to Nick's wife, Carolyn.

On returning to the UK Joe needed a way to make a living and opened Magic Mountain, a climbing gear shop in the Derbyshire village of Hope. He held great parties in his apartment above the shop. Throngs of drunken climbers pogoed and jived the night away causing the floor to bounce up and down, apparently risking collapse. Though Joe was a great host and relished the craziness of the climbing social scene, he never lost control, always watching, chatting and planning. He had a single-minded approach and was first to rise in the morning, walking through sleeping bags of party-goers dossing like slugs on his sticky carpet, readying to drive into Manchester to see a climbing equipment manufacturer, then to London to give an evening lecture. He was the first of my contemporaries to succeed as a professional mountaineer.

Immediately after K2, Doug Scott asked Joe if he fancied going to Nuptse, one of a trio of giant peaks surrounding the Western Cwm, including Everest and Lhotse. He could not resist and, within three months, despite just opening his store, he joined Doug and American climber Mike Covington in Nepal. Unfortunately, due to appalling weather, they abandoned the expedition. That winter, he started preparing for the next trip, this time to Kangchenjunga, the third highest mountain in the world. With little time for anything other than mountains, unsurprisingly his relationships were in turmoil, and he split from his latest girlfriend, Louise Beetham (whom I would later marry).

'I'd had enough of a boyfriend who was absent half the year and, when at home, was only preoccupied with going away again,' she remembered. 'He was annoyed – sad as well, tearfully pleading that I change my mind. But I think that was because I had made the decision and in doing so controlled the situation.'

Joe became guilt-ridden with that side of his life, writing, 'To what extent could I expect a girl to wait for me for three long, anxious months while I took part in such a dangerous pursuit?'

Doug Scott led the trip in the spring of 1979 to Kangchenjunga and again brought together Pete Boardman and Joe, this time with Georges Bettembourg. The four climbers all had different stories of what happened on Kangch.

When I later talked to Georges on Nuptse he spontaneously exclaimed that it was an unhappy expedition for him. In contrast, Joe wrote glowingly of a harmonious expedition, modestly doubting his ability to keep up with the other three. When I was together with Joe on Everest in winter, he never talked about Kangch. Perhaps he was tired of retelling the story so many times during public lectures, although I suspect he did not want to reopen old wounds, knowing that I was close to both Georges and Doug. Who knows what happened? Sadly, all four are now gone.

Regardless of their differences, their ascent was one of the most courageous and significant of the era. It was the first time such a small team had climbed a new route on a mountain so high without bottled oxygen and was, perhaps, the highlight of Joe's string of achievements.

Of all my contemporaries there was no one else so completely consumed by mountains. They were magnets to Joe. He began making plans for a return trip to K2 in the summer of 1980 and Everest in the winter. He also started a strong relationship with Maria Coffey. Right from the onset, Maria understood that she was living with an addicted mountaineer. 'He longed for the simple, uncluttered existence that he found in the mountains. It was a place where he was happy, in some ways much happier, I suspected, than he ever was at home.'

Maria compared him to a latter-day Ulysses; six weeks after they met, he left for Pakistan.

'Whenever Joe set off on one of his frequent Himalayan expeditions, I used to think that this was what wartime must have been like for my mother and grandmother. I felt like a war bride, left at home for long and uncertain periods, waiting for news and praying that it would be good.'

When he returned from his second unsuccessful trip to K2, at the end of the summer of 1980, she found him physically, mentally and emotionally wrecked.

'Suddenly, this different person arrived back. I felt I had to care for him and get his weight back up. He was having nightmares of being avalanched, waking up in the middle of the night shouting. In hindsight, I think he may have been suffering from post-traumatic stress.'

At the end of November 1980, Joe Tasker, John Porter, Paul Nunn and I landed at the small grass airstrip of Lukla. It took two days to walk to the village of Khumjung, at the heart of the Sherpa community in the Everest region of Nepal. The plan was to meet with the rest of the British Everest Winter Expedition: the Burgess twins, Pete Thexton and Alan Rouse, and a three-person film crew. Surprisingly, they were not there, having been delayed on their walk from the roadhead with the 150 porters who were carrying our loads. Finally, they arrived, and a week later than planned we set off on the remaining four-day trek to Everest Base Camp.

Joe Tasker and I were walking together in a world of our own when, an hour along the track, we stopped at a tea shack. The morning was warming, and it was time to take a few layers off. Across the valley, highlighted by shafts of golden sunlight, Tengboche monastery stood below the spectacular chiselled peak of Ama Dablam.

'How was K2?' I asked, but there was no reply. Joe loved light-hearted banter, discussing plans and arguing about current affairs, but when asked personal questions always clammed up. Talk had not come easily between us after I left a party with a girl he had invited. He was seething and did not speak to me for ages. From my point of view, it was accidental. Joe was delayed in arriving and, by then, I had already started a friendship with this apparently single girl. Deep in the past as this was, he never forgot that incident.

'What was it like climbing with your old mate Dick Renshaw again?' I enquired.

This piqued Joe's interest, and he opened up in a way that surprised me, explaining that he had been worried about going back to the same route on which the avalanche had killed Nick Estcourt in '78 but was determined to try K2 again. Pete Boardman and Doug Scott were also convinced that a small team could climb K2 without oxygen. Dick's frostbitten fingers had recovered, and he was the obvious choice to complete the group.

We sat and drank tea while Joe explained how they tried K2's West Ridge and got higher than before, but the weather was poor, and Doug decided to leave. So, they moved around the mountain to try the Abruzzi Ridge, the original ascent route, climbed in 1954 by an Italian expedition.

'Why did Doug leave?' There was a stony silence, so I changed the subject. 'Why didn't you keep trying the West Ridge.'

'We realised that it was too difficult to do it in alpine style with a team of three. We needed to fix ropes and establish camps that would have required more climbers or the help of high altitude porters, perhaps even oxygen.'

'Do you think there is a barrier to climbing alpine style on eight thousand metre peaks?'

'For sure, I can't climb difficult ground high up.'

'Even with oxygen?

'I don't know. I've never used oxygen. Have you?'

'No. Do you think we stand a chance on this Everest trip?'

'I hope so. We only have one bottle for an emergency, so we're stuffed if we need oxygen.'

'We'll soon find out. You have more experience above eight thousand metres than the rest of the team.'

'I suppose I do. After climbing high on Kangch and K2, I would be confident at climbing Everest without oxygen in the normal season. Who knows whether it's possible in winter?'

The question hung in the air as we set off walking. I was intrigued to know what had happened on K2, and that evening we continued our conversation. 'What stopped you getting up K2?' I asked.

'The usual. The bloody weather.'

At eight thousand metres, a vicious storm, diminishing supplies and weakening strength forced them to give up after ten hard days on the mountain. During the night, an avalanche hit their tent.

'I don't know how we survived. The snow pinned me down, I couldn't breathe and I blacked out.'

With his face etched in painful memory, he recalled how Dick's stoic determination and Pete's strength had saved the day, and how he followed in their footsteps to safety as they descended over the next three days in horrendous storms.

'We were exhausted by the thigh-deep snow and could have been avalanched at any time. It brought home to me how helpless we were, how tiny and insignificant our lives were on that mountain.'

I was speechless. He had kept this story to himself. No wonder he looked so gaunt; it was only five months ago. Previously I thought Joe had a detached air of arrogance. Now, I could see a gentle, more humble side to his character, one that in his early life might have led him to the church. As he described their epic, he seemed to desire atonement, berating himself for failure, thinking he should have tried harder, done things differently or taken greater risks.

Delays on the Everest walk-in had wasted a week of perfect weather. So, after establishing Base Camp and a few days of acclimatisation, we started on our first objective, climbing to the Lho La. This col on the border of Nepal and Tibet was situated a kilometre north of Base Camp but was guarded by seemingly impenetrable six hundred metre walls of dangerous ice cliffs on the right and vertical ramparts of granite on the left. Four Sherpas and a French climber had perished on these walls in 1975. However, the year before our attempt, a Yugoslav expedition found a cunning way up the rock walls on the left.

It seemed a forbidding place as we scrambled up the loose but easy lower rocks. To the right ice cliffs creaked and groaned and regularly unleashed thunderous avalanches of snow and ice. After several days of preparing the lower slopes, we reached the steep upper section where old, frayed rope marked the line of the Yugoslav route. I was partnered with Pete Thexton, but bouts of dysentery impaired both our attempts to support the lead climbers.

The main obstacle was a two hundred metre steep and danger- ously loose corner. Huge blocks were delicately wedged, poised to fall at any time. These 'Swords of Damocles' were impossible to avoid. The only way was to take a deep breath and carefully tip-toe over or around them, constantly yelling, 'Watch out – Below – Keep clear', as any falling rock could crush someone below or sever a rope from which a climber hung. Eventually, ropes and electron caving ladders were fixed to the corner where another area of unstable rock blocked our way. The only possibility was to traverse right along a horizontal line of rock flakes, hung by a quirk of geology, appar- ently totally detached, like a line of giant rock butterflies. Below was a sickening drop to the glacier. After this 'heart in mouth' passage, easier snow slopes thankfully appeared. The sobering fact was that we would have to climb this route not once, not twice, but fifty times to carry a ton of supplies to the Lho La.

After a week, I felt much better and partnered with Joe and Paul on the crucial day when we hoped to reach the col. We set off with tents and enough supplies for a few days of survival, hoping not only to finish fixing the rope to the col but also to dig a snow cave for Camp 1. It was late in the day when we finally stood astride this great watershed. Beneath my right boot was snow which would avalanche south, into Nepal, under my left the snow which would make the long journey north, down the easy slopes of Rongbuk glacier to Tibet

Paul was not feeling great, and decided to abseil back in the fading light while Joe and I pitched a small tent. The wind picked up after dark, and our shelter was exposed to its full force. During the night we became unwell and had little sleep so all thoughts of staying longer evaporated, and in the morning we returned to Base. That evening the whole group sat in the kitchen tent eating Wang Chop's noodly stew and drinking mugs of sweet tea. The wind howled and the tarpaulin flapped alarmingly.

'What were the conditions like up there?' Al asked, keen to know what we had discovered.

'The Lho La is more exposed to the wind than we are down here. There's no way we can use tents for Camp 1,' I said.

'Just a few hundred metres down the other side, into Tibet looked like good snow to dig a cave,' Joe added.

'If the weather had been better we would have started digging but we could hardly stand up,' I replied.

'What does the way across the col to the start of the West Ridge look like?' Pete Thexton asked.

'From what we could see, easy and no crevasses,' Joe answered.

'I wish we could have done more but we both developed terrible headaches and vomited all night. We felt so bad, regardless of the weather we had to come down,' I added.

'I was not ill. How dare you insinuate I had altitude sickness! Don't blame me for coming back down.' Joe exploding with rage. He abruptly stood up and stormed out of the tent.

The whole team sat in silence. Obviously, I had hurt his pride.

For me, nobody had been at fault, we had simply been ill, but it was as if he could not accept any weakness in himself. It was common for Joe to berate himself, but this time it was directed at me. We never partnered again and, sadly, a cold feeling appeared that was never reconciled.

Joe's role on the expedition extended to organising a film produced by Chameleon, a documentary company headed by Allen Jewhurst. Several of our team were also interested in making movies, and helping the film crew was a welcome distraction. Paul Nunn and I had recently worked on *The Bat and the Wicked* shot on Ben Nevis. The film had been shown to great acclaim at the Kendal Mountain Film Festival during a raucous weekend a month before we left for Nepal.

Jewhurst had been with Joe on his two expeditions to K2 and was always joking and telling wild stories in his cockney accent. Constant sub-zero temperatures made filming difficult yet he, Mike Shrimpton, the cameraman, and Graham Robinson, the sound recordist, were forever optimistic, though I very much doubt they knew what they'd let themselves in for. Joe was a driving force in making the film, and even in the most extreme conditions shot most of the high-altitude footage. He also looked after the safety of Mike Shrimpton who, on one notable occasion, reached the Lho La ice cave to document the front end of the climbing. Helping the film crew had a flip side as the effort occasionally distracted his energies from the climbing, and we had to remind Joe where his priorities lay.

Al Rouse and I were the closest of friends, and he confided that he was upset at the way the expedition was going. 'Joe is continually arguing with me. If I suggest anything it always seems to be wrong,' he complained.

'Yes, he likes his own way, but that's true with everyone.'

'I know we said we would decide on strategy by democratic discussion, but we all seem to be getting irritated by the never-ending talk.'

'I think the cold and illness is affecting everyone's mood.'

'I wanted this trip to be like before, a happy bunch of mates.'

Al had recurring dysentery, a persistent sore throat and a terrible cough, whereas Joe bounded around with health and energy. Al cut a dejected figure as he sat forlornly around Base Camp, trying to regain his mental and physical strength.

Al wrote to his girlfriend Hilary, 'I have had amoebic dysentery, as have half the team. I thought I had recovered and went to the Lho La Camp at six thousand metres. I was to have carried another load this morning but I was too sick. Illness is becoming a major problem with half the team always laid out.'

Because of his past relationship with the film crew, Joe was able to influence the outcome of the documentary. He also controlled the television news reports which we had been contracted to send out at regular intervals. Separately, he had gained a contract to write the expedition book. Although the expedition was Al's idea, he came to realise that the film and book gave Joe influence, possibly even control, over how the outside world would judge the expedition. This exacerbated matters. It was not just Al that resented Joe creating the narrative around the expedition. Most of the team were more than capable of writing about the expedition and John, Paul and I were making forays similar to Joe, into the film world. These sour relationships within the group, and Al's sickness, had far-reaching effects on the outcome of the expedition.

Communications with the outside world were via a mail runner who would arrive every two weeks. Everyone was pleased to get one or two envelopes, but it seemed to be even more significant for Joe who received dozens of letters. He was the star of a large family, and much of the post was undoubtedly news exchanges but, as soon as Allen Jewhurst found out that many were from Joe's girlfriends, he would joke and mock as Joe disappeared, embarrassed, to secretly read his mail in his tent.

Joe was an enigma like no other climber I knew, and it was a mystery how he kept fit. In the UK he was always busy on work projects and never appeared to climb or exercise. Yet partway through the Everest expedition, he and Aid Burgess were the fittest members of the crew. Even in the '70s, mountaineers trained, but Joe seemed to rely on his schedule of two expeditions a year to maintain his athletic prowess. Undoubtedly there was another key ingredient to his success, a phenomenal mental drive that could push his body to the limit.

The weather through January was awful, and progress on the mountain was slow with the team widely spread over the mountain slopes. There was no plan or routine, no leader, just everyone working at their own pace and initiative. Time was rapidly running out, and there was a resigned feeling amongst most of us that the conditions had beaten us. Yet every time the clouds parted, and the wind dropped, our hopes lifted.

At the end of January, Pete and Joe were poised at the highest camp, ready to break a trail to a new high point when disaster struck. Wang Chup, our cook, became ill, and Pete had to descend to Base Camp to treat him, leaving Joe alone. Aid Burgess and Paul Nunn set off up the dreary treadmill of fifty-two rope lengths to support him at Camp 3.

The next day Paul worked tirelessly on improving the crevasse cave while Joe and Aid pushed the route out to 7,400 metres along the relatively easy rounded dome that led to the crest of the West Ridge. It was a rare, magical and windless day. Most of the surrounding white mountains sparkled below, and the sky was an intense ink blue. They made steady progress, their crampon points biting into the firm wind-packed snow. The good conditions and easy terrain required no rope and, if they could establish a fourth ice cave five hundred metres ahead, near where the Americans, in 1963, had climbed to reach the Hornbein Couloir, they thought there was a chance of attempting the summit.

By late afternoon a strong wind picked up, buffeting them from side to side, and a white plume of wind-whipped snow spun away from the high slopes. It became imperative to descend. This section would be exposed to the winds and needed the safety of fixed ropes. Unfortunately, we had used more rope than expected lower on the mountain and had little left. Originally, we planned to use rope only on technically difficult sections, but we had not anticipated being blown off the easy slopes.

The trio were cooking in Camp 3 as the sun set when they heard a noise.

'Any room in there?' Al Rouse's voice came from outside. Despite illness, he had made a two-day effort to reach the expedition's highest camp.

After a poor night's sleep they rose, as yet another storm wrapped its arms around Everest. In frustration, Al and Paul made a harrowing descent to the valley. Aid and Joe were determined to stay, knowing how close we were to the last leg of our climb, the summit pyramid.

'We are established on the West Shoulder but if it were up to me alone I would probably pack in, as I think that our chances of success are slim indeed,' Al wrote in a letter to his girlfriend. 'The winds were truly infernal and the cold down to −40°C. Conditions were the worst any of us had ever encountered. Everything was okay but when I got down my throat was very bad and then I developed a cold from which I am now recovering. I seem to be ill too often on this trip. I have gone incredibly thin, far too thin in fact.'

Our permit to climb Everest expired at the end of January so, just like the Poles the year before, we applied and got a two-week extension. Sadly, John Porter and Paul Nunn had to leave due to work commitments, exacerbated by the constant worry of the dangers and prolonged debilitating illness. 'I'm disappointed that we seem to have hit a brick wall. We still might succeed, but I will not be playing any part,' John said as he left.

For three days a large plume cloud constantly trailed from the summit and the wind blew worse than ever, difficult as that was to believe. A tense three-way radio conversation served only to increase the confusion and isolation between the three groups poised at separate camps. It would be the final act of the expedition.

At Base Camp, Pete Thexton was recovering from cracked ribs, accompanied by the film crew. In the Camp 1 snow cave, Alan Burgess, Al Rouse and I were trapped by the ferocious winds that forever blew through the Lho La, all three of us utterly spent by the inactivity of lying in the sub-zero tomb for days on end. Aid Burgess and Joe Tasker were impatiently waiting high on the mountain in Camp 3.

Joe on the radio: 'Aid and I have been here for three days. We gather there's some doubt about going on, but Aid and I are quite certain we could make it along the ridge and find a place to dig an ice cave for Camp 4, but we need support – over.'

Alan Burgess from Camp 1: 'There are high winds here, and

waiting days in the cave has wasted us. Even if we could reach you at Camp 3, I am not sure we would be of any use – over.'

Joe: 'What's the point in us carrying on if you feel unable to support us? We will be exposing ourselves to needless risk – over.'

Pete at Base: 'You don't think it is worth trying for a few more days? – Over.'

Al Rouse from Camp 1: 'None of us have been able to move. You say it is possible to go along the ridge, why don't you go and have a look? The three of us are unanimous; we are not prepared to come up because we don't think it is worth the risk of climbing above 7,500 metres in the current weather conditions – over.'

Pete: 'From my perspective at Base Camp, it seems a pity to be giving up – over.'

Joe: 'It's more than a pity! Aid and I are prepared to stay here as long as it takes, but no one else is prepared to come up and help. You have asked for us to give a demonstration of what is possible by going along the ridge and digging a Camp 4 ice cave.' After an uncomfortable radio silence, he continued. 'But we gave a demonstration yesterday by going partway along the ridge. At the same time, you were not prepared to leave the snow cave at the Lho La – out.'

Aid recalls, 'Joe was into using guilt and coercion to bring them up to us, but I knew it wasn't going to work with my brother.'

Pete tried to continue the heated discussion, but Joe cut off the call.

At Camp 1, Al Rouse was upset. 'Joe's living in a fantasy world. He knows we have run out of fixed rope, and he knows that he and Aid are the only fit climbers left.'

'He can't blackmail us into risking our lives when there are such overwhelming odds against success,' I replied.

From Joe and Aid's perspective, what they said was logical. Unfortunately, the rest of us had reached our physical limit. With the continuing high winds and lack of support, they made the only sensible decision and descended. Back at Base Camp, there was a bitter reunion, especially and unusually, between the Twins.

'If you had gone along the ridge, we would have come up,' Alan said.

'No way! If you had come up, you would have done nothing the next day. Al Rouse went up there, had no strength to do anything, and came down the next day,' Aid replied.

'So, what could we have done?'

'You have to get up there and have a rest day. Then you will feel like doing something.' Aid was getting angry. 'It was an hour from Camp 3 to the West shoulder. Somebody could bomb along it and start digging a snow cave while the others lay rope; you can't do both. We need to spread the effort because Joe and I can't do it all!'

There was an uncomfortable silence before Aid continued, obviously wanting to get his feelings off his chest. 'It's the mind that drives the body, and when the mind gives up, the body ceases to function well.' I remained silent to let the brothers clear the air.

Later Aid wrote in the book, *The Burgess Book of Lies*, 'I had not thought about how the body forces the decision on the mind. This was what happened during the last weeks of the expedition. It is a delicate balance between driving oneself to exhaustion and listening to the body as it strives to survive without oxygen, food and heat. A year later, Joe miscalculated the fine balance and paid for it with his life.'

That winter everyone had their own view on what should be done. I thought we should end the expedition as I could do no more. Fortunately, we had lived to tell the tale. I was happy with my caution without having to spread the blame, make excuses or berate myself. I had suffered enough that winter.

At the end of the expedition, we took turns to speak to the film camera. Joe's summary reflected his character. 'I do not think we tried to the maximum; physically. I don't think we pushed ourselves to the limit, and I don't think we stuck our necks out as regards danger.'

There is now a body of scientific evidence showing that the apparent height of Everest's summit, in winter, could be over 10,000 metres. The cold wind and lowering of the troposphere reduce the atmospheric pressure, which increases the effective altitude (see Appendix 2). Even Base Camp feels higher than in the regular climbing season of May and October, which reduces its effectiveness for rest and recovery and severely handicaps mountaineers prepared to suffer some of the most unbearable conditions on earth.

We all thought that the West Ridge was possible in winter, and if we had got Camp 4 established, might have been able to reach the top from there in one long day. Illness and the lost week of good weather at the start of the expedition was undoubtedly crucial. Other than Joe and Aid, we thought that even another month of trying was futile unless the weather changed dramatically. We later heard that none of the much larger expeditions trying peaks that winter had got any higher than us.

'No matter how many climbers we had or what system of organisation, I think the outcome would have been the same,' Al Rouse said to the camera as we packed to leave.

Our sights had been set high and to this day, the only winter ascent of Everest without supplementary oxygen was in 1987 by Ang Rita. An unbelievable feat by this remarkable Sherpa who, during his lifetime, climbed Everest ten times, all without oxygen. His winter ascent required a rare adaptation to altitude, perhaps only found in the Sherpa people. Even this ascent was made within the parameters of a large Korean expedition preparing the route using oxygen.

Within four months, Joe was back in the Greater Ranges as part of a British team attempting to make the first ascent of Kongur Tagh (7,649 metres) in China. Chris Bonington led, and brought together the well-proven pairing of Joe and Peter Boardman. Also on the team was Alan Rouse, ideal from a climbing point of view but strained socially by his underlying rivalry with Joe. They attempted Kongur, a complex and massive mountain that seemed to be continually enveloped in storms and, after several attempts, persistence paid off. All four climbers reached the summit after a week-long alpine style ascent.

Between expeditions, Maria Coffey remembered Joe's intensity and crazy drive. 'He would not talk about risk or death; he said that if he thought about what would happen, he would not be able to go – so he did not think about it . . . He seemed driven to cram as much into his life as possible as if he accepted that it could be cut short at any time. It made for a challenging relationship. He was a

26 The author on the summit of Jannu. (Roger Baxter-Jones).
27 Nuptse, Everest, and Lhotse viewed from Kangtega.

28 Georges Bettembourg approaching the summit of Nuptse, 1979.
29 The Nuptse team at Base Camp after their epic climb.
30 Doug Scott climbs a crumbling serac while escaping Nuptse down the Khumbu icefall.

31 Pete Thexton abseiling after completing the first ascent of Thalay Sagar (Roy Kligfield).

32 Nuptse on the right, then Everest with the West Ridge descending to the Lo Lha with Changtse the peak in the background.

33 Aid Burgess outside the Lho La ice cave with Nuptse in the background.

32

33

34 Joe Tasker climbing the rocks walls of the Lho La to Camp One on Everest's West Ridge.
35 On a rare good day, Joe Tasker at the high point of the attempt on Everest's West Ridge in winter. (Aid Burgess).
36 Joe Tasker battling a storm high on Everest in winter.

36

37 Paul Nunn dressed for filming a TV documentary on the history of climbing.
38 Paul Nunn load carrying up to Everest's Lho La.
39 Al Rouse, Andy Parkin and Paul Nunn bivouacking with the Ogre and Ogre 2 in the background.

40 Al, Paul and Andy on the glacier below Ogre 2 with Death Alley on the left.
41 Choe Brooks climbing a serac on Chamlang with Makalu behind, 1984.
42 Makalu Base Camp showing the West Face with the South East Ridge on the right.

41

42

43

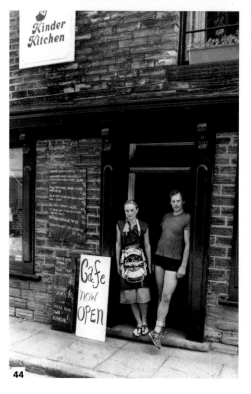

44

45

43 The author's portrait of Aleister Crowley, the image that haunted him on Chamlang.
44 Brian and Louise Hall outside their Kinder Kitchen Café in 1985.
45 Andy Parkin approaching the summit of Broad Peak in 1983. (Alan Rouse).

46 Andy Parkin with Greg Child on a climbing trip to Vietnam, 1997.
47 Voytek Kurtyka.
48 Approaching K2 Base Camp with Broad Peak on the right.
49 K2, the Abruzzi Spur on the right skyline.

48

49

50 Alan Rouse at the Gilkey Memorial in the shadow of K2.

strange mix – he would be tender, gentle and generous, then morph into an extreme and excluding focus.'

The following year, Bonington had the unclimbed North East Ridge of Everest booked with the same team, but to avoid conflict between Al Rouse and Joe, wisely changed the personnel and broke the news to Al that it might be better if he did not join them. In March 1982, they left for Everest, with Dick Renshaw replacing Al.

Joe went on four expeditions when he was with Maria. 'It was a crazy relationship as I had to completely bend my life around his; even when he was at home I used to have to wait around until he had time for me. He was very guarded about his emotions – he never said he loved me. He would say, "Why do you need to hear the words? Can't you tell how I feel about you by the way I look at you, and touch you?" When he turned his focus on me, he was very tender and loving. But I knew all along that his first commitment was to the mountains.'

As with all mountain accidents, Joe and Pete's disappearance high on Everest had far-reaching effects on their loved ones and friends. Deep feelings of grief never disappear and are only smothered by time. 'Joe's death completely shattered me,' Maria said. 'For the longest time I kept wondering why he, and Pete, pushed themselves so far beyond their limits on the North East Ridge. Why they didn't turn back, towards life and the people who loved them?'

They did not retreat because elite climbers like Joe show unwavering confidence in their own strength, a belief that they can succeed and a drive that keeps them going against the worst that the mountains can throw at them. An elusive, difficult to reach top is more attractive than one easily attained. The more effort required and the greater the danger undertaken the sweeter the success. This hard-fought achievement creates a euphoric feeling and a unique satisfaction in the mind. An addiction to risk? Joe's ambition and drive were unbounded, ultimately killing him.

But in the end, we are all just chasing dreams.

Paul Nunn on Everest, winter 1981.

12

INTELLECT AND ART

Paul Nunn

Paul Nunn returned to Sheffield from St Moritz after working on the Fred Zinnemann film *Five Days One Summer* at the start of autumn in 1981, full of tales of wild shenanigans and drinking with film stars in the exclusive resort. On the set, he looked after glacier safety and doubled for Sean Connery, who had a similar build and the same taste in whisky.

Paul was a big man in every way, with a huge presence. He would arrive in the pub with a great guffaw, the hand on the shoulder, the sideways glance to check who was present. Conversation lifted with him around, laughter grew louder, and the darts match became more competitive. A beer glass looked tiny in his massive hand and, after a few draughts, he was back at the bar for another round while everyone tried to catch up. As the evening grew old, his high forehead would sweat, and he would swipe his receding ginger brown hair and stroke his mutton-chop sideburns. At late-night parties, he was usually at the centre, speaking rapidly and incomprehensibly, punctuating his speech with huge laughs and animated actions followed by silence, as he waited for everyone to grasp the thread or get the joke. He often spoke of academics or politicians, which was hugely entertaining although much of it passed me by. As an evening wore on, he would inevitably trip over chair legs or knock beer glasses over, leaving a trail of devastation. Always gregarious, he was habitually the last to leave. There seemed to be limitless energy within his frame. Did he ever sleep?

One time at a party Louise and I hosted in Hayfield, at around 2.00a.m., Paul announced he was going home, got up and walked back to Sheffield via the summit of Kinder Scout and along Stanage Edge. A walk of fifty-five kilometres!

In the late '70s, a period in my life when I was in the doldrums and drinking too much, I was arrested for drunken behaviour. On another occasion I was breathalysed behind the wheel and banned from driving. When I became homeless, Paul kindly invited me to stay for several months in his family house with his lovely wife Hilary and their two daughters, Louise and Rachel. Ten years older, he became a mentor to me, and his gentle but shrewd advice helped bring me back on track.

As I got to know him better, more layers of his complex character were revealed. He was proud of his Irish heritage, born in Abbeyleix, Co Laois, Ireland, in 1943. He had the joyous traits of an Irishman, even though he was adopted and brought up in Macclesfield, Cheshire. The Scout movement introduced him to hillwalking and rock climbing at the age of twelve, and his natural talent was soon revealed on the nearby crags of The Roaches and Hen Cloud.

In the 1950s, the Rock and Ice Club dominated climbing with Joe Brown and Don Whillans its leading lights. The Alpha Club emerged in the late 1950s, which Paul joined, and was the spur for him to climb harder. With other members, he provided a leap forward in standards by producing a string of hard new rock routes in the Peak District and beyond. During this period, he attended the Catholic Xavier College in Manchester before studying at Sheffield University and completing a Ph D. He had a formidable intellect and became Principal Lecturer in Economic History at the University of Hallam. One of his key interests was researching where the capital originated that financed the Industrial Revolution. He was an astute political animal with deeply felt socialism, making him a staunch defender of student welfare.

We often shared a rope on the Derbyshire gritstone edges, and I was always impressed by his neat and precise technique. Although a big man, he had honed his gift through years of pioneering climbs the length and breadth of the British Isles.

He first went to the Dolomites when he was only sixteen and, incredibly, climbed the *Cassin route* on the Cima Ovest in under five hours. At twenty, he made the first British ascent of the

Philipp-Flamm route on the Civetta with Martin Boysen, then considered to be the most challenging rock climb in the Alps. Unfortunately, four pitches from the top, Paul was hit by a rock which broke his leg. Boysen, with assistance from other British climbers in the area, managed to rescue him.

During the ten weeks we spent together on Everest in winter, Paul became the elder statesman who would mediate an argument or take time to have a quiet chat about personal problems. Although only thirty-seven, his wise head enabled him to deal with day-to-day existence in harsh conditions better than everyone else.

He was a close friend of Al Rouse, living around the corner from him in Sheffield and, without his support, I doubt whether Al would have endured the hardships of illness and personal conflicts with some of the team members while maintaining his role as expedition leader. Paul understood that there were younger and fitter climbers on the team who were prepared to stick their necks out and operate at the limit. Still, he was always in the background helping and had a prodigious ability for hard work when loads needed carrying. Interviewed by the film crew, he emphasised the need for caution. 'What keeps exercising my imagination is what it will be like descending from the Lho La with a hundred mph winter storm whipping across and snowing as well – and you are on your last legs?'

He was also pragmatic. 'It's not important that I reach the top, but very good if I do succeed as it sets an example. If eight of us can get up Everest in winter, is it necessary for these regiments of people to keep coming here and despoiling the place?' It was a canny prophecy considering the vast armies of 'mountaineers' who now queue to be guided to the summit of Everest.

However, Paul was also very independent. One day at the end of January on Everest, he decided he had reached his limit, thinking there was an accident waiting to happen if we continued. He confided his thoughts to John Porter, and the two decided to go home.

After Everest, Paul, Al Rouse and I were disillusioned with expeditions to high profile objectives and vowed that our next trip would be back to our roots in style. To go with a small group of mates to a lower peak that we could enjoy by climbing in alpine style. We started planning and, to make a foursome, Andy Parkin joined us. He was also part of the Sheffield clan but, being younger, had never been to the Greater Ranges. Our intention was to go and climb a mountain for fun without all the hullabaloo of it being the highest, hardest, fastest or most difficult ascent ever made. Nor would we put pressure on ourselves with media publicity or by making grandiose claims to gain sponsorship. It would be a low budget climbing holiday paid for by ourselves.

The peak we found to climb in the Pakistan Karakoram was ideal. Explorers had called it Point 6960, simply its height, but that did not do justice to its impressive beauty, or its location next to the, better known, Ogre (Baintha Brakk, 7285 metres). Mountaineers had elevated its status by naming it Ogre 2 (Baintha Brakk 2). The Ogre itself had been climbed in 1977 in an epic, during which Doug Scott broke his leg and Chris Bonington his ribs while they descended from the summit. Ogre 2 was unclimbed.

When we set out, Paul was just shy of forty. Al and I were ten years younger and of a different generation, while Andy at twenty-six was the youngster.

Paul had already visited Islamabad many times and when we arrived in early June 1982, we were welcomed into the home of Jean and David Corfield. This couple were members of the British Embassy staff who had nursed Paul back to health after he contracted hepatitis during the 1980 Royal Geographical Society Karakoram Scientific Project. We had warned Andy of all the dangers and hardships of eastern travel, but sipping cold beer by the poolside of the British Embassy club, he probably wondered what all the fuss was about. Paul was a good friend of Nasir Sabir, the first Pakistani to climb K2, who speedily massaged us through government bureaucracy, helped with food purchases, and organised a minibus to transport us up the Karakoram Highway to the remote Baltistan capital of Skardu.

Our accommodation was the K2 Motel, a grandiose name for a series of half-finished huts. In classic Asian style, it was made from concrete blocks with metal rebar sprouting in all directions, topped by a corrugated tin roof which ensured temperatures inside stayed at a steady 40°C during the day and plummeted to freezing at night. In front, on a sun-scorched patch of yellowed grass and weeds, three Baltis stood to attention, dignified and clothed in the local dress. Traditional Nating wool hats sat at a jaunty angle atop their sun-ravaged faces, with shalwar kameez long shirts hanging over voluminous trousers – all newly washed and pressed, coloured in cascading shades from walnut, hazel, and almond. Paul embraced Fadah Hussein as a father would his child.

'Mr Paul, we heard you were arriving.'

'Good to see you again. News travels fast around here.'

'It is four years since we were together on Latok.'

'Too long.'

'Remember my son Fadah and our cook Ali Mohammad.'

'I am looking forward to Ali's food – it is the best in the world.' Paul spread his arms wide and gave a great belly laugh. 'Can you work for us?'

'Inshallah.' Three heads bowed in unison.

We enrolled the trio, with Fadah Hussein in charge as our sirdar. On the outside of the Motel's high fence was a throng of hundreds of porters. Word had got around that there was an expedition in town. It was bedlam, and at one point, Captain Ali, our Liaison Officer (LO), had to get his pistol out as the men, desperate for work, became an unruly mob and started to push and fight. Finally, he regained a semblance of order and got them into line. The captain, who had been seconded from the army to help our expedition, was a real asset, helping whenever he could and keeping Paul's hyperactive brain occupied by discussing the politics and cultures of our different nations.

'Andy, can you help me choose the forty porters?' I asked.

'Sure, what can I do?'

'Write their names down and give them one of these numbered tickets. I'll go around with this stethoscope and pretend to listen to their lungs. We'll choose the strongest-looking ones.'

'OK, but isn't Fadah Hussein choosing who he wants anyway?'

'Yes, and the LO will also help, but the medical tests will give us some respect.'

All afternoon Paul, Fadah Hussein and the captain lounged on chairs behind mirrored sunglasses as the porters trooped past, sagely nodding to accept one or shaking their heads to reject another.

An assortment of battered ex-army Jeeps took all morning to drive us along a dusty dirt track to the roadhead village of Dasso. At first, the walk to the mountains wound through a hot and barren landscape where hamlets were built on rare patches of flat land, set like garnets in a kaleidoscope of earth shades. Necklaces of bright green poplars lined the irrigation channels that provided the life-blood of water to the jigsaw of terraced wheat fields and apricot orchards. Fadah Hussein was held in such respect by the porters that the four of us had freedom to relax, stride out in front or lag behind, photograph, snooze at will, listen to headphone music, or read a few pages of a book. Each evening we arrived at a camp where our tents were already erected and dinner on the stove. I felt embarrassed at being so privileged in this penurious land. However, I reconciled my guilt with the employment and cash we brought to a subsistence community. Paul had walked this path many times, but he stopped part way through the gigantic canyon which scythed into the foothills through which the River Braldu's mud and moraine-clouded waters raced.

'This was where Pat Fearnehough was swept away.' Paul pointed at the path squeezed between the spuming water and the mud bluffs.

'It looks no different from what we have been walking through all day,' I replied.

'Death comes in all manner of places.' Paul bowed his head before continuing along the twisting trail.

Askole was the final village before we entered the high mountains. The mud-brick walls of some buildings had collapsed, and dirty plastic sheets covered holes in their flat roofs. Through the small glassless window of one squalid hut I saw a cooking fire burn with acrid wood smoke filling the air. Crushed plastic bottles, torn paper and food scraps lay everywhere, and open sewer ditches brimmed with stagnant black water buzzing with flies. As we approached, a woman fled indoors, hastily veiling her face with a brood of mangy chickens clucking in her wake.

The village's headman was called Haji Medi, which indicated he had made the long pilgrimage to Mecca. Of smallish stature, he looked better fed than his fellow villagers. In a land of no schools, he could read and write in both Urdu and English, and education gave him power. He ran the village like a business, the foreign expeditions his wealthy customers. Allegedly, he took a toll from every porter who passed through and sold the village flour at inflated prices – adding sand to increase its weight. No wonder the chapatis were full of grit and the porters had only a few black stumps for teeth. Paul knew Haji Medi well, and they met like long-lost friends.

'My house is your house,' Haji cried.

'We have a gift for you.' Paul pointed at five porters carrying coils of black Alkathene plastic water pipe.

Haji's beady eyes widened, and he spread his arms. 'Praise and thanks to Allah.'

As the official leader of our expedition, Al thought it time to interject. 'They are a thank-you from Doug Scott for your help, after his accident on the Ogre.'

Scott had organised this charitable donation through the Aga Khan Rural Support Programme to provide fresh drinking water for the village. A vital improvement after discovering that fifty per cent of the children in the community died before their fifth birthday, mainly due to diarrhoea and enteritis caused by polluted water.

'Mr Doug is too kind. We must have a feast to celebrate.' The gift merited the slaughter of a rather forlorn and skinny goat.

Andy was looking forward to the festivities until he realised that, in this remote Baltistan Muslim culture, there would be no alcohol available or women present. Still, in this community, where happiness was at a premium, it was a carefree scene as the village men and our porters danced, rhythmically clapped and sang around an open fire. It was a rare treat for them to eat meat with their chapatis and vegetable broth. In the darkness, mongrels barked, and shadows moved. As the embers flared, occasional glimpses of a woman's shawl or the dirty face of a wide-eyed child were momentarily illuminated.

Early next morning, as we left for the mountains, Fadah Hussein whispered to Paul. 'Do you know Haji Medi charged us for the goat, three chickens and a camping fee for the porters – even the five who brought the water pipes.' We were glad to get out of the filthy village and head into the mountains.

Our approach was along small paths and over endless moraine whalebacks, followed by the rock-covered ice of the Biafo and Uzzun Blakk glaciers. Paul and Fadah Hussein knew the way as they had used the same Base Camp on trips to Latok 2 in 1977 and 1978. Alas, both were tragic trips for Paul. During the first, Don Morrison died in a crevasse fall, and on the second there was Pat Fearnehough's accident on the walk-in, when he was swept away by the River Braldu.

Finally, on the third day from Askole, we reached the top of a lateral moraine ridge and looked down at a welcoming green ablation valley no bigger than a playing field. The porters pointed and whistled as a herd of a dozen ibex crossed a scree slope high above. The temperature rose as we dropped into a sheltered oasis of sedge, alpine flowers and moss with a pool reflecting the snowy mountains in its still waters. We slid a plastic sheet over the old stone walls of the cookhouse left by the previous expeditions and settled in to relax, acclimatise, and recover from the journey This would be our home for the next month.

'Bhalu, Bhalu.' A smiling porter pointed at the large prints of a bear in the mud around the pool.

Characteristically, Al soon dragged us away from our idyll to walk around the flanks of the mountain, searching for a feasible line to the summit. Gazing at the impressive bulk of the Ogre, we could follow Bonington and Scott's route to the summit. On the right, our slightly lower peak was plain to see. Joined at a high col like conjoined twins, below which ran a narrow glacial valley christened *Death Alley*. Recently, Ogre 2 had been unsuccessfully attempted by a lightweight British team and a large Korean expedition. Both followed a route up *Death Alley* to the high col before attempting the North Ridge. The two-kilometre long *Alley* was threatened on both sides by walls of tottering seracs, with debris below suggesting they fell at regular intervals. We all agreed that it looked dangerous, and were reluctant to follow in the footsteps of the earlier expeditions. To the right, on the North-West Face, we spied a potentially complex way to the summit. We returned to Base Camp and, after a few days, set off before dawn, unladen, for a recce of the heavily crevassed approach to our proposed route.

It was then time for a training climb which would aid fitness and acclimatisation at these higher altitudes. We packed large rucksacks and set off for an unclimbed and unnamed aiguille on the other side of the Uzzun Blakk glacier. It was a beautiful peak that could have easily warranted a full-scale expedition to reach its elegant needle-like summit. The peak was shaped like an antelope, and the first day we climbed the snow and rock of its *back legs*. The following day, Al and Andy took the lead. They were well matched and going like thoroughbreds while Paul and I followed at a more sedate pace, traversing a narrow icy ridge along the *spine* of our geological animal with great walls on either side plunging down its *ribs* to the glaciers far below. After a long day, we reach a flat area below the *neck*. On our perch, we put on a brew and settled into our sleeping bags. We were alone, surrounded by a stupendous mountain vista with the Ogre and Latok groups to our west and, to the east, Sosbun Brakk, below which the Biafo glacier flowed, like a massive serpent, from the distant *Snow Lake* and the Hispar La. Magical names from Sir Martin Conway's writings who, in 1892, was the first Westerner to tread this stunning landscape.

Above our bivouac, a rock ridge rose half a dozen rope lengths up the *neck* to the summit. 'We'll be on top by lunch tomorrow,' Paul said.

'That'll give us time to get down in the afternoon,' I replied.

'More tea?' Andy offered me a mug, his face bathed in custard yellow light from the sun setting behind a bank of clouds on the horizon.

I awoke in the night with a sense that all was not right. There was resistance as I tried to turn over, and any sounds were curiously muffled. I drew back the Gore-Tex cover of my sleeping bag and felt cold, wet snowflakes land on my nose. We were in a world of swirling snow. Without tents, there was no possibility of sitting out the storm. So, unanimously, we decided to retreat. It was a disappointment not to climb our antelope aiguille, but we had gelled as a team, shedding the rust of travel and recent inactivity. The four days together had been full of happiness, and we were brimming with confidence and enthusiasm for our main objective, the Ogre 2.

While recovering from our first climb we sat in the cook tent after dinner. Paul suddenly stood up. 'I've got a surprise,' he said and disappeared outside into the cold night air. He came back clutching a bottle of malt whisky he had secreted in his baggage. 'Did any of you meet Tom Patey?' he asked, a huge grin on his face.

We all shook our heads. Paul was the most interesting and wonderfully generous companion to share a camp with. If Ireland was Paul's motherland and Sheffield his base, then the North-West Highlands of Scotland was his spiritual home. He explained his special relationship with Tom Patey, the Ullapool doctor and mountaineer. 'I was younger by a decade and one of his disciples.'

We sat in awe as Paul told tales of the legendary Scottish climber who had pioneered scores of routes north of the border and went on successful expeditions to Rakaposhi and Mustagh Tower.

'We were in this small Scottish pub that smelt of burnt peat, cigarette smoke and wet wool pullovers,' Paul said, pouring the malt into four plastic mugs.

'Patey sat on a stool in the corner, regaling the drinkers crammed into the bar. He squeezed his accordion while singing songs, reciting poetry and telling tales of daring ascents on sea cliffs, icy gullies or far off mountains.' He paused with a wistful look. 'Of course, I enjoyed the climbs we did together, but it was as a raconteur and confidant that I will remember him most.'

Paul kept us entertained all evening, describing hot summers and snowy winters exploring Scotland's remote glens, hills, and coastline in search of exciting challenges. 'Patey became known as "Doctor Stack" when he initiated the ascent of The Old Man of Hoy in '66,' Paul continued. 'I got carried away in the sea stack mania and was with his group that made the first ascent of the Old Man of Stoer.'

Paul's mood changed, and he quietly described how he had been part of a five-person team that climbed The Maiden, a sea stack off the Sutherland coast. How, on this adventure in 1970, Patey was tragically killed as the result of an abseiling accident.

'Every barman in every pub greeted Tom like a long-lost friend.' Paul stared ahead with tears in his eyes. 'I saw him as an older person, yet he was only thirty-eight when he died. I think of him a lot.'

Patey instilled a deep love of Scotland in Paul, and every Whitsun holiday, his family and friends drove north to explore and enjoy the Highlands.

It was well past midnight when we retired to our tents. The whisky bottle stood empty on the table. With all the sentimental talk I went outside, feeling a long way from home. The crisp night was ablaze with the Milky Way slashed across the sky and, with the drink singing in my head, I thought of my loved ones in a far distant part of the world looking up at the same shining stars.

There is always a balance between relaxing at Base Camp and laziness. After three days, Al was impatient to have a serious attempt on the Ogre 2. As usual, our climbing rucksacks were enormous. Packed with a week's food and gas, technical climbing gear, ropes and bivouac gear, they each weighed thirty kilos. The misnomer of 'lightweight' alpine style!

In the morning, heavy clouds hung over the peaks, so we delayed our start. Having no contact with the outside world and only an altimeter to measure the atmospheric pressure, we had no way of predicting the weather. We went back to our tents to wait out the day when, Sod's Law, by mid-morning the clouds parted and we were bathed in sunshine. With a spare afternoon, I settled down to read my book, *The Magus* by John Fowles. Paul challenged Al to a game of chess although the result was never in doubt. Al always won. With his Cambridge maths degree and as a junior county chess champion, he could think many moves ahead and knew all the fancy gambits. Nevertheless, we kept trying to beat him, and it was an enjoyable way to pass the time.

Andy disappeared for a long walk and to sit on a rock, drawing the landscape. I did not know he was interested in art until I saw him unpack a sketchbook, pencil and crayons. He was very private about his work but, on this occasion, I surprised him. On the paper I could see matchstick figures busying themselves at base camp to a backdrop of abstract coloured crayon lines slashing the shade and light of bold mountain tops. Few would have predicted that this hobby would turn into a profession, and he would become a mountain artist and sculptor of the highest calibre.

Lean and taller than average, Andy had long light brown hair that dropped over his hollow cheeks, and piercing narrow eyes. A perfect build with an ideal power to weight ratio for high-level rock climbing, his bony torso seemed to survive on fresh air and water. At dinner, he would eat half the amount of my plateful. When he was not drawing, he would be climbing on the boulders surrounding the Base Camp. These granite blocks were three or four metres high and perfect for bouldering. Short enough to fall or jump from without a rope, yet of sufficient height to provide a strenuous workout. Andy and Al were the maestros and would create all manner of problems up the arêtes and walls. It was fun for everyone, and Paul and I would join in, usually failing where the other pair had so deftly led.

On 28th July, we finally set off for the Ogre 2, its summit over two thousand vertical metres above. The sky was full of stars which, with our pools of torchlight, illuminated the way up the steep glacier. In the frigid night air, the surface was bullet hard, and the snow bridges were safe to cross. A lemon light caressed the high tops as we reached a snow shelf. Above, an icy couloir promised straightforward access to a shoulder and the steep walls of the upper section of the mountain. We soloed for speed, hugging the shadows. The couloir was longer than I expected, but it was one of those days when my body felt full of vigour, and despite creaking calves, I was first to reach the shoulder. The others arrived as the sun hit the slopes. Even at that altitude the snow softened rapidly and, with each step, we sank to our knees. We decided to stop for the day. Tents had been rejected because of their weight. Instead, we had packed a lightweight shovel, and in unacceptably hot temperatures, laboured to construct a snow cave.

There was no possibility of climbing the overhanging and featureless rock walls behind our bivouac, but to the left the rock walls did look climbable. However, to reach them we had to traverse under an enormous bulging serac comprising of house-size blocks of aquamarine ice at crazy angles. At dawn, Paul led a lung-bursting dash across the mounds of avalanched debris, a deadly lottery during which an awful expectancy accompanied each step as we eyed what hung above. Sometimes you have to accept the risk and go for it.

There was a tangible release of tension two hours later when we were out of the firing line and making our way to the base of the steep walls. Here we found a perfect site for a second snow cave. Paul and I dug all afternoon while Andy and Al climbed and fixed a rope on several pitches up the steep icy cliffs to speed our ascent the following day. That evening we all had altitude headaches after our efforts, but were in high spirits, storytelling and eating our rations.

Paul had brought a small movie camera and filmed us cooking in the cave. Before leaving the UK he had, at the last minute, negotiated a deal with the BBC to provide regular news reports. It helped with the finances, but it took effort and rubbed against our original idea of a simple, non-commercial trip.

Paul and I had developed a growing interest in cinematography since working together on a film on Ben Nevis in 1979. The filmmakers, our mutual friends Jim Curran and Tony Riley, were inspired by the tale of the first ascent of *The Bat*, a challenging route climbed by Scottish climbing legends Dougal Haston and Robin Smith in 1959. We had recreated the story with Rab Carrington playing Smith and me taking Haston's role. Paul did all the rope safety and made sure nobody was injured in the name of art. Our biggest obstacle in making the film was persuading Rab to get his hair cut and bushy beard shorn off. The clean-shaven Rab was barely recognisable to his wife Sue, and I was shamed into visiting the barbers to get a short back and sides to fit in with the period look.

After waiting three days for torrential rain to stop, we slogged up the Allt a'Mhuilinn bogs (Paul three times), carrying mounds of equipment to camp below the Ben's cliffs. In the loads was enough beer and whisky to stock a bar. Rab was convinced that we had more gear than we took to climb Jannu, but it did enable us to get all the footage in a manic three days. The highlights were three staged falls, the first taken by me, which was nearly a disaster and could have ended Paul's burgeoning career in film safety. Before we started, there was a lively discussion about the lack of helmets in the 1950s but Paul reckoned that the fall would be into space and head injuries were unlikely – he hoped.

He had managed to get Tony Riley onto a ledge halfway up, to film close-ups of the action, leaving a rather hungover and emotional Jim Curran at the base to film from a tripod. I climbed twenty metres to an overhang, the climb's crux where the fall would start.

'Brian, pull some rope up,' Paul yelled. 'Rab, payout some slack.'

It was remiss that we did not measure the amount of slack rope more carefully, but we just wanted it to be spectacular! Rab expectantly held the old hawser rope in a traditional waist belay.

'Everybody ready? Cameras running . . . ACTION!'

I scrabbled for effect and let go, parting company from the rock and went screaming down, feeling the sudden adrenaline rush of falling. I expected to stop – but didn't!

'OH Noooooooooooooo . . .' The rock flashed past in a blur and I got a subliminal glimpse of the three of them on the ledge.

Something's wrong! The thought flashed through my mind.

Just as I was about to smash through Tony's camera lens, I jerked to a halt, and Rab shot into the air. It was chaos, with ropes everywhere, Tony was lying down, giving a good impression of a heart attack victim. Paul was laughing, and Rab and I were swearing. When the film was finished, Robin Smith's lyrical words from his classic article 'The Bat and the Wicked' described my bungled fall.

Then his fingers went to butter. It began under control as the bit of news, 'I'm off', but it grew like a wailing siren to a bloodcurdling scream as a black and bat-like shape came hurtling over the roof

with legs splayed like webbed wings and hands hooked like a
vampire . . . I could have sworn that his teeth were fangs and his
eyes were big red orbs.

High on the Ogre 2 the ground above the cave looked steep, and as
we set off the following day I wondered where we would be sleeping
next. The plan was for Al and Andy to lead and Paul and me to
follow, hauling the packs with our provisions. Each pitch took
hours of ferociously hard rock and ice climbing with loose sections
to add spice to the challenge, but the weather held fine. With less
than five hundred metres to the summit we were confident that we
would reach our goal in a day or two.

A smooth wall halted our progress. Al searched for a solution and
was forced rightwards onto chalk-like rock covered by great blankets of ice. The three of us stood like puffins balanced on a small
ledge, watching as he tiptoed across. The ice was barely attached to
the rock, and his axes boomed as they hit the hollow veneer. There
was hesitancy and doubt in his every move. It was midday and the
sun that had hit the face, usually welcome, was now our foe. Soon
the air was filled with a confetti of ice particles, then cascades of
water. Al hastily retreated to the ledge. We were conferring when
the massive plaque of ice he had been standing on creaked and slid
from the rock, falling into space and sending a fusillade of ice and
rock missiles to smash around us. With nowhere to hide and waiting
for the sun to disappear, and the ice to refreeze, we were forced to
retreat with all thoughts now on survival. We hastily abseiled back
to the snow cave, ducking and weaving to avoid the whistling
barrage. The sun was setting as we regained the cave, and ironically
the face fell ominously silent. The Ogre had fallen asleep.

'I've never known it so hot in the Karakoram,' Paul said.

'I don't want to climb in those conditions again,' Al replied.

'I was in a waterfall on that last abseil,' Andy remarked as he got
the stove going. 'Everything's soaked. The rope weighs a ton, and
when it freezes tonight, it will be unmanageable.'

'I'm not going up there again,' I added, 'but we can't go back
under that serac in these warm conditions. We need to find another
way down.'

It was deflating to descend in good weather when we had climbed three-quarters of the mountain. The only alternative retreat was to traverse a hanging ice shelf toward the col at the top of *Death Alley*. It was far more complicated than we thought and, as we descended, the whole mountain seemed to be falling apart in the heat, creating a worrisome orchestral cacophony of thunderous avalanches, whistling stone fall and crashing seracs. As we abseiled into the narrow glacial canyon of *Death Alley*, we knew we were committed to running the gauntlet of this giant, frozen gutter, overhung by tottering ice cliffs a hundred metres high, with the valley floor littered in their debris. Any avalanche would crush us like ants under a giant's boot.

Fortunately, the sun was still low in the sky, and the *Alley* now lay quiet in the shade. We continued our way through the litter of shattered ice blocks interspersed with knee-deep powder snow, mindful of what lurked above. Suddenly there was a deafening crack. Fearing the worst, I didn't know which way to run. High on the slopes there appeared a colossal spume of snow. The serac we had traversed under two days before had collapsed. Open-mouthed, we watched as the debris fell, thankfully far from where we stood but giving us a new sense of urgency. Finally, exhausted, we reached safety. Despite agreeing that we would be crazy to follow the same route again, we discussed whether our next attempt be the elegant North Ridge. Apart from the initial section up the *Alley* to the col, it looked appealing, snow-free granite and out of stone fall danger.

Al was determined to find an alternative to going up the *Alley*. On an exploratory excursion he spied a couloir coming down from the West Summit, and suggested this could be reached by following the South-West Buttress. He was sure this *Couloir Route* would be successful, but Paul and I thought it would suffer from the same meltwater and dangerous stone fall of our first route. We suggested trying the North Ridge. Al would have none of our protests. It was the first and last bad words of the expedition and Paul backed down in the face of his belligerence. After two days of rest, we would try his line.

While relaxing at camp, we often talked about our exploits. So, when Paul began storytelling we knew we were in for some entertainment. It was like listening to a eulogy for the climbing heroes of my youth.

'My first big trip away in 1970 was with Hamish MacInnes in the Caucasus.' Off he went, telling stories about a different world. 'Hamish led up this steep new route on the North Face of Pik Schurovsky. He used his latest invention, which he had just named the *Terrordactyl* ice axe.' Paul started laughing and became very animated, swinging his arms as he re-enacted placing the steep angled pick of this short axe into the ice. 'Our Russian friends were astonished by how fast we climbed.'

'Did the Russians copy the tools?' Al asked.

'Hell, no. The canny Scot kept them well hidden.'

'What was it like behind the Iron Curtain back then?'

'Bloody miserable and awful food – but the Russian climbers were great.'

'When did you go to Baffin Island?'

'In '72, that was my second expedition. It was brilliant climbing in the Arctic with Paul Braithwaite, Dennis Hennek and Doug Scott. So remote and we climbed a big thousand metre rock route on the east pillar of Asgard. Completely different to the Caucasus.'

His stories then moved to Russia in 1974, and a new route on the 7,135 metre Peak Lenin.

'The trouble was I got altitude sickness, and had to descend from 6,500 metres. I didn't get to the top.'

'Didn't you acclimatise properly?'

'Probably, but I've noticed that I acclimatise slowly. The trouble is that I got a reputation for not performing at altitude, and when all my mates were getting invites to Annapurna and Everest, I was ignored.'

'You were fine on the trip to Everest in winter,' Al said.

'Yes, I know, and that has given me a lot of confidence for future trips, Though I prefer to go to lower peaks – below 7000 metres. The trips are shorter, and I am away from the family for less time. As you know, I've been away most years to Pakistan and India. It helps that their summer season coincides with the academic holidays. Nepal's spring and autumn seasons clash with work.'

'It's bad when you get a reputation for something; it sticks with you for the rest of your life,' Al said. 'I got known as a party animal, drinking, smoking and taking drugs. I am sure that was a major reason why Boardman and Tasker were asked on trips to Everest and K2 by Bonington, and I was ignored.'

'Hey, after what happened between you and Joe Tasker on Everest in winter, I was amazed you went to Kongur together,' I said.

'That was a hard trip. I suppose I should have expected Bonington to tell me I couldn't join Joe and Pete on Everest's North East Ridge this year but, even so, I was pissed off. I am still annoyed.'

'At least you're still alive!' Paul laughed, and a hint of black humour lightened the conversation. We had heard the news of Tasker and Boardman's disappearance high on Everest just a few weeks before setting off on our journey to the Ogre 2.

With our rucksacks packed and ready to go the next day, we enjoyed a few hours bouldering around Base Camp. Paul lay on a foam mat watching the three of us climb, sensibly saving his energy for the mountain tomorrow. The banter was good, and inevitably the bouldering became competitive. Andy somehow managed to levitate himself onto a sloping ledge halfway up a boulder. Lying horizontal, he precariously pushed on one arm and, with a grunt, reached the top. A challenge had been set. Al was next and, with consummate ease, gymnastically completed the problem. My effort was less graceful but, after the third attempt, I lay on the ledge. I pushed with my arm and reached up. Suddenly my lower hand slipped and I fell in a horizontal position, hitting the ground with my outstretched arm. There was a sickening crunch, and a searing pain went through my collar bone. I writhed in agony as the three comforted me. Paul opened the medical kit, gave me some strong pain killers, and performed a weird manipulation shown in a diagram in our first aid book. I all but passed out when my collar bone relocated. I was angry, embarrassed and felt so stupid at injuring myself in pursuit of something so trivial. It would put me out of action for the rest of the trip.

In considerable pain, I wished them well as they set off in the pre-dawn half-light the next day. Envious, as I was sure they would reach the summit this time. Two days later, they arrived back, wide-eyed and full of tales of falling rocks and near misses.

'What happened?'

'Bloody stupid – I'm a clumsy bugger. I broke my crampons,' Paul said, wearily taking off his pack.

'The route was suicidal, so it was a good excuse to bail out,' Andy added.

'I can't believe how hot it was,' Al said. 'Same as last time, the mountain was falling apart. I'm soaked, and falling rocks have damaged the ropes.'

'Is that it then? Or are you going to have another attempt?'

'I need a good night's sleep and some food before I can think straight,' Paul replied.

Over a breakfast of porridge, chapatis and jam, we discussed a plan. 'I'm keen for one more try,' Al, optimistic as ever suggested. 'We have five days before the porters arrive and we must leave Base Camp.'

'We should go up *Death Alley* and try the North Ridge,' Paul suggested.

'It can't be as bad as the route we just tried,' Andy replied. 'There might be gear left from the Korean's, which could speed things up.'

'Good luck,' I said, troubled at what might await them. 'While you have the last attempt, I'm going to start walking out. I'll be slow, and if you do not catch me up before Skardu, I'll wait there.'

The rest of the day was a flurry of activity as the climbing team prepared for the last attempt, and I packed to leave. I was unable to carry a rucksack, so our cook, Ali Mohammad, accompanied me. Walking down the glacier, I looked back on the Ogre 2 and *Death Alley*, worrying about what lay ahead for my friends. Being separated gave me a different perspective, an acute awareness of the risk they were taking – far more than if I was with them, at the heart of the action. It made me realise how helpless our friends and loved ones must feel when we depart for the mountains.

After six weeks on the mountain, Skardu's K2 Motel seemed like the height of luxury. I stood in a hot shower for an age as the spray caressed my body, and a pool of scum sloshed around my feet.

Finally, I dried myself on clean towels that felt rough on my skin and sank into a padded mattress with a pillow to rest my head.

I awoke with a start. Ali stood by the bed with a tray of food. 'Do you want to join me for a beer, Ali?'

'Oh no, Mr Brian – it is forbidden for a Muslim in Pakistan; the penalty is eighty lashes.'

The light was fading as the haunting voice of the mu'addin's call to pray for Salat al-'asr echoed from a nearby mosque's minaret. A harmony that was a coincidental welcome for the three old jeeps carrying the team, which drove through the hotel gates. I was elated. They had made it, but had they reached the summit?

Covered in dust, like a group of wild-west desperados, they greedily drank their first bottles of beer for weeks. A pungent animal odour surrounded them, an odd assault on my senses, accentuated by my recent re-acquaintance with soap and water. Between gulps of beer, they related their last attempt.

'As we reached the end of *Death Alley*, a huge serac collapsed. It was weird because we saw it before we heard anything. It was like a gigantic bomb.' Al spoke with a manic stare piercing his glasses.

'We all ran sideways to get out of the fall line, but the rope caught on blocks of ice,' Paul explained. 'We were like chained dogs as this white veil swept towards us, filling the whole width of the narrow glacier. I thought – this is it.'

'I don't know how it missed us,' Al continued. 'There was no time to think – a wave of cold powder snow swept over us. I expected pain, but everything went still and, as the mist settled, we stood amongst all the debris, bewildered, covered from head to foot in fine white powder snow.'

'So, was that the end of the attempt. Did you come down?'

'It sounds stupid, but no – we had almost reached the col at the start of the North Ridge, so we carried on. It was the fastest way to get out of danger and have a think,' Paul replied.

'Did you climb the Ridge?'

'Hell, no! As soon as we reached safety, my legs went weak. I'd had enough. I told Al and Andy to carry on without me, but we stuck together and stumbled back down the *Alley* as fast as we could.'

We had open tickets for the flight back home, but the seats were booked solid for weeks. I was getting married in two weeks but, having bowed to my parent's wishes for a church ceremony, was now worried I would not make it. Guests had been invited, party venues booked, and, of course, Louise had planned a fantastic honeymoon to Sri Lanka . . . but here I was, stuck in the steaming heat of Islamabad.

'Don't worry. Delays always happen,' Paul reassured me as we walked into the air-conditioned bar of the British Embassy Club. 'I need to get back to work, so we will have to make plans.'

'Four beers, please,' Paul asked the barman. I greedily drank from the cold glass as he left to sit in a corner with three middle-aged gentlemen sporting smart shorts (with creases) and polo shirts.

'Cheers,' said Al, realising that Andy had disappeared outside, next to the swimming pool with a group of women looking gorgeous in swimwear. I heard laughter as he settled into a story.

'Another round of beers,' Al suggested, when Paul returned.

'All sorted,' Paul announced with a cheeky grin. 'The British Airways Captain over there said if we turn up at the airport tomorrow he will make sure we get on the flight.' With that joyous news, we joined Andy and the female cabin crew with the prospect of some serious fun.

At the airport, the captain was true to his word, and we got on the flight. As we boarded, we all turned right. 'Mr Nunn?' The stewardess asked, and led Paul to the front of the plane. The cunning bugger had wrangled a Business Class seat.

Back at home, it usually took me weeks to become accustomed to civilisation, but I had no time to adjust to the wedding. Louise was relieved to see me and had a long list of jobs for me to do, but was dismayed that my injury stopped me. I had lost a lot of weight, and my only suit for the wedding hung off me like a poorly dressed charity shop dummy. I was comfortable with my long hair, but Louise told me that it was too unkempt. Back to the real world!

The wedding, the party in the pub and the honeymoon were perfect, enjoyable and memorable. Al Rouse was my best man, with Andy and Paul at the heart of the celebrations. After taking risks, the world takes on a different perspective, and provides a sense of what is important and the futility of trivial arguments. The deprivation of living in the mountains reinvigorates the appetite for enjoyment and somehow makes life more relaxing and fulfilling.

Paul slotted straight back into the centre of British climbing affairs. It amazed me how he could juggle so many balls in the air: father, husband, senior lecturer at university, rock climber, mountaineer and writer. In addition, he sat on many important committees at the Alpine Club, the Mount Everest Foundation and the British Mountaineering Council. Habitually he would spend the weekends away in a climbing area such as Snowdonia, the Lake District or Cornwall along with visiting his spiritual retreat of the Highlands of Scotland during Whitsun.

The climbing press had a crucial role in the development of climbing through the '70s and '80s. They spread news, opinions and hosted articles from the worlds top climbers. Paul was a vociferous supporter and on the editorial team of the influential British magazine *Mountain* from its conception in 1969. At first, alongside the founder, Ken Wilson, then later, with his close friend, Tim Lewis, when he took the helm. *Mountain* became the bi-monthly bible for climbers, promoting debate on the important climbs of the day with analysis of style and ethics. As a result, there was a significant shift in the way climbs were viewed. The method of ascent became as important as the ascent itself.

Typically, a phone call from Ken Wilson would be long and like an inquisition from a private detective. 'Did you use any aid? How many pitches did you fix? So, was it a *capsule* ascent or alpine style? Have you got photos of the face you climbed? A summit shot?'

Mountain also stimulated rock climbing and mountaineering development by publishing photo spreads of cliffs, mountain faces, and unclimbed summits. For example, a series of panoramic shots showed the North faces around Chamonix, with lines marking all the routes. Implicitly, these photos indicated all the gaps where nobody had climbed, encouraging new routes.

I frequently met Paul on Stanage Edge for a relaxed evening of gritstone climbing. On one occasion in the autumn of 1994 he was cock-a-hoop. He had just returned from his seventeenth expedition, this one to the remote Kinnaur region in the Indian Himalaya, where he'd had a renaissance at the age of fifty. It was an Anglo-Indian trip jointly led by Harish Kapadia, the driving force in Indian mountaineering, and Chris Bonington, who, at almost sixty, was still committed to exploratory mountaineering. They made the first ascent of the *Unknown Mountain*, which they christened Rangrik Rang (6,553 metres and an ascent of Manirang (6,593 metres). He regarded this expedition as one of his most fulfilling times in the mountains, particularly the rapport with the Indian mountaineers.

Life was good for Paul. He was thrilled to have been elected President of the British Mountaineering Council, one of the leading roles in climbing management, and was bursting with ideas to make it a friendlier and more democratic organisation. With one of the brightest minds I have encountered and a prodigious ability for hard work, I had no doubt he would succeed.

Despite travelling the world over, the Karakoram remained Paul's favourite mountain range. The trip in 1995 to the unclimbed Haramosh II (6,666 metres) was a low-key affair by a group of experienced mountaineers: Paul Nunn, Geoff Tier, Brian Davison, Colin Wells and Dave Wilkinson. Apart from Paul, two others were close friends; Tier lived in the same village as me, and I had spent the summer of '86 on K2 with Wilkinson. They were a mature group, continuing their enthusiasm for the major mountain ranges by attempting smaller unclimbed peaks on a relaxed lightweight holiday style expedition. Unlike many better funded super-trips, they organised it all themselves, with no costly agents to buy supplies, arrange transport and hire porters. It was a proper and fulfilling adventure filled with elation at exploring unknown valleys and mountains with no trails or habitation.

Wilkinson remembers them figuring out whether they could afford the trip. 'We worked out the cost by a straightforward calculation which was termed *Nunn's Law*. Paul proposed that the net cost per head of any expedition is about "a thousand quid". Of course, bigger and more distant objectives were more expensive, but *Nunn's Law* recognised that the scope for external funding was also greater, thus leaving the net cost roughly constant. Paul was insistent that if a trip costs more, then there's something wrong with its objective, style or planning.'

On the way to Skardu, he met one of his old and trusted Balti friends, Ghulam Nabi, touting for work. They had found the sirdar for their expedition and hired twenty-four porters. The four-day walk-in was through beautiful ablation valleys full of woods and pastures along the edge of the Chogo Lungma glacier. Then, a trying ten-day wait for bad weather to clear at Base Camp was enlivened by their home-brewed beer reaching its alcoholic state, even though it tasted of vinegar.

Wilkinson shared a tent with Paul. 'This did not give me a relaxing period of stasis, but an interesting one. Paul's convoluted arguments and credibility-stretching opinions were, at the same time, a bizarre mixture of mental stimulation and an infuriating drain on my patience.'

Eventually, they set off up a snow ridge with heavy loads, traversing under several seracs which they thought looked of little consequence. The ground levelled, and they bivouacked in two small tents. A snowstorm enforced a rest day, but by evening the weather had cleared. They left camp at midnight in two teams planning to push to the top and back in one day. The first group of three reached the unclimbed summit at 10.00a.m. and the second pair of Nunn and Tier arrived a couple of hours later. They descended slowly on the sun-softened snow, reaching their previous night's bivouac by mid-afternoon. After a brew, they decided to continue down. Nearing the mountain's base, the two groups were descending separately, out of sight but within earshot and the first rope of three reached the safety of their small Advanced Base Camp in the late afternoon sun. Exhausted but content after the day's efforts, they quietly relaxed in their tents, dozing and drinking tea while waiting for the other pair to appear.

Suddenly the peace was broken by the crash of falling ice. At first, it seemed a routine matter but, when the noise died away, the silence was ominous. With mounting worry, the three hurried to a ridge where they could view their descent route. Scanning the slope, they could see their footprints crossed by a mass of car-sized ice blocks below a serac high on the mountain. There was no sign of Nunn or Tier. Their fate was clear.

'The light faded as we stood in dumb witness to this icy grave of our friends,' Wilkinson wrote later. 'If mountaineers must die in action, this wild spot would be a fitting burial place.'[1]

Nunn and Tier would have been safely back in Advanced Base Camp if that avalanche had broken a few minutes before or after. The team considered their route no more dangerous than a classic alpine route. This accident was sheer bad luck, for these men were older and conservative, not driven to take undue risks.

Wilkinson continued, 'Unlike some types of climbing, big mountains have not been made safe by technology; they remain an adventure. We would not wish it otherwise. Paul and Geoff were intelligent men; they knew the risks and accepted them as part of something they loved. So, sad though we are, we also must accept the consequences of their adventuring.'

When I received the news of Paul's death, I was devastated. With his generosity of spirit, his wily and shrewd judgement, he was the least likely person to die in the mountains, which made it all the harder to accept.

---

1. Alpine Journal 1997 'Success and Tragedy on Haramosh II'

Alex MacIntyre at Leeds, early 70s.

LIGHTWEIGHT REVOLUTION
Alex MacIntyre (Part 2)

While I had been climbing in the Andes and Himalyas through the late '70s and early '80s Alex MacIntyre had been constantly active in the high mountains.

With heavy loads shouldered, John Porter, Voytek Kurtyka and Alex MacIntyre walked to the head of a remote Afghan valley where they traversed a desolate glacier to pitch their Base Camp. Their objective was the obelisk of Koh-e Bandaka, a mountain made of dangerously rotten rock capped with icy slopes overhung by a huge cornice. When the morning sun hit, a bombardment of falling stones whistled down the 2,800 metre high North East Face, the teams' intended route, triggering Alex's, long held, morbid fear of rockfall.

The expedition in the summer of 1977 had its origin two years earlier, when the British Mountaineering Council (BMC) and the Polish Mountaineering Association held two international exchange meets in North Wales and the Polish Tatra. Porter helped organise these meets and became friends with Voytek Kurtyka and Andrez Zawada. Kurtyka was already an outstanding Polish alpinist and Himalayan climber at a young age, while Zawada was the leading expedition organiser in Poland. They dreamt up the idea of an Anglo-Polish expedition to Koe-e Mandaras (6,625 metres) in the Hindu Kush of Afghanistan. Five Brits, including Alex MacIntyre, who had just graduated from university, were invited. It would be John Porter's and Alex MacIntyre's first expedition.

It was a mutually beneficial exchange as the British supplied the cash, which was changed on the Polish black market to pay for transport and food, Their ten-day journey to Afghanistan was far from easy, travelling via Warsaw and Moscow in dirty Russian diesel trains followed by battered ex-military trucks across Afghanistan. Because the route was banned to foreign travellers outside the Iron Curtain, the British were smuggled across the Soviet Union on false papers disguised as Poles. The omens did not improve as they watched Russian tanks gather on the Afghan border.

Voytek had become frustrated by the heavy-handed methods of large expeditions and wanted to encourage small, lightweight alpine style trips. Negotiating with the leader, Zawada, he arranged a breakaway group, persuading Porter and MacIntyre to join him on Koh-e Bandaka (6,812 metres). The splinter group reached Base Camp and nervously readied for their climb.

Examining the vast face over three days they began to doubt their sanity until, slowly, Porter and Kurtyka came to terms with the dangers. Alex was still worried. At home he had frequently talked about his fear of falling rocks as though foreshadowing death, as if he knew the gods wanted him for their own, and he could not escape his fate.

Porter described his mood. 'Alex seemed to be in a state of near panic. He sat in his tent much of the day listening to music, rocking back and forth. He described his fear of falling stones to me several times. But, of course, I tried to laugh it off.'

They decided to start and packed the minimum of food and equipment. Even so, they struggled under the weight of their ridiculously heavy rucksacks, with every step taking them closer to the continuous onslaught of bullet-like stones. Porter was troubled. 'The opening couloir was a gateway to a hellish world, one of darkness, fear and continuous threat.' Kurtyka described it as, 'the gates of Mordor.'

The next day Porter considered the risks to be barely justifiable. 'Like old marble cake, without doubt, the most dangerous climbing any of us had ever done – an entire twenty-foot rock rib suddenly dissolved beneath Alex's feet and the crumbs fanned out across the wall beneath.'

Relief came each day at 1.00p.m., when the sun moved off the face and the temperature plummeted, freezing the stones in place. They climbed in a rhythm of Porter and Kurtyka leading and Alex at the back, seemingly content to follow. There was some respite on the fourth day when the rock quality improved and the angle eased. Every night was full of stars, and with each dawn the sky turned deep blue. They reached the top ice fields, overhung by the ominous cornice but, by the sixth day, their strength and food were almost at an end. The ice field was straightforward, alas, the daunting cornice of ice hung above them. Kurtyka craned his neck, searching for an alternative way through the impasse, and Alex joined him at the stance.

Porter relived the moment, 'Alex clipped onto the ice screw belay, smiled and looked up, saying, "My turn, guys". Alex had woken up. We were now in his domain.' He set off to tackle the formidable cornice and, after much grunting and cursing, was seen high above, in profile against the sky.

'Then Alex rolled onto his back, swung his Terrordactyl and took a comforting bite into the hard ice above. His arse hung in space for a moment, then he gyrated up and out of sight, and we heard a distant, muffled shout of elation.'

For Porter, his first Himalayan climb was a baptism of fire. 'We almost didn't climb Bandaka because Alex was not mentally prepared. Kurtyka and I had to help him through. He was not ready for the Himalayas. Strangely, I was more adapted, despite not having climbed as many hard alpine routes.'

In Alex's case, never had Nietzsche's words been more apt: 'What does not kill me makes me stronger.'

On returning from the Hindu Kush, Alex teamed up with talented American climber Tobin Sorenson in an attempt on the 1800 metre *Harlin Direct* route on the North Face of the Eiger. The harrowing first ascent in the winter of 1966 was siege climbed over a month with the aid of fixed ropes but, tragically, the American lead climber, John Harlin, was killed when a falling stone cut the rope he was hanging from. MacIntyre and Sorenson planned to make the first ascent in alpine style, deciding to make an out-of-season attempt in the autumn and so avoid the stone fall of summer and the deep freeze of winter. This timing proved to be fortuitous, and they climbed the route over five days, setting a precedent as, nowadays it is the norm to climb the North Face in spring or autumn. Of the dozens of routes on the Eiger, many people regard the *Harlin* as the hardest, and the pair's achievement was recognised as an advance in alpinism. Alex planned many more adventures with his new friend. They were not to be. In 1980 he was stunned to learn that Sorenson had fallen to his death while climbing alone on Canada's Mount Alberta.

About that time, Pete Boardman left his post as the National Officer of the BMC and some of the top young British mountaineers were interviewed for the vacancy, including Porter, MacIntyre and Rouse. The BMC chose MacIntyre and, at the time, I thought, 'How could *Dirty Alex* take a proper white-collar job?'

After graduating, he had enjoyed a lifestyle of late-night drinking, mixed with full-throttle climbing in Afghanistan and on the Eiger. Somehow he made it work, proving us all wrong and taking a huge stride in his quest to become a professional mountaineer. The post afforded him respectability and gave him a voice that reached far beyond his personal circle.

I was not the only one surprised at how well Alex fitted in. The General Secretary, Dennis Gray, remembered, 'He was so different to his predecessor, Boardman; he was more up front, more argumentative in stressing his views, and more aggressive. But, on the other hand, his background of being a law graduate was good at helping to form direction and policies, and he had a very sharp intellect. He was easy to work with, and many of the younger generations of activists appeared to agree that if someone like *Dirty Alex* could work for the BMC, it was a body worth supporting!'

He moved to Manchester in 1978 and rented a room from Maria, the sister of Irish climber Mick Coffey, so she was familiar with the social side of climbing. 'A good friend got in contact. He said a mate was looking for a room and heard I might have one to rent. He added he was a really good bloke, and by the way, he's called *Dirty Alex*!'

Not surprisingly, Maria thought the worst but, when he came

round, 'We got on like a house on fire. I loved his energy and cheekiness. He had twinkly eyes and the best grin. He was just very smart and funny.' They became close friends. 'Alex was very sweet to me but also extremely argumentative. He would argue the back leg off a donkey about nothing. He had very strong opinions and a lawyer's clever incisive wit and intelligence. Most of all, I found him kind, and many people did not see that side of him. They just saw the cheeky wild Alex.'

Maria had started a relationship with mountaineer Joe Tasker while, at the same time, Alex's relationship with his long-term girl-friend, Gwyneth, was disintegrating. One evening, while Tasker was away, they were having dinner together when, out of the blue, he said: 'Your bloke's away, and I'm single, so why don't we get together and you can use my car!'

Maria started to laugh and immediately he retorted, 'What's funny? My car's a lot better than yours.'

'He was totally serious.' Maria recalls fondly. 'He felt like an annoying little brother. But I had no interest, apart from friendship.'

After Afghanistan, John Porter moved to the Lake District where he organised gatherings of the Leeds alumni. Alex gave me a lift on one occasion, and we climbed on the nearby crags, followed by the usual alcoholic evening and an all-night poker game. The weekend ended when we were both worse for wear after the Sunday lunch-time session. He put his foot down on the road home, turned up Led Zeppelin on the cassette player, and drove too fast. There was a loud thump as we hit some debris on the road and punctured both front tyres. Applying inebriated logic, he continued driving for ten miles to a friend's house in Kendal. It was a rough ride with an acrid smell of burning rubber and a lot of noise. The following day we completed the journey by train.

Although we were in the same circle of friends, there were wheels within wheels. Alex shared his aspirations with Porter and the Poles, whereas mine were with Rouse, Carrington and Baxter-Jones. As it turned out, both teams were going through the laby-rinth of bureaucracy to secure permission to climb separate peaks in the autumn of 1978. Alex and Porter dealt with the Indians to climb Changabang, whereas we contended with the Nepalese for Jannu.

John Porter and Alex eventually got permission to climb the stunning granite tower of Changabang in the Nanda Devi sanctuary. It had its first ascent in 1974 when Chris Bonington, Doug Scott and Dougal Haston reached the summit by a snow and ice route up the south-east side. Two years later, Pete Boardman and Joe Tasker took almost a month to ascend the West Face in a revolutionary ascent that overcame sustained difficulties and showed what was possible for a two-person team on a high Himalayan face. The Anglo-Polish expedition would try the South Buttress in alpine style, which looked like an even steeper and harder challenge.

The trip was organised in a similar fashion as their Afghan expedition of the previous year, reuniting Alex and Porter with Kurtyka, together with a new addition, Krzysztof Zurek, a compact and powerful Pole with unkempt black hair and an impressive climbing pedigree.

This time they managed to fly and did not have to face the overland ordeal, but had a real struggle with the Indian authorities in Delhi, who surprisingly revoked their permission. The Indians had unexpectedly closed the area after discovering that a 1960's American expedition, in collusion with the CIA, had secretly placed an electronic listening device high on Nanda Devi. It was nuclear powered, and they thought an avalanche had swept it into the sacred River Ganges. After a week of delicate negotiations, the team regained permission and set off in the monsoon. At the roadhead, they hired local porters and walked the remote and challenging approach through the precipitous Rishi Gorge.

Over eleven days, they climbed their highly technical route. Unlike on Bandaka the year before, the rock was solid granite and the line followed tenuous cracks separated by blank walls that demanded some of the most difficult rock climbing ever attempted at high altitude. Some nights they found small ledges to sleep on, and three nights in a row used hammocks, specially designed by Alex, suspended from the vertical walls. Hanging in space, they cooked their frugal meals on experimental gas stoves. The weather was clear in the mornings, but it snowed most afternoons. At least the wall was south-facing so, when the sun shone, its warmth made a considerable difference to the ambience and to climbing conditions.

On the seventh day Alex, exhausted, clipped into the wrong end of a rope while shuttling loads up and down and fell the entire fifty metre rope length. He was lucky to survive. By the eighth day, Zurek became delirious and weak with an undiagnosed illness that rapidly deteriorated. With the barely conscious Zurek a passenger on the edge of survival, they struggled to the summit totally spent. It took two more days to get down and, after a few days, they recovered enough to walk back to civilisation.

At the BMC, Alex continued the tradition of inviting foreign climbers to Britain, this time a French group. Whenever British alpinists met their French counterparts, they were taunted with: 'How do you climb so well when you have no mountains?' Alex hoped they would find out on a fortnight's marathon of ice climbing in Scotland.

On the drive up, when our French friends were asleep in the back of the minibus, he quietly explained to me. 'The first night, we'll drink in the Clachaig, in Glencoe.'

'It will be interesting to see how they like the beer. Scottish heavy is not like French beer,' I replied.

'We'll not bother cooking. A fish supper from the Fort William chippy should be fine. Then an early morning fried breakfast at the cafe.'

'I wonder whether they know about the knee-deep peat bogs on the walk-in to Ben Nevis?'

'That should sort them out, and none of this fine wine, croissants, espressos and cable cars!' Alex laughed and drove into the night,

The six French lads, mostly Alpine guides, proved to be made of sterner stuff. So much so that we struggled to keep up with their incendiary pace on the walk-in, but what a week we had climbing classics and finishing long multi-route days by the light of head torches. Though the trip had a competitive edge, the teams won each other's respect and lifelong friendships were made on the ice of Ben Nevis, Creag Meagaidh and Lochnagar.

Alex climbed with an extremely fit young Chamonix guide named René Ghilini, forging a close relationship that led to ascents in the Himalayas. Taller than Alex but just as muscular, he had a thin face with a handsome aquiline nose and mid-length fair hair.

Our newfound friends now understood how we could suffer the cold and climb so adeptly in torchlight, but never converted to the local cuisine of deep-fried food and warm pints of beer.

Among Alex's many friends was an Irish climber called Terry Mooney, a well-built, square-jawed Belfast man. Terry was a barrister of the highest calibre, called to the Irish bar in 1971[1]. Their friendship grew with mutual admiration and a brotherly bond. Alex admired Terry's legal mind, and Terry was smitten by Alex's mountaineering exploits. He specialised in criminal law and walked a dangerous tightrope, working with Catholics and Protestants, being either their best friend or worst enemy. This conflict led to a secretive life requiring a certain amount of protection from big men with guns due to the longstanding sectarian Troubles.

On occasions, Terry invited us to visit Northern Island, where he was an ideal host due to his profession bestowing a deep pocket to meet the bar bills. In those days, the city's roads were strewn with barricades, soldiers stood on every corner, menacing armoured trucks patrolled the streets, and buildings were daubed with political graffiti. On our first evening, Terry took us to a bar, the front of which was entirely covered by a metal grill and barbed wire. He knocked on the steel door, and a letterbox slit opened. Two wide eyes peered out and a bout of Irish banter was followed by the sound of bolts being slid open. The bar was mayhem, full, exclusively of men, singing, shouting, jostling and drinking Guinness like there was no tomorrow.

The next day we set off on a drunken, climbing, road trip, starting in Ballycastle, where we visited the fantastic cliffs of Fairhead before moving to Donegal. I climbed with John Porter

---

1. In 1985, Terry became one of Britain's youngest QC's but still kept in touch with the mountaineering world, becoming a trustee for Doug Scott's charity, Community Action Nepal (CAN).

and later met up with Alex and Terry, who had spent all day in the bar. It was a strange trip with a continual feeling of embarrassment at being English, and an undercurrent of danger although everyone seemed friendly. Especially when holding a pint of Guinness in their hand with a lively Irish fiddle band playing in the corner.

Later in 1979 I stood, balanced on the back of a smoke-belching brightly painted cattle truck with Al Rouse by my side, next to crates of squealing guinea pigs ready for market. We were heading to the mountain town of Huaraz, a scruffy but friendly place ideally situated in a beautiful wide valley below the Cordillera Blanca of the Peruvian Andes. We'd been on a French expedition, further south in the Andes, with the ridiculously hard objective of traversing the entire skyline of the Cordillera Huayhuash. In this we failed, but did make the first ascent of Sacre Grande Oeste (5,774 metres) and two satisfying new routes on Trapecio (5,664 metres) and Ninashanca (5,610 metres). With spare time before flying home we hitched to Huaraz and the half-finished Hotel Barcelona.

The ground floor entrance had a semblance of normality, but the open top floor consisted of concrete walls sprouting metal rebar, bare electric wires, with a single cold tap and a toilet that did not flush. It was here that the hotel owner, Pepe, let the *andinista* climbers stay for a pittance and here that I immediately spotted Alex asleep on a foam mat dressed only in a discoloured pair of underpants. His boney torso was surrounded by climbing gear, empty glasses and a half-eaten rotisserie chicken carcass. Next to him lounged Terry Mooney, reading a paperback with a beer bottle grafted to his hand. The hotel had become like an enclave of Chamonix due to many of our climbing friends coming to the Andes that year including Tut Braithwaite, John Porter and Choe Brooks.

For our generation, the Andes were a crucial step between the Alps and the Himalayas. Treks were relatively short and the peaks, at around 6,000 metres, were high enough to experience altitude depravation but not so high as to occasion serious illness. Elegant summits with new and exciting unclimbed objectives added spice to our visits.

Alex and John Porter had just climbed a new route on the South

Face of Nevada III on steep waves of fluted snow. Beautiful on postcards, but a nightmare to climb.

John mused, 'It's difficult to explain how it forms, and how it sticks to the face, but the snow in the bed between these flutes usually has the consistency of feather pillows, while further out is like cane sugar.'

Alex, a magician on snow, suggested, 'Think light . . . like a fairy.'

New to the higher peaks, our group soon realised that climbing at altitude was incredibly debilitating. Alex demonstrated his wonderful writing style in his *Mountain* magazine article 'Broken English', amusingly explained his favoured way of acclimatising: by drinking large quantities of beer.

> The alternative approach and one better founded in reason, if not in medical opinion, concentrates on the brain. Brain training should not be undertaken lightly. I have heard it said by cynics that the only people who benefit are the breweries. Not so, sir! Climbing at altitude is somewhat akin to going to work with a monster hangover. Once the art of operating under such conditions has been mastered, the problem is licked. Otherwise known as Mooney's Law, this approach carries other benefits. The mass destruction of brain cells prior to one's arrival in the Zone of Death leaves less for the non-atmosphere to work on, and the general state of ill health attained throughout the year ensures that the body is well accustomed to the notion of oxygen deficiency, bordering on asphyxiation. Brain training is, unfortunately, expensive.

Although he persisted with his hangover theory, Alex was fastidious in his acclimatisation. On reaching a base camp, he would ascend as high as possible on easy training climbs, forcing his body to adapt and stimulating the creation of red blood cells. After all, the tactic of the alpine style climber was to get up and down as fast and light as possible before body and mind succumbed to oxygen starvation.

In 1980, Alex left the BMC for a life as a full-time mountaineer, planning to make ends meet by working as an equipment design consultant, giving public lectures, and writing articles. He also hoped that his silver tongue would persuade companies to sponsor expeditions such as his next project, the first ascent of the East Face of Dhaulagiri (8,167 metres) in Nepal with Voytek and another Pole, Ludwik Wiczyczynski. The fourth member of this international team was the Frenchman René Ghilini, with whom Alex had climbed in Scotland. It was the beginning of Alex's ventures above eight thousand metres, a height which has been labelled the death zone, where oxygen pressure is so low that the human body cannot survive for more than a few days.

After two lightweight attemps they reached the summit, Alex's first success on one of the world's fourteen peaks above eight thousand metres. It also consolidated his penchant for climbing with foreign climbers, an unusual practice in a time of mainly national expeditions.

The life as a top mountaineer now consumed him although, on the exterior, he appeared to be the same *Dirty Alex* of university days. In truth, he had become fastidious about preparation, understanding that he had to put in long hours of effort outside his comfort zone. Not only that, but he became convinced that each climb needed to be harder and longer, with a greater physical or mental test requiring more self-belief. Adventures had to be undertaken regularly to adapt body and mind to the challenges of the mountains. Unfortunately, the rollercoaster of one expedition after another exposed him to greater risks, and he would have to rely on the help of something outside his control: luck.

After Alex's relationship with Gwyneth floundered, while at Maria Coffey's house in Manchester she introduced him to Sarah Richards ' . . . a close friend, and we all went out for a drink.'

'Alex asked if we could meet again, and for some reason I agreed,' Sarah recalls. 'I cannot say he made much of an impression on me. He was little, scruffy and a bit brash.'

Maria remembers differently. 'The spark between them was incredible. I watched them fall in love. It changed him.'

Sarah moved into Alex's small *chalet* in Hayfield, in the Peak District. 'He was very hedonistic. Exciting to be around,' she says, 'but it was a good mixture because he could also be very driven and focused.'

Alex again joined Kurtyka in the spring of 1981, together with his compatriot Jerzy Kukuczka, a formidable mountaineer and grandee of Polish climbing [2]. The trio's objective was one of the great prizes of world mountaineering, the unclimbed West Face of Makalu, fifth highest mountain in the world at 8,485 metres. They were going into unknown territory on an icy granite wall, of a greater level of difficulty than anything attempted previously. The two Poles had more experience in the *death zone* than Alex, but they knew his rare talent would complement their experience.

Their pre-monsoon attempt was a failure. A combination of poor weather and poor conditions forced them to abandon below seven thousand metres. In the autumn they returned with renewed determination, acclimatising for a month on the avalanche-prone, normal route, eventually bivouacking at eight thousand metres and placing a supply dump on their descent route.

They climbed the lower part of the West Face but, on the evening of the third day, Alex received a severe blow to the head from a falling lump of ice. His helmet saved him but, soon after, the attempt was halted at 7,900 metres. Six hours of sustained effort had yielded only forty metres of progress and they had fallen seriously behind schedule. The steep rock and ice required more technical equipment than they could carry. They had, quite simply, reached a barrier. The increased weight of their rucksacks slowed them, hence more supplies were needed to sustain the extra time spent on the mountain, slowing them down further. Had they, perhaps, found the inevitable limit of alpine style climbing? For Alex, it was a problem to solve, not an endpoint.

At home though, Sarah noticed that successive trips without sufficient recuperation were starting to tell. When he told her about the narrow escape when he was hit by falling ice she ' . . . took

---

2. Kukuczka was locked in a battle with Reinhold Messner to become the first person to ascend all the world's 8000-metre peaks. Messner won the 'race' in 1986, but some hold Kukuczka in higher esteem due to many of his ascents being new routes or climbed in winter.

the piss out of him at first, which was part of our way with each other,' but he replied, 'You don't realise what it is like being hit on the head. It's not funny.'

He was diagnosed with concussion and shock. Sarah saw that he was tired and depressed and pondered whether this was because of his torment with falling stones and ice or because Makalu had been his first big failure.

Alex confided to her that before this injury he had never understood or had truck with people being depressed and low, which he saw as self-indulgent. 'I think after the blow to his head he became more aware of his fallibility and more understanding and empathetic to others' foibles.'

The debate in the press, particularly in *Mountain* magazine, raged between the old school and the new wave. Alex was pragmatic and accepted that many people favoured heavyweight expeditions, but it was not for him. His challenge was in alpine style. By operating at the limit, failures were inevitable.

Fifteen years later, in 1997, the Makalu's West Face was climbed by a large Russian expedition. They had won the race using fixed rope and nine camps. Many would argue it was an inevitable conquest, succeeding because they threw enough resources at the problem. Morally though, it gave the mountain no chance. The view that climbers needed to treat mountains with respect became a basic premise of the alpine style ideology. MacIntyre and Kurtyka thought mountains had a persona and should be treated like friends, or sometimes as foes, but always with reverence, a partner in the exploit.

Kurtyka, the idealist, was passionate about this, 'For Alex and me, alpine style meant a way of life and a state of consciousness that allowed us to fall in love with the mountain and, in consequence, trust our destiny to it unconditionally.' Later he would call that the *State of Nakedness*, which meant lightness, defencelessness and confidence, adding, 'This moment of entrusting was usually preceded by a torment of doubt and fear. But even this gave an enriching experience and insight. Perhaps this is why, paradoxically, alpine style in the Himalayas results in comparatively few mishaps.'

It was true that until the 1980s, there were few deaths while alpine style climbing, whereas the heavyweight expeditions were littered with fatalities and we naturally thought our lightweight method was the way forward. Sadly, in the first half of the '80s, this view would be challenged as numerous individuals died climbing alpine style in the high mountains.

Alex was realistic, and in an interview published in the magazine *Alpinismus*, said, 'Climbing a virgin wall in the Himalayas is like breaking through into the enemy trenches, trying to choose that path which avoids a bullet, an explosion, a mine or a sniper. You know you have to run, be skilful and brave, but you don't know if it is in your own hands to survive.'

The huge unclimbed face on the remote south-west side of the 8,012 metre Shishapangma in Tibet was next on his agenda. He told Sarah, 'Don't worry about this one. It's my next trip (Annapurna) that you need to worry about.'

He was invited to join Doug Scott, Roger Baxter-Jones and Tut Braithwaite in the spring of 1982 to try an alpine style ascent. The expedition totalled six members, but two were less experienced, which caused some friction when they attempted to join the main climbing group.

Alex was blunt, 'They had not logged enough hours slogging through Scottish bogs in winter blizzards, lumbering through the frantic, non-stop twenty-four-hour exhaustion of the Alps, I'm sorry, but charity ends at five thousand metres.'

To make matters worse, Braithwaite became ill on the acclimatisation climb with pain in his lungs. After a lifetime of climbing, worried about the risks, and now with a family at home, he realised his high-level mountaineering days were over. 'We have all lost friends, which deeply affected us in the mountains, but you've got to accept the fact. That's the risk, the game you play, and get on with it. If you don't, then you may as well not take part.'

In the expedition's book , Alex mused about packing the bare minimum and the commitment to climb Shishapangma [3]. 'Above all, cunning is the lot of the alpinist. The term *lightweight* is not enough to describe his activities, for it encompasses a much wider

3. *Shisha Pangma, first alpine style ascent of the South-West Face.*

brief than he entertains. The key to this alpine style is the intent with which the alpinist approaches his proposed route, the intention to climb it in one single push without previous knowledge or camps placed prior to the final venture. The commitment is total, the calculations crucial, the freedom exhilarating, and the weight of the sack still crippling!'

They knew they would only succeed by going light and carried only two ropes, six pitons, four ice screws and a few gas cartridges to melt snow, but their packs were still too heavy. Alex explained the solution. 'In the end, we hit on a masterstroke – we ate the food. When you might have expected us to force a worried way on and up the face, we called a halt, had a brew, and decided to bivouac there at the very foot of the wall. We sunbathed, relaxed and ate the food!'

Their amazingly rapid ascent and descent took four hungry days. Alex wrote that 'the wall was the ambition; the style became the obsession.'

Through the winter, not only did he plan his expedition to Annapurna, but he also designed mountaineering equipment and immersed himself in work for the manufacturer, Karrimor. Their CEO, Mike Parsons, held him in high esteem. 'I could see that going lightweight was for him about going with less than you are mentally comfortable with. His audacity astonished me and set him apart from all others.'

Reinhold Messner also respected him, saying he was, 'The purest exponent of the lightweight style now climbing in the Himalaya.'

At the start of the '80s our generation was aware of the innovations required to move forward, and that we were part of a continuum of development, mentally, physically and technologically. Alex though, had a canny knack of looking into the future, writing in the Karrimor technical brochure, 'As we pack our gear for Annapurna, we do so in the sure knowledge that one day, in the not too distant future, some lad will be packing half as much or less and set off to climb the wall in a time beyond our comprehension, backed by a methodology and an understanding of the environment that we do not have today. Our lightweight sacks will be like the dinosaurs.'

In his biography, *One Day as a Tiger*, from which I have quoted extensively, John Porter points out that Alex's predictions were correct. In 2007, Slovenian Tomaz Humar made the first solo ascent of the South Face of Annapurna in just two days. In 2017, the young Swiss alpinist, Ueli Steck, the *Swiss Machine*, soloed up and down in the astounding time of twenty-eight hours. Both died soloing in the mountains: Humar on Lantang Lirung in 2009 and Steck on Nuptse in 2017.

Also in the Karrimor publication, Alex was prophetic about future media developments. 'One day, we may be sitting in our base camp trying to choose between watching *Dallas* or some lad soloing Makalu live while keeping in touch with the progress of other expeditions by the press of a button.'

Remember, this was said long before the internet, satellite phones, laptops, digital cameras, drones, streaming, and instant weather analysis.

Alex and Sarah were very much in love. Sarah wanted to have children, to which Alex said, 'We'll have to get married because my mother would not have it otherwise.' After Annapurna, Sarah planned to accompany him on his next expedition. She had a live and let live personality and was content for him do what he wanted. 'Because I didn't restrict him, he had nothing to rebel against. We felt very happy together – a sense of calm with each other that felt right.' She added, 'I thought Alex would climb for another five years then become a television pundit.'

As the time to depart for Annapurna got closer, Sarah noted that he was tired and lacked confidence. 'On the other hand, he was more self-reflective. Discussing the risks, as we worried that something might happen, one of his thoughts was that when climbers fell in love, they were more vulnerable, distracted by having too much to lose.'

Sarah clearly remembers his fatalistic words, 'Even if I knew I was going to die, I would still go,' and he made a point of saying, 'We're together now – just remember that.' At the airport he told his mother, 'Please keep in touch with Sarah.'

I can only imagine what occurred on Annapurna.

The starlit night had been still and bitterly cold. The snow, ice and rock frozen together by the nocturnal deep freeze. Gradually, as the sun rose above the horizon, the dawn rays brought warmth to the face. There would be a crack, a drip, a whisper of wind, as the bond that held the icy slopes together began to loosen. High on the mountain, a small flurry of snow started to slide, at first no bigger than a cup of sugar. Barely a sound, a quiet whoosh as it funnelled into a snow fluting and, as the ground steepened, grew in force, dragging more loose powder off the surface to cascade down a small rock bluff. The snow flowed, gained pace and mass, poured over a larger cliff and exploded on the precipitous slope below to create a maelstrom. Clouds of airborne snow billowed upwards as the first avalanche of the day snaked and bounced down the slope, destroying everything in its path.

Alex MacIntyre and René Ghilini were cramponing upwards at the start of their new route when, from the corner of his eye, something caught Alex's attention. There was a second's delay before he heard the growl that turned to thunder. Alert and wide-eyed, he looked at René for only a moment. For ten years they had lived in the mountains and adapted to their moods and secrets. The avalanche passed harmlessly down a natural depression to their side. They had chosen their route wisely.

At twenty-eight, Alex was at the height of his mountaineering prowess. His cream fleece climbing suit cloaked his taut, athletic physique; his Mac-Pack, the rucksack which he had specially designed, clung to his back as though it was an evolutionary extension of his body. From the sides of his red helmet sprung unruly locks of black, curly hair. A matching black beard, strangely without a moustache, framed a smile of perfect white teeth, jet-black glacier glasses covered his inquisitive eyes, a heroic look that was undermined by the white sun cream daubed on his nose and cheeks.

A few weeks earlier, in late September 1982, they had arrived at Base Camp accompanied by John Porter who, at thirty-six, was the *old man* of the team. The gigantic South Face of Annapurna 1 overshadowed their camp, at five kilometres wide and 2,500 metres high, one of the most impressive mountain walls in the world. On the corniced summit crest line, above the ramparts, curls of wind-blown snow streaked the ink-blue sky. It looked impossible.

This Nepalese peak is one of the world's fourteen eight thousand metre peaks and was first ascended by Maurice Herzog and Louis Lachenal in 1950, by the easier, though highly avalanche-prone slopes on the opposite side of the mountain. Since then, the South Face had become a fulcrum for high standard Himalayan ascents. Chris Bonington's expedition was first, when Dougal Haston and Don Whillans reached the summit after two months of hard effort. In 1976 a Japanese expedition succeeded in climbing the central buttress and, in 1980 a Polish group climbed the right-hand pillar. All three were big national expeditions using fixed ropes, porters and camps. Partly due to the avalanche danger, Annapurna had a reputation as one of the most lethal mountains in the world. For every three climbers who reached the summit, one had died.

Alex, René and John planned an ambitious minimalistic ascent on a new line. At their isolated camp, they were the only climbers in the vicinity. For a weather forecast they looked at the sky and their barometer. Self-reliant, alone with precious little chance of rescue.

During the first weeks they trained and acclimatised on the nearby peaks of Hiunchuli and Tarke Kang. Alex and René displayed an extra level of fitness, perhaps because they were younger, and John feared he was being left behind. To make matters worse, he contracted dysentery. Impatient to start the main climb, Alex and René suggested they leave without him and, weakened by his illness, John had no option but to remain. He was hurt by their attitude, particularly by Alex whom he felt had betrayed their bond.

The pair set off with only the bare essentials: one rope, one ice screw and three pitons, food and fuel for four days, a sleeping bag each and a two-person bivouac tent. Their rucksacks weighed eighteen kilos, and they hoped to be up and down in five days. It was an audacious plan.

John accompanied them to near the bottom of the climb and, with mixed emotions, watched as they climbed over the large bergschrund crevasse at the base of the face, and rapidly up the steep snow slopes. All went well till they reached 7,200 metres, where a band of rock thirty metres high blocked their progress. From a distance, the vast scale had dwarfed this seemingly insignificant barrier, which repulsed their repeated attempts and by afternoon the slopes were alive with avalanches. They decided to find a sheltered place to bivouac for the night, before retreating the next day. At dawn, the face was still frozen and they began down an eight hundred metre gully, planning to go back to Base Camp, where they would rest and reconsider. By 10.00a.m., they were halfway down, and soon would be safely off the mountain.

Feeling much stronger, John walked to a vantage point on the moraine where he could see, through his camera's telephoto lens, the two figures descending, apparently unroped.

High above, the snow softened in the morning sun. I imagine the natural world at work as a solitary, fist-sized, stone became detached. Millions of years ago, this stone had been formed by coral and plankton under the sea to become a minute part of the tectonic plates that folded skywards as part of the mighty Himalayan chain. At this random moment, the law of gravity took over, and this single rock slid, bounced, and became airborne. It whistled through the air and reached terminal velocity in a moment of time, fate and place. It struck Alex and he fell like a rag doll, his life extinguished in an instant.

Confused and horror-struck, John watched a tiny body cartwheel the remaining four hundred metres to the bottom of the gully. 'I did not know for sure, but instinct told me the falling form was Alex.'

A spectator to the unfolding tragedy, he watched the second climber descend, almost out of control, rushing to the lifeless body and, a few hours later, watched him approach. 'Of course, it was René who appeared out of the ominous glacial mist that clung to the hollows of grey moraine.'

René had lost his climbing partner, John his best friend, and Annapurna had kept its grisly, statistical promise. Three climbers arrived, but only two were going home.

It snowed all next day, and all they could hear was the mountain riven with avalanches, thwarting their plans to recover Alex's body, which would soon be taken by the elements. Instead, they sped to Pokhara, the nearest town, walking non-stop for two days. René, seemingly distant and indifferent, joined a group of his countrymen on Everest that winter, leaving John to wonder whether his attitude was a reaction to the shock, a cultural trait, or if he had already become inured to death in the mountains.

Many years later, René, clearly still devastated, wrote in the prologue of the French edition of John Porter's book *One Day as a Tiger*, 'Thirty years of silence. Thirty years of denial, perhaps. Thirty years of absence of a smile that I still miss – Thirty years that I regret having untied the knot.'

In haste to relay the awful news to Alex's family and friends, John caught the bus to Kathmandu and spent twenty-four frustrating hours before making a connection on the archaic Nepalese phone system.

Sarah had taken a job at a theatre in Newcastle and spent her weekends in Hayfield. 'One night at our chalet, I was lying there, and a shadow went through my vision – it was really odd, I didn't realise till later it was the day he died – the 15th October.' After going back to work on Macbeth – of all plays – and a few days later, on her birthday, she heard the awful news. Because of the expedition's remote location, a poignant letter arrived from Alex weeks later. Sarah read how difficult the expedition was, that he was cold and the weather had been bad and he was so looking forward to getting back, dreaming of hot baths and home comforts and me. Ending – 'Just remember, I love you.'

A remote memorial headstone of Lakeland slate was erected the following year, near Base Camp, by Alex's mother Jean, sister Libby, Sarah and Terry Mooney. On the carved epitaph to Alex reads the Tibetan proverb:

Better to live one day as a tiger than to live a lifetime as a sheep.

Andy Parkin and Brian Hall
bivouac on The Ogre 2, 1982.

14

RISK AND CONSEQUENCES
Brian Hall and Andy Parkin

The twenty-five-member international expedition to Makalu in the spring of 1984 was a mix of climbers, Sherpas, trekkers, couples, and family groups with children, brought together by leader Doug Scott's hippie roots and gregarious nature. Unusually for an expedition of that time, it included nine women.

Doug brought his wife Jan and their three children Michael (twenty-one), Martha (eleven) and Rosie (five). From France, Jean Afanassieff (Afa), was accompanied by his wife Michelle and their daughter Jeanne (nine). From the USA came mountaineers Steve Sustad plus Larry Bruce and partner Molly Higgins. Individual UK climbers included, Colin (Choe) Brooks, Richard Chaplin, Dan Boone (aka Jim Fullalove), Nick Learning and me. From Ireland came Terry Mooney and from Switzerland, Arianne Giobellina.

The trekkers, who were friends of Doug's, included Clive and Sue Davies together with Arthur and Rita Lees. It was like a *camp,* akin to our gatherings in the Alps every summer on Snell's field in Chamonix, from which small teams made forays into the mountains, climbed, returned to a friendly atmosphere and recovered for the next sortie. Over the previous few years, particularly on Nuptse and Broad Peak, Doug had developed this communal approach to Himalayan expeditions.

His opinion was that it was a waste of time and money organising travel to the Himalaya for just one climb. So, he got permission to climb Baruntse (7,220 metres), Chamlang (7,319 metres), and the unclimbed South East Ridge of Makalu (8,485 metres and the world's fifth highest summit). As two of the three tops of Chamlang were amongst the highest unclimbed summits in Nepal, the government required that we form a joint expedition with Nepali climbers. So, we invited three Sherpas to join us as equal climbing members, rather than fulfilling their typical role of (at that time) support by load-carrying or fixing ropes. It was a lucrative invitation with good pay and all equipment provided. Doug invited Ang Phurba, a trusted friend, who had been sirdar and support climber on a number of his previous expeditions, and he, in turn, recommended two of his Sherpa mates, Saele and Pasang, assuring us that they were competent mountaineers.

It was early April when we began the two-week walk-in through the isolated and lovely region of north-east Nepal. Having travelled across hot, dusty plains from Kathmandu we arrived at the charming roadhead Tibetan settlement of Hille, perched high on a ridge. The first days were hot and arduous and, with few tea (rest) houses en route, meant a more demanding trek than to Everest Base Camp.

In a letter to Louise, my wife, I wrote, 'Lots of people have dysentery and, to make matters worse, Molly is a keen first-aider who never stops talking about illness and hygiene. Many of the team have never visited Nepal, and the remoteness has brought on anxiety and mass hypochondria. Also, with Dan Boone's alternative medicines (he's ill, by the way) and the hardcore vegetarians, it's getting a bit mad.'

On the seventh day on the trail, below Num, we crossed the Aran River via a rickety old iron and wood bridge. From there we slowly gained height through terraced fields of millet and maize where the farming people were less attuned to tourists. Doug and Afa had been held up by bureaucracy in Kathmandu so, as deputy leader, I led the group.

'Make sure we help the trekkers and porters on the difficult parts of the trail,' I said at breakfast. 'Choe, can you count the porter loads and make sure they're all there.'

'Brian, why the hell are you telling us the obvious,' Steve answered back. 'We've been on expeditions before.' Steve Sustad, the laconic American, was the same age and build as me. He had lived in the UK for some time as a climber-come-cabinetmaker and was taking on the habits and language of a true anglophile. We had similar mountaineering experience and he had been with Doug on Broad Peak. Although he had a calm and philosophical personality, he also had relentless drive and would make his opinions abundantly clear.

'You sound like Lord Hunt pontificating on Everest,' Choe joked.

Chastened by these comments, I realised that I was fulfilling my temporary role in an overzealous fashion, and with a lack of humour. I should keep my mouth shut – listen rather than speak out but, as we got to know each other's eccentricities, sharp words softened and arguments became more light-hearted.

Again, in a letter, 'Terry is keeping care of the money and is great company. Dan Boone is *as mad as a hatter* and asked Terry how to re-seal a sardine tin, then he asked me for help to load a film into his camera! He's a hindrance rather than a help – goodness knows why Doug invited him. Jan Scott can get a bit heavy at times as Doug has not caught us up yet. It is always the case that *Doug does this – and Doug does it that way.*'

I was particularly impressed by Arthur Lees, who was physically disabled with cerebral palsy. He was first to leave at dawn, and I would pass him struggling along the muddy trails with his wife, Rita. It was an inspiration to see him take this trek as a personal challenge, simply to prove that he could do it, with no thought of publicity or sponsorship. Every evening we worried that he would not make it, yet against all odds, Arthur, Rita and a trusty porter would arrive just before dark, and slowly he would lower his aching body onto a camp chair. Hardly able to speak, he would sip at a large mug of sweet tea with the biggest smile on his sweat-beaded face.

Most days the sun shone as we passed through groves of marijuana plants where the team harvested enough leaves for a happy stay in the mountains. At the last village of Tashigang we said goodbye to civilisation, and took the rough trail as it rose into a blaze of purple-flowered rhododendrons, eventually climbing higher through pungent smelling pine forests. Soon we were above the tree line in colder air, travelling across slopes of stunted juniper patched with remnants of winter snow. The icy Shipton La at 4,200 metres was the most challenging part of the walk, after which we dropped into the Barun River Valley with its dense lichen-encrusted virgin forests.

It was a hidden world: a rare undisturbed ecosystem with a high diversity of flora and fauna due to the range of altitudes. Colossal rock walls formed ramparts that rose above the woods to snow-covered summits, the isolated home of snow leopards, red pandas, wild boar, and musk deer. Traversing unstable moraine shelves above the river we eventually reached higher ground, where the valley opened. On the last patch of the grassy alp, we pitched Base Camp at 4,900 metres, where rugged ice and rock rose to the amphitheatre of majestic peaks that line the Nepal–Tibet border. A world dominated by the vast bulk of Makalu, the highest point in the Mahalangur Himalayas, twenty kilometres southeast of Everest.

I spent a lot of time with Choe Brooks, one of my main rock-climbing partners at home. We knew each other well and, with mutual trust, anticipated climbing together on the expedition. Of a similar age to me he had been brought up in Oldham, and had a broad Lancashire accent. Tall and lanky with a mop of curly black hair he was one of the few clean-shaven guys on the trip. Like most of us he was a full-time climber, but made pocket money as an electrician. If anything was broken, Choe relished the challenge of repairing it, and he always had a collection of head torches, stoves and sunglasses he was working on. He was generally easy going but very particular about what he ate, carefully examining the food in case it contained an ingredient he did not recognise.

The walk-in had been good for fitness and acclimatisation, and our new home was at an ideal height for recovery between bouts of climbing. From experience it was better to have a low Base Camp on *warm* grass rather than *cold* ice. Physiologically, the body steadily deteriorates when living higher than five thousand metres. A bonus was the proximity of forests with supplies of dead wood for fuel. With the nearest village of Tashigang days away, on the other side of the Shipton La, there would be no conflict with locals.

Time allowed a catch up with Arianne, whom I met first when she visited our Nuptse Base Camp at the invitation of Doug in 1979. She seemed young then, and still affected by the death of her close friend, mountaineer Dougal Haston, who was a fellow inhabitant of the Swiss village of Leysin. Five years later, on the Makalu expedition, she had matured into a beautiful, confident, and independent woman with a passion for mountaineering. She would hang out with Choe, Terry, Steve, and me, planning to start climbing as a team.

I was continually surprised by these diverse characters, and even started to appreciate Dan Boone's bizarre traits – though I never discovered the roots of his nickname. He was a rascal from Bradford who had been a good climber, making the third British ascent of the Eiger *Nordwand*. Sadly, his life descended into drug induced chaos from which he found peace by following Indian gurus. He had the gifts of a photographic memory and a fine voice, and in the dining tent would entertain us with Bob Dylan songs and Shakespeare recitations.

We started acclimatisation forays on small peaks before shifting our attention to Baruntse, at 7,220 metres. The only possible route from Base Camp that suited our purposes was the relatively straightforward, snowy South East Ridge. It had been climbed before, but it would be the first time over seven thousand metres for many of the team, and we did not want to over-extend ourselves with more difficult climbs ahead. We also had to consider that our next climb, on Chamlang, had to be a joint ascent with the Nepalese. So, the three Sherpas, as well as acclimatising, had to be given a quick apprenticeship in alpine style mountaineering.

The climbing members of the group organised themselves into self-contained teams. Afa would accompany Doug, having climbed together on Broad Peak two years previously. Ten years older than the rest of the team, they had far more experience of high altitude, having been the first English and French persons to climb Everest.

Afa lived in Chamonix and we had become friends as a result of my many visits there. He was tall with shoulder-length, light brown hair and a distinguished Roman nose, and spoke a number of languages, including fluent English and Russian. In addition to working as a mountain guide he had become a talented adventure sports film maker, and he had a wicked sense of humour. Up until this point on the expedition I had only passing contact with him as he had been keeping his wife Michelle and daughter Jeanne company. I also knew Michelle well. Tall and slender, she had striking French looks, was a talented ski instructor and totally at home in the mountains. Unfortunately, their young daughter Jeanne became unwell and distraught in the remote Base Camp environment and needed constant comforting.

Baruntse was not the simple climb we planned, and of the sixteen that set out on 29th April only six got to the top. Arianne and Michael became ill on the first day and, accompanied by Nick, returned to camp. After the second night at Corner Camp, I developed bronchitis and, at 6,700 metres, had to retreat, accompanied by Choe. Richard succumbed to an altitude headache, and, when Pasang failed to climb a short icy section, headed back to Base with him. That left Afa, Steve, Terry, Saela, Ang Phurba and Doug, who reached the top on the fifth day amidst swirling clouds and falling snow. Dan Boone got lost before reaching the first camp and from then onwards spent most days alone in his tent, smoking dope and reading *The Whole Earth Catalog*. His only social interaction was when our cook passed him cups of tea, rice and dhal and emptied his pee-bottle.

With everyone safely back at Base Camp the celebrations began. Terry ecstatically announced that he was the first Irishman up any Himalayan peak. He had commissioned a porter to carry two gallons of rakshi (the local homemade spirit) and fifteen bottles of whisky to Base Camp. The party lasted late into the night and, as Terry got drunk, sorrowful tears ran down his cheeks as he began a rambling eulogy to Alex MacIntyre. We had all loved Alex but, whenever Terry had a few drinks, he would talk about him over-effusively. Still grieving over his friend, he felt he owned his memory. It was not until some days later that anyone was fit to climb.

I worried that the expedition would be like a utopian experiment in the vein of Orwell's *Animal Farm*, but it was far from that. More akin to regular civilised life, we were a happy mix of both sexes and families with children. At the time it was the stereotypical norm for expeditions to be all male affairs, and I had no experience of climbing with women in the Alps nor on expeditions to the Greater Ranges. Thankfully everyone got on well, apart from at dinner time which was like feeding time at the zoo. We had plenty of food, but the poor Sherpa cook-team went bonkers trying to fulfil the special requests.

There had to be two different menus as some people enjoyed meat while others were strict vegetarians. Afa had brought two big hams with him, which were dangling from the kitchen ceiling. Dan Boone and Doug were not happy about that, so Afa took great delight in taking one down, slowly slicing the meat and passing it around the carnivores of the team. Other members only drank green tea, while the regular Nepalese tea included milk with copious amounts of sugar. Some liked to smoke handpicked local marijuana to relax before sleep, while others got withdrawal symptoms if they did not have a daily alcoholic drink. Predictably, choosing the music playlist on the large cassette player in the dining tent caused daily tantrums.

We eagerly awaited news from the outside world but, for reasons that remained mysterious to us, the weekly mail runner was not delivering letters. Keeping in touch with loved ones was hugely important and we worried that our letters were not reaching home.

Continuing to send letters, I wrote to Louise, 'Expeditions are OK, but when I am so much in love with you, it takes the edge off them. I'm always thinking I want to be with you rather than getting on with the expedition. It's not that I'm homesick (although I miss home); it's that I'm Louise sick – lovesick.' I wished she could have joined me, but the timing was crucial for her with a career change from British Airways cabin crew to establishing a cafe in our village.

Chamlang was our next objective, an impressive mountain whose magnificent summit ridge touches the clouds at 7,000 metres along its entire eight-kilometre length. At its south-west end lies the main summit at 7,319 metres, which a Japanese team had first climbed using fixed ropes in 1962. At the opposite end was our objective, the North East summit, unclimbed at 7,290 metres. On 12th May, I joined Choe, Terry, Steve, Dan Boone, the two Sherpas, Saela and Pasang to leave Base Camp for an attempt. Within an hour, the unreliable Dan Boone returned to camp with a severe headache. Initially, we took the same route to Corner Camp at 5,600 metres as we had on Baruntse, situated at the confluence of Chamlang and Barun glaciers. It was a long day, and we spent the next resting while the second team of Afa, Doug, Michael and Ang Phurba caught up, having set off a day later. The first team climbed the steep ice the following dawn, towards a prominent shoulder below the virgin North-East summit. Unfortunately, the two Sherpas proved to be so inexperienced at technical climbing that they slowed our group down considerably. By early afternoon the late-rising second team caught us beneath a twenty-metre ice cliff that barred the way.

Choe went at the overhanging ice like a squirrel up a tree trunk, but it took a huge effort to haul up the Sherpas, and several more hours before everyone reached the slopes above. By then, it was early evening, and we bivouaced at the first opportunity, which was on the lower lip of a bergschrund at around 6,100 metres.

The next day the first team was again slowed by the Sherpas on snow and ice slopes leading to a shoulder at 6,705 metres. We decided to pitch our three lightweight tents while the second team overtook us and carried on towards the summit. I sat outside the tents, cooking and chatting to Choe, watching as our friends climbed strongly up the steep ice bulges on the ridge above, assuming they would reach the top before dark. That evening we had a grandstand view of Everest, Lhotse and the peaks of the Hunku silhouetted by the setting sun, and were full of confidence that we would follow to the summit the next day.

We were wakened by our tents flapping in a fierce wind. As we got the stove going to melt snow, Steve poked his head out through the tent door.

'What do you think of the weather?' I asked.

'It's okay. Once you're out of the tent, the wind's not too bad.' Steve continued with some bad news. 'Terry's been awake all night with incredible eye pain. I think it's snow blindness because he said he took off his sunglasses yesterday while we erected the tents. He's in a bad way and can't see anything.'

'What are we going to do?' Choe exclaimed.

The two Sherpas remained in their sleeping bags, not keen to continue, suggesting they wait with Terry whilst Choe, Steve, and I tried for the summit. We dismissed the idea, but then Terry joined the debate. 'I would prefer to rest today. Hopefully, I'll be better tomorrow. You have plenty of time to get to the summit and return.'

There were many objections to this plan but, in the end, we agreed. 'Should we take our helmets?' Choe asked.

'It's a ridge and there should be no danger,' I replied.

'We want to carry as little as possible so we can get up and back for mid-afternoon.' Steve was keen to get started once the decision had been made.

Surprisingly, the wind dropped as we gained height. Sure that we would reach the summit in a few hours, we kept the rope in our pack and soloed until the ridge steepened and we found ourselves shouting and laughing, full of confidence on an idyllic, cloudless Himalayan day. Steve and I were a few hundred metres ahead of Choe and decided to rope-up at a bulge of blue ice at 7,100 metres, just below the summit. I sat and belayed while Steve surmounted the obstacle. When he was forty metres above and out of sight, fragments of ice chipped off by his axe and crampons bounced down the bare ice and whistled past. I was admiring the view when suddenly a searing pain shot through my head. The next thing I remember was hanging like a rag doll from the belay.

Confused and panicked, I became dizzy and vomited into the snow. I tried to shout, but only a slurred 'Help' came out. Eventually, I caught Choe's attention. At first, he did not understand but when he saw me slumped in the snow, he rushed up to me.

What happened? was all I could think. A veil of darkness enveloped me and I cannot remember much more, other than that Choe was holding my head. *They'll never get me down if I pass out.*

By now Steve had rejoined us and was arranging an abseil. Waves of panic washed over me as blood ran down my cheeks and everything blurred again. Worse was the double vision that made me feel sick. *What a place to have an accident, and why the hell did I leave my helmet behind?* I thought.

I have no recollection of what happened next, but I must have managed to stagger, enabling Choe and Steve to lower me down the slope to the tents on the shoulder.

Our situation was desperate, with Terry blind, me with a severe blow to the skull from a block of ice, and the two Sherpas needing constant supervision. We had no radios, and there was zero chance of summoning outside help. We knew the other team would not return, as they had planned to traverse Chamlang and descend by a different route. Our debilitated group was totally in the hands of Choe and Steve who, after debating several options, suggested that we stay in one group. As Terry and I could both stand, they proposed to lower us down the mountain's steep fifty-degree icy slopes using our two, fifty-metre ropes. It was an ambitious plan with a very uncertain outcome and could take days.

With that decision I started to feel better, and began to wonder what all the fuss was about. Worse, I had the deranged idea that we should go back and climb to the summit. Of course, this was illusion. Suddenly I felt faint again, and everything was doubled. I heard echoes of voices, but had little comprehension and doubted whether we would make it. My mind spun with negativity. *Will my end be a sudden black out? Could the belay fail and we all fall to our deaths? How long can I carry on, I'm so exhausted and cold?*

With little choice, Terry and I were being lowered on the rope. It was a gruelling ordeal but, although I felt wretched, I could still help to guide the blind Terry. 'To the left – watch that ice – slowly step down,' I directed.

Terry overbalanced and fell sideways. 'When's this going to end. What's happening now?' he asked, floundering around, confused in the snow while attempting to stand. I felt my energy wane with each rope length. *Will I ever see Louise again?*

It was a complicated and time-consuming procedure but it worked and, with these incremental lowers, eventually we reached the bergschrund bivouac.

By the following day my double vision and blackouts had stopped. I still felt nauseous and had a very sore head, but could just about manage without help, so I took charge of the Sherpas and continued the descent with them while Choe and Steve patiently lowered Terry. In the evening, two days after the accident, we reached the Corner Camp as a very relieved team of climbers.

We were getting comfortable in our sleeping bags when Choe sat bolt upright. 'Did you hear that shouting?' He unzipped the tent and pointed his head torch in the direction of the noise to see Doug and his team staggering out of the darkness towards us. We got up, put the stove on, and sat late into the night while Doug's party quenched their raging thirst with cups of tea. Neither group knew anything about the others' struggles. In fact, both had endured epics.

Two days before, they had been slowed by Ang Phurba's crampons continually falling off. They had an uncomfortable bivouac on the ridge, a hundred metres below the summit, exposed to a strong and cold wind. On the morning of the 16th, they reached the virgin North East summit (7,290 metres) and continued traversing to the unclimbed Central summit (7,235 metres). They decided not to continue to the distant main summit of Chamlang, at the westerly end of the horizontal ridge five kilometres away, and their two-day descent proved to be harrowing. Making dozens of abseils, they had downclimbed loose rock and crumbling ice to bivouac between two dangerous seracs, eventually reaching the glacier. They were lost in the dark when they saw Choe's torchlight.

The next day, the two teams left Corner Camp, heading for Base Camp with Terry still in excruciating pain. 'It was like having needles pushed into my eyes.'

I had a throbbing headache, and my hair was matted with blood, but I could walk under my own steam, albeit unsteadily. Everyone else was exhausted, and the Sherpas could barely talk, looking dejected and overwhelmed by the whole experience. It took all day to get to Base Camp, where there was more bad news.

When we left for Chamlang, Arianne had felt unwell and decided not to join the ascent. Now she lay in her tent, barely conscious and with a yellow pallor. By chance, a doctor accompanying a trekking group visited Base Camp and diagnosed her with hepatitis, which she must have contracted from a meal on the walk-in. All he could suggest was two weeks rest, keeping warm and hydrated. We had no radio to summon help and, even if we had, in 1984 there was no helicopter rescue available. Nor were there any medical facilities within a week's walk of our camp.

The last few days had exacted a significant toll on the physical and mental health of the whole team. At Base Camp, the inquest into what went wrong carried on long into the night.

'If only I'd worn my helmet,' I said.

'Not as stupid as not wearing sunglasses,' Terry replied.

'Small things can have big consequences,' Doug responded.

We agreed that we were lucky to all come back alive, and further agreed that joint Nepalese expeditions with inexperienced Sherpas on difficult mountains was not ideal. Almost forty years later it was heartening to hear about the remarkable first winter ascent of K2 in 2021 when an independent team of Sherpas reached the summit, demonstrating how much their skills have improved and showing their true status as climbers.

No matter how many pills I swallowed my head remained wracked with pain as I repeatedly went over the events on Chamlang, concerned that my head injuries were severe . . . all the *what-ifs*. In periods of lucidity I realised that hours had gone by of which I had no recollection. Concussion exacerbated by altitude was the obvious diagnosis but, whether it was the injury or the drugs, I could remain neither awake nor asleep and had recurring intense dreams and weird thoughts.

Doug tried to comfort me. 'Don't worry about it, youth, I have dreams all the time at altitude.' I agreed that it was the same for me. 'You should read these books, youth.' He handed me *The Teachings of Don Juan* by Carlos Castaneda and *The Tibetan Book of the Dead*.

Thanking him, I was bemused as to how these tomes might help. I had empathy with Buddhist teachings and was keen to know more, but my condition precluded reading, and most of my day was spent in a torpor.

One hallucination haunted me that was both a nightmare and a daydream, episodic and menacing. Writing it in my diary, I wondered if the recording of it would somehow prolong and entrench it further in my mind.

A giant man clothed in burnished armour stood guarding a high mountain pass wielding a long sword and a heraldic shield. His face was invisible, encased in a steel Armet helmet. Out of nowhere came a violent storm from the mountains, but his metal suit protected him from the tempest. Next, a foe dressed in chain mail came charging down the slope above, but the knight felled him with one swipe of his mighty sword. Then a beautiful queen approached and tried to lure the guard away from his sentry, but he repelled her advances with his magic shield. Suddenly, there was a crash of thunder, and lightning struck the ground above, rocks and ice avalanched down towards the knight. Try as he might, he could not repulse the mountain slide and was knocked off his feet, pinned down by rocks and the weight of his suit. I walked slowly over to the twitching body and saw that his metal suit was partly open; inside was not a giant, but a body of a wizened dwarf. I released the leather straps of the weighty helmet and opened the visor. Manically staring back at me was my own face.

Aghast, I would awake sweating and breathless. Back asleep, the nightmare continued.

From the stomach of the sprawling knight came a tube, like an umbilical cord. I followed the snaking cord to a building and opened two massive oak doors with a creak of hinges. It took an eternity before my eyes became accustomed to the light. I saw rows of pews on which sat more knights dressed in damaged armour but without protective helmets. It was freezing, and everywhere was covered in a fine dusting of snow. As I walked down the aisle I saw the faces of Mallory, Boardman, Thexton, Buhl, Tasker and Haston. All staring forward to the end of the building, where a giant icicle hung illuminated by a single shaft of dusty sunlight. I followed the cord to below the icicle and saw it was attached to the stomach of a naked corpse hanging on a crucifix on the downward pointing ice. The unrecognisable face was frightening – old cracked leather, no eyes and protruding teeth. I looked to the right and saw an old man, hunchbacked and portly, dressed in a dinner jacket, tending candles. He turned his large bald head – and I stared into the demonic eyes of Aleister Crowley – the Great Beast 66.[1]

A few years before I had painted Crowley's portrait and always thought he was an odd subject. In his day he was regarded as the most wicked man in the world. He must somehow have invaded my mind at a much earlier time but, without a clue what all this meant, I felt deeply disturbed.

To worsen matters, I started having panic attacks, which I felt self-conscious and embarrassed about and, irrationally, hid from the others by staying inside my tent. Depressed, hardly sleeping, with no appetite, my mental state was impeding my physical recovery. Almost certainly, I was suffering from either post-traumatic stress or post-concussion syndrome. With such an injury, I decided it would be best to leave for home.

I needed medical attention but had insufficient confidence to walk out alone. Fortunately, when Clive, Sue, Larry and Molly decided to leave, I was able to join them. By then, Arianne was able to get out of her tent and go for gentle walks. Still very frail, she had little appetite but was determined to get back to civilisation. I have only fleeting memories of the last days at Base Camp and no recollection of the walk-out, the return to Kathmandu, or the flight home.

When the others returned to the UK, I learnt that Terry had regained his sight, and Steve and Choe recovered their strength, and that, on 24th May, Terry, Dan Boone, Michael and Choe had unsuccessfully attempted Makalu by the North-West Original Route. Still exhausted from their earlier efforts, they abandoned the climb. Meanwhile, Doug, Steve and Afa set off on an ambitious alpine style attempt to traverse the mountain along its unclimbed, ten kilometre South East Ridge and down the Original Route.

---

1. Crowley, the bisexual English occultist, ceremonial magician, poet, spy, painter, novelist, and mountaineer. He made early attempts on K2 (1902) and Kangchenjunga (1905) and wrote many books, including *Diary of a Drug Fiend* and *The Book of the Law*. He said his purpose in life was 'to bring oriental wisdom to Europe and to restore paganism in a purer form.'

Four days later, they had come within a whisker of success, reaching 8,400 metres. Unfortunately, due to extreme fatigue and Afa suffering from oedema, the party was forced to turn back just a hundred metres short of the summit. Difficulties on the descent, into and out of the East Cwm, meant they encountered the most strenuous climbing Doug said he had ever done. If they could have climbed the final section, not only would they have completed one of the most incredible ascents in Himalayan mountaineering but it would also have enabled them to descend the easier slopes of the Original Route.

While I was writing this book Doug passed away of natural causes, aged 79. With his roots in an earlier generation, he was one of the greatest mountaineers of all time and as a driving force his influence throughout this period was unparalleled.

'A traverse as planned would have been far easier,' he wrote in his typically understated expedition report. 'Of course, there were personal disappointments which seemed to be felt by everyone. But all in all, this was a good expedition. No doubt there will be other occasions to take that extra step into the unknown, which the traverse of a big mountain entails. We learn as we go along, each trip building on its predecessor. Every expedition can be seen as an experiment with the aim not just to push back the limits of human endurance, survival and mountain exploration but also to find solutions to the problems of human relationships. By observing ourselves in action around Makalu this year, we have come to know a little more about the problems all of us have whenever we join together.'

I am sure all alpinists would agree that failures are inevitable but, paradoxically, are part of the challenge.

Soon after I returned home I heard that another of my friends, Andy Parkin, had been involved in a horrendous climbing accident. After our Ogre 2 expedition he had moved to Chamonix and started working as an alpine guide. He had travelled to the Swiss town of Zermatt and taken a client up a minor practice peak called the Riffelhorn. Partway up his client fell and the belay pitons pulled out, catapulting Andy ten metres onto a ledge, inflicting horrific injuries. The client escaped unhurt and managed to raise the alarm for a helicopter rescue.

The doctors told his family he would not survive injuries that included a ruptured spleen, displaced heart and shattered bones. They flew to Andy's bedside to say their final farewells while his life hung in the balance. The Swiss hospital in Berne did wonders, and he survived, but his body suffered life-changing injuries.

Six months after Andy's accident I went to see him in Sancellemoz, the rehabilitation hospital in Plateau d'Assy, near Chamonix. I looked on in horror as he showed me his elbow fused at a right angle and when he got up, he shuffled ungainly as his hip joint had been broken in thirteen places

'Waiting a year and a half in hospital I thought I was going to come out completely healed,' he told me recently, 'but calcification of my hip joint meant there was no hope from medicine.' The doctors had saved Andy's life, but they could not repair his body.

'I was psychologically crushed . . . this is what I'm going to be like for the rest of my life. Can I deal with it? I went through a period of depression, then realised it was just up to me, and putting my energy into painting was therapeutic and I came out of it mentally stronger.'

We continued to talk about the trauma and the recovery. Aged just 29, it looked as if he would never have an active life again.

'I was ashamed to be an invalid and I tried to hide it. Even when I started climbing well again, I was self-conscious. I wanted to pretend that I was normal, almost in denial. But perhaps that is what shaped my new mentality to carry on and push myself.'

In 1986, two years after the accident, he continued his love of art and started sculpting using detritus he found in the mountains. His movement severely restricted, he would go on solitary forays searching for material. Remnants of an Air India plane crash of 1950, partway up Mont Blanc, became a rich source of artefacts. He made headline news when he created a huge face on the Mer du Glace glacier: hair made from cans threaded on wire with a white wall tyre as an eye. A temporary sculpture, a metaphor for pollution and global warming, it slowly collapsed as the glacier melted. When I moved to Chamonix in 1987, Andy became one of my closest friends. His art was going from strength to strength but, although he received deserved critical acclaim, he never had any money.

'I tried not to talk about the accident for ten years, like it never happened. I can talk about it better now. Nobody discussed post-traumatic stress back then, it was not on the radar. There was no counselling – you dealt with it yourself, or were supported by friends and family. Disability was like a taboo area – *poor Andy, etc*. I wanted to forget it as though it never happened and get on with my life. But I've got the stigma of what happened for ever ... my body is still fucked.'

Quite miraculously, Andy gradually rediscovered his ability for cutting edge climbing. With few material possessions and little responsibility for other people's emotions and lives, he pursued the purest, most aesthetic, and riskiest style of climbing by going into the mountains alone and soloing new routes without the safety of a rope. Despite the pain of permanent disabilities, his story must be one of the most courageous in any sport.

'I felt happy alone, soloing because no one could see me and judge me. No one to compare myself with – like an able-bodied friend. Who could I trust to climb with? There are not many, they have to understand me and put up with my disabilities and take a share of the work that I'm not as good at. Above all I have to feel good with them.'

He started climbing with Mark Twight, the top American alpinist and, in the winter of 1992, they climbed one of the most sensational new routes in alpine history on the Aiguille des Pélerins above Chamonix, which they called *Beyond Good and Evil*. Twight was also acutely aware of the close link between between risk and consequence. 'To do extraordinary things in the mountains when I was younger, I had to be 100 per cent in the mountains, I had to cut away all relationships to things in the valley. I could not do it with an anchor. I needed the freedom. Later, with a wife, a house and a dog I had too many things binding me to the ground and I gave up climbing.'

During the same period I climbed with Andy many times, including in Patagonia in 1993. He was an inspiration, climbing at the highest standard on mixed and ice, equally well as any able-bodied climber in the world.

In Andy's words, 'I've died once already – what have I got to lose? I was conscious of how near I was taking it to the limit. But I'm quite good at blocking things out like danger. I just turn it off and keep going. Before the accident I was never conscious of risk . . . I was young and ignorant. I didn't feel immortal and that's why now I do not like to talk about my climbs. I don't want to believe in my own myth. Keep it private, keep it secret, above all keep the outward pressure away.'

Two years later, Andy went to Patagonia again, this time with one of the top French alpinists, Francois Marsigny. Their epic new climb on Cerro Torre became one of the greatest survival stories of modern mountaineering, for which they were awarded the Piolet d'Or – the Golden Ice Axe.[2] It was a testament to Andy's unquenchable spirit.

'The distance of the art is very important. It is important that I can paint and switch off from the objective of climbing . . . after all, it could be my last climb. I paint as a barometer to judge when I am ready to go. When soloing I have nobody to discuss it with and if I mess it up that's it. I paint the mountain and become familiar with it, with the climb. I contemplate and when I am ready, I will go. The art keeps me sane. Keeping me away from this awe-inspiring idea of soloing.'

His independence and mental desire to climb is unbelievable. Because of the high risk, many view soloing as irresponsible, but self-determination is a person's ultimate right.

'You're going to die if you mess soloing up. I pushed it to the limit but unlike before the accident I got to understand myself. Before I took it for granted that I could climb well. After the accident every climb was a healing climb. I was discovering my capacity again. I thought my climbing was finished and I would become an artist. But it was strange; I was becoming better as a climber. I was caught up in the question – how far can I go? I was very vulnerable because I was an invalid and I knew full well there could be a situation I could not deal with. There were one or two occasions where I put my head in a noose like the climb on Mermoz in Patagonia. That

2. The Golden Ice Axe is mountaineering's highest honour and is considered to be the 'Oscars' of alpinism. It is a French award given jointly by magazine Montagnes and the 'Groupe de Haute Montagne' since 1992.

was stupid. I pulled off a move on that climb and thought ... I'm still alive! I can't believe it. I went through four clicks of the barrel.'

Having narrowly escaped death, on several occasions, it somehow released his fear. Andy was skilful, and lucky enough to survive and, although age and the consequences of disability have tempered his climbing, he still spends much of his time in the mountains. He has also developed into an extraordinary artist, and each year goes to Nepal to teach art to village children. He brings back their work to sell in his Chamonix studio, raising money for Doug Scott's Community Action Nepal (CAN) charity.

In April 1984, when I left for the Makalu expedition, Louise and I had just bought a semi-derelict shop in the centre of the village of Hayfield. All our energy was devoted to renovating the property and converting it into a cafe. I also helped Doug organise the expedition and worked as a design consultant for Berghaus, the outdoor gear manufacturer. The last few weeks before setting off were unusually chaotic, but it was a fulfilling time, and Louise and I grew closer. Expeditions were exciting, but my departure put a tremendous strain on our three-year relationship. There was never a right time to sit down and discuss the risks in the mad rush of leaving, and it was an uncomfortable subject. What must Louise have thought while I pursued a dangerous activity, always wondering whether it would be good or bad news she might receive while I was away?

'By the time Brian went on Makalu we had already had the deaths of Alex MacIntyre, Joe Tasker, Peter Boardman and Pete Thexton to contend with, so the alarm bells should have been ringing but they weren't,' Louise remembered. 'Many times I have asked myself why not? Did I think my so very capable husband was invincible? Of course he would come home! Looking back, I am shocked at my insensitivity, my hardness and my lack of awareness during these times but equally I know that there would have been nothing I could have said nor done to stop Brian going on his beloved expeditions.'

In my twenties, as a mountaineer without a regular partner, I rarely discussed the topic of death. However, when I fell in love with Louise in '81, I became aware that my attitude to risk was changing. In the first delicate years of romance, the thought of prolonged separation preyed heavily on my mind, as did the consequences my death would have on Louise. Previous short- term, casual relationships did not have that effect. Marriage in '82 further triggered my conscience, and I began to realise that my high-risk mountaineering days were finite. We never had children, but I can only imagine that parenthood would have added another unbearably heavy load of responsibility.

Louise still ponders those days. 'I always knew when I hooked up with Brian that life would never be boring! That was a big part of what attracted me to him. Our first few years together were a whirlwind. He was at the top of his game in the mountains, I was flying round the world as international cabin crew and later opened a village cafe.'

Her father had been a climber. 'All his life and throughout my childhood I had grown used to my dad's long forays away on the Munros of Scotland, which were his true love. There were very few phone calls home from these wild places and Mum accepted his absences . . . *just getting on with things*. I guess that rubbed off on me. Also, I climbed myself, and circulated socially on the climbing scene, so it wasn't as though I was entering an unknown world when we married.'

Before marriage, I had been blasé about the risks of mountaineering. My accident on Chamlang changed all that. Probably the recent deaths of friends in the mountains had also altered my perception. In my mind, the mountains changed from friends to foes. After that, I seemed to wake up to the dangers, and my past attitude surprised me. I became convinced that my previous disassociated attitude to risk was a requirement for success as a high-level mountaineer.

I had not worried about how the consequences of my death would affect my parents and, with a sense of everlasting guilt, I regret that cavalier attitude. When I sorted out my mother's belongings after her death, I realised how close and intimate her memories were. Hidden inside a chest I found a collection of clothing, toys and drawings belonging to my younger brother, Stephen, who died of a heart condition when he was eight. I unashamedly cried. How could I not see that high-risk mountaineering and the well-publicised deaths of some of my friends would have been an unbearable torment to her? Losing another son would have destroyed my mum.

When I got back to Hayfield, Louise, with the help of friends, had transformed the building site I had left her with into a thriving village cafe. She had employed staff, painted the inside a gorgeous green and burgundy and had a menu influenced by her travels around the world. It was more San Francisco than English village. I loved what she had done and settled down into recovering from the expedition. My headaches disappeared, and I got back into the rhythm of midweek visits to Newcastle, working for Berghaus.

One day, at an important meeting with the managing director, I started to feel unwell. I became hot and sweaty, dizzy, and started gasping for breath. I made excuses and went to sit in the toilet with my head in my hands. My doctor reassured me that nothing was physically wrong and gave me exercises to help stop the panic attacks, but they arrived without warning, and the condition remained a curse over the next few years. I enjoyed rock climbing and skiing and, on regular occasions, worked as a mountain guide in the Alps. There did not seem to be an association between mountaineering and anxiety, but I felt there must be a link with my accident.

Our minds react differently to accidents. For Andy Parkin it seemed to act as a spur to greater things; for me the event reined in my ambitions. For sure we are different people with our own soul and spirit, but was it also because I was older, in a permanent relationship and settling down, where Andy was younger, single, and living in Chamonix, the fulcrum of world alpinism?

The big question I now faced was, would I be comfortable returning to climbing in the Greater Ranges?

Al Rouse in his tent during the last days
of the K2 expedition, 1986.

15

THE END OF AN ERA
Alan Rouse and K2

I have spent a lifetime mentally chipping at a block of stone and still not produced a sculpture of Alan Rouse.

He was my closest friend for fifteen years and my best man when I married. We met as boys just out of school and parted as men on the icy slopes of K2. Between times we travelled the world climbing mountains. He was the halyard that enabled me to reach such heights, my cord through the chapters of this epoch. I remember the mischievous grin that belied his complex character, and a generous front of bravado and laughs behind an independent nature full of paranoia and self-doubt. Yet he achieved so much.

He and his younger sister Susan were raised in a middle-class family living in a semi-detached house in Wallasey, near Liverpool, by their parents, John and Eve. His father died when Al was nineteen and later Eve married Dick Rooke, who was a close family friend.

Susan wrote in *Alan Rouse – A Mountaineer's Life*. 'As Al grew up, he developed a deep-rooted wanderlust. No sooner had he learnt to walk than he would wander off on his own exploring the local streets, too young to know fear.'

As a child, he disliked team sports. His bedroom became a laboratory where he experimented with chemicals, built complicated *Meccano* models, and attempted to make a computer out of old televisions. At fifteen, he started playing chess and competed in national competitions. With a keen interest in mathematics, he would explain the philosophical implications of nuclear physics and relativity to his confounded mum and sister. The collecting of rocks, minerals and stamps were added to his long list of hobbies.

'He was a strange mixture of ingenuity and impracticality,' Susan told me. 'He began to discard convention, growing his hair longer than either his school or his father thought desirable and generally became involved in all the subversive activities of youth. He started to drink, smoke and listen to Jimi Hendrix.'

Much to his parent's horror he began potholing and regularly, with single-minded enthusiasm, disappeared alone into the depths of Yorkshire caves. At fifteen, he started climbing with his school friend Nick Parry, and joined the Wirral-based Gwydyr Mountain Club, underage drinking in the pubs where the club met. Soon he was living for climbing, spending his weekends on the crags of Snowdonia.

Near his family home was a small cliff called the Breck, which he visited most days, developing a training regime to hone his finger strength. On one visit in 1969, he made the first ascent of *Bluebell Buttress Traverse,* now graded V7 6b, in hindsight regarded as one of the world's hardest boulder problem climbs of the time. Later, at nearby Helsby, he made the first solo of a difficult E5, *The Beatnik*. In his last year at school, he journeyed to Chamonix, serving an alpine initiation by climbing classic routes on the peaks around Mont Blanc.

He was very gregarious and often mixed with members of Liverpool's Vagabond Climbing Club, particularly being led astray by an older, unruly scouser called Pete Minks. His rise was meteoric, and his strength and confidence sky-high. Aged eighteen, he succeeded on an audacious unroped solo of *The Boldest* (E3 5c) on Clogwyn Du'r Arddu (*Cloggy*). He wrote, *Mad? Probably, but what a superb form of madness to engage in,*[1] and, shortly afterwards, made the second ascents of *Our Father* (E3 6a) and *Wee Doris* (E3 5c), two of the hardest climbs on the limestone cliffs of the English Peak District. The raw teenager had already become one of Britain's top rock climbers.

When I first met him in 1969, he was a wayward young adult looking for fun, as I was. He had stayed on at school to take his Cambridge University entrance exams and regularly hitched to

---

1. Ch 34 'The Boldest and West Buttress Eliminate' *Extreme Rock*, Wilson and Newman, Diadem Books, 1987.

Leeds University to meet Nick Parry, with whom, by chance, I shared lodgings. We soon became close friends and, from the start, I could see that he was incredibly bright but with a beguiling two-sided character: very composed, introverted and calm when climbing but, once in the bar, extrovert, carefree and animated. When he started at Emmanuel College, his visits to Leeds increased in frequency, as there was little climbing to be found on the flat-lands around Cambridge.

I introduced Al to my university climbing friends, and he enjoyed a friendly rivalry on the local gritstone crags with John Syrett, the most talented climber at Leeds. Mike Geddes was his roommate at Cambridge and, in winter, they would join us on ice-climbing forays to Scotland. Al would arrive on my doorstep wearing his mother's dishevelled fur coat and Geddes in a threadbare army greatcoat. With Geddes, he emulated his success on rock by making ascents of numerous new ice routes.

Al gained a reputation for solo climbing, having the gift of remaining calm and detached when faced with apparent danger. On one occasion, after a lunchtime drinking session, a group of climbers visited the roadside cliff of Tremadog in North Wales to solo climb. Al encouraged me to join in, but I froze halfway up a middle-grade climb called *One Step in the Clouds*. Fearful of falling, I could not make the next move and, embarrassingly, had to be rescued by a top rope. It seemed that the others were pushing the boundaries, soloing routes that I could barely climb. I watched with a mix of horror and admiration as Rouse and Minks climbed the extreme route, *Vector*, Al with the Rolling Stones' *Get Yer Ya Ya's Out* blasting from a cassette player strapped around his back. Minks smoked a large joint as he laughed and joked his way up the climb.

They did it, I suspect, for the thrill of living on a knife-edge, stimulating an addictive adrenaline rush, but Al also had a deter-mination to succeed regardless of what others thought or wanted. As they reached the top, I felt left out and isolated by the peer pressure. With hindsight, I am amazed that nobody died.

In 1970, Rab Carrington walked into the Padarn Lake pub in Llanberis, Wales, on a midweek April day.

'I saw a tall and gangly teenager with long dark brown hair stood at the bar wearing loons and horn-rimmed glasses,' Rab remembers, 'We had never met, but I immediately recognised him as Al Rouse. I sidled up to him and casually asked him what he was doing. He said he was looking for someone to climb with. Neither of us had transport so, at closing time, we walked an hour up the road to Humphries Barn, a scruffy bunkhouse in Nant Peris. Next day we went onto Snowdon, to the cliffs of *Cloggy* and had one of those wonderful effortless climbing days.'

Rab was no stranger to cutting-edge climbing in Scotland, having made the first ascent of the *Pinch* on Glen Etive's granite slabs and a first winter ascent of *Gargoyle Wall* on Ben Nevis. His last two summers had been spent in the Alps, where he had succeeded on an impressive list of climbs.

Rab knew of Al's reputation. 'He was the guy in the lights. I looked up to him even though he was only nineteen, four years younger than me. He had such ability and all the ideas of where to go. He gave me the world.'

That chance meeting between Al and Rab evolved into a formidable climbing partnership throughout the '70s. 'I began to realise that Al wasn't out in front of me, rather that we had become equals. In fact, in certain things, I had taken over, such as organisation and better stamina on the mountain. So, my early respect disappeared.'

Al went back to the Alps in '71 with Rab and they progressed to more challenging climbs. On one occasion, Al went off on his own to rope-solo the extremely difficult South Face of the Fou. Full of confidence, he was making good progress when a piton pulled out. The fall was only a few metres but, unfortunately, he hit a small ledge and broke his ankle. Forced to self-rescue, he made seventeen abseils down the rock face, for much of the time using only his knees for support. Eventually, he managed to alert another climbing party and was winched to safety by a helicopter.

Undeterred by the accident, he returned to the Alps with Rab the following year and made ascents of more challenging routes, including the second ascent of the *Lesueur Route* on the Dru. In 1972, after their second Alpine season together, they flew to

California's Yosemite Valley, but disagreed over what to climb. Al wanted to aid-climb the famous Big Walls whereas Rab wanted to free climb shorter routes. Al's obstinance prevailed.

'We set off to do the *Leaning Tower*. I had hardly done any peg climbing and never used a *Jumar* rope ascender. It took three uncomfortable days. I hated every fucking second of it,' Rab remembers.

For the rest of the trip, they went their separate ways, Al attempting the North Face of Half Dome with an American he had just-met. Five pitches up he fell, again fracturing his ankle. His partner was of no help, and Al had to organise all the abseils. Eventually, they reached the base from where he was stretchered down by the Yosemite rescue team which, much to Al's surprise, included Rab who had joined to earn some extra cash.

Extravagant ideas came naturally to him and, on his return, he proposed that I join him on what would be our first expedition together, to Fitzroy in Patagonia. I couldn't afford to go, but Al still managed to put together a team of six, including Carrington and Geddes. Their trip seemed fated, gear was impounded by customs and the weather was atrocious. Unsuccessful from a climbing point of view and a complete waste of time and money. Expeditions may sound exotic and exciting, but for every successful one, there are many failures.

During 1984, when I shared a farmhouse near Bangor, North Wales with John Whittle, the nearby Gogarth sea cliffs on Anglesey were fast becoming one of the UK's major climbing areas, enjoying better weather than Snowdonia's mountain crags. One winter weekend when Al was staying with me, we decided to climb at Gogarth, the weather being poor inland.

Al knew the area well from his first ascent of *Positron*. The guidebook described the climb as – *An extremely strenuous and sustained route up very steep rock. The top pitch is phenomenally impressive and one of the hardest pitches at Gogarth.* And Rouse as – *The most brilliant young climber in the country.* It was given the hardest grade of the day, *Hard Extremely Severe* and, fifty years later, is still regarded as a test piece.

On this occasion, we planned a complete sea-level traverse of the main cliff, which Al, forever the optimist (and fantasist), convinced me would be a doddle, even though there were some sections he had never seen. We looked at the cold sea with its heavy swell and made our first mistake by assuming that flared jeans, tie-dyed tee-shirts, and wool pullovers would be sufficient clothing. Grabbing a rope and a couple of slings for an emergency, Al was confident it could be done in a couple of hours, and there would be no need for food and water. He had a strange Svengali influence over people, and stupidly I trusted him.

As usual, the previous night we had drunk too much beer. Al suffered horrendous hangovers and would carry his special remedy of tinned pea and ham soup wherever he went. That morning though, even a bowl of his magic potion would not assuage his illness.

'Have you got any paracetamols?' he asked.

Sorry, no. Is the tide going in or out?

'I forgot to look.'

'It'll be a lot easier if it's a low tide.'

At that, Al slipped and went flying onto boulders covered in barnacles, sharp mussel shells and slippery seaweed. A seal's head bobbed out of the water nearby, its big round eyes staring at him, bent double, puking into the water, blood oozing out of his gashed hand.

After a few hundred metres of good progress, we found our way blocked by a steep wall that gave exhilaratingly steep climbing, but it should have been obvious that the tide was coming in. Looking back along our traverse, the easy ledges we had just crossed were disappearing underwater. With our retreat blocked, we were forced to continue with increased difficulty into the *Easter Island Gully* area.

'Should we put the rope on in case we fall into the sea?' I suggested.

'We can, but I don't intend to fall.'

I looked at the foaming water, insisted we tie onto the rope, and keeping just a few metres above the sea, started to lead across a series of greasy grooves. Twenty metres out, the rope started to drag under the water. 'Al, let more slack out! The rope's pulling me off.'

'Okay!'

A large swell rose and, as it sunk again, pulled at the rope and the inevitable happened: I was yanked off the rock. Pulled under by my wet clothes and the rope, I spluttered and fought to swim in the freezing water. Fortunately, after a few vigorous strokes, I flopped onto the ledges, the barnacles having ripped my jeans, and with blood pouring from my knees. Al laughed at my misfortune and followed until, precisely where I had fallen, the rope pulled him into the sea. I started hauling as he was not a strong swimmer, but the rope jammed.

'Throw the spare end. I'm being pulled under,' Al yelled.

I threw the rope, but it didn't reach. I tried again, and it disappeared under the waves. Meanwhile, Al was being dragged under by the swell and was having difficulty swimming wearing his rock-boots. 'Untie your rope,' I shouted.

There was a lot of frantic splashing and treading water before he managed to remove the rope from around his waist. When a wave swept him towards me, I grabbed his outstretched arm and pulled. Amazingly, his horn-rimmed glasses were still cockled on his nose, a blessing as he was almost blind without them. We were shivering as the late afternoon winter light dimmed and the beam of the South Stack lighthouse appeared.

'Wish I'd brought a torch,' I said.

'Did you tell anyone what we were doing?'

'No'

'Did you leave a note on the car windscreen?'

'No'

Climbs in this area were highly difficult, accessed only by abseiling, thanks to the ubiquitous overhanging walls. With no rope, climbing out was impossible. Therefore, we had to keep traversing, realising that our light-hearted adventure had turned into something a lot more serious.

A couple of years previously, we had climbed in this area on a hot summer day. We did *Wonderwall* in fancy dress for a laugh, Al as a pirate and me with a top hat, and we knew from this experience that, a short distance further on, was a steep-sided inlet where there was a mid-difficulty climb called *Wen*. If we could get to the inlet, even though our rope was lost to the sea, we might be able to climb out. So, we started traversing the rock walls in the dark but, with numb hands and wet boots, inevitably fell into the freezing sea. Thankfully our eyes had become accustomed to the gloom and, after what seemed a marathon swim, we identified the start of *Wen*.

'I'm not sure I can climb this,' I called. 'Perhaps you climb out and call for help.'

'You'll be fine. Just take it slowly.'

My rock boots were soaked and had little grip, and I was chilled to the bone, shaking uncontrollably with little feeling in my fingers. Without the safety of a rope, we groped up the hundred-metre climb. Now Al was in his element, encouraging me by pointing out holds. In one way the darkness helped, by hiding the sickening drop. Eventually, more by feel than sight, we reached the top, but that was not the end of the escapade. The two-hour walk back to the car in tight-fitting rock boots was purgatory. I had never felt so cold, and when we reached my old Morris 1000, we were staggering like two drunks and slurring our speech.

It was another of Al's wild ideas to climb in the Alps in winter, persuading Carrington, Whittle and me that we could afford to rent an apartment for three months in the Chamonix valley. We approached the Alpine winter very scientifically, testing gear and starting on minor routes to gain experience for bigger challenges.

Following all our careful planning, Al was incensed when Dave Robinson and James Bolton, friends of ours from Bangor, came to stay at our apartment and, without any preparation, succeeded on the prestigious first winter ascent of the North Face of the Droites. His competitive spirit was further heightened when we heard that Joe Tasker and Dick Renshaw had made the first British winter ascent of the North Face of the Eiger. This began a rivalry with Joe (and later with Pete Boardman), which simmered in the background till their deaths in 1982. What annoyed Al was that he felt he was the better climber.

His favourite climbing was the technical hard mixed type found in the Alps in winter, such as the *Rebuffat-Terray* on the North Face of Pélerins. 'At one stage I had to negotiate a vertical arête with ice on each side, nasty and uncompromising, twenty-five metres above the last runner. My feet skated a little and my arms tensed with effort. Eventually I passed the last stage of fear and switched onto a kind of automatic. It was as if the subconscious had decided to kill the fear and devote everything to movement. It proved superb, the most exposed ice climbing I have ever encountered.'[2]

That winter had many other highlights. Rab remembers, 'One route stands out as the best climb Al and I ever did. It was not our first winter ascent on the Pélerins as many people would expect, but the *Gervasutti Pillar* on Mont Blanc du Tacul. It took three days of the most impeccable climbing.'

After I finished my degree in Bangor, I became part of a small group who gravitated to Chester and worked as supply teachers to finance our climbing habit. I shared a small one-bedroom flat with Al and an eccentric, foul-mouthed Welshman called Davvy. Al slept in the entrance passage, squeezed under a wrecked piano. I was in the lounge behind the sofa while Davvy, the tenant, had the bedroom. Rab and his girlfriend Sue had their own flat, as did Al and Aid Burgess with their partners. We followed a routine of teaching during the day, climbing or running in the early evening, then going to the pub. At weekends we hitched to Snowdonia or the Peak District. It was a very sociable time that often got out of hand.

The Twins and I had just come back from a training run around Chester's medieval walls. Al's ankle injuries precluded such exercise, and Rab thought running unhealthy, saying, 'There isn't enough time between drinking and climbing.' Davvy's only running was from restaurants where he had not paid the bill. Our first-floor flat was accessed by open steps and, after the run, we took turns to hand-over-hand up the underside of the stairs. Rab, Al and Davvy joined and soon we were bare-topped, dressed only in shorts, pumped-up and sweating. Suddenly there was a stampede of feet up the stairs, and someone stood on Al's fingers.

2. 'Wintering Out' *Climber and Rambler* magazine April 1976.

There was a loud commotion, and three scruffily dressed blokes with a large Alsatian dog appeared at the top of the stairs.

'What's going on?' the Twins shouted as they rushed up the steps, bristling for a fight. They were about to lay into the uninvited guests when one shouted 'Police' and held out his warrant card.

'Stay there, or we'll let the dog loose.' Now confronting six athletically built young males, he ordered, in the usual police monosyllabic language, 'Inside. Sit down. Do not talk. It's a drug raid.'

More police arrived, some in uniform, and proceeded to search the flat, the crackle of their walkie-talkies occasionally interrupting. We were interviewed and strip-searched, which became comic when visiting friends began to arrive. First, a climbing mate and his girlfriend popped in to be greeted by an aggressive copper. 'In there and take your clothes off.'

They did not grasp the situation fully and shouted at the policeman, making matters worse. By now, there was hardly room to stand in the small flat. Second to arrive was the respectable lady from downstairs, who often came round to find out what we were doing. This time she got an unwelcome surprise as she was ordered into the bathroom and searched. Half an hour later her disgruntled husband arrived complaining that the dinner was burnt and he was hungry. He was also strip-searched and interviewed.

Meanwhile, his small yappy Scotty dog which, to Carrington's annoyance, was called Rab followed him upstairs. I have never seen such a mismatch between dogs as when Rab (the dog) attacked the Alsatian. The supposed highly trained police dog went berserk, howling and crashing around the room as our neighbours looked on in dismay.

Even though our flat was opposite the police station and the least likely home for a drug cartel, they pulled the place apart until, under the piano, near where Al slept, they found a half-smoked joint. Al was partial to a smoke, and I had been with him a couple of years before, when he was arrested at the Kendal Rock Festival. While listening to the music, he'd offered the undercover cop next to him a drag on his joint. Al was arrested and spent the night behind bars. The Chester bust was therefore more serious for him, as it would be his second offence, and he was treated in a heavy-handed way, handcuffed and taken to the police station. These arrests only confirmed his anarchistic view of the law and increased his rebellious streak.

In the Alps, a counterculture thrived in the valley where all nationalities of alpinists gathered as a shady community, where the theft of a rotisserie chicken or a bottle of cheap wine did not feel like a crime. It became the norm, and we were no different to the rest. True to character, Al took this to excess on a climbing trip to Switzerland, where he was caught stealing, deported, and banned from entering the country ever again. He would have been unperturbed except that it stopped him climbing one of the routes on his wish list, the North Face of the Eiger.

Our debauched lifestyle of the mid-1970s was orchestrated by Al Harris, a slim, good- looking, guy with wavy fair hair and a mild cockney accent who was also the wild man of British rock climbing. A hedonist in every way, he was a talented climber who set up Wendy's cafe in Llanberis, from which he ran a climbing school. By the time I got to know him, he had virtually given up climbing but maintained an infamous party cottage called Bigil.

Al and I would travel to Snowdonia determined to climb, only to be hijacked into Harris's den of iniquity. All-night parties, excessive drinking and drug-taking, dancing and driving fast cars down winding lanes drained our energy for climbing. Visiting American climbers such as Henry Barber, who climbed hard and played harder, would disappear into the black hole of Bigil only to surface a month later, not having touched rock. At 4.00a.m. we would find Rouse dancing with six cigarettes or a foot long joint between his lips, completely out of his head. He said he did it for a laugh, which was part of his crazy, loveable character.

However, the constant high octane party life had a detrimental effect on his fitness and health. He also kept injuring himself. One evening on the gritstone edge of Stanage in the Peak District, he unexpectedly started shouting for help near the top of a climb he was soloing. We rescued him with a rope, but he was yelling in pain. His shoulder had dislocated, which blighted his climbing until he had it pinned. This was Al's third significant injury, after which it became apparent that he was losing ground to the more abstinent climbers.

In tandem with the party life in Wales, a group of approximately twenty climbers, mainly from Derbyshire and Yorkshire, formed an unofficial drinking group called the Piraña Club. The difference with Bigil was that we would choose a venue for the weekend and actually climb or go caving, before getting wasted in the evening. Al would generally think up crazy adventures while John Sheard, a talented Yorkshire climber, became the driving force as he owned a large Ford Transit van. We became friends for life which, for me, emphasises how, at that time, climbing was a culture rather than a sport.

Eventually, it became time to move into a new phase of our lives. On 5th November 1976, Rab and Sue got married, and we had a leaving party in Chester before our first expedition together, a super-trip to South America that Al had devised. His overall vision was for three pairs of climbers, some accompanied by partners, to travel for a year, starting in Patagonia but heading northwards as the seasons changed. The pairs would operate independently and choose their own objectives. So, in December, the Burgess twins, John Whittle and I, together with Al and Rab, found ourselves in Parque Nacional de Los Glaciares in southern Argentina.[3]

'Al was the inspiration, doing all the research and choosing the routes,' Rab says. 'I was enjoying the climbing, doing the moves, it didn't really make any difference which mountain it was. I was the complete opposite of Al, and that's perhaps why we made a good team.'

We had the time of our lives, and all made significant ascents, with Al and Rab making a fitting crescendo to the trip with three outstanding new climbs in Peru's Cordillera Huayhuash on Rasac, Rondoy and Yerupaja Sur. Al had lists of climbing objectives written in his spidery hand and, after South America, a major new route in the Himalayas became his next plan.

In 1978, Al, Carrington, Baxter-Jones and I set off for the unclimbed East Face of Jannu in Nepal. However, our proposed route was too dangerous. Instead, our epic ascent of the original

3. See Chapter 6

French route became a significant landmark in climbing alpine style in the Greater Ranges. We kept strictly to the idea of climbing as two independent pairs and did it in one single push without outside help.[4]

As the expedition progressed, I grew into the landscape, better understood my three partners and shed the lethargy of urban life. At the end we were lucky to get away with something so near to the edge of life and death and gave all of us a feeling of long-lasting contentment.'

'At our peak, most of us never thought we were going to die; we hadn't room for that,' Rab explains. 'You had to have a clear mind, and Al and I felt we were invincible and just kept doing it.'

On occasions, Al would work as a climbing guide for Jon Fisher's Palisade School of Mountaineering in Bishop, California. The American West Coast lifestyle suited him, and he wrote to me saying he was thinking of moving there permanently. Impressed by the company, he suggested emulating their business model in the UK, thinking it may be a way to make a living out of climbing. So, after returning from Jannu, we formed Mountain Experience, a partnership between Al and me along with two Scottish climbers, Mal Duff and Robert Bruce. The bulk of the money needed to kick-start the business came from Bruce, who tragically died, in July 1979, in a storm on the summit of Mont Maudit, above Chamonix.

Nevertheless, we decided to continue the business. The following year we devised a complete programme, including guiding The Old Man of Hoy, holidays in the Alps, and longer trips to the Peruvian Andes. As Al and I were away mountaineering most of the time, Mal did the office work.

Just before we went to K2 in '86, Al and I took full control and drafted plans for guided trips to Himalayan peaks. If successful, it would have been a forerunner of mountain adventure tourism, where companies specialise in climbing Everest and the Seven Summits. After Al's death, I successfully continued the company out of Chamonix, but only ever organised one commercial trip to the Greater Ranges. I was left to ponder *what if*?

4. As recounted in Chapter 7

By the '90s, guided ascents of Everest had started, notably with
Rob Hall's Adventure Consultants and Scott Fischer's Mountain
Madness.[5]

Eventually, Al's voracity was the undoing of his relationship with
Rab, who says, 'He wanted all the labels and to be seen. He had
ambitions and lists: climb Everest, be the next Chris Bonington, the
youngest President of the Alpine Club and a key decision-maker in
BMC.'

When Al, Rab and I went to Kangtega in 1979, I sensed the
atmosphere was strained. Rab explains: 'It is not a good idea going
to the Himalayas in the wrong frame of mind. You don't have the
will to make the right decisions – to carry on or turn round. The
split with Al was my fault. I recall the specific moment on Kangtega.
We had an argument, a shouting match from one end of the rope
to the other. I thought he was faffing around and not climbing fast
enough.'

Rab's perception of what was happening to Al at that time
cannily augured his demise. 'When we parted, I think Al's life was
becoming chaotic, and he was unhappy. He was juggling so many
balls at that time. He started drinking and smoking a lot, as well
as taking drugs. As a result, his fitness level went down.'

By the time we trekked up the Khumbu Valley to attempt a new
route on the North Ridge of Nuptse, Al appeared to have put the
split with Rab behind him. After we got down we all agreed that it
had been among the most exciting ten days of our lives and we were
lucky to have survived the descent through the Khumbu Icefall.

Al's romantic life was always a rocky road. In the winter of 1980,
he moved to Chamonix to live with his long-term French girlfriend
Gwen who one day fell while skiing the precipitous ENSA couloir
on the Brévent, above Chamonix. Al rushed to the hospital to be by
her side but was ushered into the mortuary rather than a hospital
ward. Due to a miscommunication, nobody had told him she had

---

5. Scott and Fischer died while guiding Everest in May 1996, an epic
   described in Jon Krakauer's book Into Thin Air. In 1997, Mal Duff died
   in his sleep of a suspected heart attack at Everest Base Camp while
   guiding the mountain.

not survived. After that tragedy, a bitter edge appeared in his character. He moved back to Sheffield, where he met Hilary Ramsay, who had just moved from Bristol and was grieving after her boyfriend, Arnie Strapcans, who was killed while soloing a climb on the Brenva face of Mont Blanc.

Hilary remembers, 'Al called around very soon after Arnie's death, mostly to talk about Gwen, as he said he knew about losing someone, especially as their relationship had been on and off. He was full of guilt, and looking back, he found it difficult to accept.'

Finding solace together, they started a relationship, but Al began planning an ambitious expedition to Everest in winter almost immediately.

'All of a sudden, he was gone, and I was alone for three months. I was really excited, anticipating his homecoming but was shocked when I saw him. He was quite ill, very underweight, sad and withdrawn. He also talked a lot about his fear of dying in the mountains, and the failure on Everest upset him. On the trip he was constantly sick and had a miserable trip, affected by his conflict with Tasker, who he felt mentally bullied him.'

Over the next few years, they seemed to be a contented couple and bought a house but, coming from Bristol, Hilary found it tough moving into the cliquey climbing scene in Sheffield.

'It made economic sense for Al rather than a sign of us settling down. It was a happy period even though Al wanted me to decorate and sort the house out while he went away on his adventures. It was like having two lives, I had a routine of living on my own, and then Al would come back, and suddenly everything got complicated, and the house was full of gear as there was always another expedition on the horizon. He was quite old fashioned in his attitude to women, perhaps demeaning but never unkind. So, I felt I was a good practical solution for him. He would have his little chauvinistic jokes, which he would see as funny, but I thought they were irritating.'

Although on his next expedition, led by Chis Bonington, Al reached the summit of Kongur, Hilary said he was paranoid when he got back. 'He felt uncomfortable and sidelined after conflicts with Tasker and Boardman, the latter who had a clean-living image and was part of the establishment. Fearful that he would be judged on his performance, frightened that he would lose respect if he failed.'

He started rock climbing again in '81 with Phil Burke. 'Al went back to his roots, started training, and still had phenomenal finger strength, allowing him to succeed on hard rock climbs again.'

Burke remembers how days on the crag were good fun. Although Al was charismatic and had a big reputation, he seemed lost with no regular climbing partner, but as soon as they climbed, it was as equals. 'He was fantastic company, and I would only think positively about Al. But he could always be led astray and loved staying up all night drinking and telling stories.'

Back in a stable relationship, I could see Al was shedding his worrisome cloak and becoming optimistic about the future. Public lectures and working as an equipment consultant started bringing in cash, and he took a rung up the political climbing ladder when he was made Vice President of the BMC.

After our unsuccessful trip to the Ogre 2, he returned to the Karakoram in '83 on Doug Scott's multi-peak expedition on which he summited his first eight thousand-metre mountain, Broad Peak. The tragic death of Pete Thexton clouded the expedition. They then tried K2, but bad weather frustrated the attempt.

Hilary really wanted to join him on that trip, 'I thought it could be my great adventure. I started to get fit, walking as fast as possible in the hills to show Al I was good enough. But he was absolutely against it. He did not believe in wives and girlfriends going on an expedition and said it had ruined everything when Sue accompanied Rab to Kangtega.'

Disappointed, she decided to go to Australia for six months and, on her return, told him that she'd had a holiday romance. They tried to patch things up, but it was never the same. 'The trip away felt liberating, and I did not want to go back to the same lifestyle,' she said. Al was devastated when she moved out in June '84. However, within a few months, he met and started a new relationship with Deborah Sweeney, which undoubtedly improved his mood.

To his friends, Al was a confident, happy-go-lucky person, but it was a crumbling facade to those who were closer. When we met on my frequent visits to Sheffield, he was drinking heavily and suffering wretched hangovers, and I was concerned about his mental health.

'I haven't slept for three days. I'm awake all night pouring in sweat,' he complained.

'Have you seen a doctor?'

'No, do you think I've got malaria?'

Buying a bigger house that he could not afford increased his worries. Having invented a fictitious income for his mortgage application, he filled it with tenants, most of whom turned the house into a twenty-four-hour party venue.

I was having my own mental problems, after being injured on Chamlang and, when Al talked to me about going on another expedition, I was still coming to terms with that accident, wondering whether I even wanted to return to the Himalayas. He was very persuasive, and while drinking in one of the pubs in Sheffield's Nether Edge, asked, 'Wanna come to K2?'

'Yeh.'

'Two more pints, please.'

'Fancy a game of darts?'

That was about as formal as it got. I still needed to *feed the rat*[6] but naively thought I had committed to a small expedition to make a lightweight alpine style ascent.

When a child draws a mountain, it looks like K2, a steep triangle with a pointy top. Never like the rolling bulk of Everest. By popular opinion, K2, the world's second-highest mountain at 8,611 metres is deemed the most challenging of mountains although accomplished climbers know of more difficult and steeper peaks. Before our 1986 expedition, thirty-nine climbers had reached its summit at a cost of twelve lives. There had been no British ascents. Known as the *Savage Mountain*, it is regarded as the greatest prize in mountaineering.

The first serious expedition was in 1902. Led by Oscar Eckenstein, it included the occultist Aleister Crowley. The next,

6. *Feeding the Rat:* Al Alvarez, Harper Collins, 1989

abortive, attempt was in 1909, organised by the Italian Duke of the Abruzzi, on the South East Spur, now known as the Abruzzi Ridge, which, many years later, would become the standard route to the summit. After that, the Americans had three serious, though failed, attempts in 1938, 1939 and 1953. Finally, on 31st July 1954, the Italians Lino Lacedelli and Achille Compagnoni reached the summit by the Abruzzi Ridge.

Al was fixated with the idea of making the first British ascent and wanted to give it another try after his failed attempt in 1983. He applied to the Pakistan government for permission in 1986 but, unfortunately, his personal life descended into chaos and he asked me to take over leadership. I declined, having my own work commitments as well as helping Louise develop our cafe in Hayfield.

Out of the blue, he passed the administration onto John Barry (JB), a relative stranger with whom neither of us had climbed before but whose quick Irish wit and love of banter helped in coordinating the trip. JB had a record as an excellent mountaineer and mountain guide. Formerly a Royal Marine captain and then director of Plas y Brenin, the National Outdoor Centre in Snowdonia. He was also commissioned to write the expedition book *K2 – Savage Mountain, Savage Summer*. In the book, he wrote, 'I didn't know Al well at this stage, but I was beginning to see his genius was frantic, frenetic and flawed – and that his dealings wavered extreme to extreme, from rigorous to random, superficial to sedulous.'

Every time I met Al and JB, the expedition personnel had changed, with more people added. Our good friends from the Everest winter trip joined us, John Porter and the Burgess twins, along with Phil Burke and Dave Wilkinson (Wilkie). It was the first time Burke had been to the Himalayas, but he was a lean and extremely fit climber, runner and caver who had been on an audacious expedition to Cerro Torre in Patagonia. With a dogmatic attitude and a love of good debate he fitted in well with the rest of the single-minded and opinionated team. Wilkie was his opposite. Squat and powerful, beneath a quiet and reticent nature hid the determined expedition climber who had made the first ascent of Rimo 3. A mountaineer who preferred slogging up mountains over gymnastic rock climbing.

Bev Holt, a doctor, and Jim Hargreaves as Base Camp manager were appointed. As the expedition grew, it became too expensive to fund with only personal contributions, so it was decided that a film would attract sponsorship. This would be made by our friend, Jim Curran, who lived near Al in Sheffield. I had filmed *The Bat* with Curran a few years previously, and he had helped John Porter and me set up the Kendal Mountain Film Festival. He had also made a string of expedition films, including a documentary on the first ascent of Kongur. He worked as a fine art lecturer but, as he spent more time writing, filming and painting, his girth increased and his climbing standard dropped. He was a raconteur with an ironic sense of humour, always guaranteed to entertain. A warm and thoughtful man and one of Al's closest friends, he was also concerned about Al's health.

When JB got involved he was amazed to hear Curran, of all people, counsel Al over his love life. 'Though he purported to be an expert on women, his only qualification to help seemed to be a lengthy string of broken relationships.'

JB had excellent organisational skills but, unfortunately, the rest of the team were not too happy about being treated as foot soldiers. Somehow, without making a conscious decision, we had become a heavyweight traditional expedition of eleven people using fixed ropes and camps, albeit without bottled oxygen or high-altitude porters. This was a style I had been trying to avoid since I started climbing in the Greater Ranges.

Al's mental health improved as his relationship with Deborah blossomed and, a few months before departure, he came to believe that he was well enough to take back the leadership. JB was not convinced and suggested joint leadership. I was dismayed, as were some of the rest of the team. Rarely do such compromises work.

Then, unexpectedly, Al announced, 'I'm going to be a dad. Deborah's pregnant, and the baby is due soon after we return from K2.'

'How do you feel about that?' I asked.

'It hasn't really sunk in. It all seems unreal. I'll sort it out when I get back home.'

Again, his hyperactive brain was in turmoil, but there was no suggestion that he might not go to K2. He had complex and confusing sentiments towards women, but I knew that, once he was in a relationship, he was faithful and loving with one huge proviso: everything came second to climbing. He certainly had an outdated and dismissive attitude of women climbers, saying to me, 'If a woman climbs better than me today, I will give up tomorrow.' So, since a British woman, Julie Tullis, would also attempt K2 that season, there was an intriguing situation developing. I became convinced that Al was paranoid that she might beat him to his coveted first British ascent of K2.

I had my own issues to contend with. In the spring before our planned departure to Pakistan, on a relaxed skiing holiday with Louise in Chamonix, as I traversed a slope of fresh snow, my skis caught on a rock and I fell in agony. Gingerly, I managed to descend to the valley with my knee the size of a balloon. A visit to the doctor diagnosed knee ligament damage which needed further investigation and I feared that it would end my dream of climbing K2. A scan was inconclusive but the swelling came down, and I convinced myself that it would be okay to go.

With only a few months before departure, a lack of funds seriously jeopardised the expedition. We stepped up our fundraising efforts claiming that *we were the strongest expedition team to leave British shores to climb the world's hardest mountain*. The publicity made me cringe with embarrassment, but it worked, and JB persuaded the beer manufacturer, Fullers, to sponsor. The day before we left was full of festivity as we drove around London in the brewery's red double-decker bus while sampling their fine ales.

Our troubles began before we arrived at Base Camp on 23rd May. Our original application was for a new route on the South Face, but there were so many expeditions on that side, we instead received a permit for the North-West Ridge on the Chinese border, the opposite side of the mountain to our Base Camp. With no possible chance of negotiation, it meant a mammoth approach, through an icefall and across an interminable glacier before we could even start. Nor was the route suitable for our favoured alpine style ascent. The attraction was that it remained unclimbed despite attempts by the Americans in 1975 and a sizeable Polish group a few years later.

During the first weeks, we enjoyed focus and harmony. Filled with pent-up energy, everyone was keen to get to grips with the mountain. However, throughout the trip, the long approach remained a nightmare. 'I've never been so hot in my life.' I lay exhausted in the tent at Advanced Base Camp, red-faced and pouring in sweat after a day load-carrying.

'It was like skiing through glue,' Al replied.

'I've got a splitting headache.'

'Probably dehydration or the strong sun.'

'Or the altitude.'

The next day our load-carry to Camp 1 was aborted in a whiteout as a snow blizzard filled all our hard-won tracks. The storm lasted three days. 'I'm not enjoying this expedition. It's boring and a hard slog,' I told Al.

'I agree but, now we are here, we have to make the best of it.'

'All these camps and fixed ropes are not our style.'

'Our main aim is to get to the top of K2,' Al said.

'For me, it's not.'

During the initial stages of the expedition, I was not happy and wrote to Louise, 'Jim Curran and I are suffering from terrible colds. I've never been so ill in my life, I've had a succession of ailments, and now my knee is bad after load-carrying yesterday.'

As our energy flagged, we needed Al to be a confident leader but, conversely, it was not in any of our natures to lead or be led. While sitting around at Base Camp, there was pointless bickering about the best way to climb the route.

Burke recalls, 'In Britain Al was a laugh to rock climb with but, on K2, I saw a different side of him. He was ruthless and wanted to get up the mountain at any cost. So, he divided the team up to his best advantage, separating the Twins whom he thought were a power block who were strong enough to do their own thing.'

In my view, Al's insistence on dividing the party into two teams was okay, but calling them A and B was a mistake, predictably creating rival cliques who spent much of the expedition competing and blaming each other in equal measure.

I wrote in my diary:

> June 5th. Thursday. After taking painkillers, I felt better this morning but still difficult to get to sleep. Very bad weather with lots of snow. Al, Aid, Phil and John came down from camp one where they achieved very little apart from personal acclimatisation. They want the others to go up today, which seems impractical and a waste of time. It's a bit like Everest in winter. I expected an argument, but there was none, though Rouse and Aid had a bit of a set-to.

After a month, my knee had not improved, and despite the doctor's treatment, the cold I had been fighting had migrated to my chest. I was coughing incessantly, the headaches and panic attacks that had plagued me on Chamlang started to re-occur, and I hardly slept. Feeling useless and depressed, I decided to leave. As soon as I made the decision, I slept well and woke in a better frame of mind. With a clear head, I reconciled that Al and my ideals were at loggerheads. All that mattered for him was reaching the summit, after which he thought all his problems would evaporate.

As I left, the miserable weather continued to hamper progress. Al and Porter were climbing together, but spent many days sheltering in a tent at Camp 2 on the ridge at 6,800 metres. Porter told me, 'Al was a very different person from the carefree youth I first met in Leeds. He was morose, constantly talking about his troubled relationships and confusion about fatherhood.' Porter added that he told Al, 'You are going to have to face up to it. For God's sake, it's a baby. There are lots of them. Every man has his doubts.'

Eventually, the ropes were pushed out to 7,400 metres. Snow conditions were hazardous, and Burke narrowly escaped with his life when an avalanche swept down the route. In one brief clearing of the weather, when Al and Porter were at the high point, they considered a sprint to the summit, estimating they could reach the top and get back in two days. They decided not to risk it, worried by ominous clouds on the horizon. A day later, a vicious storm hit the mountain, killing two people making a summit attempt on the other side.

At the beginning of July, Porter and Base Camp manager Hargreaves departed, the pressure of work commitments outweighing the trials on K2. They waved goodbye as, to their frustration, the weather improved. Under a calm blue sky, the remaining six moved up the mountain: Rouse with Wilkie, Burke with Aid Burgess, JB with Al Burgess. It took almost a week of determined efforts in deep, new snow to regain the high point. Exhausted, JB and Burke retreated and, shortly after, the Twins, even though they were going strongly, pronounced the route unclimbable that year. Faced with a fait accompli, Rouse and Wilkie had no alternative but to descend and the team abandoned their primary objective, the North-West Ridge.

The international village of nine K2 expeditions was housed in a colourful assortment of tents pitched on a strip of moraine. On rest days, it became a social pastime to cruise the camps, chatting and sampling the hospitality in the kitchen tents of Americans, Italians, Poles, French, Koreans, Germans, Swiss and Austrians, catching up with what was happening on the other parts of the mountains. It was a harrowing season during which there had been triumphs, failures, epics, and deaths.

It started when two Americans, John Smolich and Alan Pennington, were swept away by a colossal avalanche on the South West Ridge. Two days later, a Pole, Wanda Rutkiewicz and a French team of Michel Parmentier with Maurice and Liliane Barrard and two Basque climbers reached the summit via the Abruzzi Ridge, which was notable for the first female ascents, but tragedy struck on the descent when the Berrard couple disappeared. Nevertheless, this ascent confirmed that if the top of K2 was the main objective (rather than a new route), then success was more attainable by the Abruzzi than any other route in the short windows of good weather.

Two weeks later, four Italians, a Czech, a Frenchman and two Swiss climbed the Abruzzi. Unbelievably, the Frenchman, Benoît Chamoux, made a twenty-three-hour ascent. Soon after, the Poles Jerzy Kukuczka and Tadeusz Piotrowski climbed a major new route up the central rib of the South Face in lightweight style, but disaster struck on the descent when the exhausted Piotrowski fell to his death.

Against this background the remaining six of the British team changed plans and in good weather on 15th July, they set off on the Abruzzi, deciding it was the best chance of reaching the summit. The start was adjacent to the Base Camp, and the lower section was fixed with ropes from previous attempts. Al was confident they could achieve it in four days, taking a minimum of gear.

'I was surprised by how easy it was, and the renowned House's Chimney was rigged with a caving ladder,' Burke confided later. 'I was sure we would get to the top but, for Al, it was shit or bust. He had to get up the mountain to further his career in the path he had chosen or die in the attempt.'

They climbed strongly for two days, with the Twins leading the charge but, on reaching Camp 3 at 7,350 metres the weather deteriorated, and they were forced to descend.

After this effort, resting at Base Camp, they heard that the renowned Italian solo mountaineer Renato Casarotto had fallen into a crevasse just above Base Camp, only minutes from safety, after attempting to solo a new route. He was still conscious as the rescue team pulled him out with his wife, Goretta, standing at the lip of the crevasse talking to him before he died of internal injuries.

For the Twins, Burke and JB, it was the final straw, and they decided to leave, accompanied by Holt. Hollow-cheeked and with matchstick legs, the two months' toil had emaciated their bodies. Emotionally drained, they'd had enough and packed in readiness for the arrival of the porters.

During our stay at K2, we were always made welcome at the Polish Base Camp. Over the past ten years, there had been a growing rapport and respect between our two climbing communities. Janusz Meyer was leading a seven-person Polish team trying a new route on K2's South Pillar. As the British team prepared to leave, Al spent more and more time at the Polish camp and started dropping Meyer hints that he should join the Poles. His overtures fell on deaf ears.

However, he met one of the three female expedition members, Dobraslava Miodowicz-Wolf, nicknamed Mrufka. A short woman with dark hair, piercing blue eyes, and a mischievous smile, who spoke only pidgin English, she was married to Polish mountaineer John Wolfe, and they had two young children. She was disillusioned with the South Pillar, thinking it was too hard for her, and the catalogue of deaths further increased her hesitancy. However, she felt that she stood a higher chance of success on the Abruzzi and suggested to Al that they join forces. He considered the idea, especially as most of the remaining British members had decided to leave.

However, Wilkie was determined to give K2 one last go, and assumed that he would climb with Al. Unfortunately, no concrete plans had been made and, when he heard that Al had agreed to climb with Mrufka, he was incensed. To make matters worse, Al, as usual, would not admit his mistakes and tried to justify himself, suggesting they climb as a threesome. Wilkie rejected that outright, thinking it logistically cumbersome. Their relationship was now in tatters, and Wilkie joined the exodus.

As one of Al's closest friends, Curran says, 'I found Al intensely irritating at times, but he, more than anyone else on the expedition, had an awesome determination to climb K2.' Even so, he became concerned when Meyer expressed his surprise that Al intended to climb with Mrufka, worried that he had overestimated her ability to keep up.

On 28th July, there was an acrimonious parting before the small group of British climbers and their porters wove their way down the moraine of the Goodwin Austen Glacier, disappearing into a greyness where the leaden skies melted into the high summits. Given the context of that season, our trip was lucky to escape without any significant injuries or fatalities. Of the British climbers, only Al remained, although Curran stayed at Base Camp to support him, being the filmmaker and not a lead climber. The teams waited for a weather window and a final attempt on K2, the Austrian, British and Korean teams poised to attempt the Abruzzi and the Poles on the South Pillar.

The management and petty arguments of expedition life had lain heavily on Al, and when the main team left, Curran noticed a marked change. 'Almost immediately, the strains and tensions that had so obviously been affecting him for the previous weeks dropped away. He became his normal boyish self again, bubbling with enthusiasm and self-confidence.'

A few days later, the barometer unexpectedly rose, and the clouds cleared. It was a siren call for feverish activity as the teams readied to take advantage of the good weather. Al could now attempt a fast ascent of the Abruzzi, in the way he knew best, without the trappings of a big expedition. Curran was concerned that he was run down after two months on the mountain, but Al was typically optimistic. If he felt tired, he would simply turn round, come down, and they would head for home.

Al and Mrufka wasted no time and set off that evening to ascend through the night to Camp 1. Three members of the Korean expedition were already on the move, as were Kurt Diemberger and Julie Tullis, together with three members of the Austrian expedition: Alfred Imitzer, Willi Bauer and Hannes Weiser.

Diemberger and Tullis were an affable pair, filming on the mountain, and had a disarming belief that it was their destiny to climb K2 that summer. Austrian Diemberger at fifty-four, notwithstanding his bald head and lined grey-bearded face, was a phenomenal high-altitude climber, filmmaker and author. A legend of mountaineering, he had made the first ascents on two mountains over eight thousand metres: Broad Peak in 1957 and Dhaulagiri in 1960. With shoulder-length fair hair and a smiling face, Julie Tullis also had a steely determination and extraordinary depths of physical reserves. At forty-seven, she was married with two children and was regarded as the most successful British female mountaineer of the time, being the first British woman to summit an eight thousand-metre mountain, Broad Peak.

Curran noticed that there now seemed to be a herd instinct running through the groups, a feeling probably exacerbated by the season coming to an end. If one group was going up, it must be okay. The teams flocked upwards with one thing in common, an obsession for the summit of K2. Mentally they had fallen into what today are called heuristic traps.

The weather was perfect for the next four days, and reports suggest that good progress was made by everyone. On 3rd August, the sky was cloudless when Curran visited the Korean Base Camp expecting news. Intermittent radio communication reported that the three Koreans were out in front, heading for the summit, aided by supplementary oxygen, and Curran assumed the other seven climbers on the Abruzzi would follow in their tracks. They would be slower as they were not using oxygen, but they could step in the Korean footsteps, saving considerable effort. The six Poles were also making good progress on the South Pillar.

Later in the day, a conflicting radio message came through saying Al and Mrufka had stopped for a day at Camp 4 at eight thousand metres. Jim was perplexed because they should have been heading for the top that day with the Koreans. If the radio message was correct, he and Mrufka were spending a rest day in the death zone where they could not recover any strength as the body deteriorates rapidly in the reduced oxygen pressure.

That evening the Korean camp erupted with joy as they learnt that their three climbers had reached the summit. Strangely, nobody had followed. The day after, 4th August, Jim was wakened by the Polish Pakistani Liaison Officer bearing bad news. Although the three lead Polish climbers had reached the summit, an accident had occurred as they descended the easier Abruzzi Ridge. Wojeich Wroz had abseiled off the end of a fixed rope and perished. The remaining pair were resting at Camp 4. There was a lot of radio chatter in Polish, making it difficult for Jim to understand what was happening with the other seven climbers on the Abruzzi.

Meanwhile, banks of mackerel cloud formations rolled in from the south, and a malevolent torpedo shaped cloud sat on the nearby summit of Broad Peak. Thankfully, K2 remained clear.

The following day, Curran peered out of his tent at falling snow and a constant roar of winds. Conditions would be ferocious on K2. How could anyone survive? Thankfully in the afternoon, the successful Koreans and Poles returned after descending the Abruzzi, the Poles shattered and distraught at the death of their compatriot. They brought more disturbing news.

When they left Camp 4, menacing clouds filled the sky, and they watched as Al, with no rucksack, wearing his red one-piece down suit, broke trail, heading for the top, ahead of Mrufka, Imitzer,

Bauer, Weiser, Diemberger and Tullis. They added that Weiser had
returned after a hundred metres with wet gloves, fearing frostbite.
There was no more news. What had become of them, and could
they survive the storm?

A sense of gloom and foreboding spread around Base Camp as
the storm continued. Curran was distraught. By 9th August, the
chance of survival seemed all but gone for the seven climbers. He
had started the sad task of packing Al's gear on 11th August when,
suddenly, there were shouts and people pointing towards the ridge.
In a brief clearing of wind-driven snow a figure had been seen.
Surely after seven days, this was impossible but, then, the clouds
parted to reveal a figure slowly descending out of the storm.

'My heart burst with hope and apprehension,' Curran remembered. 'I rushed with everyone towards the apparition. But it was
not Al, and I felt guilty as my heart sank; it was Bauer, the Austrian.
He was speechless with exhaustion and dehydration and quite liter-
ally on his last legs.' He whispered that Diemberger and Mrufka
were somewhere behind. Weiser and Imitzer had collapsed immediately after they left Camp 4. Tullis was dead, and he had left
Rouse in his tent, unable to move, delirious and drifting in and out
of consciousness.

The remaining people at Base readied for a rescue mission and
Curran arrived at Advance Base Camp at 11.00p.m. He collected
meltwater and noticed a few stars in the sky, then heard a repetitive
noise that piqued his interest. Setting off upwards in the dim light
of his head torch, the noise got louder, and suddenly he bumped
into Diemberger, painfully climbing down.

'Kurt, it's Jim! You're okay. You're nearly safe.'

'I thought I saw lights, but am I imagining things?' Kurt said
uncomprehendingly. 'I have lost Julie.'

Despite horrendous frostbite, Bauer and Diemberger had survived
one of the most incredible ordeals in mountaineering history. They
had endured a week at high altitudes in sub-zero temperatures and
hurricane winds with no food or water. Eventually, the pair were
helicoptered to safety on 16th August, both losing multiple fingers
and toes to severe frostbite.

From the base of the mountain, Curran witnessed the tragic

events that were to leave thirteen dead that season. In his book *K2, Triumph and Tragedy*, he pieced together what happened on those fateful days from interviews with the two survivors.

Bauer said they did not follow the Koreans because they needed a rest day. They waited for the trail to be cleared to the top. Al had been the strongest on 4th August and made a heroic effort to break trail for most of the day, but probably at the cost of all his energy, and survival later in the storm. The two Austrians caught him up at 4.00p.m., just before they summited. On the descent, they met Mrufka, exhausted but determined to carry on. Al persuaded her to retreat and helped her down, the four climbers getting back to Camp 4 at 6.30p.m. The delay in aiding Mrufka would have sacrificed Al's usual strategy of immediate and rapid descent. Diemberger and Tullis did not reach the summit till 7.00p.m. and, on the descent, Tullis fell, pulling Diemberger a hundred metres before he arrested the slide. Overtaken by darkness, they survived the night in a makeshift snow hole before making it back to Camp 4 the following day, exhausted and frostbitten.

As they clung to life, disaster struck. In bitter hurricane winds, snow engulfed and destroyed their tent. The others managed to dig them out, and Diemberger squeezed in next to Al and Mrufka in their tiny bivouac shelter. They had difficulty getting Tullis out. She had hardly any clothes on and had suffered terrible frostbite, but they got her into the Austrian tent, where she died the next morning. For three days the weather was so bad it was impossible to get out of the tents. Exhausted and without food or liquid, Al's condition deteriorated, and on 10th August, he was barely conscious. Hypothermic, frostbitten and suffering from seven days of reduced oxygen in the death zone, the surviving climbers realised that they must descend. It was now or never. Weiser and Imitzer struggled for a few hundred metres before collapsing.

It was impossible to see anything as Diemberger, Mrufka, and Bauer struggled down in whiteout conditions. 'Mrufka was helping me break trail,' Bauer recalls. 'She was really fantastic, and we managed to reach Camp 3 at 7,300 metres in darkness. But the camp wasn't there. The tents had been swept away by the wind.'

There were fixed ropes below, which aided their descent, and they thought the worst was over. They continued through the night, but Mrufka had problems using her abseiling device with her frostbitten hands. Bauer made it to the comparative safety of the lower camp stocked with food and fuel, but Mrufka failed to arrive. A few years later, her frozen body was found by a Japanese expedition, still in a standing position and attached to the fixed ropes. Only Diemberger and Bauer survived.

K2 had received its first and second British ascents, but at what cost? As Curran wrote, 'Both had perished in their triumph.'

Returned from K2 in August, I visited a knee specialist who confirmed that I had torn my anterior cruciate ligament and needed an operation, which helped justify my decision to leave and assuaged my guilt at abandoning my mates. On the other hand, it felt strange to be safely back while they were still on K2. Perturbingly, there were mixed messages and rumours from Pakistan. Some said that everyone was safe and on their way home. Others that some members had stayed for a last try at the summit.

At home in Hayfield, I was digging the allotment to take my mind off the worry when I saw Louise running towards me, still wearing her purple cooking apron. As she got closer, I could see she was crying. With trembling hands, she gave me a piece of paper.

'There's been an accident on K2. You need to phone this number.'

Was it a premonition or a hunch? Either way, I knew what had happened before I made the call. It was written in the script that Al would die but, when I pieced together the events, I was distraught at the circumstances and the awful death toll.

The newspapers were full of analysis and retribution, using the futile tool of hindsight, creating a blame game that dictated someone had to be at fault. It was only when Curran returned that we achieved any kind of understanding. He was a witness, albeit at the base of the mountain, to the horrendous reality of those last days on K2. A story that unfurled like the smoke of a funeral pyre.

Once the storm stranded those six brave climbers at eight thousand metres, it was a miracle that anyone had survived. They didn't know the severity of the oncoming weather, but how many times do clouds gather only for the next dawn to rise clear? Where would we be if everyone turned around when a problem arose? Stripped of sense and logic, climbers in the death zone can be overtaken by summit fever.

If an explanation has to be found, it lies in the desire for human beings to succeed and reach the top, whether it be in sport, adventure, work or life.

On another day, they would have been hailed as heroes. Despite Al's worrying mood swings and difficulties coping with the stresses and strains of expedition life, through pure self-centred determination, he reached the top. The courageous climbers endured, despite the risks, ignoring the well-known motto, *Reaching the summit is optional. Getting down is mandatory.*

A year earlier, Al had prophetically written in the Alpine Club Journal, 'In the future, we are bound to see a competent alpine style party stuck somewhere above eight thousand metres because of bad weather. Its chances of survival for more than a few days will be slim.'

That summer, sixteen mountaineers reached the *Savage Mountain's* summit, and thirteen more died. I've danced around the timeline of Al's life, but K2 was his last waltz. I still scratch my head to figure out why one of the apostles of alpine climbing decided to organise a trip with many of the traits of an old-style heavyweight expedition. It was a betrayal of a lifetime of beliefs. In retrospect, my participation was equally a mistake. Even the most admired and influential characters have their worries and, undoubtedly, he was scared and bewildered at what his new life back home would bring. Sometimes I dreamt that he surreptitiously descended K2 and made his way to his spiritual home in California, where he lived as an eccentric old hippie, a fantasy that is a sure sign of my enduring grief.

There is no better remembrance than from his family.

From his mother Eve: 'I am writing this on Alan's birthday. I went out shopping but had to come back as I couldn't stop crying. I have just got a beautiful bouquet of flowers from Jim Curran and am so very touched to know that Alan was so well thought of, and I am so proud of him. I don't think I will ever get over it but know that time softens most things, and I am sure this will be the same.'

From his sister Susan. 'He came home with an unlimited repertoire of stories and anecdotes; he was like a breath of fresh air in
the house. He often returned ill, injured or without money, but
never with his spirit dulled. I shall remember him not only as a
brother but also as a happy companion and eternal optimist and
someone who made me feel glad to be alive.'

On 5th September, a month after Al passed away, Deborah gave
birth to Holly. I cannot imagine the emotional turmoil that she
endured as she nursed her baby and brought her up alone. Life
carried on, but sadly their daughter was raised without ever
knowing the love of her father. When Al was younger, and his reputation and fame were growing, I could never see him changing
course from the buccaneering life of an elite mountaineer. He never
wanted the norm but, under new circumstances, I think he would
have been able to navigate from his old life, treating fatherhood as
his next challenge.

When he climbed, he ring-fenced his emotions to concentrate on
the task at hand. Elan and temerity moulded his success. Obsession,
the single-minded pursuit of his interests made him a top mountaineer and why he could be an infuriating character. He knew
what he wanted to do and did it regardless of other opinions.
Despite his emotional problems and because of his mischievous
character, he was my closest friend. His death signalled the end of
an era, destroying my love of mountaineering on the highest peaks.

Fixed ropes on the Abruzzi Ridge of K2.

AFTERWORD
The Course of Time.

I lived through a golden age of Himalayan exploration, and when I ceased climbing in the Greater Ranges, in 1986, the world of climbing was in a buoyant state. I'd been part of the transition from heavyweight to alpine style and observed the mountaineers who drove the sport forward into the new millennium. The impetus continued with small international teams using impeccable style to make ascents that were unimaginable to my generation.

The Italian Reinhold Messner had been at the forefront. Victorious after sixteen years of dedication, in 1986 he was the first to complete all fourteen eight-thousanders, including the first ascent of Everest without oxygen. The Pole Jerzy Kukuczka donned his mantle and was second to succeed on all fourteen in 1988. Admirably, most of Kukuczka's ascents were by alpine style new routes or in the grip of winter as one of an elite group of Polish *ice warriors*. On Broad Peak, then on Gasherbrum 1 and 2, he was joined by Voytek Kurtyka, who, more than anyone else, shaped the rise of alpine style. The idea of minimal equipment and support even on the most challenging walls and highest peaks became Kurtyka's philosophy. His ascent of the West Face (Shining Wall) of Gasherbrum 4 in 1985 with Austrian Robert Schauer is still regarded as a high point of world mountaineering history.

Speed, facilitated by high technical ability and fitness, allowed Swiss climbers Erhard Loretan and Jean Troillet to take alpine style to the extreme, developing what they called *night-naked*. In 1986 they climbed, alone, up and down Everest's North Face, through the night in an astounding, lung-bursting forty-three hours.

International co-operation within mountaineering was plain to see when Kurtyka joined the Swiss pair on Cho Oyu and Shisha Pangma in 1990. Their tactics became a model for the next generation, with the young Swiss alpinist Ueli Steck soloing the South Face of Annapurna in 2013, one of the most impressive Himalayan climbs in history, completed in twenty-eight hours. He also set records in 2015 by soloing the North Face of the Eiger in two hours and twenty-two minutes. Even top climbers usually took twelve hours.

The risk of climbing at the limit was exemplified in 2017 when Steck fell to his death on Nuptse. More recently, fatalities to David Lama, Jess Roskelley and Hansjorg Auer on Howse Peak, Kyle Dempster and Scott Adamson on the Ogre 2, Rick Allen on K2 and Corrado Pesce on Cerro Torre illustrate that accidents continually occur amongst the world's top mountaineers.

Since inception in 1992, the Piolet d'Or is awarded annually for impressive ascents. It was evident at the time, from this barometer of excellence, that the focus for modern alpinism was (and still is) on the six thousand and seven thousand metre peaks, with the high difficulty of steep and extended faces providing the challenge rather than the struggle with reduced oxygen levels above eight thousand metres.

The British pair of Mick Fowler and Paul Ramsden have won an unprecedented three Piolet d'Or awards. In 2002 they succeeded on Mount Siguniang in China then, in 2013, climbed the Prow of Shiva in India; lastly, in 2016, they summited Gave Ding in Nepal. The crucible of mountaineering now lies with small teams, working on shoestring budgets, while seeking out challenging unknown walls on remote but slightly lower peaks.

1978 saw a sudden increase of climbers in Nepal when the government opened eighteen *trekking peaks*. All were below 6,654 metres and without the onerous regulations and expense of higher expedition peaks. However the term was misleading as most of the mountains were too dangerous for the average trekker. What it did do was open objectives in Nepal to mountaineers who wanted a taste of the Himalayas without going on a full-scale expedition. Most of these summits have steep and difficult faces, ideal for alpine style mountaineering. *Trekking peaks* also have relatively easy aspects that provide mountaineers of modest ability the opportunity to attain a Himalayan summit. This provided the catalyst for the growth of commercial mountaineering. Many guiding companies, including my own, seized the opportunity to offer regular alpine clientele a dream trip to Nepal.

Who could have imagined the consequences when, in 1992, the New Zealand company Adventure Consultants organised the first commercial Everest expedition? It was a raging success with guides Rob Hall, Gary Ball and Guy Cotter reaching the summit with six clients and four Sherpas. The guides were an enthusiastic group of top climbers wanting to earn extra cash, using a concept no different from guiding clients up Mont Blanc or Mount Rainier ... but what a monster was born. Soon, other Western guiding companies joined in the fray but, in May 1996, tragedy became headline news when eight climbers died descending from Everest's summit, including Rob Hall and fellow guide Scott Fischer. The accident highlighted the vulnerability of climbers when an unexpected storm hits a high mountain. The fallout from the tragedy was understandably immense, but it did not end the desire of people to climb to the top of the world.

In the competitive world of commercial guiding, there is little regard for ethics and mountaineering style, just a hell-bent drive to put as many people on the top by any means possible for monetary gain. On 23rd May 2019, a staggering 396 people were photographed snaking up the fixed ropes to the top of Everest, taking advantage of a brief weather window. An attempt costs a client between $20,000 and $100,000, depending on the level of service and whether the attempt is from Nepal or the more expensive Tibetan side, and whether a client pays for a local Nepali company or a foreign operator.

Each season Everest Base Camp becomes a temporary village that struggles to contain rubbish and sewage yet has both internet and mobile phone coverage, with the first phone message sent from the top of Everest in 2011. However, the unique feeling of isolation is being destroyed. There seems to be poor control over the use of helicopters, both to ferry clients to and from base camps and to supply higher camps. The latter an especially controversial practice, with rope and oxygen bottles having been flown to Camp 3 at seven thousand metres on Annapurna in 2021.

Guided attempts on Everest, Cho Oyu and Ama Dablam account for well over half the people presently climbing in Nepal. Underpaid Sherpas encourage clients upwards as they labour, carrying all their paymasters' kit, food, and spare oxygen on these three trophy peaks. The buffoonery that goes on cannot be described as a fair ascent.

'What is now going on in the big mountains is tourism,' Reinhold Messner told me recently. 'It has nothing to do with alpinism – I would not go back to Everest if they paid me.'

Mountaineering should not be about the summit but about the way, and it is a sad state of affairs when commodification removes much of the adventure, harms the environment and destroys the reputation of mainstream mountaineering. Most guided clients appear to be blind to the ethics, heritage and heartbeat of mountaineering, egotistically only wanting the prize of the summit.

Paul Nunn wrote prophetically in a 1973 *Mountain* magazine.

> Little expeditions are more likely to be good expeditions – the battle for Everest seems to me to have undermined the very term 'expedition', which now implies multiple forms of exploitation and rigid organisation for which the only compensation for many individual climbers is pretentiousness. The alienation of the heart, combined with extreme graft involved, seems to me to be the complete antithesis of what mountaineering is all about. So a small group of climbers, friendly, intimate, motivated but not utterly achievement-orientated, promised to get away from all that.

That said, generalisations often overlook the exceptional individuals that stand out from the norm. In 2019 an ex-Gurkha and UK Special Forces member Nimsdai Purja attempted all fourteen, eight thousand metre-peaks within seven months (the previous record being eight years). Most thought his *Project Possible* was crazy, and he got little support in advance of his efforts. Nevertheless, he claims to have achieved his goal, helped by strong support from a team of fellow Nepalese and utilising helicopter transport between base camps. However, rumours abound that he stopped short of the highest point of Manaslu. Regardless, it was an unbelievable feat, illustrating the developing ability of local climbers, combining their natural strength and adaptation to altitude while using the latest technology. It is heartening to see a growing number of qualified Sherpa mountain guides, and that a nine-strong Nepalese team (including Nimsdai) succeeded on the long awaited first winter ascent of K2 in 2021.

Typically though, Sherpas receive little recognition for their climbing achievements. Lhakpa Sherpa has climbed Everest nine times, a women's world record, but she still receives no publicity or sponsorship and lives in the USA, raising her three children alone, working as a house cleaner between trips back to her homeland and the more lucrative job of guiding Everest.

In the past, mountains were viewed as wild and forbidding places where demons lived. In much of Asia, peaks are holy places representing deities in Buddhist and Hindu religions. In Europe, at the end of the eighteenth century, the Romantics such as Byron, Coleridge and Rousseau called their artistic and semi-religious contemplation of the mountains *the sublime,* and mountains came to be viewed as beautiful and majestic. Later, powerful Victorian ideals suggested that facing the dangers of the mountains made one a better person. There was a growing concept that the possibility of death was an essential part of an adventure, especially in mountaineering.

'If somebody says climbing is fun then they have not been mountaineering,' Reinhold Messner pointed out. 'I don't like suffering, but it's part of exposing yourself to the power of nature – no sleep, headache and far away from safety. The art of adventuring is not to die, and yet near death experiences are the most important experiences.'

The Himalayas followed after the Alps both in exploration and mapping, the first ascents of the peaks, and the development of *directissimas* on the unclimbed faces. Guiding was first practised by local hill folk, but then specialist mountain guides led the cartographers, crystal hunters, scientists and amateur mountaineers into the hills. Love of the mountains eventually led to today's multi-sport adventure playground, encompassing trekking, climbing, skiing, mountain biking, trail running, paragliding and BASE jumping. The reality is that commercialisation is inevitable.

The first quarter of the twenty-first century brought a more risk-averse society to which the sport of climbing adapted and became safer. Bolt protected sports climbing in the sun is booming, and guided treks with luxury accommodation flourishing, whereas high-risk mountaineering is losing popularity. I suppose we should applaud democratisation, and development of the outdoors as an easy and predictable venue for the enjoyment of the masses. What I could not predict when I first went to the Greater Ranges was how mountaineering would divide into two separate activities: alpine style that my group passionately followed, which in my opinion, is still the preferred way for ardent mountaineers, regardless of the high levels of risk, and commercial mountaineering using heavy-weight expedition tactics which improves safety and helps ensure success. Adventure versus tourism?

The risk of dying while mountaineering is at the heart of this book. The youthful arrogance of the characters in these pages gave us confidence that our high levels of climbing skill and experience would improve our safety. However, research shows that a seasoned elite mountaineer has the same risk of dying as a first-time amateur.

'It is time to put a stop to the belief that serious accidents only happen to beginners or ill-shod tourists. Accident statistics state the exact opposite,' wrote Sébastien Rigault, Commander of Isère PGHM Rescue Team.

Well-known American mountaineers David Roberts and Ed Viesturs explored this issue in their memoirs. Roberts viewed the risks of death as uncontrollable, simply a result of chance, like the analogy with Russian Roulette. However, Viesturs disagreed, maintaining that most accidents on the high peaks are due to human error and that his experience made his ascents less risky than those of the typical climber. 'If I learn something from a previous climb and become a better mountaineer – smarter, faster, stronger, more efficient – then the next climb will be safer,' Viesturs writes. 'The risk actually goes down!'

Conventional wisdom agrees with Viesturs, believing that Darwinian adaptation is associated with improved survival. There are obvious parallels in sports where training and game time improve skills, fitness, and mental attitude. However, elite mountaineers are usually high-level risk-takers, countering the benefits of their experience. Additionally, any advantage that greater expertise offers is overwhelmed by objective dangers such as avalanches, crevasses, falling rocks and storms.

It is now believed that heuristic traps significantly influence accidents in the mountains. Heuristics are mental shortcuts that are part of how humans make subconscious daily decisions. For example, heuristics guide our behaviour in familiar terrain. Rather than figuring out what is appropriate every time, we behave as we have before in that setting. When nothing happens we stop being attentive to the dangers and do not apply risk reduction measures. Thus, the avalanche or falling stones were not the killers, it was the compelling heuristic traps that deceived the victim into thinking that the terrain was safe.

Avalanche experts Henry Schniewind and Ian McCammon concluded that two-thirds of avalanche victims ignored obvious signs of danger regardless of a victim's skill and experience. There are six heuristic traps commonly identified:

Familiarity: I've done it before.

Consistency: I'll do it the same way as last time.

Acceptance: Fitting in with the social scene or norms.

Expert halo: I know best; I'm the leader.

Social: Other people have done it; therefore, so can I.

Scarcity: We have a good weather forecast. We must use it.

Heuristics have analogies in other areas of social psychology. Where *optimistic bias* explains that people think that their own risk is less than that of others. A *false sense of control* proposes that the more people think they are in control, generally, the less worried they are. *Confirmation bias* occurs when people confirm their preconceived ideas by seeking favourable evidence. *Outside pressures* underlines the debate between the reward you'll receive outweighing the risk. Sponsors, media, peer pressure, social standing and status or ranking within a sport all associate with winners, which puts pressure on an athlete to succeed, which undoubtably alters their decision making.

Avoiding stupid mistakes is why the World Health Organisation implements Surgical Safety Checklists on invasive procedures. It is why pilots complete inventories before every take-off, lest they forget or ignore the obvious. Nobel Prize-winning psychologist Daniel Kahneman states, 'We trust our intuitions even when they're wrong.' To me, the evidence is clear: on the peaks my generation strove to climb, our skill did not provide any survival benefit.

At the start of this book I asked: were we the *generation that climbed themselves to extinction*? A clear picture is difficult to discern while the governments of India and Pakistan issue only limited figures. Most of our information comes from Nepal, extracted from learnt papers based on the Himalayan Database. Annoyingly, their focus has become skewed towards Everest and commercial expeditions. Mixing such data with alpine style climbs is confusing – as I explained earlier they are different games.

Nevertheless, in my first years of Himalayan climbing, between 1978 and 1982, there was a fourfold increase in the number of deaths. This could simply be explained by four times the number of climbers visiting Nepal, chiefly due to accessible air travel and the increased popularity of small alpine style trips. The actual chance of dying remained the same. Despite our initial optimism, the mortality rates of alpine style climbing proved to be similar to those of heavyweight expeditions, the lower risk bestowed by reducing the time spent on alpine style ascents cancelled out by climbing on more challenging terrain and going on a greater number of expeditions.

By the start of the '90s, the commercialisation of Himalayan peaks had one significant advantage: the death rate more than halved, particularly on Everest where it was ten times safer in 2020 than in 1980. Any lower skillset and lack of experience in the clients was balanced by using supplementary oxygen and fixed ropes all the way to the summit, along with improved weather forecasting, equipment, communication and careful management strategies devised by highly experienced operators. Moreover, the two easiest ascent routes were used: via the South Col on the Nepalese side and the North Ridge from Tibet. Alan Arnette, the Everest expert, gave a fascinating insight, finding that of the ten thousand plus summiteers, only 3 per cent used routes other than the two 'trade' routes and 2 per cent did not use bottled oxygen.

In the past two decades, under the watchful eye of professional guides and Sherpas, the overall success rate has doubled on commercial expeditions. There is also evidence of lower death rates and improved success in alpine style climbing in recent years, with advantages bestowed by technological improvements and collective *herd* knowledge.[1] Yet there are fewer people climbing seven thousand-metre peaks today than in 1980.

Overall, the records show that the era from the mid-'70s to the mid-'80s, when I climbed, was more dangerous than the periods before and after.

There are many ways to die, and predictably the most significant is getting old, with one's risk of dying doubling every eight years. After that sobering statistic, the mortality leader board is topped by heart attacks followed by strokes and cancers.

By comparison, the risk of dying in popular sports is low. However, it is difficult to compare sports empirically, due to the various metrics used in the statistical analyses. The problematic issue is defining the 'population'. In climbing there are so many games (bouldering, sports climbing, alpinism etc.) each with different risks, but how do you measure participation in climbing – per route (but what about multi-pitch versus single pitch), per day, or the number of climbers in each country? Each nation seems to have a different system and in most of the world numbers are only estimated. Similar issues confront other sports, such as swimming, which is subdivided into indoor, outdoor, wild water or in the sea (with sharks!). BASE jumping, usually cited as the most dangerous

---

1. On the 7,000 metre peaks often attempted by alpine style teams, death rates between 1950 and 1989 were 3.03% and from 1990 to 2019 they had dropped dramatically to 0.89%.

sport, measures its risk per jump, with a 1.6 per cent chance of participants dying each year or a death every 2,300 jumps.

Fortunately, the analysis in *The Himalayas by Numbers* by Salisbury, Hawley and Bierling, 2021 provides a consistent picture of mountaineering in Nepal. They use numbers of climbers above base camp as their population. Far from perfect but better than the eye-catching statistics frequently used by the media, which calculates risk of death related to summit success. Surely all climbers should be counted whether they reach the summit or not.

In Nepal the statistics show that death rates on peaks over six thousand metres between 1950 and 1989 (the era when I climbed) stood at 2.60 per cent; then between 1990 and 2019 they dropped to 1 per cent. A small cohort study of mountaineers climbing within New Zealand confirms this extraordinary high risk, finding that over a four-year period, 8.2 per cent of the participants had died in the mountains, a risk of 2.05 per cent per year. Undoubtedly, mountaineering is a high-risk sport, with a death rate thousands of times more dangerous than the estimates for swimming, cycling and rock climbing.[2]

The debate on whether the dangers are manageable runs through the mind of every mountaineer. By using the analogy of Russian Roulette, I hoped to emphasise the high risk of death while mountaineering and convey my dismay at losing so many of my climbing friends.

What makes us go mountaineering and take these risks? For some, ambition overrides caution. Successfully pushing the boundaries creates euphoria and a unique satisfaction, which can result in an addiction to risk. Others feel a spiritual preference for the solitude of the mountains and want an escape from the pressures of mundane and urban life.

I chose to be a mountaineer because I wanted adventure. Attracted to a lifestyle of physical challenges and the mystery of travelling through the unknown, my spirit was lifted by wild and beautiful places. I kept climbing, death after death, as it became all

2. 1.77 (0.0017%) deaths per 100,000 swims; cycling: 1.8 (0.0018%) deaths per 100,000 rides, and rock climbing: 0.13 (0.00013%) per 100,000 climbs.

I knew, a habit and an addiction. My entire life revolved around expedition mountaineering, and for a dozen years I loved it regardless of the risks.

One cannot compare mountaineering to a simple game of chance, rather it gives the opportunity to learn about oneself when overcoming obstacles on a journey. It is also about the comfort and stimulation of being part of a group with a shared purpose. Days of adversity, time in the wilderness, exploring strengths and weaknesses, brings an astonishing closeness to friendships.

Talking with fellow climbers, I found a common thread. In our youth we felt that we were immortal. Yet after the age of thirty, two things happen: the body slows down, and the appetite for risk-taking diminishes. A stage of life that is coincidental to increased social responsibilities with relationships, children and work.

'As your friends die you begin to assess things differently,' John Porter believes. 'As soon as I had children, I heard little voices in my head saying, *Daddy Daddy* when I was climbing.'

Some friends reviewed the fragility of life after a traumatic accident or a near miss; a condition now diagnosed as post-traumatic stress. Others were affected by survivor guilt. For all those reasons, many of us reached a time in our lives when we chose safer objectives, reducing the frequency of our participation or giving up entirely.

'Mountaineering is a vibrant expression of the spirit – going towards the sky and the sun – going to the top,' Canadian alpinist Barry Blanchard explained to me, reflecting his Métis heritage. 'I have been affected immensely by the deaths of two of my climbing partners, Dave Cheesmond and Alex Lowe, my whole being, my spirit, my soul, my everything. I quit climbing for a year. It was largely David's spirit that took me back into the mountains, realising that he would still want me to climb. There was something so wild inside both of those guys and I do not know how much choice they had.'

Too many of my companions have perished before their time. It was only fate that three of the people I write about died of natural causes, with another so tormented that he took his own life. The seven who were seduced and then taken by their lover, the mountains, knew and accepted the risks. They just happened to be in the wrong place, at the wrong time. Suffering and the possibility of death was the price paid for leading such a fulfilling life.

If we do everything right, the unpredictable still happens, and when it does there are no clear-cut answers to the question why, which is part of the mystery and attraction. If it had been me, would I have made different choices to those who succumbed to rockfall, avalanche, exposure, or altitude sickness? I'd like to think so, but that implies they made mistakes and, in some cases they did, but surely they made the best decisions they could in the circumstances. Ambition, ego, financial pressure, the distractions of fame, mysterious individual motivations and drives can warp our capacity to make *good* decisions but, as much as we try to stack the deck in our favour, there is always an element of luck, or fate, involved.

Mountains are geological undulations without emotion, and they do not care who succeeds or fails, who lives or dies. You really do roll the dice, and perhaps an accident is, in the end, only an appointment with time and place. Friendship with these colourful and courageous characters has made my life so much richer. Reminiscing about them in bygone days, in a different age, has been a pleasure, and I will remember them forever as vibrant and young.

APPENDIX 1

Winter seasons in mountaineering

What constitutes the mountaineering winter season? In Nepal it used to be from the 1st December to 31st January but in 1980 when, during the first winter expedition to Everest, the Poles ran out of time, the authorities gave them an extra two weeks, until 15th February. By the time they reached the summit on the 17th they had been granted a further extension. The Nepalese have now altered the definition to 1st December to 28th February.

Usually, the weather is good before Christmas, a colder version of the settled post-monsoon season. Normally, it is in late December that the vicious weather arrives, lasting through February. The Poles endured horrendous storms in both January and February so, having noted this, following expeditions have arrived early, to prepare and acclimatise. Subsequent Everest winter ascents have all been in December. To prevent early starts, the regulations now forbid climbing above base camp until 1st December.

The regulations differ in Pakistan, with the first winter ascents of Broad Peak and Gasherbrum 1 recognised as having taken place in March, on the 5th and 9th respectively. In the European Alps, the winter mountaineering season is 21st December to 21st March.

There seems to be no consistency in the dates of the winter mountaineering season, which begs the question of whether these dates should be defined by mountaineers, bureaucrats or historians.

APPENDIX 2

The Problems with climbing Everest in winter

There are several reasons why it remains a daunting task to climb Everest in winter as a small team with no supplementary oxygen, as we tried in 1980–81. The hurdles include reduced oxygen pressure, the cold and the wind.

It is a common misconception that there is less oxygen at high altitudes. In fact, the ratio is the same as at sea level. It is the atmospheric pressure that is lower at high altitude. When we breathe air into our lungs, the atmospheric pressure pushes oxygen through the alveoli into the bloodstream. As air pressure at the summit of Everest is about one-third of that at sea level, less oxygen is pushed into our blood. Athletic performance is severely impaired, and cognitive functions deteriorate. Clearly, the oxygen pressure on the summit of Everest is only just high enough for human survival. If dwellers from sea level were rapidly transported to the summit of Everest, they would be hypoxic within minutes, lose consciousness and die soon after. Acclimatisation and using bottled oxygen significantly helps humans to perform at these heights.

Since our attempt on Everest, more has become known about the science of acclimatisation. A measure of how well the body performs at a given altitude is the blood oxygen saturation levels. The Caudwell Xtreme Everest team of climbing doctors in 2007 evaluated blood samples taken close to the summit. The expedition found the average arterial oxygen level to be 3.28 kPa (kilopascals); the normal value in humans is 12–14 kPa. Patients with a level below 8 kPa are considered to be critically ill. It shows that humans can only stay in the 'death zone' above eight thousand metres for a few days. Even for a well-acclimatised person, it is incredible that they can climb Everest, and it is beyond the physiological limits of most people without supplementary oxygen.

In winter, a mix of environmental conditions makes it harder to climb above eight thousand metres. Low temperatures cause air pressure to drop, effectively increasing the apparent height of the mountain. When gas molecules cool, they move more slowly. This decreased velocity results in fewer collisions between molecules, and barometric pressure decreases. In January, the estimated temperatures on the summit varied from −36°C to −60°C. In May, by comparison, the summit averages hover around −20°C. Base Camp in January averages a chilly −19°C at night and −6°C by day; in May, it is −4°C at night to 6°C during the day.

It is not just temperature that affects air pressure. The troposphere (the lowest layer of the earth's atmosphere containing the gases we need for life) is as thin as seven thousand metres near the Poles and as thick as twenty thousand metres at the equator. Because this layer has a mass, the thinner the layer, the lower the barometric pressure. For example, at the same height, the oxygen pressure is lower on Denali in Alaska (at sixty-three degrees north) than on Everest in Nepal (at twenty-eight degrees north). The troposphere also thins significantly in winter. The boundary between the troposphere and the stratosphere is called the tropopause, and it is here that the jet stream winds circle the earth. Usually, Everest's 8,848 metre summit sits just below the tropopause but, in winter, and on occasions in the pre- and post-monsoon seasons, it lowers onto the mountain causing ferocious storms.

In an article in *New Scientist* in May 2004, Kent Moore reported that a temporary weather station, near the top of Everest in 1998, measured a dramatic fall in pressure during a storm of sixteen millibars caused by a lowering of the tropopause and was the equivalent of raising Everest's height by five hundred metres and cutting the amount of oxygen the mountaineers were breathing by about fourteen per cent. This phenomenon is normal in winter but is thought to occur at any time of year. In May 1996, eight people were killed in one of these storms (described in Jon Krakauer's book *Into Thin Air*).

The summit of Everest in winter could well be the windiest place on earth. In February 2004, a wind speed of 280 km/h (175 mph) was recorded. Winds of over 160 km/h (100 mph) are normal in winter when the jet stream hits. These have the power to blow climbers and tents off the mountain. The wind also lowers atmospheric pressure. Bernoulli's principle explains that faster-moving air has lower air pressure than slower moving air; the same theory explains how heavier-than-air objects can fly. Kent Moore calculated that jet stream winds typically reduce the partial pressure of oxygen in the air by about 6 per cent, which translates to a significant reduction in oxygen uptake for the climbers, in addition to the lower pressures caused by the lower tropopause and cold temperatures.

ACKNOWLEDGEMENTS

The germ of the idea to write a book started in the spring of 2019 and at that time I had no idea what I was letting myself into - neither did my wife, Louise. It is only through her help and support that I managed get it past the finish line. Not only keeping me sane but also reading my work, offering opinions, and correcting my hundreds of mistakes. In the end I think she preferred to be married to a mountaineer than an author.

The crucial event that committed me to this book was acceptance on the Banff Mountain and Wilderness Writing Programme in the autumn of 2019. I cannot imagine completing *High Risk* without the help of Tony Whittome, Marni Jackson and Harley Rustad who guided and mentored nine prospective authors through the daunting (for me) steps of writing a book. Without doubt Louise Blight, Maria Coffey, Gloria Dickie, Martina Halik, Michael Kennedy, Kate Rawles, Rhiannon Russell and Katherine Weaver and myself became close friends during our stay in Banff. To such an extent that afterward we kept in regular contact through unofficial on-line meetings across the globe where we discussed and critiqued each other's work. An invaluable process for my confidence to continue.

After a false start with one UK publisher, I was introduced, by my good friend Keith Partridge, to Robert Davidson of Sandstone Press, who commissioned my title and has since guided me through the labyrinthian process of producing a book. Patiently editing my clumsy prose and keeping my ramblings to the point.

Special thanks go to Joe Simpson, who generously provided the foreword.

I have had help from friends who have read extracts and made constructive comments; in particular Vanita Warden, Tim Rhodes, Colin Maber, Michael & Jan Anderson and Dave Postlethwaite.

It has been crucial to contact the families and friends of the eleven climbers who are the core of this book. It must have been very difficult for those so close to re-live the past. I have done my best to remember accurately my lost friends and I sincerely apologise if my writing does not do justice or portray these characters to the high standards which you rightly expect. I also appreciate the photographs that have been sent; they really do stir my heart. Thank you: Nigel Abbott, Steve Arsenault, Sue Barker, Christine Baxter-Jones, Mélanie Baxter-Jones, Dave Binns, Geoff Birtles, Paul Braithwaite, Choe Brooks, Gwyneth Brooks, Jan Brownsort, Alan and Adrian Burgess, Phil Burke, Rab and Sue Carrington, Greg Child, Carol Cochrane, Matthew Cochrane, Maria Coffey, Nick Colton, Caroline Coppock, Dick Croft, Leo Dickinson, Ed Douglas, Sarah Ferguson, Helen Geddes, John Given, Dennis Gray, Pete Gray, Lindsay Griffin, Hilary Hamper, Leo Houlding, Roy Kligfield, Dai Lampard, Howard Lancashire, Kev Martin, Mike Mortimer, Bernard Newman, Hilary Nunn, Mike Owen, Andy Parkin, Mike Parsons, Nick Parry, Dick Peart, John Porter, John Powell, Sarah Richards, Doug Scott, John Sheard, John Stainforth, Mike Swain, Phil Swainson, Pol Syrett, Deborah Sweeney, Paul Tasker, Terry Tasker, Mike Thexton, Stephen Venables, Jess Whittle, Dave Wilkinson, Noel Williams and John Witcombe.

Many of those listed above have taken the time and effort to be interviewed and I have also discussed the topics within this book with several prominent mountaineers and experts, including, Barry Blanchard, Will Gadd, Michael Kennedy, Reinhold Messner, Geoff Powter, Mark Twight and Ian Wall. I have also had much help from learned books and journals mentioned in the Bibliography.

If you have helped me and you are not mentioned above, I apologise for your ommision and add my thanks, but these words are my last and tomorrow I am going out climbing.

Brian Hall - February 2022.

SELECT BIBLIOGRAPHY

Adams, John: *Risk*. Routledge 1995

Bandolier website: *Risk of dying and sporting activity* 2007

Barry, John: *K2: Savage Mountain, Savage Summer*. Oxford Illustrated Press, 1987

Bettembourg, Georges & Brame, Michael: *The White Death*. Reynard House, Seattle, 1981

Birtles, Geoff: *Alan Rouse. A Mountaineer's Life*. London, Unwin Hyman, 1987.

Boardman, Pete: *The Shining Mountain: Two Men on Changabang's West Wall*. 1984 by Dutton Books

Bonington, Chris: *Heroic Climbs: A Celebration of World Mountaineering*. Mountaineers Books 1994.

Boyce and Bischak. *Learning by Doing, Knowledge Spillovers, and Technological and Organizational Change in High-Altitude Mountaineering* 2010

Burgess, Adrian & Alan: *The Burgess Book of Lies*. Cloudcap 1994

Cheng & Edward: *Is high-altitude mountaineering Russian roulette?* Journal of Quantitative Analysis in Sports 2012.

Cave, Andy: *Thin White Line*. Cornerstone 2009

Child, Greg: *Mixed Emotions: Mountaineers Books* 1993

——— *Thin Air: Encounters in the Himalayas*. Peregrine Smith Books 1988

——— *Postcards from the Ledge*. Mountaineers Books 1998.

Coffey, Maria: *Fragile Edge: A Personal Portrait of Loss on Everest.* Trafalgar Square Publishing 1990

—— *Where the Mountain Casts Its Shadow: The Dark Side of Extreme Adventure.* Hutchinson 2003

Curran, Jim: *K2: Triumph and Tragedy.* Hodder & Stoughton Ltd 1987

—— *K2: The Story of the Savage Mountain.* Hodder & Stoughton Ltd 1995

Czech Mountaineering Association Medical Commission: *Medical Aspects of Mouintaineering.* UIAA Mountain Medicine Conference 1998.

Fanshawe, Andy & Venables, Stephen: *Himalaya Alpine Style: The Most Challenging Routes on the Highest Peaks.* Hodder & Stoughton Ltd 1996

Franco, Jean & Terray, Lionel: *Battle for Jannu.* Victor Gollancz, London, 1967

Grocott and Montgomery: *Risk of dying and sporting activities and Mountain mortality: A review of deaths that occur during recreational activities in the mountains.* Bandolier 2009 ResearchGate

Huey, Caroll, Salisbury and Wang: *Mountaineers on Mount Everest: Effects of age, sex, experience, and crowding on rates of success and death.* Plos One 2020

Krakauer, Jon: *Into Thin Air.* Macmillan 1997

Leeds University Climbing Club journal 1971 & '73

McCammon, Ian: *Heuristic Traps in Recreational Avalanche Accidents: Evidence and Implications.* Avalanche News, No. 68, 2004

Macdonald, Bernadette: *Freedom Climbers.* Vertebrate Publishing 2012

—— *Art of Freedom: The Life and Climbs of Voytek Kurtyka.* Vertebrate Publishing 2017

McDonald, Bernadette: *Winter 8000.* Vertebrate Publishing 2020

Macfarlane, Robert: *Mountains of the Mind.* Pantheon 2003

MacIntyre, Alex & Scott, Doug: *Shisha Pangma: The alpine-style first ascent of the south west face.* Vertebrate Publishing 2016

McCammon: *Heuristic Traps in Recreational Avalanche Accidents: Evidence and Implications.* Avalanche News, No. 68, 2004)

Messner, Reinhold: *Murder of the Impossible.* Mountain #15 1971

Monasterio ME. *Accident and fatality characteristics in a population of mountain climbers in New Zealand.* N Z Med J 2005

Nunn, Paul: *At the Sharp End.* Unwin Hyman 1988

Petzl Foundation: *Accidentology of mountain sports.*2014

Pollard, A and Clarke, C: *Death during mountaineering at extreme altitude.* Lancet 1988

Porter, John: *One Day as a Tiger: Alex MacIntyre and the Birth of Light and Fast Alpinism.* Vertebrate Publishing 2014

Prichard, Paul: *Deep Play: A Climber's Odyssey from Llanberis to the Big Walls.* Baton Wicks 1997

RAC (Royal Automobile Club) Foundation: *Traffic Accident Statistics* 2021

Roberts, Dave: *On the Ridge Between Life and Death.* New York: Simon & Schuster 2005.

Salisbury R, Bierling B & Hawley E: *The Himalaya by the numbers: a statistical analysis of mountaineering in the Nepal Himalaya 1950-2019.* Kathmandu, Nepal: The Himalayan Database; 2021.

Schniewind: *Decision-making, risk and crisis management from an avalanche point of view.* On line lecture https://henrysavalanchetalk.com/author/rob-stewart/2019

Scott, Doug: *Makalu-Nearly.* The Himalayan Journal #41 1985.

——— *Up and About: The Hard Road to Everest.* Vertebrate Publishing 2015

——— *Kangchenjunga: The Himalayan giant.* Vertebrate Publishing 2021

Simpson, Joe: *Touching the Void.* Random House 1988

Stainforth Gordon: *Fiva: An Adventure that went wrong.* Golden Arrow Books 2012.

Syrett, Pol: *Searching for my brother.* 2021. Blurb self publish ISBN 978-0-473-57770-4

Tasker, Joe: *Savage Arena.* St. Martin's Press 1982

———— *Everest the Cruel Way.* Methuen Publishing 1981

Tejada-Flores, Lito: *Games climbers play.* Ascent 1967

Thexton, Mike: *What Happened to the Hippy Man? Hijack Hostage Survivor.* Lanista Partners Ltd, 2006

UK Office for National Statistics. *Mortality and Suicide.* Website 2021

Viesturs, Ed. and Roberts, Dave: *No Shortcuts to the Top: Climbing the World's 14 Highest Peaks.* New York: Broadway 2006.

Ward, Mike: *The Commoditisation of Climbing.* UKC website 2020

———— *How the Leeds Wall Changed Climbing History.* UKC website 2018

Wells, Colin: *A Brief History of British Mountaineering.* The Mountain Heritage Trust, 2001

Westhoff JL, Koepsell TD, Littell CT. *Effects of experience and commercialization on survival in Himalayan mountaineering* Br Med J. 2012

Westman, Rosén, Berggren & Björnstig. *Parachuting from fixed objects: descriptive study of 106 fatal events in BASE jumping 1981–2006:* 2008 British Journal of Sports Medicine

Whittle, John. *Standhardt.* Crags Magazine #1 1977.